THE COMPLETE COLLECTION

IMPERFECT LOVE *Series*

USA TODAY BESTSELLING AUTHOR

NIKKI ASH

IT'S NEVER TOO LATE
TO LIVE HAPPILY EVER AFTER...

THE PICKUP

IMPERFECT LOVE SERIES: BOOK ONE

PROLOGUE

*N*ICK
    Twenty years old

I'VE JUST GOTTEN BACK to my dorm, and I'm fucking exhausted. I'm ready to take a hot shower then go see my girlfriend, Samantha. I throw my gym bag on the bed and grab a change of clothes and a towel. Stripping out of my sweatpants and shirt, I turn the water on as hot as it can go and wait for it to heat up. Once I can see the fog filling the bathroom, I get in. Standing with my back toward the hot water, I let it rain down on my sore muscles. Between sitting on a crowded, uncomfortable-as-fuck bus for the ten-hour trip to and from D.C. for our first football game of the season, the lumpy king-size bed I had to share in the hotel with my teammate Killian, and the two-hour meeting I had to attend once we returned to go over the game tapes, a hot shower is exactly what I need.

I grab my shampoo and wash my hair, then squirt some body wash into my hands. As I scrub the dirty feeling from the nasty bus off my skin, I try to think of everything I need to get done. With it being the beginning of my junior year at North Carolina University, it feels like my to-do list is never ending. I need to pick up the text-book I ordered for the British Literature class I'm taking, go by the library to see if I can check out *The Hobbit* and *The Neverending Story* for my Fantasy Lit class... Shit! I also need to go by the writing lab to schedule the required tutoring session. Some days it feels like there aren't enough hours in the day, and today is definitely one of those days.

After rinsing off, I get dressed and head to the writing lab. "Excuse me, my name is Nicholas Shaw. I'm taking Professor Hughes's creative writing course, and he said we have to schedule a tutoring session."

"Yep! Let me pull up your name. What's your student ID number?" I give her my ten-digit number, and she types it into the computer. "Hmm...it seems you're no longer enrolled in that course." She types some more on her keyboard. "It actually shows you've dropped the course and switched your major." She prints something out and hands it to me. I read over it, and sure enough, my degree seeking states business and not English Literature. My classes are all basic accounting and business management shit. What the hell? I just picked my damn major not even two weeks ago when I met with my advisor.

"Okay, thank you. I'll get this figured out." I fold up the paper and put it into my back pocket and start heading toward Samantha's dorm, furious as hell. There's only one person who would do this. I hit his name on my cell phone, and not even one ring later, my dad answers.

"Dad, we need to talk."

"Nick, I'm glad you called. I saw your game, and I'm not the only one. There's chatter from several teams. If you continue to play the way you did yesterday, you'll be entering the draft this year instead of next, and most likely go in as a first round—"

"Did you change my major?" I ask, cutting him off.

"What?" my dad responds incredulously. "Did you hear what I said? There's a damn good chance you will be drafted this year."

"Yeah, I heard you. But I thought I was going to stay in college all four years so I can graduate with my degree."

"We talked about this, Nick," my dad says, frustration evident in his tone. "Football comes first. Your coach called and told me that you asked for permission to leave your practices early this semester because you need to attend some writing bullshit."

"Writing lab." I sigh. Since I was little, I've always felt a pull toward literature. When I'm not reading, I'm writing. Horror, Mystery, Fantasy, Nonfiction, I don't care what it is. When I was a kid and didn't really believe I stood a chance at playing pro ball, my dream was to one day delve into the world of books. My second grade teacher gave me a writing journal, and that year I filled the entire thing with story after story. Growing up, I read everything from *The Boxcar Children* and *Harry Potter* to *1984*. As an adult, I'll give anything a try. From James Patterson to Stephen King. Hell, I've even given Nicholas Sparks a go-round. I'm not sure, if given the opportunity, what I would do in the field—maybe write or edit. All I know is I love books.

Not that it matters at this point. I'm not being given the opportunity, and I won't be in the future. How many football players do you know of that have written a novel? And I'm not talking about the millions of autobiographies. Exactly...

"I don't give a shit what it is!" my dad yells. "We talked about this. You're majoring in business." I stop walking and sit down on the bench outside of Samantha's dorm. With my face in my hands, I close my eyes and take a deep breath.

"Does it even matter what I'm majoring in if I'm not going to graduate anyway?"

"It does when you're having to cut out of practice early." I want to argue with my dad, but I don't. It's pointless. It was stupid of me to sign up for those courses in the first place. When I met with my advisor, I thought maybe my choice of major would go under my dad's radar, and truth be told, had the creative writing class not required a tutoring session at the same time as practice, I might have gotten away with it. But it does, and I didn't.

"What if I can save that class for another semester?" I ask as a last-ditch effort to convince my dad to let me keep my major as English Lit. When he sighs, I think for a moment that maybe he's going to relent. *How stupid am I?*

"Nick, you go to North Carolina for football. Your scholarship covers your classes and dorm. I pay for everything else. Your books, your food, your car, insurance, cell phone, clothes. Are you prepared to pay for all of that?" He already knows I can't. Not if I want to graduate debt free. What if football doesn't work out? Then I'll be stuck with loans, and who's to say I'd even be approved for a loan big enough to cover everything. And getting a job is out of the question. I can't even attend a damn tutoring session twice a week.

Without waiting for an answer, my dad continues, "Besides, an English degree is a waste of time and money. I went to law school, and so did your grandfather. The men in our family don't major in English," he scoffs. "Your coach has notified your professors that you'll be starting your new classes on Monday, and they know to give you time to get caught up. I need to go; I have a client calling.

Don't forget we're having a dinner at the house for your mother's birthday next Sunday." And with that, he hangs up.

Just as I'm about to stand, my phone rings. Surprise, surprise, it's my mother. I consider not answering but figure I might as well get it over with, so she won't continue to call me while I'm hanging out with Samantha.

"Mother."

"Nicholas, please tell me your majoring in English was a joke." C'mon, who the hell picks a major as a joke? Clearly her question is rhetorical, but fuck...

"Yeah, Mom," I say dryly. "It was a joke." *And so were all of the books I had my nose stuck in throughout my entire childhood...*

"And what exactly would you do with that degree? What if, God forbid, you got injured? What would you do with a degree in English?"

Oh, I don't know...maybe write a book...work in publishing... maybe I could teach English...Of course, I don't say any of that to her. Speaking to her is the same as speaking to my father. A waste of time and energy.

"According to Dad, I won't even be getting my degree."

"I heard!" she exclaims. "Can you believe it? Not many football players get drafted their junior year. I told all the women at the country club today. Helen Grotowski, of course, tried to trump my news with news of her son's early admittance to law school. But I heard from Bertha Stein her husband had to make a rather large donation to the school." I sit back on the bench and close my eyes, knowing my mom won't be done gossiping any time soon. Once she starts, she can go on for hours.

I grew up in Piermont, a small town in North Carolina. It's split down the middle by a set of railroad tracks. On one side is where my dad grew up, in a wealthy gated community. On the other side is where my mom grew up—in a rundown trailer park. My parents met when my mom was eighteen and my dad was twenty-five and fresh out of law school. He had just moved back to Piermont and had begun working at Shaw Management—a sports management agency my grandfather started. He met my mom when she was waitressing at a restaurant he stopped into one night after a meeting ran late. They hit it off immediately. While my grandparents weren't thrilled about my dad and her dating, she apparently adapted into my father's life quickly, and soon she was the perfect Stepford wife—although, I'm pretty sure her getting knocked up by mistake has something to do with why he married her. I also think he loved that he was able to mold her into what he wanted her to be. I imagine when you come from nothing, if given the opportunity, you'd do whatever it takes to become something.

"...so then I told Bertha that if Sherry plans to come to my birthday dinner with her mother, she needs to leave that good for nothing boyfriend of hers at home. All those tattoos. It's a disgrace. I can't believe she's dating him."

"Hey mom," I say, cutting in before she can continue. "I need to get going. I'm sorry. I'll see you Sunday, though, for dinner."

"And will you be bringing Samantha?" If my mother had it her way, Samantha would be out of the picture. While she approves of her coming from wealth, she hates that Samantha wants to work. According to my mother, women belong in the home. Which is ironic since my mom was home my entire childhood, yet I spent more time with my nanny than with both of my parents combined.

"She'll be there, Mom. Please be nice." She lets out an annoyed huff but agrees. We say goodbye then hang up. Standing, I take one more calming breath before I head into Samantha's dorm. We've been dating for the last year, and she's a junior like I am. She's majoring in business and planning to work for her father's company after she gets her MBA. Hence, the reason my mom isn't thrilled about us dating.

When I get to Samantha's door, I wiggle the doorknob, and when it doesn't open, I knock. I hear shuffling and then she opens the door slightly. Her hair is messy, and her lips are puffy. She looks like she always does when we finish having sex.

"Nick! Wh-what are you doing here? I thought you had a game."

"I did have a game...yesterday. We got back a couple hours ago, so I came to see you." Samantha's features contort into a pained expression, and I'm slowly putting the pieces together. Pushing the door open, I walk into her room to find Jesse, a friend of mine, shirtless and sitting on Samantha's bed.

"Are you guys serious?" I ask even though it's a dumb question. There's a fucking condom wrapper on the nightstand. It doesn't take a genius to figure out what the two of them were doing.

"I'm sorry, Nick, it's just that you're always playing football, and even when you're not, you never have any time to hang out." I thought she understood how important football is to me. It's not like I suddenly started playing. I've been playing since the day we met. *Hell, I've been playing pretty much since the day I could walk.* I'm attending NCU on a football scholarship, which means on top of taking a full load of classes, I have practice every day and games every weekend during season.

"How long has this been going on?"

"Since the beginning of summer. You're just always so busy and—"

"And instead of talking to me about it, you decided to fuck my friend?" I yell before I look over to Jesse. "Way to have my back, *bro*." I cut across the room and deck him straight in his face. He falls backward onto the floor, then stands but doesn't attempt to retaliate.

"I swear, we didn't mean for it to happen," Samantha cries, but I'm already halfway out the door.

"Spare me. As far as I'm concerned, you're both fucking dead to me," I shout before I walk out of her room, slamming the door behind me.

I get back to my dorm and see my friend Celeste is waiting for me. Growing up, Celeste was always around. When my mom left the trailer park, she left everyone from her old life behind, except for her best friend, Beatrice. Beatrice and my mom grew up next door to each other—two peas in a pod. The only difference between them is while my mom got knocked up by my dad and crossed over the train tracks into a life of luxury, Beatrice fell in love with a biker in a motorcycle club. The story I've heard is that he told her he had something to take care of and promised he would return. Over the years, Beatrice had the opportunity to be with several wealthy men, thanks to my mother, but she's chosen to pine after Celeste's dad, hoping one day he will come back. Seventeen years later, and he still hasn't returned.

For whatever reason, she doesn't seem to care that she's living in a trailer park, and Celeste resents the hell out of her for that. She doesn't understand why her mom would choose love over money, especially choosing to love a man who left and never returned. Her mom might be content living in a trailer park and pining after the love of her life, but Celeste isn't. While she's sixteen and still in high school, because she looks a lot older, she only gives her attention to wealthy guys. Her goal is to marry a man who is the opposite of what her mother fell in love with—wealthy and emotionless. Her plan is to show her mom that money, and the comfort it brings, is more important than love.

Celeste is beautiful, and she knows it. She's five-ten with jet black hair and big black eyes. She has a model's body—thin and leggy with minimal curves, but a decent rack—and she wants a modeling career. I don't doubt one day she'll have it. She's determined. She's already been in several commercials and ads for local stores and such.

"I saw you play on TV. Good first game." She's sitting on my bed in a pair of tiny shorts and a low-cut shirt, despite it being chilly outside. "Did you go see Samantha?" Her voice is smug, which means she already knows.

"Yeah, I caught her cheating with Jesse."

"Don't worry...I won't say I told you so." She lays back against the headboard. "I saw them last night at the club all over each other. Smart girl, Jesse's loaded."

"Whatever, Celeste." I sit on my bed next to her. Between Samantha cheating and my dad fucking up my major, I'm annoyed as hell and not in the mood for Celeste's shit. Some days, despite our four-year age difference, she's my best friend; other days, she's more like the annoying little sister I never had. "And why the hell were you even at a club? You're sixteen years old."

"It's called a fake ID. And even if I didn't have one, every bouncer in North Carolina thinks I'm of age." She rolls her eyes. "Don't change the subject. Everyone knows Jesse got his trust fund at eighteen, and he has no problem spending his money on whoever he's fucking. Maybe you should come with a warning label: I'm rich but broke." She cackles at her dumb joke. She's right, though. My dad is rich, but I'm not, which means that while my parents have always provided for me, I don't have a stuffed bank account I can access anytime I want. Hell, even after being married to my dad for over twenty years, my mom still doesn't have her own bank account. She might spend her days socializing at the country club, dining at expensive restaurants, going to the spa, or shopping for shit she will never use or wear, but it's all done with my dad's credit cards. Henry Shaw lives for control. Giving my mother or me money would mean losing a slice of that control, and that's definitely not happening.

In all honesty, I've never really cared. I have everything money can buy. I drive a nice-ass Audi A4, courtesy of my father. I have unlimited funds for food and clothes. My schooling is paid for. What I don't have is money to spend on women, and apparently, that's all women seem to care about. All through high school and college, it's been the same shit with every female. They hear I'm rich, so they expect me to be their meal ticket. They hear I'm the quarterback, so they want to latch on to my status. I'm so fucking sick of all the fakeness.

"I refuse to believe money is all people in this world care about.

I'm going to find someone who couldn't care less about money, and when I do, I'm going to love the hell out of her." Celeste cackles again and shakes her head. Since we were old enough to understand the difference between our living situations, we've had an ongoing debate. She believes money trumps love, and I believe money destroys it. My parents have a ton of money and they're miserable as fuck.

"You've always been so naïve, Nick. This isn't some fairytale. This is real life. Love is nothing more than a wasted emotion. One that only gets in the way of the important things like nice houses and cars and clothes...and eating at expensive restaurants! Oh! And vacations! And don't get me started on social status..."

"There should be more to life than all that." I grab the remote and switch the television on to Sunday football. "Money doesn't buy happiness. It just buys shit."

"You wouldn't understand," Celeste says, her voice serious. "Because you've never been without money. You've never had to worry about the electric or water being shut off. If you want to go to Colorado to ski, you go."

I don't even know why I bother to argue with her. It's always the same shit. I'm rich and my life is perfect...She's poor and her life sucks...

Celeste continues, "You'll see. All those broken hearts you've had because you keep thinking with your heart. Once you're in the NFL and making bank, you won't have to worry about all that. I guarantee once you're making your own money, girls like Samantha will be begging to be with you, but it won't be your heart they're after."

"They can come after me, but that doesn't mean I'll be with them."

"Let's be real here, Nick. Those that are poor, want to be rich, and those that are rich, only want to be richer. Plus, you've had how many failed relationships in high school and college? You should just quit while you're ahead."

I turn my head to Celeste and glare at her. "When I throw a shitty pass, I don't quit playing. I keep throwing until I get the pass right."

Celeste laughs. "You know what they say the definition of insanity is? Doing the same thing over and over again and expecting different results."

"You're such a bitch." I laugh, and Celeste hits me in the face with my pillow. "I'm going to find *her*...One day I'll find a girl who'll love me and won't want shit from me other than me."

"Okay...how about we make a pact?" She smirks. "If you haven't found love by the time you turn thirty, you'll admit I'm right. Money makes the world go round."

"Okay..." There's got to be more to this.

"And we get married."

At this, I crack up laughing. "Wasn't that in a movie once?"

"So?" She hits me with another one of my pillows.

"I'm pretty sure it didn't work out for them..."

Celeste rolls her eyes. "It was a movie. What do you have to lose? You have ten years to prove me wrong."

"Are you serious? You and me get married?" I rake my eyes down her body. Sure, Celeste is hot, in a Victoria Secret model sort of way, but she's not exactly my type. I prefer my women with a little more T and A if you catch my drift.

"Don't give me that look. I'm not attracted to you, either. If I haven't found a rich guy yet, we get married and do it my way. Not for love, but for money. I mean, c'mon...just about every NFL player you know has a model attached to his arm."

Before I can respond, my best friend, roommate, and teammate, Killian Blake, walks into our dorm, slamming the door behind him.

"What's up?" he asks, throwing his gym bag onto his bed.

"I caught Samantha fucking Jesse. Apparently, she's been cheating on me with him all damn summer."

"I told you that bitch was money-hungry." Killian shakes his head as he plops down on his bed across from us. I groan internally because apparently everyone saw it but me.

"And Celeste wants to make a pact." I laugh. "If I don't find love before I'm thirty, I marry her."

"You can't seriously be considering this?" Killian sits up, his eyes trained on me, not even acknowledging Celeste is in the room. Killian and I met our freshman year of college, when we were assigned to the same dorm room, and clicked immediately. He's a wide receiver, and I'm the quarterback. This will also be our third year sharing a room, and if my dad has it his way, it might be our last. "You realize you're making a deal with the she-devil, right?" he adds, and Celeste glares at him.

The two of them have never gotten along. Celeste has never hidden the fact that she wants a man who has money, and for that reason, Killian thinks she's a gold-digging bitch. The funny thing is, she's never denied it, never once tried to be someone she's not, and oddly enough I respect her for that. At least she isn't constantly getting her heart smashed on like I do.

I let out a low chuckle as I consider her proposition. For years, my mom and Beatrice have said Celeste and I will one day get married. I think deep down my mom is rooting for Celeste to get out of her situation like she did, but only because she's her best friend's daughter. Any other girl in Celeste's situation, my mom would be looking down on. But Celeste, she's always had a soft spot for. Like the daughter she never had.

"And what if I do find love?" I challenge Celeste.

"Well, then you'll restore my faith in love, and I'll stop looking for a rich guy and find myself a man to love." She snorts in disbelief at her own words.

"Yeah, right," Killian scoffs. "You wouldn't know what love looks like if it smacked you in the head with your high heel." I laugh, and Celeste shoots daggers his way.

"You're too young to be this jaded," I say to her.

"I'm only four years younger than you, and if we go by life experience, I'm actually ten years older."

Killian groans and falls back onto his bed, covering his face with a pillow.

"So, do we have a deal?" Celeste grins, extending her hand out to me.

"Fine," I say, and we shake hands. If by thirty, I still haven't found the one, maybe it will be time to admit Celeste is right...but I'm not ready to give up on love yet. Plus, the thought of finding love and Celeste having to give up on her 'marry-a-rich-man plan' to find her own true love will make it well worth it. "Better be ready." I smirk.

"For what?" she questions.

"To find your happily-ever-after. Once I find true love, it will be your turn." I shoot her a wink, and she rolls her eyes.

"You guys have lost your minds." Killian laughs. "Party tonight at Jase's new place. You down?"

"Hell yeah," I tell him. Jase Crawford has been a friend of mine since high school. We played football for two years together at Piermont Academy and then another two years at NCU before he graduated last year.

"I'm down," Celeste agrees, and Killian gives me a hard stare, telling me to shut it down.

"Not tonight," I say apologetically to Celeste.

"Really?" She scoffs. "It's like that?"

"Yeah, little girl, it is," Killian says. "You might have a fake ID that says you're older, but you're still only sixteen, and we're not going to be responsible for you. This is an adult party."

"Whatever." She stands. "I'll catch you later. Have fun at your *adult* party." She saunters out of the dorm room with an extra sway to her hips.

"That girl is nothing but trouble," Killian says as we watch her close the door behind her.

"Don't I know it."

ONE

"IT'S *all going to come down to this final play. If Nick Shaw can pull off this touchdown, North Carolina will be the Super Bowl champions for the fourth time since Shaw was picked up eight years ago."*

"If anybody can do it, it's Shaw."

"And he has a lot on the line. This has been a rough season for Shaw, and with his contract up this year, I imagine this will make a difference when the owners reevaluate whether to sign him again."

"It's almost as if he's a completely different guy out there. Now, I'm not saying he isn't good. We all know he is. But his numbers have steadily declined this season, and with three interceptions during this game alone, Shaw is in the spotlight."

"All right, here we go. With ten seconds on the clock, they're on Pittsburgh's ten-yard line—there's no room for error. North Carolina either scores a touchdown or Pittsburgh will be the new Super Bowl champions."

"They snap the ball...there's nobody open! The pocket's collapsing. Shaw better make a decision quick."

"He's scrambling toward the end zone!"

"He's reaching toward the goal line...he's been hit!"

"Did he get in?"

"I don't know. It's going to be close."

"It appears Shaw is still down. He's grabbing his arm, John. This can't be good."

"The ref is saying the touchdown is no good."

"They have the trainers coming out. He's still holding onto his arm."

I cringe as I watch the replay over and over again. Even with a broken arm and a dislocated shoulder, another few feet before getting tackled and we would've been the Super Bowl champions. Instead, I not only let my team down but my parents as well.

Not able to watch the video for a fifth time, I put my phone away and turn on the television. Of course, every sports station is analyzing the game. They all have opinions, assumptions, and predictions. I stop on a station that has the headline: **Will Nick Shaw be re-signed?**

"It's a tough loss, but Nick Shaw has earned them three championships. That's more than most players ever get in a career. He deserves a chance to come back."

"You're ignoring the fact he just broke his throwing arm and dislocated his shoulder. That's a lot to come back from. Plus, there's the fact he was showing a decline this year with a career high of fifteen interceptions."

Not able to take another second of listening to this shit, I turn the television off and toss the controller across the room. It hits the door and crashes down, the batteries spilling out and rolling across the floor.

The door opens and in walks my mother. Her heels clack across the tile as she flits across the hospital room like she owns it—and in her completely selfish, self-absorbed mind, she probably believes she does. Dressed impeccably in only designer labels—from her Chanel glasses to her Saint Laurent heels—you would think Victoria Shaw actually worked for a living. Well, I guess she does...if you count running my life and spending my dad's money as a job.

"Throwing another hissy fit, Nicholas?" She comes to the side of my bed and pats my arm like I'm a fucking dog. "Stop watching those shows. They thrive on negativity." One might think she's trying to give me some motherly advice, a pep talk of sorts to help me stay positive during the most fucked up time of my life, but I know better. She's trying to convince herself that her now imperfect son isn't about to disgrace the family name by becoming unemployed at twenty-nine years old.

"Would it be so bad if I did get released?" The words come out before I can stop them, and my mother looks like I just told her I'm having a limb cut off. And I guess in her eyes, it would be the equivalent, since all I am to her is the golden-boy child who plays professional football. Without my career, what would she have to brag about? What would she say to her stuck-up country club friends? And my dad, if I'm released, he'll lose his twenty percent agent fee he makes off me. What would we even have to talk about? I mean, without football, what else is there?

"Nicholas! Don't say that!" my mom shrieks. "This is because of your girlfriend, isn't it? I know she hates you playing. We didn't come this far for you to just give up now..." I tune her out as I think about how everything I've worked my entire life for is about to go down the drain, but for some reason, I'm not worried about what I'm about to lose, what my parents are about to lose, but rather what I might gain.

My girlfriend, Fiona, has made a few comments about wanting to get married and settle down. She doesn't like how often players are away from their families and said she would feel like she's a single parent. Maybe now would be the right time to settle down and start a family.

As my mom continues to nag me over my comment about getting released, I pray the nurse will come in soon to give me more pain meds. I was transported back home to North Carolina—from Baltimore—where the Super Bowl was held—immediately after I was taken off the field. Once the team doctors assessed and prepped me, they performed surgery on my arm. Then we had to wait for the swelling to go down enough for the doctors to see how it went. So here I am, stuck in this fucking hospital, living on pain meds and waiting for the doctor to make an appearance to read me my future.

The nurse, who was here earlier flirting with me, said she'll be back with the doctor in a little while when he makes his rounds. It doesn't matter what he says, though. Mandatory surgery due to a broken arm plus a dislocated shoulder can only mean two things: time off and physical therapy. And at almost thirty years old, even with three Super Bowl wins, there's no way North Carolina is going to renew my contract.

I replay my mother's words in my head. *We didn't come this far for you to just give up now.* What a fucking joke. My parents have ridden my ass for as long as I can remember. From playing pee-wee football to high school ball. From playing College ball to me dropping out of college a year early to enter the draft. I've done everything their way, worked my ass off, made choices I didn't want to make, and I'm fucking exhausted. *We* haven't come anywhere. I've come this far. Not my mom. Not my dad. Me! I'm the one who practiced every damn day. I chose football over having a life. And what the hell for? My mom wants me to play for the status and fame. My dad wants me to play for the money. What I can't seem to remember at the moment is why the hell I want to play.

"Are you listening to me?" I open my eyes and see my mother glaring at me, her resting bitch face even more prominent than usual. I can't even recall the last time she smiled. She's so concerned over the possibility of me choosing my girlfriend over football. She's my mom. Shouldn't she want her son to put his girlfriend first? Isn't that what you do when you love someone? Ha! Love...I don't think she's capable of such an emotion. At least not by the definition most would go by. Does she love her home? Yes. Her car? Definitely. Does she love shopping? Without a doubt. Does she love my dad? Or me? I think once upon a time she did...but now the only thing she loves is what we can do for her.

Before I can answer, my father strolls through the door. "Victoria." He gives her a chaste kiss on her cheek before approaching my bed. That's the extent of their affection. "How're you feeling?" he asks me.

"Shitty," I answer honestly. The door opens again and in walks my girlfriend. She smiles sadly as she approaches my bed.

"Hey." She leans in and gives me a kiss. Her lips are soft and sweet, and for a brief moment I feel like everything is right in the world. "How are you feeling?"

"Okay. Waiting for the doctor to come in and tell me my fate."

"If you can't play again..." Fiona swallows thickly. "It won't be the end of the world."

"You can't be serious!" my mom hisses.

"Mom, stop," I say, hoping to prevent an argument between my girlfriend and my mom. It won't be the first one.

"No, Nicholas! She doesn't want you to play, yet she has no problem spending the money you make from playing."

"I don't spend his money, Victoria," Fiona shoots back.

"Your school? Apartment? All the bills?" my mom volleys.

"Enough, Victoria," my dad snaps. "The doctor will be here soon. Please get control of yourself. Fiona, it's probably best if you leave. Nick can call you with an update."

Fiona's eyes widen.

"Dad," I hiss.

"Nick, we have a lot of shit to figure out. I don't have time for your mom and girlfriend to be going at it like children. I have a business to run. So, it's either your mother or your girlfriend."

My dad doesn't say another word—already back on his phone, furiously typing away.

"Fiona," I say with a sigh, and she shakes her head. "I want you here." I take her hand in my good one. "I just don't want to argue with them."

"You never do, Nick." She walks out of the door, and I wish I could chase after her, but I can't.

"Knock, knock," the doctor says before the door is even finished closing. His lips are upturned in a sympathetic smile as he walks into the room, the nurse from earlier following behind him. "How are you feeling, Mr. Shaw?"

"I'm in a bit of pain," I answer truthfully, hoping they can give me something to knock me out so everyone will leave me the hell alone.

"Nurse Karson can take care of that for you." He nods toward the nurse who then scurries over to my bedside and switches something on to release more meds into my IV.

My father gets straight to the point. "What's the prognosis, doc?" It's always about business with him, and since right now, I'm the highest paid quarterback in the NFL, if I can't play, my dad will be losing a shit ton of money. Because at the end of the day, twenty percent of zero is zero. With my contract being up this year, I don't see them keeping me on. There's a lot the team can do with the millions of dollars they pay me.

I glance toward my dad, who has a worried look marring his features, and feel a twinge of sadness. In my father's eyes, all I am is a football player. If it weren't for me playing, we wouldn't even have a relationship. And if I can't play, where will that leave us? I won't be bringing anything to the table, and as a result, he'll no longer have any use for me.

"The surgery went smoothly. My recommendation is time off for ten months to a year, minimum. He's going to need extensive physical therapy..." He continues on with his doctor talk, but I'm no longer listening. I'm looking at the disappointment on my father's face. The sadness in my mother's eyes. Other than football, I can't remember a single thing I've ever done to make them proud. It didn't matter that I was a straight A student, or that I volunteered after school for the literacy program to help kids who couldn't read. They never went to any of my Math Elite matches or attended any of my engineering competitions.

But every Friday night, they would be in the stands to watch me play. My mom would cheer for me throughout the entire game, and my dad would spend the entire next day strategizing for the next game. And it was during those moments, I felt like they actually saw me—that they actually cared. I thought her cheering me on and him strategizing with me was us being a family. But now I'm starting to wonder if it was love or greed. My guess is toward the latter.

As I stare at the both of them, I consider telling them to go fuck themselves. That they can take my money and status and shove it up their asses. But I can't do that. Because at the end of the day, they're my parents, and like any child, I want them to love me and be proud of me. I let out a heavy sigh, my heart cracking as I come to the realization it might not even matter. Without my job or income, neither of them will need or want me.

"Nick." I snap back to the present to see the team owner, Edwin Smith, and my coach, Reggie Frazier, standing in front of me. The doctor has apparently left, and everyone is staring at me. "You okay?" Coach asks, and I lift my chin up and down robotically.

"We need to talk," Mr. Smith says, and I nod again. "The doctor filled us in..." Of course he did, because he's the team doctor. They probably knew my prognosis before I did. "It's not personal..." Like fuck it's not. I give them eight fucking years and three super bowl rings, and the minute I'm no good to them, they drop me like a bad habit. "We just feel at this time it's best to part ways. After careful consideration, we've made the decision to take the team in a different direction."

Fuck, have I always worn rose-colored glasses? How did I not notice all of the greed and selfishness around me? Probably because up until this moment, it's been smooth sailing. My numbers have only increased. My income and bank account only growing. I allowed everyone around me to use me while I basked in the artificial feeling of being wanted and needed while believing I was making everyone happy.

My mom starts to frantically argue and beg. She doesn't give a shit about my job, or about the fact that my entire life has been about ball since I was a kid and my father realized I could throw like a pro. She doesn't give two fucks that I'm not even thirty years old and my football career might be over. She cares about one thing: how this will look to her stuck-up country club friends.

"Mom." She ignores me. "Mom!" I yell louder, but she just keeps going on and on. "Mom!" I shout, and everyone looks at me. "Stop!" I glare at her and see she has actual tears in her eyes. I don't think I've ever seen her cry before. "Coach, Mr. Smith...thank you for coming by to let me know."

"If anything changes..." Mr. Smith starts to say but doesn't finish. We both know my career with North Carolina is over. There's no point in making false promises he can't—and won't—keep.

"Thank you," I respond politely.

They leave, closing the door behind them, and then my father starts. "This is just a temporary setback. This isn't the end, Nick. Rest up, do your physical therapy, and next year we'll get you back on a team and making money again." He says all this while he's typing away on his phone. "I need to take this. It's Roger Cedarbeck, the rookie offensive tackle. We're in negotiations." Bringing the phone up to his ear—not even bothering to look at me—he walks out, leaving only my mother and me in the room. *Guess some things never change.*

"Well, since you'll be available, we can schedule luncheons and charity events. We can find ways to make you look good in the public eye. As soon as you get out, we'll go over the social calendar." She gives me a kiss on my forehead, and then she's gone, leaving me alone.

The doctor comes back in and lets me know I'll be discharged from the hospital by the end of the day tomorrow. Not wanting to text Fiona and ask her for a ride since she left here upset, I put a call in to the car service I use often and arrange for someone to pick me up tomorrow.

"I DON'T LOVE you anymore, Nick, and I can't be in this relationship another damn day." I'm sitting on the couch in my apartment, listening to my girlfriend explain why she's leaving me. When I arrived home, I found all of her stuff already loaded into a U-Haul truck. The only reason why we're even having this conversation is because she thought I wouldn't be home for another couple days. She was planning to leave with nothing more than a note and her apartment keys on the counter.

"Okay, so let me get this straight. You loved me a week ago...hell, supposedly you loved me two days ago...but now you no longer love me?" I ask, confused as fuck. "So, all the talk about wanting to get married and have a baby...it was what, just talk?"

"It was me being stupid. I have no family or support, and your parents, they would make horrible grandparents." She cringes. "Plus, you always put them and your job first. I need a man who actually puts me first."

"I'm right here. I'm putting you first." *Was my paying for all of our bills and her schooling not putting her first?*

"Until next season...then you'll be back to playing football, and I'll be stuck here by myself. I have dreams, and I need to follow them, and starting a family with you is no longer one of my dreams. To be honest..." Fiona pauses. Her eyes close, and a second later they reopen with a look of such contempt, I can feel it down to my bones. "I would consider it a nightmare." She lifts her purse over her shoulder and says, "Honestly, Nick, I don't think I ever really loved you" and walks out the door, slamming it behind her.

Well, damn...okay, then.

My head hits the back of the couch as I think about how much my life has already changed because of my injury. My dad hasn't once called me since the doctor gave us the verdict—not even to see if I made it home okay. My mom's one and only text was regarding the charity functions she thinks I should attend to keep myself in the public eye. And Fiona, as you can see, just walked out the door and out of my life.

Maybe it's time for me to make a change. Time to put myself first. There's no way I'm staying here for the next year and attending charity functions with my mom. Grabbing my phone from the coffee table, I shoot a text to Killian. The year after I was drafted, he was drafted to New York. We might not be roommates anymore, but we're still best friends.

Me: I'm out. Minimum 10 months. They let me go.
Kill: Fuck. What are you going to do?
Me: If it were up to my mom… charity functions.
Kill: Fuck that.
Me: You up for some company?
Kill: Fuck yeah! But what about Fiona?
Me: Apparently she's looking for her next meal ticket.
Kill: Bitch. Where are you now?
Me: Home
Kill: Get your ass up here!
Me: I'll get everything settled here and be on my way in the next few days.
Kill: I'll get a room ready.
Me: And the women.

One thing that I've learned from Fiona is that it doesn't matter how much you give or try, it's never enough, and I'm done doing both. Fuck my parents, and fuck Fiona, and fuck love. It's time to get fucked.

Kill: That's a given.

He says women are a given, but the truth is, I haven't seen Killian with a woman in years, not since our sophomore year. The guy went from practically sleeping his way through the student body to barely looking at a woman. I'm not sure what happened, but he refuses to talk about it. Anytime I see him at a football function or charity event, he always has a woman on his arm, but in all the years I've stayed with him or vice versa, I've never seen him bring a woman home or spend the night out with one.

TWO

NICK
   Fourteen Months Later

WE'RE SITTING in a booth in Club Envy, partying like we do most nights. Only tonight, we're partying with a purpose.

"Bro! You fucking nailed those tryouts. You and me," Killian shouts over the music. "You and me! We're going all the way!" We clink glasses, and Killian announces "My boy is back!" before we both throw back our shots. It takes everything in me to tamper down the nagging feeling that once again somebody is after me for what I can do for him. But I remind myself that Killian isn't like that. He's not like my parents, who both went radio silent—after my mom threw a fit—when I up and moved to New York, or the women who only want me for what I can give them: materialistic possessions, trips, nights out at expensive restaurants. The tabloids say I'm a manwhore, a playboy of sorts, but you know what? Those women who spread their legs with dollar signs in their eyes aren't any better. I tried the hearts and flowers route and look where it got me...so don't judge me when I finally come to my senses and give everyone what they want.

For the last year, Killian is the only person who has had my back. After putting my condo on the market and having my shit shipped to New York, I chartered a plane and refused to look back. I've been living with Killian at his place, and it's been like one long party. On the days he's home, he helps me with rehab, and he's done it without knowing if I'll ever be able to play again. So, no, Killian isn't like that. I know that, but sometimes I have to remind myself. When it's all you know, it's hard to accept otherwise. I heard through the grapevine Fiona is still attending dance school and living it up in North Carolina in a nice as hell apartment. Seeing as she was broke as fuck when we met tells me one thing: she did, indeed, find her next meal ticket.

"I think I spot Melissa. I'll be back." Killian fist bumps me before walking away to find his friend. They hang out more often than not, but nothing seems to ever come of it. I look to my left and then my right. I've got a woman on each side of me, both fake blondes, and both vying for my attention. One is rubbing up on my dick while the other is licking down my neck. I bring another shot to my lips as I ignore the buzzing in my pocket indicating I have a phone call coming in—most likely one of my parents who are back to acknowledging I exist since there's a good possibility I'll be getting my career back tomorrow. I wouldn't be surprised if they're both on a plane heading to New York right now.

I press my finger against my pocket to stop the vibration, and when it starts up again, I pull it out and shut off my phone. Tomorrow, I'll deal with them. Tonight, I'll pretend they don't exist. After all, they spent the last year pretending I don't exist.

When I look up from my phone, I spot the most gorgeous fucking woman I've ever seen, standing at the bar. She's wearing a black lacy top and matching shorts. Her brown hair is down in waves, and she's sporting the most adorable pout as she tries to get the bartender's attention.

Not giving the two women on either side of me another glance, I shoo them off me and make my way to the bar. "Can I buy you a drink?" I whisper into the woman's ear as I approach her from behind. She angles her head to look at me then graces me with the most beautiful, shy smile before she shakes her head no.

"No, thank you. I can buy my own...if the damn bartender would ever look my way." Her face scrunches up in anger, and I have to hold back a laugh. She waves her hand out with a bill between her fingers, and I can't take my eyes off her. Dark brown hair, chocolate-brown eyes, and creamy, porcelain skin. Her natural beauty stands out like a shiny diamond in a room filled with dirty stones. Amongst all the fakeness in New York, this woman screams, 'real.' Of course, that's what I thought about Fiona and look where that got me.

I raise my finger in the air, and the bartender immediately makes her way over. "What can I get for you, baby?"

I turn toward Brown-Eyes. "What would you like to drink?"

At first, she looks stunned, but then her face contorts into a look of annoyance mixed with anger. "Seriously?" She rolls her eyes, and I shrug. I don't know why she's shocked. Everyone knows who I am here in this city. "I'll take two vodka cranberries," she says to the bartender then places a twenty on the bar top. The bartender nods, then she turns her attention to me. "What're you having?"

"Her...I'm having her." I point to the woman next to me. This time, the bartender rolls her eyes, unamused, while Brown-Eyes snorts in amusement. "But for now, I'll take a couple shots of Patron."

"Sure thing." The bartender goes to grab the woman's twenty, but I pull out a fifty before she can. She takes my bill—leaving hers —slips it into her bra, and walks away to make the drinks.

"So, two vodka cranberries?" *Please don't let her be here with another guy.*

"One is for my friend. She's somewhere around here. She ran into a guy she knows when we were walking in." *Thank God!*

She looks around in search of her friend before her brown eyes come back to me, giving me a once over. This is where I expect her to recognize me, figure out who I am and milk it for all its worth, and believe me, I most definitely will.

But instead, she gives me a small smile, takes her twenty off the bar top, and says, "Thank you," shrugging nonchalantly.

"No problem. But now you owe me." I shoot her a playful wink.

"Oh really...even *after* I tried to buy our drinks?"

"Yep." I hold back a grin.

"And what is it I owe you?" She cocks her head to the side, a small ghost of a smile playing on her lips.

The bartender comes back over and sets our drinks down in front of us. I grab one of the shots and hand it to her. "A shot."

She throws her head back in laughter, and I know I've got her. And fuck, if her sexy laugh doesn't have me.

"SHOT! SHOT! SHOT! SHOT!" Lifting the shot with my mouth from the middle of Brown-Eyes' perky tits, I tilt my head back and swallow it in one gulp. The Patron burns going down, the warmth settling in my stomach. I hold the shot glass up for everyone to see, and the crowd erupts in cheers and applause. We've been drinking for the last hour, and I still don't even know the woman's name. But what I do know is, I'm deeply and madly...in lust with everything about her.

She grabs her shot and downs it, her slim sexy-as-fuck neck on display, begging for my lips to kiss it. Closing the gap between us, I pull her tiny waist into my body. My arms wrap around her backside, and my hands land on her tight little round ass. "Dance with me," I murmur into her ear. My tongue darts out to lick the bottom of her earlobe. Chills rush down her arms as I feel her physically shiver.

She nods in agreement, and I pull her in closer. Our bodies are flush against each other. Our skin sweaty. I'm not quite drunk, but I'm definitely tipsy, enough that I'm nuzzling my face into her hair and sniffing her sexy perfume. It's sweet and has my dick twitching, wanting to know what else on this woman is sweet. My lips move to her neck, and I trail kisses downward toward her collarbone. Her head rests on my shoulder as our bodies grind against one another to the pulsating dance music that's infiltrating the club's speakers. It's loud, and we don't speak, allowing our bodies to do all the talking for us.

"Yo, bro!" I hear Killian yell to me over the loud music and chatter in the club. "I'm out." I look up long enough to lock eyes with him. I was curious as to why I haven't seen him much tonight, but the doe-eyed woman by his side answers my question. He found Melissa. I tilt my chin up in acknowledgement then bring my attention back to the woman in my arms.

Gliding my hand over her ass and up her back, I grip the back of her head, entwining my fingers in her thick mane, and pull back enough so she can make eye contact with me.

"Are you drunk?"

She looks up at me and shakes her head. "No."

"Want to get out of here?"

Her lids are hooded over with lust, and she bites down on her bottom lip as she considers my question. What I thought was an act —her not knowing who I am—I'm starting to think isn't one after all. Because let's be real, if she knew who I was, she wouldn't even be contemplating whether or not to leave with me. I'm Nick fucking Shaw. Any woman who knows who I am would be begging *me* to leave with them. I have a reputation of being stellar in the sack, which I take seriously. And even if I sucked in bed, they would still come because money talks. Now, with all the buzz about the possibility of me signing a multi-million-dollar contract tomorrow, women are all over me trying to get on this money train. So, as I watch this woman consider whether it's a good idea or not to leave with me, I'm thinking she has no clue who the hell I am.

"Okay," she finally says, a small smile playing on her deliciously bee-stung lips that look like they were made to be wrapped around my cock. "Let me text my friend and let her know I'm leaving." Her friend and the guy she ran into joined us earlier for a quick drink, but then they excused themselves to dance.

Grabbing her by her hand, I guide her toward the side exit of the club. I'm going to have to hail a cab since we've both been drinking. The last thing I need is to get a DUI when I'm about to be back on a team playing ball again.

Just as we're about to leave, I spot Celeste, and her eyes meet mine. I give her a chin-jerk toward the door to let her know I'm leaving, and she rolls her eyes at me. She's used to me leaving with a different woman from the club.

"I'm staying at the Ritz," Brown-Eyes says once we're outside. "It's only one block over."

"Sounds good to me."

We head to her hotel in silence. We walk through the lobby, and she presses the button for the elevator. Once we're inside, she says, "I know it's probably going to sound cliché, but I've never done this before." Her honesty paralyzes me. She's a complete contradiction to everything I've ever known. I'm used to women who make a career out of bedding guys like me.

Pushing her gently against the elevator wall, I brush my lips against hers. They're soft and plump and taste fruity, and they have me craving more. "I'll take care of you." I give her another kiss, this time my tongue pushes into her mouth. Our tongues swirl against one another as our kiss deepens. She pulls back slightly, her chest rising and falling quickly as she catches her breath.

"I don't even know your name." Her words come out breathless, and I find myself wanting to know what she'll sound like when she's calling out my name. Then it hits me. She just said she doesn't know my name, confirming she has no idea who I am. I look into her eyes, trying to find some type of untruth in her words, but all I see is a beautiful, brown-eyed woman staring at me with want in her eyes. Not want for my money or status or fame, but just plain and simple want. This woman is either going to win an academy award for her acting skills or she's telling the truth.

"I'm Cole."

"I'm Liv." Her lips upturn into a small, shy smile as I take her in. She's fucking beautiful. From her silky brown hair to the slight pink tint on her cheeks that tells me she really is this innocent. The elevator dings, and I follow her lead, not knowing where we're going. Once we get to her room, she pulls a key out of the back pocket of her short shorts, which show off her toned legs, and walks in first. I follow behind, my eyes raking down her body, landing on her muscular calves and her sexy fuck-me heels.

She stops in the center of the room and catches me checking her out.

Averting my eyes, I notice this is a multi-room suite. "Is your friend staying here with you?"

"Yes, the one you met briefly at the club. She's still there catching up with her friend, but she'll be back later." Smart woman...letting me know someone will be here soon.

"Got it."

Placing her hand in mine, she guides me to her room, closing the door behind us. The room is dark, the only light shining in through the curtains from the New York City skyline. The light hits her face, and she looks worried.

"You okay?" I ask, framing the sides of her face with my hands. Her cheeks are warm, and if it wasn't so dark, I would bet they are flushed pink with need.

"Yeah."

"You sure?" I ask again, wanting to make sure we're on the same page.

"I'm sure. I want you. I want this." Her hands grip my shirt, lifting it over my head. Her fingers trail down my torso, landing on my belt. When I don't move, she stops. "Do you...want this?" Her question is filled with self-doubt. She thinks I've changed my mind. Has this woman lost her damn mind?

"Fuck yes, I do. I've wanted you since the moment you walked into the club."

Instead of continuing with my belt, Liv steps forward and places a soft kiss on my pectoral muscle right above my heart. I stand there, frozen in my spot, watching her place kiss after kiss along my chest and down my torso. She kneels down so she's parallel to my crotch and looks up at me, her brown eyes connecting with my green. She has a look of mischief on her face as she places an open-mouthed kiss right where my dick is bulging through my boxers and jeans.

"Fucking tease." I laugh, and she giggles. Her eyes break the connection as she becomes a woman on a mission. She unbuckles my belt, unbuttons my pants, then pulls the zipper down. When she yanks my jeans down, she takes my boxers with them, and my hard cock springs to attention. Toeing off my shoes, I kick them, along with my pants, to the side.

My eyes stay trained on her as she takes my shaft in her hand. She lifts it up until it's almost hitting my stomach and then she languorously licks the entire underside like she's savoring every fucking inch of me. I let out a groan at the feeling of her wet tongue running along my flesh. When she gets to the head, a bit of pre-cum is beaded over. Her tongue darts out and licks the cream, and I about lose my shit. I grab her by her hair, my hand fisting her mane. Pulling her up, I lack all the patience she possesses. She pulls her top off and unclasps her bra. I toss her onto the bed, then yank her shorts and panties off.

I push her legs back, and my head is between her thighs in mere seconds, lapping at her wet fucking cunt. The heady moan she lets out in response only spurs me on. I lick and suck on her clit, but it's not enough. I need more. I need to feel her. I push my fingers inside her. She's warm and wet, and fuck, she's so goddamn tight. I want to be inside her, but I need to make her come first. I lap and lave up her slit, my tongue pushing on her clit, and finally, she fucking comes all over my tongue and fingers, her juices spilling onto the bed sheets.

Not able to wait another second, I'm up on my knees, condom ripped open and rolled on, and pushing into her. Her head rolls back, her chin lifting, as her back arches. And then she's meeting me thrust for thrust as we chase our orgasms.

"I. Need. It. Harder," she groans out. Grabbing her ass, I flip her over onto her knees, her round ass in the air. I give it a hard smack, and then I'm pushing back into her from behind. My fingers dig into her hips as I piston in and out of her, bottoming out. I can feel her trembling around my cock in pleasure, and then her cunt starts to choke my dick like a goddamned vice grip as she comes for a second time. Not able to last a second longer, I pull out and rip the condom off my dick, preparing to come all over her ass. But before I do, she turns around, and taking my dick in her hand, strokes me up and down until I'm releasing my seed all over her luscious fucking tits. And holy hell, if the sight of my jizz dripping down her breasts doesn't have me hard all over again. I swipe my finger across her taut nipple, and her body shivers.

"Open your mouth," I demand, and she obeys. I run my cum-covered finger over her lips, painting them a creamy white, then I push my finger inside her mouth. Her tongue darts out and her lips close. She sucks my finger clean, her eyes closing as she lets out a breathy moan. When her eyes open back up, she grants me a mischievous grin.

"How about a shower?" I suggest, and she nods in agreement.

Once we're both cleaned up, we lay down in her bed. Usually this is the moment when I make up some bullshit excuse as to why I need to leave, but for some reason, I don't want to go anywhere.

"Tell me about yourself," I find myself saying.

"What do you want to know?" she asks.

"Tell me something you love."

"I love art." Her smile is bright and wide. "What about you? What do you love?"

"Playing football." The words are out before I can stop them. I expect her to ask me about it, but she doesn't.

"Tell me something you hate," she asks instead.

"Playing football."

She gives me an incredulous look. "Explain."

And for the first time, I tell Liv something I've never told anyone. "I love playing football because I'm good at it. I love the rush I feel when I'm out on the field. The thrill of the plays. What I don't love about football is everything else."

"Like?"

"Like the fact that if football didn't exist, my parents probably wouldn't know I'm alive." And now I sound like a whiny little bitch... "Tell me something you hate," I say, changing the subject.

"Switzerland."

We both laugh. "Switzerland? What the hell did Switzerland ever do to you?"

"A guy I was dating left me to move there." She shrugs. "I gave him three years, and he didn't even give me a second thought as he packed up and left."

I pull Liv closer and into my arms. "It's his loss, trust me." I bring my lips to hers and thank my lucky stars for that dumbass leaving her. His loss is definitely my gain.

MY EYES OPEN SLOWLY, but quickly close when the sunlight shining through the window adds to my fast-growing headache. I groan as my head throbs. It takes me a second to remember where I am and what I did last night—or I should say *who* I did last night. The sucking, the fucking, the talking for hours, the falling asleep with Liv in my arms. Waking up and needing more of her. Pulling her on top of me, and her riding my cock until we both came. Falling asleep sticky and satiated.

Some would think I'm crazy, but I think I could fall in love with this woman. What started out as lust turned into something more as the night went on. Between the fucking and talking, I found myself craving Liv in a way I haven't wanted a woman since Fiona left me. And if I'm honest, I don't even think I ever wanted Fiona like this.

I roll back over, feeling for Liv's warm body, wanting to hold and touch her. I want to ask her for her phone number. One night wasn't enough. I need more time. More nights and days. Only there's no warmth. It's cold. My eyes dart open, and I glance around until I spot a note on the pillow.

> ***Have a flight to catch. Check-out is 10:00. Thanks for last night. –Liv***

My heart constricts as I crumple up the note and throw it onto the floor, suddenly feeling pissed off and used. Why doesn't it surprise me the one woman I've met in the last year I thought might be different, isn't? Just like everyone else, once I was no longer of use to her, she walked out without even a backward glance, showing me once again people are only in it for what they can take from you.

After I'm dressed and make sure I have everything I came with, I head out. As I'm snagging a cab, Celeste texts me, asking to meet up for breakfast. She moved here after she graduated from high school in hopes of having a career as a model. Using my connections, I was able to get her into a summer internship program with a modeling company, which got her foot in the door. She now makes a more-than decent living and her name is definitely out there. You can find her picture on several billboards throughout the city. She also has her own successful makeup and accessories line and has been on shows like America's Elite Model as one of the judges. But she's still not satisfied. She's always striving for more. She's one of the most hard-working and determined women I've ever known.

When we were younger, I thought for sure she would latch on to some rich guy and ride his coat tail, but I was wrong. Celeste is independent and career-focused. Don't get me wrong, the men she dates are always wealthy, and if it's possible she's even more cold and emotionless than she was when she was younger, but since she moved here, she's different. She no longer comes across like she needs a man. Maybe it's because she has her own money. I don't know. As close as we are, she doesn't open up to me about that kind of stuff. She travels a lot for work, but when she's in town we hang out often.

We meet at Buvette in West Village and are seated immediately. After she orders a mimosa, and I order a coffee, she says, "So today's the big day, huh?"

"Yep, I find out in a couple hours if New York is going to take a chance on me."

"You nervous?"

"I guess." I shrug. The truth is my mind is still on the beautiful brown-eyed woman who rocked my world and then skipped out.

"You guess? What's up with you?"

The waiter sets down our drinks, and Celeste takes a sip of her mimosa while I pour a bit of milk into my coffee.

"That woman last night..."

"The one you left with?"

"Yeah. She skipped out on me this morning."

Celeste cackles. "Aww...you poor baby. You got left before you could do the leaving."

"It's not that." I take a sip of my coffee. "I thought maybe..." I shake my head. "I thought maybe there was something there. Something more." I cringe at my confession as I wait for Celeste to give me shit.

And of course she does. "Oh God, Nick. You didn't really think a woman you met at a club was going to fall in love with you. You're an NFL player."

"She didn't know that, though," I point out.

"Oh, c'mon! Of course she did." Celeste laughs. The waiter comes back over, and we order breakfast. Once he leaves, Celeste says, "Sometimes I wonder if you're really related to Henry and Victoria. You're so damn gullible."

"Because I wanted to fall in love instead of being in a money and status driven marriage like my parents?" I volley back.

"No, because even though you've had your heart stomped on and used repeatedly by everyone around you, you refuse to see life for what it really is." I notice when she says this, her lips turn down into a frown, and I wonder if maybe Celeste has had her heart broken. I don't bother asking, though. If she has, she would never admit it. She hates appearing weak or vulnerable.

"Well, then you'll be happy to know I've given up. Money

makes the world go round. Women are heartless, and my parents don't know the meaning of love. You win, I lose."

"Are you saying what I think you're saying?" Celeste leans in toward me, and I'm confused by her question.

"That I'm done with love? Yeah." I shrug. "I mean, I pretty much gave up on it after Fiona left me. And after Liv left me a note this morning..." I release a humorless chuckle. "I think it's time I throw in the towel and admit defeat."

"No, not all that." Celeste shakes her head. "Although, that information definitely helps. But what I meant was..." She bites her bottom lip nervously. "You're thirty."

"Yeah, so?" I shrug. "And you're twenty-six," I point out, not understanding her need to remind me of my age. The waiter sets our food down in front of us, and I grab my fork to dig in.

"Our pact when you were in college," Celeste says. "If you didn't find true love by thirty, you would marry me."

My fork falls out of my hand and clatters against the plate.

THREE

*N*ICK

"YOUR TRYOUT and evaluation were top notch, and the doctor signed off on your physical..." I'm trying to focus on what's being said in probably the most important meeting of my career, but my mind is completely fucked up at the moment. First off, I can't seem to get Liv off my mind, which is really fucking stupid because other than knowing her first name, nothing else I know about her will help me find her. She said in her note she had a flight to catch, which most likely means she doesn't even live here...or maybe she does and she's leaving on a trip. But then why would she be staying in a hotel? I tried to get the front desk to give me some information on her, but they wouldn't budge. I shouldn't have even tried. If she wanted to see me again, she would've woken me up or left her number. She did neither.

And then there's the fact that I'm actually considering making good on the pact I made with Celeste all those years ago. When I agreed to her terms, I imagined by thirty I would be married with kids. But after having dealt with Fiona, my string of one-night stands this past year, and then Liv leaving this morning, I'm beginning to think maybe Celeste has the right idea. Fiona said it herself, I would make a horrible father, and the one woman in the past year I actually wanted to get to know better left without a trace the morning after. Clearly, I'm doing something wrong here, so maybe it's time I do things Celeste's way... Jesus, to even be considering this must mean I've lost my damn mind.

"We would like to offer you a one-year contract, ten million—"

"Absolutely not!" my father booms, cutting off Declan Thomas, the owner of the New York Brewers. "You know damn well Mr. Shaw is worth double those numbers."

"If he's successful," Stephen Harper, the new coach, points out. "It's a risk, but one I'm willing to take."

"He's hardly a risk," my dad says. "You saw him out there with your receiver. This team's about to get its first Super Bowl win in over a decade."

"Henry, let's not get ahead of ourselves here," Declan says.

"I'll take it." Everybody's gaze swings to me.

"What are you doing?" my father hisses. It's been over a year since I've even seen the man who walked out the door at the hospital and has barely spoken five words to me since then. When Killian mentioned our college playing days to the new coach, he asked to meet with me. Of course, that meant contacting my agent on file. My dad was on the next flight out, dollar signs flashing in his eyes—my mother right beside him. For a while there, I forgot why I was playing football. I was so caught up in trying to make my parents proud of me, I lost my love of the sport along the way. This last year has been eye-opening.

Now, playing football is about me—what I want. If I'm going to bust my ass, it's going to be because of my love for the game and not because of the money, status, or fame. And it's definitely not going to be to make my parents give a fuck about me. Being with Liv last night, I thought maybe was a sign—reminding me love could still exist—but her walking away only reconfirmed why I'm done. Football is the only damn love I have left, and I'm going to give it my all.

"We're coming up to the end of free agency. I'm happy here, and I want to play." This past year has been fun, like an extended vacation. I've worked hard in physical therapy, and I've partied even harder. But now I'm ready to get back out there and play again. I didn't bust my ass this last year rehabilitating my throwing arm to be out for another year because I refuse to take a deal from a team who's willing to give me a shot.

Sure, with a month left of free agency, there's still a chance another team will offer me a deal, but what if they don't? And even if they did, that would mean moving. Plus, signing with New York means playing on the same team as Killian.

"Does your ass hurt?" my dad asks. I know he's pissed because, for once, I'm actually going against him. Up until I was injured, I've done everything he's advised. Where to go to college, what to study, when to leave college, who to play for...but I'm done going along with everything he says.

"I'll make sure to ask for some lube." I shoot him a condescending smirk, and he throws his hands up in the air. He's only peeved about this deal because the less I accept means the less he pockets. He doesn't give a shit that I'm actually going to be on a team and able to play. He doesn't give a fuck that I busted my ass day after day in physical therapy. Most guys at my age would've said fuck it and retired. I've made enough in the last eight years to last me a lifetime. I'm no longer playing for the money—I'm playing for the love of the game.

"There is one condition," Mr. Thomas says slowly.

"Okay."

"We need you to settle down."

"What?" I ask, confused.

"This past year you've managed to party in probably every club on the East Coast, as well as screw most of the female population. You've lost most of your endorsements, and nobody is going to take you seriously if you don't start acting like the thirty-year-old man you are."

"I lost those endorsements because of my injury," I point out.

"True, but you won't get them back if you keep acting like the playboy of NYC."

"What are you saying?"

"I'm saying, it's time to settle down."

"What the hell does that mean?"

"It means no more partying. No more drinking. No more one-night stands." Mr. Thomas places a piece of paper on the table. "You were seen leaving a hotel this morning in the same clothes you were seen in last night."

I pull the paper closer to examine it. It's a printout from something a trashy tabloid posted online. In the image my tall frame is hovering over Liv's petite body, hiding her face.

"I didn't know we were being watched."

"You've spent the last year being filmed and photographed while partying. We can't have that if you're playing for this team."

Coach Harper adds, "You're going to be the face of this team, the man who's hopefully going to lead us to a championship, and you're going to need to act like it. Nobody wants to root for a guy who's spending his time sleeping with half of New York. Got it?"

"Got it," I agree.

"Excellent!" Mr. Thomas clasps his hands together. "Now that we have that figured out, let's get this contract signed."

FOUR

*N*ICK
  Nine months later

"ALL RIGHT, guys. This is it. We've worked too hard not to make it to the playoffs now. Let's finish this." We're huddled up on San Francisco's twenty-yard line. There's only twelve seconds left in our season, and we're down by four points. As I look around at all the cheering fans in the stadium, I have a bout of déjà vu. Only this time, I'm not playing for North Carolina but instead for New York. We get this touchdown, and we make the playoffs. We don't, and there's a chance this is the last game I'll ever play. I feel a twinge of pain radiate down my arm, reminding me this game has to end differently.

The guys are all pumped up and ready to win this game. I call out the play, "FB West right slot 372 Y stick on three, break!" And then we take our positions on the field. On my three-count, the center hikes the ball. Taking a three-step drop, I find Killian and see he has a step on the defender. I throw the ball to him, a bit too high —my nerves getting the best of me—to avoid the interception—and like always, he comes through in the clutch, catching the ball in the end zone for the touchdown. The rest of the team joins him as we celebrate our win and our spot in the playoffs.

Every game we win leaves me feeling exhilarated. I've learned over the last several months my one and only true love is football.

It's all I need. Sometimes when I wish for more, I remind myself of what *more* means in my life. And then I accept my life for what it is. I'm damn blessed, and it would be selfish of me to want more.

We head back to the locker room to shower—adrenaline still coursing through our veins from our win. The guys are shouting and joking. It's the week before Christmas, and this is without a doubt the best gift I've ever been given.

"Reservations at El Tao," Brian McCaldon calls out to the team.

"We fucking did it!" Killian jumps on my back. Then as he comes down, he pulls me in for a side hug.

"We still have a long way to go...but yeah, we fucking did!"

"You going to El Tao?" he asks.

"Yeah, might as well. I'm alone for the night." I shrug. "Want to play some Madden at your place afterward?"

"Hell yeah."

A few months ago, I moved out of Killian's condo and into my own place. I didn't want to, but I had to. After accepting the contract with New York, my life changed drastically, and while I know it's what needed to be done, sometimes I wonder if I made the right decision.

"When does she—" His words are cut off when I hear a version of my name being called. The version I have only told one woman. I put my hand up to stop him from speaking and look around, wondering if I'm hearing shit. Wondering if it's possible, after all this time, I'm imagining *her* calling my name.

"Cole," I hear again, and my eyes swing over to the woman who's calling me. And sure as shit, standing there in the locker room is *her*.

"Brown-Eyes." I say the nickname I gave her. So many times I've tried to remember what she looks like, but my memory of her didn't do her justice at all. Her hair is a bit longer, a little lighter. Her eyes are still a beautiful shade of brown that remind me of melted chocolate—sweet like the taste of her pussy on my tongue.

My eyes move downward, lingering on her voluptuous breasts, before I continue farther down, stopping on her...stomach. What the fuck! She's...pregnant? "You're pregnant?"

She follows my gaze down to her protruding belly and then gives me a *duh!* expression.

"What're you doing here?" I ask a bit too coolly as I suddenly remember the note she left the morning after the night we spent together.

"Well...I saw you playing..."

Coach Harper cuts in, making his presence known. "How do you two know each other?"

Liv darts her gaze from Coach to me and then back to him. "He's the father," she says softly. Her eyes close slightly, and the guys gasp and curse around us.

Coach makes eye contact with me, his glare like nothing I've ever seen before. It's a look that says he's about to kill me, and it has me repeating what she said over and over again in my head, hearing the words but not comprehending them. Why the hell is she saying I'm the father? And why is she telling my coach?

"You're...the father?" Coach asks, but I don't answer him. I've lost my voice. I'm in shock. A minute ago, I was remembering how this woman was the best damn lay of my life, how I woke up wanting more, wanting to get to know her, how she walked away without looking back, and now she's trying to fuck me over. She didn't want anything to do with me the morning after when she thought I was a nobody, but now that she knows who I am, she wants to cry baby?

"Bullshit!" I say, finally finding my voice. "We had a one-night stand." I turn to Liv. "If you think you're getting a dime from me, you've lost your mind."

"Son, what did you just say?" Coach's face is turning beet red. I've never seen him this pissed. I'm not sure why he cares, but he needs to have my back or mind his own business. "I would watch what you're saying."

"What the hell, Coach? You expect me to just stand here while this gold-digger tries to fuck me over?" I nod toward Liv who looks like she's not sure whether to be mad or upset. "You're supposed to have my back."

Without saying a word, Coach cuts across the room, and before I can duck, he punches me in the face. My back hits the wall as the guys all jump into action, pulling him off me.

"That *gold-digger* is my daughter!" Oh, hell...shit just got real.

And this is when I should close my mouth, but I'm too worked up—too pissed because I thought she was different, too disappointed that she's like everyone else in my fucking life. "That may be so, but can't you see this for what it is? She's a fucking groupie." I turn to Liv. "What do you want? Huh? Money? A house? A car?"

Coach pushes through the guys, but Killian grabs him before his fist can connect with my face for a second time.

"Nick, stop!" Killian shouts, but I don't listen.

"C'mon, you come at me, what—" I quickly do the math in my

head "—nine months later. What do you want? And don't tell me nothing. *Everybody* wants something."

She stares at me for a minute, her face bright red with anger and her hand resting on the top of her swollen belly. "I didn't know...I lived in Paris...I didn't know who you were that night, *Cole*." She emphasizes my name to prove her point. Anybody who knows me calls me Nick. My mother calls me Nicholas. I told her my name was Cole.

Coach goes to his daughter's side. "Olivia, honey, what the hell happened?"

FIVE

OLIVIA
  Nine months ago

"OLIVIA, I hate that you wouldn't let me fly over for your graduation." I'm sitting on my terrace, talking to my dad, but my mind and heart are a million miles away as I stare at the Eiffel Tower. It's nighttime, and the beautiful tower monopolizes the area. The twinkling lights glitter, making it look like a white Parisian Christmas tree.

"You came for my graduation when I got my bachelor's degree. You didn't need to come for my master's as well. Plus, I was thinking of coming to visit you." I wasn't really, but in light of recent events, I'm thinking a vacation across the Atlantic is just what I need.

"Yeah?" My dad's voice raises several octaves in excitement. "I haven't seen you since the wedding. I would love for you to come and visit." My thoughts go back to the day my dad married my step-mom, Corrine. The way he smiled with unshed tears in his eyes. After losing my mom—his soulmate—to breast cancer seven years ago, he didn't think he would ever fall in love again. Then he met Corrine. I remember when he called me. His voice wavered, scared I wouldn't be happy for him. How could I not be? He loved my mother until she took her final breath. Nobody deserves to live the rest of their life alone because they lost the love of their life too soon.

"I would only be able to come for a week, though. The museum has asked me to come on fulltime as their Arts Education Coordinator now that I've graduated."

"That's amazing! I'm so proud of you. You took your passion for education and your love of art and seem to have found a job you really enjoy."

"Well, I have to make a living somehow."

My dad chuckles. The truth is, my mother was an extremely wealthy woman, and when she died, she left everything to me. I have enough money to never have to work a day in my life. When I asked my dad why she didn't leave it all to him—he was her husband after all—he told me his job was to take care of her. She never had to touch the money while she was alive, and it was her last wish to know I would be taken care of.

"I miss you, Olivia," my dad says. "I would really love to see you, even if it's only for a week." Six months after my mom died, I turned eighteen and received my inheritance. I made the decision to leave New York and attend college in Paris. My mom was from there, and I wanted to spend some time seeing for myself all the stories she used to share of her childhood in France. And if I'm honest, I needed some distance from the home I grew up in. My mom was my best friend, and losing her hurt my heart beyond belief. Everywhere I went, it reminded me of my mom and the fact that I would never see her again.

So, I moved to Paris to attend college, which is where I met my best friend, Giselle Winters, my freshman year. She had a horrible flat mate and was looking to move. I had an extra room, and we hit it off immediately. A bachelor's and master's degree later, and we've created a home here. I never thought that six years later I would still be living here, but I love it, and so does Giselle. The funny thing is, we're both from New York, but because we're from different areas, we never met until we were going to school in Paris.

"Are you excited to be starting your new job?" I ask my dad.

"Yeah, I am. I loved coaching college ball. I've been doing it for the last fifteen years. But I'm excited to take this team on. You know I love a good challenge."

"Yes, I do."

"How is Victor?" And this is the part of the conversation that I've been dreading. I don't lie to my dad. I don't keep secrets from him.

"We broke up."

My dad is silent for a moment before he asks, "What happened?"

"He was offered a job in Geneva."

"Switzerland?"

I laugh softly. "Yes, Switzerland. He didn't ask me to go. Not that I would have…but he didn't even ask. Didn't even consider me when making his decision."

"He's a dumbass."

I love that my dad always has my back. "It hurts. I gave him three years, and he gave me a thirty-hour notice he was moving out."

"I bet Giselle is thrilled," he points out.

"She is." Giselle and Victor never got along. Last year, after dating Victor for two years, he suggested we move in together. My flat was the obvious choice. Giselle swears he only asked so he could crash somewhere in luxury. She might've been right, especially since he made more excuses than not to keep from contributing on a monthly basis.

"All right, well, you talk to Giselle, because I know you won't be coming here without her, and let me know the dates. I'll make sure I'm available to you. We can stay at the house in the Hamptons. It will be great."

"Sounds good, Dad. I love you."

"Love you, too."

IT'S our last day in New York. We've been here for nine days. Five of them spent at our beach house in the Hamptons, two of them exploring all the museums I love to visit while here—during which time my dad mentioned a million times I could do the same job I'm planning to do in Paris, here in New York. Yesterday was spent at the spa with Giselle, Corrine, and her daughter, Shelby, who is in town visiting from Connecticut, where she lives with her father and his family.

Earlier today, I met my dad for breakfast, and then I spent the rest of the day doing some shopping since he had to attend a meeting for work and Giselle was visiting with her family. Tonight, Giselle and I are meeting my dad, Corrine, and Shelby at a new club my dad heard about.

After we've perfected our hair, makeup, and outfits, we walk the few blocks over to Club Envy. I'm about to call my dad to see where we should meet them when my phone pings with an incoming text. It's from Shelby, letting me know her dad needed her to babysit for him and her stepmom, so she had to drive back early. She says she's going to try to come back tomorrow for breakfast. I text her back that it's okay and if she can't make it, I understand. Her dad relies on her a lot to help with her half-siblings.

Just as I'm swiping out of the message, my phone rings.

"Hey, Dad! We just got here. Where are you guys?"

"Hey honey! I'm at home. Corrine thinks she might've gotten food poisoning from the sushi she ate earlier. She's been hugging the toilet for the last hour."

"Oh, no! Do you want me to go over there?"

"No, no. You should still go to the club and have a good time. I heard it's all the rage." I laugh at my dad trying to sound cool.

"Shelby had to cancel too. Her dad needed her to babysit. Are you sure you don't need me to come over?"

"No, there's nothing you could do here, and I'm almost positive Corrine would kill me if I allowed anyone to see her in her current state. Besides, there's no reason for you girls to be stuck in on your last night in New York. Go. Have a good time...but not too good of a time," he adds, and I roll my eyes.

"Fine, but we'll see you before we leave tomorrow, right?"

"Damn right you will. We're still meeting for breakfast after you check out. I moved my meeting back to the afternoon, so I can take you to the airport myself. You know I'm still annoyed you insisted on staying at a hotel instead of with me."

"Dad..." I groan. "You downsized. Your two-bedroom condo is beautiful, but it's not big enough for us women and our luggage." I giggle, and he grunts. My dad finally made the decision to sell our family home and buy a condo closer to the stadium in Lower Manhattan since he will be spending a lot of his time there.

"I know, I know. I'll see you in the morning," he says.

"Okay, Dad. Tell Corrine I hope she feels better soon."

"Will do."

"What happened?" Giselle asks once I end the phone call.

"Corrine has food poisoning, and Shelby is stuck babysitting. I guess it's just us."

"Well, that sucks! But we're going to have a fabulous time."

We approach the bouncer and, after paying the cover charge, enter the club. We aren't even down the hall when Giselle's name is called.

She turns around, yells, "Oh my God," and then runs into a man's arms.

"Christian, this is my best friend, Livi; Livi, this is Christian. We dated for a while in high school." Her cheeks flush pink, and I remember her telling me about the guy she left in New York to move to Paris. He's now the lead singer of some huge band here in the U.S.

"Nice to meet you." Christian shakes my hand. "Are you back for good?" he asks Giselle.

"Actually, this is our last night here."

"Then you have to give me tonight," he says forward as ever, causing Giselle's pink-colored cheeks to deepen to a dark crimson.

She glances my way, and I nod my encouragement. "Go and catch up. I'll order us a couple of drinks and bring them over."

"Are you sure?" Giselle asks.

"Yes! Go! Christian, would you like something to drink?"

"I'm good, but thanks," he says, "I have my beer over at my table. It's in the back corner just behind the bar. I spotted Giselle and didn't want to take a chance of losing her in the crowd." Christian gives her a soft smile. "I can't believe after all this time we ran into each other here."

Giselle smiles back. "I know...it's been a long time."

"Okay, I'll get us drinks and then find you guys," I say, wanting to give them some privacy. They obviously have a lot of catching up to do.

Giselle throws her arms around me in a tight hug and whispers, "Go find a guy to get under." I just shake my head. Earlier, she told me the best way to get over a breakup is to get under someone else. I love Giselle to death, but she's freaking crazy.

She and Christian head to a booth nearby, and I go to the bar to order us a drink. The club is packed, and the bartenders seem to be picking and choosing who they're serving. I attempt to get their attention, waving my bill in the air, but it's not happening.

Just as I'm about to give up and go beg Giselle to dance on the bar to get their attention, I feel a whisper of a breath in my ear. "Can I buy you a drink?" I turn slightly to see who the owner of the voice is and find myself staring at one of the sexiest men I've ever laid eyes on. Messy light brown hair that looks like he just climbed out of bed, dark green eyes that scream trouble, and day-old scruff that has me clenching my legs together as I imagine his face buried between my thighs. I back up slightly to get a better look at him. He's built but not bulky—lean and fit. He's dressed in an expensive light green button-down shirt that makes his eyes pop even more.

My eyes drag back up to his face and land on his cocky grin, telling me he knows how hot he is. He knows he can get any woman he wants, and that look has me wanting to show him that not every woman bows down to guys like him. When I politely tell him I can buy my own drink, he laughs, and the melodic yet masculine sound has my insides melting. He shoots one glance over to the bartender near us, and she comes running our way. Of course he has no problem getting the female bartender's attention.

We order.

We drink.

We dance.

And several hours later, I do the craziest thing I've ever done in my twenty-four years. I invite him back to my hotel room, where we have the hottest, most passionate night of sex I've ever experienced. Our chemistry is undeniable and off the charts, and for a moment I think about what it would be like to be with this man again. But I quickly check that thought, remembering what this was about. *My attempt at getting under someone to get over someone else.*

The next morning, I wake up and leave him sleeping in my bed.

I check-out.

I have breakfast with my dad.

I board my flight.

I arrive home.

My luggage gets lost.

A week later it's found.

Three weeks after that I find out I'm pregnant.

Giselle and I search the football roster for a Cole, hoping we might find him on there. He did mention he loves—and hates—to play football. Giselle calls Christian to see if maybe he's heard of him. They only briefly met, but it's worth a try. Unfortunately, he doesn't know who he is.

I ask my dad—as nonchalantly as possible—if he knows a Cole. He says he doesn't.

I search the headshots on the ESPN sites. What I don't take into account is that because he's a free agent, he hasn't been put on the roster since the season hasn't officially begun.

So, I do the only thing I can do. I move on with my life with my growing baby inside me. I don't tell anyone how much it hurts every time I think about my baby never knowing his father. I keep it to myself how much my heart breaks whenever I think about being a single mom. Not because I can't do it, but because that's not what I want. I wanted the fairytale like my parents had. I wanted the happily-ever-after. There's no Disney book where the mom gets knocked up from a one-night stand and raises the baby alone.

When my dad asks who the father is, I tell him the truth. It was a one-night stand. I can hear his disappointment. I was raised to believe in the power of love. He's been with two women his entire life: my mom and my stepmom.

He asks me to come home.

I agree to come back temporarily.

Giselle graduates in December, and we pack up the flat and head to New York.

I've been here for three weeks, focusing on buying a place and then getting it ready for my baby.

My dad asks me to attend a game since I haven't been to one all season.

I look out from the owner's suite and see *him*.

The father of my baby.

SIX

Nick

"OLIVIA, HONEY. WHAT THE HELL HAPPENED?" Coach Harper asks his daughter.

"He..." She points directly at me, her perfectly manicured fingernail pressing into my chest. "He said his name was Cole! Not Nick!"

"My name is Nicholas," I point out, "and what does it matter what I'm called?"

"It matters—" her voice raises several levels "—because I looked for you! I searched the roster for Cole! I asked my dad if he knew of a Cole!" This woman is so mad right now, I'm thankful she doesn't have a weapon in her possession, because if she did, I would be a dead man. I can't imagine her getting this worked up is good for her, and really...what is she so mad about? I'm the one finding out a one-night stand I had nine months ago—who I might add, left me— might've left me a father. Something I've decided this past year I'm not at all interested in becoming.

"First of all, you're the one who walked out the door the morning after, leaving me with nothing but a 'thanks for the fuck' note. Second of all, I'm not sure you should be yelling and screaming and getting all worked up in your condition."

And I don't think that was the right thing to say because that finger that was in my chest a moment ago becomes several fingers as she pushes my chest in frustration.

"It was a one-night stand! What did you want from me? To ask you to marry me? I was leaving back to Paris! And this..." She points to her belly. "It's not a goddamn condition! It's called pregnancy, you moron!"

I hold my hands up in a placating manner. "Okay...but I don't get why you're yelling at me. You left me that morning. I woke up, and you were gone. I didn't do anything wrong."

She looks around the silent locker room as if just now realizing our conversation is taking place in front of the entire New York Brewers football team. Using a lower, more controlled tone, she says, "Umm...maybe because you said your name was Cole when everybody else calls you NICK! And...you're the one who put me in this *condition*, as you call it."

Oh. Hell. No. "Like fucking hell I did...we used protection. You better go figure out who else you slept with that you didn't use protection with." I shrug. *Glad we cleared that shit up.*

I turn to walk away not wanting to continue this pointless conversation. The locker room is still radio silent, and then I hear a loud screech. I turn back around to see what the hell that noise is when I'm decked in the head with a hard object. I grab the side of my face as it radiates with pain. "What the fuck!"

I look down, and there's a water bottle rolling across the ground. "Did you just throw that at me?"

"You're lucky that's all I did!" she shrieks again, this time grabbing a Gatorade bottle off the table and chucking it at me. I duck out of the way this time as the bottle hits the wall with a bang.

"Coach, get your crazy fucking daughter away from me."

"I'm going to kill him," she says to her dad, and then she's coming after me. Thankfully, her father pulls her back before she reaches me.

"Olivia, calm down, please." She relaxes slightly at his words, but then her eyes go wide, and she looks down. There's liquid dripping down her leg. Is she so upset she peed herself? My conscience gets the best of me, and I almost feel bad. I didn't want to upset a pregnant woman. She's clearly distraught over not knowing who the father of her baby is.

"Dad," she whispers, her voice coming out soft, reminding me of the woman I met at the club and spent the night getting to know in the most intimate way. "It's too early." She shakes her head then glances toward me, tears welling up and glossing over her brown eyes.

Her dad looks down at the puddle, and he must know something I don't, because he says, "Let's get you to the hospital." Our argument completely forgotten, she nods in agreement. Holding onto her arm, he walks her through the locker room while pulling out his cell phone and calling someone. "Corrine, can you pull the car around? Olivia is in labor." Well shit, apparently peeing yourself means you're about to have a baby.

Killian's eyes meet mine with shock and worry. "Are you going to go to the hospital?"

"For what?" I step around the mess on the floor as the janitor comes over to mop it up.

"She's about to have your baby." He says the words slowly like I'm an idiot.

"She's about to have *a* baby." I shake my head. "Not mine."

"Nick, is there any chance that kid could be yours?"

I think back to that night. I was tipsy, but I wasn't drunk. I'm positive we used protection: in the bed, against the dresser, me on top, her on top...Fuck! Did we use one when I woke up in the middle of the night and pulled her on top of me?

"Nick." Killian pulls me out of my memory. "Are you one hundred percent sure?"

"I-I'm pretty sure." But as I say the words, I know they might be a lie.

"If there's any chance you could be the dad, you need to go to that hospital. You don't want to live with that regret, man." His words sound ominous, almost like he can empathize with what I'm going through.

KILLIAN DRIVES me to the hospital in his car, since we drove together this morning. I was hoping to get in the doors without being seen, but it's just my luck the fucking paparazzi followed us here. It shouldn't surprise me, though. With Killian driving his fucking Bugatti, we stick out like a damn sore thumb. He drives me around to the side, but there's no way to get in other than through the main doors or the emergency room entrance.

"Fuck it. I'm just going to have to make a run for it."

"Good luck, man. I'd wait in the waiting room for you, but I don't want to draw any more attention to you. Text me once you know anything." Killian pats me on my back before I jump out of his car.

Photos are taken and questions are slung my way, but I ignore them all. When I get inside, I'm met by none other than my dad and Amber, my publicist. They pull me into a private room where nobody can overhear our conversation.

"Dad? What are you doing here?" My publicist, I understand, as it's her job to keep my name squeaky clean. Plus, I called her on my way over here. But I'm not sure why my dad would fly all the way from North Carolina when he could just call me or Amber. And how the hell did he get here so fast?

"Your mother and I flew in last night for the game!" he barks. "In case you forgot you're in the middle of the goddamned playoffs!"

"Yeah, I'm well aware," I snap.

"So, is it true?" he asks. "Did you knock up this woman?"

"I-I don't know. She says the baby is mine, and we did spend the night together..." I can't believe this is happening. The last thing I wanted was to be a dad. I had it in my head being a father wasn't in the cards for me.

"Damn it, Nick! Have you not listened to a single word I've said to you over the years!" My dad shakes his head in disappointment. He's engrained it into my head a million times over the years to be careful. Too many guys end up paying half of everything they've earned by being cavalier when it comes to wrapping their dicks up. I also think, while he's never said it, him knocking up my mom meant he was forced to marry her. I've never asked them, but I'm almost positive my dad has cheated on my mom several times over the years —and vice versa.

"You have everything going for you," he continues. "You have your career back; your personal life is on track. I can't believe you would be this careless." He curses under his breath as he storms out of the room.

Jesus, he's acting like I'm the first guy in professional sports to get a woman pregnant by accident. He's a damn sport's agent. Half his clients probably have kids from one-night stands.

"Did you call my dad on your way here?" I ask Amber once my dad is gone.

"No, but I'm pretty sure it got leaked by a fan or someone. There's footage of the pregnant woman and Coach Harper leaving the stadium, and then you and Killian following almost directly after."

"Her name is Liv...Olivia. She's Coach Harper's daughter."

Amber's eyes go wide. "I'll make a statement right away. I'll keep it simple. We don't know anything at this time, and you're requesting privacy while you get it sorted." She gives me a sympathetic smile.

"All right, thank you."

SEVEN

OLIVIA

MY FEET ARE in the stirrups, and the doctor is sitting between my legs. When we arrived several hours ago, I was checked in and then brought back to labor and delivery. The nurse hooked me up to several monitors and took my blood. When I requested an epidural for the pain, she frowned apologetically and said I was already too far along for it, but she could give me some pain reliever. Once I was situated, I called Giselle to fill her in, and she immediately left her mom's house to meet me here. The doctor has come by numerous times to check on my progress, and my family has been in and out of my room to make sure I'm okay throughout my labor. A few minutes ago, after checking on the baby's status once again, the doctor informed me it's time to push.

Since I made the decision to only have Giselle in the room with me when I give birth, my dad is outside with Corrine and Shelby, while Giselle is next to me currently holding my hand.

"Okay, Olivia. Here comes a contraction," the doctor says. "Push for me." I push through the contraction, and the pain is like nothing I've ever felt before. I almost feel bad I might break Giselle's hand from squeezing it too hard. "That's good...and relax." This process goes on and on and on for God knows how long. Each push hurts worse than the last. My body is tiring out.

And then finally in the middle of another push, the doctor says,

"I see hair. You're close." I stop pushing, taking a small break, and wait for the next one to hit. My throat is dry from screaming and exerting myself, and I'm seriously questioning this so-called pain reliever the nurse insisted she gave me.

"Sir, you can't go in there!" the nurse shouts, and I look over to see Cole's large frame filling the doorway.

"I might be the father," he says, ignoring her and walking inside. I'm about to kick him out when another contraction hits, and I find myself pushing.

"Oh my God!" I scream in pain.

"Keep going. Keep going," the doctor commands. "There he is!" My body finds relief as the doctor holds the baby up. "Congratulations."

The nurse comes over and cleans up my baby boy, then she sucks all the stuff out of his nose. He's screaming and crying, and it's the most beautiful sound I've ever heard.

"Would you like to cut the umbilical cord?" the doctor asks Nick, and I shoot him a warning glare, which he ignores—Nick, not the doctor.

"Oh, I'm not a doctor." Nick shakes his head, and the doctor chuckles while I roll my eyes.

"I know, I am. Sometimes the dads like to cut the umbilical cord that connects the mother to the baby."

Nick nods and slowly steps forward. The nurse holds my baby while the doctor hands Nick the scissors to cut the umbilical cord. I want to yell at him and tell him not to touch anything involving *my* baby. Not even a few hours ago he was accusing me of lying and saying the baby isn't even his. But I don't say a word because I can't. My heart is pained, and there's a huge lump in my throat. This was supposed to be my husband cutting the umbilical cord. I read about this in a baby book. It's a tradition for men to feel like they're part of the delivery—to help establish an emotional connection between the father and the baby. Tears blur my vision as I watch Nick carefully cut the cord. I feel Giselle's hand on my shoulder, and when I look up, she's snapping pictures with her phone camera. I, both, hate and love her for that.

"Good job!" the doctor says, taking the scissors back from Nick, who nods once and backs up out of the way. The nurse finishes cleaning off my still-crying baby, then she wraps him up in a blanket and places him on my chest. "Shh...it's okay," I coo. "Mommy has you." I bring my hands up to hold him as his warm body rests against mine. "I love you, baby boy." I place a kiss on his forehead.

"I'm going to get him checked out," the nurse says, taking him from me far too soon. "As soon as you're stitched up and moved to recovery, I'll bring the baby to you."

I watch as she takes my entire world away from me. "Is he okay?" I ask another nurse. "I wasn't due for a few more weeks."

"We'll know more once the tests are run, but he seems perfect." I close my eyes in relief as everybody bustles around me getting the room cleaned up. The doctor lets me know the placenta has passed, then he stitches up a cut he had to make so I didn't tear. I'm lifted and transferred to a clean bed, given a fresh gown, and moved to a new room.

The entire time I feel Cole still lingering in the background, but I ignore him. I have nothing to say to that asshole. He might've been the best sex of my life, and I'll never regret that night because it gave me the most precious miracle in the world, but still...fuck him.

Once I'm situated in my new room, my dad, Corrine, and Shelby come in and join Giselle and me. That's when I notice Cole isn't here anymore. Well good fucking riddance. "We saw the baby being brought to the nursery for tests. He's beautiful," Corrine gushes, and I smile.

"I took like a million pictures." Giselle holds her phone out for me to take.

"Thank you!" I pull her in for a hug before I begin swiping through each photo.

"Is that Nick?" my dad asks when I stop on the one of him cutting the umbilical cord.

"Yeah, he snuck in and declared himself *possibly* the dad, and the doctor asked if he wanted to cut the umbilical cord." I swipe to another photo.

"I can still remember when I got to do that with you." My dad smiles at me. "One of the greatest moments of my life."

"Yeah, well, I doubt Nick felt the same way." Fresh tears surface, and I will them away. *Damn hormones.*

"Okay, here he is." The nurse comes in, pushing my baby in a rolling bassinet. "His Apgar scores were perfect." She hands me a piece of paper that shows the tests which were given, along with the scores. "His lungs are fully developed. It says in your birthing plan that you're planning to bottle-feed. Here are a couple different kinds." She pulls the bottles out. "This one is good, but if he has reflux or a sensitive belly, try this one." She points to the different formulas.

"Thank you." She picks him up and brings him to me. I shake

the bottle gently like I read in the baby books and bring the nipple to his mouth. He starts sucking and drinking immediately. Giselle comes over and snaps another picture. A few minutes later, there's a knock on the door and the nurse opens it. Nick walks in and glances around the room.

"Now's not the time," my dad says.

"Dad, it's fine." I lean over and give my baby boy a soft kiss on his forehead before I pick him up to burp him. "Can you guys give us a few minutes, please?" It's best to get this over with. Reluctantly, everyone leaves.

"Sorry for barging in earlier. I was waiting outside your door, but when I heard you scream, I thought something was wrong."

"It's called giving birth," I say dryly. "Why are you even here?"

"I'm not really sure."

"Look, if you don't want to be a dad, you don't have to be."

"And what is it you want?" He stands at the end of my bed, his arms crossed over his chest. His question comes out cold and distant. He's nothing like the man I spent the night with all those months ago. Or maybe I just convinced myself it was more than what it really was.

"It doesn't matter to me..." I start to say, but he shakes his head.

"No, I mean what do you want in order for me to sign over my rights? How much? You're right, I don't want to be a dad." My heart breaks when he says this. My mind going back to my fantasy—the one where I have a baby with a man who loves me. We would get married, buy a house with a backyard like the one I grew up in, and we would start a family together. I didn't realize it until right now, but when I watched him step forward and cut that umbilical cord, something in me felt a sense of hope that maybe he wanted this too.

My little man burps. When I lower him from my shoulder to take a good look at him, his eyes are already fluttering shut. I swaddle him in his blanket, but instead of laying him in the bassinet, I hold him, hoping that having him in my arms will help heal my broken heart.

Just as I'm about to respond, a woman comes barreling through the door. "Ugh! Do you know how hard it was to get through the hospital without being photographed?"

Having no clue who this woman is or why she's in my room, I say, "Excuse me?"

"Celeste, what are you doing here?" Cole walks over to her. *Okay... I guess he knows her.*

"It's all over social media! Do you not understand how bad this looks? And I'm your fiancée! A phone call to let me know would've been nice." Taking a closer look at the woman, I spot a gigantic engagement ring on her left hand, the hand that's waving around in frustration as she drones on about being blindsided. She's skinny and tall and lacks any major curves, yet she's stunningly beautiful. Her hair is long and black and smooth. She's wearing what I recognize as a Valentino dress from his couture winter line, and her makeup appears to be professionally done. I can't put my finger on it, but I recognize her from somewhere...

"I was forced to leave the shoot, and now it will need to be rescheduled for another night." Oh, yeah! She's a model. I've seen her on billboards. And...wait a second...holy shit! She's Celeste Leblanc. I only purchase my makeup from her line. It's the best. Jesus, Olivia...now is not the time to fangirl over her and her amazing makeup line. She's your baby-daddy's fiancée for God's sake.

"I didn't ask you to come here," Cole points out. "And I was going to call you, but everything happened so fast."

"Ahem." I clear my throat, and both of them whip around to acknowledge I'm in the room. "If you guys wouldn't mind, maybe you could discuss this...oh, I don't know—" I lift my shoulders in a shrug "—out of my room." I hold my sleeping baby up slightly. "I just gave birth, and I'm a bit tired." I'm aware my words come out bitchy, but we'll blame it on the new mom hormones. Okay, no, screw that. I'll take responsibility. I just don't want to hear them.

"Look, Celeste. I didn't know she was pregnant. I just found out. And I didn't know the press and paparazzi figured it out until I got here." He looks at me. "I'm going to call my attorney and find out about having a paternity test done."

I would rather not do this with an audience, but I guess I have no choice.

"You said you didn't want to be his dad," I point out.

Celeste's eyes swing from him to me, and she gives me an incredulous look. "Wait a second, you're not pushing for Nick to be the father? Then what's your angle?"

Refusing to discuss this with a woman I don't know—and also mentally making a note to throw away all of my makeup—I say to Cole—or shit, I guess it's *Nick*, "I told you, you're the father. If you don't want to be the dad, you don't have to be." I try my best to keep my crazy emotions from leaking out. "I don't know what happened that night, but I didn't get pregnant on purpose. I'm not going to force you to want our son." I hear my voice crack on the last word, but I will myself not to cry. It's not like I'm in love with the man—I don't even know him. I just always thought I would raise my children in a two-parent loving home like my parents gave me. I never thought at twenty-five I would be a single mother.

With his eyes trained on my baby in my arms, he says, "I still want to know."

Celeste steps closer to him and says, "If you take that test and it proves you're the dad, there's no going back. You're the one who said you don't want to be a dad. The last thing that baby needs is a father who doesn't want him."

He nods once and then says, "If I'm the father, I'll pay you whatever it is you want."

"Will you stop saying that?" My voice comes out harsh, and my baby jumps in his sleep. "I don't want or need your money, and if you don't want to be this baby's father then I don't want you to be. If you want a paternity test, fine. I know he's yours. Now both of you... *get out.*"

Nick opens his mouth to argue but closes it. Both of them walk out and close the door behind them.

A few minutes later, my dad, Corrine, Shelby, and Giselle all come back into the room. Nobody asks what happened. Instead, we focus our energy on the beautiful, healthy baby.

"Do we have a name?" Giselle asks.

"Yes, we do. Reed Cameron Harper." I look to my dad, and he gives me a warm smile.

"Oh, sweetie!" Corrine coos. "That's perfect. Both of your parents' middle names." Tears well in her eyes as my dad cuts across the room to my bedside.

"If your mom were here, she would be loving on her grandson. She'd be so proud of the woman you've become."

"What is there to be proud of? Getting knocked up from a one-night stand?" I joke, but even I can hear the embarrassing truth in my words.

"No, for taking responsibility. You're going to be an amazing mom just like yours was."

EIGHT

NICK

IT'S BEEN a week since I walked out of the hospital with Celeste and argued with her for hours over the Olivia and baby situation.

"I can't believe this is happening," she says. "Everything was going perfectly fine. And now it's all about to be destroyed because of your one-night stand. I shouldn't be surprised." She throws her arms up in exasperation. "You're a man, which means keeping your dick in your pants is impossible."

"This happened before we got together!" I shout in frustration. She's acting like I asked for this to happen. "You knew I was sleeping around. It's part of the reason I agreed to make good on our pact."

After I was told I needed to settle down, figuring I had nothing to lose, I called up Celeste and agreed to go through with our pact. At least with her, I knew what I was getting myself into. A business arrangement. We dated for a couple months and then announced our engagement. Celeste let the lease on her apartment go and moved in with me once I purchased a place in Lower Manhattan near the stadium—and directly above Killian.

"I know." She nods. "I just...I thought being with you would be safe," she whispers.

"I'm sorry," I say, "But it's not as if I cheated on you." Despite the fact that Celeste and I have never once had sex, I've been one hundred percent faithful to her. It's not that we didn't try. We did.

But the foreplay was robotic, and neither of us could get into it. After getting her off, I ended up finishing in the shower using my hand. We've never spoken about it or tried to have sex again.

"I know that," she says, her voice rough with emotion. "That's not what I meant." She swallows thickly.

"Celeste, what's going on?" I've never seen her like this. Celeste doesn't do emotion. She doesn't get her feelings hurt. "Talk to me."

She opens her mouth to speak then closes it. She stands taller, straightening her back and squaring her shoulders. "Nothing is going on," she says. "I just meant that I thought you would be safe for my reputation. I guess I was wrong."

"I can't change what happened," I tell her, "but this doesn't have to change anything between us."

"Don't you get it?" She shakes her head. "This changes everything." She sighs in defeat and sits down on the couch. I walk over and sit next to her. "I didn't sign up for this, Nick."

I know from the outside it may seem like Celeste is being a bitch, but she's right. She didn't sign up for this. In the beginning of our relationship, we hammered out all the details. Celeste wanted to make sure we were both on the same page. She told me she didn't want to have kids and I agreed. I feel bad that my past is complicating what we have. Celeste doesn't deserve any of this.

The truth is, from the beginning, being with Celeste has been easy. Because of our high-demanding careers, we're rarely ever home, both busy living our lives. There're no expectations. No emotions involved. She's more like a roommate than my fiancée.

We both sit in silence for a few minutes, and then she asks, "What are you going to do?"

"I don't know," I admit. "I don't know what the right answer is."

"You said you didn't want to be a dad," she says, "You told me you felt like you were never good enough in your parents' eyes. And you said that Fiona not getting pregnant was for the best."

"I know." She's right. I did say all that. But at the time I said all that I didn't think there was a chance of me actually becoming a dad. Now, there's a baby who I might share DNA with.

"And what about Olivia?" she asks.

"What about her?"

"You said it yourself the morning after you two hooked up that you thought there could be something more between you guys. Are you telling me you honestly haven't thought about how she plays into this picture?"

I let out a low groan, regretting my decision to confide in Celeste *the morning after. "She walked away that morning, leaving me with nothing more than a note. Her only role in my life would be as my son's mother." As I say those words, my heart strings feel like they're being tugged. Watching her deliver the baby was probably the single most amazing thing I've ever witnessed. She was so strong through it all. And then when she held him in her arms...the love that shown through in her eyes... In all my years growing up, I don't think I ever saw my own mother look at me the way Olivia looked at her son. Had she not left without giving me her number, who knows how things would be different right now. But it doesn't matter because she did leave, and now I'm engaged to Celeste. It's pointless to focus on the what-ifs.*

"She probably wants to trap you."

"Did you not see her in the hospital? She can barely stand to be in the same room as me."

"Then she's doing it for the money," Celeste states.

"I don't think so," I say honestly. "She said she doesn't want my money."

"There you go being all naïve once again."

"I'm not being naïve," I argue.

Celeste turns her body slightly in my direction and our eyes lock, neither of us saying a word as she tries to determine if there are any hidden emotions behind my features. She's trying to figure out what I'm thinking but not saying. Finally, she sighs and says, "It's like we're teenagers all over again. How many times are you going to let a woman manipulate your emotions?" She gives me a pointed look. "You said it yourself. She's the same woman who left you the morning after with nothing more than a note. Who knows what her angle is now that she knows you're a professional athlete."

I hear everything she's saying, and had she mentioned all this before I watched Olivia give birth I probably would've agreed, but the problem is I saw the little boy who might be my son. Hell, I even cut his damn umbilical cord. I saw the way Olivia's love for her son shone through. And while I won't admit this to Celeste, it made my heart feel something I haven't felt in a long time. Does that scare the shit out of me? Hell yes, it does. But it also feels damn good to feel something, anything, again.

"I really don't think she has an angle."

Without her eyes leaving mine, she says, "You want her." Her tone as she says those three words contain zero emotion, as if she's simply stating a fact. A fact I'm not ready to deal with yet. Because those three words, if they are true, will change everything, just like Celeste said.

"This isn't about her," I say, deflecting. "This is about a baby who might be my son."

"Yeah, okay, Nick. We both know you think with your heart. It won't be long until you've ditched me to play house with your baby mamma."

"Celeste..." I begin to say, but she cuts me off.

"Don't 'Celeste' me. Just think about this before you make any rash decisions. You agreed to give this relationship a chance, not only because of your reputation but because you were tired of getting your heart stomped on. Since we've been together, how many times has your heart been broken? Zero." I don't point out that my heart can't be broken if it isn't on the line.

"You want to go play Daddy to this baby, fine." She lets out a frustrated sigh. "I'm not going to stop you. I would never try to stop a father from taking responsibility. But don't be so naïve to think this woman is your one true love. You aren't going to find out you're the dad and live happily-ever-after, Nick."

I can hear the fear in her voice. She won't ever admit it, but one of Celeste's biggest fears is not being put first. Her dad never came back for her mom or her, and in her eyes, he chose someone else over them. And then for years, her mom put her love for her dad above her own daughter. Beatrice chose to stay in that trailer park and work at that diner over creating a good life for Celeste. Now she's afraid I'm going to choose my son and his mother over her, leaving her once again on her own. She comes across so tough on a day-to-day basis that sometimes I forget how insecure Celeste really is.

"All I want to do is find out if that little boy is my son."

"And what if he is, Nick? What then? What will that mean for us?"

"I'm not breaking off our engagement," I tell her.

"Yet." She huffs and snatches her purse off the table. I know I should stop her and convince her she's wrong, make her feel secure about us, but for some reason I can't bring myself to do it, to say the words she needs to hear.

"I need to get going," she says. I watch her walk to the door, but then she stops and turns around. "You might not see where this is all going, but I do. And as your best friend I'm going to warn you just like I did when we were younger. She's going to break your heart." I open my mouth to argue, but she doesn't give me a chance. "And when she does, this time I will say I told you so." And without

waiting for me to respond, she swings the door open and then slams it shut behind her.

I hate to admit it, but on some level Celeste is right. Olivia walked away that day. She didn't want a future with me. If she did, she would've stuck around or left me her number. She did neither. I was nothing more than a one-night stand to her that left her knocked up.

The next morning I called my attorney, and he put a petition in to the courts to establish paternity. I went to the hospital, got swabbed, and left. Now, I'm just waiting to find out the results.

Yesterday, my mom called to find out when she would see me for Christmas—which really meant she wanted to find out my side of what's going on. Luckily, we had an away game, so I was able to put off her inquisition temporarily. But at some point I'm going to have to deal with her. There's no way she's going back to North Carolina until she gets some answers. My dad has already mentioned them finding a short-term lease here in New York. I'd like to think it's so they can be near me for moral support, but I know better. I've been spending every day at practice or in the gym to keep busy. I need to stay focused. We're too damn close to becoming champions for my drama to fuck it all up now.

The negative tension between Coach and me has been awkward to say the least, and I was worried it would rub off on the rest of the team, but we made it through our game—winning 24-21. We already clinched a spot in the playoffs, but this game determined if we would have home-field advantage. It was a close game, and it had the commentators talking, questioning if I'm regressing with the new weight and stress on my shoulders. Celeste was right in that regard. The tabloids and gossip rags are all talking, and none of it is projecting me in a positive light.

I was hoping when we returned today, I would come home to a quiet house, but instead, I walk into the opposite. Groaning when I spot everyone, I consider sneaking back out and heading to Killian's place, but before I can, Celeste spots me and calls out my name.

"Thanks for letting me know everyone is here, *babe*." I glare at my fiancée, and she shoots daggers back at me. Nobody besides Killian has any clue about our pact-slash-fake relationship.

"Of course we're here!" My mom huffs. "Yesterday was Christmas and you were away. I was thinking we can open gifts. Celeste said your results are back. They came in this morning. Has this *woman* told you what she wants yet?"

I grab the envelope off the counter and notice it's been opened. "Really? You guys opened the results for me?"

"We need to know what we're working with, Nick," my dad says. "I saw your game yesterday. You can't let this baby news affect your game, and if you don't nip this shit in the bud, she'll be suing you for child support."

"So, I'm the father?" I ask, pulling the papers out to read them myself.

"Yes," Celeste answers, zero emotion showing through her rough exterior. "But this doesn't have to change anything." She comes over to me and puts her hands on my arms.

"I need to think about all this," I tell her honestly. Now that I officially know I'm the father, there are a million different thoughts swarming around in my head. It was one thing to consider the possibility, but now it's fact. I'm someone's dad.

Not liking my answer, Celeste squeezes my arms. "What is there to think about?"

"A lot, actually," I say, moving my arms out of her grip.

"Like what?" she presses.

"How about the fact that I have a child with my coach's daughter, for starters?" That's not really high on my list of worries, but it's the safest thought to say out loud.

"That's hardly a concern," my dad says. "Your season is almost over, which means so is your contract, and with the way you've been playing, every team is going to want you."

"Like who?" Celeste asks.

"LA for one," my dad says. This gets Celeste's attention. I can already hear the ideas forming in her head of moving across the country and away from Olivia. LA isn't really where Celeste wants to live, but since she sometimes travels there for work, it wouldn't be the end of the world.

"I don't know what the future holds. For all we know, I could end up in Michigan or somewhere." I name the last place in the world Celeste would want to end up just to fuck with her, and it works. She shudders then glares.

"Don't be ridiculous, Nick," she seethes.

"I need to go speak to Liv about the paternity. Now, as my fiancée, do you want to go with me?" I know she won't want to go, but at least I can say I tried.

"I need to catch my flight soon."

"Mom, do you want to go with me to meet your grandchild?"

My mom scrunches up her nose. "How about you send me a picture? At that age, all they do is eat and sleep anyway."

"Dad?" I ask stupidly, but before he can answer, my mom cuts in.

"Can we please open presents?"

"And that's my cue to leave," my dad says. "Money doesn't get made by itself. I have a meeting with a potential client." He glances down at his watch to check the time. My mom doesn't even ask him to stay, like it's perfectly normal for her husband to choose work over spending Christmas with his family. And I guess it is. It's how it's always been.

Once he's gone, the three of us make our way to the living room, and my mom grabs the gifts under the small tree Celeste paid to have brought in.

Both women open their gifts, squealing with delight. Celeste throws herself into my arms, giving me a kiss on my cheek. "Thank you so much." She puts the stainless-steel Tiffany watch on her wrist then shows it to my mom. "Isn't it gorgeous?" *I'm not sure why she's acting so shocked, she picked the damn thing out herself.*

My mom agrees. "It is. Thank you, Nick." She holds up the certificate for the week-long cruise I purchased for her and my dad. That gift I did pick out myself. Regardless of how frozen my heart has become, I don't think I'll ever stop trying to help my parents rekindle the love they once had for each other, even if I've accepted it's most likely not going to happen. I figured a cruise would be a good place for them to get away and enjoy each other's company.

"You're welcome, Mom."

She leans over and gives me a kiss on my cheek. "I love you, sweetie."

I nod absently as the women open up the other gifts I got for them, the smiles on their faces never faltering, and I wonder what it would take to put a smile on Olivia's face. Most women are simple. Expensive jewelry, clothes, vacations, and they're good to go. Olivia, on the other hand, that day in the locker room and then in the hospital room, didn't want anything I had to offer. Then I question why I'm even thinking about what it would take to make her happy. It's not my job to make her happy. I shouldn't *want* to make her happy.

Celeste may think I'm going to end up with Olivia, but she's wrong. Olivia chose to walk away that morning after. She's one of the reasons I agreed to the pact with Celeste in the first place. No emotions. But even as I try to convince myself what I'm thinking is how I really feel, I can't overlook the fact that Olivia has crossed my mind a dozen times since Celeste and I talked. I may not want her to be in my thoughts, but that isn't stopping her from being in them.

"All right, I need to head over to Olivia's."

"Wait, I have a gift for the two of you." My mom runs to her purse and pulls out an envelope.

Celeste opens it then jumps up off the couch. "Oh, Victoria! Thank you!"

"What is it?"

"It's an appointment with Dedra Fray, one of the most elusive wedding planners in the world! How did you do this? I heard she has a wait list a mile long."

"I've become close with Kelly Parks."

"The mother of Zack Parks, my teammate?" I question.

"Yes, she's so sweet. Anyway, his wife used Dedra, and when I mentioned Celeste would be looking for a planner soon, she called in a favor. Turns out Dedra is a huge fan of yours, Celeste."

"Oh, wow! Thank you. I can't wait to start planning our wedding. You'll come with me, right?" she asks my mom.

"Of course. Maybe we can finally get your mom to fly up with me so she can join us."

"I doubt it," Celeste says with a frown. "It's been ten years since I moved to New York, and she hasn't once agreed to leave Piermont. Not even for a weekend."

"I know, but maybe I can convince her," my mom says.

"Yeah, maybe." Celeste shrugs.

"You know, when I spoke to Dedra, she mentioned a few locations that have availability. She thinks the Seversky Mansion might even have an opening for a summer wedding."

"This summer?" I choke out. My throat feels like it's tightening and blocking my airflow.

"Yes, Nicholas. This summer." My mom shoots me a hard glare.

"I thought we were going to do a longer engagement," I mention to Celeste, who is now shooting daggers my way. *I guess the excitement over the gifts has worn off.*

"Are you having second thoughts?" Celeste asks. She raises one brow, challenging me to lie to her...or maybe to admit the truth. The problem is I don't know what answer would be a lie or the truth.

"Can we please talk about this when you get back?" I ask. "I really need to head over to Olivia's to discuss this paternity situation."

Celeste nods once. "Of course." The hurt that comes through in her voice is evident, and I hate that I'm the reason she's hurting, but I don't know how to fix any of this.

"Don't be like that." I attempt to grab her hand as she turns to walk away, but she yanks her hand out of my reach. "I'll see you when you get back," I say to her as she walks down the hall toward our room.

She ignores me, and knowing how stubborn she is, I don't attempt to apologize. Instead, I say goodbye to my mom and then head out.

NINE

Olivia

"DO you think the couch would look better against this wall?" Giselle points to the wall across from the fireplace. "Or maybe this wall?" She points to the wall adjacent to the one she just pointed to. We've been settled into our brownstone in Brooklyn Heights for close to a month, but I'm beginning to think Giselle will never be settled with our décor. We put up a small Christmas tree in the corner, and now that it's gone, Giselle's back to rearranging our furniture. The woman didn't even wait until New Year's Day to take the tree down.

When I found this brownstone online, she insisted we keep all the furnishings in our flat in Paris there. She claimed it was because she didn't want us to spend the money shipping it all to New York, but we both knew she just needed an excuse to decorate while she's job hunting. With a bachelor's and master's degree in Interior Design, my best friend better know everything there is to know about decorating a place. Who even knew you could go to school for six years to learn how to decorate a room?

"I think it should stay right where it is." And yes, my answer has everything to do with the fact that I'm currently sitting on the couch in question. Giselle pops her hip out and glares, knowing me way too well. I laugh, setting Reed down in his bassinet.

Her phone beeps indicating an incoming text. When she looks at it, her face lights up.

"Christian?" I ask.

"Yeah." She grins, typing something back. "I just can't believe we're back together again."

"Why? Because he's a famous musician now?"

"No...well, yeah, I guess that's a little bit of it." She giggles, throwing herself onto the couch next to me. "I'm just so happy. You would think after not seeing each other for six years, it would be awkward. But it's not. It's like we picked right back up where we left off all those years ago. It just feels so surreal, like any moment I'll wake up and it will all have been a dream. When I left for Paris, I honestly never thought we would be together again, and I had accepted that, you know? Christian needed to follow his dreams, and I needed to chase mine."

"But you guys found your way back to each other. You deserve to be happy." Giselle doesn't talk often of her home life, but from the little bit she's mentioned over the years, she didn't have it easy growing up.

"I know, but sometimes I feel guilty."

"You can't feel guilty for living your life. Your mom has your dad, and it's his job as her husband to help her. You visit all the time, and you're there for your sister. You can't do it all."

"I know. I know you're right, but it doesn't stop me from still feeling that way."

"Well stop feeling that way!" I pull Giselle into a hug. "You know if you ever need anything I'm here, right?"

"You do enough, but yes, I know. Thank you."

"I'm going to take a quick shower before we head out to brunch. Can you keep an eye on little man?"

"Of course."

Yesterday was Christmas, but because my dad was away for a game, we're all getting together today to celebrate. As I stand, the buzzer goes off indicating someone is downstairs, so I press the button. "Hello?"

"I have a certified letter for Olivia Harper to sign."

"Okay." I buzz him in.

"Paternity results?" Giselle questions.

"I'm sure." I roll my eyes as I walk to the door to wait for him so he doesn't knock and wake up Reed. We're on the third floor, so the courier will have to take the elevator up. When I see him walking down the hall,

I notice he's not alone. Cole—shit, I mean Nick—is with him, and holy hell does he look hot. He's standing to the side of the courier in a baby blue collared Lacoste shirt that fits his arms and chest way too well, distressed jeans, and a pair of Nikes. The guy definitely knows how to do casual—No! No! I will not go there. He's a dumbass who doesn't even want his own baby and that makes him ugly as fuck, NOT hot.

"Hand delivering your own paternity results?" I say to give him attitude, and he actually has the nerve to sneer at me.

"He was coming up at the same time I was, so I tagged along." His lips contort into a *fuck you* kind of smile that has me wanting to slap the smirk right off his too good-looking face.

"Next time, buzz." He gives me a confused look. "That way I can deny you access," I explain. He hits me with a hard glare, and I shoot one right back.

"Real mature," he mutters. I ignore his jab and take the envelope from the poor kid who looks unsure of what to do. I show him my identification and sign, then give him a tip. He thanks me and scurries off. *Smart kid...*

Before I can invite Nick in, he takes it upon himself to walk through my door. "Sure...come on in." I slam the door behind me in frustration and immediately regret it when Reed starts whimpering. "Damn it."

"What's he doing here?" Giselle hisses, her nose scrunched up in disgust. Have I mentioned how much I love my best friend who totally has my back?

"I'm the dad," Nick states matter-of-factly.

"No, you're the sperm donor," Giselle lobbies back. "A dad is a man who claims his baby and cares for him. You simply shot your load into her vagina. X plus Y equals baby. You're the sperm donor, not Reed's father."

Nick lets out an annoyed huff, and I stifle a laugh. Reed's cries quiet back down, telling me he's fallen back asleep. "Would you like something to drink?" I ask Nick, my manners winning out over my desire to tell him to go jump off the GE building. He shakes his head, and I head to the kitchen to grab myself a bottle of water. Untwisting the cap, I chug half the bottle down, dying of thirst. Giselle and I just finished doing some yoga. I've been doing it since I was a little girl with my mom. It's a great stress reliever, and a good way to slowly begin to get my body back in shape. I'm still in my workout clothes, and I'm hot and sweaty.

When I walk back out to the living room, Giselle is standing near the bassinet looking like a human watch dog, and Nick is on the other side. "Everything okay?" I come up next to Nick, and he's looking down at Reed sleeping.

He clears his throat and steps back. "You named him Reed?"

"Yes, Reed Cameron *Harper*." I make it a point to place emphasis on the fact our son has *my* last name. "Reed is my dad's middle name, and Cameron was my mom's." He nods, and we both stand here staring at each other. I don't know what to say, and he's not saying anything either.

"Why are you here?" Giselle asks, breaking the silence. Nick ignores her question, glancing back down at Reed. Giselle and I lock eyes, and I shrug.

"I'm going to shower," she says, but it comes out more like a question, asking me if I want to be alone with Nick.

"Okay." I give her a tight smile. Once she's down the hall, I turn to Nick. "Why are you here?" I repeat Giselle's question, only this time he doesn't ignore it.

"I never thought I would become a dad."

"I never thought I would get pregnant from my one and only one-night stand." I lean against the arm of my sofa, not leaving Reed's side.

"I really thought we used protection."

"Look—" I tilt my head toward our sleeping baby and give Nick a sarcastic grin "—it really doesn't matter now. I'm assuming the results state you're the father."

"Yeah."

"Great, glad we got that sorted out without having to go on Maury."

Nick sighs in frustration, his eyes briefly closing. When he opens them, he hits me with a hard stare. The bright green in his eyes remind me of the fresh green grass in Central Park, the first sign of spring and warmth after a long, cold, white winter. Reed has his eyes. They're still dark since he's a newborn, but the emerald is already shining through.

I should say something, but I don't. I refuse to make this easy for him. I didn't ask to get knocked up, but here I am with a baby. I don't regret having my son. I love him with every fiber of my being. But I didn't plan or ask for this. My life has completely changed while Nick's has remained the same. Every day I live in fear I'm going to mess up my son's life. Make the wrong decision. What if he one day blames me because he doesn't have a dad? Being a new mother is a lot of work. I'm exhausted. I'm emotionally and mentally drained. I'm doing the best I can, but I'm scared my best won't be good enough.

"I don't know what to say, Liv," he finally says, using the name I gave him, and I have to force myself not to go back to that night all those months ago. When everything between us clicked. When his kisses alone had the ability to drive me insane.

"You don't have to say anything, Nick." This is so freaking awkward. You would never know less than a year ago, the man standing in front of me fucked me just about every way possible and then held me in his arms while we talked for hours.

"I wouldn't make a good dad." His lips turndown into a frown, and the sadness in his voice has my heart tightening. My natural instinct is to reach over and comfort him, tell him he can do it, just like I would with one of my art students when I give classes and they feel like they're failing. When they're afraid they can't draw or paint good enough. But I don't because he's not a student or a child, and it's not my job to comfort him. My job is to care for Reed, and if Nick doesn't want to be his dad, that's his choice. There's a reason why adoption is an option. Not everybody is cut out to be a parent.

"Now that paternity has been established, you can have your attorney draw up papers to relinquish your parental rights." Nick flinches slightly, almost like the words I just said pained him, but I ignore it. "Once you do, have them sent to my attorney. I gave Reed's and my information to your attorney the other day at the office when I brought Reed in to be swabbed. There's no reason for you to come back over here ever again."

"I can give you money..." he begins to say, but I put my hand up to stop him.

"We already had this conversation. I don't want or need your money. Does it look like I'm living on the streets?" I glance around my home to make my point. We're standing in a multi-million-dollar brownstone for God's sake, in one of the wealthiest areas in New York. "I can afford *my* son just fine."

"I didn't say you couldn't." His jaw clenches. "I just—I'm just trying to do the right thing here."

"Well, you don't have to worry about doing the *right thing*. I walked away that morning without telling you anything about me or getting your information. You didn't have a say in any of this, and I'm not going to force anything on you."

He sighs in frustration and then says, "If it's not money you want, then what is it?" He runs his fingers through his already messy hair, messing it up some more. "Damn it, Liv. I don't know what you want from me." His eyes are pleading with me to give him the right answer, but I can't do that because what I want isn't possible.

What I want to tell him is that I want to give Reed a family. One with a mom and a dad who love him and love each other. I want to be able to tell my son he was conceived out of love and not from a half-drunken one-night stand. I want to beg him to change his mind about wanting his son. But I don't tell him any of that. Instead, I say, "I don't want anything from you. Now if there's nothing else, I'm stinky and sweaty—" I glance down "—and I could really use a shower before Reed wakes up. I think it's best you go." I shrug my shoulders in total nonchalance when really, I feel the complete opposite. He has me riled up and wanting to punch him while also wanting to crawl into my bed and ugly cry.

"Okay." He nods slowly, his eyes darting from Reed to me. He turns and walks to the door. He opens it then twists back around like he wants to say something. And a small part of me—the part that stupidly still believes in fairytales—holds on to the hope that maybe he has changed his mind. While another part of me considers, even for a brief moment, blurting out everything I just thought and seeing where the chips fall. But the biggest part of me wants to push him out and lock the door behind him so he can't hurt me any more than he already has.

Okay...and maybe, just maybe, there's a small part that wants to pull him back in because holy shit! The man is swoon-worthy... Nope! Not going there...he's engaged and doesn't want his kid. He's off limits!

However, I neither push nor pull him anywhere. Instead, I stand frozen in place, waiting to see what he does. His mouth opens and closes like he's at war with himself, and for a second I think he's actually going to say something, but he doesn't. He lifts his hand, and with a sad smile, gives me a small five-finger wave before walking out the door.

I don't realize until the door is shut that I wasn't breathing, and I let out a much-needed breath, the tears releasing I didn't know I was holding in. They race down my cheeks one after the next until Giselle comes out and finds me. She holds me to her chest as I let out every emotion I have had locked up inside of me.

As I come to accept every dream I ever had as a child, and even as an adult, of finding the kind of love my parents had—the kind of love I long for—won't be coming true.

TEN

Nick

WELL, that sure as shit didn't go as planned...Then again, what the hell did I think would happen when I showed up at Olivia's home unannounced? It's not as if I exactly had a plan. I went there with the intention of discussing me being Reed's dad, but then I took one look at him and choked. And Instead of doing what I set out to do, I once again, like an idiot, offered Olivia money. I knew in the back of my mind she wouldn't accept it, but I had to try. Because for the first time in my life I'm at a complete and total loss as to what somebody wants from me. I have no clue how to make any of this right. She's just so...mad. It's obvious in the way she looks at our son and talks about him, she loves and wants him. But then why is she being so hostile toward me? God forbid she just tell me what the fuck she wants from me. And despite her denial, I know damn well she wants *something* from me...

Just like she wanted something from me nine months ago...That night I knew exactly what she wanted and gave it to her...but then again that want was mutual...fuck, was it mutual—until she walked away. I guess what has me going crazy is that when she showed up in the locker room, I thought for sure she wanted something from me. Everybody wants something. My dad wants money and respect. My mom wants to be accepted through status. Celeste wants to be financially stable, to feel taken care of while still feeling independent. But Liv's a whole different story because according to her, she wants nothing. But if that's true, then why the hell did she seek me out?

As I walk down the sidewalk away from her home, I think about how angry I made Olivia when I offered her money. I tried to explain I was just trying to do the right thing, but she wasn't exactly understanding.

Liv reminds me of a mystery novel. One that keeps you guessing the entire time. The more I read, the more clues she lays down for me to find. But with every clue, I'm left even more confused. At least with a novel, you know when you get to the end, the author will tie all those clues together in a neat package. Everything that was confusing will finally make sense. And, with a novel, if you lack patience you can always flip to the end to see how it all turns out. But with Liv, there's no end to turn to. I'm trying like hell not to run out of patience, but I'm afraid I may never figure out the mystery that is this woman.

I stop at the corner and pull the paper out of my pocket, needing to read the paternity results again. Like somewhere on this paper is the answer to all of my problems. I still can't believe I'm actually a dad. A week ago, I was a football player, a son, a fiancé... Now, I'm a fucking dad. I shake my head in disbelief. What the hell do I even know about being a dad? Giselle wasn't too far off base with what she said. The results may label me the father, but I haven't the slightest clue as to what to do with a baby. And then what happens once he's older? I grew up wishing for a dad who would love and pay attention to me. Wishing for a mom who would put me above herself just once. I grew up spending more time with Ms. Kelley, my nanny, than I did with my own parents. The day Fiona left, she looked at me and said having a baby with me would be a nightmare. A woman who had the shittiest life out of anyone I've ever known—raised by a drunken and drugged up mother in the worst part of North Carolina—actually left me because the thought of marrying and having a family with me was so terrible in her eyes.

I glance up and spot the old movie theater across the street. It reminds me of when I was younger and would ask my dad to take me to see the latest Star Wars film, but he would tell me he was too busy. The only time he would ever say yes to spending any time with me was when I would ask to play catch. I remember throwing the ball and his face lighting up. It was the only time I ever saw him truly get excited. The only time he would praise me. My heart constricts as I think about how good it would make me feel. I would've thrown that ball a million times if it meant having his attention. If it meant him telling me I was doing a good job. I didn't want shit from him. I just wanted my dad.

My mind goes back to what Fiona said: "*You always put your parents first.*" She walked away because she needed someone who would put her first. It's the same thing Celeste is afraid of—not being put first. Is that what Olivia needs? For me to put Reed first?

I lean against the brick wall, watching a family walk down the street. A flashback surfaces of my mom and me walking hand-in-hand through the park. I couldn't have been more than eight years old. We stopped at the ice cream truck, and she bought us the biggest ice cream cones. We sat on the edge of the sidewalk, talking and laughing, as we ate our cones. I smile, remembering that day like it was yesterday. She may not have ever looked at me the way Olivia looks at Reed, but I would like to believe in her own way my mom does love me. I just think somewhere along the way she got sucked up in the life of the rich and famous. And she was so scared of going back to where she came from, she ran as far as she could in the opposite direction—losing herself along the way.

A father and son pass by, and the dad grabs him in a chokehold, making the boy laugh. I try to recall even a single memory of my dad and me acting like that, but I can't. Celeste's recollection of what I once told her comes to the forefront of my mind: *You never felt you were good enough in your parents' eyes.* I don't want a child to ever experience the heartache I've felt over and over again, every time my parents have let me down, or when, in their eyes, I've let them down. All I wanted was for my parents to put their wallets and expectations away and love me.

And yet, here I am with a son of my own, who's not asking anything from me, and I'm walking away. And why? Because I'm scared of the idea of failing my son? While I'm over here judging my parents, they're exactly who I've become—only worse. I threw money at Fiona, paying for her school and the bills, and justified it as loving her. I've seen Olivia three times, and every time I've offered her money to make things right. I've agreed to a relationship of convenience with Celeste just so neither of us has to deal with any real emotions. Holy shit! I've literally become my father. But I can still change this. I can give my son the love and attention without the expectations and strings attached. I can show my parents what it looks like to simply and unconditionally love someone else.

My feet start moving of their own accord, and before I know it,

I'm buzzing the intercom. Giselle—with contempt dripping from every word she speaks—lets me up. And once I've taken the elevator up to their floor, I'm knocking on their door.

Giselle swings the door open, eyeing me up and down with disgust. "Livi is in the shower. Didn't you do enough damage?"

"Damage?"

She holds the door open, and I walk inside.

"You're so fucking blind. Livi might be selfless, letting you off the hook, but I'm not her. You come up in here, waving your dollar bills around like it's going to make up for the fact that you knocked her up and want nothing to do with being a dad. Your money means jack shit to Livi." I listen to her as she confirms everything going through my head, but also adding to what I was thinking. Olivia does want something from me. She wants the same damn thing I've wanted from my parents my entire life.

"She wants me to be a dad," I confirm, and Giselle gives me a *duh!* expression, reminding me of Olivia. Well shit, I can do that. That's why I came back here. She looks at me like I'm crazy, and I realize I'm grinning. But I can't help it. It feels like a huge weight has been lifted off me. Olivia doesn't want anything from me except for me to be a dad to our son, and not one like my father is to me, but one that's hands-on. Reed whines, so we walk over to his bassinet. "Can I hold him?"

Giselle gives me a hesitant look, but after a few beats, relents. "Fine. Have you ever held a baby before?"

"No." The little guy's cries pick up.

"Reach down and pick him up, but when you do, make sure you hold his head and neck steady. Newborns don't have control of their neck muscles yet."

Reaching down into the bassinet, I pick him up the way Giselle said to. He's tiny in my hands, yet solid. Definitely my kid. When I lift him up, I hold the back of his head in one hand—the rest of his tiny body resting on my forearm—and he stops crying for a second, confused.

Giselle's phone rings in her pocket, and she pulls it out. "I need to take this. It's the interview I've been waiting for. I'll be right out there." She points to the patio. "Be careful with him." She gives me a pointed look. I hear her answer the phone as she closes the door leading to their outside patio.

I watch Reed as his eyes work to focus, and once they're open, I can see the dark green irises that match mine. His lids flutter a few times, his eyes moving all over— not quite sure what he's looking at —and then he lets out an ear-piercing wail.

"Oh shit!" I'm not sure what the hell to do. I look over at Giselle, and she's still talking on the phone. Not wanting to interrupt her interview, I make my way down the hall with the crying baby. "Liv!" I whisper-yell, having no clue which room she's in. My eyes stay trained on the screaming baby, making sure he doesn't fall out of my hands.

Olivia opens the door, and holy shit, she's a fucking wet dream, standing there in only a small plush towel with her wet hair pulled up in a messy bun, the ends dripping wet. I watch as the droplets run down her neck—that same neck I spent hours sucking and kissing on—over her collarbone, and disappear down into her luscious tits.

"What the hell are you doing?" She cuts across the hallway and plucks Reed out of my hands. "Who let you in here?" She glares my way while she rocks him gently, his cries lessoning by the second.

"Giselle let me in. She had to take a call...an interview, I guess, and he started crying."

She huffs loudly in frustration, then walks down the hallway toward the kitchen, her ass swaying in the towel as I follow behind her. She stops at the counter and grabs a can of something with one hand. When she reaches for what looks like a bottle, it falls to the ground. She sighs, the baby still crying in her arms. She bends down to pick it up and the bottom of the towel rises, giving me a peek of her ass. *Jesus, I'm going to hell...*

"Here! Let me help." I reach down, needing to focus my attention on something other than her sexy-as-sin body, but she snatches the bottle off the ground before I can grab it. Once she's standing upright again, I reach for the baby in an attempt to help her.

"What are you doing?" she snaps.

"I'm trying to help."

"I don't need your help." *Alrighty then...*Olivia finishes making the bottle one-handed then sticks the nipple-looking thing into Reed's mouth. He immediately stops crying and starts sucking. She carefully wipes the tears from his eyes, gives him a kiss on his forehead, and then looks at me. We stand in the kitchen, staring at each other for a moment, neither of us knowing what to say. These awkward moments just might be the death of me. I've only known Olivia for a second, but she has got to be the most challenging person I've ever met.

"He has my green eyes," I say, trying to break the silence. She glares, and I close my mouth. Just as I'm about to say what I really came here for, there's a knock on the door.

"Jeez!" she huffs out. "It's like Grand Central Station over here." Still holding the baby and the bottle, and still in her towel, she opens the front door.

And it's her dad. His gaze moves back and forth between Olivia and me. "Why are you standing in a towel with Nick here?" Olivia's eyes dart down to her lower half then back up to me, embarrassment coloring her cheeks.

"Oh my God!" She carefully thrusts the baby with his bottle into her dad's arms before scurrying out of the living room and back into the bathroom, slamming the door shut behind her.

I chuckle, and her dad hits me with a hard glare. "Why are you here with my daughter while she's in a towel?"

"The baby was crying, and she just got out of the shower."

He lifts the baby up, burping him like he's done this a million times. "Doesn't explain why you're here." Reed burps, and Coach lays him back down across his arms, giving him some more of the bottle.

"I came here to see Reed." I study Coach for a few moments, comparing him to my father. I would bet my dad never fed or changed me. He probably never even held me. Ms. Kelley was a part of my life from as far back as I can remember. I doubt either of my parents actually took care of me more than they were required to. Meanwhile, Liv is doing it all on her own here—with the help of her friends and family. Not with the help of her baby's father.

"You okay?" Coach asks, concern evident in his eyes. I glance from my son to him, and I know what I need to do. My words aren't going to make a difference with Liv or her dad. I need to show them through my actions.

"Yeah."

"We're going out for brunch to celebrate a belated Christmas. Would you like to join us?"

I consider it for a moment, but then Olivia walks back out, dressed and shooting daggers at me, and I figure it would be best not to upset her further.

"That's okay. There's something I need to take care of. I'll see you tomorrow at practice." I'm about to walk out the door, but before I do, I stop and lean down and give my son a kiss on his forehead.

When I get home, I put a call in to my attorney with my request. He says he'll file the paperwork today, and Olivia should receive the papers in the next two to three days. Next, I call Celeste, not wanting her to hear it from anyone else. When it goes straight to her voicemail, I remember she's on a plane to Los Angeles.

I text Killian and ask him to meet me at the baby store, and he agrees. I'm scared as shit at the idea of being someone's dad, but I'm confident that with time I'll get the hang of it. Practice makes perfect, right?

I'M PRETTY sure we purchased every item imaginable at the baby store. Luckily, they deliver, and I won't have to deal with any of it until tomorrow when it all arrives. I have practice in the morning, so I scheduled it all to arrive in the afternoon. Seeing that it's almost nine o'clock here, I call Celeste since she more than likely arrived in LA a couple hours ago.

"Nick," she answers.

"How's it going in LA?"

"Good. It's a quick visit for a last-minute shoot for my spring line. I'll be back tomorrow."

"I need to talk to you."

"Look, if it's about me not going with you to see Olivia..."

"I've decided to file for joint custody. My attorney is filing the paperwork today."

When she doesn't say anything, I continue. "I want to be Reed's dad."

"Reed?" Her voice is soft, very unlike Celeste.

"That's his name. I saw him today, and he has the most beautiful green eyes and a thick mop of brown curls. He deserves to have a dad. I know you of all people can understand that." Celeste stays quiet, so I keep talking. If we're going to work in any way, she's going to have to be on board with my son staying here in our home. "I got a bunch of baby stuff today. It's all being delivered tomorrow."

"Where's it all going to go? We only have three bedrooms."

"Killian is helping me move my desk and files into your office. I figured we can just share one office. And that will open up a room, so that I can turn it into a nursery for when Reed comes over." When Celeste doesn't say anything, I pull the phone away from my ear. It shows she's still on the line. "Celeste?"

"Yeah," she says quietly. "I need to run."

"Okay...have a good night."

"You, too."

ELEVEN

Olivia

"THAT MOTHERFUCKER!" I throw the papers onto the table, and Giselle swipes them up. I'm so pissed I could murder him!

"He filed for joint custody?" she questions after reading the top document.

"Yep! The last thing he said to me was that he didn't want kids! He said he wouldn't be a good dad! Now...he wants shared fucking custody! Fifty-fifty!"

I sit down at the table, my head resting in my hands. I don't know what happened, what changed his mind, but he could've let me know. "We could've discussed this. I don't understand what happened that made him not only change his mind but file for joint-fucking-custody."

"It says he agrees to pay child support as well." Giselle sets the document on the table. "Maybe he's just trying to do the right thing."

Do the right thing...those are the same words Nick threw at me the other day.

"I should've known he was up to something when he came back the other day." I pull out my phone and call my attorney. His assistant puts me through.

"Olivia, I just received the petition."

"He said he didn't want kids." My voice cracks at the thought of my baby having to go with him and his evil fiancée—which reminds me that I still need to throw away all of the makeup with her stupid name on them! "He didn't want Reed. Why is he doing this?"

"I'm not sure. But as a father who has established paternity, he's within his rights. You have thirty days to respond, but he's requested he be given visitation in the meantime."

"How long do I have before I need to respond to his request for visitation?"

"Fourteen days for the temporary visitation and thirty days for the shared custody."

"Okay, can you please hold off until the last day? Maybe he'll change his mind."

We say goodbye, and I call my dad. When he doesn't answer, I remember it's Friday. Tomorrow is game day. I look online and see it's a home game. Good! That means I won't have to wait for Nick to get home to kill him. Then an idea forms. He wants to fuck with me, well two can play this game.

I'VE RALLIED up my girls—Corrine, Shelby, and Giselle—and we're in the owner's box getting situated. I didn't tell them my plan, in fear they would try to stop me, but I still wanted them with me in case anything goes down. I know they'll have my back regardless if they think I've done something stupid. Reed is sleeping, and I'm looking around for my target. If she's not here, my plan won't work. I spot her, and when she notices me, I set my plan into action. Immature, sure. Dirty, definitely. But so was Nick filing for custody without telling me!

Gently, I shake Reed awake—don't judge me. He begins to cry, and everyone's eyes start darting over to us. Giselle shoots me a confused look, but I ignore her, standing up and pretending to soothe him. The truth is, he hates it when you rock him too much. He prefers to be swayed. His cries continue to get louder. Out of the corner of my eye, I see Nick's fiancée staring at Reed in horror, her mouth pinched in annoyance and her eyes squinting in pain at the loud cries coming from my baby. I hold back my grin, pretending to look concerned, meanwhile Reed is now pissed off and wailing at the top of his lungs. I want nothing more than to soothe him, and I will soon.

Celeste continues to glare daggers my way, her eyes squinting from Reed's ear-piercing screams. And then when she can't take it any longer, she swipes up her purse and stomps out of the room. As soon as the door closes behind her, I immediately slow down my rocking, and my baby boy instantly lowers his cries. "Shh... Mommy's sorry, baby," I coo softly, wiping his tears away. His eyes begin to flutter closed.

"You're bad." Corrine smirks knowingly.

"I don't know what you're talking about." I play stupid, trying to hide my triumphant grin.

"I've seen her here several times. She shows up once in a while to support her fiancé. She's always dressed impeccably and always makes sure to speak to the media."

"If I've learned anything from watching my dad with my mom and then with you, it's that men follow their woman's lead. If he's filed for custody because she wants to play house, hopefully this will have her thinking twice."

"And if he filed because he wants to be a dad?" I still at her question. I hadn't thought about that. I've been so mad over the fact that he filed behind my back, I never considered his motives, or that they might be pure.

"I'll cross that bridge when I get to it. Based on her reaction to Reed crying, if she did want to play house, she'll more than likely be begging him to drop his petition for joint custody. I guess we'll find out soon enough what his motives are."

Corrine gives me a soft smile, the one moms give their kids right before they're about to give them advice. "I know you're hurt, and nothing is happening how you imagined it. But the one thing I learned from my divorce with Shelby's dad is that it's better to get along and play nice than to piss everyone off. If he's serious about being a dad, you both will be raising Reed together for the next eighteen years."

WE STAY for the entire game. Eventually Celeste returns, but I don't play any more games—not wanting to upset Reed again. New York wins, and after the teams make their way off the field and into the locker rooms, Giselle and I take off. I had wanted to confront Nick, but Corrine's words have me wanting to avoid him while I come to terms with the harsh reality of this situation. If he's filed because he wants to be a dad, I'm going to have to share my son...*our* son with him—as well as with his soon-to-be wife.

We get home and I lay Reed down to sleep in his crib. Grabbing a glass of wine and my laptop, I pull up a couple museum sites in the area. While I love being home with Reed, one day I'm going to want to find a job doing what I'm passionate about—sharing my love for art with others. I had planned to go back to France one day, but now I'm not sure that will be possible.

Giselle has taken off to go have dinner with Christian, so when there's a knock on the door, my thoughts are that it's probably my dad. Corrine asked if she could tell him about the petition Nick filed, and I told her she could.

I look through the peephole, and when I see it's Nick, I swing the door open. "Don't you know how to use the intercom system downstairs like everyone else?"

He shrugs. "I figured Reed might be asleep, so I followed someone in." He steps into my home without invitation. "Have you received my petition yet?"

Guess we're getting right to it. "Yep, thanks for the heads up." I go to slam the door but catch it. My anger isn't worth waking up my newborn baby.

"I was going to tell you, but you weren't in a good mood. I figured it would be best to show you through my actions."

"Oh, you sure showed me." My hands go to my hips.

"Okay..." He gives me a confused look, and I glare at him, silently wishing for a space shuttle to come down and kidnap him. "Well, I haven't heard back yet, so I wanted to ask if I could see Reed."

An oversized lump forms in my throat, and I have to swallow several times before I speak. "I just got the papers. I have fourteen days to respond."

"Yeah, I know, but I was thinking I could spend some time with him while we wait for it all to go through the courts and become official."

"No." The word is out before I can stop it, and Nick's confused look morphs into anger.

"No? You're going to keep my kid from me?" His eyes glance over my shoulder and around the room for Reed.

"He's sleeping. I think it's best if you go. As I said, I have fourteen days to respond, and until then there's no agreement." My palms are sweaty, so I rub them down my jeans to calm my nerves.

Nick gives me an incredulous look. "I don't get it." He scrubs up and down his face with his hands and then locks eyes with me. "You gotta give me something here, Liv. You can't really be considering fighting against me for wanting to spend time with our son. You came to me. That day in the locker room. You came in there and flipped my world upside down. You said you didn't want anything from me. You just wanted me to know I'm the father. What did you think the outcome would be when you told me? If you didn't want me to be a dad, you shouldn't have said anything when you recognized me. You fought for this, and now you're fighting against this. What you're doing doesn't make any sense."

He's frustrated and confused, and I don't blame him. He hit the nail directly on the head. I didn't think any of this through. I saw him playing, and all I thought was that I would be able to give my baby his father. I never imagined that he would be engaged, and we wouldn't be a family. I never considered I would have to give up my son fifty percent of the time. I was blinded by wanting that stupid effing happily-ever-after. But none of this is Nick's problem. He's doing the right thing, and he's right, I can't keep our son from him.

After I take a calming breath, so I don't cry in front of him, I force my tears back and say, "You're right." I nod once. "It's late, and like I said, he's sleeping. Would tomorrow be okay?" I only suggest this because tomorrow is New Year's Eve. There's no way he'll agree to take a baby on one of the biggest partying nights of the year. I'm sure he and his fiancée have plans.

Nick's shoulders sag in relief. "Yeah, I'm off tomorrow since we played today. I can come by in the afternoon."

"It's New Year's Eve," I point out, but he simply shrugs.

"I'm pretty sure our only plans were to go to the team party, but I'll cancel them, or she can go alone."

"And when would you bring him back?" *Please say in a few hours. Please say in a few hours.*

"I bought a crib and stuff, so I can keep him for the night and bring him back in the morning. We don't have practice until the following day." Not able to speak, I nod again, then walk over to the door, opening it up to indicate I want him to leave. He gives me a quizzical look, but I avert my eyes, not wanting to look at him. "Okay. Well, I guess I'll see you tomorrow."

He shoots me a small smile, thanks me, then leaves. When he's just on the other side of my threshold, he turns around like he's going to say something but changes his mind. *He seems to do that a lot.* I shut the door, lock it, and close my eyes, wishing that this entire ordeal is one big nightmare that I'll soon wakeup from.

TWELVE

NICK

IT'S CLOSE TO NOON, and I'm lying in bed, half-awake, when the bed dips down slightly. By this time of the day, I've usually gone for my daily jog and been to the gym to get a workout in, but with everything going on, I've taken the day off. I roll over and Celeste is facing me. She had to attend a photo shoot last night after my game. Because it ran so late, she ended up staying at a hotel near where they were shooting.

"What are you still doing in bed? It's almost noon."

I sit up and take a sip from my water bottle I left on the night-stand. "I took a day off. What's up?"

Her eyes go wide, and her grin is huge. "I heard back from Richard Ford."

"The designer?" Celeste has been looking into expanding her company. As of right now, she has a makeup and an accessory line, both of which are excelling far beyond what she'd ever imagined. Now her goal is to start her own clothing line. She's been pitching said line to several different investors, but who she really wanted to partner with is Richard Ford. According to Celeste, he's one of the top designers in the world.

I offered to lend her the money to make it happen, so she wouldn't have to partner with anyone, but she told me this is some-thing she wants to do herself. I had invested in the initial startup of her company a few years back and was shocked when she'd paid off her loan in full—interest included—sooner than what we'd originally agreed upon. To say that I'm damn proud of her is an understatement. From the outside, Celeste may *look* like she's nothing more than a beautiful model, but don't let her cover fool you. Inside is a damn smart and savvy businesswoman.

"Yes! He's all in!" she squeals. "I can't believe it, Nick." She clasps her hands together in excitement. "Production will start early spring."

"That's amazing!" I pull her in for a hug.

"And there's more. Several of the department stores and boutiques I reached out to have verbally confirmed that they're interested in carrying my line. If all goes well, my clothes will be in stores next Christmas! And not just in the United States! I'm talking international...Milan and Paris...Italy!"

"Look at you, conquering the world." I give her hand a squeeze.

"My dreams are finally coming true." She looks at me with a watery smile, and before I even know what's happening, her mouth crashes into mine. I back up quickly, confused. "What are you doing?"

"Kissing my fiancé," she says, hurt evident in her tone.

"Since when?" I ask. We've been together for the last nine months, and aside from the one time we tried—and failed—to have sex, Celeste has never once kissed me in any way other than as a friend.

Celeste lets out a soft sigh and then follows it up with a loud huff. I watch as her eyes go from appearing hurt to being cold. "Do you not understand how bad this all looks, Nick? You're going to be raising another woman's baby."

"No...I'm going to be raising *my* baby."

"That you had while engaged to me!"

"No," I repeat. "He was created before us. He was *born* while engaged to you."

"Everything is about to be destroyed."

"Nothing is going to be destroyed."

"You don't know that." She shakes her head. "If a scandal arises, Richard might change his mind about wanting to partner with me, or the department stores might decide that carrying my name isn't in their best interest."

"It's hardly a scandal. I'm not the first guy to find out he has a son. The stores aren't going to think like that about your name. They want you because you're the best. And Richard Ford isn't going to change his mind. He would be stupid to." I take another sip from my water bottle and then add, "I thought I had your support, Celeste. You told me Reed deserved more than to have a dad who doesn't want him."

"I do support you," she insists.

"Okay, good. I really appreciate it." I throw the sheets off me and get out of bed. "I need to get ready. I'm having lunch with Killian and then going by Olivia's to pick up Reed."

"What? Why?"

"I'm assuming that you're referring to me picking up my son and not me having lunch with Killian." I smirk, and Celeste rolls her eyes. "I told you earlier in the week, I petitioned for joint custody. The room is ready."

"It's New Year's Eve," Celeste deadpans.

"And I'll be bringing in the New Year with my son. You're more than welcome to join us."

"I saw her at the game. That baby...it kept crying!" Her eyes go wide.

"She was at the game?"

"Yes! And the baby was screaming his head off. Maybe you should suggest she hire a nanny," she says, scrunching her nose up in disgust.

I internally groan. Every time I've seen Olivia, the baby is fast asleep or being cared for. "Babies cry. What's really going on?" I cross my arms over my chest and stare down at Celeste.

"I-I..." She throws her arms up in frustration. "I can't do this! I can't be the other woman." Tears prick her eyes, and I know there's more to all of this than what she's saying. But Celeste is a vault, and she'll never open up to me—or anyone.

"You're my fiancée."

"Exactly! So can we maybe...try for real?" She gets up from the bed and approaches me. "I know you went from getting laid on the regular to not at all. I don't want you to be unhappy." Her hand moves to my dick, and she grips it through my boxers. She's right. I did spend a lot of time inside women, and obviously sex is on my mind. For one, I'm a man, therefore, it's pretty much always on my mind, but also, ever since Olivia came back, I can't get our night together out of my head. She was the last person I was with before I agreed to this pseudo relationship with Celeste. She was the last woman I sank my dick into, and I can still remember the way her tight cunt felt... *Fuck!* I can't think about Olivia like that.

Removing Celeste's hand from my crotch, I back up slightly.

"We already did once and there was nothing there. As a matter of fact, I'm pretty sure your exact words were, 'I can't do this. It feels like I'm about to fuck my brother, if I had one.'"

"Well, maybe we didn't try hard enough. What does she have that I don't, Nick?" *Oh, hell no...there's no way I'm going there, not even with a ten-foot pole...*

"Celeste, you're a beautiful woman. You know this. But you're my friend, and I can't see you as anything more than that. Just like you don't see me as anything more. If you're scared I'm going to cheat on you, I wouldn't do that. You know I've been cheated on, and I wouldn't do that to someone else." I walk over to the bathroom door.

"I'm not scared of you cheating," Celeste says, but the way her voice cracks as she says the words tells me otherwise. "It's just...you spent an entire year only having one-night stands, and not once did you want more...until her."

"That might be true, but she left," I point out, opening the bathroom door.

"And now she's back."

Celeste doesn't wait for me to respond. She walks out of our room, and I watch her walk away, having no clue what to say to her to ease her mind. Closing the bathroom door behind me, I strip out of my clothes and jump into the shower. Celeste was right. I slept with way too many women last year, but it wasn't until Olivia that I found myself wanting more. Fuck, how could I not? The chemistry between us was like nothing I'd ever experienced.

Reaching down, I fist my cock as I think about her, my mind going back to our one and only night together. How brazen she was. The way she sucked and fucked me like a woman on a mission. How responsive her body was to my touch—the way we connected on a deeper level. My fist tightens around my hard shaft, stroking it up and down as I recall Olivia's mouth around my cock. The way she took me with abandon.

My fist pumps harder, my grip tightening. I can feel the pull in my balls beginning. My forehead hits the shower wall as I recall the way she rode my dick in the middle of the night. The way her tits bounced up and down. Her hands splayed across my chest as she milked my cock until it was completely drained. My fist tightens, my strokes get more frantic, as I chase my release. I remember the way she kissed me with such passion. The way her body felt against mine. The way we fit so goddamned perfectly together. Letting out a low groan, I watch my cum shoot out and coat the wall before the water washes it away.

Letting go of my cock, I feel a sense of relief for about a minute, until it hits me that I just got off to the visual of Olivia, the mother of my son, the woman who *isn't* my fiancée. And with that thought comes the sobering realization that this engagement isn't going to last. So much has changed in the last couple of weeks. Everything I thought I wanted, I'm quickly realizing isn't actually what I want at all. I've been living in denial, not wanting to deal with the reality of this situation—that when I got together with Celeste, it was because she was the safe choice. Olivia had just walked away, the New York Brewers' owner and coach had said I needed to settle down, and Celeste was there, ready to make good on our pact. We were on the same page. But now, in light of recent events, I don't think we're even reading the same book.

Finding out about my son was eye-opening, a game changer of sorts. I've spent all these years wishing things would change between my parents and me, but when I was injured and then Fiona left, I gave up. I took the easy way out. From the one-night stands to agreeing to the arrangement with Celeste. But now that I have my son to think about, I'm ready to try again. I'm ready to open my heart and be the type of father he deserves. The change has to start somewhere and what better place to begin than with my son and me.

I flip the switch to turn the water off, grab a towel and dry off, then get dressed. Once I'm ready, I head out to the living room. Celeste is on the phone making plans, so I slip out quietly. Usually I'd call for a car service to keep it simple, but since I'm picking up my two-week-old son, I decide to grab one of my vehicles from the garage.

The valet brings around my BMW X6—and even helps me install the car seat—and then I'm heading out to meet Killian. We meet at one of our favorite hole-in-the-wall cafés. New York may have many big-named restaurants, but it's the small ones that nobody's ever heard of that are actually the best.

"Olivia is letting me take Reed tonight," I say after the waitress sets our drinks down.

"By yourself?" Killian looks at me incredulously.

"Yes, by myself, *dick*."

Killian chuckles. "Calm down, I was just asking. So you're not going to the New Year's Eve party tonight?"

"Nah, I know Olivia did that shit on purpose. Told me I could take him on one of the biggest party nights of the year."

"Hoping you would say you couldn't," Killian adds with a smirk.

"Yep." I take a sip of my water. "But I'm not about to choose a party over my son. That's the shit my parents did, and my new goal in life is to be the opposite of them."

Killian nods in agreement. "Can't go wrong there. I bet Celeste is pissed."

"Yeah, but I can't really blame her. This isn't what she signed up for. We agreed to no kids, and now here I am with one."

"Can you imagine Celeste with a baby?" Killian laughs so loud that people look our way. "I would pay half my salary to see her change a shit diaper!"

I laugh along with him as I try to picture it—I can't. The waitress comes over and takes our order. We both go with a Club sandwich and a salad.

"Are you bringing Melissa to the New Year's party tonight?" I ask Killian once the waitress walks away.

"No." Killian takes a sip of his drink. "She actually met someone, and I guess it's serious." He rolls his eyes. "She's talking about moving across the country with him or some shit." Killian's been friends with her for years, and while I'm almost positive she's always had a crush on him, he's never shown interest in being anything other than friends with her. Guess she finally moved on.

"So, who are you bringing then?" I ask.

"Nobody special." He shrugs nonchalantly then changes the subject, just like he always does when the topic of him dating gets brought up. "Are you heading over to get Reed after lunch?"

"Yeah, wanna join me?" I'm only joking, but the truth is that I could definitely use the moral support when dealing with Olivia. Between her and her friend, I don't stand a chance.

"Hell no!" Killian laughs. "That's all you. I have an appointment with Jase to get some ink added to my sleeve." Killian lifts his shirt sleeve to show me where he's planning to get the work done.

"Damn, I need to go by and see their shop soon. That's awesome that he and Jax opened a tattoo shop here in New York." Jase Crawford is an old friend of mine and Killian's from back home. Even though Jase was a couple years ahead of us, because we all played ball together, we ran in the same circles. While in school, Jase was also apprenticing to become a tattoo artist. Shortly after he graduated, he got a job at the same shop his brother Jax was working at. They always said their dream was to open their own place. But when Killian told me a few months ago that they opened their shop, Forbidden Ink, in East Village, I was surprised. Jase and Jax always seemed like the type of guys who'd prefer to live in a small town over a big city. New York definitely isn't for everyone. It's fast-paced and will eat you alive if you aren't quick enough.

"Planning to get some ink?" Killian jokes. While his body looks like an art canvas, I've never really considered getting a single tattoo. Guess there wasn't ever anything worth putting permanently on my body.

"Who knows?" I laugh. "If I were going to get one, he's the guy I would trust to do it."

After we're done having lunch, and Killian tells me he's only a phone call away if I need any help with Reed, I head across the Brooklyn Bridge into Brooklyn Heights. I find fifteen-minute parking in front of Olivia's brownstone and then head up, buzzing for her to let me in. *See? I know how to work the intercom…*

When I get to her front door, her dad opens it up. He's dressed to the nines in a three-piece tux. He must've stopped here on his way to the team party. He enters the hallway and closes the door behind him instead of letting me inside. "Do you know what you're doing?"

I'm confused as to what he's talking about. "Coach—"

"Not here. Outside of the locker room, I'm not your coach. I'm Stephen Harper, the father of the woman you created a baby with… a baby you initially said you didn't want. I'm the grandfather to the baby you're now demanding to take."

We commence in a stare-down for a few moments before he closes his eyes and sighs. When he opens them back up, he says, "Just tell me this, are you taking him to prove something? To punish my daughter?"

I take a second to think about my answer. Growing up I never had a man to look up to. When I was in college and then playing pro for North Carolina my coaches were assholes. It wasn't until I was picked up by New York I felt like I truly found my place in the world, a place I felt at home, and a lot of it has to do with the man standing in front of me. The day we found out I slept with his daughter, our relationship changed. We should've had this talk a couple weeks ago, but like the men we are, we both avoided it.

"I didn't know she was your daughter." I blow out a harsh breath. "I never would've slept with her had I known. I'm sorry for all of this. I never wanted to hurt her. You of all people know the shitty relationship I have with my dad. My initial response toward becoming a father was out of fear that I would end up like him. I shouldn't have reacted the way I did. I know my word doesn't hold a lot of weight right now, but I'm going to do everything in my power to make sure the relationship I have with Reed is nothing like the one I have with my parents. So, to answer your questions, I guess I'm trying to prove something to myself, but it isn't to hurt Liv. I want to be a good dad."

"Okay," he says, "as a father, I can respect that." Without waiting for me to respond, he opens the door wide, allowing me to walk through first. There are several people here: Olivia, Giselle, her stepmom, and stepsister. They're all sitting around her and appear to be comforting her.

"Is everything okay?" I ask, suddenly worried something has happened to Reed. The women all turn to face me, four pairs of glaring eyes that have me taking a step back.

Olivia stands, wiping her eyes, her chin raising in defiance. "Yep." Giselle goes to say something, but Olivia stops her. "No." She shakes her head.

"Is Reed okay?" Something is going on, but nobody is saying anything.

"Yes." She hands me a diaper bag. "Reed's formula and bottles are in here, as well as a change of clothes and diapers and wipes in case you don't have any yet. He usually eats every three hours, and he was just fed." Her voice cracks, and I want to ask why she's crying, but I don't. "Do you have a car seat?"

"Yeah, my car is parked in the short-term parking in front of your building."

She nods and heads down the hallway.

"You're such an asshole," her stepsister hisses, but before I can ask what the hell I did, Olivia reappears holding Reed.

"Okay, sweet boy," she murmurs to him. "Mommy is going to miss you so much." She gives him a kiss on his forehead, her eyes closing and her lips lingering. When her eyes open, the tears she's trying to hide, escape. "I love you," she whispers to him.

She hands him over to me, and looking me dead in the eyes, she pleads, "Please take care of him."

"Of course." I take him from her, and when he squirms slightly, I tighten my hold on him. "I'll bring him back in the morning."

Since I'm almost positive every person in the room hates me, I quickly say goodbye as I head straight for the door.

"Wait!" Olivia runs over and hands me a piece of paper. "This is my number. Can you please text me yours in case of an emergency? This paper also has Reed's doctor's information and anything else you need to know about him."

I take the paper from her. "I'll text you once I get him settled in the car."

"Thank you."

The car ride back to my condo is uneventful, and after pulling up to the valet, the attendant informs me I can keep Reed in the car seat to bring him up. I give him a large tip in appreciation, and he laughs, telling me he has four kids and if I need any help, to ask.

When I get inside, I see Celeste is dressed in a floor-length silver gown. Her hair and makeup are done, and she looks beautiful as always. I set the car seat down on the coffee table, and she comes over to check him out.

"He looks just like you, Nick." She smiles, but it's sad.

"Yeah, he does, doesn't he?" I grin. "You look beautiful."

"Thank you. I spoke with Mercedes, and she referred me to Quality Nanny. I wasn't sure with it being New Year's Eve, but they were able to find a nanny who's available." Mercedes is a model Celeste is friends with, who recently had a baby. She's also the wife to Brandon Evers, one of the linebackers on our team.

Carefully taking Reed out of his car seat, I place him into the swing and click it on just as the YouTube video I watched showed me how to do. "I told you I'm not going out. Olivia let me take him for the night. I'm not leaving him with a nanny."

"You act like nobody leaves their children with a nanny. You loved yours growing up," she insists, and she's right, I did love Ms. Kelley. She was beyond sweet and maternal in a way my mother had no desire to be. When Celeste would come over after school, Ms. Kelley would make us snacks and take us to the park and on picnics.

"I know they do, and you're right, I did love Ms. Kelley. But I saw more of her than my own parents. It's not happening. I can't let it happen. You want to go out, go."

"We were supposed to go together. As a *couple*. It's your team party. I can't believe you're really going to make me go alone." She snatches her handbag off the table, and with a huff, swings the door open and slams it shut behind her.

The loud sound reverberates through the walls and Reed starts to cry. "Hey there, little guy." I stop the swing and pluck him out, giving him his pacifier since it's not quite time for him to eat yet. Sitting down on the couch with Reed, I set him between my legs and create a vibrating motion with my thighs by shaking my feet back and forth. I read that a lot of parents do this to help calm their babies down. Within minutes, his cries cease and soon after he's asleep. Afraid that if I move in any way he'll wake up, I carefully reach for the remote control and turn the television on and then switch the channel to ESPN.

I'm not sure how long I watch the highlights of today's game for, but when Reed starts to stretch his tiny little body, I glance outside and see it's already dark out. His pacifier drops out of his mouth as he starts to cry. Taking him with me, I grab a bottle from the diaper bag to feed him, but it's empty. Then I remember Olivia had to put stuff in it. With one hand holding him, I use my other hand to sift through the bag. I find a can of formula and pop the lid open. It's powder and smells like shit. *Do I add water or milk?*

Reed's cries get louder as he grows more frustrated by the second. "Hold on, little guy." He was asleep for a while, so I imagine he must be starving. I read the back of the can and it says to mix with water, but it doesn't state how much he should take.

Remembering I have Olivia's number, I dial her. It barely rings once before she answers. "Everything okay?" She sounds distraught.

"Yeah," I answer her over Reed's crying. His face is now red, and hot tears are pouring down his face.

"Nick, why is he crying?"

"He's hungry, but I don't know how much he takes."

She's quiet for a second, and I think I hear her sniffle. Then she says, "I included it all on the paper I gave you." The paper! I should've read the paper. I only glanced at it long enough to get her number from it.

"Okay, thanks! I'm sorry for bothering you."

"You're not a bother. You have our son. Please call me if you need anything."

We hang up, and after reading the directions on the paper she gave me, I make Reed a bottle and feed it to him. His cries stop immediately, and a few minutes later, his entire bottle is gone and he's content once again. Laying him down on the ottoman in front of me, I snap a few pictures of him and send them to Olivia, figuring she might enjoy seeing them. She texts back a thank you.

"All right little man, it's just you and me bringing in the new year together. What do you want to do?"

Reed kicks his feet out.

"Sorry, buddy. No partying for you, you're too young." Reed's feet start kicking faster and faster. He looks like he's becoming agitated, and then a second later he starts to cry. I pick him up and walk him over to the swing. He seemed to like it earlier. I set him in it and try to give him his pacifier, but he immediately spits it out, his cries getting louder. Well, hell. He can't still be hungry. Maybe he needs to be changed?

Taking him out of his swing, I bring him into his room and place him on the changing table. I go about changing his diaper, and after several attempts of trying to get the tabs to stick, it works and he's in a fresh diaper, but the crying continues.

Not wanting to bug Olivia—and if I'm honest, I want to prove I can handle being a dad on my own—I pull up a baby site the sales associate told me about and search reasons for babies to cry. Holy fuck! There's like a hundred different reasons!

"Okay, let's go down this list," I say out loud to Reed, who isn't listening. I go through each reason, one by one: Hungry, wet diaper, fever, teething, constipation...the list keeps going. I haven't the slightest clue about half this shit. One reason for a baby to cry is being overtired. He just woke up from a nap, but then again, I have no idea how long babies stay awake for. Could he already be tired again? A mom mentions that she takes her baby for walks or for a drive when he's tired and needs help going to sleep. Spotting the car seat in the corner, I set Reed in it and buckle him in.

About two minutes into our drive, Reed's cries get louder, angrier. It sounds nothing like his cry of hunger. It's painful to listen to. I glance in the review mirror into the mirror facing his seat. His face is bright red, and my heart begins to pound as I consider something might be wrong with him.

Putting my pride, as well as the need to prove I can do this by myself, aside, I grab my cell phone and call Olivia while turning the car around to head toward her place. "I think something is wrong." I explain everything I did—from feeding him, to changing his diaper, to taking him for a drive. While we're talking, his crying never once lets up.

"I'll be right there."

"I'm already on my way."

We hang up, and roughly ten minutes later, I hand Reed over to her. She takes him out of his car seat, sits down on the couch, and starts checking him out. Then she places him on his belly across her lap and starts patting his back.

Within minutes, his crying has ceased. She glances up at me with a ghost of a smile playing on her lips. And it's then I notice her nose is red, her cheeks are blotchy, and around her eyes are puffy. She's been crying.

"He's gassy, but it's trapped. When you press on his belly, it helps release the gas. You have to make sure when he eats, you stop him several times to burp him. He's a little pig and will suck it all down too fast."

"Fuck!" I say aloud, "I forgot to burp him." I'm already sucking at this parenting thing.

"You'll learn," she says, "it just takes time."

I sit down next to her and glance at Reed, who is still on his belly across her lap. His eyes are open, but he's totally content. "Why didn't you go out tonight?" I ask her. She's sporting a pair of fleece sweatpants and a matching hoodie. Her hair is up in a messy bun, and her face is free of any makeup.

"Umm... maybe because I just had a baby a couple weeks ago." She nudges me playfully. "I was surprised you wanted to take him on New Year's. My dad and Corrine are at the team party."

"Yeah, Celeste is there too. I don't really care about that stuff."

"That's not what google says." My eyes meet hers, and she immediately tries to backpedal. "I mean..."

"You googled me?" I waggle my eyebrows playfully, and her cheeks turn an adorable shade of pink.

"I wanted to know about the father of my baby."

"And what did you find out?"

"Nothing I didn't already know." Reed makes a cooing sound, and she picks him up.

"Tell me why you were crying." She averts her eyes, but I'm not having it. "Liv, talk to me."

"He should be good now." She ignores my question and hands him back to me. I notice she has a movie going, but it's been paused.

"What're you watching?" When she doesn't answer right away, I look at her and see that she's blushing. "What is it? Porn?"

She slaps my arm. "No! Here." She hands me the pacifier, and I put it in Reed's mouth. His eyes roll back, and I laugh.

"He loves that thing. So, what are you watching?"

"Titanic."

"Ahh...good old Leo." I glance around the room. "Where's your roomie?"

"I made her go out." That's when I notice on the coffee table is a box of Kleenex and a tub of ice cream.

"Liv, why were you crying?"

She huffs. "You can't be that oblivious, Nick." She hits me with a pointed look, but I have no clue what she's talking about. "I was crying because you took my baby. My very new, very fragile, newborn baby," she whispers, her eyes shooting up toward the ceiling as she tries to stop the tears from falling.

"I told you I'd bring him back tomorrow."

"I've never been away from him." Her voice cracks. "I wasn't prepared for this, prepared to let him go. I went from thinking my son would never have a father, to you saying you didn't want to be a dad, to being blindsided with a petition for joint custody. I just gave birth a couple weeks ago for God's sake. It's just..." She swipes at her eyes, but the tears come anyway. "It's just a lot. I'm a new mom. I don't want my baby out of my sight."

"Fuck..." I was so caught up in trying to do the right thing, I didn't even think about how my taking our son would affect her. Most women in my life wouldn't care. Look at Celeste. She was trying to hire a nanny before she even officially met Reed. My mom had a nanny hired before I was even born. I spent more time with her growing up than I did with my own parents.

"I didn't think any of this through. I grew up with a nanny who was more of a parent to me than my own parents. Unless it was football related, my dad didn't know I existed. And the only time my mom showed me any attention was when she would drag me to family functions."

Olivia's eyes meet mine, and I can tell she's paying attention—actually listening to what I'm saying—so I continue. "You were so mad that I didn't want to be a dad. When I realized I could do this, and that I wanted to do it better than my parents did, I didn't stop and think about your feelings, or what all of this would mean for you. I'm sorry. We'll figure it all out. I promise."

"Thank you." She grants me a sincere smile.

We look down at our son and see that he's fast asleep. "I should get going. Let you get back to your movie."

Her lips turndown into a slight frown, but she nods. "Or we can watch the countdown," she suggests.

"I'm leaving Reed here with you, Liv. He's exhausted and finally asleep."

She bites down on her lower lip for a second and then softly says, "You could still stay and watch the ball drop. I mean, if you want to...or you could still make it to the party."

"I'll stay here," I tell her without giving my decision a second thought.

Our eyes lock for a brief moment and then she nods. "Okay." She switches the movie off and finds the New Year's Eve show on the television. "Have you ever been?"

"To Times Square for New Year's? Once. It's a damn madhouse. You?"

"Growing up, my parents would always stay home. They said there were too many drunks on the road. My dad would pick up take out, and they would let me stay up to watch the ball drop on TV. Once I was old enough to go out, New Year's Eve was the only night they would make me stay home, but I didn't mind. It had become a tradition of sorts, plus they always let me pick the food."

"Where's your mom now?"

Olivia frowns. "She passed away from breast cancer when I was seventeen. She was born and raised in France until she came here at eighteen to meet with a photographer. She was a model. She met my dad on the subway on the way to her meeting." She laughs. "It was love at first sight."

"Is she why you were living in Paris?"

"Yeah...after she died, it was hard to be here without her. I moved over there after graduation in hopes of learning about my roots and ended up staying there."

"What made you move back?"

"Reed. My dad wanted me to be near family. Giselle graduated a few weeks ago, and since she's from here as well, she agreed to move back here with me. She's the best friend a woman could ask for."

"She hates me."

Olivia giggles. "With good reason."

"Hey, you're the one who left me."

"It was a one-night stand!"

"Says who? It was never specified. I woke up and you were gone. If you wouldn't have hightailed out of your room the next morning, I would've asked for your number."

"Oh God! You're so full of it, *Cole!*"

"Okay, *Liv.*" I chuckle, and she snorts.

"Just watch the show."

THIRTEEN

Olivia

THE DOOR SLAMS closed and I jump slightly, my neck groaning in pain. My hand comes up to massage the kink as I attempt to sit up, only I can't. My body is overheated and I'm being weighed down by... Nick? I glance around. Why the hell is Nick's body wrapped around mine on the couch?

"Oh shit!" Giselle shrieks, and Nick rolls off the couch, landing on the wood floor with a loud thump.

"What the hell?" His voice is husky and has me tightening my thighs as I remember the last time I heard his voice like that—when he was pulling me on top of him at three in the morning, so I could ride his hard...Shit! I can't think about that night. He's freaking engaged!

"What's going on here?"

I sit up and notice Giselle has her hands on her hips, and she's still wearing her clothes from last night. Her makeup is also completely messed up like she's been crying.

"What's wrong?" I ask, rubbing the sleep out of my eyes. "And what time is it?"

"It's four in the morning. I spent the night at Christian's hotel..." Her words drift off, and her eyes brim with tears.

"Giselle, what happened?" I've never seen her look this upset.

"Christian and his friends threw a party. Before the clock even struck midnight, they were completely wasted and I had enough, so I went to bed alone. I woke up around two to go pee and he was still partying hard. He had left his phone on the counter and it went off several times. I couldn't help being nosy, so I checked it. It was from another woman."

"Oh no! He's seeing someone else?" Giselle was just saying she felt like it was too good to be true. *Dammit, Christian!*

"Not someone...some-*ones*. Plural. I could tell that he's changed, but I didn't want to admit it to myself. He was drinking a lot, and I caught him with drugs. He kept making excuses, but I knew deep down that's just what they were...excuses. I ran out of his room upset, but after thinking about it, like the idiot I am, I went back up to his room to talk to him. I guess I was hoping he would convince me it wasn't what it looked like. I wasn't even gone an hour and he had already replaced me with some groupie-whore. I'm so stupid. I walked in and caught him fucking her in his bed. I should've known. He's a damn musician who travels around the country on tour. Of course he has a different woman waiting for him on speed-dial in every city."

"Hey now, that's not fair," Nick cuts in. "Not every guy who travels, cheats. I've never cheated while on the road."

Giselle glares down at Nick who is still on the floor. "That you'd admit to," Giselle hisses. "But there's more, and it's not about me." She frowns.

"Jesus, what else happened?" I ask.

"While I was waiting for my Uber to arrive, I was checking my social media and saw something..." She glances toward Nick, who has moved from the floor to the couch and is sitting next to me. "You know what. We can discuss what I saw later. What I'd like to know is what your baby daddy is doing here and not at home with his fiancée."

"We must've fallen asleep while watching the countdown. Nothing happened." I stand. "Now tell me what's going on. You have me freaking out and assuming the worst." Her eyes dart toward Nick. "Is it about Nick?"

"No." She shakes her head.

"Then just tell me!"

"Fine. Victor the asshole posted on social media."

"My ex?"

"Do we know any other asshole named Victor? Yes, *that* Victor. He announced his engagement to Heather."

"Heather? Our friend from college?"

"Yes! And according to their post, they've been together for two years."

"But that would mean..." I do the math in my head. "He cheated on me?"

"Apparently they were keeping it all under wraps the entire time. Nobody knew."

"Wow, I guess that explains why he didn't ask me to move with him to Switzerland."

"He was a self-absorbed dickhead anyway," Giselle points out. "Plus, he was shitty in bed. Remember you said you didn't know how bad Victor was until..." Her eyes glance toward Nick, and I will her not to finish her sentence. The last thing I need is for Nick to know that the night I spent with him was without a doubt the best sex I've ever experienced. I had no idea how crappy my sex life with Victor was until Nick and I spent the night together.

Reed lets out a wail, and I get up way too quickly to grab him, needing to end this potentially awkward moment. I change his diaper and clothes, and when I come back out, Nick is still sitting on the couch.

"You okay?" he asks.

"Oh yeah." I wave him off. "Nothing I can't handle. We've been over for a while. Before you and I—well, anyway, I should've known, but I was too blinded by trying to find that stupid happily-ever-after. Speaking of which, shouldn't you get home to your fiancée?"

He looks like he wants to respond but thinks better of it. "Yeah... umm...is it okay if I come by Tuesday to see Reed? It's my day off from practice. Once you respond to the custody petition, we can figure out a set schedule."

"Sure." I leave the living room and head to the kitchen to make Reed a bottle, and Nick follows. "Reed has a doctor's appointment tomorrow afternoon. It's just a routine check-up. I don't know what your plans are but—"

"I only have practice in the morning. I'll go." Nick takes Reed from me so I can make the bottle, and I let him.

"Right...okay." Nick is standing close to me, our son nestled in his arms. He smiles softly, and I allow myself a minute to check him out. Reed has a lot of his features. From his bright green eyes, to his messy hair, which curls at the ends. His jaw is chiseled with day-old scruff. He's a handsome man, and my son will most likely look similar to him. He leans over and gives Reed a kiss on his forehead, and the beauty in the moment sends shivers down my spine.

To an outsider, we look like a family. A mother and a father looking down adoringly at their baby. The false illusion has me frowning. All my life I watched my mom and dad live in a fairytale. I imagined one day I would have that. Instead, I'm a single mom with a baby by a man who's engaged to another woman. It sounds like the making of a Lifetime movie instead of Disney.

I finish making the bottle then take Reed from Nick, situating him into my arms and giving him the bottle. We're walking out of the kitchen and into the living room when Giselle comes running out from her room, freshly showered and looking like she's ready to take on the world.

"I got the job! I got it! Lydia emailed me last night! I'm officially employed by one of the most elite interior design firms in New York. I mean, it's only an internship, so I won't get paid much, but it's a start."

"Fresh Designs?"

"Yes! This is a dream come true. Do you know what this job will do for my resumé?"

"I'm so happy for you! When do you start?"

"Next Monday. They're off for the holidays. She said to come in early Monday morning to get all the paperwork filled out. We need to celebrate. Let's go out for lunch."

I glance down at Reed. "I'm not ready to bring him in public yet."

"You brought him to the game," Giselle points out.

"Yeah, but that was only..." My eyes dart to Nick, remembering he's still here.

"To scare the hell out of Celeste?" he says dryly, and I flinch.

Giselle giggles, and I do my best to hide my grin. If Nick knows, that means Celeste went home and told on me.

When I don't answer right away, Nick says, "I don't know all the details, other than the fact that Celeste thinks you should hire a nanny."

"What?" I screech. That wasn't my intention!

Nick smirks. "That poor baby was crying and being neglected."

"He was not! He is perfectly taken care of." My heart starts racing. Is that why he's here? Does he think I'm incapable of taking care of our son? "I just let him cry for a few minutes. I was hoping she would freak out and run back to you, and you would go away!"

Nick's grin widens. "Nice try. I'll give you credit, though. Your plan worked...partially. She wants nothing to do with a baby unless it comes with someone else to handle the crying, but you aren't getting rid of me that easily." He taps my nose with his pointer finger and chuckles. Then he says goodbye to Giselle and gives Reed another kiss. "See you tomorrow."

"Yep," I say, watching him walk to the door.

"Well, well, well," Giselle says slowly, once Nick is out the door. "I must admit, I didn't see this change of events coming, but now it makes sense."

"What are you talking about?"

"You and Nick." She nods slowly.

"I wasn't trying to break them up. I was hoping to scare her, so she would convince Nick not to seek custody. I was desperate. It was stupid." I sit on the couch and continue to feed Reed his bottle.

"But did you hear what he said? His fiancée won't be getting anywhere near the baby. I give that engagement two more weeks tops. He's committed to this daddy gig, and she's committed to the runway." Giselle plops down on the couch next to me.

"And if they split up, that will be their issue. It has nothing to do with me."

"So, you haven't thought about what it would be like to give Reed a mommy and a daddy?"

"I am giving him one of each." Setting the bottle down, I lift Reed up against my shoulder and pat his back until he lets out a loud belch.

"You know what I mean."

"In the beginning...when I first found out I was pregnant, all the time. Then when I spotted him playing football, the thought ran through my head...until he spoke." Giselle laughs. "We have nothing in common other than one night of hot sex."

"Explain."

"He's a freaking pro football player who's engaged to a gorgeous, successful supermodel. I bet they jet off on his days off to the Caribbean or some shit. Nick probably lives an extravagant, over-the-top life while I prefer mine to be more...low key. Sure, right now he says he wants to be a better parent to Reed than his were to him, but that's only because Reed is like a shiny new toy. Once Nick gets bored of playing dad, I'll be the one who is left to pick up the pieces of our son's heart when I have to explain to him why his father doesn't want him."

Giselle gives me a pointed look. "Your mom was a model, in case you forgot, and your dad played football before he became a coach." My heart tightens at the mention of my mom.

"Are you defending them? Because she's nothing like my mom, and he's definitely not like my dad."

"No, I'm simply pointing out that you're making a lot of assumptions and judgements without knowing all the facts. In case you forgot, you're rich. You could out-vacation both of them."

"Whatever..."

"Don't 'whatever' me. What if Celeste wasn't in the picture? Could you see yourself with Nick?"

"No way. My life might've taken a detour, but I'm not giving up on true love. I want what my parents had. I want a man who is in love with me."

"You had to have seen something in Nick to bring him back to your hotel room that night..."

"Victor had just broken my heart, and Nick was nothing more than a hot guy who helped me get over him." But even as I say the words, I know they aren't completely true. That night with Nick felt like more than just a one-night stand. It felt raw and real, like we connected on a whole other level—something I never felt with Victor. It scared me, and I ran.

"Judging by your expression, I think I've made my point." She puts her hands out wanting to hold Reed, so I hand him to her. "What your mom and dad had was beautiful and magical, but you're never going to find your happily-ever-after if you keep comparing every guy to your dad, and every relationship to the one your parents had. What they had was theirs...maybe it's time you find your own."

"Enough about me. I'm sorry Christian ended up being a cheater," I say, changing the subject.

"It's not your fault, but I can tell you one thing. I'm never dating another musician again. And while I'm at it, I'm banning all athletes too! Who else travels?"

"Pilot," I say, going along with her rant.

"No pilots! Who else?"

"Umm...Military guys travel, right?" I ask.

"Yeah, but don't they go to like Afghanistan? Do you think they cheat with Afghani women?"

"I'm not sure," I say. "We could look it up."

"Well, to be on the safe side, I'm banning all men in the service! Oh! And truck drivers too!" I bite my bottom lip to stop from smiling, but when Giselle cracks a smile, I can't help but giggle.

"You're banning everyone!" I say through my laughter, and she throws her head back in a fit of giggles. "There's going to be nobody left."

"Maybe I'll turn lesbian like my sister!" She laughs.

"What? Since when is Adrianna gay?"

"Since she called me last night and told me she wants me to meet her girlfriend!"

"My goodness. This New Year's is jam packed full of surprises!" I say. "Speaking of your sister. How is she doing? Aside from her switching teams?" I wink dramatically, and Giselle laughs.

"She's good. Living and enjoying the college life. She was accepted into some sorority, so she's ecstatic."

"And how's your mom doing?"

Giselle sighs. "It's a good thing we came back. My mom has gotten worse, and my dad is almost never home. I've been visiting her, trying to help around the house, but she's just too much to be around sometimes. I asked my dad about getting her help, but he doesn't want to deal with it. Every psychiatrist she sees says the same thing. She's depressed."

"I'm sorry, sweetie." I pull my best friend into a hug. "If you need anything, all you have to do is ask...no, not ask, just tell me."

"I know, which is why you're my best friend and I love you."

"Love you more."

FOURTEEN

NICK

AS I'M LEAVING Olivia's place, my mom calls me. I've barely said hello when she starts ripping into me.

"Nicholas, you weren't at the party last night." Immediately, I regret answering the phone call. Before I can respond, my mom continues, "That was a team party. There was a lot of press there. It looks bad when the face of the team doesn't show up." Stopping in front of my car, I close my eyes and lay my head against the side. Holy shit! I'm a thirty-year old man whose mom is still keeping tabs on him. It was so nice during the year I wasn't playing and they left me alone. The holidays need to seriously be over so she and my dad can go back to North Carolina.

"Mom—" I'm about to tell her I need to call her back when she puts my dad on the phone. *Great...*

"Nick, I have three contracts for endorsements, which need to be signed. I've already okayed them all. I'll bring them to you later today with all the details. I had Amber make sure the commercials and photoshoots will take place after your season is over."

Before I can ask any questions or even say okay, he's already put my mom back on the phone. This is what he always does, though. He handles my career. My mom rattles on about the next function and how important it is for me to be there, and just like my dad, when she's done saying what she needs to say, she hangs up. Unlocking my door, I get in my vehicle, feeling suddenly drained. Has dealing with my parents always been this exhausting? And yet, it doesn't even feel like I've participated in the conversations with them. What exactly did I say? Hello?

Needing to let off some frustration, I head over to the stadium. There's no practice today, but the gym is always open for us. When I walk inside, I spot several of my teammates working out. Not wanting to talk to anyone, I change into my workout gear and head out to the field. My workout of choice for today is sprinting up and down the steps. Plugging my ear buds into my ears, I start jogging upward. The music is playing, but I can't focus on the lyrics. My mind goes back to my non-conversation with my parents and then to last night with Olivia. The two of us watching the countdown—talking and laughing and getting to know each other. I've never felt that at ease around someone. When I talked, it felt like she was actually listening.

Since as far back as I can remember, everybody in my life has talked at me instead of with me. They've always wanted something from me. From my parents, to my coaches, to my girlfriends. Everybody has these expectations that are exhausting to live up to. But when I was sitting on the couch with Olivia, watching television and eating her microwaved snacks, something felt different. Real.

We fell asleep on the couch, and even without anything sexual happening, I felt closer to her than I have felt to anybody I've ever been with. It has me wanting to find out where things might lead to, but I know I can't do that as long as I'm engaged to Celeste.

Fuck...Celeste. I hate that I agreed to this pact and to this engagement, and now I want out. I never should've agreed to it in the first place, though. It doesn't matter how many times I get hurt, I don't think I can give up on love. Sure, I took a break from it. I had my fair share of meaningless hookups, but I never really gave up on the idea of love. I'd just accepted that it probably wouldn't happen for me. When Fiona told me the thought of having a family with me was the equivalent of a nightmare, I took her words to heart. And I don't blame her...I know I put my parents and my career before her. But now that I'm recognizing that, I'm hoping I can change things. It wasn't until I walked away from both of those things that I found some happiness. Now I have my football career back, but with it came my parents. I'm not about to let history repeat itself, which means I have some tough decisions to make. First one—being honest with Celeste.

"OH GOOD! YOU'RE HOME!" I'm not even through the door and Celeste is on me. "I leave for Milan in an hour. I've been thinking about our conversation yesterday, and I know I had said that I only viewed you as a brother before, but I really think—"

Grabbing Celeste's hand, I pull her to sit next to me. "We need to talk," I say, cutting her off. Her brows furrow with worry. "Last night I was—"

"Nick, whatever it is you're about to say, don't. I don't want to know."

"I spent the night at Olivia's place."

"I said I don't want to know!" Celeste stands.

"I'm not going to hide shit from you."

"I can't handle knowing if you cheated on me. Please, just don't tell me," she pleads. Tears fill her lids, but she quickly blinks them away. "Don't tell me," she whispers.

"Celeste, did someone cheat on you?" I ask. Her eyes go wide for a split second before she schools her features. "You know you can talk to me," I add.

"There's nothing to talk about," she says, her voice now completely devoid of all emotion. I assess her for a moment, but when it's clear she's not going to open up to me, I give up on trying to get anything out of her.

"Nothing happened," I say, needing her to know that I would never cheat on her.

"Okay, good." She nods her head up and down several times. I stare at the beautiful woman I've known my entire life. When I was told I needed to settle down and Celeste had reminded me of our pact, I thought it was fate. I was done with love and relationships. We agreed on a marriage of convenience with a prenup and no kids. She knew exactly what she wanted, and I thought it was what I wanted as well. But now as I look at her, I know all I was doing nine months ago was taking the easy way out. I didn't want to go up against my parents. I didn't want to risk letting another woman down. Celeste was safe. But the truth is, I never would've lasted in a loveless marriage, and Celeste deserves so much more, even if she doesn't realize it.

"Celeste."

She grants me a small smile, one that most don't see. It's one that screams vulnerability. When she's unsure of how to make something right. When the situation is out of her control. The fact is she's not a bad person. She's one of my best friends. When she lets you in, she is sweet and kind and supportive. She was honest with what she wanted, and none of this is her fault.

"Don't do this, Nick. Please." A single tear escapes, rolling down her cheek. "We have a good thing going."

"This type of relationship isn't for me. And it shouldn't be for you either. We both deserve more. To be with someone who we love and who loves us back."

"So, what? You're in love with Olivia?"

"No, but I want to find out if I could be. What if she's the one?"

"You thought Fiona was the one, and she—" Before she can finish her sentence, there's a knock on the door. She walks over to it, and my parents are standing there. That's when I remember my dad had mentioned he was going to bring the papers by for me to sign.

"Celeste, what's wrong?" my mom asks.

"Nick believes he could be in love with Olivia."

"Wait, is this over the baby?" My mom gives me a confused look. "Celeste said you chose to stay home last night instead of going to the party even though she found a nanny."

"I don't want a nanny. I want to raise my son myself."

"You had a nanny," my mom points out.

"I don't want my son to have the same kind of life I had." The words are out before I can stop them, and my mom flinches as if she's been slapped.

"You had a good life."

"According to who? You? Dad?"

"You were given every damn thing you wanted," my dad says, joining the conversation. "Most would kill for your damn life. So stop acting like a spoiled brat."

"Yeah, I was given materialistic shit, but neither of you actually raised me. If it wasn't football related, you didn't even know I existed."

"Oh, Nick, stop acting like a damn little girl," my dad scoffs.

"Tell me this. Other than football, what did I participate in, in high school?" I turn to Celeste. "Don't say a word." She might sometimes be self-absorbed, but she was still my best friend growing up, and unlike my parents, she actually knows me. And even when I had no one else at my various school events, Celeste would always be there.

"Nicholas! Why are you acting like this?" my mom screeches, avoiding the question she can't answer. "Your father and I have done everything in our power to make sure you had your future paved for you. You should be thanking us, not judging us. You have no idea what the real world is like."

"What I do know is that growing up, all I wanted was to make both of you happy. I busted my ass in football to the point where I lost my love of the sport and my girlfriend left me. Did you know that when she left me, she said I put you guys first? And what sucks is that while I was putting you two before my girlfriend, you were putting yourselves first! It's the parents' job to put their child first, not the other way around."

"This is all about that flighty waitress?" my mom asks. "She was a waste of your time."

"That flighty waitress? She was in dance school. Holy shit! Can you be any more stuck up and judgmental? Do you not remember that you used to live in a trailer park?" I point to my dad. "Until he got you out! I loved her and was going to marry her. But she left me!" My voice booms. "She left me because she said it would be a goddamn nightmare to have a family with me because I put you guys first!"

"Stop!" Celeste yells, and everyone turns their attention to her. "I'm not going to let you believe that."

"Celeste, don't," my mom hisses.

"No, it's enough. Look, Nick, that woman you loved. She didn't leave you because you put your parents first. She left you because—"

"Celeste!" my mom yells.

"Your mom paid her off. She gave her five hundred thousand dollars to walk away."

My head jerks to my mom. "Is she for real?"

"I did it for you. She didn't love you! She wanted you to quit playing and start a family. And then you got injured. I knew if she had it her way, you would never play again."

"Are you out of your mind? You didn't do it for me!" I nod toward my dad. "You did it for him and for you. So he could keep making money off me and you could continue to brag about your NFL player son! That's all I am to you people!" I shake my head then turn to Celeste. "And where do you fit into all this?"

"I didn't know, Nick. I've always been upfront with you. She just told me this last night at the party."

"So, this entire time, I thought she left because she no longer loved me, but it was because she was paid off."

"You know what, Nick? Your mom might've paid her off, but Fiona took the money." Celeste puts her hand on my arm. "You chose love, and she chose money. You walked away heartbroken, and she walked away hundreds of thousands of dollars richer. I told you years ago, the world revolves around money, not love."

"Maybe so, but in my experience, money destroys the world. I'll take love over money any damn day." And that's without truly experiencing it firsthand.

"Nick, stop being dramatic," my dad says.

"Did you have anything to do with all this?" I ask him.

"No, I didn't. It was all your mother. But let's be real. Had she stayed, you wouldn't be playing. So, I have to say I think she did what was in your best interest at the time." He pulls the papers out of the envelope. "I need to get going. I need to talk to you about a possible new contract at the end of the season, but it can wait. I just need you to sign these papers." He hands me a pen, and I quickly sign them.

When I hand him back the pen and papers, he heads toward the door, my mom following on his heels. As he opens the door, I call out my mom's name. "Let me tell you something. Olivia is my son's mother, and she'll be around in some shape or form for the rest of my life. If you try to mess with her in any way, I'll make sure your status and reputation are the least of your concerns."

"Nicholas!" my mom cries, "are you threatening me?" It's the first time I've ever seen tears actually appear from her.

"No, Mom. It's a goddamn promise. Either you accept Olivia and Reed or you're dead to me."

Once my parents are out the door and it's closed, Celeste says, "I have to leave, but when I get back, I'll move my stuff out."

"You don't have to leave right away. If you need time to find a place, it's okay."

She comes over and hugs me. "I appreciate that, Nick, but it's time. You're my best friend and I'm not about to lose you because of my issues. I'm sorry for asking you to own up to that pact."

"You didn't make me do anything. But you know..." I laugh, thinking about the other half of the pact. "I really do think there's a good chance Olivia could be the one."

Celeste rolls her eyes. "Yeah, yeah."

"And I met her before I turned thirty."

"Okay..."

"So, if we end up falling in love, technically that would mean you would have to pay up."

"What are you talking about, Nick?"

"We agreed...if I found love before thirty, you would do the same."

Celeste suddenly looks crestfallen. Her eyes go glossy and she averts her gaze away from me. She clears her throat and swipes away the tears. "Sorry, there's something in my eye."

"Yeah, you've had a lot of *somethings* in your eye lately," I say. "Want to tell me what's going on?"

"Nope, it must be something in the air...pollen or dust..."

"Yeah, okay. Have it your way. But I'm not letting this pact go. You better get ready to find your true love."

"Talk to me once you're actually in love and in it for the long haul, lover boy." She pats my chest playfully, but the sadness in her features remain. "I need to catch my flight." She leans over and gives my cheek a kiss. "I'm sorry for what your mom did. Please believe me when I say I never wanted to see you hurt."

"1-RIGHT, 11 BELLY, PASS ON 2." The guys scramble, and I completely forget the play I just called. Luckily, Craig Stratum, one of the wide receivers, is open, and I throw it right into his awaiting hands.

"That wasn't the play!" Coach yells, not missing a beat. "Where's your head at? That's the fifth play you've messed up!" On any given practice, we'll go through over a hundred different plays, and I always get them right. Today, my head isn't in the game.

"All right," Coach yells. "Head on over to the weight room and give me an hour and then we're done for the day. Nick, wait back a minute." I jog over to Coach Harper, and he waits until everyone has cleared the field to speak. "You're not yourself today. How's your arm feeling?"

"It's solid," I answer truthfully.

"Good. Then what's going on?"

"Just some personal shit. I'll get my head back in the game."

"Okay," he says, not pressing me for more. "After your workout, want to get a session in?" Coach Harper has been my biggest supporter since he picked me up last year. He's stayed after everyone's left to help me more times than I can count. I've missed working out with him these last few weeks.

"I would, but I told Liv I'd pick her up for Reed's check-up." Coach nods, a hint of a smile playing on his lips.

"I heard what you did on New Year's Eve." Unsure of what he's referring to, I give him a puzzled look.

"You spent the night so Reed would be home."

"I fell asleep..."

"You didn't have to do that. You have no idea how much that meant to Olivia. I know the day will come when you'll pick up your son, and she'll have to accept that she's in a co-parenting situation, but thank you for giving her a little bit of time."

"What if it didn't have to be that way?"

"What do you mean?" He cocks his head to the side.

"What if I wanted to be more than parents with her?"

"Are you asking my permission to date my daughter? While you're engaged?" He shoots me a look of disappointment.

"I called off the engagement. Celeste is moving her stuff out when she gets back from Milan." Coach nods slowly, taking a second to think about what I've told him.

"I've never been in this situation. The first time I fell in love was with Olivia's mom, and I loved her until the day she died. The second time was with Corrine. It was a few years after Francesca died. I never imagined I would fall in love again, and at first, I felt so damn guilty for moving on. But when I called Olivia and told her, she said, 'Dad, we don't decide who we love; the world decides for us. And if Corrine is who you love, you can't turn your back on it. Nobody should be without love.'"

Coach Harper smiles in memory. "My daughter has always believed in true love, probably more than most. She believes in the happily-ever-after—the fairytales you see in the Disney movies— and it's my fault. What her mother and I had was pretty damn close to what you see in those movies, and even when times were tough, we never let her see those moments. She grew up believing that's how love should be. Now I'm afraid one day she'll wake up and lose her belief that true love exists. She's already made comments about that dumbass Victor cheating on her. And then to top it off, she's being so hard on herself over how Reed was created." He shakes his head, and I'm stunned by the turn this conversation has taken. This is the same man who drills us every day on the field, and he's talking about Disney movies and fairytales and shit.

"I guess what I'm trying to say is before you make a move on my daughter, you need to figure out if you believe in love. If you're willing to give her, her happily-ever-after. Because if you aren't, stick to co-parenting. Let her find the guy who can give her what she deserves. My daughter deserves her fairytale ending."

I know exactly the kind of love Olivia wants because it's the same kind I want.

"Regardless of what happens, I'm here for you. You're the father of my grandson. No matter where you end up at the end of this season, or in life, I'm only a phone call away."

"Thank you, Coach."

FIFTEEN

OLIVIA

BECAUSE OF NICK being well-known in the area—and the fact that he's three games away from bringing the team to their first Super Bowl game in well over a decade—the nurse had to rush us back to a room. I didn't even think about it when I made the appointment as I didn't plan on him attending.

"If you could please fill out this paperwork, I'll be back in a few minutes to collect it and then the doctor will be in to check out your son." The nurse hands me a clipboard of papers and walks out, closing the door behind her. Nick is standing against the counter, holding Reed in his arms, and I can't help but smile at how adorable they are. Our son looks like a tiny little peanut when he's laying against his father's muscular forearms. Nick is wearing a New York Brewers T-shirt that accentuates his muscles in all the right places, and Reed is in a matching onesie. When Nick arrived to pick us up, he handed me a small bag with the onesie inside. Since I hadn't gotten Reed dressed yet, I put it on him. We both took several pictures, and I sent one to my dad.

I get busy filling out the paperwork while Nick talks to Reed. "...so then I threw the ball to Killian for the touchdown, but the ball slipped out of his fingers like his gloves were lined with butter. He better get it under control..." I glance up, and Reed is staring at his father like he knows what he's talking about. My heart stutters and then flutters at the beautiful sight in front of me. Without Nick seeing, I pull my phone out and snap a picture of them.

Putting my phone away, I go back to filling out the paperwork, when I hear Nick say, "Whoa there, buddy. What did your mom feed you?" When I glance back up, his face is contorted into a look of disgust.

Setting down the clipboard, I reach into the diaper bag and pull out a diaper and wipes. "I can do it," Nick offers, taking the items from my hand. I'm about to argue with him but instead hand over the items.

"Thanks," I say, then go back to filling out the paperwork. A minute or so later, I hear "Holy shit! Dude, what the heck did you do? It's like a shit bomb blew up in here." I giggle softly but continue what I'm doing.

"Umm...Liv, can you get me more wipes?" His question comes out muffled, and when I look up, he appears to be paler than a few minutes ago. The bottom half of his face is hidden under the collar of his shirt, and he's making a gagging sound.

Grabbing the wipes container, I jump up to help him out and about die at the scene in front of me.

"Oh my God!" I crack up laughing. There's shit everywhere! All over the baby, the table, Nick's hands. "What happened?" I cackle, and Nick glares.

"What the heck are you feeding this kid, Liv?" He gags again, grabbing the wipes from me.

"It's just formula." I shrug. I pull some more wipes out and start wiping up the poop, which is everywhere. I strip down Reed, who doesn't seem fazed at all by any of this. Nick grabs the diaper and gags again while wrapping it up.

"Bad gag reflex?" I joke.

"Oh, c'mon! That smell should be considered toxic. Did you see the fumes rising from his ass?" Nick says as he washes his hands in the sink. He's dead serious and that only makes me laugh harder.

We get Reed cleaned up and get a fresh diaper on him, but I don't bother dressing him, knowing the doctor will just ask to remove his clothes. Instead, I wrap him up in a blanket and hand him back to Nick so I can wash my hands and finish filling out the paperwork.

"Knock, knock." The pediatrician comes in, closing the door behind her. "My name is Dr. Fox." She shakes Nick's hand then mine. I've met her a couple times before, but this is her first time meeting Nick. She has Nick lay Reed on his back. "And how is

Reed doing?" She begins to examine him, taking his temperature and checking his heartbeat. Nick stands over her the entire time while I answer the questions. We go over how much he's eating and what percentile he's in for height and weight—he's above average for both.

When she's all done, she says, "Okay, he's getting three shots today. The nurse will come in and explain what they're for. Once she's done, you can check out in the front and make his next appointment."

She shakes both of our hands one more time and then leaves.

"What does she mean three shots?" Nick looks at me horrified. It's then I remember he wasn't there at Reed's post-birth appointment a couple weeks ago.

"Babies get a lot of shots their first year." Nick picks up a now-whimpering Reed and holds him close to his chest. He's still in only his diaper.

The nurse comes in with the syringes on a tray. She explains the three shots he will be getting and gives me a pamphlet of information for each one. "Okay, Dad. You can hold him just like you're doing, and I'll get the shots in from right here." Nick's eyes shoot to mine, the first look of fear I've ever seen from the man. I haven't spent much time with him, but when I have, he's full of confidence in everything.

The nurse sticks Reed with the first shot and his whimpering turns into a high-pitched scream. Nick backs away from the nurse before she can get the second shot in. "Nope! Not happening." He backs up a little more until he's in the corner, comforting Reed.

"You're just going to let her do this to our son?" he says to me, accusingly. I let the judgment go because he's only being a protective dad.

"He needs these shots to protect him. Do you want me to hold him?" I put my hands out, and he shakes his head.

"No, forget this. He's crying." Tears are racing down Reed's face, and Nick is trying to soothe him.

"It will be over quick, I promise," the nurse says, and Nick shoots her a glare that has her flinching. If he wasn't so serious, this entire situation would almost be comical.

"Easy for you to say." Nick's hands tighten around Reed's tiny body. "You're not the one being stabbed with needles." I grab his pacifier from the diaper bag and use it to calm him down. He immediately stops crying, and the room goes quiet.

"Ready?" the nurse asks Nick, who looks like he's a wild animal trapped in the corner with nowhere to go but into a cage. He nods slowly and starts talking softly to Reed about football like he was doing earlier. The nurse pricks Reed two more times and he lets out another cry, his pacifier falling from his mouth. I catch it and push it back in while Nick continues to sway him gently in an effort to calm him.

———

"SURELY, with all the medical advancements they've made, they can find a better way to give a baby a shot," Nick drones on over the entire shot experience that he's clearly more traumatized over than the baby who actually got the shots and is sound asleep in his car seat.

We're sitting in one of the more well-known restaurants in East Village. As we were leaving the doctor's office, Nick mentioned lunch, and I reluctantly agreed. Then Giselle called at the same time Killian did, and Nick suggested they join us. So here we are, the five of us—including Reed—eating a late lunch at the French Bistro.

Because it's January in New York and freezing, we have to eat inside. Nick called ahead, and once we arrived, we were whisked back to a private room that looks like it usually holds fifty people. He definitely gets good dad points for this one. He's sitting next to me, and while I know it's wrong, I can't help pretending that instead of us being here as just Reed's parents, we're here as a couple. I've seen a different side of Nick today. Not the same guy as the night I met him—who was straight up sexy as hell—but a softer, gentler side. The kind of guy I see in my father.

"Don't kids get like a hundred shots over their lifetime?" Killian points out, and if I knew him better, I'd kick him from under the table. Giselle, on the other hand, doesn't seem to care that she doesn't know Killian, because a couple seconds later he screeches like a little girl. "Oww!! What the hell!" His eyes dart around the table until they land on Giselle. "Did you just kick me?"

"Not helping," she hisses, and I laugh.

"So, game two of the playoffs," I say, changing the subject.

Nick grins ear-to-ear, nodding and reminding me a lot of my dad when football is mentioned. "Hell yeah. We got this!" Nick exclaims. His arm goes around the back of me, his forearm resting on the top of my chair.

"And we're going to be in Miami. We're definitely going to be getting lit after we win that game," Killian adds, raising his fist to hit Nick's, but Nick shakes his head. Killian lowers his fist and takes a sip of his drink.

Giselle shoots me a look, and I shrug.

Nick leans in close to me, his cool breath hitting my neck. "Don't listen to anything Killian says, ever." Then he leans in even closer. "I was actually thinking that maybe you and Reed could join me. Eighty degrees and sunshine." I turn my head and have to back up slightly, so our faces don't bump.

Nick waggles his eyebrows, and I'm at a complete loss. I know his offer is innocent, but my body doesn't necessarily understand that.

"I—" I clear my throat. "I don't think that's a good idea. Giselle's birthday is this week, so we're going to do a girls' day." Giselle gives me a confused look but goes along with it. It really is her birthday, but we hadn't solidified any plans yet.

"Yeah, I'm turning the big two-five," she says. "We're going to spend the day at the spa."

"Okay." He nods in understanding. "Next time."

SIXTEEN

NICK

IT'S BEEN a little over a month since my life was forever changed with the birth of my son. We've won all three of our playoff games, which means this coming weekend we'll be playing in the Super Bowl. Because the game will be in Denver, I won't be able to see Reed or Olivia this weekend. I haven't taken him for the night since New Year's Eve, and we haven't discussed it, but I make sure to see him several times a week. I usually come by every Tuesday and Thursday and one day during the weekend depending on which day we're playing or if we're out of town.

Olivia has put up an impenetrable wall when it comes to me. It's tall and concrete, and I haven't got a clue how the fuck I'm going to break it down. Sure, she'll send photos of Reed when I ask, but if I try to find a crack in her wall, try to sneak in through a crevice, she's right there, spackling the shit out of it, making sure I have no way in.

I've tried to text her several times, asking how she's doing or what she's up to, but she keeps it all about Reed. When I ask her to lunch or dinner, she comes up with some excuse as to why she can't go.

After practice, I'm planning to spend the afternoon with her and Reed, and I'm hoping maybe while he's napping, we can discuss the possibility of us. I've thought long and hard about what her dad said. And I know, had she left me her number that morning in the hotel room, I would have sought her out. That night was completely different than anything I've experienced, and I want to see if given the chance, we could work.

Since I needed clarification on what Coach meant, I made Killian watch a Disney princess movie with me. His niece owns a bunch of them, so I had him snag one and bring it over. He thought I'd lost my mind, but I needed to know what I'm working with here. Which play is going to land me the touchdown.

"Here ya go!" He flings the DVD at me. "Planning to become one with your inner-princess self?" He chuckles and plops his ass onto the couch.

"Fuck you. I need to see how it goes."

"How the movie goes? I can give you a play-by-play. My niece makes me watch this crap every time I babysit, so my brother and his wife can go out for some adult time. The girl seeks love, there's an evil queen who tries to fuck it up, there's a throw down of some sort, the prince saves her, and they live happily ever after. The end."

I stare at him in silence. Clearly, there's more to this shit than that. "Let's just watch the damn movie."

"First tell me why," Killian insists.

"Liv's dad said she wants the fairytale. He even compared it to a Disney movie. Usually the key to a woman's heart is through my bank account, but not when it comes to Liv. She's not letting me in. So, I'm going to figure out how to give it to her."

"The bank account?"

"No! The fairytale!"

"You're fucking nuts, man. Fairytale's aren't real. What you need to watch is Daddy's Home." He cackles, and I lift one brow, silently asking him to explain. "You know...the one where the dad and the stepdad are forced to get along. It's hilarious and more accurate in our generation."

"What happens in the movie?"

"The stepdad wants the kids to love him, but the real dad comes in and messes it up. Eventually they all co-exist."

I grab my pillow and throw it at him. "I'm not preparing for Olivia to end up with another guy!"

"You really like this woman, don't you?"

"Yeah, I do. I really liked her when I spent the night with her, but as you know, she left without leaving her number. Now I feel like I've been given a second chance, and I don't want to fuck it up. She's not like anyone I've ever met."

"Damn...going soft on me." Killian laughs.

"Shut the hell up. Now watch this fucking movie with me or leave."

"Fine...but after your fairytale shit doesn't work, we're watching Daddy's Home."

We watch the movie, and I take notes. Here's what I've learned about fairytales through Sleeping Beauty:

The princess is beautiful yet helpless—Olivia isn't helpless.

There's an evil bitch who—like Killian mentioned—fucks shit up —kind of reminds me of my mom.

The parents send Aurora away—which is nothing like Olivia's life—unless you count her leaving for Paris after her mom died.

There's a whole lot of singing—I wonder if Olivia can sing, and I hope she doesn't want me to.

Princess Aurora sees the prince and falls in love with him after they dance together—I can handle that.

She's being forced to marry the guy she doesn't love—Olivia would never do shit she doesn't want to do.

She pricks her finger on a needle and passes out—fucking needles! Nothing good comes from those fuckers.

The prince does all the hard work, defeating the evil bitch and winning the battle—I need to convince Olivia to let me do some of the work.

The prince saves the day by kissing the princess, and they live happily-ever-after—I got this shit.

Now, I don't know anything about the other fairytales, but from what I gathered while watching that one, Olivia wants me to show her I can be her Prince Charming. The problem is, like in football, a quarterback is only as good as his receiver. I can throw perfect passes all day, but if I don't have someone there to catch the ball, it's pointless, which is why Olivia and I need to talk. I need to find out if she's going to be a team player or if I'll be throwing incomplete passes.

I'm about to head out the door when my phone rings. I see it's my attorney, Dylan Blake, calling. Dylan is Killian's brother and a sports attorney. He doesn't usually do family law, but he's familiar with it, and he's the only person I trust to handle this shit with Olivia.

"Hey, Dylan. How's it going?"

"Good. I just wanted to let you know Ms. Harper responded." Shit...I completely forgot about the petition I put in for joint custody.

"And...?"

"She countered. She wants legal custody, giving you visitation. You had requested fifty-fifty joint. This would mean sixty-forty with her legally being allowed to make all final decisions."

"What about the child support?"

"She's okay with it, but she did make a few revisions. All expenses are split down the middle including health insurance and educational expenses."

"She's something else..." I laugh to myself.

"She had to submit her bank information to the courts. Are you aware this woman could probably buy the team you're playing for?"

I chuckle. I knew she had money, but I didn't know she had that much. The brownstone she's living in has to be worth a few million, but I kind of assumed her dad might be helping her out. Apparently, I was wrong. "She's definitely not the helpless princess," I say more to myself than to my attorney.

"What?"

"Nothing...go ahead and approve her request. I agree to all of the above."

After practice, I get to Olivia's place, and she lets me in. "I wasn't sure if you were still coming over."

"Why wouldn't I?" I walk in behind her.

"Well, my attorney called and said you approved the custody agreement. Today is Monday, and your days are Tuesday and Thursday."

"I leave tomorrow to go to Denver for the Super Bowl." And then an idea forms. "Why don't you and little man join me?"

"Umm...I'm not sure that's a good idea." A beeping noise comes from the kitchen, and she runs that way, pulling a pan of brownies out of the oven. The house smells like a bakery, and my stomach rumbles.

She places the pan onto a rack of some sort, then goes about cutting up another pan of brownies into small squares and placing them on a plate. I grab one and pop it into my mouth. They're cool, so they must've been sitting there for a little bit. The brownie practically melts in my mouth. "Jesus, woman. That's some good shit." I grab one more.

"Thanks! Are you umm...are you taking..." She gulps loudly, looking everywhere but at me. "Are you taking Reed with you today?" She asks this same question every time I come over, and every time I make up some lame excuse as to why I'm just going to chill here.

"Nah...like you said, it's not my day. I'll just hang out here if it's okay with you." I move closer to her, and she backs up slightly. She has a spatula of brownie batter in her hand, and she nibbles down on the plastic nervously.

She moves the spatula from her mouth, leaving a bit of batter behind. "Yeah...that's fine. I imagine we'll have to work around your football schedule."

I close the distance between us. This is the closest we've been since New Year's Eve when we fell asleep together on the couch—the closest she's allowed me to be. We're standing only inches apart, and when I glance down, I can see her nipples are pebbling through her top. She wants me.

"What?" she asks shyly, watching me watch her.

"You have a bit of..." Without finishing my sentence, I lean down to make my move. It's risky as fuck, but I'm all about the gamble. My hands come down onto the counter, bracketing her in my arms, and I notice she stills, frozen in place. My lips brush against the corner of her mouth, my tongue darting out to swipe the bit of batter. She sucks in a harsh breath, not reacting but not pushing me away either.

Taking it a bit further, my lips move down, and I tug on her bottom lip softly with my teeth, my tongue licking across her flesh. When she doesn't move, I open my eyes and see she's staring at me, watching me with wide eyes. I move my lips up and place a gentle kiss on hers. But when my tongue seeks entrance, the trance she's in is broken.

"Stop, please." Her voice is breathy—full of want, a complete contradiction to her words. "I'm not a cheater."

I back up slightly, but my hands stay pressed against the edge of the counter, my arms caging her in. "Are you seeing someone?" Surely, I would've seen someone hanging around.

"No, but you're engaged. You might be okay with cheating, but I'm not, and I imagine your fiancée wouldn't be okay with it either. As you know, I've been cheated on and it sucks, and while it's true, I don't exactly like your fiancée, I'm not about to become the other woman." *Whoa...what?*

"What are you talking about? Celeste and I broke up weeks ago." Olivia's hand comes up to my chest and pushes me back slightly. "Don't you read the tabloids or go on social media?"

"I've been a little busy taking care of our baby. I don't stalk your social media or look at tabloids. Maybe if I did, I would have found out who you were sooner." She moves out of my hold and sticks another brownie pan into the oven. "Regardless...I can't be your rebound."

She sets the timer to forty-five minutes and makes her way out of the kitchen and down the hall to check on Reed. "Who said anything about being my rebound? In case you've forgotten, I was with you before I was with Celeste. Technically, she was the rebound." I shrug, and Olivia laughs.

"Very funny." She grabs the baby monitor and walks out onto her terrace, sitting down on the outdoor sofa set and flicking on the electric heater. I sit next to her, and she moves to the corner.

"Look," I say, my palms going up in a placating manner. "I know what it is you want."

"Oh really?" She bites her lip to hold back her smile. "Please, Nick, tell me what it is I want." She brings her legs up to her chest, and her chin rests on her knees.

"You want me to defeat the evil queen and kiss you awake."

"What?" She throws her head back in a fit of laughter, and fuck if I don't want to kiss my way down her throat.

"You know? Like in the Disney movies. You're looking for a Prince Charming, and I can be him."

Olivia's expression sobers. "Are you making fun of me?"

What? "What? No, I'm being serious. You don't want money or materialistic shit. You don't need me to buy you anything. You're looking for your magical kiss, and I can be that guy."

"What do you know about Disney movies?" She eyes me skeptically and an idea strikes. I pull my phone out and scroll through my play list, finding the perfect song. I hit play and turn the volume up.

"Dance with me." I stand and put my hand out for Olivia to take.

SEVENTEEN

Olivia

ALL-4-ONE'S "I can love you like that" plays over the speaker on Nick's phone. I haven't heard this song since I was a little girl. The words hit so close to home when it comes to what I have wished for that I have to wonder if it's a coincidence or if he picked the song out on purpose after telling me he knows I'm looking for my Prince Charming.

I stare at his proffered hand, and for some reason it feels as though this moment is monumental. Like if I take his hand, I'm agreeing to so much more than just this dance. I'm agreeing to give him a chance at making my happily-ever-after fantasy come true.

He stands in front of me, his face devoid of all emotion as he waits for me to make my decision. He's allowing me to be in control. There are so many reasons why I shouldn't do this, why this can end in disaster. Each of them running through my head on repeat. But instead of listening, I push them aside, ignoring them all, and go with my heart. If it doesn't work out, at least I can say I tried. And if it does—my mind goes to our one night together, to the way he's been around Reed—there's a chance it could be amazing.

Taking Nick's hand, I rise to my feet, and he shows his first sign of emotion—a small smile ghosting upon his lips. Pulling me into his arms, his hands trail down my sides, resting on my lower back. My hands move up his chest, over his shoulders, and circle around his neck.

The music plays in the background, the guy telling the woman he will make her his world, and after a minute or so, I allow myself to relax—my head comes down and rests against Nick's chest. Our bodies sway to the music in silence, until about halfway through the song when Nick murmurs, "I can love you like that." I know it's the lyrics to the song, but he doesn't appear to be singing them, but instead telling me. I don't know what to say, so I nod into his chest. As the music continues to play, Nick's hands tighten around me, and he pulls me in closer to him, his lips brushing against my ear as he softly sings the lyrics to me. Each word shattering a piece of the wall I've been trying to build in order to keep my heart safe from this man.

The song ends and another begins. It's Imagine Dragon's "Thunder." Nick laughs as he reaches into his pocket and stops the song. "It must've switched to my pre-game music." He shrugs. "Thank you for the dance."

"What does this mean, Nick?" We're still standing in each other's arms, neither of us making the first move to separate.

"Your dad said that according to you, people don't make the decision to love; it just happens. But I don't agree, Liv. I believe love is a decision. Who we love, how we love. It's in our hands. I grew up having no clue about the true meaning of love. When I was little, I thought it meant bicycles and PlayStations. And when I got older, I thought it meant cars and houses. To my mom, it means vacations and jewelry and status. To my dad, it means power and money. I grew up with everything a kid could ask for, yet nothing a kid really needs. It wasn't until you gave me Reed that I learned love can be more...so much more."

"What does that mean?" I rasp.

"I can't explain it." Nick shakes his head. "It's"—he backs up slightly, loosening our connection—"in here." He points to his chest. "It's not any of those things I mentioned. It's so much more power-ful. When Reed cried from those shots at his check-up, my heart... fuck, it felt like my heart was going to explode. It's like nothing I've ever felt before. My parents choose to love the way they do, and I'm choosing to love my way, with my heart. And if you could give me a chance, I would love to love you the same way."

His words are so unexpected, and they frighten me because they hit all the right places. But what if this is just a phase? What if he thinks because he loves his son with everything in him that means he can love me the same way? What if he can't? A parent's love isn't the same.

Two minutes ago, I was willing to take the leap, but now listening to how strongly he feels, I'm scared. If it doesn't work, Nick just might leave me broken beyond repair. And who will be there to pick up my pieces?

"Did you love Celeste?"

Nick sighs, and taking my hand, guides us to sit. "Celeste and I have been friends since we were little. Her mom and mine are best friends who grew up next door to each other in a trailer park. Both of them dreamed of getting out, but unlike my mom who married a rich guy and created a whole new life for herself, Celeste's mom fell in love with a guy from a motorcycle club who left, promising to return, and never did. Celeste grew up poor. Her mom loved that guy, and even though she had several opportunities to be with wealthier men over the years, to provide Celeste with a better life, she chose to stay single and struggle. To this day she's never left that trailer park. She's still waiting for Celeste's dad to return. She literally chose love over money, and because of that, Celeste resents her mom for everything she didn't have growing up."

Nick takes my hand in his and massages circles into my palm with his thumb and fingers while he continues to speak. "When I was in college, we made a pact. If I didn't find love by thirty, I would marry her and give her way a chance."

"Which was?"

"A business arrangement. No love or emotions." I'm shocked at what he's telling me. You see stuff like that in books or movies but never in real life. And at thirty?

"But thirty is still so young. You were willing to give up on love at thirty?"

"I was twenty when I made the stupid pact. I was young and didn't, for a second, think I would end up thirty and alone. But over the years I allowed football and my parents to run my life, and the results were a lot of failed relationships. That morning I went to meet with Declan Thomas, the Brewers' owner, and your dad." He laughs. "It's kind of ironic actually."

"What?" I ask.

"Your dad and Declan sat me down and told me I needed to settle down. They had a photo from an online tabloid of you and me walking into the hotel, but because I was towering over you, they couldn't see your face."

"Oh my God!" I jump to my feet and gasp in shock. "Had my

face been in the image, my dad would've known we hooked up that night."

"Exactly," Nicks agrees. "But they couldn't tell who the woman was. All they knew was that my partying was a bit out of control, and they needed to clean up my image so I could be the face of the team."

"So you agreed to the pact you made with Celeste."

"Yeah," Nick admits with a nod. "I guess I just needed a break from it all, and being with Celeste forced me to settle down and focus on football again...without putting my heart on the line."

"So, what's changed?" Why is he suddenly willing to put his heart back out there?

"You. Reed. I felt something for you the night we were together before I even knew we created Reed. But you left. So when I felt like my back was against the wall, I took the easy way out and agreed to give Celeste's way a chance."

"And what? You told Celeste you've changed your mind? I can't imagine that went over well."

"She's been one of my best friends for years. Yeah, she's hurt, but she understands. We've never even slept together."

Whoa! Okay, then. So it really was all business.

"I think right now she's more upset about her half of the pact." Nick smirks.

"What do you mean?"

"If I find love, she has to stop looking for a rich guy to be in a business arrangement with and try to find love as well."

"But you didn't find love. I mean, what we had...that night..."

"It was more than a one-night stand, Brown-Eyes. It might not have been love, but it was more, and if you give me a chance—*us* a chance—it can grow into love. What we have is different, and I think you feel it too." He's right. The night we spent together, the chemistry we shared. It was more, which is why I ran scared the morning after.

"I need some time to think." His face falls, and my heart cracks. "I'm not saying no. I've just...I've been hurt, Nick. I thought someone loved me and it turned out he didn't. Then to find out he cheated...it really hurt."

"I understand," he says. "I've been there, but I'm not him, Liv."

"I know you're not. But what if you're only doing this because I'm the mother of your son? Or what if I only say yes because I want the fairytale. I just need to think about everything. Had I not come back, you would still be with Celeste in a relationship of convenience. Now you're telling me you want the real deal."

"Celeste and I wouldn't have ever worked out." He stands and walks the short distance over to where I am. "It was nothing more than a temporary band-aid." His arms encircle my waist, his face nuzzling into my hair. "But I get it. You think, and I'll be waiting." He gives me a soft kiss on my cheek and then backs up slightly. "I have to get packed for Denver. We leave tomorrow. If you're willing to give me a chance—to give *us* a chance—come with me. The team charters a private plane there, so Reed won't be on a commercial flight. You can stay in the same hotel we stay in, and after the Super Bowl, we can spend some time together, the three of us."

"I don't think I can decide that quickly," I admit. "This is a big decision to make."

"If you need more time then that's fine too," Nick assures me. Then he steps back into my space once more and gives me a kiss on the corner of my mouth. "I'll be here," he murmurs, "if or when you're ready. If you don't go to Denver, I won't hold it against you. Just promise to put Reed's swing in front of the TV so he can watch his dad kick some ass." He backs up once again and shoots me a playful wink.

"Now, that I can do for sure."

Reed wakes up shortly after our conversation ends, and Nick spends the rest of the afternoon with Reed and me. While he's awake, Nick does everything for him, from changing his diaper to feeding him. He's become ten times as confident at being a dad than he was the first time he showed up on my doorstep with our son crying. It's only a matter of time until he starts taking him for the night, and I've come to accept it.

What I didn't expect was for Nick to show up here today and ask for me to give us a chance. Most women in my position would jump at the chance to date Nicholas Shaw, especially given the fact that we have a baby together. But I'm not most women. Call me crazy but I'm looking for the forever, and I'm not sure Nick can give me that. I know the man can give me the for-now. He gave that to me over and over again the night we spent together.

But I want more. I want what my parents had. I want what my dad was able to find for a second time with Corrine. Nick joked about giving me the fairytale, but does he really understand all that it entails? And then there's the fact that if we don't work out, we're stuck co-parenting together. He and Celeste might be over, and their relationship might not have been real, but if we don't work out there will be more women. Do I really want to put myself in that position? When I was in his arms, it felt so right, but once our connection was broken, my mind started to race. I wish I could be back in his arms, thinking with my heart instead of my head.

Nick leaves after giving Reed a bath and a bottle and putting him down for the night, but not before reminding me that he leaves tomorrow morning for Denver. Grabbing a glass of wine, I sit on the couch to unwind, and shortly after Giselle comes home from work.

"How was your day?"

"Amazing!" she gushes. "I am literally living out my dream. I had a meeting with Lydia, my boss, and she loves my ideas. She mentioned that she can see me one day moving into a real position there." She pours herself a glass of wine and joins me. "Of course, that won't be for a while. Most internships at Fresh Designs are for at least a year."

"I'm so happy for you. The year will fly by, you'll learn a lot, and soon enough you'll be running the place."

Giselle laughs. "I don't know about that, but at least once I get through the internship, I'll be able to finally pull my weight around here."

"Stop!" I hate when she brings up money. Money simply pays the bills. Giselle being in my life is worth more than any dime she ever pays toward the bills. Her friendship is invaluable.

"Whatever. So, how was your day?"

"Nick and Celeste broke up," I say nonchalantly.

Giselle gives me a *duh!* look. "Yeah...like weeks ago."

"And you didn't think to tell me?" I give her the side-eye as I take another sip of my wine.

"Everybody knows. It's all over the tabloids. I just assumed you knew." She shrugs.

"You came home at four in the morning to tell me Victor cheated on me when we were together, but you didn't think to mention Nick is no longer engaged?"

Giselle laughs. "I came home to comfort you because you were at one time in love with Victor. I didn't think I needed to comfort you regarding Nick. Why would you even care..." She stops speaking and tilts her head to the side, giving me a curious look. "Livi, why would you care?"

I let out a loud sigh. "He wants me to give us a chance." I throw back the rest of my wine like it's a shot.

"No way! And you said yes, right?" I avert my eyes to the picture hanging on the wall. "Livi, you said yes…"

"I said I would think about it. He wants Reed and me to go to Denver with him for the Super Bowl, but there's a lot to consider. If we don't work out, we can't simply go our separate ways. We're Reed's parents until we die. And then there's the fact he might get bored of me or meet someone else. Or he might get bored of being a dad…"

Giselle sighs and sets her glass down. "You know what I don't get…you talk all this shit about wanting your fairytale happily-ever-after, but you never let anyone in enough to actually allow it to happen. Did you see Cinderella come up with excuses? No! She wore that glass slipper like a fuckin' boss." I can't help but giggle at her words.

"And Belle… you didn't see her doubting the Beast. She went all in. Accepting him the way he was and falling in love, despite him looking like a scary monster. Oh! And Jasmine! She fought right alongside Aladdin against that asshole, Jafar. Aurora in Sleeping Beauty; she was strong until she pricked her damn finger and passed the hell out."

Giselle scoots closer to me and pats my leg. "You want this fairy-tale, but no one said it would be easy. You may have seen your parents in love, but you didn't see the hard work that went into their relationship. We always remember the happily-ever-after in these movies, but too often we forget the effort and struggle and heartache the characters have to endure in order to get that ending."

"When did you get so wise?" I joke, and Giselle pulls me into a hug. "I'm going to do it." I nod emphatically into her neck before pulling back. "I'm going to go all in. Consequences be damned."

"That's my girl."

I stand and grab my keys, then remember I drank some wine. "I'm going to call a Lyft. Can you watch Reed?"

"You're going to Nick's now?"

"He told me to let him know, and he leaves in the morning. I don't want to tell him over the phone. When I get back, I'll pack for Reed and me. Any chance you want to take a trip to Denver with us?"

"Oh no…you aren't using me as your buffer." Giselle shoots me a playful wink. "Besides, I love my job, and I'm pretty sure it's too soon to request time off." She laughs. "Go…go tell your baby daddy what he wants to hear."

I give her a hug then call for a Lyft. I've never been to Nick's home before, but I know what his address is from when he gave it to me. I tell the driver where I need to go, and about fifteen minutes later, I'm outside of his building. It's a nice skyrise condominium in Lower Manhattan. I walk through the marbled lobby and press the intercom for his number. Without him saying a word, I'm buzzed up.

The elevator doors open and his door is the only one on the floor. I knock once, and the door swings open. Only it's not Nick, it's Celeste.

She's standing in the doorway—all six feet of legs—in a pantsuit and heels, her makeup done to perfection and not a single hair out of place. And then I glance down at myself...I ran out the door without even thinking. I'm in sweats and a hoodie, and I'm almost positive there's some stupid logo or saying scrawled across my ass. I have zero makeup on, and my hair is up in a messy bun—and I'm not talking about those 'cute' messy buns. I'm talking the real ones that look like a rat has made his nest up in there.

"Can I help you?" She stands taller—if that's even possible—her chin jutting out.

"I was hoping to..." But I stop speaking because suddenly it's all pointless, my reason for being here. If they're back together, I'm here for no reason. Just as I'm about to turn around, Giselle's words come back to me. *"We forget the struggle and heartbreak..."*

"I was hoping to speak to Nick," I say with more confidence than I feel. He asked me to give him a chance, and if something has changed then he can man up and tell me himself.

"I figured as much when I saw you on the camera asking to be let up. He's not here." She closes the door in my face. Okay then...

I make my way back to the elevator, shooting a text to Nick.

Me: Where are you?

The bubbles appear instantly.

Nick: Killian's

Nick: Everything okay?

Me: I came by your place...

The bubbles appear and then disappear, and a second later, my phone rings.

"Hello?"

"What did Celeste do?"

"Slammed the door in my face."

Nick sighs. "This is the part of the story where you come across the evil witch." I can't help but laugh at his Disney story reference. "But have no fear because your prince has already taken her down."

"Are you still going on with that stupid fucking analogy?" I hear Killian yell in the background. The phone is muffled for a few seconds and then Nick comes back on the line.

"So, does you coming by my place mean you've decided?"

"Umm...can we get back to you taking down the evil witch? She's in your home..."

"She got back from Milan today. I was just kidding about taking her down. She'd probably kick my ass with those ten-inch heels of hers. She's moving her stuff out, though, as we speak. Now, back to us..."

"There's a really good possibility I'm going to regret this."

"There's a really good possibility you won't."

"What if we don't work?"

"What if we do?"

"I don't remember any of the Disney movies having this plot," I joke.

We both go silent for a moment, and then Nick says, "How about instead of trying to copy stories that have already been told, we write our own?"

I take a deep breath. "I can do that."

"Good. Chapter one begins tomorrow morning. I'll pick you and Reed up at seven to catch our flight."

"I'm pretty sure chapter one was our one-night stand."

He laughs. "Fuck no, it wasn't. That was the prequel. Our story doesn't begin until now."

We hang up, and I lean back against the wall next to the elevator, closing my eyes for a few seconds while taking several much-needed calming breaths. It's really happening. I'm actually going to attempt to date the father of my son. Not so long ago I didn't think I would ever even see Nick again. He's right, though. This is our story, and therefore, we get to write the chapters. Pushing off the wall, I press the button for the elevator. I'm watching as the numbers slowly increase when Nick's door creaks open.

"So, I'm not sure what the hell Nick is talking about, but I believe he just called me an evil witch." I turn around, and Celeste is leaning against the doorframe. "Although, it might have been an evil *bitch*." She shrugs, and her head tilts to the side slightly. "I think we got off on the wrong foot." She steps out of the doorway and walks toward me. I hear the elevator open, but instead of getting in, I meet her halfway.

She extends her perfectly manicured hand. "I'm Celeste Leblanc, the *friend*."

I stare down at her proffered hand for a second before I take it in mine and shake hers. "I'm Olivia Harper, the...*baby mama*." Yep, I totally just said that.

She throws her head back in laughter. "If you ask Nick, I think he would call you more than that. Why don't we go inside? Nick called, and after yelling at me for closing the door on your face, said he'll be home soon. But I don't think he realized you were still here. Otherwise, he'd probably be hauling ass home sooner."

I take her up on her offer for no other reason than curiosity. I've never been in Nick's place before. We walk inside, and there's a woman taping up boxes and stacking them in the hallway. Celeste doesn't say a word to her, but instead grabs a bottle of wine and two glasses and nods toward the back of the room. There's a set of French doors, and when she opens them, they lead out to a terrace. It's smaller than mine, but large enough to have a table and a few chairs. We both sit, and Celeste pours us each a glass of white wine.

"I'll get straight to the point," Celeste says, handing me one of the glasses. "I don't know you, and I wouldn't know the first thing about being a mom or what you're going through. I had no right to judge you, and for that, I'm truly sorry."

"Damn it!" I take a sip of my wine.

"Excuse me?"

"I said 'Damn it.'" I shake my head. "I was prepared to hate you...hell, I did hate you. You're beautiful and elegant and success-ful, and you talked shit about my parenting. You were engaged to the father of my child, and did I mention you're beautiful? I was supposed to hate you. I even threw away all the makeup with your name on it." I take another sip of my wine. "And that shit isn't cheap." I raise a brow and she cracks a smile. "Then you had to go and apologize. So yes, 'damn it'."

"My makeup is worth every penny." She winks playfully. "And apologizing is a bad thing?" She laughs.

"Well, yeah...because now I'm going to have to forgive you, and since I don't have a lot of girlfriends, we're totally going to click and become besties. Then my best friend Giselle will wonder why I'm constantly ditching her for someone else and insist on meeting you, and the three of us will all have to hang out, and you're totally going to be that friend who brings us free makeup and jewelry from all your current lines and introduces us to all of the famous people you know." I shrug, and Celeste laughs harder.

"What are you? A fortune teller? Care to tell me my future while you're at it?" She smirks, taking a sip of her wine.

"Oh, that's easy!" I giggle. "Nick is going to hold you to the pact you guys made, and Giselle and I will bug the shit out of you to find a guy for you to fall in love with. You'll argue you aren't capable of falling in love, and we'll argue you are. Then one night when we're all out, you'll meet him and fall in love. You'll resist at first, but we'll be there to push you. You'll finally come to your senses, and we'll all live happily-ever-after."

"Oh my God!" Celeste cracks up. "Who is this woman?" I'm confused as to why she's referring to me in the third person until I see her eyes trained on something—or someone—behind me. I turn around to find Nick standing in the doorway, a huge grin splayed across his lips.

"She's the woman I'm going to fall in love with, and who's going to fall in love with me." He smiles warmly at me, and my heart picks up speed. Unsure of what to say, I chug down the rest of the wine in my glass, and Nick chuckles.

"How did you get here so fast?" I ask.

"Killian lives one floor below me." He shoots me a wink that has the muscles between my legs clenching. "I didn't realize when I was talking to you that you were still on my floor. I thought you had already left to go back home. Otherwise, I would've come right up."

"Told you," Celeste says as she stands. "Well, this has been fun, but I need to get going, and I'm almost afraid the love in the air might be contagious." She scrunches her nose and mock-gags.

I stand with her, and the three of us walk back into the apartment. Celeste takes my empty glass and places it on the kitchen counter next to the wine bottle and her now-empty glass. "Everything of mine should be packed. The movers will be by in the morning to pick it all up." She leans into Nick, giving him a hug and a kiss on the cheek before she turns to me.

"I'm assuming since you know about our pact, you know Nick and I have been friends our entire lives. You got one thing right. I don't have a lot of friends, so if it's possible I would like to be friends. Nick's important to me, and I know you're important to him."

"Of course, we're going to be besties." I wink. "How else am I going to make sure you find true love?" I grin, Nick laughs, and Celeste groans.

"And that's my cue to leave." She pulls her purse over her shoulder and walks toward the door. But before she opens it, she turns around and says, "By the way, when I was on my fact-finding mission to dig up dirt on you in hopes of getting you out of the picture, I read that Francesca Harper was your mom. Is that true?"

The mention of my mom has my heart tightening. "Yes, she was."

"She was my idol." Celeste smiles. "I *literally* wanted to be her when I grew up. She was walking the runway at the show I was at when I was twelve years old. Nick was there, too. Every person watching was captivated by her beauty and elegance. When I came to New York right after I graduated from high school, I was lucky enough to meet her... right before..." As Celeste's words trail off, a lump forms in my throat because I know the words she can't say: *she was diagnosed with cancer and then died.* It all happened so quickly. One day she was healthy and the next she wasn't. Less than a year after she was diagnosed, we lost her.

"I swear I cried for a week when she passed away," Celeste admits, "which says a lot since I don't cry." She sniffles and then smiles softly. "I'm sorry for your loss. I can't even imagine what it was like to have her as a mother."

"She was amazing..." I bite my lip to keep myself from crying. "But not because of how famous she was as a model, but because as a mother and a wife, she was the best. She always put me first and loved me unconditionally. She would let me play with all her makeup and clothes." I laugh, recalling all the times I would get into her stuff and she would never get upset. "Some of her model friends had kids, and they would come over to visit occasionally. The other moms were so stuck up. One time while they were having brunch, we got into all of her clothes and makeup to put on a surprise fashion show." I smile at the memory. "The other kids' moms freaked out. But not mine. She pulled out her camera and took pictures, and then told the other moms to pull the stick out of their butts." Celeste laughs.

"And the love my parents had was like no other. Every Friday night was date night. Even when she was away, they would video chat and pretend to be on a date. She used to tell me that just because they were married didn't mean they stopped dating."

"She sounds like she was a truly wonderful person," Nick says.

"She was...and she was a beautiful model," I tell them, "but only because she loved with everything she had." The tears that were threatening to spill over, fall, and Nick pulls me in for a hug. When we break apart, Celeste is watching us. She doesn't comment on anything I said, but I can see it in her eyes. She's absorbing the meaning behind my words.

"I better get going," she says softly. "I'll be at the Super Bowl, but in case I don't see you before you're on the field, good luck. Let's try to do lunch soon." She looks at me. "All of us." And then she's gone.

"I thought you said she was the wicked witch." I wink at Nick.

"Good thing we're writing our own story," he volleys back.

EIGHTEEN

WE ARRIVE IN DENVER, and it's as cold here as it is in New York. Reed is bundled up in his car seat, and the media is waiting to bombard us. Olivia handles it well, smiling politely while ignoring the questions that are flung at her. She covers Reed's car seat with a blanket and heads straight to the car while I stay back answering various questions. Reed's face hasn't been seen in public yet, but it's only a matter of time. I've been approached by several magazines, but it's not happening without Olivia's consent. My publicist put out one of those cookie cutter public statements to let the world know Celeste and I feel we're better as friends and our engagement has been called off. She also stated I'm Reed's dad and that I'm asking for time while I get to know my son. Obviously, based on the amount of press here throwing questions my way, they ignored my request—not that I ever really thought they would listen.

The players usually take the team bus to the hotel to check in, but today I'm going with Olivia. The car service takes us to the Four Seasons, and then I have to leave Olivia and Reed to go to the stadium for our scheduled media day. I'm glad her stepmom and stepsister are both here, so she won't be alone. Not that she can't take care of herself, but it makes me feel better to know she has other people around her.

Questions about my injury, the upcoming game, and my future

are tossed at me for hours by reporter after reporter. When seven o'clock rolls around, I can't get out of there fast enough. Tomorrow is the first day of practice, which means I need to rest up, but before I do, I'm going to spend some time with Olivia. The players are required to share rooms, and I always share with Killian. I was able to book Olivia a suite on another floor, and as much as I'd like to spend my free time there, I'm not going to make any assumptions. She did give me a keycard, though, so there's that.

"Brown-Eyes, I'm—" I haven't even finished my sentence when Olivia flies through the main room and covers my mouth with her hand.

"Shh...he's finally asleep. I don't know if babies can have jet lag, or if it's the time difference, but he was so cranky tonight."

She moves her hand from my mouth, and my eyes dart to her plump, pink lips. Damn, I want to taste her. Instead I give her a peck on her cheek. "Have you eaten? I was thinking we could order some room service and watch a movie or something."

"Disney?" she teases.

"Funny." I have Olivia order some food while I jump in the shower to rinse off. When I'm done, I return a call from my publicist and confirm a couple endorsement deals with my dad. He's been rather quiet lately. Now that I think about it, both my parents have been. And neither of them has once asked about meeting their grandson. Not that I should be surprised. What could he possibly do for either of them?

When I come out, Olivia is dressed in tiny cotton shorts and a long sleeve Henley—sans bra. She's closing the door and has a couple bags in her hands.

"Food's here." She places the bags on the table and grabs the boxes of food, bringing them to the coffee table so we can eat while we watch TV. I sit down before her and pull her between my legs on the couch. Her body is stiff at first, but she quickly relaxes her back into my front.

"Here." She hands me my chicken sandwich. "I got a parfait. I ate a bigger meal earlier." Grabbing the remote, she switches through the channels stopping on *That 70's show*. "I love this show!" She throws the top of her parfait onto the table and takes a bite of her yogurt.

We eat and watch the show in comfortable silence. I'm starving, so my sandwich is gone in minutes. "Want some of my parfait?" she asks. "It's the perfect sweet after your sandwich."

She turns slightly and pushes the spoon toward my lips. I open wide, and she thrusts the yogurt into my mouth, the sweetness of the strawberries and vanilla yogurt hitting my taste buds. "Good?"

"Yeah." I nod in agreement, swallowing my bite. She smiles before turning back around. We continue to watch the show, and every few minutes Olivia reaches back to give me a bite of her yogurt and fruit until it's all gone. Once she places the empty cup on the table, she settles back farther into my hold. We're in between sitting and laying down. Her head is resting on my shoulder and her ass is perfectly placed in front of my dick. My top leg parts her legs and my knee and thigh rest in between her thighs. I try to remember the last time I cuddled with a woman. Then I do remember; it was with Olivia on New Year's Eve when we fell asleep, and before that...the night we hooked up.

My right arm is situated under her—my fingers running up and down her arm. My other arm is wrapped tightly around her waist. There's no doubt about it, this woman's body was made perfectly to fit with mine.

The show ends and another episode begins. I'm not paying attention to what's happening, my focus completely on the woman lying in my arms. Her hair is up in a messy bun and her face is free of any makeup. She's the perfect mix of sexy and adorable. I lift my head slightly, and she tilts hers to give me access. My nose brushes against her exposed neck, and when she feels my skin touch hers, she releases a small shiver, reminding me how responsive she is to me.

When she doesn't stop me, I take a moment to inhale her scent. She smells sweet. It's the same perfume she was wearing during our one night together. Don't ask me how the hell I even remember that, but I do. I find myself latching on to every detail when it comes to this woman, not wanting to forget a single moment I spend with her. My nose brushes across her neck again and then my lips land on her sensitive pulse point. She lets out a soft sigh, and my dick twitches as a result.

"If you want me to stop, tell me," I whisper into her ear.

She stills and then says, "I can't have sex...I haven't been given the okay from the doctor yet." I'm not sure how long a woman has to wait before she can be sexually active after giving birth, but for some reason this tidbit of info has me smiling. For one, I wasn't planning on having sex with her yet. Olivia needs to know I want more than just sex from her. She needs to know I'm serious about us. And two, sex is great, but the foreplay—the buildup—can be even better, and once I'm done with her, when the doctor gives the okay, she'll be begging me to make love to her.

"That just means we get to do everything but..." My lips go back to her neck as I trail open-mouthed kisses downward. My fingers brush across her taut nipples through her shirt, and Olivia's soft sighs turn into moans.

"Everything but..." She repeats my words, turning her face toward me and pressing her lips to mine.

NINETEEN

OLIVIA

NICK'S long fingers rub back and forth across my hardened nipples. His lips trailing kisses all over my neck. But I need more. Tilting my neck to the side, I cover his mouth with mine and kiss him eagerly. He kisses me back, his tongue passing through my lips and groping mine. And then he's moving us. His body is hovering above mine, my back now flat on the couch. Our kiss deepens, our tongues hungrily meeting thrust for thrust. We kiss passionately for God knows how long—until Nick breaks the kiss.

With one hand holding himself up, he uses his other hand to pull my shirt over my head, my heavy breasts hitting the cool air, and my nipples hardening to the point it's almost painful. Nick brushes his lips against mine once more before he trails kisses downward, stopping on my breasts. He kisses everywhere but my nipples, teasing me until I'm squirming with want. It's been almost a year since I've been with this man, since I felt his touch.

"Nick, please," I beg. He obliges, his lips parting slightly and wrapping around my nipple. He sucks on it for a few seconds before his teeth gently clamp down. My back arches and my hands go to his head. My fingers entwine in his hair. His tongue darts out and licks the areola before moving to the other breast. He sucks and bites, teasing me and turning me on. Foreplay seemed like a good idea...until now.

I can feel his bulge through his sweats rubbing against my thigh, and remembering how well-endowed he is, I raise my leg slightly, rubbing his cock through his pants. Nick lets out a moan, his teeth biting down on my nipple harder. I yelp, and he chuckles mischievously.

His lips leave my breasts and move down farther. He rains kisses on my soft belly, giving extra attention to my stretch marks. "Our son did this to you." His tone conveys pride mixed with awe.

"The downside to carrying a football player's baby. He was nearly a month early and still a solid seven pounds."

He lifts his head to lock eyes with me, laughter shining in his beautiful green irises. "I love these. They're a reminder that you carried our baby."

"I'm pretty sure the baby sleeping in the other room is reminder enough," I volley back, and Nick laughs. He kisses a couple more of the silver marks before he pulls my shorts and panties down, putting my entire lower half completely on display.

"You still have the same landing strip that you had before." His face lowers until he's face to face with my pussy. He kisses the landing strip, and I run my fingers through his soft hair, needing to touch him in some way.

His fingers part my lips, and his tongue delves into my folds, landing directly on my clitoris. My bottom bucks against the couch, and Nick's hands come down to my hips to hold me in place. His face ducks lower and then his tongue laves up the entire length of my seam before settling back on my clit. He licks and sucks and nibbles, successfully working me into a frenzy. I watch as he feasts on my pussy like it's his own personal dessert. My orgasm builds, and I'm forced to bite down on my bottom lip to keep my screams down. I can see my juices coating Nick's lips as he lavishes my pussy, working me up higher and higher. I've never felt this way with anyone I've been with. This instant connection. It's been months since we were together, and it was only that one night, yet it feels like I've been with him a million times.

His eyes lock with mine. His tongue licks. His lips kiss. He laps at my juices, and then I'm coming. My butt tries to lift off the couch, but Nick's hands grip my hips harder, his tongue and lips not slowing down at all, not letting up a single bit as my climax rips through me wave after wave. Only when I've come down from my orgasm, my lids barely able to stay open, and my head slightly fuzzy, does he remove his mouth from between my legs.

"I've been wanting to have another taste of you since the

morning you left me." He gives the hood of my pussy one last soft kiss before he climbs up my body, his face intimately close to mine. He debates whether to kiss me with my juices still lingering on his mouth, but I make the decision for him when I pull his face to mine and kiss him hard. The tanginess of myself mixed with Nick's own personal taste has me wanting him something fierce.

Reaching down, I rub my hand up and down the outline of his rock-hard cock. His moan rumbles and vibrates into my mouth before he pulls back. He licks a trail back down my neck, stopping at the pulse point to suck on it. My hand makes its way to his sweatpants and boxers, and I begin to push them down. I feel Nick's hand grab mine, and what I think is him helping me is actually him stopping me.

"We were supposed to take things slow," he murmurs against my lips.

"Says who?" I ask, pulling my head back slightly.

"Me. I wanted you to see that it's not just sex I want from you," he admits sheepishly.

"Oh, okay, duly noted. Now move your hand, so I can *slowly* suck your dick." Nick laughs under his breath as he lets go of my hand, so I can finish pushing his boxers down the rest of the way. My fingers wrap around the shaft, and his dick thickens under my touch. I stroke it slowly at first, then pick up the pace. His face burrows into my neck, his breathing rapidly increasing. I love the feel of his dick in my palm, but I need to taste him. I need to feel more of him.

Pushing him back slightly, I let go of him as I slide down the couch until my head lands on the sofa pillow and my back hits the cushion. "Come here." He looks confused at first, but when my hands go to his butt and I pull him closer, he catches on quickly, all too willing to comply. He's on his knees, one leg on either side of me, his hard as steel dick bouncing in front of my face. I lift my head and take him into my mouth, circling the swollen tip with my tongue. He tastes fresh and clean—from just having showered— mixed with a tad bit of saltiness from the precum dripping out of his slit. Grabbing him from behind, I pull him closer, his dick thrusting into my mouth and down my throat as I swallow almost all of him. He's too big to fit his entire length down my throat, but it's not from lack of trying.

"Fuck, Liv. I'm never going to last...it's been...fuck, it's been too long." He groans and his words spur me on, wanting to pleasure him that much more.

I tilt my head back slightly releasing him completely. Then I lift up, inserting his entire length back into my mouth. I pull back again, and he moans in frustration. "Fuck my mouth, Nick." His eyes dart to my face, his brow raising in a silent question. "Please."

His hips begin to thrust slowly at first. My tongue swirls and licks his hard shaft. My cheeks hollow to create a suction. My fingers dig into his flesh, pulling him closer, silently telling him to give it all to me.

Nick picks up the pace. His cock driving in and out of my mouth. It hits the back of my throat over and over again, and my pussy clenches in response. I can feel it when he's about to come. His shaft begins to throb, and his thrusts become frantic. I'm ready to take it all, every ounce of his cum, when his dick leaves my mouth. Before I can protest, Nick's large hand grips his dick, and less than two strokes later, his cum shoots out and all over my breasts, warm seed coating my nipples.

"See what I mean about writing our own story?" Nick grins. His fingers come down and swirl a bit of his cum around my nipple. "This chapter never would've made the cut in those Disney books."

I COME out of the shower to find Nick feeding Reed a bottle. He's sitting up against the headboard in nothing but his boxers, and I have to remind myself I can't go there, yet. After Reed finishes his bottle and Nick burps him, I take him to change his diaper. Then I rock him back to sleep before placing him back into his crib and checking to make sure the monitor is on.

I get back to my room, and Nick is still in my bed. He's reading something on his phone that has the corners of his mouth turned down into a frown. Not knowing what's wrong makes me realize how little I truly know about Nick. Sure, I know him sexually, and the night we spent together we talked for hours, but we kept it at a surface level. I know his favorite food is Chinese, his favorite color is blue, and his favorite animal is a dog—he hates cats. I know his favorite movie is The Blind Side, and he loves to go snowboarding every winter. I know his relationship with his parents is strained to say the least. But I want to know more. I want to know what makes him laugh, what makes him smile. I want to know why right now he looks so sad.

When he hears me come in, he sets his phone down on the end table to give me his attention.

"Reed asleep?"

"Yeah. Everything okay?" I nod toward his phone as I lay down in bed.

"Yeah, my mom and dad are here for the Super Bowl and want me to attend a breakfast with them and some of my dad's clients.

"And that made you frown?"

Nick scoots down the bed until he's lying on his side facing me. "My relationship with my parents is kind of tense right now."

"Because of Reed?" He hasn't once asked me if his parents could meet our son, which seems so crazy to me. My dad and Corrine can't get enough of their grandson.

He shakes his head. "It's more complicated than that."

I wait for him to elaborate, and when it's clear he's not going to, I tell him what I was thinking a moment ago. "I want to know every-thing about you. Talk to me. Tell me what's going on."

Nick is silent for several long seconds before he says, "You said you went to college in Paris, right? What was your major?"

"Art. I used to work at a museum over there."

"Well, my degree would've been in business."

"Would've?"

"I didn't graduate." Nick grimaces. "I wanted to major in English Literature, but my dad told me it was a waste of time, and it interfered with practice. Not that it mattered because I went into the draft at the end of my junior year, so I never graduated." I can't imagine my dad ever telling me what to major in. He's always been so supportive of whatever it is I've wanted to do in my life. Both my parents were.

"Who was he to tell you what you could or couldn't major in?"

"The school paid for my education, but my dad paid for every-thing else, therefore he got to have the final say in my major. I was so busy trying to make him and my mom proud, I didn't see how badly they were always trying to manipulate me."

Nick laughs softly, but it's a sad laugh. "Want to know some-thing really fucked up? I found out recently my mom paid off my last girlfriend. Five hundred thousand dollars to leave me because she didn't want her to convince me to retire and start a family after I was injured."

My hand comes up to my mouth in shock. *What the hell!* "And she took it?"

"Yep. I came home from the hospital and found a note on the counter. Only I got there before she could leave, so she was forced to face me. We argued, and she told me that having a family with me was her idea of a nightmare."

"Oh, Nick. Is that why you didn't want to have kids? Why you didn't think you would make a good dad?" My palm rests on his cheek as my heart breaks for this man. It's easy to forget that not everyone was raised in a loving home the way I was. I know Giselle's parents have issues, but she never wants to discuss them no matter how much I beg.

"I had failed my parents and team by getting injured. I failed Fiona by putting my parents and football above her." He turns his face slightly and gives the inside of my palm a kiss. "I think I was afraid of failing Reed, of failing you."

We lay here for a few minutes in silence, both of us lost in our own thoughts, when Nick says, "You know...that year after Fiona dumped me I was with a lot of women."

I groan, not wanting to know about his previous conquests. "Do you have to remind me?"

"Let me finish," he says. "I was with a lot of women, but it wasn't until that night with you that I even considered putting myself out there to try again. I knew the moment you told me you could buy your own drink you were different."

I roll my eyes, remembering that night. "You still ended up getting your way and paying."

"That I did." He grins. "Best fifty bucks I've ever spent."

"I still can't believe I actually had sex with a guy I didn't know. I wasn't lying that night when I told you I'd never done that before."

"You were so fucking sexy." He gives me a soft kiss to my neck. "It was obvious from the get-go that hooking up with a strange guy wasn't your norm. I could see it in your eyes how nervous you were, but then when we got to your room, the way you let loose and opened up to me...fuck...I knew one night with you wouldn't be enough."

"Why didn't you say anything?" I question. We talked for hours that night and he never once mentioned wanting to see me again.

"I didn't know you were going to disappear the next morning. If I would've known I was going to wake up to an empty bed and a note, I would've tied your wrists to the headboard so you couldn't leave." He winks playfully. "I'm just glad you went to my game and spotted me." He kisses the tops of my knuckles. "Had you not been at that game who knows if we ever would've found each other." The thought of never seeing Nick again makes my heart hurt.

"Is that why your parents and you are on the outs? Because of me?"

"I don't think it's any one thing," Nick says. "Ever since you showed back up and Reed was born, I've started to see things differently, more clearly."

"How?"

"All of the shit my parents have pulled over the years, they've always acted like it was done out of love and in my best interest. Now, though, I'm beginning to think their motives are less out of love and more out of greed. Pushing people I care about away, bribing them with money to leave, forcing me to change my major... those aren't things parents do when they love their children. I will *never* be that kind of parent to Reed."

"I think it says something about you as a person and especially as a father that you recognize that. Have they asked to meet Reed?"

"No, and that's why I was upset when you walked in. My mom implied I should show up alone, knowing you and Reed are here with me."

"I'm sorry." I scoot closer to him to give him a kiss. "I would say we don't need to go, but I'm thinking that's not exactly the point here."

"No, it's not. I wouldn't ask you to bring Reed. He's too young, and we're not showing him to the public yet. But they're acting like he doesn't exist. Other than them worrying about you distracting me from football or trying to take all my money, they haven't acknowledged Reed being my son at all."

"Well, maybe they will come around once they see I'm not going to steal all your money, and the only time I will distract you is in the bedroom." I waggle my eyebrows playfully, and Nick smiles. "Now tell me about this English Lit degree. I had no idea you liked to read."

"I do," he admits, "but lately I've been thinking about trying my hand at writing."

"Like taking a writing class?" I sit up, shocked.

"Yeah, I mean I know it's too late to get my degree, but—"

"Wait! Who says it's too late? You only had a year to go... you could easily go back and finish. And now with online classes, you could switch to English Literature like you wanted."

Nick's face lights up like a little boy who has just been told he can stay up late and eat too much candy. "You're right...I can. And I have plenty of money now, so there isn't a damn thing my dad could do to stop me."

"Of course he can't! Are you going to still major in English Lit?"

"Hell yes! And the first class I'm going to take will be the creative writing class I never got to take."

"You can totally do it!"

I lay back down and wrap my arms around him. We lay together in silence for a few minutes, and I think about Nick and me and how far we've come from being the people we were in that hotel room almost a year ago.

"Hey Nick..."

"Yeah?"

"I'm sorry I left with only a note to say goodbye." And I am sorry. If I would've known he was looking for more, I never would've left the way I did. Yes, I was only looking for a one-night stand, but once we were together, I felt something more, and the thought scared me into running, never for a second believing he felt something as well.

"It's all good, Brown-Eyes." Nick gives me a kiss on my forehead, then on my nose. "Just please...in the future, if you're going to leave a note, always tell me where you're going so I can find you."

"Deal! Now let's look up colleges. With football ending this week, you can probably take an express spring class or even take a couple summer classes."

TWENTY

Nick

I'VE YET to take Olivia out on a date, and having her family here means we have willing babysitters. It's Thursday night and we're free for the evening after practicing all morning and going over tapes and plays this afternoon. I shoot a text to Stephen and ask if there's any way he and Corrine can watch Reed. He texts me back that they would love to.

I put a call in to a recommended restaurant to see if it's possible to have private seating. With the Super Bowl in three days, anywhere we go we'll have fans trying to get photos and autographs. The paparazzi and media are everywhere. The manager tells me they can get us into a private booth near the back at seven o'clock, so I let Stephen know to come over to Olivia's room at six.

I get back to her room—which might as well be mine since I've slept here every night—and she's on the floor with Reed singing to him about baking a cake. He's lying on a large blue blanket and his legs and hands are flailing every which way. Every day he becomes more alert...more like a real person. I can't believe I almost gave up my right to watch him grow up.

Olivia looks up when she hears the door close. "Hey you. How was practice?"

"Good." I drop onto the floor next to her and give her a quick kiss before leaning over and giving one to Reed. His face moves side to side as he makes a soft cooing sound that has me grinning. These two are quickly becoming my entire world.

"Why don't you go shower while I watch him?"

Her nose scrunches up. "Do I smell that bad? I showered this morning."

My fingers grip her nape, and I pull her into me, my mouth slanting over hers. "No, you don't smell. We're going out to dinner."

"I thought you said you didn't want Reed going out too much because of the media."

"Not Reed. Just us. I'm taking you out on a date, and before you argue, your dad and Corrine are coming down to watch Reed while we go."

"Hmm..." She taps her finger against her bottom lip. "A date, huh? Why do I feel like we've done this all wrong? Sex, pregnancy, foreplay, and now a date?" Her eyes light up telling me she's joking, but I also know deep down the way all this played out bothers her.

"We're not doing anything wrong. We're doing things our way... our story, remember? We get to write the chapters. And this is chapter two: Date night."

While she's getting ready, her dad and Corrine show up. They take over with Reed, so I can get dressed. Once I'm ready to go, I rejoin them in the living room to wait on Olivia. She comes out of the bathroom about thirty minutes later, dressed in a pair of tight—extremely tight—dark jeans. She's been working out every day—switching between yoga and Tae Bo—with Giselle in their living room, and it's showing. The woman almost looks like her pre-pregnancy self. Her hips are a bit wider now, but there's nothing wrong with giving a man something to hold onto. She's wearing a teal off-the-shoulder sweater and some fuzzy-looking boots women always wear when it's cold outside. Her hair is down in loose waves, and her makeup, like always, is the bare minimum. She looks breathtakingly beautiful except...

"Why are you wearing the other team's colors?" Stephen scowls, and Corrine laughs.

"Oh, stop! I swear, every time I go to put on an outfit, if it doesn't support New York, I never hear the end of it," Corrine says, rolling her eyes. "You look lovely, Olivia."

Olivia looks down. "Thank you. I don't own anything in that ugly grass color, so this is going to have to do." She shrugs and walks over to Reed to give him a kiss goodbye. She explains everything to her parents, and they listen even though I'm sure they've heard it all a million times.

We head downstairs to the valet, and they point us in the direction of the car service. I could rent a car, but it's easier and safer to hire someone else to drive us around.

Twenty minutes later, the car service drops us off in downtown Denver. He opens the door, and Olivia gets out first. Before I can get out, I see the lights of the cameras flash. For a second I worry how she's going to react, but she handles it like a pro. She locks her arm into my elbow and smiles softly up at me, allowing the media to snap pictures.

"I'm sorry about this. I made sure to get us a private booth," I whisper into her ear. She nods, her smile never wavering. I imagine, because her mom was one of the biggest international models of her time, and her dad was a huge college football coach, Olivia's experienced the paparazzi at some point during her life. Luckily, for the most part, they really only follow athletes during the weeks of the big games. Sure, in New York, you'll get an occasional paparazzo snapping photos, but it's not like it is when you're an actor or singer living in Los Angeles.

We start walking toward the restaurant and several fans stop us so I can sign stuff for them. Olivia offers to take pictures using their phones. We easily ignore the comments and questions about Celeste and my called-off engagement, but when a question is asked about Reed, I almost answer.

"Nick, is it true your son is the result of a one-night stand?"

Olivia's fingers dig into my arm to stop me. When I look down at her, she smiles then comes up on her tiptoes to give me a chaste kiss. "Ignore them," she murmurs against my lips before pulling back.

When we finally reach the restaurant, we're seated immediately. The waiter takes our drink order and then drops off some bread.

"Wow! Walking with you reminds me of being in high school and dating the star quarterback." She giggles, and I glare at her.

"You dated the quarterback? Who? Does he play now?" Olivia throws her head back with laughter, but I'm not laughing.

"Oh my God! Stop!" She continues to laugh. "I don't know what happened to him, but I can assure you, you're way more popular and get so many more girls than him." Her tone is playful and mocking, and it makes me crack a smile.

"Damn right I'm better, but the only woman I need to get is you. This is why you should be wearing our team colors. So everybody knows you belong to me."

"Aww...maybe you should buy me a letterman's jacket with your number on it...or better yet, I can get your number tattooed right above my ass." She laughs some more.

I, on the other hand, imagine her naked in nothing but my jersey and have to block the visual out before I'm sporting a hard-on right here at the table. Good thing the table is blocking anybody's view from seeing my crotch.

"Both those ideas sound great to me."

We spend the rest of our time at dinner getting to know more about each other. It's nice getting to know Olivia as a woman, as more than just Reed's mom. She tells me about her mom and her childhood, about her time in Paris, some more about her career in the arts. You'd never guess she's worth millions of dollars. She's down to earth and sweet, and she lets everything roll off her back. She listens to everything I say, like she's genuinely interested, asking questions and adding in her own thoughts. And with every word she speaks, and every smile she grants me, I find myself falling harder for her.

We get back to the hotel room and thank her parents for watching Reed. Olivia tells me she needs to run downstairs and grab something, so while she's gone, I jump in the shower to rinse off.

When I get out, I wrap a towel around my waist and head into the room to grab some clothes. Before I can make it out of the doorway, I'm stopped in my place. Because standing in front of me is Olivia in nothing but my jersey. I recognize them from downstairs in the hotel giftshop. They're selling them for the Super Bowl. The jersey is too big on her, exposing her bare shoulder. Her creamy legs are bare, and I wonder if she's wearing panties underneath.

Her mouth twitches into a shy smile as she waits for me to say something. "Fuck" is the only word that comes out of my mouth as I close the distance between us. My one hand cradles her face as my other one moves down the jersey and lands on her smooth thigh. My mouth crashes into hers. It's not sweet or romantic. It's raw and needy. Urgent and demanding. My tongue duals with hers, and she moans into my mouth. My fingers glide back up her thigh, under the jersey, and when I feel there's nothing underneath, I let out a low groan.

"You're killing me, woman," I murmur against her lips. My hands grip her ass cheeks, and I lift her and bring her over to the bed, laying her down under me. My mouth goes back to hers, kissing her with everything in me. Her soft, plump lips have me addicted.

We kiss until she pulls away slightly. "I feel like we really are teenagers. I'm wearing your jersey...we're making out like we're in high school." She giggles, and I shake my head at her playfulness.

"What am I going to do with you?" The question is meant to be rhetorical, but when I speak the words, Olivia's eyes widen.

Her voice is soft. "Maybe...one day love me." She shrugs her shoulders shyly.

Stick a damn fork in me because I'm fucking done. This woman is everything I need in my life, yet I had no idea I was missing.

"That's definitely a huge possibility," I say before my lips capture hers once again, and we continue to make out like horny teenagers.

TWENTY-ONE

OLIVIA

IT'S SUPER BOWL SUNDAY, and I'm sitting up in the friends and family suite with Corrine and Shelby, while Nick and my dad, along with the rest of the team, are in the locker room getting ready for the biggest game the New York Brewers have faced in over a decade. The game is being played in Denver, but the team we're up against is none other than Nick's old team, North Carolina. They made it to the playoffs last year without him but lost. This year they're favored to win it all.

The last few days have been nothing short of amazing. During the day, Nick has been with the team, practicing. It's a huge game, even bigger because he's playing against his old team. They let him go, thinking he wouldn't bring them another championship, yet here he is, hopefully about to prove them all wrong.

Every evening Nick has spent his time with Reed and me. While Reed is awake, Nick's and my attention is on our son, but once he's asleep, it's a whole different ball game. I've never experienced such closeness with a man without having sex. The foreplay with Nick is out of this world, but more than that, it's the time afterward—before I fall asleep in his arms, when he talks to me.

After our conversation about Fiona and me both leaving him a note, an idea sparked. I wanted to turn something negative into a positive, so a couple nights ago I snuck out of bed, wrote him a note, and stuck it in his gym bag. Then last night I did the same thing—unsure if he even saw the first one. Only this morning, I woke up to a note as well, telling me he not only saw it, but it meant a lot to him. He promised to always leave a note, so his words are the first thing I read when I open my eyes, and in return I made the same promise.

"Excuse me." A soft voice brings me back to the now. Reed is awake in my arms, but it won't be long until he's asleep. It's 4:30 here, but he's still refusing to conform to the time zone in Denver. In New York, it's 6:30, and Reed's internal clock has him passed out by seven o'clock every night—waking up every four hours to eat and getting up for the day at six. I love that my son is already on a routine, but here in Denver that means he's up at four in the freaking morning!

"Excuse me," I hear again, and this time I look up to see if someone is speaking to me. With Corrine and Shelby to the left of me, I look to the right. It's an older woman who looks to be around the same age as my stepmom, maybe a little younger. Her hair is dyed in perfect highlights and is tied up in a tight ponytail. Her dress is Stella McCartney—a designer my mom used to love. Her lips are pursed into a half smile-half grimace, and I glance down at my son to confirm he's not crying. I learned from my stunt a few weeks ago, people don't like babies who cry in public.

When my eyes move upward, they land on her eyes—emerald green like Nick's...like Reed's. My gut tells me this woman is related to Nick, and then I recall our late-night conversations where he confided in me about his childhood and lack of relationship with his parents. How he never understood the different kinds of love until Reed was born. My initial instinct is to hate this woman, but instead I choose to pity her, because she's the one missing out on having an authentic relationship with her son.

"Can I help you?" I finally say, and her lips twitch slightly into a shell of a smile.

"I just wanted to introduce myself. I'm Victoria Shaw, Nicholas's mother." She puts her perfectly manicured hand out to shake mine, and I meet her halfway.

"I'm Olivia Harper." She obviously knows who I am or she wouldn't be standing here introducing herself to me.

Reed chooses this moment to make his presence known. He squirms slightly, his arms coming up, and when I lift and turn him around to face me, his mouth morphs into a smile—a new milestone

I can't take enough pictures of. "And this is Reed," I add, my eyes staying trained on my baby boy.

Corrine reaches over and tickles his belly. "I can't get enough of those smiles," she says, joining the awkward conversation. "Every time I see him, I swear he's grown another inch." She lightly pinches Reed's cheek then glances up at Victoria. "I'm Corrine, but you know that...we've seen each other at several team functions this year. I'm also Olivia's stepmother." Corrine stands and walks around the back of the couch over to Victoria. "I've watched how you treat those around you. And I'm warning you right now, if you treat my stepdaughter with anything other than respect, I'll have you removed from the premises." She smiles saccharinely and excuses herself to the restroom with Shelby following behind.

I hold back the tears that want to break free. I miss my mom every day, but having Corrine in my life almost makes up for not having my mom here. She's everything a woman could ask for in a stepmom, and I'm so blessed to have one more person in our lives who loves Reed and me.

After a few seconds, Victoria says, "He looks just like Nicholas."

"Yeah, he does. Would you like to hold him?" I hold Reed out, but when Victoria shakes her head, I bring him back against my chest.

"I better not. This is a new dress, and I would hate to have to go back to the hotel and change if he..." She scrunches her nose up in disgust. "Well, you know." She smiles a pained smile, and it has me wanting to find Nick and hug him tightly. The stories Nick has told me about the type of relationship he has with his parents didn't fully sink in until this moment. I mean, what grandmother doesn't want to hold her own grandbaby? I can barely keep Corrine and my dad from hogging Reed when they're in the same room as him.

"Okay..." I give her a plastered-on smile and turn back to watch the pre-game ceremony. Corrine and Shelby return a few minutes later, and we chat about the upcoming game as we wait for it to begin. Our conversation is interrupted when Nick's dad, Henry, shows up. Victoria introduces us, but just like his wife, he has no desire to hold his grandson, and they both choose to sit elsewhere instead of near us. Nick mentioned that the majority of the time they live in North Carolina, and I've never been more relieved to know they won't be around fulltime.

Just after half-time, Celeste walks in. I only know this because I hear Victoria gush over her. "Oh, Celeste! Sweetheart! I'm so glad you're here." Corrine makes eye contact with me and rolls her eyes. I roll mine back, but deep down I'm sad Nick's parents are behaving this way. I can't imagine not having the support and love I have with my family and friends. I haven't known Nick for long, but other than Killian, I haven't seen anyone else have his back. I know he and Celeste are best friends as well, but I haven't yet to witness their actual friendship.

I hear Celeste politely say hello to Nick's parents, and I hold my breath, afraid our truce was only temporary. A minute later, Celeste sits down next me and says, "About time you got control of that baby." I take a calming breath and turn to her to say something back —what, I'm not sure—but when I look at her, she's grinning ear to ear.

"Ugh..." I groan. "I'm never going to live that down, am I?"

"Probably not, but on the flipside, after hearing him cry, it cemented my decision to never have children." She laughs. "Crying babies are the perfect way to control the population if you ask me. Five minutes of hearing him cry, and I was double checking that my birth control was up to date." She shoots me a wink, and I laugh.

Celeste sits next to me for the entire game, and the more we talk, the more I find she's actually a very likable person and can see why she and Nick are such good friends. Underneath her flawless makeup and designer clothes is a sweet and funny woman. She shares hilarious stories of Nick growing up that I stow away to later rib into Nick about. Corrine and Shelby join the conversation, and we make plans for a girls' night. Corrine says she's too old to go out but would love to watch Reed. I text Giselle, and after she about dies through text over the fact I'm making plans with Nick's ex, she, of course, agrees to go out as well.

All of our talking ceases as the game winds down. New York has intercepted the ball and there's only enough time for one, maybe two plays. The next play, if done right, can mean we're Super Bowl champions.

TWENTY-TWO

*N*ICK

HALF THE CROWD erupts into an explosive roar of cheers as our defense intercepts the ball at the forty-yard line with under a minute remaining, no timeouts left. This is exactly what we needed, what we were banking on. The game has been close the entire time. If they would've scored, we would need this touchdown to stay one up on them, but because they didn't, if we score, we win. Our entire season is on the line, the entire game coming down to this next play. Everyone is counting on me. I glance up at the owner's box, not that I can see Olivia, but knowing she's up there calms my nerves.

The last time I was in this position, I was with Fiona, but she wasn't there. I know a lot of what went wrong between us had to do with my mother, but I hope what I'm building with Olivia is stronger. While I'm pissed at my mom for what she did, what Celeste said rings true. Fiona made the choice to take the money. She chose to walk away. She could've come to me and I would've given it to her, but she didn't. I'd like to believe everything happens for a reason, and Fiona and Celeste were merely stepping stones that led me to Olivia and Reed.

Offense makes their way onto the field, huddling together and waiting for me to call the play, so I jog over to join them. "All right, guys. We got this. One play...maybe two, and we'll be Super Bowl champions. We have zero timeouts, so the clock will be ticking."

Here's the play: West right slot, seventy-two, z bingo U split, dummy snap count on three." The huddle breaks, and everybody lines up.

On my three-count, the center hikes the ball. Taking a three-step drop, I find an available receiver, but just as I'm about to throw the ball, he's covered by the fucking cornerback. Defense is rushing me, and I know I've got to make this throw before I'm tackled. I spot Killian sprint left. He's open—just barely. I throw the ball to him, and it's a shitty throw at best, too far to the left, just before I'm knocked to the ground. Killian catches the ball one-handed and runs. I watch with bated breath as he passes each yard line—thirty... twenty... ten... with the safety on his ass every step of the way.

A safety comes from the right, and Killian, like the crazy ass he is, leaps over the guy into the end zone.

"Touchdown!" The crowd screams, and the entire team congregates into the end zone, celebrating. Brian Peters, our kicker, makes his way out onto the field for the extra point. Then, with only twenty seconds left on the clock, the special team's unit comes onto the field for the kick off. Peters, once again kicks the ball, and the other team receives it. Their kick returner runs up the field, but he's immediately taken down by one of our players. With no time left on the clock, the game is over, and we're Super Bowl fucking champions.

Coach Harper makes his way over to me and pulls me in for a hug. "We did it!" he shouts into my ear, and I hug him back. "Hell yeah, we did." The confetti falls from the sky, and the media makes their way over to us in a frenzy, surrounding us like vultures.

Killian jumps up against me and pulls me into a hug. "Fuck yes!" We're both crying as hats are handed out. Several of my teammates come over and hug me. I place my hat on my head as one of the reporters sticks a microphone in my face. Her name is Jennifer, and she's one of the sport's channel's main reporters.

"Two years ago, you were on the other side. Now here you are with your fourth Super Bowl win; first one with New York. To get this win today, what does that mean?"

"It means everything, Jennifer. This season wasn't easy by any means. It doesn't surprise me we had to fight every step of the way through this game, until the very end." The reporter laughs. "It was a team effort. It tested every one of us, but we came through in the end."

The reporter moves on to her next question. "It's public knowledge that you're in New York on a one-year contract. Can you tell us your plans for next year?" I want to say I'm not going anywhere, but the truth is contracts haven't been discussed formally yet, so I have to go with a politically correct response.

"There are definitely a lot of decisions to be made, but I have some priorities I need to get to first, starting with finding my girlfriend, Olivia, and kissing the heck out of her. Then I'm going to celebrate with my team and thank God we won so Coach Harper doesn't have a reason to ban me from family holidays. After that, I'm taking my girl and son on a much-needed vacation." I glance over at Coach Harper who throws his head back in laughter, shaking his head in understanding. I just went on record, on live television, and admitted to the world that Olivia is my girlfriend.

Jennifer and I go through a few more questions and once we're done, I make my way down the field to meet up with the rest of my team, so we can celebrate our win.

TWENTY-THREE

NICK and I are cuddling on the couch at his place, watching shit television while Reed is napping. I'm laying horizontally across the couch, my head resting in his lap, and Nick is running his fingers through my hair. The last two weeks since we've returned from the Super Bowl have been spent with Nick either at my place or Reed and me at his. The team is on break until the end of June when their training camp begins, and we have somehow created our own schedule of pure laziness. Nick and I haven't discussed his plans in regard to his contract with New York, but I think he's just basking in the glory of his win right now—he's had to make appearances on several daytime and late-night shows—and enjoying the downtime. We rarely go out in public, and if we do, it's to grab something to eat. My dad and Corrine are away in Italy. They left the day after the Super Bowl. Corrine is from there, and my dad surprised her with a romantic trip, just the two of them.

Nick pauses the show, and I turn over onto my back to look at him. "I have something I want to ask you, but I'm going to need you to be openminded."

I sit up, intrigued. "Okay."

"I want us to go away."

"Where do you want to go? Somewhere warm would be fabulous, so Reed can wear less than three layers of clothing outside."

"Actually, that's where the open-mindedness comes in. I was thinking we could go away...just the two of us."

I sit up, confused. "What would we do with Reed?"

"Giselle said she could watch him."

"You already asked her?"

"I didn't want to bring it up if she couldn't. I was going to ask Shelby if Giselle said she couldn't, but she said she can."

I stand and begin to pace the living room. Reed will be two months old this week. Am I ready to leave him for the night?

"Liv, it would only be for two nights. It's Valentine's Day weekend."

"Could we stay local?"

"Like stay at a hotel in the area?" He eyes me incredulously.

"My dad has a house in the Hamptons. It's only a couple hours' drive from here, so we wouldn't be far if something happened."

Nick chuckles. "How about I'll agree to the Hamptons, but I'm picking the place. I'm not spending the weekend under Coach's roof with his daughter."

I roll my eyes. "Deal." And then it hits me Valentine's Day is *this* week, like in two days. "Wait! We're going this weekend?"

"Yeah...we'll drive up Thursday after Giselle gets off work and stay through the weekend."

"That's hardly any time to prepare." I feel myself getting worked up.

Nick gets up off the couch and moves toward me. His arms encircle my waist, and he leans down and places a calming kiss on my lips. "Brown-Eyes," he whispers. He moves his lips to my neck and kisses the sensitive flesh just under my ear. "There's nothing to prepare for. You don't even have to pack. If I have it my way, we won't even be getting dressed." He lifts his head, and with a wide grin, waggles his brows suggestively.

"LIV, WE'RE HERE." I feel Nick gently shake me, but my eyes refuse to open. "Liv, baby. You have to wake up." Reluctantly, I open my eyes and stretch my arms as I remember where I am. One minute I was talking to Nick about Reed's growth spurt and the next I'm waking up in the car. I sit up and glance around. We're in the driveway of a beautiful three-story cottage. I can't see the ocean from where we are, but I know it's back there because the home is sitting on top of a dune.

"Nick...this place is huge. Did you invite more people?"

He laughs. "Actually, I did..."

"Oh." I had assumed when he mentioned clothing was optional, he was implying we would be alone. Maybe he wanted Reed home because there would be a party going on...

"Not right now. For the next two nights, it's just you and me. On Saturday, however, we'll have a full house. Giselle is going to bring Reed over, and Killian is joining us. Shelby can't make it because she has a birthday party to attend for her stepmother, but your dad and Corrine will be coming...and..." He pauses, worrying his bottom lip, nervously.

"And?"

"Well, Celeste mentioned she wanted to join, and since you guys seem to be getting along...texting and planning a night out, I said okay, and your parents said they'd have no problem watching Reed while we all go out. Is that okay?"

"Yeah! That sounds really great. How long are we here for?"

"Only five days...but then we're going away on another trip, and Giselle and Killian will be joining us for the second half of that trip."

Turning in my seat to face Nick, I place my palms on his cheeks. "You know you don't have to take us away, right? I don't need surprise trips; I just need you."

Nick frowns. "I know, but I only have so long until football starts back up again." He takes my hands in his and brings them up to his lips, kissing the inside of each of my wrists. "I want us to make the most out of it. It was only going to be us, but then Giselle mentioned she could help babysit, and once Killian caught wind of where we're going, he begged and said if I didn't let him go, I was choosing your best friend over mine."

I laugh, imagining Killian pouting like a child.

"What are you thinking in regard to your contract?"

"It's kind of out of my hands. I'm waiting to hear from my dad if New York wants to re-sign me. If they don't, I have to hope another team will pick me up. I would like to think I've proven my worth this season."

I hadn't considered New York might not re-sign him, and if they don't, he would have to move to wherever the team is that does sign him. Would he ask us to move with him? Would I be willing to move somewhere else? My thoughts go back to a year ago when Victor left me to move to Switzerland. Of course, him not asking me makes more sense now that I know he was cheating on me for a year with my so-called friend.

"Hey, I can see the cogs in your head turning. It'll all work out. We'll figure it out together. But first, let's enjoy ourselves. We have this house—" he points toward the beautiful cottage "—and it has a hot tub and a heated pool."

"Do you want me to talk to my dad? I know he's not the owner but—" Nick leans over the center console and kisses me. His tongue darts out quickly, massaging mine, but then he backs up leaving me wanting more.

"No. One, all negotiations need to be done through my agent, and two, I want to keep us separate from business. I want to have a good time this weekend. No talking shop." I nod in agreement.

After dropping our bags in the foyer, Nick and I take a tour of the cottage. It has at least seven bedrooms and even more bathrooms, a huge kitchen, and several sitting rooms. We find the bedroom we're going to be staying in, and Nick brings our bags up.

Afterward, we make our way outside. It's fifty degrees out today, so we're both dressed comfortably in jeans and a hoodie. There's a huge back patio with tons of seating and a humungous pool. Just past the pool is a wooden bridge that leads down to the beach. The sun is shining, and it helps offset the cool air.

"Let's go inside. I brought a bottle of wine, and I was thinking we could go to dinner tonight."

"Sounds good. I'm just going to go up to the room and freshen up. You pour us a glass, and I'll be right back down."

I start to walk away, but then remember something I wanted to tell him. "Oh, Nick..."

"Yeah?"

"Remember when I went to the doctor for my check-up?"

"Yeah." He nods.

"He okayed me to have sex." I shoot him an overly dramatic flirtatious wink, and Nick throws his head back with a laugh. I start to ascend the stairs when he calls out my name. I stop on the first step and turn around to find him right in front of me. He pulls me into his arms, and his lips brush mine softly before he pulls back and smiles, his green eyes shining bright. "Thank you for coming away with me. I know it was hard to leave Reed."

"Thank you for bringing me. Now let me go make myself presentable. I feel gross from sleeping in the car."

Nick lets go of me, and I run up the stairs to our room. I jump in the shower to rinse off then brush my teeth. I'm debating whether I should go down there dressed, in a robe, naked, or in lingerie when my phone dings with a text from Giselle: **Are you busy?**

Me: Nope. Everything okay?

It takes her a few seconds to respond, so I wrap the fluffy white towel around me and sit down on the bed.

Giselle: Yes...Reed took a bottle a couple hours ago, but now I think he's wanting another one. He's really fussy. I just wanted to check with you before I go off your feeding schedule.

And this is why I fell asleep in the car. My baby boy is going through a growth spurt, which means he has been getting up every few hours all night long to eat. The pediatrician said it's normal, but I was nervous about leaving Giselle to deal with it. Up until a few days ago, he's been on a great eating and sleeping schedule.

Me: Go ahead and give him half a bottle. If he doesn't take it, he might just be tired. He's been up a lot throughout the night. Oh! Can you take his temperature? I just want to make sure he's not sick. Can you please text me and let me know?

I debate whether to send that entire text, but with me over two hours away I need to make sure Reed isn't catching a cold or something worse. After hitting send, I lay back in the bed to wait for her response. The pillows are comfy, and the down blanket is super soft. Maybe I'll just close my eyes for a few seconds while I wait...

TWENTY-FOUR

*N*ICK

MY PHONE RINGS, and when I look at the caller ID, I see it's my dad. Since the only time he ever calls is when it's work related, I let it go to voicemail. Right now my priority is Olivia. Speaking of which...it's been a while since she went upstairs to freshen up.

Leaving the bottle of wine, along with the glasses where they are, I run upstairs to check on her. Immediately, I spot her on the bed, passed out. When I get closer, I can see she's in a towel. Her phone dings in her hand, but she doesn't move. She's snuggled up in the sheets and snoring softly.

Taking the phone from her, I check it and see a photo of Reed sleeping with an accompanying text from Giselle saying he doesn't have a temperature and that he ate and fell asleep. I text her back a quick thank you and place her phone, as well as mine, on the night-stand. After stripping off my jeans and sweater, I climb in with Olivia—she's in the center of the bed, so I slide in behind her, my arms encircling her body. She makes a soft sighing noise as she settles into me.

Pressing a small kiss to her check, I lay my head down on the pillow, and for a few minutes I enjoy holding this beautiful woman. The last few days she's been supermom. Reed's been up at all hours, and while I try to help, she insists on getting up no matter what. My goal is to get her to understand I want us to be a team. She doesn't have to do this all on her own. Letting my eyes close, I drift off to sleep.

I'M NOT sure how long I was passed out, but what I do know is that Olivia is awake. How do I know that? Because her towel-clad ass is rubbing against my front in a way that has my dick hardening. My hands are still wrapped around her waist, and I can feel her shifting in the bed. Pressing my face into her nape, I tighten my grip on her. She sighs and moves her ass up and down my front again.

"Liv." I say her name to make sure she's awake.

"Mmhmm" is all I get.

My hand moves up the towel, and finding the knot holding it closed, I loosen it until I feel the two sides of the towel part ways. Grabbing the material separating us, I tug on it slightly until it unravels off Olivia's body. I throw it onto the floor then bring my hand back to her body. My fingers stroke and tweak her pointed nipples. My lips trail kisses down the back of her shoulder, and I feel her shiver at my touch.

"Liv, you awake, baby?"

"Yes," she breathes. I love the affect my touch has on her.

My hand glides across her smooth skin, down her hip, and around her front between her thighs. She parts her legs enough for my fingers to slip into her tight cunt. When she lifts slightly, I slide my other arm under her. Sticking one finger, then two, inside her, I fingerfuck her, getting her wetter and wetter. The room is silent, the only sounds coming from the slickness of her pussy, and from her mouth as she lets out moans of pleasure.

Using her juices, I move my fingers to her clit, circling and massaging the swollen nub. One of her hands goes to her breast, and I can see her pinching her nipple. Her moans get louder. Her other hand comes around behind her, finding my dick and stroking it. It's already hard, but with her touch, it's granite.

"Fuck me, Nick, please," she begs, turning her neck enough to lock eyes with me. Shifting her ass up slightly, I guide my hard cock into her pussy from behind. It's warm and wet and so fucking tight, and all fucking mine. Once I'm completely seated inside her, I give her neck a kiss. Then I start moving in and out of her. My fingers are digging into her side, and Olivia's meeting me thrust for thrust.

It feels so damn good from behind, but I can't kiss her or see her. Reluctantly, I slide out of her, and she lets out a disappointed whimper. She rolls to her back, and I crawl up her body, quickly pushing back into her. My hands are on either side of her face, and as I lean down to kiss her, I see her chocolate-brown eyes sparkling with pleasure. I kiss her with every ounce of want and need I have inside me as I make love to her.

Her legs part a little more, and I'm able to go deeper. I can feel my cock rubbing against her clit. Her body tightens in anticipation of her impending climax. Our kisses turn ravenous, frantic. We're all lips and tongues and teeth. My thrusts get harder, rougher. I can feel sweat beading above my brow. It's been too fucking long since I was inside her. I'm never going to last.

And then Olivia's walls tighten. I feel her pussy contract, and I know it's about to be over. She lets out a long, breathy moan into my mouth, without breaking our kiss, as she comes so damn hard around me I about lose it. My hands find their way to her head, and my fingers grip her hair as I pump into her with abandon, finding my own release. I hear myself let out a groan as my seed shoots into my woman's pussy, filling her with every fucking drop of cum I have in me.

TWENTY-FIVE

Olivia

NICK'S BODY STILLS, and I can feel his cum inside me. We stop kissing but Nick's lips stay pressed against mine for a few more seconds before he backs up. He pulls out of me, taking his warmth with him. When he doesn't say anything at first, I get worried. What if being with me again wasn't as good as the last time? I've had a baby, so maybe I don't feel as good to him.

"Whatever you're thinking, stop." He presses a kiss to my lips then to my cheek and last to my neck. "No, I take that back. Tell me. I can't fix it or tell you you're wrong if I don't know what it is you're thinking."

"Was—was it as good as before I had a baby?" Nick's brows pinch together. I can feel his semi-hard cock rubbing against the top of my thigh, but I block it out.

"I don't think you can compare the two. That night we spent together was incredible. Mind-blowing fucking amazing." I feel myself frown at his words, but then he continues. "But that night, it was strictly physical. You had me addicted to your body within seconds."

He holds himself up on one forearm. "Brown-Eyes," he says softly, and my stomach knots up. I love when he calls me that. "You can't compare a night of lust to what we just did. The sex that night was off the charts hot, but now so much has changed...the way you make me feel. It's what I was talking about before...so much fucking more. It's not just your body I'm addicted to. It's also your heart and your mind that's got me hooked and craving more." And in those couple of sentences, he's managed to tame down all of my fears and insecurities.

He gets off the bed and pulls me up with him, giving me a quick kiss before we go to the bathroom to clean up. Once we're done, we get dressed and head downstairs. Nick pours us each a glass of wine, and we sit down on the sofa facing each other. For a few seconds, we're both silent. Then Nick says, "Liv, I came in you...I know it's too late now, but we probably should've discussed this first." My body freezes, and I force the sip of wine down as he continues. "I don't know what happened when you got pregnant with Reed, if a condom broke, or if we didn't use one once and I didn't pull out, but—"

"I lost my luggage and my pills. I didn't take them for almost a week," I blurt out. Nick's brows raise at my admission. "I'm so sorry. The entire plane's luggage was put on the wrong plane. You can ask Giselle. I didn't do it on purpose. I wasn't trying to trap you...I mean, how could I? I didn't even have your information. And just so you know, I'm on the pill. I promise I'll be more careful this time." I stop speaking long enough to catch my breath. "If you want to use condoms to be on the—"

"Whoa, calm down." Nick laughs. "If we would've used condoms every time, you not taking your pills wouldn't have mattered. It takes two. I don't for a second think you tried to trap me, and I don't regret whatever happened because it got us our son. And—" Nick grins wickedly "—there's no way in hell I'm using a condom with you. I've felt your pussy raw, and there's no way I'm going back to having latex between us."

His words have my cheeks heating up, and of course it only has him grinning wider.

"MY BABY!" I screech as I run out the door. The last couple days alone with Nick has been nothing short of amazing. The fucking and sex and lovemaking—and yes, I'm listing them separately because when Nick took me from behind in the shower, that was definitely fucking, and when he took me on top of the table, it was sex, and when he woke me up this morning, the way he languorously pumped in and out of me, well, that was most certainly making love. I feel caught up on my sleep and like a whole new person. And now I'm missing the heck out of my son.

Giselle takes his car seat out and Nick takes it from her. "I need him now," I state matter-of-factly, which makes Nick laugh.

"Let's get him inside where it's warm and then you can have him," he says, carrying Reed inside. Killian follows Nick inside, but I hang back to help Giselle with her bags.

"How was the ride?" I take one of her bags, and she grabs the other.

"Too long."

"Oh no! Was Reed cranky?" We walk up the sidewalk and are almost to the front door when Giselle stops.

"He was a perfect angel. Killian, on the other hand, drove me nuts. I might have to drive back with your parents because another two hours in the car with that man, and I might end up in jail for murder."

"Really? He seems so nice every time we hang out with him." I shrug. "What did he do?"

"Olivia, Giselle, let me help you with those." Killian pops out from behind the door and takes the bags from both of our hands. He smiles sweetly at me, but when he smiles at Giselle, it's almost *too* sweet.

She groans and rolls her eyes, pushing past him. "I need a drink."

We head inside, and Nick already has Reed out of his car seat and is making him a bottle. Giselle grabs a bottle of wine and two glasses and brings them over to the table. "This place is unbelievable. Maybe I need to go against my rule of never dating an athlete again." She waggles her eyebrows playfully.

"You have a rule against dating athletes?" Nick asks, sitting down next to me and feeding Reed. "I thought it was only musicians."

I laugh. "Nope, she's included athletes in her ban as well."

"And why is that?" Killian asks Giselle.

"Because they think because they can throw and catch a ball, they're above God." She winks my way, telling me she's just messing with the guys. "No offense, Nick."

"No offense taken. Besides, you're not far off. Only it wasn't me throwing a ball this morning that had Olivia screaming 'Oh god' in bed."

"Nick!" I screech, and he cackles.

"Nice!" Killian reaches over and gives Nick a fist-bump.

"Pigs," Giselle huffs.

"She was just kidding!" I exclaim. "She's really just against dating in general." Giselle and I laugh.

"And what about you?" Nick asks, lifting Reed up to his shoulder to burp him. "I know you mentioned dating a quarterback, but were there any types of guys you preferred to date?"

"I'm an equal opportunist...but there is something about a tall, tan, muscular man who knows how to use his hands...to throw that gets me all hot and bothered."

Nick chuckles. "You better equally remember I'm the only one allowed to get you hot and bothered." He leans over and pulls me into a kiss before getting up with Reed. "Kill, want to grab a beer outside so the women can gossip?"

"Sure." Killian laughs, then stands and follows Nick out of the room.

"Wait!" I yell, and Nick stops in his place. "Hand over my baby." He laughs as he hands Reed over to me. Then he and Killian grab a couple of beers from the fridge and head out back.

"That guy has it bad," Giselle comments once the backdoor is shut.

"It's definitely mutual. Now tell me what happened with Killian that has you drinking before noon."

She drinks her glass of wine slowly until it's completely drained. "The guy is just such an asshole," she finally says. Seeing her glass is empty, she refills it. "Now, tell me about your romantic getaway." And I know that's all I'm getting out of her right now.

A little while later, my dad and Corrine show up. Nick and Killian run to the store to buy groceries and when they return, Nick grills up some burgers and steaks while Corrine and I make several side dishes. We all congregate to the dining room to eat. The guys banter back and forth about their Super Bowl win, and the women discuss Giselle's latest job with some high-class executive who is having his entire place redecorated. It's the most content I've felt in a long time, like everything is finally falling into place.

Just as we finish cleaning up from dinner, there's a knock on the door. Since Nick is laying Reed down, I run to the door to quickly answer it, and standing there is Celeste with a single suitcase. She smiles wide at me, and I smile back.

"I'm glad you could make it."

"Thank you for having me." She leaves her luggage by the stairs, and we join everyone back in the living room. I make introductions around the room even though she knows my dad and stepmom.

"I love that everyone is here," I say. "I was so scared when we closed up our flat to come back here, but I'm glad we did."

"I was about to drag you back myself," my dad jokes.

"Speaking of which, have you decided if you're going to sell or rent it out?" Giselle asks.

"You own a place in France?" Celeste asks, joining in the conversation.

"I lived there for six years. It made more sense to buy than rent. Giselle and I went to college there and then both got our master's. I haven't decided if I'm going to sell it, though."

Nick and Killian walk into the room as I'm finishing my sentence. "Sell what?" Nick questions as he sits down on the couch. He lifts me slightly then snuggles me into his side.

"My flat in Paris."

"You should keep it, so we can visit. I've never been. You can show me your home away from home." He presses a kiss to my neck.

"True, but we could always stay in a hotel. The market is flourishing, and I could make a decent amount on it. It's in a college district."

"Does that mean you're staying for good?" Giselle asks, and I shoot her a glare.

"What do you mean for good?" my dad jumps in, confused. I didn't want to get into this now, but it seems I don't have a choice.

"Are you planning to move back?" Nick asks, his voice devoid of all emotion.

"When I came to visit it was only for a week because I was offered a position as an Art Education Coordinator. When we left to come here, I took a leave of absence with the Museum I was working at. You get two months of maternity leave, but I put in a request for additional time."

"How much extra?" Nick asks, his tone now ice cold.

"If I plan to keep my job, I have to return in four months."

"Olivia!" my dad exclaims. "You didn't mention this when you agreed to *move* home."

"I know. I wanted to keep my options open. I never imagined I would find Reed's dad. Obviously, a lot has changed."

Celeste's eyes are trained on me when she says, "You agreed to shared custody. You can't just leave with Nick's baby." If Nick's tone was ice cold, his friend's is equivalent to an arctic glacier, and in this moment, I can understand why they're such good friends. They might not see eye-to-eye on everything, but she one hundred percent has his back.

"I'm not going anywhere. I was just keeping my options open," I repeat. "I love my life here, and I love being near my dad."

"What happens if Nick ends up on another team? Like in Florida or Texas?" Celeste pushes, and I stop myself from telling her to mind her own business. It's clear she's only being protective of Nick.

"And this is where the conversation needs to end," my dad says. "As the coach, I can't discuss this with my player, especially with his contract up in the air."

Nick agrees, and the conversation shifts to another topic, but my mind is stuck on Celeste's question. If Nick leaves, would I go? Would he ask me to go?

He must sense my confusion because he dusts my hair over my shoulder and whispers into my ear, "I'm not going anywhere, and if I have to, we'll discuss it together. Just don't go and leave the country without me." He kisses my temple then my earlobe. "Okay?"

"Okay," I agree.

"Are you kids going out tonight?" Corrine asks, changing the subject.

"Yes!" Celeste answers before I can. "I've been wanting to check out AM Southampton!"

"Giselle?" I ask. "You down?"

"Hell yes."

"Well I'm definitely down," Killian adds.

"I guess that's a yes then," I say through a laugh.

After we spend the rest of the afternoon hanging out, Giselle, Celeste, and I go upstairs to get ready. We're all dressed in slinky, way too tight dresses, and as I stand next to Celeste in the floor length mirror, I get choked up. The woman reminds me so much of my mom. She must be almost six feet tall in heels with a slender, yet feminine body. She's tanned and...perfect. I clearly got more of my dad's genes than my mom's since I'm only five foot five and curvy.

"We look hot," Celeste winks as Giselle walks over to join us.

"You remind me of my mom when she was younger."

Celeste's face whips around to mine. "Really?"

I nod. "I used to wish I could have had her height and body."

"You might not be tall, but you're beautiful, Olivia. Trust me.

You look a lot like your mom. You have her eyes and nose, and when you smile you light up the same way she used to in her photos."

"Really?" I ask as tears fill my lids. It's the first time anyone besides my dad has ever told me I look like my mom.

"Really! Now wipe those tears, and let's get this party started!"

TWENTY-SIX

Nick

"HOLY SHIT, BRO." Killian's eyes dart over my shoulder, and when I turn around, the women are standing at the bottom of the stairs. All of them in dresses that I'm almost positive are illegal in several countries and high heels that could kill a man—figuratively and literally. They're all wearing makeup and look beautiful in their own way. But my eyes zero in on Olivia, who looks devastatingly fucking gorgeous.

Closing the gap between us, I pull her into my arms and give her a kiss on the corner of her mouth so I don't ruin her lipstick. "You look stunning, Liv," I whisper in her ear.

"Thank you."

"All of you look beautiful," Killian adds. "Now let's go."

We pile into the SUV I ordered, and about twenty minutes later, we're at AM Southampton night club. Of course the bouncer recognizes us right away, and we're let in and brought over to the VIP section.

"Let's dance." Olivia pulls me onto the dance floor before we can even sit down. The music is thumping, and the club is crowded as hell. I pull her into my arms, and she grinds her body against mine to the music.

"It's like we've come full circle," she yells over the music, and I laugh. She's right. A year ago, we were at a club dancing just like this. I thought back then she was the one for me, but now I know she is.

We spend the next few hours drinking and dancing, and only when Olivia is so drunk and horny that I fear for the pictures that might surface, do we call for the car service to come back and pick us up.

"I need you to fuck me good and hard," Olivia slurs as we walk up the steps to our room. I chuckle at her brazen remarks. Killian, Giselle, and Celeste all laugh, and it's then Olivia remembers we aren't alone. We reach the landing, and Olivia throws her arms around Celeste.

"Thank you for not having sex with my boyfriend. If you did, we wouldn't be able to be friends and then you wouldn't be able to one day be a princess like me." Celeste shoots me a *please help me* look, but I just shake my head. My woman apparently has no filter when she's drunk.

"And don't you worry. When we get back from vacation, I'm going to find you a prince to love. I'm Princess Aurora, but you can be..." Olivia backs up, swaying slightly, and looks at Celeste for a moment. "You can be Belle." She nods, agreeing with herself. "She's not born into royalty and has no desire to marry Gaston, but when she meets the beast, she can't help but fall in love. While some would say the beast saved her, I think they actually saved each other. You're going to meet a man, and you'll both find love in each other. Yep! You're definitely Belle."

"And which one am I?" Giselle asks, of course playing along.

"You're..." Olivia taps her bottom lip in concentration. "Rapunzel."

"Rapunzel? But I have brown hair."

"It's not about how she looks. Rapunzel is strong and brave and knows how to stick up for herself." Olivia crosses the landing, and when she's only a few inches away from Giselle, she places her hand on her cheek. "And one day you're going to meet a prince you will trust with all of your secrets and he's going to save you just like Flynn Ryder saved Rapunzel."

The room goes quiet, quickly realizing Olivia's drunken silliness has turned serious. "All right, my drunken princess. Let's get you to bed before your chariot turns back into a pumpkin." I grab her hips and guide her toward our room.

"Yes!" she squeals. "But that's Cinderella! I'm Aurora!"

TWENTY-SEVEN

OLIVIA

I WAKE up with the most intense, pounding headache I've ever experienced in my life. When I open my eyes, I glance next to me and see the bed is empty. Noticing a ripped piece of paper on the pillow, I snag it, and with only one eye open, read it.

Good morning Princess Aurora, I've left you a glass of water and two Advil in case you need them. I have Reed with me. Take a bath and relax. Come down when you're ready.

–Your Prince ;)

After I've taken the pain meds he left for me and soaked in a hot bubble bath, I make my way downstairs. Everybody is sitting around the table talking, and when they see me, they all go quiet and then crack up laughing.

I look down to make sure I'm dressed appropriately. No nip slips... "What?"

"Nothing, Princess Aurora." Giselle giggles, and Celeste throws her head back in laughter.

"Ha ha. Very funny," I say dryly, which only has them laughing harder. Why? I'm not sure.

Giselle's phone rings, and she stands up, excusing herself to the other room to take the call.

I walk over to Nick to sit down next to him, but before I can sit, he pulls me into his lap. "Good morning, baby," he murmurs into my neck.

"Morning. Where's Reed?"

"Taking a nap." He sniffs my hair. "You smell good. Did you take a bubble bath?"

"I did. Thank you. So, why was everyone laughing?"

"You don't remember last night?" Killian asks.

"Going to the club?" I question.

"No." He shakes his head. "When we got home."

I try to remember, but I can't. "The alcohol must've hit me hard since I haven't drunk in over a year," I admit.

"Don't worry about it, babe," Nick says. "All you need to know is that you, Celeste, and Giselle are all princesses and—"

"Umm...Olivia...I need to go." Giselle comes back into the dining room, looking pale and worried. "And I don't have a car. I came here with Killian...Shit!"

"What's going on?" I ask.

"My dad left my mom. My sister just texted me that she came home for the weekend. She planned to leave this morning, but when she woke up, my dad was gone. I need to get there. You know how my mom is..."

"I know. Why don't you take Nick's car? We can ride home with Killian or my parents..."

"I'll drive you," Killian offers.

Giselle gives him a once over. "I have to go to my parents' house in Rye. It's going to be a good two-hour drive there, and another hour drive back to Brooklyn, and I don't even know how long I'll be there for. Could be a few hours... if she lets me in, that is." She cringes at her last sentence, and my heart breaks for Giselle and the rocky relationship she has with her parents.

"Then we better get moving." Killian walks back out of the room without waiting for Giselle to respond.

We spend the rest of the day out back. It's warm enough to grill outside, so my dad and Nick grill up some chicken and steak while Corrine, Celeste, and I make up some sides. We eat outside on the back patio while Reed naps. Afterward, Corrine offers to watch Reed while Nick and I go for a walk.

"I love the ocean, but I hate the sand and the salt water," I admit as I toe the sand.

Nick chuckles. "I'm pretty sure without the salt water and the sand you have a pool."

"Oh...well, whatever." I laugh.

"I looked up some schools this morning while you were asleep." Nick reaches down and picks up a stick that's washed ashore.

"And what did you find?"

"A couple schools where I can take all my classes online, but I was hoping to take the writing classes on campus. The problem is I don't know where I'll be, so I'm going to have to wait until I find out who I'm playing for next season."

"That makes sense." I sit down while Nick, using the stick he picked up, writes in the sand. "Until then you could do something you enjoy, like writing for fun."

Nick stops drawing in the sand. "What do you mean? Like write a book?"

"Sure, why not? You don't need a degree to write."

Nick comes over and sits behind me, his legs outstretched on either side of my body and his arms wrapping around me. "I also think I'm going to get more involved in the charity my mom runs for me."

"You have a charity? What is it for?"

"Promoting literacy in kids. I started it a few years ago when my publicist said it would look good. I used to go to different schools and read to classes in lower income schools."

"That's amazing, Nick! Why did you stop?"

"The short answer is I got busy, but the truth is, looking back, once it was established, my mom stopped scheduling events, and I didn't push her to do it."

"Well, if you want, I can take a look at it. I ran the youth program at the museum I worked for in Paris. I worked with several charities and organizations." And then an idea hits me. "What would you think about expanding the charity? I've always wanted to start one. What if we combine both of our passions by having one charity that helps promote the arts and literacy?"

"Absolutely. I'll text my mom and let her know you'll be contacting her. She can give you whatever information you need."

We stand, and I brush the bottom of my jeans off. When I turn around, I look at the writing in the sand.

"Umm...Nick, did you write that?" I ask dumbly as I look over my shoulder to find Nick smiling at me. I know he wrote it because I watched him.

"Yeah." He grins. "I did. I love you, Brown-Eyes. It's probably too soon to be saying those words, but they're exactly how I feel. I love you." My heart tightens and then expands. It has never felt so full in my life.

Throwing my arms around Nick's neck, I pull him down for a kiss. I'm not quite ready to say the words back yet, and he doesn't push for them. So for now, I just show him how I feel.

TWENTY-EIGHT

NICK

"CLOSE YOUR EYES, LIV."

"Is this really necessary? First, you wouldn't tell me where the plane is flying us, now you're not going to let me see where the driver is taking us?"

"It's a surprise."

"Fine. I know we're in another country, though. That flight was way too long to still be in the U.S."

"I'm not telling you anything. Now shush." I put Reed's pacifier in his mouth. He's getting a bit antsy, but surprisingly he did well on the flight over here. I can't imagine having to fly commercial with a baby, though. I give major props to the moms and dads who do. It was enough work on a private plane.

Olivia rests her head on my shoulder while the car service takes us to where we'll be staying. I wanted to get away with her and Reed for a couple weeks. No media or paparazzi. Just us on a sandy white beach under the warm sunshine, where our son can—as Olivia put it—wear a single layer of clothing. She doesn't know it yet, but I've left all of our electronics at home. I gave her dad the number to the resort we're staying at in case of an emergency and gave Giselle and Killian our info for when they arrive. They'll be joining us the last half of the trip, and we'll all fly back together.

We pull up to the resort, and the driver opens Olivia's door while the valet opens mine. She steps out of the car, opens her eyes, and glances around. "I can smell the beach," she says, sniffing the air.

A Hawaiian woman comes over and says, "Aloha" while placing a pink and yellow flowered lei over Olivia's head.

"Are we in Hawaii?" Olivia asks excitedly. She runs around the car and jumps into my arms. "I've never been here before! Oh my God! It's so warm here! Thank you!" She plants a wet kiss to my lips before dropping back onto the ground.

She fiddles through her purse then looks up with a frown. "I don't have my cell phone. I wanted to take a picture."

"No cell phones." I hand her a digital camera I picked up for the trip. "You can take photos with this."

"Where's your cell phone?" she questions.

"Back in New York. We're electronic-free for two weeks."

"A girl can get used to this kind of treatment: a week in the Hamptons, two weeks in Hawaii. Where are you taking me next?"

"Unfortunately, this is our last stop. After this trip, I have to go home and get my contract situated for the season. But once that's taken care of, we can plan another trip before the season starts."

"Are you staying with New York?" Olivia asks.

"I would like to, but you know it's not up to me. So, for now, let's enjoy ourselves."

"But what if you have to move?"

I've only known Olivia for a short time, but this is the first time I've seen any type of real insecurity shine through her tough façade. I was worried about tearing down her wall, the one she keeps erect to protect herself. But as I stare at her, I see that somewhere along the way she lowered her gate and willingly let me in.

Sliding my arm around her waist, I pull her into my embrace. Leaning down, my green eyes meet her brown. "We'll figure it out together." I place a soft kiss to her forehead and another one on her plump, pouty lips. "I promise."

We grab Reed's stroller and car seat and let the valet grab our bags. After checking in, Olivia insists we bring Reed down to the beach. I've rented a cabana on the beach and by the pool for the entire two weeks, so after getting changed into our swimsuits— thanks to the hired personal shopper who did some last-minute shopping—we make our way down to the beach.

"This place is beautiful, Nick." She plops down onto one of the lounge chairs under the cabana and lays out a blanket for Reed. I hand him over to her, and she lays him down against her stomach so he's able use her like his own personal lounge chair. The waitress comes over, and we order some drinks and food.

We drink, eat, and watch the waves hit the shoreline the entire afternoon all the way through the sunset. Reed naps occasionally on a blanket, on the lounge chair, or in one of our arms. It's relaxing and exactly what we needed. Eventually, we make our way up to the room, and after settling Reed down for bed, settle into bed ourselves. And this repeats every day for a week until Giselle and Killian arrive.

TWENTY-NINE

*N*ICK

"THIS IS SO COOL!" Olivia removes her snorkel and mask from her face and finds me. "Did you see all the fish?! The one that looks like Nemo! And the shark looking one!"

Giselle and Killian are keeping an eye on Reed this morning while I take Olivia out. Last week, we stuck to the beach, the art museums, and finding the local marketplaces—all things we can enjoy with a baby in tow. We spent a lot of time talking and getting to know each other. This week, we're taking advantage of having help with Reed, and exploring the outdoors. We had surf lessons yesterday, and today we're doing some snorkeling off a private island we took a yacht over to. It's just the two of us here on this beach. Tonight, the four of us—and Reed—will be attending a dinner and show. And tomorrow, as a surprise, I've booked a day spa for Olivia and Giselle.

"It's cool as hell. I've never seen water so clear before." We wade through the water until we're back on shore. Setting our gear down, we both grab a towel to dry off before taking a sip of our waters. There's usually staff down here to wait on people, but I requested for them to stay at the restaurant, and if we need anything we'll come up.

I sit down on the beach chair, and when I look up, I see Olivia is right above me. She straddles my lap, a sexy leg on either side of me, and her hands come up to my cheeks. "I love when you don't shave," she says with a smile.

"Oh yeah, and why is that? Because when I don't shave, I look closer to your age?" I joke, and she shakes her head.

"No." Her hands move up and down the sides of my face along my stubble. "Because when you go down on me your hair tickles the insides of my thighs." She blushes pink, and I laugh. Then I imagine my face buried between her thighs, and I groan, my dick enjoying the visual as well.

Her eyes widen slightly when she feels my bulge pushing through my board shorts. "Are we...completely alone here?" She glances around. Even if we weren't alone, the cabana we're in blocks anyone from seeing inside unless they're standing directly in front of us.

"Yep."

"So if I wanted to pull your shorts down right here and ride you, I could?" Her eyes are hooded with lust.

"Fuck yes, you could, and I fully encourage it."

Olivia backs up slightly, her ass coming off me long enough so I can pull my shorts down. My dick bobs between us, but I'm only semi-hard. When she looks down at it, she frowns for a second before she gets a mischievous glint in her eyes. She lifts each of her legs up as she pushes her bikini bottoms off her, exposing her delicious cunt. Then she pushes the triangles, which cover her tits, to the side.

My dick is getting harder by the second. My mouth goes to her perky tit, and my lips wrap around her pert pink nipple. My hand goes to her other tit as I massage it. Olivia lets out a moan, the outside of her pussy grinding against my shaft. Her back arches slightly as I suck on each of her nipples.

"Jesus, Nick. I want you inside of me," she groans. My lips move upward as I trail kisses along her breasts and neck. She grinds harder, and I can feel the wetness from her pussy against my dick.

"Are you wet enough?" I ask. She nods, but I don't take her word for it. Instead, I push two fingers into her. She wiggles her ass, needing more, and lets out a growl when it's not enough.

I swallow her frustration with a kiss to her lips. It's filled with lust and want. She quickly attacks my mouth with fervor I've yet to see. Her thighs clench on either side of me as I continue to finger-fuck her, her pussy grinding down on my fingers.

"Please," she begs. I pull my fingers out of her wet and ready cunt, and within seconds she's guiding herself onto my dick. When

I'm all the way inside her, my head goes back, hitting the back of the chair. It's never felt as good with any other woman as it does with Olivia. I know that sounds fuckin' nuts. Like she has some special pussy that's unlike any other woman's. But it's the truth. Every time I'm with her, I feel it. I don't think it's her pussy per se—although, it really is a great fucking pussy. It's the connection we share. When I'm with her, it's more than just sex. It's every-fucking-thing.

She begins to move up and down—her arms wrapping around my neck, her fingers threading through my hair. She pushes her tits into my face as she comes almost completely off my dick before grinding back down and taking me all the way back inside her.

"Suck on my tits," she moans, and I about come right here on the spot. I love when Olivia lets loose, when she turns into a sex-crazed wanton woman. My lips suck on her nipple, and I bite down hard. She moans loudly, picking up speed. My fingers make their way between us, landing on her soaked pussy. I gather up her juices then circle my arm around her back side, pushing a finger into her tight hole.

"Oh my God," she screams as she picks up the pace, her ass bouncing up and down on my dick, her juices dripping down my balls. I'm mesmerized by the way she moves on top of me. Rolling and shifting her hips in such a way that has me ready to come. I continue to suck her nipple and finger her tight hole as she rides me harder and faster. When I feel her getting close, her walls tightening like a goddamn vice grip around my shaft, I glide my lips to her neck, sucking on the sensitive flesh. Olivia moves forward slightly, her pussy grinding me, her clit getting the friction it needs to get her off.

"Nick...holy shit...I'm. Going. To. Come." I push my finger a bit farther into her ass, and she loses it. Her movements turn desperate, her clit grinds harder, her cunt begins to pulse around my dick, and then she's coming all over my dick and balls. I pull my finger out and grip her hips, taking over. Her head is thrown back in pure ecstasy as I push her down, bottoming the fuck out in her tightness as I come inside her.

We both come down from our highs, and she looks at me with tears in her eyes. "What's wrong? Did I hurt you?" I've used my finger in her ass before, so I can't imagine it hurt, but you never know...

"Nothing's wrong." She begins to sob. "Everything is perfect. I-I love you, Nick."

"I love you too, Brown-Eyes, so goddamn much."

THIRTY

Nick

IT'S the last day of our trip, and we're packing to go home. It's an eleven-hour flight, so we're getting everything ready to take on the plane for Reed so it goes as smoothly on the way back as it did coming here. The bellman knocks on the door, and we head out. We stack all of our luggage on the cart then make our way down to the valet.

Once we're seated on the plane, and Reed is sleeping in his portable crib, Olivia comes over and sits next to me. "Thank you for this, Nick." She gives me a kiss on my cheek. "I had a really good time." She wraps her arms around my neck. "I love you."

"I love you, too."

I don't think I'll ever get tired of hearing those words from her. The night we got back to the hotel, after she told me she loved me, I made love to her several times, demanding each time she tell me again. She thought I was joking at first, but once she realized I was serious, she complied, screaming and moaning the words every time I made her come.

WE HAVE LESS than an hour left of our flight, and Olivia is playing with Reed on a blanket she has spread out on the floor.

Killian and Giselle are sitting next to each other, looking at Killian's iPad. I told them no cell phones allowed on the trip, so of course he found a loophole and brought his iPad.

"Everything okay?" I ask when I notice they're talking in a hushed whisper. Just the fact they're sitting next to each other without killing one another should be a red flag. Giselle looks up at me and glares, and Killian gives me a wounded look.

"Damn, man...you could've at least told me," Killian says, and I'm confused as hell.

"Told you what?"

He throws the iPad into my lap, and when I read the headline, my heart stops.

Nick Shaw signs five-year contract with Los Angeles

I scroll down and read the story. It says I signed the contract a couple weeks ago and will be their starting QB. "This doesn't make any sense." I click out of the article and google my name. Article after article all say the same thing.

"You're saying you didn't sign with LA?" Killian asks, and I see Olivia's head pop up out of the corner of my eye.

"You signed with LA?" she asks, hurt evident in every word.

"No." I shake my head. "This doesn't make sense."

"They can't just print something like that if it's not true, Nick," Giselle points out. And she's right. There's no way LA would announce something false, nor would ESPN.

I go to call my dad but remember I don't have my cell phone and we're thousands of feet in the air. "I didn't sign with them," I state again. Olivia gives me a sad look but doesn't argue.

We land and head to our vehicles. After we get all the luggage put into our trunks, Killian comes over to me and says, "Listen, if going to LA is what's best for your career..."

"I didn't sign with them," I say. "And if I had, I would've told you."

He sighs but nods his head in acceptance. "Okay, let me know if you need anything." We bump fists and take off in our own vehicles.

The entire drive to Olivia and Giselle's place is done in silence. I don't know what to say or do, and I know I need to first figure out what the hell happened before I attempt to say anything. When we arrive at their place, I help the women get all their luggage and Reed's stuff inside. "I need to go speak to my dad," I tell Olivia. "I'll call you as soon as I know what's going on." She nods, and I give her a kiss. "I love you." She nods again, and it doesn't go unnoticed that she doesn't say it back.

I get back to my place and grab my cell phone, powering it on. A million texts and missed calls come through. I ignore them all and call my *agent*.

"Son," my dad says when he answers on the first ring.

"Don't fucking 'Son' me," I growl. "What the fuck did you do?"

"Why don't we meet to discuss this in person?"

"Are you in town?" Because his cliental has increased in New York, he's expanded his company here and has purchased some office space in the Financial District. He said he's only planning to stay here long enough to make sure everything is in order, then he and my mom will be going back to North Carolina. That day can't come soon enough.

"Yes, I'm at my office. They completed the renovations last week."

Twenty minutes later, I'm standing in his office. "I didn't sign a contract with Los Angeles" are the first words out of my mouth. My dad is sitting in his chair, typing away on his laptop. He takes his time before looking up at me.

"Actually, you did." He pushes some paperwork at me, and I grab them off his desk. My eyes scan the documents. It's a contract between LA and me, and sure enough, on several of the pages is my signature.

"What the fuck did you do?" I throw the papers back at him.

"I did what was in your best interest."

"When the fuck did I sign these? You never said a word to me!" I boom.

"Right before your trip to Hawaii."

My mind goes back to our brief visit before I left.

"Any news about New York?" I ask, sitting down on the couch with Reed in my arms. Olivia had a doctor's appointment, so I offered to keep Reed with me so she could go by herself.

"That's not why I'm here. I need your signature on a couple of papers...endorsement contracts and such. I'll make it quick so you can get back to your son." My dad hands me the documents as Reed starts squirming and getting fussy. He's due to be fed, so he's cranky. I grab the pen and flip through each page quickly, signing and initialing where the yellow arrow sticky notes point to sign.

Once I'm done, he snatches the papers off the coffee table. "Enjoy your trip. We'll discuss your contract when you get back."

"Holy shit, you had me sign a fucking contract with LA without my knowledge. You realize I'm going to fight you on this, right? And after I win, I'm going to destroy any credibility you have. Fuck, if I have to, I'll go after your license."

"Did you not read the contract? Five years, one hundred and sixty million dollars. As your agent, and your father, I did what was best for you. I wasn't going to let you throw away your future for that woman!"

"I don't give a fuck how much it's for! You went behind my back! You didn't do what was best for me. You did what was best for you." I slam my fist down on the desk. Then it hits me. "Did New York not want to re-sign me?"

"Not for what you're worth."

"But they would've signed me," I clarify.

"For fucking pennies!"

"You're going to fix this, or I'm going to sue you."

My dad stands. "You're thinking like a pussy-whipped fool!" He leans over his desk, challenging me. "If Olivia wants to be with you, she'll move to California. You're not going to stay in New York to make her dad happy and get paid half. That's ludicrous!"

"It's my choice to make!"

"You're making the wrong choice. Choosing love over money will get you nowhere fast."

Realizing nothing I say to this man will change his money-hungry mindset, I stalk toward the door. "I'm giving you an hour to fix this shit and then I'm coming after you." I slam the door behind me and head to the elevator. Once I'm to my car, I call Olivia, but her phone goes to voicemail. I try again, but it does it again.

Next, I try her dad.

"Nick," he says when he answers.

"I need to talk to you about my contract."

"Son, you know we can't discuss this." *Fuck!*

"Okay, can you at least tell me if you've spoken to Olivia? I can't get a hold of her."

He's silent for a second, and my heart starts racing, the hand holding my cell phone getting sweaty. "Stephen, where is she?" There's no way she would've taken our son away from me. "She didn't go to Paris, did she?"

"No! No," he says, finally speaking. "I think she's headed to our place in the Hamptons. She said she needs some time."

Fuck that! She's not getting any time. "Stephen, in those fairy-tales, I highly doubt when the princess runs, the prince sits back and gives her time."

Stephen chuckles softly. "That's probably true." Just as I'm about to say goodbye, he adds, "Like I told you before, Nick, regardless of what happens in this business, you're part of our family. That will never change. I don't know what happened, but I'm always here if you need a friend...or some fatherly advice."

"Thank you."

I hang up and turn my car toward 27-W toward the Hamptons when my phone rings. Olivia's name pops up on Bluetooth.

"Liv," I answer.

"Hey, can you come over? We need to talk."

THIRTY-ONE

OLIVIA
One hour ago

NICK DROPS me off and the first thing I do is call my father. When he answers, I breakdown. "Is it true? Did he sign with Los Angeles?"

"He did, sweetheart. He didn't tell you?"

"No! He didn't say a word." I start to gather Reed's clothes, throwing them into a small suitcase. "I asked him so many times and he said we would figure it out together." I shove diapers and a container of wipes into a bag.

"We just don't have the money they have. We offered what we could, but it was still only half of what LA could offer him."

My body freezes in place. "This is about money? Are you serious?" A lump lodges in my throat. "One of his biggest concerns was that everyone around him was money hungry, and in the end, he chose money over his son and me?"

"You don't know that. He could want you to join him." My dad, always the optimist, always seeing the best in everybody.

"Then he should've asked before he signed the contract."

"Do you want me to come over?" my dad asks, concerned.

"No, I'm leaving." There's silence over the phone.

"You're not going back to Paris, are you? Because I would really miss you and my grandson. I feel like I just got you back."

"No, I'm not going to Paris. Probably just to the Hamptons. I'll call you once I'm on the road."

"Okay, sweetie. I love you."

"Love you too, Dad."

Just as I'm ending the phone call, Giselle comes down the hall. "Reed's asleep." She assesses the situation in front of her. "Where are you going?"

"To our place in the Hamptons."

"Wow! You're running again?" She snatches the luggage and throws it to the side. It hits the floor with a thud. Giselle has never been mad at me before, never raised her voice with me, so her actions have me frozen in place.

"What do you mean, *again*?"

Giselle scoffs. "You ran to Paris when your mom died. Then you ran home when Victor dumped you. *Then*, you ran home again when you found out you were pregnant. And two out of three of those times I ran with you. Well, I can't run, Livi." Tears threaten to spill from her lids, but Giselle is too strong to let that happen.

"I can't run anymore. It's not that I don't want to...but I *can't*. And if you stop for one damn second and think about this, you don't really want to run either. It's just what you're used to doing, and up until now, you've never had a good enough reason to stay because everything you were running from you had already lost. Your mom died. Victor broke things off. We graduated. But now—"

"Now I have Nick," I finish her sentence for me. She's right. I always run. I want the fairytale, but I never fight for it. I want the happily-ever-after without wanting to work for it. I don't know what is going to happen with Nick or what's going through his head, but instead of running, I need to face this head on because he's worth fighting for. I ran when I felt like my life was out of my control, but now it's time to stay and fight. Then it hits me...

"Giselle...what if in order to be with him, it means having to move to California?" She knows what I'm asking. *Does this mean I'll be living across the country from my best friend?*

Fresh tears brim over as she opens her mouth to speak, but no words come out. Then she closes her eyes for several beats before opening them back up. "Then I'll come and visit you and Reed every chance I get." My heart tightens. I can't imagine my life without Giselle in it. I shake my head, not liking her answer.

"Livi..." Her tears fall like a waterfall down her cheeks. "My mom...she's not doing so well, and I don't know how to help her.

And now with my dad gone and my sister away at college, I have to stay here."

I hug my best friend. "I'm so sorry. I completely understand."

"Thank you. I probably shouldn't have left for Hawaii, but I just needed a breather from it all, to escape from reality for a few days, and since my sister was off of school for spring break, she offered to keep an eye on our mom, so I could go."

"I hate that you're going through this. What can I do?"

"You can go figure out what's going on with you and Nick. One of us deserves a goddamned fairytale ending." She laughs softly, trying to play off the seriousness of what she just told me about her mom. "Go! Go call him." She stands and grabs her keys. "I have a couple errands to run, but I'll be back later."

Before she makes it out the door, she says, "Oh! By the way, this came for you." She hands me a large envelope.

"Thanks." I open it and inside is all the information I requested from the accountant who handles Nick's charity, Touchdown for Reading. Apparently, the original accountant retired, and Nick recently hired someone new. When we spoke, I asked him to go through and let me know how active the charity has been these last few years, so I know where to begin. I pull the papers out of the envelope and a note falls out.

You might want to check the charges I highlighted.

I flip through until I find the highlighted amounts. I read over them several times. This can't be right. There's no way...

My intercom buzzes, so I put the papers down. "Hello."

"It's Victoria."

"Okay, I'll buzz you up."

Knowing it will take a minute for the elevator to make its way up to my floor, I call Nick.

"Liv," he says when he picks up.

"Hey, can you come over? We need to talk."

"I'm on my way now. I should be there in two hours." *Two hours?*

"Where are you?"

He pauses for a second. "Where are you?"

"Home...where else would I be?"

"Your dad said you were going to the Hamptons. I was on my way there." *Oh no!*

"I was going to, but Giselle talked some sense into me."

"I'll be there in a few minutes."

"Okay, good, because your mom is on her way up."

I end the call just as Victoria knocks on my door.

"Victoria, come in."

"Thank you." She steps into my home, and I close the door behind us. "Well, this is a beautiful home you have here," she says, her gaze darting around my living room.

"Thank you. Would you like something to drink?" I ask, trying to be polite, but also wanting to stall so Nick has time to get here.

"No, thank you. I won't be here long."

"Well, I'm thirsty," I tell her. "Feel free to get comfortable while I grab a drink. You sure you don't want anything?"

"I'm sure," she snaps, losing a bit of her patience.

While in the kitchen, I read through the documents once more just to make sure what I'm looking at is correct. Unfortunately, it is.

After grabbing a bottle of water, I head back out to the living room to find Victoria is still standing where I left her, texting on her cell phone. When she hears me enter, she puts her phone away and looks up.

"So, to what do I owe this pleasure?" I ask.

"I'll cut right to the chase," she says. "Convince Nicholas to keep his contract with LA, and I will make sure you're taken care of."

"Excuse me?"

"This home you're living in runs roughly three million dollars. If you want to continue to live a life of luxury, convince Nicholas to keep the contract with LA. I'll make sure your home is paid off, and on top of whatever child support he's agreed to pay, I'll double it so you're living more than comfortably."

I stare at this woman for several seconds. I can't believe she raised Nick. But then I remember, she didn't. His nanny did.

"You are really something else—" But before I can say anything more, there's a knock on my door. I open it, and Nick saunters in.

"You're just in time. Your mom was just offering to pay off my home." I laugh humorlessly. "Which by the way—" I turn back toward Victoria "—is actually worth four-point-two million. You underpriced it. If you're going to be so generous and offer to pay off someone's loan, you should at least look it up, so you know how much to offer."

Her eyes are wide as saucers as she looks between Nick and me, knowing she's been caught.

"You know how I know that? I own it," I tell her. "And if you did your research, you would know that too."

"You offered to pay her off like you did to Fiona?" Nick eyes his mother incredulously. "What the hell is wrong with you? First of all, Olivia is worth millions more than I am!" His mom gasps in shock. "And second of all, didn't you learn your lesson from paying off Fiona?"

"Oh, it gets better...or I should say worse." I grab the papers from the table and hand them to Nick. "Your mom not only used your charity to pay off Fiona, but she's been siphoning money from the account to pay your parents' bills."

"I was going to put it all back!" she screeches. "Mind your own business!"

"What the fuck." Nick takes the papers from me and scans through them.

"I contacted the accountant directly when Victoria refused to let me have access to anything. I thought something might be up when you mentioned she pushed you away from being actively involved. Since you gave him the go ahead, he sent these over to me. She paid off Fiona through the charity funds, and she's been using the funds to pay several of their bills, including their mortgage and car payments, claiming them as business expenses directly related to your charity."

"Nicholas," his mom pleads. "A few of the investments your father made didn't pan out. We were upside down and just needed a little bit of help to get through. With your new contract, we'll be able to pay you back."

"I'm done." Nick throws the papers onto the table. "You and dad are dead to me. I've already told him he's going to fix my contract, or I'll sue him. Get out of this house and out of my life."

"You don't mean that!" Victoria cries.

"Yeah, I do. You are so far gone, there's no saving you. You aren't my family, and you have no idea what it means to love someone. Now get out." He swings the door open.

With tears streaming down her face, Victoria walks out. Once she's gone, Nick closes the door and comes over to me. He pulls me into him, his arms enveloping me. "Thank you for not running, Liv," he murmurs into my ear.

We have a seat on the sofa, and Nick takes my hands in his. "Remember when Celeste was at my place and I told you that was the part of the book where the evil witch had to be beaten?"

I try to hide my smile, but I can't contain it. He's just too fucking adorable. "Yes."

"I guess it was actually my mom who was the evil witch. Talk about a plot twist."

"I'm sorry, Nick." I know he's trying to turn this into a joke, but it's only because he's attempting to cover his hurt.

"It's her loss. I never really had a mom to begin with. Unfortunately, though, this part of the story isn't over yet. We still need to defeat the villain...like in Sleeping Beauty."

"What happened?"

"Apparently, my mom wasn't the only one fucking me over. My dad came by to see me before we took off on vacation and had me sign some papers. I didn't look at them. I was busy with Reed, and I trusted him. Turns out he was having me sign a contract to play for Los Angeles for five years."

My hands come up to my mouth. "Oh my God. You didn't know?" That's what his mom meant by convincing Nick to keep the contract as-is.

"Nope." He shakes his head. "New York could only offer me half of what LA was offering, and my dad knew I would choose New York, which would mean less money in his pocket. He's so money hungry, Liv. It's insane. He can't see anything besides the potential dollar bills in his pockets. But now it makes sense. If they spent too much money, they needed the percentage my contract would bring in to pull them back up."

"How much was the offer for?"

"One hundred and sixty million."

"Damn, that's a lot of money."

"I don't give a fuck about the money. I meant it when I said we're in this together. I'm not going anywhere without you." His lips meet mine for a kiss, but before it can go any further, his cell phone rings. "Speak of the villain." He answers the phone. I try to move off him, but his fingers grip my hips, silently telling me not to go anywhere.

"Dad, I'm assuming you're calling to tell me you fixed the mix-up." He pauses for a long moment while he listens to whatever his dad is saying. "That's good for you, since you're going to need to keep your license to make more money to get yourself out of the hole you created. All the money Mom stole from me, you two will be repaying."

I don't hear what his dad says on the other line, but Nick shakes his head. "You know, Dad, you spent so much time chasing all the wrong things in life: money, respect, success. And while you were so busy chasing those things, you didn't even realize you were leaving your son behind. I kept chasing you, trying to catch up, but you never once stopped for me. So, now you have not only lost all of your money, but you've lost me, and let's be real, you barely even have mom now that you're broke. I hope it was all worth it. The one thing I've learned is all of those things you were chasing aren't worth a damn if you don't have anyone to share them with. Good luck in life, *Dad.*"

He ends the phone call and drops it onto the couch cushion, his head falling against my chest. My fingers run through his hair while I wait for him to gather himself together. I can't even imagine what's going through his head right now. He's disowned both of his parents in a matter of minutes.

"He got me out of the contract. I'm a free agent. LA said the offer is still on the table, though, if I want it. I have twenty-four hours to decide what I want to do, but there are a few other teams who have made offers as well."

"And what is it you want to do?"

"I need to know something...before we go any further." He moves me off his lap and sets me on the sofa next to him. Then he pulls something out of his pocket...a box...a ring box! He kneels in front of me on the floor, his bright green eyes sparkling as he smiles nervously up at me. "If I have to move, whether it's to California or Texas or...I don't know...Florida. Will you go with me? Will you continue writing this book with me as my wife? Because Liv, I'm not ready for our story to end yet. Olivia Harper, will you marry me and keep our story going no matter where it takes us?"

He opens the box, which holds a beautiful diamond ring, and his eyes lock with mine as he waits for my answer. My brain tries to think logically—rationally—weighing the pros and cons to determine the right decision. But my heart speaks louder, winning over. The fact is I would follow this man anywhere he goes because I love him. He's buried himself deep into the valves of my heart, and it can't beat without him. He makes me want to fight.

"My happily-ever-after is wherever you are. If it means we move, then Reed and I will be right there beside you. Yes, I'll marry you." I throw myself into his arms, and he kisses me hard.

Then he pulls back and puts the ring on my finger. "Good because we're moving to Montana."

"Montana?" I question. "They don't even have a football team."

Nick's shoulders shake with laughter. "I'm glad you know your football. I'm just kidding. We're staying right here in New York. But I should warn you...money is going to be a bit tight. New York could only do a five year, eighty-million-dollar contract."

I sigh. "However will we live off that? It's a good thing your soon-to-be wife is loaded. Don't worry, baby, I'll be your sugar mama." I give him an over exaggerated wink, and he throws his head back in laughter.

"I've never had a sugar mama before. What do I have to do in return?" Nick pulls me down onto the floor with him, my legs straddling his lap.

"In return?"

"You know...in exchange for you taking care of me. What do you want?" His lips move to my neck, and I tilt my head slightly to give him access.

"Hmm...sex. Whenever I want."

"Mmm...I like the sound of that." He continues kissing upward, landing on the sensitive flesh behind my ear. "What else?"

"I want a house. A big one with at least five bedrooms."

"Oh, really? Do we get to fill this bigger house with more babies?"

"Umm..." I try to focus, but his lips wrap around my earlobe, and it's hard to think. "Yes," I moan out. "Yes, more babies."

"What else?" he asks, his tongue circling the inner part of my ear, eliciting a chill down my spine. "What else do you want, Liv?"

"I want to get married soon and for the three of us to have the same last name." Nick stops his assault on my body momentarily and looks at me.

"That can definitely be arranged." His lips touch mine, and his tongue sweeps into my mouth before he pulls back. "What else?"

"I don't know. I can't think with your mouth all over me." He chuckles. "Let's just start with number one. Sex now."

"Sounds good to me." Nick picks me up and carries me to the bedroom where he proceeds to make good on my first demand of being his sugar mama.

EPILOGUE

Nick
  One Year Later

"DO YOU REALIZE HOW THIS LOOKS?" Olivia laughs as we look down at the home pregnancy test.

I know where she's going with this, but it's her own fault. I've brought up getting married several times, but she keeps saying, "Soon." Right after I proposed, she accepted a job at the local art museum as an Art Educator Coordinator. She organizes and teaches art classes to children a couple days a week. Between her working part-time, my playing football, and us raising our now one-year-old son, we haven't done anything we said we were going to do...well, except for the *have sex* part. So now here we are. Expecting our second baby and still not husband and wife, and still living in separate places.

"Like there are two lines indicating I got my fiancée pregnant?" I answer her question jokingly, earning me a slap to my chest.

"No! Like you keep knocking me up out of wedlock!" She giggles and throws the test into the trash.

"It's not my fault my super sperm overpowers any birth control."

She snorts, rolling her eyes. "Now we *really* do need to get married...and buy a house!"

I chuckle because she's said this too many times to count. I've finally gotten her to agree on a date to get married. Now we just need to buy a home. "Whatever you want, my beautiful brown-eyed girl." I pull her into my embrace. We're standing in the bathroom, and Reed is sleeping. "But right now, I think we need to shower together." She nods emphatically, liking my idea, so I turn the water on to hot.

We both undress at the same time, our clothes flying to the floor. I open the shower door then shut it behind us. We're at her place, and the shower has an extremely convenient bench running along the back. Sitting down on the bench, Olivia straddles my lap, her warm cunt rubbing friction against my semi-hard cock. Her lips press against mine and her tongue pushes through. Her hands entwine in my hair as she moans into my mouth.

"I need you inside me," she pleads. She rains kisses all over my face then moves to my neck, sucking on my flesh. She lifts slightly, and I guide my dick into her until she's filled completely.

"Oh God, Nick." She doesn't move for a second, her body adjusting to my size. Then slowly, she begins to rock her hips up and down and side to side. The feeling of being inside my woman, this closeness we share, is fucking unbelievable. Her ass moves as she rides me faster and faster, taking what she wants—what she needs—from me.

I bend my head to snag a nipple between my teeth, and she thrashes against me. "Oh shit! They're so sensitive." I still, afraid I've hurt her. "Don't stop!" she commands, her voice wild, out of control. I bring her nipple back up to my lips, licking and sucking on it before giving the other one equal attention.

My other hand rests on her ass, making sure she doesn't fall as she continues to ride me, bouncing up and down on my cock. Her clit is rubbing against my front. I feel her muscles tighten and know she's close but not quite there.

Lifting her off me, I turn us around. "Hands against the wall, now," I demand. Her delicate hands slap the wall and her ass juts out on display. I separate her thighs and watch the water drip down her perfect round ass. I give it a good slap, and she lets out a soft moan, her ass squirming with need. She turns her head slightly, about to say something, but before she can say a word, I grip her hips and thrust into her from behind.

She lets out a loud groan as her head falls forward. Gripping her hip with one hand, I pump into her over and over again. My other hand skirting around to her clit, massaging the swollen nub as Olivia meets me thrust for thrust.

"Oh God! Harder, please." I've never seen her this starved for sex, this needy, but her every wish is my command. My fingers dig harder, holding onto her tighter as I move in and out of her tight pussy—my fingers stroking her clit simultaneously. She's so close I can feel her tight cunt squeezing around my cock.

"Come on, baby. Come for me."

She's panting and moaning. I press my thumb down harder on her clit as I push into her from behind, hitting her G-spot over and over again, building her up until she can't take it anymore. And then she's falling. Her body trembles. Her legs shake. She whimpers loudly as she comes all over my cock. My orgasm follows right behind. I pull out of her, and she releases a shiver.

"Come here." I pull her into me, so she's under the hot water. "What was that?"

She smiles sheepishly. "I think that was a very horny pregnant woman."

Extended Epilogue

OLIVIA

I'M SITTING at the table feeding Reed some sweet potatoes and fish when Giselle makes her presence known, slamming the door behind her. She's been acting strange lately, and she won't talk to me about anything. I know she has a lot going on, but she won't let me in, and as her best friend, it hurts my heart.

"That motherfucker!"

"Who?" I ask, feeding Reed another bite.

She notices Reed is now staring at her. "Shit...I mean, shoot! I didn't mean to curse." She gives Reed a kiss on the top of his head. "Hey, handsome."

"Who were you cursing about?" I ask again.

"It doesn't even matter. I was just having a bad moment." She shrugs. Her phone dings, and she glances down at it. "I need to get going. I just came home to change."

"Another date?" I ask, concerned. Ever since Giselle found out Christian cheated on her and broke things off with him, she's gone from zero to one hundred. Whereas before Christian, she rarely dated at all, post-Christian, she's going on dates several nights a week, none of which she ever brings home or introduces me to. And the weirdest date of all was when she showed up with Killian to our charity fundraiser we hosted to announce the expansion of Touchdown for Reading, which is now Touchdown for Reading and the Arts.

"Yep!" She doesn't say anything else before she disappears into her room.

Reed slams his hand down wanting another bite, and I turn my attention back to him. A few minutes later, I hear Nick come in from outside on the terrace. "Hey, babe." He presses a kiss to my temple. "There's something you need to know about Giselle."

My hand freezes in place. "Okay."

"Killian said he paid—"

"Don't you dare finish that sentence!" Giselle yells, cutting him off just as Killian walks through the front door. "This is none of your business." She glares from Nick to Killian.

"Somebody tell me what's going on, please," I demand.

"Either you tell her, or I will," Killian threatens.

"I hate you!" Giselle shouts, and I notice tears are now streaming down her face.

"No, you don't, but if you continue this, you're going to hate yourself," Killian says to her.

"I already do," she whispers before she runs out, slamming the door behind her.

GOING DEEP

IMPERFECT LOVE SERIES: BOOK TWO

PROLOGUE

GISELLE

"I KNOW you're cheating on me! Admit it!" Mom chucks a vase across the room at Dad, who doesn't duck quick enough, and it hits his shoulder before it crashes onto the tiled floor, breaking into a million pieces. "I hate you!" she shouts with tears streaming down her cheeks. She turns around, her possessed eyes searching for another item to throw. My dad uses that moment as an opportunity to wrap his strong arms around her tiny, fragile body from the back. She kicks and screams, trying to get out of his hold, but he's stronger. "Let go of me! I'm going to kill you! You're such a piece of shit liar!"

Ignoring the hateful words she's spewing, he pulls her down onto the couch as I pop the lid to one of her prescription bottles and shake out two pills. While he's holding her down, I pry her mouth open and push the pills down her throat. She tries to gag, her manic gaze hitting me with so much hate, it sends chills racing up my spine. She continues to kick and thrash around while Dad holds her tight, waiting for the pills to make their way through her system and temporarily calm the beast inside her.

She was doing so well the past few months, I thought for sure this time the therapist got her meds right. She was so happy and cheerful. It was as if she was on cloud nine. Until she wasn't. And now, once again, it seems we're back to where we started.

Once Mom's lids begin to droop, Dad lessens his hold on her, and my sister makes her presence known. "Is Mom okay?" she asks quietly, afraid if she speaks too loudly, she might poke the beast, which in our many years of experience is never a good thing.

"She's okay, Addy." I cut across the room and pull my scared sister into a tight hug. When she was little and Mom would lash out, she would hide in her bedroom until one of us would come and get her. Now that Adrianna is older, she no longer hides. She's too worried about our mom hurting herself or one of us. But because of how violent mom can get, Dad and I make her hang back while we get her under control.

"Dad, I think she needs to see a psychiatrist again," I say to my father. "Her pills aren't working. We can't keep drugging her like this." My eyes dart to my mother who is lying lifeless on the couch, still in my father's arms. My heart breaks every time we have to sedate her, but we don't have any choice. It's either that or she will end up hurting one of us, and then when she wakes up and realizes what she did, she will sink even further into depression. It's a shitty no-win situation.

Dad silently shakes his head in frustration as he lifts my mom and carries her to their bedroom. Once he comes back out, he grabs his briefcase and cell phone and heads toward the front door without saying a word. This is what he always does when she gets like this. Hides away at his office. Sometimes he'll be gone for days at a time, but it's pointless to call him out on it. He's the only breadwinner in this family, which means we need him. He pays the bills and attempts to take care of our mom. And I love him, even if many days I also hate him. When he comes home and smells of another woman's perfume, I want to smack him senseless, yet at the same time, I can understand why he does what he does. He's married to a woman who is so far gone most days, he spends more time taking care of her than actually being with her. Their kisses have turned to tears, and their love that once upon a time shined through during even the darkest of days has been covered by a dark, black cloud that has been stagnant directly over our life for too many years.

"Dad," I call out, refusing to let him run this time. We can't keep doing this. "She needs help."

"What do you want from me, Giselle?" he snaps. "Our insurance barely covers the appointments, let alone the medications. The doctor has tried every drug imaginable, and nothing fucking works. I'm doing the best I can." And without waiting for my response, he's out the door.

"I found this," Adrianna says softly once the door has slammed shut. I turn around to see what she's talking about, and in her hands is my acceptance letter to NYU Paris I received in the mail last month. The deadline to accept is coming up.

"How many times have I asked you not to go through my stuff?" I swipe the paper out of her hands. She frowns, and I immediately feel bad.

"I was looking for your eyeliner. I'm sorry. Now, tell me you're going." Her voice is demanding, and her hand goes to her hip. I have to bite down on my bottom lip to stifle my laugh at my little sister's attitude. "Giselle, tell me you're going," she repeats.

"Addy..."

"No, don't you dare 'Addy' me. I don't want to hear some bullshit excuse about you needing to stay here for Mom. She's been like this for as long as we can remember, and it's never going to get better. This is your out." She snatches the paper back from me, waving it in the air. "Run, Giselle, and don't look back."

"One, you're thirteen, don't say bullshit." She rolls her eyes and tilts her head to the side, waiting for me to continue. "And two, I can't leave you—" Before I can finish my sentence, Adrianna cuts me off.

"One, you're not my mother, and mine is too depressed and out of it to give a shit what language I use." She purses her lips together in defiance, daring me to argue. I know her words aren't meant to be hurtful. We've grown up taking care of one another. But with my being five years older, I've always tried to be the mother she's never really had. However, as she gets older, she often says she prefers me to act like her sister and not her mom, which is understandable. But that doesn't stop me from trying.

"And two," she continues, "this is your dream, to study interior design in Paris, and there's no way you're not following it, just to stay here in this hellhole for me. I'll be fine. You're going to do whatever you're supposed to do to let them know you'll be there, and then you're going to get on that damn plane after graduation and get out of here."

Tears prick my eyes as I stare at my beautiful, grownup sister. Sure, she's only thirteen, but because of the life we've had to endure, she's been forced to grow up twice as fast as other kids her age. I can't imagine being across the pond from her for a week, let alone for years, and with us having no money, who knows when I'll be able to come back and visit. But for her, I will find a way. If I have to work full-time while going to school, I will. I'll do whatever I have to do to make sure she's okay.

"I'm going to miss you," I tell her.

She snakes her arms around my waist and rests her head on my shoulder. "And I'm going to miss you, but in five years I'll be out of here as well, and I can tell you one thing. I'm not staying here for mom. I love her with everything in me, but I can't live like this forever."

"Promise me that if you need me, you'll call. I don't care what I'm doing, I'll come home," I murmur.

"I promise. Now, can I borrow twenty bucks? I'm meeting some friends at the movies." She backs out of our hug and bats her lashes innocently. I sigh dramatically then giggle.

"Sure, how about I drop you off on my way to Christian's house?"

Adrianna rolls her eyes. "I don't need my big sister to hold my hand on the subway."

"I know you don't *need* me to, but I would feel better if I did. I'm heading that way anyway."

Adrianna huffs in annoyance. "Fine, but only because I know you'll withhold the money until I agree. Let's go."

After checking on our sleeping mom, we head out to the Rye Metro station. After making sure Adrianna makes it safely to the IMAX theater in Rochelle—and only once I see her and her friends go inside—I head back to the station, jump on the 6 and take it to Lafayette. I get off then take the F to the Lower East Side. The entire trip is a good seventy minutes, and I'm lucky enough to get an actual seat, so I use the time to pull up the online application to NYU Paris. Without giving myself time to second-guess my decision, I click accept. Even with the help of financial aid, I'm not sure how I'm going to be able to afford it. But my sister is right, this is my dream, and I will always regret it if I don't follow it.

When East Broadway lights up, I stand and make my way to the doors, so I can exit. I climb the steps and glance around for Christian. He said he would meet me here. I spot him across the street and wave. I know he sees me when his face breaks out into a huge grin. With black curly hair, onyx eyes, and dozens of tattoos running up and down his arms, he is the epitome of a bad boy. He's also my best friend and boyfriend. I run across the crosswalk and throw myself into his awaiting arms. He lifts me up, twirls me around in a circle, and kisses me passionately.

"Mi Amor," he murmurs against my lips. It's been almost a

month since I've seen him, and I've missed him like crazy. Because he's a year older, he graduated a year before me and attends NYU's School of the Arts. His dream is for his band, Down Coyote, to one day get signed. We've been dating for close to two years now. I hate that in order for both of us to follow our dreams, it means we'll be living four thousand miles away from each other.

"What do you want to do today?" he asks excitedly, and my heart fractures.

"I was thinking we could go back to your dorm. I need to talk to you."

His steps falter, and he eyes me skeptically before he says, "You've decided to go." It's not a question, he knows I've already made the decision. He knows me that well.

"I have," I say. "It's just that—"

"You don't have to explain, Giselle, I get it. It's a once in a life-time opportunity and a chance for you to break away from your mom for a little while. You deserve this. But what does that mean for us?"

"It means we enjoy the next couple of months together, and once it's time for me to go, we say goodbye." I've always been a real-ist, and I'm not about to hold either of us to being in a long-distance relationship. While Christian was my first kiss, my first love, the first guy I had sex with, it's not fair to expect him to remain faithful to me while I'm overseas for school for the next four years, if not longer.

"Okay," he agrees, "but promise me one thing."

"What?"

"When you return to New York, I'm the first person you look up after you see your sister." He pulls me into a hug and gives me a soft kiss on my lips.

"I promise."

"I know this isn't the end for us, Giselle. This is just a minor detour. One day you'll return, educated and cultured, ready to take the design world by storm." A grin splits across my face. "I'll be a famous musician, making millions and living in a penthouse apart-ment on the Upper East Side." He waggles his eyebrows. "We'll be a power couple, baby."

He kisses me again, and I nod in agreement. Is it possible? Everything he's saying about our future...can we really have it all? I guess only time will tell.

ONE

GISELLE
  Seven years later

"FUCK YES. You like it when I ram my cock into you, don't you? Scream my name when you come all over my fucking cock."

I refrain from rolling my eyes as Paul 'rams' his cock into me. And I'm using air quotes to emphasize the word *rams*, because let's be real here, when the guy is only working with a four—maybe five —inch dick, he isn't ramming anything into anyone. But he thinks he is, so I guess it's the thought that counts. Not that it matters. He's Paul Cohen, a multi-billionaire real estate tycoon who owns a good portion of the Upper East Side. I wouldn't care if he had a one-inch dick and wanted me to call out his mother's name as long as he keeps wanting to fuck me.

"Oh, Paul," I call out dramatically. He looks down and grins at me as several beads of sweat fall from his face and land on my chest. And because we're fucking missionary, and he can see every face I make, I have to force myself not to cringe. But internally I'm scream-ing, "Ewww! Fucking gross!"

How someone is able to work up that kind of sweat in only—my eyes dart to the clock and see it's 9:08 p.m.—seven minutes is beyond me. But if his nasty sweat and breathless grunting is any indication, we're going to call this a wrap in under ten minutes. Not a record time, but pretty damn close.

Wanting to speed this along, I squeeze my vaginal walls together in an attempt to grip his dick—not that it does much good. His groans get louder, his thrusts turn frantic.

"I'm coming," he grunts out, and my eyes go to the clock again. 9:10 p.m. Damn, I'm good. Just under ten minutes like I predicted.

"Oh yes, Paul," I call out, putting all the years of my doing Kegel exercises to use as I force my muscles to clench around him and fake my orgasm. He stills on top of me, pulls out, and climbs off the bed, going to the bathroom to dispose of the condom. I wait until he comes out, then grabbing my clothes off the floor, head inside to quickly clean up. I'll shower once I'm home, but I hate the lingering smell of latex. After washing my face—because eww, sweat!—and hands, I make my way back out to the bedroom. Paul is in only his boxers, and is laying on the bed, scrolling through his phone.

"Have you called Henry?" I ask, referring to his driver who always brings me home.

"Any chance I can talk you into spending the night?" He looks up from his phone and shoots me a playful grin. He may have a small dick, but he's not hard on the eyes. Between his mop of blond curls, his striking emerald eyes, and the adorable dimple that peeks out of his left cheek when he grins, he's extremely good-looking in that boy next door sort of way. And if I were any other woman, that grin would have me climbing back into his bed. But I'm not, and his grin does nothing for me.

"Sorry, it's already after nine. I really need to get going. I have work in the morning."

He nods, knowing there's nothing he can say that will convince me to stay. I've been there and done that, and it will never happen again. Sleeping together leads to feelings, and feelings lead to your heart being shattered into a million pieces.

"See you Wednesday night?" he asks, getting out of bed to walk me to the door.

"See you then." After grabbing my clutch from the table in the foyer, I turn the knob to open the door, when Paul's arm snakes around my waist, and he pulls me in for a kiss.

"Goodnight," he whispers against my lips.

"Goodnight."

It's a thirty-minute drive from the Upper East Side—where Paul lives—to Brooklyn Heights—where I live. I use the time to check my text messages and emails. I see one marked as urgent from my boss, so I click it open first.

Giselle,

please advise. Mr. Caprice has forwarded his wife's requests, and she would like to discuss them with you tomorrow. Please confirm a time. He has listed times that will work for her.

Thank you,
Lydia Strickland
CEO
Fresh Designs, Inc.

I scroll through the requests and grin when I see everything Elizabeth Caprice is requesting are all the suggestions I made when we did a walkthrough of her home a couple weeks ago. With a degree and master's in interior design, my dream was to land a position with the largest interior design company on the East Coast, and I actually achieved it. I've only been working under Lydia for just over a year now, and while the pay is downright embarrassing since it's an internship, I'm confident if I keep going the way I am, I'll land myself a permanent position, with decent pay, soon enough. Most internships here last between one year and eighteen months. I just need to hold on a little bit longer.

After checking my schedule for tomorrow, I email Mr. Caprice back to confirm a time. When I feel the car come to a stop, I look up and see we're here.

"Thank you, Henry," I say before jumping out of the backseat like I always do before he can get out to open the car door for me. The poor guy must be in his eighties, and there's no reason why I can't open my own door.

"Goodnight, Miss Winters," he calls out as I shut the door.

It's a good ten-minute walk to the building I live in, so I pull up my sister's name on my contact list and call her to see how she's doing. She's a sophomore at the University of Boston and lives in a sorority house, so there's a good chance she'll still be awake.

"Giselle!" she shouts into the phone when she answers, and I pull it away from my ear. A few seconds later, the noise is gone. "Sorry about that. It's the Spring Social. The entire campus is like one giant party. How are you?"

I smile on the inside at how happy my sister sounds. She deserves to be carefree and enjoy her four years of college. I was worried when, during her senior year of high school, she came out that she's gay. Not because I care which sex she prefers, but because I was nervous others might not be as accepting, and she would feel like an outcast at her school. I worried for nothing, though, because she's excelling both socially and academically, and even has her first serious girlfriend.

"I'm good," I tell her. "How was your first week back to school?" Adrianna has just begun her spring semester.

"So good! I got into the lab I was telling you about. It will mean taking fifteen credits instead of twelve, so I'll have to work twice as hard, but I'm so excited."

"The microphysics lab you told me about?" I confirm.

"Yes! It's extremely rare for a sophomore to be approved to take the class, but Professor Gent said with my grades and the fact that I was the top scorer in her chemistry class, she feels I will be successful."

"That's amazing, Addy. I'm so proud of you." My words come out slow, so she can't hear the emotion laced in them. I swallow down the lump in my throat and swipe a falling tear, reminding myself this is why I'm doing what I'm doing. For Addy. And for mom.

"Thanks, Sis."

"How's Stacey?" Stacey is Adrianna's girlfriend. They met in one of their science classes and hit it off right away. They've both picked the same major, which I imagine gives them a lot to talk about.

"She's great. Busy with school and softball."

"I look forward to meeting her."

"Yeah, maybe over spring break."

"Sounds good."

Adrianna's quiet for a moment, and when she does speak, her voice is soft and hesitant. "Umm...listen." I hear the nervousness in her tone, and I'm instantly worried. "The registrar's office sent a final notice. If I don't have the remaining balance paid by Monday, I'm going to have to withdraw from my classes...I know I was just going crazy over the lab, but I can take less classes if you need me to. I don't want—"

"Stop it! I'm sorry. I've just been so busy at work, it slipped my mind. I'm walking inside my building right now, and as soon as I get to my room, I will pull it up and pay the bill."

"Are you sure?" she asks, and my heart tightens in my chest. It wasn't supposed to be like this. Damn my father!

I inhale deeply then exhale to collect myself. The last thing Adrianna needs is to hear me crying. "I am one hundred percent sure."

"Okay, thank you."

"You're welcome. Hey, I'm about to get on the elevator, and I don't want to lose you. Have fun at your party tonight, and we'll talk soon."

"Okay! Love you."

"Love you too."

We hang up, and before I get into the elevator, I type out a quick text to my *other* boss and hit send.

Me: I need more hours.

Bianca: Noted.

I take the elevator up to the third and top floor of the brownstone I share with my best friend, Olivia Harper. And by share, I mean she owns it, and I pay pennies to live here with her. I met Olivia our freshman year of college in Paris. I was assigned a flat mate, and after only one week of living with her, I was almost positive I was going to kill her in her sleep. While most students spent their first week of school trying to figure out which classes they wanted to keep or drop, she spent the week sleeping her way through the entire lacrosse team...in the middle of the night...while I was trying to sleep.

As fate would have it, Olivia and I were in the same Art History class. She mentioned being lonely in her two-bedroom flat, so I offered to move in. We lived together during all four years of college and two years of getting our master's degrees. During which time, our friendship went from flat mates, to best friends, to sisters. She is the yin to my yang. Which is why when she said she needed to move back to New York last year, I packed up my stuff and followed her home.

I'm quiet as I open the door, unsure of who's here and not wanting to wake anyone up if they're sleeping. But when I walk inside, I see Olivia is sitting on the couch watching television with her sweet baby boy in her arms. He's drinking a cup of juice, but when he hears the door creak open, his head pops up, and he grants me the most adorable toothy grin.

"Hey, how was your night?" She pauses whatever she's watching to give me her full attention.

"Good." My answer is too vague for her liking, and she frowns.

"Were you on a date or working late?" Knowing she won't stop until I give her the information she wants, I sit down next to her and put my arms out for Reed. He drops his cup and climbs into my lap. I give him an extra tight hug, inhaling his baby scent, and he giggles.

"Hey there, my little love muffin. Did you miss me?" I coo. Reed plants a big, wet kiss on my cheek, and my heart soars. "I missed you too." He scoots out of my lap and slides down the couch and onto the ground, toddling over to where some of his toys are. I watch him for a second before I realize Olivia is still waiting for me to answer her question.

"I was on a date."

"With who?"

"Just some guy."

"What's his name?" she presses.

"Paul." I give her a look that says I don't want to discuss him, but she ignores it.

"That's a nice name. Is it serious?"

"Not really. Where's Nick?" I ask in an attempt to change the subject. Olivia grins at the mention of her baby daddy-slash-fiancé, momentarily forgetting about my date.

"Jacksonville. They've made it to the playoffs. We're flying out Saturday for the game." Nick Shaw is the starting quarterback of the New York Brewers. While he has his own place in the Lower East Side, he's more often than not wherever Olivia and Reed are.

"That's awesome!"

"They might be Super bowl champs for the second year in a row." Olivia beams. "How's work going? Anything new on the big account you've been working on?" she asks.

"Actually, yes!" I get excited thinking about the email I read earlier. "The client loved all of my suggestions, and we're meeting tomorrow morning to discuss moving forward."

"That's fabulous! One day you will be the most sought-after interior designer on the East Coast, and I'll get to say I'm your best friend." She grins, and my heart swells at the way my best friend always sees the best in me. She has no doubt in her mind that one day I will achieve my goals and dreams. If only I was as optimistic as she is.

"Now, let's talk about your birthday." She claps her hands together in excitement.

I groan. "Livi, c'mon! Can't we just pretend I'm not getting any older and forget my birthday altogether?"

"Nope and nope! I know you're crazy busy these days between work and making up for all the years you haven't dated..." She gives me the stink-eye, telling me she isn't happy with my lack of details. "So, I'm calling dibs on you next Friday night. Birthday dinner followed by a night out. Corrine and my dad are watching Reed."

When I open my mouth to argue, she shoots me a rare glare that has me cringing slightly. She's not going to accept any excuse I try to give her, so I don't bother. I'll just need to let Bianca know I can't work next Friday, which sucks since I literally just asked her for more hours—and more importantly, I need them.

"Okay, Friday." I nod with a smile, and Olivia squeals in excitement.

"Yay! We're going to have so much fun!" Her phone goes off, and when she checks to see who it is, her smile widens. "Reed, Daddy is calling. Come say hi." She hits accept and Nick's face appears on the screen.

"Hey buddy," he says as Reed crawls over to the couch to see his dad on the other end of the line.

Figuring Olivia will be busy on the phone for a good while, and wanting to give her some privacy, I sneak away into my room. After taking a long hot shower and getting dressed into my comfy pajamas, I open my laptop and pull up my bank account information. Then I open another window and log into Adrianna's school site. It's going to be tight, but if Bianca can give me some additional hours, I think I can swing it without going into the negatives. Not that I have a choice, since the alternative is my sister not taking all the classes she's signed up for—and that's definitely not an option.

I click on her semester bill and type in my credit card information then hit submit. I refresh my bank site and the balance drops from five figures to four. I type another text to Bianca with an apology that I can't work next Friday night then remind her I can work any other day.

Closing my laptop, I turn my light off and crawl into bed. Then I remember I never called my mom tonight. *Damn it.* I look over at the clock and see it's too late now. I'll just get up a few minutes earlier tomorrow and call her before I get ready for work.

TWO

KILLIAN

"WING T 69 BOTTLENECK RIGHT!" Nick yells, announcing the next play we're going to run through. During any given practice, we'll go through dozens of different plays. With our team making it to the playoffs for the second year in a row, all eyes are on us—many wanting us to succeed, but a lot wanting us to fail. When you become the Champions after not even making it to the playoffs in over a decade, it's a given everyone will be ridiculing every move your team makes, questioning if you can do it again, or if it was just a one-time deal. I've been with the New York Brewers since I was drafted my senior year in college, and after finally earning a ring, I can tell you, one isn't enough. Especially when my best friend Nick has four of those damn things—three from the team he previously played for, and one from last year when we won during our first season of playing together since college. The Super Bowl was almost a year ago, and I'm still high on the win and craving another one. It's what keeps me motivated every game as we get closer to the Super Bowl once again. We won our first playoff game against Jacksonville last weekend. That's one game down. Only three more standing in the way of us getting that ring.

We break into formation and then the ball is hiked. Everyone scrambles to their position on the field. Nick steps into position and throws the ball right into my awaiting arms, which of course I catch, and run down the field for a touchdown.

Coach Harper blows the whistle, and everyone congregates around him. "Good practice, everyone. You have the next two days off to rest. Practice Saturday and we play Pittsburgh Sunday. Don't get into any trouble. I don't need to remind you we're only three games away from being Super Bowl champions." Everyone cheers at his words then head into the locker room to shower and change.

Coach Harper pats Nick on the shoulder. "See you Friday, Son."

Nick nods and smiles. "Yes, sir." Coach Harper is the father of Nick's fiancée, Olivia, and the grandfather to their son, Reed. You would think it would be awkward for Nick to be playing on the same team his future father-in-law coaches, but the truth is, Stephen Harper is more of a father to Nick than his own father is. He never gives him special treatment, but it's clear they have a good relationship. When Nick was picked up last year, Coach spent every day helping him work out and get back into shape after his injury.

Once I'm packed up and ready to go, I turn my cell phone back on and see a missed call from my publicist. I give her a call back. "Amber, how's it going?"

"Good, thanks for returning my call. I just wanted to remind you tomorrow night is the party with Bugatti to announce your endorsement deal with them. Several major investors will be there."

I grin at the thought of signing a deal with Bugatti. My first big purchase I made after I signed with New York was a Bugatti Veyron, my dream car. I've owned several others since then, but the Veyron will always be my favorite. So when my agent, Mike Miller, was approached about me signing an endorsement deal with them, it was a fucking given. It's common for football players to endorse various items and companies such as insurance agencies, clothing lines, and different health food companies. But being named MVP of the Super Bowl last year has opened endorsement gates I never imagined possible—including getting a special edition made of my favorite car.

Amber continues. "I'll email you the details again, just in case you lost them." The woman knows me way too well. I suck at remembering anything other than when to catch a ball. "Will you need a date?" she asks.

"Yeah, thanks."

We hang up, and as I'm grabbing my gym bag, I spot Nick

walking over to me, his own bag slung over his shoulder. "Ready to go?" I ask.

"Hell yes." We head out of the stadium and toward my car. Because we live in the same building, we often ride together. Driving in New York sucks, which is why we only live about ten minutes from the stadium. "So listen, there's a little get together Friday night for Giselle's birthday. We're going to dinner and then out afterward. Olivia knows we have curfew, so we won't be out too late. I know you and Giselle aren't exactly friendly, but it would mean a lot to Olivia if you'd go. Giselle doesn't have many friends."

"How is that my fault? Maybe if she wasn't so unpleasant to be around, more people would like her. Then you wouldn't need me to increase your number of guests." I know I sound like a dick, but I'm not lying. I have no clue how Olivia and Giselle are even friends, let alone best friends. While Olivia is sweet and soft-spoken and just an all-around nice person, Giselle is the complete opposite in every way: blunt, loud, and not at all nice.

"She's not really that bad. You just have to get to know her. She's like a Pitbull. She looks vicious, but once you pat her head, she'll roll over, wag her tail, and lick you to death." Nick shrugs.

"You realize you just compared her to a dog, right?" When Nick's brows furrow in confusion, I shake with laughter. "A bitch?"

His eyes widen. "That's not what I meant!"

"Well, if the shoe fits...or should we say paw?" I laugh harder at my own joke. "So, who else is going?"

"Her sister might come down, and Celeste will be there." I start laughing all over again at the mention of Celeste.

"What?" Nick asks.

"I just can't get over the fact that your current fiancée is friends with your ex-fiancée." Nick glares, and it only has me cackling harder as I press the ignition and head out of the parking lot.

"Bro, shut the fuck up. Celeste was barely my fiancée." He's right, but I still have to give him shit about it. I met Nick and Celeste our freshman year of college. Nick and I shared a dorm, and Celeste was his childhood friend who was a few years younger but always hung out with us. She was and still is a gold-digger. She might be hot as fuck, and a huge model who owns a few successful businesses, but that doesn't change the fact that her entire goal in life is to make money and marry a guy who will give her more money. I will never understand how in the world Nick has not only remained friends with her over the years, but almost married her last year.

"Whatever you say. Have you guys found a home yet?" Nick groans, and I laugh some more. I shouldn't get such a kick out of this man's life, but I can't help it. Nick and Olivia are the only two people I know who are engaged to be married, can afford to purchase a new home—hell, fifteen new homes if they want to—but instead live separately.

"I think Olivia is putting off moving because of Giselle. Since they've met, Olivia has always found ways to take care of Giselle without making it look like she is, and if she moves out, Giselle will be more or less homeless."

"What do you mean?" I ask, turning onto our street. Olivia owns a beautiful brownstone in the heart of Brooklyn Heights, and there's no way she would kick Giselle out. Those two women are closer to being sisters than best friends.

"If Olivia moves out, Giselle will never stay living there knowing her friend is only continuing to pay the mortgage for her, and there's no way she can afford to take over those payments." That's for sure. You would never know it, but Olivia's mother, who died when she was younger, left Olivia a huge inheritance. The woman could probably afford to purchase the entire building she lives in. Giselle, on the other hand, comes from the same background as me: middle-class working family who live paycheck to paycheck.

"I could be wrong, but I don't think it's normal to be married and live in separate homes," I joke.

"Which is probably why we still haven't gotten married. I love how selfless Olivia is, and that she wants to put her best friend first. And I get it. Giselle moved back to New York just for Olivia. But fuck, I just want to marry her and live under one damn roof. I feel like a kid in a divorced home, bouncing back and forth between our places."

"Well, then Giselle is just going to have to do what everyone else does and stand on her own two capable feet." I pull into our parking garage and turn the car off. When we get to the elevator, Nick presses the button for my floor then the one directly above for his. "I'm sure you guys will figure it out. It will suck once you do move, though. How will you come down to play Madden with me?"

Nick laughs. "Don't worry, honey, I'll always find time for you." He winks.

The elevator door opens on my floor. "I have that endorsement party for Bugatti tomorrow night, so I won't see you until Friday. Text me when and where to meet you guys and I'll be there."

Nick nods. "Thanks, man, and congrats on your deal."

I thank him then step off the elevator, the door closing behind me.

"TABITHA, YOU LOOK BEAUTIFUL." I step out of the limousine and give my date a kiss on her cheek. She's dressed in a black floor-length gown, and her blond locks are up in a bun of some sort. Amber came through, as always.

"Thank you, Mr. Blake," she gushes as I help her inside before walking around to the other side, so she doesn't have to slide over in her dress.

"Please, call me Killian. Tonight we're going to a party to announce and sign my endorsement deal with Bugatti. They're planning to run the ads during the playoffs and Super Bowl. There'll be some pretty big investors there."

"Understood," she says with a smile. We make small talk on the way to the Four Seasons where the party is being held. Tabitha is polite and professional, and I can already tell tonight will be a good night.

Once we arrive, we're escorted back. I'm met with several people who introduce themselves, including the head of the design team who is in charge of making the special edition.

"This beautiful car will only be available to fifteen people," Travis boasts, clearly proud of what his team has created.

"I'm just honored I'll be one of those fifteen people." I shake his hand.

"That's so exciting," Tabitha whispers enthusiastically.

I begin to tell her it's a dream come true when I spot someone I know out of the corner of my eye and wonder why in the world she's here at my party. "Excuse me for a second. I see someone I know."

I make my way over to the bar where she's sitting on a cushioned stool. When I get close enough, I notice she's sipping on what looks like some type of scotch. *Of course she is.* While most women would choose a fruity drink of some sort, Giselle chooses the hard stuff. Her brown hair is pin straight down her back, and her blood-red dress fits every curve of her damn body perfectly. When I approach the bar, the bartender asks what I would like.

"Jameson whiskey sour, please." I lean one elbow against the bar top and face her. "What are you doing here?"

She takes a slow sip of her drink before she gives me any of her attention. "I'm assuming the same thing you're doing here. Celebrating the endorsement deal for a..." Her voice trails off as she realizes just who the endorsement deal is for. "You?" She shoots me a side-eye, her nose scrunching up as she takes another sip of her drink.

"Yes, me, and I'm almost positive an interior design *intern* isn't needed for any part of this deal, so I'll ask again, what are you doing here? Did you crash the party in an attempt to find some rich guy to latch onto?"

She cackles, throwing her head back like what I just said was the funniest thing she's ever heard. Then, she stands, and because I'm standing directly next to her barstool, the front of her body rubs up against mine, and her perky tits, which are overflowing out of the top of her dress, press against my chest. I force myself to keep my eyes on hers.

She leans into me and whispers, "I'm here with the man you made the deal with, silly. The man, who in about sixty minutes will be nestled between my thighs, fucking me senseless. And if I wanted him to, would give me ten of these stupid ugly cars." Giselle smirks snidely as she edges out from between the stool and me, remembering to take her drink with her.

"There you are, lovely." Roman Ette, the man responsible for this deal taking place, comes over and rests his hand on Giselle's back, giving her a chaste kiss to her cheek. "I should've known you ran off to the bar." He smiles at her, and Giselle giggles. *What the fuck!* She actually giggles. Who the hell is this woman, and if she's dating him, why is she crying broke?

"You know me too well, Roman. I was actually on my way back to find you. I was only gone but a minute." She giggles some more. "Were you missing me already?"

"Always." He shoots her a wink then turns his attention back to me. "Mr. Blake, I heard the guest of honor arrived." He extends his hand and I shake it. "Are you excited to see your special edition?"

"I am, sir. This is truly a dream come true." I spot Tabitha making her way over, but for some reason, everything I found to be beautiful about her suddenly seems so plain. I refuse to acknowledge my thoughts have anything to do with the woman still standing in front of me, currently eye-fucking a man more than twice her age.

Tabitha stops at my side and I make introductions. "Tabitha, this is Roman Ette."

"Nice to meet you, sir." She smiles politely.

"And this is his date." I make it a point not to mention Giselle's name, refusing to give her any importance, just to piss her off.

So, I'm shocked when Tabitha says, "Nice to meet you, Giselle." My eyes dart over to Tabitha first, who doesn't seem to notice her slip-up—maybe she knows her?—but then my gaze goes to Giselle. Her glacier-blue eyes which normally appear cold, go wide with what looks like worry, and I know right away something is up.

"Do you two know each other?" I ask.

"We do." Giselle quickly speaks first. "We went to school together."

"Oh, really? Where did you go to school, Tabitha?" Her eyes are now as wide as Giselle's.

"We went to NYU—" Giselle begins to say, but I cut her off.

"I asked Tabitha."

"We went to NYU," Tabitha says.

"Really?" Roman says, joining the conversation. "I thought you went to school in Paris?" His question is aimed at Giselle.

"I did. NYU Paris," she says, her perfect smile never faltering. But as I rake my eyes down her body, I notice she's wringing her hands together—something I'd seen her do a few months back when she was worried about her mom. It's her telltale sign she's nervous. Why would Giselle be nervous? Unless she has something to hide...

"Yes, NYU Paris," Tabitha agrees, but unlike Giselle, she isn't as good at faking it. Her voice wavering with each word she speaks.

Roman smiles, none the wiser, but something feels off. My gaze meets Giselle's, and for the first time since I ran into her, she isn't glaring at me. Instead, it's almost as if she's pleading with me to drop it. Her eyes are no longer icy—they're vulnerable, exposed. I've seen this look from her before. I remember it well because it's not often Giselle allows herself to appear weak.

My thoughts go back several months to the night we spent in the Hamptons with our friends. We had been partying at AM Southampton until Olivia got too drunk and Nick felt it was time to head home.

As we were all climbing the stairs, Olivia, in all her drunken glory, decided to assign each woman to a princess. Celeste was labeled Belle, and Giselle was Rapunzel, but that wasn't the part that got my attention. What did was what Olivia said afterward:

"And one day you're going to meet a prince you will trust with all of your secrets, and he's going to save you just like Flynn Ryder saved Rapunzel."

Giselle's eyes went wide, much like they are now, as she silently pleaded with her best friend to shut up. But her eyes weren't angry...they were scared. She's always been a damn contradiction: strong, yet she relies on her best friend to support her. Hard working, yet she dates rich men who want nothing more than a trophy wife on their arm. Maybe I was focusing on the wrong part of what Olivia said. On the part about her needing to be saved, when what I should've been paying attention to was the part about her having secrets. Is it possible there's more to Giselle than what meets the eye?

The rest of the night goes smoothly, and I force myself to push any more thoughts of Giselle out of my head. It doesn't matter what she's hiding. None of it is my business. Giselle isn't my business. And the last thing I need in my life is a lying, sneaking, secret-keeping woman. I've dealt with those type of women more times than I can count, and I've learned my lesson the hard way. I'll be damned if I put my hand on the hot stove after getting burnt.

Once the night comes to an end, Tabitha and I say our good-byes. When we're a few minutes away from her apartment, I can't help myself. I told myself I didn't care what Giselle is hiding, but I can't get her off my mind.

"What did you major in at NYU?" I ask. Tabitha flinches.

"I...um...I didn't make it that far." She shrugs. "I dropped out." Her eyes dart everywhere in the limo but at me.

I open my mouth to ask her another question when she squeaks out, "Oh, we're here." She scoops up her clutch then quickly swings the door open. "I hope you had a good night." She smiles awkwardly then slides out, shutting the door behind her and scurrying up the sidewalk like her ass is on fire.

Oh yeah, something is definitely up.

Once I'm back home, I shower and change into some lounge pants. I try to get Giselle off my mind, but it's not happening. I lay in bed and turn on the television, willing myself to drop whatever I'm thinking. But the more I try not to think about her, the more I do. A memory surfaces from our night in the Hamptons—after Celeste, Nick, and Olivia disappeared into their rooms, and I thought Giselle had done the same thing.

"Hey! Do you mind?" Giselle snaps at me.

"Sorry, I didn't realize anyone was in the bathroom." I should've knocked, but when I grabbed the knob and it opened, I assumed it was empty. Now that I know it is indeed occupied, I should close the door, but instead my eyes are frozen on Giselle's sexy body. She's wearing a powder blue lace bra that matches her eyes. Her nipples

are hard and pebbling through the thin material. My eyes drag down her body, over her toned stomach, and land on her tiny matching lace panties. Without thinking, I lick my lips as I imagine what her cunt would taste like. It's been a long time since I—

"See something you like?" She smirks and takes a step forward. "Too bad I don't fuck athletes." Her hand lands on my chest. She pats it condescendingly, effectively snapping me out of my trance as she saunters past me, out of the bathroom, and leaves me standing there with a raging hard-on.

I think what confuses me the most about Giselle is while everyone is privy to that version of her, the beautiful woman who hides behind her ice-queen persona, I've seen another side of her. A side I'm not even sure Olivia has ever seen.

The next morning, Giselle gets a phone call from her sister that her dad left her mom. She has no way of getting there, so I offer to take her. After a completely silent two-hour drive to Rye, we pull up to her house. Giselle quickly unbuckles her seatbelt, throws open the car door, and runs up the short sidewalk to her parents' house. It reminds me a lot of the home I grew up in before I could afford to buy my parents a nicer place. A single-story home on zero lot land with paint probably twenty years old peeling off the walls. There's a beat-up looking Ford Focus in the driveway that must be at least thirty years old. I step out of my vehicle and my eyes land on some teenagers who are currently standing on the street engaging in what looks to be a drug deal. One of them gives me a curt nod, and I hit the alarm on my car, knowing damn well it won't really do any good in a neighborhood like this.

I walk into the house to find Giselle and her sister talking. Their words come to a halt when her sister sees me. "Who's this?" she asks, and Giselle introduces us. "This is Killian, a friend of Nick and Olivia's. He brought me here."

"Thank you." She wraps her arms around Giselle in a hug. "I'm so sorry. She won't come out, and I have to get back to school. I didn't know—"

Giselle pulls back. "It's okay," she says, cutting her off. "Go, and don't worry about a thing. Just focus on your classes. I will make sure mom is okay. I promise." She gives her sister another hug, then pushes her out the door. Once it's closed, her back hits the wood and she lets out a deep sigh. Her eyes close, and for just a small moment, she appears softer. She doesn't look anything like the closed-off ice-cold woman I've come to know the last couple months. That is until she opens her eyes back up and speaks.

"You can wait outside. I don't need you here." Her blue eyes are once again hard, and she glares at me like I'm the enemy. Without waiting for me to speak, she blows past me down the hall. I'm about to go back outside when I notice she's trying to pry the door open with a screwdriver.

"What are you doing?"

"What does it look like?" she snaps. "I'm having a fucking tea party? I'm trying to open the door! My mom locked herself in there."

I walk down the hall and take the screwdriver out of her hand. "That's not going to work."

"Well, I need to get in there. Can you break it down, please?"

"You sure?" I ask. "The doorjamb will probably splinter."

"Yes. My mom...she could be..." She doesn't finish her sentence with words, but instead with her terrified eyes. I tell her to stand back, then I kick the door, and just as I predicted, it opens but the frame splinters, and pieces of wood fall to the ground.

"Thank you." She rushes into the room while I stay in the doorway. Her mom is on her bed, sobbing, and Giselle climbs on to the bed and pulls her head into her lap.

"He's gone," her mom cries. "He left me."

"It's okay, Mom," Giselle says in the same melodic tone parents use when trying to soothe their upset babies.

Wanting to give them their space, I back out of the doorway and walk back down the hall to wait in the living room. I haven't even sat down on the sofa when I hear screaming and shouting coming from the bedroom.

"It's all your fault! I hate you!" The voice isn't Giselle's, so it must be her mother. I start to walk back toward the bedroom.

"Mom, please calm down."

I stop in my tracks, unsure of what I should do. Then I hear something crash, and then Giselle says, "Mom, stop, that hurts."

My feet move of their own accord into the bedroom, where I see Giselle's mother dragging Giselle by her hair to the center of the room.

"Mom, you're hurting me!" she yells, but her mom doesn't stop.

"Everyone left me! You, your sister, now your father!" When her mom turns her back toward me, pulling Giselle into a standing position, I come up behind her and cage her arms in my own. I'm not sure if I'm doing the right thing, but I can't just stand here and watch her hurt her daughter. Giselle's mom appears to be shocked at first, her head tilting back to look at me, but then she starts to fight back. For a tiny little thing, she sure is strong. She thrashes about and tries

to kick me in the groin, all while screaming for me to let her go. Giselle runs out of the room, and a few seconds later, returns. She stabs her mom with a needle to her neck, and a few minutes later, her mom's body feels like dead weight in my arms.

"You, umm...you didn't kill her, did you?" I ask nervously.

"No, it's a sedative. We try not to use it unless it's necessary. I knew there was no way I would be able to get her to swallow her pills. Thank you for holding her down. Usually her nurse is here, but she has the weekends off when my dad is home. You can lay her down."

Carefully, I lift her and set her on the bed. She's definitely out.

Giselle walks over to the dresser and opens the drawer. "Damn it!"

"What's wrong?"

"My dad really did leave. All of his clothes are gone." She slides open the closet door and there's a huge empty spot.

"What's wrong with your mom?" I ask.

"She suffers from depression, and we can't seem to find meds that work." She pulls out her phone and dials someone. "Donna, it's Giselle. Listen, my dad left. All of his stuff is gone. Until I can figure everything out, can you stay with her?" She goes quiet, listening to the person on the other end. Then she says, "Yes, of course you will be paid accordingly." She listens some more and then says, "Okay, thank you," before ending the call.

"If you're afraid of your mom being alone, we could bring her with us," I offer.

"She hates to leave her house, and since I live with Olivia, that's not an option. I'm not about to bring my shit to her doorstep. I'll figure it out. I'm sorry you had to see that." She smiles softly, but it's a sad smile, and my heart hurts for her. But then her eyes meet mine, and it's as if she's just remembered she isn't supposed to be nice to me.

"You can wait outside in the car. Once Donna gets here, we can go," she says, clearly dismissing me, and I can already see her mask rising back over her face.

The ride home was once again silent. When we arrived at her place, she quickly thanked me and got out, and since then she's never once mentioned her mom again. I have no idea what happened—if her dad returned, or even how her mom is doing. I haven't asked, and she hasn't spoken of it. I shouldn't even care. It's not my business. *She's* not my business. So *then why are you thinking about her?*

THREE

GISELLE

I'M SITTING at the table in my favorite Japanese restaurant with Celeste, Killian, Nick, and Olivia. Adrianna didn't make it down because she had an important cram session she needed to attend for an upcoming test, and I insisted she stay there to prepare. Nick and Killian are discussing their win against Jacksonville and what they need to do to beat Pittsburgh. Olivia is showing Celeste pictures of Reed since she's been out of the country the last few months. She launched her new clothing line worldwide last year, and she's been traveling all over to promote it.

We're all here to celebrate my twenty-sixth birthday, and the only thing I want to do is go home and get some sleep. I'm beyond exhausted from all the hours I've worked this week. But because I know tonight means a lot to Olivia, and I've been pushing her away recently, I keep a smile on my face as I listen to everyone around me converse.

"You ended up staying longer than planned. Did you meet anyone special while you were away?" Olivia asks Celeste, waggling her eyebrows playfully.

Celeste laughs. "Funny...actually, I am dating someone. His name is Chad Vacanti."

"Good for you," Olivia says. "Is it serious?"

"As serious as two people can be who have busy careers." Celeste shrugs.

"So, in other words, he's a workaholic like you," Olivia volleys back playfully.

"No, he's...dedicated to his job and works hard like me. He's a VP for the investment banking firm he works at. He had to fly over to the UK for some business, so we met up while I was there. It was nice."

Killian chuckles, and everyone looks his way.

"What?" Celeste glares.

"Nothing." Killian smirks.

"Just say it," Celeste insists.

"It's nothing, really. I'm just glad you finally found your millionaire." He pops a piece of sushi into his mouth and chews, then adds, "I take it you found him on Wall Street? Tell me, Celeste, does he know he's dating a gold-digger?"

"Screw you!" Celeste hisses. "For your information, my company's fourth quarter earnings grossed over six-point-five million dollars in profit, asshole."

Everyone at the table stills in shock. Holy shit! Celeste really is doing well for yourself. Go her!

"Damn, Celeste!" Nick pats her on her shoulder. "That's awesome."

"Congratulations," Olivia adds.

"Seriously!" I say, "That's awesome!"

"Thank you." She smiles proudly.

"Then why the hell are you still searching for your happily-ever-millionaire?" Killian questions.

"Killian," Olivia chides.

"What? It's just a question," he says. God, he's such a judgmental ass!

"I'm not looking for a millionaire." Celeste takes a deep breath and her eyes dart all over the place, like she's suddenly uncomfortable. "There's nothing wrong with wanting a man who's stable and has his life together...who can afford to pay his bills..." She huffs. "Never mind, you wouldn't understand." She lifts her glass of Sake to her mouth and downs it.

"So, what you're saying is if you met a guy who, let's say, works full-time, pays his bills on time, but only makes five figures a year, you would date him," Killian challenges.

Celeste shoots daggers his way, and Killian laughs. Before she can answer, Nick jumps in. "Kill...stop, man."

Killian shrugs and downs his beer. I don't know what his deal is tonight, but I do not want to be on the receiving end of his inquisition. My goal is to lay low and pray he doesn't call me out on seeing me last night. I'm already regretting the fact that I goaded him by telling him I was going to fuck Roman and that his car was stupid and ugly. It's really not either one. On the contrary, it's one of the most beautiful cars I've ever seen, and it has all the bells and whistles.

Olivia, feeling the need to change the subject, turns her attention on me. Great... "How's Paul?"

"Who?" I ask before I can catch myself, forgetting I gave her a name the other night.

"Paul, the guy you went on a date with last week."

I notice Killian sit up higher in his seat. His eyes widen marginally as he stares at me, like he's just as interested to know my answer as Olivia is. Damn it!

Ignoring Killian's stare, I focus my attention on Olivia when I answer. "I'm actually not seeing him anymore. It didn't work out."

Olivia frowns. "I'm sorry."

"How's Roman?" Killian asks. My eyes dart over to him, and the asshole is fucking smirking.

"Who?" Olivia asks, confused.

I glare at Killian, silently warning him to shut up. He's doing this to mess with me, but he doesn't understand this isn't a fucking game. He's not only messing with my life, but he's messing with my friendship with Olivia. Instead of heeding my warning, his smirk turns into a full-blown grin as he says, "The guy I saw Giselle at the party with last night." And he just had to fucking go there...

"You went on a date last night? When I asked you where you were, you said you were working." I drag my gaze from Killian to look at Olivia. The hurt in her features is evident, and I feel like the world's shittiest friend.

I consider how to word my answer before I speak, because up until this moment, I've technically never lied to Olivia, and I have no clue how to twist this so I'm not lying now. But before I can answer her, my name is called, and when I look over my shoulder, my heart drops at who is calling it. *Christian.*

Seriously, can this day get any worse?

He approaches the table, and I feel everyone's eyes on us. "Hey, I thought it was you." He grins nervously. Asshole should be nervous. The last time I saw him, he was balls-deep in a groupie in his hotel room, only days after he told me he loved me. We had gotten into a fight regarding a text I saw on his phone. I left upset and sat on the bench outside of his hotel room, trying to figure out how to handle what I saw. Not even an hour later, I made the decision to go up and talk to him about it. I think I was hoping he would convince me what I saw was a big misunderstanding. Only, when I got up to his room, he had already found another woman and was fucking her on the couch. That was a year ago, and I haven't seen or spoken to him since.

"It's me," I say dryly, not bothering to smile back. He doesn't deserve anything from me, let alone a fake emotion. He lost the right to anything regarding me the day he chose to throw our friendship and relationship out the window for some random groupie pussy.

Christian glances around the table before his eyes come back to me. "It's your birthday." It's not a question—he's just remembered.

"Yep...Happy Birthday to me," I say.

Nobody says anything for a good thirty seconds, until Killian chooses to speak up, breaking the silence. "Wait a second. Aren't you Christian Ortega, the lead singer for Down Coyote?"

"That would be me." He nods with a small but genuine smile. Christian lives for the moments when people recognize him. His dreams came true. His band was signed, and they rose to the top. It's too bad the industry destroyed him. With the fame came the parties, and with the parties came the drugs. With him being high as often as he is—or at least was during that short time I was around him again—I don't even know how he enjoys his success. The morning after I found him fucking the groupie, he called me as if nothing happened. He blamed the drugs, promised he would stop getting high. He swore he didn't even remember having sex with her.

He called several times, begging me to forgive him, but I told him it was too late. The damage was done. I can forgive a lot of things, but I can't forgive cheating. The fact is we never would've worked out anyway. Seven years apart changed us both. We're no longer the naïve young teenagers we once were, and there's no going back.

Sometimes when I think about the way Christian behaved, I wonder if that's what happens to my mom. I know the drugs Christian was on aren't the same as my mom's, but I wonder if maybe she doesn't remember what she does or if it's possible she's reacting a certain way because she's on so many different drugs. If we just took her off of everything, maybe she would see things more clearly. I can't be sure, though, and I'm too scared to find out.

"We're just finishing up dinner and are about to head out for some drinks," Killian says, snapping me out of my thoughts. "You should join us. Any *friend* of Giselle's is welcome. Or wait, are you her boyfriend?" Killian smirks devilishly.

Christian's hand grips the back of his neck nervously, unsure of what to say. Thankfully, Olivia jumps in. "You need to walk away right now, asshole. I know about you cheating on my best friend. Go back to your groupies and stay away from her." Her voice is barely loud enough for the entire table to hear, and while her intent is to sound big and bad, she just sounds adorable, but I still love her even more for defending me.

"I think it's best if you go," Celeste adds. "It's clear you're not wanted here." Celeste has heard all about Christian and what he did to me on several girls' nights out.

"Look, I'm sorry. Would it be possible for us to talk?" Christian asks, and this time Nick jumps in.

"You heard the ladies. You're not wanted here."

"This is between Giselle and me," Christian snaps.

"No, it's really not," Killian says, shocking the crap out of me. He and Nick stand, and Christian backs up. "I didn't realize when I extended my offer you were a cheating piece of shit. So, not only am I rescinding my offer for you to join us, but I suggest you walk out of this restaurant and lose Giselle's number. If she wants to call you, she'll do so. But until then, get fucking lost."

Christian's hands go up in surrender, and he looks at me like he wants to say something, but luckily, he thinks better of it and walks away.

"I'm so sorry, Giselle." Olivia gets up and comes around to my side of the table to give me a hug. "I love you."

"I love you too. Thank you, guys." Tears brim my lids as I look around at everyone who just stuck up for me, including Killian. I might not have a lot of friends, but the few I do have are pretty freaking great. And while Killian isn't my friend, it means a lot that despite how much he doesn't like me, he still stood up for me.

"Growing up I never really had any friends," I admit out loud. "My family kind of has some issues." My eyes dart to Killian who has seen them firsthand. "Christian was not only my best friend but my boyfriend. I never imagined one of the people closest to me would betray me like he did. Anyway, you guys sticking up for me like that means the world to me."

"You would've done it for us," Olivia points out.

"After that, I think we all need to get drunk," Celeste says with a laugh. "That guy was about to ruin my buzz."

"Actually, we have something else planned." Olivia grins. "It's a surprise, though."

"What happened to partying? Getting drunk?" Celeste pouts.

"We will, I promise! After we go to our next stop. But first, we need to sing Happy Birthday." She nods behind her and the waiter comes over with a candle-lit birthday cake. Everyone sings Happy Birthday, then Olivia cuts the cake. Once we're done eating it, we pile into the limo Olivia rented for the night.

Killian is sitting next to me, and I'm shocked when he leans in close to speak to me. "I'm sorry about what I did in there. Inviting that asshole out with us."

I just don't have it in me to call him out on his shit. So instead I say, "It's not your fault. You didn't know."

"True, but we both know I was only inviting him to piss you off." Killian smiles apologetically, and I laugh at his honesty. "So, I'm sorry," he adds.

"It's okay," I tell him.

"We're here!" Olivia announces, and everyone steps out of the limo onto the sidewalk in front of...

"A tattoo shop?" I ask excitedly.

"Yep! I made us appointments!" Olivia clasps her hands together and jumps up and down.

"Hell yes!" I yell, joining her.

"You, umm...you didn't make an appointment for me, did you?" Celeste asks nervously.

"Well, I told him we had a group coming and I wasn't sure who all would want one. He said a couple people would be here," Olivia tells her.

"Oh my god, Livi! This is so exciting!" I exclaim.

"A dream of yours?" Killian asks.

"Of ours." I smile at Olivia. "We both said we wanted one, but we were too scared to actually get them. So we agreed that once we graduated with our masters, we would get tattoos to celebrate. Olivia graduated before me, and by the time I graduated six months later, she was knocked up."

"Must you word it like that," Olivia says through her laughter. "Let's go!"

Linking our arms together, Olivia and I walk into Forbidden Ink, followed by Killian, Nick, and Celeste. From the outside, it looks like nothing more than a small hole-in-the-wall shop with blacked out windows. But once we open the door, it's as if we're stepping into a New York City alleyway, and I'm not talking about one behind Fifth Avenue. More like the ones from where I'm from. The walls are painted to look like graffitied CBS block, but the artwork is far better than anything you would see in the real alleyways. They are eye-catching and beautiful. The floors are concrete, identical to the sidewalks outside, but cleaner. There are a couple of black leather couches in the front area, and on a black wooden coffee table are stacks of books. In the right corner is a pool table, and to the left is the front counter. A narrow hallway goes down the middle.

"How can I help you?" the woman sitting behind the counter asks with a smile. She's pretty, with her silky black locks tied into low pigtails, perfect porcelain skin, and big onyx eyes. Her arms look like beautiful canvases of colorful artwork.

"We have an appointment with Jaxson," Olivia says.

"All of you?" the woman questions, her gaze following over each of us. Then it stops on someone, and her smile widens. My eyes follow her line of vision to...Killian.

"Kill!" She jumps off her stool and runs out from behind the counter, straight into his arms. And if I thought she was just pretty from behind the counter, I was wrong. She's wearing a flowy yellow top and tiny cut-off jean shorts that on most would look trashy, but on her look seriously hot. She's sexy and adorable, and with her arms wrapped around Killian, I kind of hate her, which doesn't make any sense. *Maybe I drank more than I thought at dinner...*

"Quinn, how are you?" Killian asks once they're done hugging.

"Same shit, different day. You here for another tattoo?" She waggles her eyebrows flirtatiously, and it's confirmed, I hate her. Why? I have no fucking clue, I just do. *Seriously, how much did I have to drink?*

"Well, since I'm here, maybe." Killian laughs, and his emerald eyes light up. "But we're actually here for those two." He nods toward Olivia and me. "Olivia, Giselle, this is Quinn, Jax and Jase's little sister. It's Giselle's birthday, so they're looking to get tattoos."

"How about you?" a deep male voice rumbles. I turn in place to see a gentleman leaning against the doorframe with his muscular tattooed arms crossed over his chest. He's wearing a fitted plain black T-shirt and ripped jeans, and he's staring at Celeste, who looks completely out of place in her expensive designer dress and high heels.

"Excuse me?" she asks, her nose scrunching up in clear disgust. The guy lifts off the wall and steps toward her until he's directly in front of her.

"The other two women are here to get a tattoo. How about you? Are you going to finally let me mark this flawless skin of yours?" His finger runs up her arm, and she visibly shivers. *Finally? Who is this guy?*

"Don't touch me," she hisses, moving out of his reach.

"Is there a problem?" I ask, not completely comfortable with this guy touching Celeste. Unlinking my arm out of Olivia's, I step between the two of them, and the guy grins mischievously, not taking his eyes off Celeste.

"Umm...maybe we should go somewhere else?" Olivia suggests.

"I agree. Let's go," I say.

"Wait," Nick says, pulling Olivia in the front of him and wrapping his arms around her waist. "Jase, I would like for you to finally meet my baby mama and fiancée, Olivia." He gives her a small kiss on her cheek.

"Nice to meet you," Jase says. "I've heard a lot about you."

When Olivia looks back at him confused, Nick says, "Jase and I played ball together in high school and college. He was two years ahead of Kill and me."

"We had some great times." Jase and Nick bump fists.

"Did you go to school with them?" I ask Celeste. It would explain why this guy Jase was acting the way he was toward her. Although, I'm pretty sure she's a few years younger than Nick.

"No." She shakes her head. "I went to public school," she adds softly.

"You met him at the party I took you to, right?" Nick asks. "I forgot about that. Do you two...*know* each other?" His eyes volley between Celeste and Jase.

"Yes, you did," Celeste says dryly, "but I don't know him."

Quinn sneers. "Oh, that's rich! What's wrong? Is my brother not worthy of your memories? Did you block out everything that happened before you ran your stuck-up ass to New York? What are you even doing slumming it in East Village? It's a far ride from the Upper East Side."

"You know what—" Celeste steps directly in Quinn's face "—I don't need to take this shit from you. I didn't know you guys worked here, and if I had, trust me, I never would've come."

"Well, now you know. And FYI, my brothers don't just work here...they own the place. Don't let the door hit you on the way out," Quinn says before turning her back on Celeste.

"All right, everyone, just calm down." A guy who looks similar to Jase steps into view. "Everybody is welcome here. Which one of you is Olivia?"

"Me," Olivia says, raising her hand.

"Nice to meet you. I'm Jaxson Crawford, but everyone calls me Jax. I spoke to you on the phone. I'm this asshole's older brother." He smacks his palm against Jase's chest. "And this spitfire is our little sister." He pulls Quinn into a playful headlock.

"Celeste, it's good to see you again," he says giving Celeste a sincere smile. "Although, with those billboards of you all over New York, I feel like I see you every day." He winks playfully, and Celeste's scowl breaks into a small grin.

"Great, if we're all done with this reunion, how about we figure out who's getting inked?" Jase says, sounding annoyed.

"I want the nice guy," I say, pointing to Jax. "It's my birthday. Livi, you can take the cranky one." Everyone laughs, and Jase cracks a small smile.

"I might be the crankier one, but I'm still the better artist. Ain't that right, Dimples?" His gaze lands on Celeste, who scowls.

"Bullshit!" Jax laughs. "I'm older, wiser, and a better artist."

"Nah." Jase chuckles lightheartedly. "Just older." Then he looks back at Celeste and his eyes turn smoldering. There's clearly a story there.

"I really need to get going," Celeste announces. Her heels clack against the cement floor as she walks over to me. "Happy Birthday." She gives me a hug.

"Wait! We're supposed to go clubbing after this." Olivia pouts. "Don't go."

"I have an early morning meeting." Celeste moves to Olivia and gives her an air kiss on each of her cheeks since Nick still has his arms wrapped around her waist. "We'll do lunch this week."

Then she makes her way back over to Jax and gives him a quick hug. "It was nice to see you again." She doesn't wait for him to respond before she's out the door.

"I'm going to make sure she gets into a cab safely," Nick says, letting go of Olivia and rushing after Celeste. When I look over to Jase, his eyes are trained on the door Celeste just exited through.

"All right, so who wants what?" Jax asks.

"I want a quote across my upper back, right below my neck," I say.

"And I want Nick's number tattooed above my ass," Olivia adds seriously.

"What?" I shriek. "No way! You're name isn't Haley, and you don't live in *Tree Hill!*"

Olivia turns around to face me with a huge grin splayed across her lips.

"Oh, thank God, you're joking." I sigh in relief. "Don't do that to me again!"

Olivia laughs. "C'mon, I totally had you there."

"Honestly, as much as you love that show, it wouldn't surprise me if you were serious."

"Kill, you getting anything?" Quinn asks.

"Nah, I think we'll keep it about the ladies tonight, but I do need to schedule a time to have some more of my sleeve done."

Nick walks back through the door. "All right, she's off." He smiles, but it almost looks sad. Olivia must notice because she goes over to him and asks if everything is okay.

"Yeah, I think so...Celeste wouldn't say much. She seemed upset she didn't know Jase worked here, but like I told her, I didn't even know they knew each other like that. Although, based on the way she hugged Jax—" his gaze lands hard on Jax "—it seems she knows the entire family more than she led on."

Quinn snorts. "Oh, we definitely know Celeste."

"Quinn, cool it," Jax chides.

Nick glances over to Jase. "Did something happen between you and Celeste the night of the party?" You can hear it in his tone, he's not being nosy. He's in big brother-slash-best friend mode.

"Nothing worth mentioning," Jase says coolly.

Nick gives him a long glance then nods, choosing to let it go. He turns his attention back to Olivia. "So, what are you thinking of getting? I remember you once mentioned putting my number above your ass." He waggles his eyebrows.

"Not happening," I tell him. "No friend of mine is getting a tramp stamp. Pick something else."

"That's what I'm talking about!" Quinn raises her hand for a high five. "If only I could say that to every other female who walks in here, asking for a unicorn above her ass."

"Hey, those unicorns helped pay your way through art school," Jax says.

"I still say a unicorn dies every time one is tattooed above a woman's ass." Quinn laughs.

"I'll go first," I offer. "I know exactly what I'm getting."

"Sounds good," Jase says, "You can come back with me."

"You better not take your crankiness out on me." I pin him with a glare.

Jax laughs. "Jase has been cranky his entire life. Well, except for when he was—"

"Enough," Jase says, cutting him off. His voice is deadly serious, but it only makes Jax grin.

"I want to watch!" Olivia says.

"You might change your mind once you hear that needle." Killian laughs.

"I gave birth to this guy's baby without any meds." Olivia points to Nick. "I'm sure I can handle a tattoo."

Everyone cracks up laughing, and Jase walks me to the third room on the right. "Write down the quote you want." He hands me a pen and paper. "Any particular font you were thinking of?"

"Well, it's from *Alice's Adventures in Wonderland,* so something fun, but not too childish. Surprise me."

"Okay." He grins wide. "I think I know the perfect one."

I hand him back the paper, and he reads the quote out loud. "I can't go back to yesterday because I was a different person then."

"Giselle, that's beautiful," Olivia says. "I remember when we read the book in our English class. You doodled the quote in your notebook for like a month."

"Everyone can stay, but you're going to have to take your shirt and bra off for the location you want," Jase says. "Go ahead and get undressed and shout once you're ready for me to come back in."

Everyone exits but Olivia, who looks upset. "What's wrong?" I ask her.

"Your quote is perfect and beautiful, and it made me realize I'm not sure what I want yet."

"We can wait," I tell her.

"No, I want you to get yours, and once I'm ready to get mine, will you come back with me?"

"Of course!" I give her a hug. "Thank you for making my birthday special."

I take my shirt and bra off and hand them to Olivia. Then I lay down on the leather chair face down. "Ready!" I call out.

"Okay, let's do this."

FOUR

KILLIAN

WE'RE SITTING in the VIP lounge in Provocative, an exclusive nightclub in the Lower West Side. With Celeste gone, it's just the four of us. Olivia is gushing over Giselle's new tattoo, and Nick, as usual, is gushing over Olivia simply being herself. I must admit I was shocked by the tattoo Giselle chose. Most women go for the cute and popular. Like Quinn said, the unicorns. Giselle's tattoo was deep. Although, it shouldn't surprise me. Giselle's actions seem to be throwing me off at every turn. I was stunned earlier tonight when I witnessed her get emotional over her ex-boyfriend showing up. I honestly didn't think she was capable of feeling anything other than what she feels for Olivia and Reed. Even when I took her to her mom's house, the entire time she was cold and withdrawn—dealing with the situation, but not appearing to be emotionally affected.

I'm beginning to think there are several different parts to Giselle, and maybe not all of them are so bad. I think back to Nick's description of her. Maybe she is just a Pitbull. One who is judged unfairly based on her looks, but isn't really as vicious as she appears. I know I've definitely judged her.

"It sucks Celeste isn't here, but since we have you both together, there's something Nick and I would like to talk to you two about," Olivia says. "Actually two things." She grins excitedly.

"Okay, shoot," I say, taking a sip of my water.

"As you know, Nick and I are planning to get married, and we've finally picked a date! We've decided to get married in June of this year!"

"Oh, Livi! That's only a few months away!" Giselle says.

"Yes!" Olivia agrees. "Also, Reed will be walking better, and football season will be well over so we can go on a honeymoon." She stops talking to give Nick a quick kiss before she continues. "We want a small, intimate wedding, and I would love it if you would be my maid-of-honor."

She hasn't even finished her sentence and Giselle is already leaping across the table and into Olivia's arms. "Yes! Yes! Yes!"

"And I'd like for you to be my best man," Nick adds. "But if you jump into my lap, I'm going to beat your ass."

"Awe, c'mere, good-looking." I shoot him a wink and stand. Nick shakes his head but stands to give me a hug. "Congratulations. I'm happy for you."

"Thanks, man."

"What's the second thing?" Giselle asks once we're seated again.

"We'd love it if the two of you would be Reed's godparents," Olivia says. "We can't imagine anyone else loving and caring for him the way you two do."

"Agreed," Nick says.

"Oh, Livi, you're killing me tonight!" Giselle hugs her friend once more, and when she sits back down, there are tears shining in her eyes. "I would be honored, even if it means sharing my godson with this guy." She nudges me with her elbow.

"I'd be honored," I tell both Olivia and Nick.

"Yay! Thank you!" Olivia squeals. "Oh! I love this song! Let's dance!" She pulls Nick out of his chair, and the two of them hit the dance floor, leaving Giselle and me at the table alone as Justin Bieber sings about not giving up on love.

"You didn't want to invite Roman out tonight?" I ask Giselle, and she glares. "What? I just figured you would invite the guy you're dating out to help celebrate your birthday." I shrug. I wasn't trying to piss her off. I really was just curious.

"Roman isn't exactly the going out to a club and getting a tattoo kind of guy," Giselle replies dryly, then takes a long sip of her Jack and Coke.

Speaking of tattoos... "Does the tattoo you got have a story behind it?" She eyes me warily, then finishes off her drink.

She sighs loudly. "It's from a book I read."

"Which book?" I ask, curious.

"*Alice's Adventures in Wonderland.*"

"The children's book?" I give her a confused look, trying to recall which book that is. I think it's the one with the little girl who falls down a rabbit hole.

"Yes," she sasses. "You would be surprised how deep the story is."

"Really?" I laugh. I've never read the book, but I've seen the movie once with my niece, and it's hard to imagine how deep the book could possibly be with talking animals.

"Every life and love lesson can be found in that story." She shrugs. "You should read it sometime."

The song changes and Giselle laughs humorlessly, shaking her head.

"Don't like this song?" I ask her.

"Are we playing twenty questions?" she snaps. I hold my palms up and she sighs again. "The song is just so fitting."

I listen to the words for a few seconds. I don't know who sings it, but it's a woman and she's singing about taking a guy home one last time even though another woman is in his heart. My eyes flit to Giselle who's frowning. She reaches over the table and grabs a shot of Johnnie Walker, downing it in one gulp then slamming it on the table.

"Have you ever cheated, Killian?" she asks. When I don't answer right away, she adds, "What? You can ask questions, but you can't answer them?" She reaches for another shot and downs it as fast as the last one.

"No," I say, answering her question, "I've never cheated."

She raises her eyebrows like she doesn't believe me, but after a few seconds, she shrugs and says, "I guess that makes sense. Rumor has it you don't do girlfriends. You can't cheat if you don't commit, right?" She reaches for the last shot, but I grab it first and shoot it back.

She glares daggers my way. "Real nice. I need to get going anyway." She stands and her body sways slightly from all the alcohol she's had to drink, so I stand as well, putting my arm out to help her.

"I don't need your help," she hisses. "I don't need anyone."

"Yeah, maybe not, but you've had quite a bit to drink. Why don't I let Olivia and Nick know we're leaving, and I'll take you home?"

She eyes me skeptically, but shocks me when she nods. "Okay, but only because I don't want them to have to leave because of me."

After I let Nick and Olivia know I'm going to get Giselle home, we head outside. Since we all rode in the limo tonight, I told Nick and Olivia they could take it home and I would call for a car service to take us home. I could call for a separate one for Giselle, but with the amount of alcohol she's consumed, I'd feel better making sure she gets inside safely myself.

The car pulls up and I open the door for Giselle. She slides in, and I go around to the other side to get in. I give the driver Giselle's address. The ride to her place is silent aside from the music playing on the radio. Giselle stares out the window, and I find myself staring at her reflection in the same window. A song comes on that catches my attention. It's upbeat...different...and the words hit me hard. I ask the driver to turn it up and he does. The guy is singing about being broken and lonely, but he isn't sad about it. He's reveling in the fact the girl he's with is just as broken and lonely. My gaze stays trained on Giselle. I can't be sure, but I'm almost positive a tear rolls down her cheek. It's hard to tell.

I glance down at her hand, and without thinking, reach for it. Her head swings my way, her glassy eyes meeting mine before she looks down at my hand covering hers. Intertwining our fingers, I pull her into my side. She stiffens but doesn't fight me as I wrap my arm around her shoulders and gently guide her head to my shoulder.

"Do you ever feel broken and lonely, Killian?" she asks softly.

"Every damn day," I admit. She looks up to meet my gaze and nods once.

"Me too," she whispers.

The car arrives at her place, and Giselle thanks me for helping her get home safely. When I offer to walk her up, she tells me she can handle it, then she leans over and gives me a chaste kiss on my cheek. As I watch her walk into her building, I can't help but wonder just how many layers of Giselle there are hidden deep down under the surface. And then I shock the hell out of myself when my next thought is that I'm pretty sure I want to see every one of those hidden layers.

***

"UNCLE KILLIAN, YOU'RE HERE!" My adorable niece, Julia,

flies down the steps and jumps into my awaiting arms. "I have a new princess movie. Can we watch it, please?" she begs.

"Not right now, kiddo," Dylan says before I can answer her. "Uncle Killian and I have business to discuss." My brother, Dylan, who is also my attorney, is all about business.

Julia pouts, and I pick her up and throw her into the air. "My goodness, I think you've gained ten pounds since the last time I was here."

"Not true." She giggles. "Do it again!" I throw her into the air one more time before I set her down.

"I think you're taller too." I tilt my head to the side. "How old are you now? Fifteen?" She giggles some more.

"No! I'm four, silly!"

"I could've sworn you were fifteen. Huh."

"Killian, congratulations on the win!" My brother's wife, Christina, gives me a kiss on my cheek.

"Thank you," I tell her. "Two down, two to go."

"You guys got this. Your brother cleared his schedule, so we'll be there cheering you on at the next game."

"Sounds good. How's little man doing?" I rub the top of her pregnant belly.

"He's content in there. The real question is, how am I doing? I'm ready for him to come out." She laughs.

"Only a couple more months, right?"

"Nine weeks, four days," she corrects me with another laugh. "Are you staying for dinner?"

"Of course. Julia and I have a new princess movie to watch, don't we?" I shoot a wink to my niece, who grins.

"Yes!" she squeals.

"Okay, go handle business with your brother. Dinner will be ready in about an hour." Her voice raises a beat louder to let my brother know that's all the time he has to hold me hostage.

"How's Nick doing?" Dylan asks, pouring us both a drink.

"He's good. He and Olivia picked a wedding date and asked me to be the best man. They're getting married in June."

"Good for them. We should all barbeque soon."

"For sure."

He hands me my drink. "All right, let's get down to business."

We spend the next hour going over several contracts, endorsement deals, my bills, and a few new investments I asked him to look into for me. He commends me on making smart choices with several investments that have made me a substantial profit. Going into my career I knew many professional athletes end up broke and filing for bankruptcy. I wanted to make sure I'm never in that situation. If my career were to end tomorrow, I need to know I'll be okay.

"Boys, dinner is ready," Christina yells from somewhere in the house.

"You heard the woman." I stand. "Dinner is ready."

"I think you use my wife for food," Dylan accuses light-heartedly.

"Hell yes, I do," I admit as we head to the dining room. "You know I can't cook, and your wife can."

"Maybe it's time you got a wife of your own," Dylan says with a laugh. He sits down at the table next to his wife, and I sit next to Julia, who is already munching on her chicken nuggets.

"Your date to the party the other night was pretty," Christina says.

"Who?" I ask, placing a piece of lasagna onto my plate and grabbing a roll.

"Well, I guess that answers the question I was about to ask..." Christina rolls her eyes. "If there's a chance she's someone serious." She makes my brother a plate of food and hands it to him before she makes herself one.

"I went to a birthday thing for Olivia's best friend, Giselle, the other night. I wasn't sure if maybe the paparazzi got pictures." I cut up my food then take a bite.

"I was referring to the woman you had on your arm at your endorsement party for that car." She's talking about Tabitha.

"Being as she was rented for the night, I don't think it's anything serious." I shoot Christina a wink, and her eyes go wide.

"You paid for a hooker," she whisper-yells. "Killian!"

"She's not a hooker." I laugh nervously, immediately regretting I said anything. "She's an escort."

"What's an escort?" Julia asks, reminding us of her presence.

"Nobody, sweetie," Dylan says. "Are you all done eating your nuggets?"

"Yes! Can I get the movie ready for me and Uncle Killian?"

"Sure, go ahead," my brother says. Being as they never let Julia leave the table before everyone is done eating, I know I'm about to get shit from him.

Sure enough, as soon as Julia has skipped out of the room, he glares my way. "Bro, you can't seriously think it's okay to hire an escort. Do you know how bad this would look if it gets out?"

"One, Amber handles it for me. It's done through my personal account and it's all handled properly. It's not like I picked her up on the street corner. The women have to sign NDAs and everything. You'd be surprised how many celebrities use escorts for different events."

"How did it come to this, Kill? How did you become the guy who rents women instead of trying to meet one the right way?" My brother gives me a concerned look. "I'm not judging you," he adds. "I'm just trying to understand. If I recall, you dated a few girls in high school, right? And several in college? What happened that scared you from settling down?"

I know he's not going to let this go until I give him something, but at the same time, I've never spoken about what happened in college. Just thinking about it has me feeling all types of shit I don't want to deal with.

"I'm not the same person I was back then." My words make me think of Giselle's quote, and it has me wondering if maybe she is the way she is because of something that's happened in her past. "I'm a professional athlete, Dylan. Every woman I meet I wonder if she's with me for my money or because I'm in the NFL. I've met women who've straight up told me they just want to fuck me." I lower my voice to make sure Julia can't hear me. "The truth is I don't know how to meet a nice woman that I'm one hundred percent sure doesn't have a hidden agenda."

I shrug and take a bite of my food. Once I swallow and take a sip of my water, I add, "I guess I just sort of gave up."

"Well, you aren't going to find a nice woman with no agenda through an escort service." Dylan quirks a brow up. "I get it, I do. I work with dozens of guys in the same situation as you. I write up their prenups, and then soon after, I help file their divorce papers." He frowns. "But you can't give up, Kill. You're thirty-one years old and you've never even had a serious girlfriend that I know of."

"I agree, Killian," Christina says. "What about letting me set you up with a friend of mine?" Christina, at one time, was an international supermodel who retired when she got pregnant, wanting to be home with her family. "I think the key is to find someone who is in a similar situation as yours, with her own money, but is also a good person."

I laugh. "Good luck with that."

"Is that a yes?" Christina beams with hope.

"Sure, why not?" I take another bite of my food.

"Yes! You boys do the dishes. I need to start scrolling through my friends list."

FIVE

GISELLE

"I'LL TAKE the BLT Club sandwich with sweet potato fries and a side of fruit. Thank you." Olivia smiles at the server, who writes everything down before he looks at me.

"And for you, ma'am?"

"Just a house salad, please. Ranch on the side." The waiter nods and thanks us, then leaves to another table.

"That's it?" Olivia's brows furrow. "You're not on a diet, are you? You look amazing." She hands Reed, who is sitting in his high chair, a toy to play with.

"I'm not that hungry." The truth is I know I'll be going on a date tonight, which means I won't have to pay for whatever we eat while we're out, so I'd rather wait until then to eat. Every dollar counts right now, and since I'm not about to let my best friend pay for my meal, I need to be careful.

"How's the charity event coming?" I ask, changing the subject. Olivia and Nick have decided to take Nick's current charity organization, Touchdown for Reading, and expand it to Touchdown for Reading and the Arts, since Olivia's passion is art. She even works part-time at a children's museum as their Art Education Coordinator.

"So good!" she gushes. "Almost everyone who was invited has RSVP'd, and those who said they can't make it, have made generous donations that will go a long way with all of our plans. You're coming, right?"

"Yeah." I nod as I try to think of a way to get out of it. "Just send me an invite to my email and I'll add it to my calendar."

"Why did you frown?" Olivia asks, handing Reed his sippy cup and some Goldfish. Only my best friend can be taking care of her one-year-old son and notice my hidden emotions. She's like Superwoman.

"I didn't," I deny.

"Yes, you did," she pushes, and I sigh in defeat.

"Look Livi, you know I support everything you do, but the entire purpose of this charity event is to get donations, right?"

"Right...and to announce the expansion."

"Tell me someone who couldn't make it."

"Umm...Nathan Fillion. He's a huge New York Brewers fan."

"The guy from *Castle*?" I'm almost positive my jaw hits the table. This is even worse than I thought.

"Yeah, he actually has a non-profit organization which provides books to children who can't afford them."

"And how much did he donate because he can't make it?"

"Fifty thousand," she says nonchalantly, like fifty thousand dollars is no big deal. She grabs a bib from Reed's diaper bag and places it around his neck.

"Livi, how much does everyone have to pay per plate?"

"Ten thousand." She pops open the top of Reed's baby food then freezes, looking up at me. "Wait a second. Is that why you're upset? You think I'm going to expect you to pay that? You're my best friend, Giselle!" She frowns in confusion. "I know you don't have that kind of money."

"Well, someone is paying it."

Olivia's mouth opens then closes as she carefully considers how she's going to word whatever she's about to say, but I don't give her a chance to speak first.

"Either you're paying for my spot, or you're giving me a plate for free, which is it?"

"I paid for your plate." I open my mouth to argue, but she holds up her hand. "It's for a good cause, and really, if I'm honest, I did it with selfish intentions. I need my best friend there. Nick will be busy with everyone, and I was hoping you would be there to keep me company." Her eyes are pleading, and I let out a defeated sigh. It's not like I'm going to say no to anything she asks of me, even if it's a reminder of how one-sided our friendship is.

"Okay, I'll be there." I force a smile on my face, mentally reminding myself to seriously look into putting my mom's house up for sale. It was one thing to live with Olivia in college. I was able to somewhat pay my way with the loans I took out. And when we moved here, she thought she would be raising Reed alone, so I justified living with her so I could help out. But now that Nick is in the picture and they're going to get married and start a life together soon, I need to get myself together. It's not fair to our friendship to continue to take advantage of my best friend's generosity.

"Thank you." Olivia grins as she feeds Reed a bite of sweet peas.

The waiter comes over and sets our food down in front of us. We eat our lunch, and when we're done, we go our separate ways. Me, back to Fresh Designs for a new client consultation, and Olivia, to drop Reed off with her stepmom, Corrinne, so she can watch Reed for a few hours while Olivia goes to the Children's Museum.

***

"MOM, DEDRA?" I call out when I walk into my mom's house and don't see anyone in the living room.

"In here, Giselle," Dedra, my mom's nurse, calls out from down the hall.

I throw my purse onto the counter and check the time on my cell phone before stuffing it into my back pocket. It's already a quarter after four and I have a date I need to be ready for by seven. I should've been here hours ago, but the consultation with Lydia and the new client ran way over the scheduled time. He's a wealthy commercial developer, which means he's very opinionated. Normally that quality would be great because opinionated people tend to know exactly what they want. However, this man isn't one of those people. He's hired Fresh Designs to decorate his new eight thousand square foot skyrise that he's had completely renovated. And while he had tons of opinions throughout our meeting, he couldn't make up his mind on a single thing.

Then, of course, the subway I take to my mom's house had mechanical issues and everyone was forced to take a detour route, which meant an additional forty-five minutes on the subway.

"Hey, sorry I'm late," I tell her as I walk into my mom's room. She's lying in bed in a fetal position with tears flowing down her face. "How's she doing?" I ask Dedra, who frowns at my question.

"Why don't we talk in the other room?" she suggests. I come

around to the side of the bed and give my mom a kiss on her forehead.

"Giselle, you're here," she cries. "I've missed you so much." My mom snakes her arms around my neck and pulls me into a hug. "Please don't leave me," she begs, and my heart fissures.

"I'm just going right outside to talk to Dedra. I'll be right back. I promise." I press my lips to her forehead once more before removing her arms from around me and stepping into the hallway.

"These meds seem to keep her anger subsided, but now she's sunken into a deep depression." Dedra sighs. "I'm afraid to leave her here alone, Giselle."

"Okay." I try to do the math in my head of what it will cost to hire another nurse for the hours Dedra won't be here. I've been getting more hours, but paying Adrianna's tuition severely depleted my funds. And I still need to pay her sorority dues and meal ticket, which will set me back a good amount.

"I have a friend of mine who's a retired nurse like me," Dedra says. "She can use the extra money to supplement her social security. I can speak to her about spending a few days a week here."

"That would be great. Thank you." I give Dedra a hug. "I've actually been thinking about putting the house up for sale. If I can make enough on it, I can use the money to get my own place in the city, so she can live with me." Of course, that will mean having to find my father so he can sign off on the sale.

"I know this is a lot, dear. You're already working too many hours. Just take it one day at a time. You are a wonderful daughter." Dedra smiles warmly. "And a wonderful sister."

"Sometimes it doesn't feel that way." Tears leak from my eyes. "Sometimes it feels like I'm really sucking at life," I admit aloud, suddenly feeling like everything that's piled on my shoulders is just too much to handle, and it's all about to come crashing down around me.

"This is a lot to deal with. You are only human."

"Thank you. I'm going to spend some time with my mom before I need to head back."

I head back inside my mom's room and spend the next hour with her. She's momentarily stopped crying while we watch some of her favorite shows she's recorded. When 5:30 hits, I have to go. I'm already going to be cutting it way too close as it is. I give my mom and Dedra a hug with a promise to visit soon. When my mom cries, begging me to stay, I consider it, but then remember I have a date tonight I can't miss. On my way out, I grab the bills on the counter I need to pay since my dad stopped paying them the day he walked out on my mom, and lock the door behind me.

The subway is thankfully on schedule, and I make it home with twenty minutes to get ready. Throwing my hair up so I don't get it wet, I shower quickly, extremely thankful I recently got everything waxed. I get dressed into a cute ivory cold-shoulder lace dress and throw on a pair of brown leather pumps. After switching out my everyday purse for a matching clutch, I head out of my room.

"Hey!" Olivia says, "I didn't realize you were home!" Her eyes skate over my outfit. "Going out?"

"Umm...yeah, I have a date." I smile hesitantly, praying she doesn't give me the third degree about where I'm going and who I'm going with. I'm already running late as it is.

"Okay, well, have a good night," she says, shocking the crap out of me.

"You too."

After walking three blocks to the corner, I find the limo waiting for me. The driver opens the door for me, and sitting inside is my date, Andrew Parker. It's our first date, but I've done my research. One of Manhattan's top financial moguls and on Forbes's list of top thirty under thirty wealthiest men. He's staring at his phone, but once I scoot in next to him, he lifts his eyes and grins, politely putting his phone away.

"You look beautiful," he says smoothly, leaning over and giving my cheek a chaste kiss. "Thank you for joining me this evening."

"You're very welcome," I say while checking him out. With a shaved head, dark brown eyes, and a strong jawline, he almost looks like a bad boy instead of a billionaire. That is until you get to his expensive suit, which probably cost more than my parents' house, and the TAG Heuer watch he's sporting, which is more than likely the price of a vehicle I can't afford. I look closely and notice a bit of a tattoo peeking out from under his dress shirt. *More like reformed bad boy.*

We arrive at the movie premiere at AMC Lincoln Square. Andrew explains that one of the umbrella companies he owns has invested some money into the film, which is why we're here. We walk the red carpet and make our way into the theatre. Andrew is stopped a few times along the way, but it's when he's stopped by one person in particular my heart just about jumps out of my chest. This seriously can't be happening.

"Andrew! How are you doing?" Killian says, shaking my date's hand.

"I'm doing well. It's good to see you. Making time to see a movie in the middle of the playoffs?" Andrew jokes.

"I figured it was the perfect way to impress my date." Killian looks over to the beautiful woman on his arm. "This is Rochelle."

"Nice to meet you." Andrew nods and places his fingers against the swell of my back. "This is Giselle, my date. We were just heading inside. Why don't you two join us?"

"Oh, I'm sure—" I begin to protest, but Killian speaks over me.

"We would love to."

The next three hours are spent with Killian shooting daggers my way while I ignore them and pretend he doesn't exist. I couldn't even tell you what the hell the movie was about, and I'm thankful when Andrew tells me he has an early meeting tomorrow, so he unfortunately has to call it a night directly after the premiere party.

SIX

KILLIAN

"THANK YOU, THANK YOU, THANK YOU!" Olivia hugs me for the third time. "I would normally ask Giselle to babysit, but well... she's been kind of busy lately, and Corrinne and my dad are having a date night."

"So, pretty much I'm your only option," I say dryly, and Nick chuckles.

"What? No!" Olivia shakes her head.

"Liv, he's joking," Nick says. "I'm going to set out some snacks and a drink for when Reed wakes up, and then we'll go." He gives her a kiss on her forehead before he heads into the kitchen.

"We'll only be gone a couple hours. We have to meet with the party planner to finalize all the details for the charity event. She called and said she needed to reschedule last minute."

"No problem. I would've just been hanging out at home anyway."

"I saw you're bringing a date." Olivia grins. "Is it the woman you were spotted with at the movie premiere?"

"No, she was nice, but we didn't really have much in common," I say, cursing my sister-in-law for setting me up with a woman who's recently divorced and still in the 'I hate all men because my ex-husband cheated on me' stage of mourning.

"Oh, that's too bad. Giselle seems to have the same problem.

The woman dates more than anyone I know, which is the complete opposite of how she used to be, yet she seems to find flaws in every guy she's with." Olivia shrugs.

"How did she used to be?" I ask in an even voice, hoping I sound nonchalant.

"For the entire six years we lived together in Paris, she maybe went on a handful of dates. The only thing I can think of is that she was pining for Christian the entire time. But then we moved back here, they got together, and he turned out to be a cheating asshole." She scrunches up her nose in disgust. "Maybe she's just done pining. I don't really know." She shakes her head. "Giselle doesn't really talk to me anymore." The corners of her lips turn down into a frown. She's obviously worried about Giselle.

"All right," Nick says as he walks out of the kitchen. "Snacks are on the counter. Juice is in the fridge. Here's his monitor so you can hear him." He hands me a walkie-talkie looking thing. "I appreciate you coming over to Liv's place last minute. Waking Reed up early from a nap is the equivalent of poking a bear in hibernation."

What's up with this guy and comparing everyone to animals? "You've poked a bear?" I ask with a laugh.

"No, but I can imagine what it's like. Scary as fuck and has you running the other way in fear for your life."

"Bro, he's only a year old." I laugh harder.

"It doesn't matter." Nick shakes his head then glances over to Olivia. "Brown-Eyes, tell him."

Olivia nods in agreement. "Yep, scary."

When I give them a doubtful look, unable to imagine Reed as anything other than adorable, Olivia adds, "Trust me, you don't want to find out."

"No worries," I tell them. "I'm just going to watch some TV while he sleeps. Take your time. We'll be here. It's all good."

Olivia and Nick head out, and I throw myself onto the couch, flipping through the channels. Practice today was brutal and I'm exhausted, but it was a damn good practice. I'm confident that if we play the way we practiced today, we'll have a good shot at beating New England this weekend. And if we do, we're in the Super Bowl. I stretch my legs and flinch at how sore I am. I don't know how Nick does it. He comes home from a grueling practice and jumps right into family-mode.

I feel my eyes begin to droop, so I stand and head into the kitchen to make myself a cup of coffee. The last thing I need is to fall asleep while babysitting. Olivia would come home and murder me in my sleep. Reed waking up early would be the least of my concerns. The coffee is brewing, when I hear the door open, and a few seconds later Giselle is standing in front of me.

"What are you doing here?" She has her hands on her hips.

"Babysitting."

Her brows furrow in confusion. "Where's Olivia?"

"She had a last-minute meeting with the event planner for the charity event."

She scoffs. "So she asked you instead of me?"

"Apparently you're too busy working your way down the most recent Forbes list of the wealthiest bachelors, so Olivia called me."

Giselle's purses her lips together and shoots me a glare. "You know what, fuck you," she hisses. "You don't know shit about me."

"I've seen enough to know you're a gold-digger." I shrug.

"Wow! You just love to throw that label around. First Celeste, now me."

"If the shoe fits...What are you doing exactly? Trying to figure out who your best option is, so you're prepared once your best friend finally puts herself before you and moves in with her fiancé?"

Grabbing my cup of coffee, I pour some milk into it and stir, then head back into the living room to sit down. Giselle, of course, follows behind, her heels click-clacking against the hardwood floor.

"What the hell is that supposed to mean?" she asks. "Nick and Olivia are taking things slow."

"Oh, c'mon, you can't be that dense." I take a sip of my coffee. "Nick has been begging her for damn near a year to move in with him! You think either of them want to bounce their son back and forth between homes? You think Olivia, the queen of fairytales, wants to wait months to marry her fucking prince?"

Giselle frowns. "She never said anything..."

"Of course she hasn't. She doesn't want to leave her best friend homeless."

"I didn't know," she murmurs.

"Well now you do."

Her phone's alarm goes off, and she pulls it from her purse. "Shit, I need to go."

"Another date?" I shake my head. "You should hang out with Celeste more. You two have a lot in common." I laugh. "Although—" I snap my fingers "—she's at least finally standing on her own two feet instead of leeching off her best friend."

Giselle flinches. "I gotta go," she whispers. "As always, it was great seeing you." She turns her back on me and heads down the hallway.

I take another sip of my coffee, *almost* feeling bad for what I said. But the truth is, everything I said is fact. It probably wasn't my place to point it all out, but how could she not have known that's why Olivia is still refusing to buy a home with Nick.

About thirty minutes later, Giselle comes out, dressed in a tight black dress and black fuck-me heels. Her hair, which was down in waves, is now pin straight, and her makeup is a bit darker. And in her arms is Reed, who is smiling and babbling like crazy at her.

"He was sitting up in his crib, so I grabbed him." She hands him over to me. "I changed his diaper."

"I didn't hear anything," I say, holding up the monitor.

"That's because you never turned it on." Giselle grabs the monitor and clicks it on, then hands it back to me. "Goodbye, my little love muffin. Be very bad for Uncle Killian." She glares at me then gives him a kiss on his cheek.

"Have fun on your date." I smirk. Giselle rolls her eyes, grabs her purse, and heads for the door. "Oh, wait, I forgot to ask you..." She stops in her place but doesn't turn around. "What number is this guy on Forbes's list?"

She swings the door open, flicks me off, then slams it closed. Guess she didn't like my question.

SEVEN

GISELLE

"IF THEY CAN GET this touchdown, they will be in the Super Bowl," Olivia tells me for the hundredth time in the last two hours. I don't call her out on it, though. She's just nervous. She paces across the room in the friends and family suite we're currently in. Reed toddles over to her and pulls on her jersey. She lifts him up so he can see the field and talks to him as if he knows what's going on. Everybody else is more or less quiet, watching down below as the New York Brewers huddle. The team breaks and gets into forma-tion. The score is tied with less than a minute left on the clock.

When I walk up next to her, Reed leans over and I take him in my arms. Olivia's eyes never leave the field as she watches Nick call the play. The players scramble, and Nick looks for an opening. Killian runs to the left and is open, but as Nick cocks his arm back to throw the ball, he's tackled. The ball falls to the ground and New England gets it.

There are collective sighs and several people in the suite curse. New England has the ball now, and if they score, New York won't be going to the Super Bowl. The players are walking off the field, and that's when I notice Nick is still down.

"Oh no," Olivia gasps. We watch as Killian kneels next to Nick. We can't hear what's being said, though. A second later the medic runs out with the coaches.

"Oh god, please no." Olivia's eyes meet mine. "He's grabbing his arm." Tears pool in her eyes. Reed reaches for his mom, but I hold him close. She's shaking, on the verge of freaking out.

"I need to get down there," she tells me. Then she turns toward her stepmom, Corrine. "He's hurt."

"Let's just give him a minute," Dylan tells her. Everyone watches in silence, until the gurney is brought out, and that's when we know it's game over.

"Go," I tell Olivia. "I have Reed."

"Thank you." She gives her son a kiss. "Mommy will be right back. I love you." Then she takes off out of the suite, along with Dylan, his wife, and Corrine.

A few minutes later it's announced that Nick Shaw will not be back in the game. New England has the ball. They score and New York is out of the playoffs.

NICK HAS BEEN in with the doctors for the last hour. Corrine took Reed back to her place since it's well after his bedtime and he was getting cranky. Olivia is sitting quietly in her seat, her eyes glued to the door, waiting for a doctor to come out so she can go back and see her fiancé. She's trying so hard to remain calm, but I know my best friend, and she's freaking the hell out on the inside. When she first met Nick, he was recovering from a shoulder injury and wasn't sure if he would ever play again—let alone come back to win a Super Bowl.

"Any news?" Killian asks, walking over and sitting next to Olivia. His hair is still damp from the shower. He's in a New York Brewers hoodie and sweatpants. He must've come straight from the stadium. A few other players sit down as well but keep their distance. Everyone wants to know how Nick is doing.

"No, the doctors are in with him," Olivia says, her voice strained from holding in her emotions. "They called my dad and Declan back about twenty minutes ago." Declan Thomas is the owner of the Brewers. When the owner is involved, it can't be good.

Killian wraps his arm around Olivia and her head lulls to the side, landing on his shoulder. "It's going to be okay," he murmurs. His eyes come up and meet mine. I shift in my seat as I remember what it felt like to be comforted by a man. When Christian and I were together, he would hold me for hours while I cried over my mom. He would tell me everything would be okay. He was wrong, though. Nothing is okay. Killian gives me a small, sad smile, and I find myself smiling back.

"Olivia Harper," someone calls out, and we all stand. It's a woman dressed in scrubs. Maybe a nurse. "Nick is asking for you. You can follow me."

Olivia nods silently then turns to Killian. "As soon as I can, I'll text you or come and get you."

She follows the nurse back. For the next hour everyone waits in silence. It's late and the waiting room is quiet. The door finally opens again, and Olivia and her dad walk out. Her eyes are puffy from crying but she forces a watery smile.

Killian and I both stand at the same time and meet her halfway across the waiting room. "You can go see him," she tells Killian, who doesn't waste a second before heading back.

"How is he?" I ask.

"He's going to make an announcement. He's retiring. It's his same arm and he would need surgery again. He doesn't want to go down that road for a second time. He wants to go back to school to study Literature. It's a dream he's had since he was little." Tears fall down her cheeks. "He wants to write a novel." She sniffles.

"Why are you crying?" I ask as I pull her into my arms for a hug.

"I don't know," she sobs. "I'm just being emotional." She cries harder through her laughter and I join in until we're both laughing so hard tears are streaming down both of our cheeks. Neither of us having the slightest clue as to why we're laughing or crying.

"I'm going to stay here with him," she finally says once she's composed herself.

"Okay, love you." I give her another hug. "If you need anything, please let me know."

I exit the hospital and grab a cab home. After showering the day off me, I climb into bed and snuggle into my blankets. My thoughts go to Killian and the way he held Olivia. It was nothing more than a friend comforting a friend. But it allowed me to see a different side of him. He might be an asshole to me and Celeste, but it's obvious that there's a softer, sweeter side to him he only allows certain people to witness.

EIGHT

GISELLE

"I'M SORRY, Giselle. I've tried to find another nurse for tonight but haven't had any luck," Dedra says through the phone. "It's Paula's night off and she's not answering her phone." Paula is the night nurse I've had to hire so my mom is taken care of around the clock. It meant adding more to my endlessly growing pile of bills, but it was necessary. Hopefully the house will sell quickly, and then I can use that money to pay off some debt and get my own place for my mom and me. I put the house up for sale a few weeks ago—after Killian pointed out what I already knew—that it's time I stop depending on Olivia and handle my shit—and we've already had quite a few people interested. No offers yet, but it only takes one.

At first when I told my mom the house was being put up for sale, she called me a selfish bitch and kicked me out, but a few days later, I was shocked when she called and told me she's excited to be moving out. She's actually been in a great mood lately. Gardening in her backyard and talking about not needing my father and being ready to move forward. I think the meds she's on are finally working. Of course I've said that before and then they stopped. The problem now, however, is when I tried to schedule for her to see the psychiatrist to get a refill, I found out my father's insurance had been canceled. And when I called his job to speak to him about it, I was told he no longer works there. *Of course he doesn't!*

So now getting my mom new health insurance has been added to my list of things I need to purchase once I have the money. I spoke to one insurance agent, but with my mom's medical history, I was quoted ten thousand for the year. It's going to have to happen soon, though, because she can't get off her meds, especially since right now they seem to be working.

"It's not your fault," I tell Dedra. "Of course you need to be there for the birth of your grandchild." My phone beeps with an incoming call. It's my sister. I unlock the door and throw my purse down on the counter. "I just got home. I'm packing a bag, and I will be over there soon. Go ahead and go. Congratulations, Grandma!"

"Thank you, sweetie."

We say goodbye, and I throw my phone onto the counter, frustrated that I need to be in so many places at once and I can't do it all. Just as the phone hits the granite, it starts to ring again, the sound sending me over the edge I didn't know I was standing so close to. "Fuck! Stop ringing!" I yell out loud, begging my phone to silence. When it doesn't stop, my hand swipes at the offending device and it flies through the air, hitting the wood floor. It goes quiet for a second but then starts up again.

I walk around and pick it up, seriously contemplating shoving it into the garbage disposal, when Olivia makes her presence known.

"What did that phone ever do to you?" she jokes, but I can hear it in her voice, she's concerned.

"I can't make it to the charity event tonight. I'm sorry." The phone starts to ring again. This time it's Bianca. I send it to voicemail and silence my ringer.

"Is this about the cost of the plate? Because—"

"No!" I snap. "I need to go see my mom. She needs to have someone there with her at all times and Dedra's daughter is having a baby. And the other nurse isn't answering her phone. They can't find another nurse last minute, and even if they could, it would cost a damn fortune! She just lives so far! I can't be everywhere at once! Once I sell her house and move her into an apartment with me it will make things a lot easier." My mouth finally stops moving as I pause to take a deep breath. My mind plays back everything I just said, and I quickly realize—too late, of course—I just word-vomited all over Olivia.

She stares at me for a second, clearly shocked I just told her more about my life in those fifteen seconds than I have in the last year. "You put your parents' house up for sale? You never mentioned that." Olivia shifts Reed on her hip, but he squirms wanting down, so she sets him on the floor. He crawls over to his toys and starts to play.

"It's no big deal." I wave her off.

"Umm...yeah, it is. You grew up in that home."

"It is what it is." I nod toward my room. "I need to go pack a bag to take to my mom's. I'm really sorry I can't make it tonight." I start to head to my room when Olivia calls my name.

"You know I'm here for you, right?"

"Of course," I say, turning around and plastering a fake smile on my face.

"Just because I'm with Nick doesn't mean you're not still my best friend." My thoughts go back to what Killian said about her putting me before Nick, and the words are out before I can take them back.

"Actually, Livi, that's exactly what it means," I say honestly. "And that's how it should be. Things have changed. You had a baby, and you're engaged to be married. I'm no longer your problem to deal with."

"Why would you say that? You've never been a problem. You're my best friend."

"Why haven't you moved in with Nick yet?"

"I told you we're taking things slow."

"No, you're not. You're only living here because I told you I wouldn't live here without you if you moved, and you know I can't afford to live in the city on what my internship pays me." My voice elevates with frustration, and Olivia flinches.

"I don't mind keeping the place for you."

"I mind!" I yell a beat too loudly, then lower my voice so I don't upset Reed. "I mind you paying for a place for me to live when you won't even be here. It's not your job to take care of me."

"I love you." She sniffles. "I don't know what I've done wrong, but I can't fix it if you don't tell me." Tears fall down her cheeks, and I hate myself for being the cause of her crying.

"You didn't do anything wrong." I step toward her as the front door opens and in walks Nick.

He takes one look at Olivia and glares my way. "What the hell is going on?"

"Nothing," Olivia says, placing her hand on Nick's chest to calm him down.

"It doesn't look like nothing. It looks like you're crying," Nick says to Olivia, then he looks at me. "What's going on?"

"I was just telling Olivia that I've put my mom's house up for sale, so if all goes well, I'll be moved out soon." The last thing I want is for my best friend's future husband to think I'm leeching off her. For Killian to make those comments, words must've been spoken between him and Nick.

"Unnecessarily," Olivia says through her sobs. Nick wraps his one good arm around her waist in a comforting and protective manner, and my heart squeezes as I wish, not for the first time, I had someone to hold me like that.

"We both know if I wasn't living here, you guys would already be married and living together." I look at Nick to deny it, and he frowns but doesn't say a word.

"I asked you to move back here and Nick understands that." Olivia steps out of Nick's hold. "I know something is up with you, but you won't let me in. I haven't once asked you to move out or even indicated I want you to. So can you please tell me why you're pushing me away?"

"I'm not pushing you away. I'm just so sick of our friendship being one-sided."

"One-sided? You don't think I've been a good friend?" Of course she would jump to that conclusion!

"No! One-sided meaning me! What have I done in this friend-ship? You've paid my way for the last seven years. You take me out for my birthdays and buy me expensive gifts for the holidays. You even have to pay for my ticket to your charity event because I can't afford it. Meanwhile, what have I ever done for you?" I throw my hands in the air in defeat and blink back my tears, willing them not to come. "Nothing! I've done nothing! And to top it off, I'm the reason why you haven't gotten your happily-ever-after!"

"Are you serious?" Olivia questions. "You were the one who pushed me not to run when I got scared. You're the reason I got my happily-ever-after. And as far as our friendship goes...When I was lonely and lost in Paris, *you* befriended me. *You* let me cry on your shoulder for months over my mother's death," she says. "And then when I was dumped by my cheating ex, it was *you* who ran away with me to New York." She swipes at her falling tears. "When I found out I was pregnant and thought nothing would ever be okay again, you held me in your arms on the floor of the bathroom and promised me it would be."

The tears I was holding back finally fall.

"And even though you hate New York, when I said I wanted to move home, you packed up your stuff without saying a word." Olivia steps forward until she's directly in front of me. "No amount of money could ever pay for the friendship you've given me. Having you in my life is worth a thousand times more than anywhere I pay for us to live, or whatever gift I buy, or the ticket I purchase for you for a stupid dinner. It's just money."

A humorless laugh escapes me. "It's *just* money to someone like you. It's *everything* to someone like me who doesn't have any."

"Is that what this is about?" Olivia asks. "Do you need money? Did something happen? I can help you. Just let me in."

My eyes widen at her words, shocked that after everything I just said, her answer is to offer me money. Having no clue how to even respond to what she said, I turn to walk away.

"I'm sorry!" Olivia grabs my hand. "I didn't mean it like that. I just—I don't know how to fix this! Tell me how to fix this, please. I just want my best friend back."

"You can't, and even if you could, I wouldn't let you." I let out an exhausted sigh. "Look, I'm sorry I've been so distant lately. I'm working a lot and taking care of my mom and sister. It's not you. I'm not moving out because I'm mad at you. Like I said before, it's something I need to do for my mom. I appreciate everything you've done for me, but it's time I stand on my own two feet."

"Wait a second," Nick cuts in. "Did Killian say something to you?" I shake my head, and Nick gives me a hard stare, silently telling me not to lie. "Damn it, he did, didn't he?"

"It doesn't matter if he did or didn't," I tell him, because it doesn't. Everything Killian said was the truth. "Look, you guys have an event to get ready for, and I need to get to my mom's."

I give Olivia a hug. "I love you, Livi."

She hugs me back. "This conversation isn't over," she murmurs into my ear.

I nod once then retreat to my bedroom to get packed. My phone vibrates for the millionth time. When I glance at the screen, it shows it's Bianca calling again.

"Hello." I nestle the phone between my ear and shoulder while I grab a change of clothes and stuff them into my overnight bag.

"I've called you a dozen times."

"I'm sorry. My mom's nurse—"

"Giselle," Bianca snaps, "I'm too busy to listen to your latest sob story. That's what you have friends for. I was calling because I'm going to need you to come in tonight."

I stop in my place. "I can't tonight." I squeeze my eyes shut as I wait for Bianca to yell at me.

"Then you're fired," she says in a calm voice which tells me she's serious.

"Bianca..."

"You can go afterward. I only need you for a few hours."

"Okay." I let out a frustrated sigh. "What time?"

"A driver will be there to pick you up at your usual spot in thirty minutes. It's black tie. I've sent you all the info you will need. Also, if it helps, because of it being last minute, you will be paid double." She hangs up without a goodbye.

I finish packing and get dressed. The place is quiet, which means Olivia and Nick must've already left to the charity function. They're bringing Reed with them, and once he's tired, Olivia's stepsister, Shelby, is going to take him home. I hate that I can't be there for her tonight, especially since she spent all that money on my plate just so I could go.

After I step out of the elevator and head down the street, I call my mom to check on her, but she doesn't pick up. I leave her a voicemail to let her know I will be by in a few hours to see her. When I see the limo parked and waiting for me, I tell her I love her and will see her soon.

I approach the vehicle and notice the driver is someone I've never seen before. And then it hits me that in my rush I didn't check the info, so I have no clue who I'm going on a date with.

"Good evening, ma'am." The driver bows slightly and smiles. I smile back before lifting my cocktail dress up slightly and sliding into the backseat. The door closes behind me, and I look to my right to see my date for the evening. Dark brown hair—thick and lustrous with blazing hazel eyes. His skin is flawless, and his face is strong and defined with prominent cheek-bones. My gaze goes to his soft, sharp lips which are turned down in a scowl. He's wearing an expensive suit that molds his body like it was made just for him, and it probably was. His tie is emerald green and gold. It brings out the tiny flecks of green in his eyes. It's also the colors of the New York Brewers, which makes perfect sense, since the man wearing the tie is the receiver for that very same team.

My eyes glide back up and meet his, and his scowl deepens. "What the hell are you doing in my limo?"

"Apparently I'm your date."

NINE

KILLIAN

WHAT IS SHE DOING HERE? In a shimmery silver dress and matching heels, why is Giselle Winters sitting next to me inside my limo? When Bianca, the owner of A Touch of Class, called my assistant an hour ago and said there was an issue with the escort who was supposed to be my date, she assured her that she would have someone else for me. My assistant notified me we would need to pick her up in Brooklyn Heights instead of in SoHo. I told her to forward the info to my driver. I was going through my emails on my phone when the limo driver parked, so I had no clue we were stopped only about four blocks from where Giselle and Olivia live. And I never imagined when the door opened who would be stepping into my limo.

"What the hell are you doing in my limo?" I ask way too harshly. But I can't help it. The woman has been on my mind way too often lately, and being forced to spend an entire evening with her won't help.

"Apparently I'm your date," she slings back with a glare. "Who would've thought Killian Blake would resort to paying for a woman?"

"Who would've thought Giselle Winters would resort to whoring herself out?" Giselle's face falls, and I regret my words. "I'm sorry," I say. "That was uncalled for."

"It's the truth." She shrugs, opening the door. "I'm a whore...just like Tabitha...you know, the woman you paid to accompany you to your event not long ago. But I bet you didn't call her a whore." Oh, shit! Now it makes sense. How Tabitha knew Giselle. They both work for the same escort service.

"I'll call Bianca and see if she can find you someone else... Someone who is less of a whore. I didn't know you were my client." She steps outside and closes the door behind her.

Flinging my door open, I go around to her side. She's dialing a number. I snatch the phone out of her hand before she can make the call. "Look, I'm sorry for what I said. The woman I was going to take didn't work out. Then the date I hired had to cancel. I'm pretty sure you're my only option."

"Great." She closes her eyes for a long beat before she opens them back up. Her blue eyes don't look cold like they usually do. Today, they look deep like the bottom of the ocean, and if I'm not mistaken, they look sad, burnt out as if the light in them faded.

"If you want to call your boss, maybe she can find someone else." I hand her back her phone. The last thing I want is to be stuck on a date with Giselle, who would rather be anywhere but with me.

"She told me if I didn't go, I would be fired." She frowns. "I can't afford to be fired."

"All right, then why don't we just go and make the best of it?"

Giselle looks up at me and nods, resigned. "Okay."

We get back in the limo, and I let the driver know we're ready to go. The drive to the event is awkwardly silent, neither of us daring to break the tension in the air. When we arrive, Giselle's head whips around to me.

"Oh my god! This is the Prince George Ballroom." She jabs her finger toward the building.

"Yeah..." I confirm, confused.

"This is *the* Prince George Ballroom," she repeats, and this time I chuckle.

"I'm aware."

"Oh my god—"

"You're not about to tell me for a third time where we are, are you?"

"This is where the charity event is. Olivia and Nick's event." Oh...now I see where she's going with this.

"Olivia doesn't know you're an escort, does she?"

"Of course she doesn't know!" Giselle shouts. "It's not exactly something I'm proud of."

"What I don't understand is if you're escorting on top of working at that design place, why are you always so broke?" I don't know how much she gets paid, but I know what I pay the company she works for, and it's a small fortune.

Giselle glares daggers my way. "You don't know shit, Killian. Don't you dare make assumptions or pretend to know anything about me or my life."

I raise my hands in surrender, not wanting to piss her off right before we go out in public. "I'm not. It was just a question."

"Whatever, let's just do this." Giselle grabs the handle, but the driver opens the door before she can, and she almost falls out of the vehicle. I circle her waist to catch her and she shakes me off with a quick "Thanks."

The moment we step out of the limo, the press go crazy. At first, I'm worried about how Giselle is going to act in front of everyone. But as we walk the carpet slowly, allowing the press to take pictures, the entire time Giselle has on the perfect game face. She links her arm around mine and smiles for the cameras. When different magazines ask me questions, she stands slightly back while I answer them.

"Can I ask you about your date tonight?" one of the reporters asks. "I don't believe we've seen her with you before." I feel Giselle's body stiffen next to me, while she waits for me to answer.

"She's actually the best friend of Olivia Harper, the woman who made this entire evening possible." I smile, and we move forward.

"Thank you," Giselle murmurs once we make our way inside.

"Outing you would only make me look bad," I say. "If anyone else asks, I'll give them the same answer I did out there."

We head through the grand ballroom and over to the table with numbers. The woman asks for my name and then hands me two place cards so we can find our seats. The entire place is decorated in gold, silver, and cream. The outer walls have tables lined with silent auctions for the guests to check out. All of the winnings will go toward Touchdown for Reading and the Arts.

We find our table and set our place cards down. Nobody is sitting at the moment, so I suggest we head over to the auctions. Giselle follows me through the room while I place bids on a few auctions. When different people stop me to talk, Giselle is sweet and charming—the same way I've seen her act when she's with her other dates. And then it hits me. All those men I've seen her with. They weren't dates. They were clients.

"Killian, I'm so glad you could make it." Olivia pulls me out of my thoughts and in for a hug. "And who's your date?" She tilts her head to the side, and that's when I notice Giselle is hiding behind me. Laughing under my breath, I move to the side.

"Olivia, I would like for you to meet my date. Giselle Winters, this is Olivia Harper." Giselle raises her head and smiles nervously.

"Oh my goodness!" Olivia claps excitedly. "I didn't know you two were coming together. I thought you couldn't make it." Olivia wraps her friend up in a hug.

Giselle's eyes bounce from Olivia to me, clearly unsure of what to say, so I answer her instead. "She's doing me a favor. My date couldn't make it."

Nick eyes me accusingly, silently calling bullshit, and I shake my head once, telling him to drop it. "We're glad you both could make it. Killian, I want to show you something. Join me?" It comes out like a question, but it's anything but.

"I think it would be rude to leave our dates—" I begin to say, but Nick cuts me off.

"It will only be a minute." He gives Olivia a kiss on her cheek with a promise to be right back.

"Where's Reed?" I ask as we walk back over to the auction tables.

"He passed out an hour after we arrived, so Shelby took him back to Olivia's place." We stop in the corner, and Nick turns to face me, hitting me with a hard stare. "Did you say something to Giselle about her moving out?"

"No," I start to say, but then I remember when I was babysitting and Giselle came home, we had words. "Yeah."

"Dammit, Kill. Giselle told Olivia tonight she's moving out."

"And that's a bad thing, why?"

"Because she's put her mom's house up for sale, and even if it does sell, she can't afford a place in the city."

"Trust me, Giselle is making more money than you think. Besides, it's not like she's your concern."

"It doesn't matter if she's a fucking millionaire. She and Olivia got into it because of whatever you said to her, and now Olivia is upset. I get you don't like Celeste and Giselle, and I'm pretty sure it's a mixture of you looking out for me and you refusing to deal with whatever you've been running from since college. But no more treating them like shit for me. I accept both of those women the way they are. Just like I don't know what's going on with you under the surface because you refuse to talk about it, the same can be said for them."

Damn it, he's right. I've been projecting my issues onto Giselle and Celeste, when the truth is, I'm not fucking perfect, and I definitely have no right to judge other people.

"I'm not sure why Giselle agreed to be your date, but maybe you can use it as an opportunity," Nick says.

"An opportunity for what?" I ask, confused.

"To actually get to know the woman you're on a date with. Who knows? Maybe Giselle will shock you. It's not often you bring a date you didn't have to pay to join you." Nick smirks. *If only he knew the truth…*

"I went on a date recently. Fuck you very much," I say in my defense.

"That model Christina set you up with? That doesn't count. We both know she was too busy modeling for the paparazzi to actually pay any attention to you. You would've been better off with one of your paid escorts."

He's got me there. Christina might be down to earth, but her friend definitely wasn't. She barely said two words to me the entire time, more concerned with who was taking our photograph or interviewing us. It was obvious she was using me to get back into the spotlight. And the few words she did speak to me were about how much men suck.

"Don't you think it's time to deal with whatever has been eating you up inside? Maybe you could give someone a chance. Let someone in. Not every woman is a gold-digger." I want to explain to him that it's more than them being gold-diggers… it's about protecting myself. But if I say that, he'll want me to explain, and I'm not prepared to go there.

"Maybe not, but most women aren't anything like Olivia," I point out.

"How would you know if you refuse to give anyone a chance?" Nick pats me on the shoulder. "I'm going to dance with my fiancée. Be nice to Giselle." He gives me a pointed look.

"Yes, sir!"

I follow him back over to where the women are standing and talking. Nick leads Olivia onto the dance floor, and Giselle is left standing there alone. I take a moment to look at her—really look at her. With her hair down in waves and minimal makeup on her face, there's no denying she's a beautiful woman. Her dress is elegant and classy, yet with the back completely bare and the front cut just low enough that the swells of her breasts peek out, it screams sexy and wild. What Nick said about not knowing what's under the surface suddenly comes to the forefront of my mind. He's right, I won't talk about what happened, and too many times since I've met Giselle, I've thought there might be more to her than what meets the eye.

Before I can question what I'm doing, I step in front of her and extend my hand. She eyes it like it's covered in shit before she looks up, silently asking what I'm doing.

"Dance with me."

"Why?" she asks with a look of disgust.

"Because I'm paying you to," I hiss. She flinches, and I curse myself. Jesus, I suck at this shit. Before I can apologize, she takes my hand and pulls me onto the dance floor. Her arms go around my neck and her eyes look anywhere but at me.

Encircling one arm around her waist, I use my other hand to steer her chin toward me, so she's forced to look at me. "I'm sorry."

"You have nothing to be sorry for. Everything you've said is the truth." Giselle diverts her eyes away.

"Hey," I murmur, "look at me, please." Her cold blue eyes meet mine and they're glossed over. "I didn't mean to make you cry. I'm sorry."

"Can you please just stop saying sorry?" She removes one hand from around my nape and swipes the falling tear away. When she places her hand back, I feel the wetness of her touch, and it sends a chill through my body. I did this. I made her cry. I'm such a fucking asshole. "I'm well aware of what I am and what I do for money. I'm nothing more than a glorified prostitute."

It takes me a second, but her words hit me like a punch to the gut. "Hold up." I stop moving. "Do you have sex with the guys you go out with?"

Giselle looks at me incredulously, and I think she's going to tell me she doesn't. But instead she glances around to make sure nobody heard me before she says, "Are you serious right now? You know I do!" she whisper-yells. "And don't go acting like you're better than me. I might get paid to fuck men, but you pay women to fuck you. There's no difference."

I open my mouth to argue but stop myself. She thinks I've hired her to get laid. I knew sex was an option with the escort service I use, the service she works for, but that's not why I use them.

"This is just a date," I tell her. "I have no intention of having sex with you."

Giselle rolls her eyes, misunderstanding the meaning behind my words. "Not up to your standards?" She eyes me up and down. "Don't worry, I have no intention of sleeping with you either." Her nose scrunches up in disgust.

"You would if I paid you to," I point out, and she glowers. *Jesus, have I always been such a dick?*

"I'm so—"

"Oh my god! If you say you're sorry one more time, I'm going to leave you here. How about you just stop talking for a while, so you won't have anything to apologize for?"

I nod once, and we go back to dancing in silence. One song flows into the next and eventually the awkward silence almost turns comfortable. At one point, I think Giselle even forgets who she's dancing with because she lays her head down on my shoulder. A lump forms in my throat at the gesture, and I try to block out how good she feels in my arms. *She isn't my date. She's here because she's getting paid to be.*

A few songs in, the music comes to a stop and dinner is announced. Of course we're seated at the same table as Olivia and Nick, Celeste and her date, and Olivia's parents. We eat and converse. Olivia and Nick speak on behalf of Touchdown for Reading and the Arts, and then they start to announce the winners of the auctions.

"...and the winner of the cruise for two donated by Global Yachts is...Giselle Winters with a bid of twelve thousand dollars. Thank you, Giselle."

Giselle's eyes bug out, but she stands to walk up to the podium, not wanting to cause a scene. "Thank you." She smiles nervously, takes the coupon, then sits back down.

Jokingly, when I filled out my bids, I put her name instead of mine. I thought it was funny at the time. Now, seeing her pissed off scowl, it doesn't seem quite as funny. "Asshole," she hisses, slapping the paper on the table in front of me.

"It was just a joke," I whisper. "I didn't really think I would win any of them."

"You're paying for this." She glares my way.

"Obviously." I hand her back the coupon. "Global Yachts has beautiful ships. Take someone and have a good time."

"I don't want anything from you," she whispers, refusing to take the paper. Not wanting to argue, I fold the paper and put it into my jacket pocket.

Once all the auction winners are announced, the deejay turns the music back on and several couples make their way back to the dance floor. Since Giselle and I seemed to have found common ground while dancing earlier, I extend my hand and ask her to dance.

Once again, she eyes my hand and asks, "Why?"

This time, though, I don't answer her like I did before. Instead, I tell her the truth. "Because you look absolutely breathtaking tonight and I enjoyed our last dance. I can't think of a better way to spend my evening than on the dance floor with you."

She appears stunned by my words, but doesn't argue. Instead she stands and takes my hand. I lead her out onto the dance floor, where I spend the next hour—with Giselle in my arms as we sway to the music.

The evening comes to a close, and after saying goodbye to Olivia and Nick, we step outside. My driver circles around to pick us up, and once we're in the car, he asks where we're headed.

"Brooklyn Heights, please," I say.

"Actually, if you could please drop me off at the subway station that would be great." Giselle glances down at her phone. "Grand Central off 42nd Street." That's when I notice she has a duffle bag with her. She must've brought it with her when I picked her up, but I was too in shock over learning she was my date, I didn't notice.

"We can drop you off at home," I insist. I know she got upset over the silent auction and some of the stuff I said, but after I apologized, we seemed to have an okay time.

"I'm not going home."

"Where are you going?"

"To the subway station."

The driver glances back at me and I shake my head.

"I saw that!" Giselle hisses. "What are you going to do, keep me hostage in your dumb limo?"

"Damn, first my Bugatti is stupid and ugly and now my limo is dumb? What have my vehicles ever done to you?" I laugh, and Giselle growls. "Tell me where you're going," I insist.

"To my mom's! And if you take me to Brooklyn, it will only make my trip longer."

"Leo," I say to my driver.

"Sir?"

"There's been a change of plans. Please stay here for a moment."

"Yes, Sir."

"Killian, I don't need you to take me. I can take myself," Giselle says, but I ignore her, stepping out of the vehicle. I dial Nick's number and he answers on the second ring.

"Did you drive here?"

"I did."

"Perfect, I need to borrow your car. I'll tell my driver to wait here for you."

"Okay, just let the valet know."

"Thanks, man."

We hang up, and I let my driver know the change in plans. Then I have the valet bring around Nick's car. After arguing with Giselle for a good five minutes, I convince her to get in the car and then we're on our way to Rye, where her mom lives. It's a good forty-five-minute drive, but I make it in close to thirty.

"Thank you," Giselle says. "You can go ahead and go. I'm spending the night."

"You're welcome."

She shocks me when she leans over and gives me a kiss on my cheek. "Despite the rocky start, I had a good time." She grabs her bag from the backseat and gets out of the car. As I wait for her to get safely inside, I check a couple text messages that came through while I was driving. I'm about to back out when the door swings back open, and she comes running out.

"Killian, my phone is dead! Call 911 now!" She runs back inside without waiting for me, and I follow her in, doing as she said. When the operator answers and asks what the emergency is, I'm not sure what to say. And then I see her. Giselle's mom lying on the bathroom floor with empty pill bottles surrounding her.

"We need an ambulance. Someone has overdosed on prescription drugs." I tell her the address then hang up. Giselle's holding her mom in her arms and rocking her back and forth, begging her to wake up. She's completely still.

I google what to do when someone overdoses. Every website says to call for help and to make sure the person's airway isn't blocked. "Open her mouth and turn her face to the side in case she chokes," I tell her. She does what I say and then continues to rock her mom while begging her to wake up.

Finally the paramedics arrive and take Giselle's mom out of her arms. Tears of devastation and fear are dripping down her cheeks as she quickly answers their questions. I gather up the pill bottles and hand them to them, and then they're leaving with her mom on a gurney.

"Let's go," I say to Giselle who is standing still in the driveway watching the ambulance leave.

"This is all my fault." Her voice is so soft, I almost don't hear her.

"Giselle, c'mon, we need to get to the hospital. I doubt it's your fault, but right now it really doesn't matter."

When she doesn't move, I walk around in front of her. Her cheeks are stained from her tears, and she looks almost as lifeless as her mom.

"I was supposed to be here." She shakes her head. "And then Bianca said if I didn't go tonight, I would be fired." Even in the darkness, I can see her throat move as she attempts to swallow her guilt down.

"I was on a date while she was trying to kill herself. I should've been here." She nods once to no one in particular then finally makes eye contact with me. "If you can let me use your phone, I can call for a cab. Thank you for calling the ambulance. When I found my mom, her phone was floating in the toilet. And when I tried to dial 911 from mine, it wouldn't even turn on. I didn't realize my phone was dead. I must've forgotten to charge it. I don't know what I would've done if you weren't still here."

"You don't have to thank me. I'm just glad I hadn't left yet. I'm not letting you call for a car. Let's go." Gently, I grip her wrist and guide her to Nick's BMW. Thankfully, she gets in without arguing, and we head to the hospital.

TEN

*G*ISELLE

THE ENTIRE DRIVE to the hospital is spent with me silently working myself up. My mom is dead. How could she not be? As I held her in my arms, I couldn't find a pulse. I couldn't feel any air coming from her nose. Her body was limp, and she was white as a ghost. I don't work in the medical field, but it doesn't take a doctor to know the odds are stacked against her. I have no idea how many pills she swallowed or how long ago she swallowed them. It'll be a miracle if I'm told she's alive. I should call my sister and tell her what's going on, but I can't do it. Isn't telling your younger sister your mom is dead something that should be done in person?

This is all my fault. I should've gone straight to her the minute Dedra said she had to leave. It doesn't matter that she's been happier lately. Laughing and smiling. I know that at any given moment she can sink back into her depression. I shouldn't have chanced it. Her life should've been more important than my job. More important than money. *But the job and the money are how you take care of her...*

Killian parks Nick's car, and I jump out, heading straight through the emergency room entrance. I find the front desk and give the nurse my mom's name. After she confirms who I am, I'm told she's been put into the system and is being worked on.

"She's not dead?" I ask.

The nurse's lips twist into something between a frown and a sad smile. "I'm not sure," she admits. "It doesn't give me any information. I've notated you're here, and as soon as there's any information you'll be called."

I thank her and have a seat. Killian sits next to me. I should tell him he can go, but I don't. As strange as it may seem, it feels nice having him here with me. He's the only person aside from my dad and sister who has seen my mom at her worst. And while he's said some pretty shitty stuff to me, he's never said a single mean thing about my mom.

I'm not sure how long we sit here, but at some point, his hand makes its way into mine and my head makes its way onto his shoulder. My thoughts go back to last week when I wished for a man's shoulder to put my head on. My eyes close and my body shuts down temporarily, needing a tiny moment of reprieve from the onslaught of emotions that are weighing down on me.

"Giselle." I hear my name being whispered. I open my eyes and lift my head to find Killian softly smiling at me. "The doctor is here to speak to you." My body shoots up too quickly and everything goes fuzzy. Killian's hands grip my waist, and I steady myself.

"Thank you," I whisper then step closer toward the doctor.

"Next of Kin to Sarah Winters?" he asks.

"Yes, I'm her daughter." I extend my hand to shake his and he takes it.

"I'm Dr. Goldberg. As I'm sure you're aware, your mother overdosed on prescription drugs. We were able to pump her stomach in time. We have her in a drug-induced coma and will slowly lower the dosage. I'm going to strongly suggest you have her Baker Acted."

"What's Baker Acted?" I ask.

"It's when you sign off on your mom to be held for up to seventy-two hours for involuntary examination."

"Like being committed?" I question.

"Yes, the doctors will be able to assess her more thoroughly. The form you filled out indicated she's been on several different types of prescriptions over the years. My guess is she's seen different psychiatrists who have diagnosed her to the best of their ability, but my recommendation is to have her evaluated more thoroughly. With this suicidal attempt, plus the scars on her wrists, which indicate this isn't her first attempt to commit suicide, and add in the different diagnoses, they may even recommend she stay longer."

My initial thought is to ask how much this will all cost, but he's only the doctor, so he won't know anyway. My next thought is that I'm a horrible fucking daughter to worry about the cost when my mom almost died. I will figure out how to cover whatever the cost is.

"Thank you. I will sign off to have her Baker Acted."

"Okay, I'll write up the referral to have her transferred." He flips through what looks like her chart. "It shows you're self-pay. I must warn you this is a private facility." This is exactly what I was afraid of. "They will bill you for the initial consultation, but if they decide to keep her after that, you will have to pay up front. You'll have a couple people come by so you can fill out and sign some forms, and they can go over everything with you."

I glance over to Killian who heard everything he said. "Can I go see her now?"

"Yes, but she's still unconscious."

I thank him one more time, and then he heads back to wherever he came from.

"You can go ahead and go," I tell Killian. "I have no clue how long I'm going to be here, but I imagine it will be a while. Thank you so much for everything you've done." I pull him into a hug, and surprisingly he wraps his arms around my waist. My face presses against his chest, and for a moment, I revel in the scent that is Killian. A hint of cologne and a whole lot of just him. I let out a deep cleansing breath. It's been a long time since I felt safe, but here in his arms, surprisingly, I feel just that.

"Are you sure?" he asks, concerned.

"Yes, thank you." I'm used to dealing with this on my own, and I can't let a friendly gesture from Killian change that. All I can count on is myself and that's not going to change. I might not be able to stand on my own two feet when it comes to living on my own yet, but I've never once asked anyone to come to the rescue when it comes to the rest of my life.

Killian nods once. "All right, but if you need anything please call me." He walks over to the front desk and comes back, handing me a piece of paper with his number on it. "Anything."

"I appreciate that."

I watch Killian walk away, then ask which room number my mom is in. The nurse directs me in the right direction, and I head back to her room. I should probably call Adrianna and tell her what's going on, but I don't want to worry her. She needs to focus on her classes. She'll just want to drive down to be here when there's nothing she can do anyway.

My mom's room is quiet with only the sound of the machines monitoring her. Her color is starting to come back, and she looks so peaceful. My heart clenches at the thought of her waking up. Why can't the psychiatrists figure out what's wrong with her? She deserves to be happy, to live a healthy life. One where she doesn't think her only answer is to kill herself.

ELEVEN

GISELLE

"THE QUARTERLY EARNINGS are projected to be up two hundred percent..." Paul, my date for the evening, drones on with his business partner over how much money they're expected to make this year. I'm trying to focus on what he's saying, appear like I give a shit about whatever they're discussing, but I'm finding it hard to focus. It's been four days since I signed for my mom to be committed to a mental health facility. I've applied to several insurance companies, but because of her situation, I keep getting denied. Nobody wants to take on someone with preexisting conditions, especially as extensive as my mom's. Because she's still legally married to my father, she doesn't qualify for state assistance and the government offered insurance won't cover her stay. I make a note to speak to an attorney about filing for divorce on my mother's behalf. If the house sells, I need to make sure my father doesn't get a dime of the money I make from the sale.

Paul's hand squeezes my thigh, and I look over to him, realizing I've been zoning out. I give him a smile, but his brows pinch together. He knows something is up. We've been out enough times that he knows me well enough to know I'm not all here. He quirks one brow up, silently asking if I'm okay. I give him another smile and then stand, excusing myself to the restroom. Paul's business partner stops speaking and looks to his wife, Patricia, to see if she needs to use the restroom…because apparently women can't use the restroom on their own. She stands as well and follows me down the hall. We both enter our stalls. I go pee and then wash my hands. While I'm drying them, I feel my phone vibrate in my clutch. I pull it out to make sure it isn't Serenity calling—the behavioral health facility my mom's in.

Unknown: "Have I gone mad?" "I'm afraid so. You're entirely bonkers. But I'll tell you a secret. All the best people are."

Glancing back, I see Patricia is still in the stall, so I text back: **Who's this?**

Unknown: The Mad Hatter

I laugh to myself. I can't be positive, but something tells me this is Killian. He's the last person I spoke to about my love for Alice in Wonderland. Instead of asking if it's him, I go along with it.

Me: Funny. Enjoying the book?

Unknown: Yep!

Me: Too bad that quote is from the movie…

I watch as the bubbles appear and disappear. Then, finally a response comes through.

Unknown: You got me. And it's Killian.

Me: I figured… go read the book! A movie should never be a substitute. First read the book, then watch the movie. How did you get my number anyway?

I input Killian's name into my contacts while I wait for him to respond.

Killian: In high school, the movie was always the perfect substitute ;) I got your number from Olivia. I hope that's okay. I just wanted to see how you're doing…how your mom is doing.

My heartrate picks up and tears prick my eyes. The truth is I'm not doing well at all. I'm scared for my mom, tired from working fifteen-hour days to try to earn the money I'm going to need to pay for my mom's treatment. I feel like I'm drowning. Every day feels like a struggle to breathe, to simply exist. But I don't tell him any of that. Instead, I text him back that I'm okay, and thank him for checking on my mom and me.

He responds with: **What are you doing right now?**

I reply with: **Working**

I regret typing the word as soon as I hit send. This late at night, there's only one job I could be at right now, and it's not Fresh Designs.

Less than ten seconds later, he responds.

Killian: On a date?

I know what he's asking. Am I working as an escort?

I type back my response with a quote from *Alice's Adventures in Wonderland*—the book, not the movie.

If everyone minded their own business, the world would go around a great deal faster than it does.

I smirk as I watch the bubbles, which indicate he's typing. Then they stop. They start again. But then stop. Immediately, I wonder if I offended him. I meant it as a joke, but even when it's put like that, in a quote from a children's book, it still means the same thing. *Mind your own business.* And even if I meant what I wrote, I shouldn't be rude to Killian. What he did for my mom... he's the reason she's still alive. Had I taken the subway that night, I never would have gotten to her in time. And once we arrived, it was his phone call that got the ambulance to her in time.

Before I can type back, a text comes in: **Off with her head.**

I let out a soft giggle at his response, then reply: **I'm sorry, that was rude... Yes, I'm on a date...as an escort.**

I throw my phone back in my clutch and make my way back out to the table. When I get there, I realize I left Patricia in the bathroom. She walks up behind me and sits down. The next hour I try to focus better, participate in the conversation more, and earn my pay. When the bill is paid, we say our goodbyes, and part ways once the valet brings the cars around.

"You okay, Giselle?" Paul asks, glancing over to me as he drives us back to his place. He's a VIP client, which means his dates always include a 'nightcap.'

"I'm just a little tired," I tell him.

"Why don't I bring you home?" he suggests. I want to tell him I appreciate that, but it will mean less money—and I need the money.

"That's okay." I give him a smile. "I'm good."

"No, you aren't," he argues. "If it's the money you're worried about, I'll notate we had our nightcap."

"I appreciate that, but I couldn't let you do that. I promise I am good." The last thing I want is another person taking pity on me. Paul doesn't argue further. He takes me back to his place where we spend the next half-hour having sex. When we're done, he thanks me for another wonderful evening and then calls his driver to take me home.

On the way, I check my messages. If I'm honest, I'm a bit disappointed to see Killian never texted me back. Not that I blame him.

Why would he want to continue a conversation with a woman who's whoring herself out? Then again, he does hire women for the same services I provide.

Once I'm dropped off, I head upstairs. The place is dark and quiet, and I assume Olivia and Reed are at Nick's. I take a hot shower, scrubbing the slut off me. It doesn't matter how much I clean myself, though. I know who I am and what I've become. I can't regret it, though. It's how I'm surviving. It's what pays my mom's mortgage, my sister's school, my school loan debt. It's how I'm going to get my mom healthy. I don't have it in me to regret my choices. But even with all the justifying I do, it doesn't stop me from feeling gross and dirty.

After putting on my pajamas, I head out to the kitchen to get a bottle of water, when I hear something. I knock on Olivia's door and she tells me to come in.

"I thought you were at Nick's," I say as I enter her room.

"I'm not feeling well," she whispers. When I step closer, I can see she's been crying. Her eyes are puffy, and her cheeks and nose are blotchy. I crawl into bed with her, and she cuddles up next to me—her head landing on my chest. My fingers run through her long strands of hair.

"What's wrong?" I ask her.

"I—I'm not sure. I've just been really emotional lately, and the last few days I've been feeling nauseous. I threw up this morning." My fingers still in her hair. Emotional. Nauseous. Throwing up. She's pregnant. She knows it. I know it. She just doesn't want to admit it. I could point it out to her, but it's obvious she's not ready to deal with it, so I'll let her remain in denial for a little longer. If I were to guess, she's nervous to tell Nick, which is why she's home instead of with him. The last time she was pregnant, he didn't handle it well at all. Of course he came around, but it makes sense that she would be nervous to tell him.

"I'm sure it's just a bug or something," I say.

"Yeah, maybe. Or maybe it's just nerves. Between the charity event and Nick getting injured, things have been crazy."

We lay in bed, not saying a word for several minutes. Then Olivia says, "I figured out the tattoo I want to get." I stifle my laugh. She won't be getting a tattoo for at least the next nine months.

"Oh, yeah? What do you want to get?" I ask, going along with the conversation.

"I want to get 'And they lived happily ever after' written across my ribs with three hearts for Nick, Reed, and me."

"That will be beautiful." But it will be four hearts and not three, I think, but don't say out loud.

"I miss you, Giselle," Olivia whispers.

"I miss you, too," I whisper back.

As we lay in bed, I consider telling her everything. She's my best friend, my sister. Olivia would never judge me. I know that. I could do no wrong in her eyes. No, she wouldn't judge, but she would want to fix it. And the thought of her paying for anything, makes me feel sick. She's done so much for me over the years. I can't let her fix this. But I also can't keep this from her any longer. It's destroying our friendship. Just as I work up the courage to tell her what's been going on, Reed cries from his room.

"He's been teething," she says, getting up. She brings him back into the room with us, and when he spots me, he gets excited.

"Gi Gi!" he exclaims in his cute little voice. Olivia lays him between us, and he pulls on my hair with his chubby little fingers. He rolls from side to side getting comfortable. Once he's settled down, Olivia rubs his back and within minutes he's passed out.

"Do you have any plans tomorrow night?" Olivia asks me. I think for a minute. As of right now I'm not on the schedule.

"No."

"I was thinking we could do a girls' night out, and I can invite Celeste. We spoke a few days ago and she's been acting weird since the night of your birthday." I stifle a laugh for a second time. She's totally avoiding Nick. "We can go out for drinks."

"Or we can stay in and watch some chick flicks," I propose.

"Reed's been acting weird. My dad and Corrine will have to watch him here. He hasn't been wanting to sleep anywhere else lately."

"What about Nick?" I ask nonchalantly.

"His arm has been hurting. I don't want him to have to pick up Reed. He'll probably just hang out with Killian, play the PlayStation or whatever."

"Sounds good." I let out a yawn at the same time Olivia does, and we both laugh. Reed rolls over and his hand comes up to my cheek. His eyes stay closed. I watch him for several minutes, realizing I never told Olivia anything I planned to tell her. Tomorrow, I think to myself. I'll tell her tomorrow. Tonight, I just want to pretend everything is right in my world.

TWELVE

KILLIAN

"SO, she's been avoiding you since you got injured?" I ask Nick, my eyes not leaving the television. The score's 28-35, and I need this touchdown to tie the game.

"Yep, I don't know why, man. Any other woman, I would say she's upset that I won't be a pro ball player anymore..." Nick's defensive team comes at my quarterback, and I throw the ball to one of my receivers.

"But this is Olivia," I say, finishing his sentence. "And the woman is richer than you are."

"Exactly," he agrees, "it doesn't make any sense. I thought she would be happy to have me home more." My guy is tackled, and the time runs down. I throw the controller onto the coffee table, and Nick laughs.

"Where is she now?" I ask.

"Right above us." Nick looks toward the ceiling. "Girls' night. Coach and Corrine are watching Reed at her place. I think the moving back and forth is effecting him. He doesn't want to sleep anywhere but at her place." He frowns.

"Who all is up there?" I ask, attempting to sound nonchalant, when what I really want to know is if Giselle is up there. The woman has been on my mind for days now. In a moment of weakness I texted her to see how she was doing only to learn she was out with another guy. It shouldn't have affected me the way it did. I know what she does for a living. I know she dates and fucks men for money. But it did affect me. And now I can't stop thinking about her. Everything doesn't add up. There's definitely more going on than she's allowing people to see. And I want to know what it is.

"Giselle and Celeste," Nick says, standing and heading to my kitchen. "Want a drink?" he calls out.

"Sure." He comes back in and hands me a cold beer.

"If you're worried about Olivia avoiding you, you should go see her."

"Right now?"

"Yeah, she's upstairs, so she can't run." I shrug, and Nick gives me a curious glance.

"How did your date with Giselle go?"

"Fine." I take a long pull of my beer.

"Fine?" he parrots.

"It started out a bit rough...I may have said a few things that pissed her off..." Nick groans. "But I apologized, and by the end of the night I have to admit I was enjoying her company." I don't mention what happened with her mom and how it made me see Giselle in an entirely new light.

Nick eyes me warily. "Are you thinking about seeing her again?"

"What if I am?" I shoot him a *what the fuck* look. "Aren't you the one who said I should give her a chance?"

"Yeah, I did, but I don't want to see either of you get hurt. She never seems to last more than a couple of dates with the same guy. I think she just has a lot of shit going on. Her dad left, and from what I can see, she's paying for her sister's school and her mom's bills. She won't discuss it and she's never confirmed it, but it doesn't take a genius to figure out that when her dad left her mom, he stopped supporting his family." I begin to do the math in my head: the mortgage, house bills, college can't be cheap. I remember that the doctor mentioned she was self-paying. Does she not have insurance? That bill would be thousands of dollars.

"You don't know shit, Killian. Don't you dare make assumptions or pretend to know anything about me or my life."

Jesus, is this why she's barely making ends meet even though she's living with Olivia rent-free? Why she's working as an escort, even though she has a job as an interior designer? She's taken on an entire family in her father's absence. All the pieces finally fit together, and fuck if I don't feel like the biggest piece of shit.

"Why don't we go crash their girls' night? You know...so you can see how your fiancée is doing."

Nick laughs. "Okay, we'll blame it on me." We stand and head toward the door, but Nick stops me from opening it. "I know Giselle comes across tough, but this morning, when I was missing Olivia and Reed, I went over there to see them. I snuck in and saw Olivia, Reed, and Giselle all sleeping in Olivia's bed together. Olivia and Reed were both asleep. But Giselle...she wasn't asleep. She was watching them both...while crying.

"I think she's in over her head, Kill, but she won't let Olivia in. I know you don't understand why I won't push for Olivia and Reed to move out, but that woman was there for Olivia when I wasn't. I owe her. She's not just her best friend. She's her family, which means she's my family."

"Got it."

We get off on Nick's floor, and without knocking, walk into his condo. The girls are on the couch laughing and talking animatedly. Giselle and Celeste have a wine glass in their hand, and Olivia is drinking a bottle of water. The three of them stop speaking and laughing the second they see Nick and I enter. Celeste smirks, Giselle's eyes go wide and then she glares, and Olivia looks like she's nervous.

Celeste and Giselle both stand, setting down their drinks while Olivia stays seated.

"You don't have to leave on our account," Nick says to the two women. "I was just hoping to see my fiancée for a few minutes. She's been...busy lately." He shoots her a pointed look, and Giselle giggles. My eyes swing to her, and she's grinning from ear-to-ear.

"I'm out of here," Giselle announces.

"Same," Celeste agrees.

"No, you aren't." Olivia stops them. "You've been drinking. Please spend the night. Nick has a spare room."

"It only has one twin bed," Nick says.

"Giselle's coming with me," I announce. Her eyes go wide. "We need to talk."

"Great!" Olivia exclaims. "Celeste, you can take the spare room."

Celeste and Giselle both look like they want to argue but for some reason, don't.

"Fine," Giselle says. "Let's go." She gives Celeste and Olivia a hug, then, after grabbing her purse, follows me out. Once we're in the elevator, before I can press the button to my floor, she presses the button for the ground floor.

"You agreed to come to my place. Like Olivia said, you've been drinking, and it's late." I press the button for my floor.

"I agreed because Olivia is hormonal and in denial. I didn't want to upset her."

I'm not sure what she means by that, but right now I need to focus on Giselle. Nick can handle his fiancée. "Well, now I'm responsible for you." The bell dings, indicating we've arrived, and the doors open. Giselle crosses her arms over her chest in defiance, and I grin.

"You coming?" I ask, giving her one chance to come on her own.

"Nope." Her lips pop at the p, and I stifle my laugh at how adorable she is when she's been drinking.

"Fine." I bend at the waist and throw her over my shoulder. She kicks and screams as I walk her down the hall to my condo. With one hand, I unlock my door and walk us inside. When I get to my couch, I drop her and she lands on the cushions with a huff.

"I want the truth," I demand. "Why are you an escort?"

Giselle glares my way, her invisible shield rising to protect her. "Because I love to fuck."

She stands and fills the gap between us. Then she runs her fingers down my chest and over my abs through my shirt. It's been a long time since I've been touched by a woman and my dick instantly takes notice.

"Do you love to fuck, Kill?" She licks her lips seductively. "I can fuck you." Her hand lands on my crotch and she squeezes my dick. A groan escapes me. "I'm good at my job."

Her words are like ice water to a flame, knocking me out of my trance. "I don't want or need you to fuck me," I growl as I back up slightly. "Now, answer me. Why are you an escort?"

She flinches at my repeated question then steps forward into my personal space. "What do the other women have that I don't?" she questions, changing the subject. "You let Tabitha fuck you. I could please you. Just ask my other clients. They all come back wanting more." I don't bother to tell her that Tabitha most definitely didn't fuck me.

Giselle encircles her arms around my nape and her lips press against the side of my neck. "Let me make you feel good," she murmurs. My eyes close as I allow her to trail soft kisses up my neck and along my jaw. When her lips press against mine, I smell the wine, reminding me she's been drinking. I can't let this happen. I have rules and I'm not going to break them now. Especially for a woman who is treating me like I'm a paying client.

Gently, I push her away. "Giselle, I'm not your client. Stop avoiding my question. Why are you selling your body for money?"

Her arms cross over her chest in what looks like a defensive move. "Why did you bring me up here if you don't want to get laid?"

"I want to talk to you. Nick mentioned you're paying for your sister's school. Is that true?"

"Since when do you want to talk to me?" She snatches her purse off the couch. "It's not your business what I'm paying for."

"Wait, please." I grab her upper arm gently but firmly to hold her in place. "How's your mom doing?"

Giselle looks into my eyes for a beat before she lets out a deep breath. And then she shocks the shit out of me when she actually lets me in. "She's still being evaluated. I have to go tomorrow to speak to the doctors."

"Stay," I say. "Not to have sex, but to talk." I don't know why I'm begging this woman to stay and talk. Maybe it's because I feel like it's possible we have something in common. We both carry secrets we aren't proud of, secrets we can't even tell our best friends and family.

"Why?" she asks, her voice small and vulnerable.

"I don't know," I tell her honestly. "Maybe it's because when I look at you, I see myself: broken and lonely." I let out a deep breath. "Stay the night and talk to me. Be broken and lonely with me." I repeat the words to the song we heard on our way to her house the night of her birthday. I've heard the song several times since that night and every damn time my thoughts go straight to Giselle.

THIRTEEN

I DON'T EVEN REALIZE I'm crying until Killian swipes his thumb across my cheek. He presses the pad of his thumb to his lips and I'm almost positive he just tasted my tears.

Be broken and lonely with me.

Can I do that? Can I let him in? I practically threw myself at him to stop him from getting too close to me, and he refused to have sex with me. Is it possible Killian Blake is just as broken and lonely as I am? I can't imagine what he's been through to feel that way, but then again, most wouldn't know what I'm going through. Suddenly, a flashback hits me hard from the night of my birthday. The drive home. I drank way too much, and Killian made sure I got home safely.

"Do you ever feel broken and lonely, Killian?"

"Every damn day."

Unable to voice my answer, I nod once, and he nods back. Then, taking my hand, he leads me into his bedroom. He opens up a drawer and pulls a couple items out, handing me a shirt and boxers. "So you're more comfortable." He shrugs. "My bathroom is through that door."

"Thank you," I tell him. After changing out of my clothes and into his, I use the bathroom and wash my hands and face. This will be the first time since I was with Christian that I'm spending the night with a man. Even the men I've been with, I never spend the night. My rule is midnight. Many have offered more money for me to break that rule, but I've never once done it. It sounds stupid, but I never wanted to be that intimate with someone. It's one thing to have sex with them, but it's another to sleep and cuddle with them— to act like we're something we're not—something we'll never be.

When I exit the bathroom, Killian is dressed in a pair of New York Brewers sweats and a plain white T-shirt. I take a moment to look around his room. The walls are a soft beige, and the furniture is a dark chocolate brown. The four-poster bed is huge and placed directly in the middle of the wall.

"Would you like something to drink?" he asks. "Water? Tea?"

"Water would be great."

I stay standing in place as he walks out of the room. I can't believe of all places to be, I'm standing in the bedroom of Killian Blake. It wasn't too long ago the guy hated my guts—and the feeling was mutual. I guess the saying is true: there's a thin line between love and hate. Not that this is love...Never mind, ignore that last thought. I've clearly had too much to drink. There's a thick line—a very thick line—and we're nowhere near crossing it.

"Giselle," Killian calls out and I follow after him. I find him in the kitchen grabbing two waters out of the fridge. He hands me one and I take a long sip. After taking a drink of his own water, he walks out of the kitchen and into the living room, sitting down on the sofa.

I study him for a long beat, confused as to how I got here. How we got here. And not just in his home, but the two of us, comfortable enough with each other that I'm wearing his boxers. "I thought you hated me," I blurt out. "Why am I here?"

"Come and sit with me. Let's talk." He pats the cushion, and reluctantly, I join him.

"Why do you work as an escort?" he asks again, getting straight to the point. We both know he already knows why, but he wants to hear it from me.

"When my dad left my mom, he stopped paying the bills. I took over, but as an intern I didn't make enough. I applied for assistance for my sister for school, but on every application they included my father's income. He didn't make a lot, but he made too much for her to get financial aid. I couldn't let Adrianna take out loans. She would graduate and be thousands of dollars in debt like me. One night while I was out with Christian, I overheard his friends talking about the escort service they use. After I caught him cheating on me, in a desperate act to make some quick money to pay for my sister's semester of classes, I looked it up. I interviewed with Bianca and was hired."

My eyes close in embarrassment. Escorting has become a part of my life, but up until now, I've never discussed it with anyone. Saying what I do out loud makes it seem more real.

"My dad didn't just leave," I add. "He also quit his job.

"So, doesn't that mean you can get her financial aid?" Killian asks.

"It was already too late to apply. There's a deadline. And on top of that, because he's no longer employed, my mom's insurance was canceled. The medications she's on cost thousands a month. I'm trying to get her insured, but nobody wants to write a policy for a woman who has the preexisting conditions my mom has. And honestly, we don't even know the extent of her condition. She's been diagnosed a million times, but nobody seems to get it right. I've watched her struggle my entire life, and I have no idea how to help her. I'm hoping the doctors at Serenity—the mental health facility she's at—will be able to figure out something the others couldn't."

Killian stares at me for a few seconds before he says, "I'm so sorry, Giselle."

"I don't want your pity," I snap before I can stop myself.

"No." He shakes his head. "I'm not sorry for what you're going through...I mean, I am, but that's not why I'm apologizing. I'm sorry for the way I treated you. I assumed you were leeching off Olivia. And once I found out you were an escort, I assumed the worst. That you were loaded and choosing to let her pay your way." Killian takes my hand in his. "Please forgive me."

My head and heart are spinning. I've spent the last several months refusing to have any emotions, and now this man is pulling them out of me. I feel like I've been exposed and laid bare, meanwhile he hasn't given me anything.

"I'll forgive you on two conditions."

He nods for me to continue.

"One, you apologize to Celeste. You've been mean to her and she doesn't deserve it."

Killian nods. "Okay, and two?"

"The night of my birthday, you admitted you were broken and lonely..." When Killian doesn't deny it, I continue, "Then, when you asked me to stay with you tonight, you said 'Be broken and lonely with me.' Tell me your story."

Killian flinches but tries to quickly play it off with a small, nervous smile. "What you said about me paying escorts to have sex with me, you were wrong. I do pay them to go to events with me, but I don't have sex with them." He pauses for a moment, then surprises the hell out of me when he says, "I don't have sex at all."

I try to contain my shocked expression, but it must seep through my features because Killian laughs softly. "I'm not a virgin, if that's what you're thinking."

"Well, yeah, it kind of was," I admit.

"I haven't had sex in over ten years."

I have so many questions, but I remain silent and allow him to tell me his truth.

"I was popular in high school. Your typical varsity football player." Killian laughs but it's not a happy laugh. "I was even crowned homecoming king my senior year."

A giggle escapes me when I picture Killian wearing a crown.

"I definitely had no trouble getting laid. I slept around like most guys my age do. I wasn't a complete manwhore, but I had my fair share of women. When I started at the University of North Carolina, I continued as I had in high school, only I became even more popular. Girls would throw themselves at me, wanting to date a college athlete. Nick was the starting QB, and when we went out together, girls would flock to us.

"My sophomore year I met this girl, Melanie. She was in a sorority and a cheerleader. We hit it off. I took her out on a few dates and one of them led to us having sex. I really enjoyed her company, but I was young and immature. She wanted more..."

"To be your girlfriend," I say, and Killian nods.

"Playing college ball took up a lot of my time," he explains. "Between going to classes full-time and practice. Add in the away games. It was just too much. I wasn't in a place to commit to one person. She said she understood, and we continued to sleep together." His eyes drop and my stomach tightens. Something in his voice tells me he's getting to the climax of the story.

"A few months later Melanie got pregnant." He takes a shaky breath. I wait for him to continue, but instead he stands, and grabbing his water bottle, chucks it across the room. It hits a picture and knocks it to the ground.

"I'm sorry. I can't do this." He storms out of the living room and into his bedroom. I wait a few minutes, unsure if I should go after him. Whatever happened can't be good. I consider leaving, but make the decision to stay. He started this. He asked me to be broken and lonely with him. I told him my truths and now it's time for him to tell me his. Judging by the way he's acting, if I had to guess, I would say he's never told anyone this before.

Standing, I head into the bedroom and find him coming out of the bathroom. He sits on the edge of the bed, his elbows landing on his knees, and his face falling into his hands.

"I have a spare room," he tells me. "I can take you to see your mom in the morning, so you don't have to ride the subway."

"Be broken and lonely with me," I say, repeating his words.

Killian looks up at me, and it's apparent from his bloodshot eyes that he was crying in the bathroom.

"Please," I add.

He stares at me for a long time, searching for what, I'm not sure, and then he nods once. I take that as my cue to sit next to him on the bed.

"Fuck, this is so hard." He closes his eyes and I take his hand in mine. I rub circles into his flesh with my thumb until he relaxes enough to reopen his eyes.

"When she found out she was pregnant, she came to me." His eyes close once more and a single tear falls. I watch as it makes its way down his cheek and lands on the front of his shirt.

"Fuck, Giselle." His voice cracks on my name. "She was scared and crying. She needed me to tell her everything would be okay."

He swallows loudly and then continues, "I had a game coming up, and finals, and I was exhausted. I freaked out. I told her I couldn't deal with it. She was on the pill. It shouldn't have happened. Looking back, I know shit happens and how she got pregnant shouldn't have mattered. Even if she was trying to trap me, it was my baby in her." He releases my hand and uses his to scrub his face.

I stay quiet, waiting to hear what happens next. Being as I've never heard of him having a kid, I have a sinking feeling his story doesn't have a happy ending.

"I left for my game without talking to her. I assumed she would be there when I got back. Only when I returned, she was gone."

I hear myself gasp.

"She dropped out of school and went to live with her aunt in Tennessee...after she had an abortion." Tears of regret and devastation prick Killian's eyes, and before I can think about what I'm doing, I climb onto his lap, my legs straddling his muscular thighs, and give him a hug. I wrap my arms around his neck and hold him tight. His shoulders shake up and down as he cries for the baby that was never born, the baby he blames himself for losing. With his head buried in my chest, neither of us say a word. There's nothing I can say that will make this go away. His baby is gone, and he blames himself. He's spent the last ten years punishing himself over it.

When his body stops shaking, he looks up at me. His beautiful hazel eyes fall to my mouth and then he kisses me. Light, feather touches. His lips are strong yet gentle. The kiss is soft and has me melting around him like a pile of goo. It's been so long since I've been kissed like this. Like I'm something more than a whore who is getting paid to pleasure a man.

When he pulls back, he sees the tears brimming my lids. He cocks his head to the side in a silent question. I'm not sure if it's that I need him to know it's not him but me, or if maybe I feel like after he's told me his deepest, darkest secret, I want him to know one of mine, but without a second thought, I tell him another one of my truths.

"It's been over seven years since I've been kissed like that," I admit. "I was eighteen years old. Christian kissed me goodbye as I boarded the plane to Paris."

"I thought you two got back together when you came back to the states with Olivia?" he questions.

"We did, but he had changed. The stardom had gotten to him. He was high or drunk all the time. We hooked up a couple times, but it wasn't good. Then I caught him cheating on me. Shortly after, I took the job at A Touch of Class."

"None of the guys you were with kissed you?" I can tell from the sound of his voice, he isn't judging me but simply trying to understand. I go to climb off him, but his hands grip my hips and he holds me in place.

"My job is to make it about them. Sometimes we kiss, but it isn't pure or sweet. It's filled with an agenda, a gateway to sex." Then I tell him something I haven't told anyone. "I've had sex with dozens of guys these last few months but I've never once orgasmed."

"You've never orgasmed?" he asks incredulously.

"Of course I have, but not by the men I've been with. It was always about them. I faked it every time just to quickly end it." I cover my face with my hands in embarrassment, but Killian isn't having it because he moves them away. Then, holding onto me, he drags us up the bed. He lays me down next to him and pulls me into his side. I lay my head down on his chest and wrap my arm around his front. He runs his fingers through my hair a few times before they move down to my back. My eyes close as I get lost in the feeling of his touch. I didn't realize how much I needed this, craved this. To be held and comforted.

And before I can second guess myself, I whisper one last truth. "It's not really the orgasms that are important," I admit. "It's the connection. I just want to feel connected to someone. I'm tired of feeling so alone."

FOURTEEN

KILLIAN

LAST NIGHT with Giselle didn't exactly go as planned—or maybe it did. I'm not sure what was going through my head when I brought her back to my place. Maybe in the back of my mind I thought I would call her out on her shit and she would open up to me about her money troubles. I'm not sure what I was expecting to happen from there, but never did I imagine that with her legs wrapped around my waist, while hugging me, I would confide in her my deepest secret. I never could've predicted she would hug and comfort me while I lost my shit and released all of the built-up guilt I've been holding onto for the last decade.

And then, when Giselle in return admitted she hasn't had been pleasured by a man in years, my first thought was to pull my boxers down her creamy thighs and eat her cunt until she's screaming my name while she orgasms all over my tongue. The only thing that stopped me was the fact that I knew it wasn't the right time. We were both too raw and emotional. When I pleasure her, I want it to be when she's of her right mind and not feeling exposed and vulnerable.

"I just want to feel connected to someone. I'm tired of feeling so alone."

While Giselle and I are different in many ways, we're actually similar in other ways. I understand exactly where Giselle is coming from. While I've spent years keeping women at arm's length, I have longed to have a deeper connection with someone. I was so stuck in my way of not having casual sex until I was in a serious relationship, I never even unlocked the door to let a woman try to step through. I was afraid of their ill intentions, their hidden motives. Opening up to Giselle last night felt completely foreign, but at the same time it felt like it connected us.

Gently moving her body off mine, I get out of bed and go to the kitchen to start the coffee. While it's brewing, I hear the sound of feet padding across my wood floor. Giselle appears in the doorway, still wearing my shirt and boxers. Her hair is messy from sleep, her face free of all makeup, and she looks gorgeous as hell. She grants me a shy, nervous smile. I know she wasn't drunk last night, but my guess is she's wondering if I regret everything we talked about. Needing her to know I don't regret anything, I grin back. Her smile widens and then she throws her head back with a laugh, and fuck if it isn't the most beautiful sound I've ever heard.

"What?" I question.

"*We're all mad here. I'm mad. You're mad,*" she says through a fit of giggles, and the melodic sound has me grinning hard.

"An *Alice in Wonderland* quote?" I ask, even though I already know it is. After she told me to read the book, I googled '*Alice in Wonderland* quotes,' and came across several. Who knew the author of children's books could be so poetic?

"Yeah." She nods with a smile.

I pull a mug down from the cabinet and hand it to her. She goes to take it, but I don't let go. Instead, I use her grip on it to pull her closer to me. Her body presses against mine, and I tilt my chin down to kiss her. Only she turns her head to the side at the last second and my lips land on her cheek. Without letting go of her, I whisper, "I'm afraid we are mad. But I'll tell you a secret. All of the best people are." I have no idea if the quote is from the book or the movie. It's one of the ones I found when I googled, but I'm sure she'll tell me.

Giselle backs up, and shaking her head with a large grin splayed upon her face, says, "That's from the movie, and I'm pretty sure, you didn't even say it right. Read. The. Book." Then, plucking the mug out of my hand, she goes about making her coffee.

I study her as she flits around my kitchen like she belongs here. She grabs the milk and sugar from the fridge and adds them both to her coffee. Then she turns around and leans against the counter. Her foot pops up against the cabinet, exposing her sexy thigh. She lifts the hot coffee to her lips and blows on it. Her eyes come up slowly, and she peers up at me through her thick lashes.

"Thank you for last night," she says softly. "It felt really good to be able to talk to someone about everything. Thank you for not judging me."

I cut across the kitchen and encroach on her space. Then, taking the mug out of her hands, I set it on the counter. She gives me a confused look, until my hands come down on either side of her, caging her in. Our faces only inches apart from each other. Her look of confusion turns to nervousness.

"Why did you stop me from kissing you?" I murmur.

Giselle's lids flutter closed. She takes a deep breath, and when she reopens her eyes it's as if she's found her confidence. Her face takes on a look of determination. "Kill...you're a pro ball player who uses escorts so you don't have to have sex. I'm an escort who fucks guys for money... and I don't date athletes. Last night was exactly what I needed. Someone to talk to. And I'd like to think it was what you needed as well. Someone to share what you went through all those years ago. If you want to be friends, I can definitely use one. But that's all I can be. Your friend."

I stare at her for a minute, deciding where to begin first, because there's so much wrong with everything she just said. Finally, I start with her issue with athletes.

"Christian is a musician," I point out. "You mentioned you don't date athletes back in the Hamptons. Did one break your heart?"

Giselle shakes her head, then lifts my arm up and ducks underneath. She grabs her coffee off the counter and sashays across the kitchen. "No, I don't date musicians, athletes, pilots, traveling salesmen, doctors without borders...anyone who travels for their job." She shrugs and takes a sip of her coffee before she continues. "I'm not about to be cheated on again, and it's been proven more times than not, guys who travel, cheat. My dad traveled with his job and he cheated on my mom. Christian cheated on me while on the road."

"Nick is an athlete and he would never cheat on Olivia," I state matter-of-factly.

"Look, it doesn't matter. That's just one part of it. Did you not hear the part about me being an escort?"

"Yeah, I heard," I tell her, "but that's going to change. Even if you want to just be friends." I want to add *for now*, but I don't. I'll take it slow with Giselle, but I'm not going to settle on just being friends with her. For the first time in years I want to see where things can go with a woman, and I'm not about to let her stubbornness get in my way. And yes, I'm fully aware just how much of a hypocrite I sound like, when just a few short weeks ago I was accusing her of living off Olivia. But that was before I took the time to find out the entire story. And now that I know, I'm going to make it up to Giselle. I'm not going to let her sell her body to take care of her family.

"That's not your decision to make." She takes another sip of her coffee. "I need to get going. I took the day off to meet with my mom's doctors." She pours the remaining coffee into the sink and rinses out the mug. Then she heads back into my bedroom.

Following her, I say, "This conversation isn't over." She lifts her arms up in a *whatever you say* gesture.

I shower while she gets dressed and then we head down to the garage so I can take her home to get dressed. When I press the button on one of my fobs, the lights to my special edition Bugatti flicker on. It's a beautiful shiny black with accented green tones to match the Brewer's team colors.

"This is what we're taking?" Giselle laughs. "Aren't you afraid your precious car might get nicked?"

"I figured you needed to experience Betty yourself. You know, she was deeply offended when you called her ugly and stupid." I pout playfully, and Giselle doubles over in a fit of laughter.

"You named your car Betty? How cliché!" She laughs harder.

"Now you're dissing her name?" I tsk. "Get in. Once you get to know her, you'll regret the name-calling and apologize." I open the door for her to get in.

"Are we seriously taking this car? We're in New York! It's kind of a waste. Isn't it known for doing like zero-to-one hundred in thirty seconds? The only thing you'll be doing on the streets of New York is wearing out the brakes."

"Actually, it's zero-to-two hundred and forty-eight in forty-three seconds." I grin. She rolls her eyes completely unimpressed. "Now get in, so I can prove to you she's not only beautiful, but also smart."

Giselle shakes her head as she gets in. "She's not a person, you know."

"Shh, stop putting her down."

The truth is, I have only driven my special edition once, and she's right, driving this car in the city is a waste of its potential, but I can't *not* drive the cars I love simply because of where I live. Now that would be a waste. Plus, fucking with her over her hatred of this car will be fun.

Once she's buckled in, I close the door and go around to my side to get in. It smells of new leather, and I can't help but inhale the scent. Giselle giggles. "Feel the leather and silver," I say as I run my fingers over the dashboard. She snorts out a laugh thinking I'm joking.

"Seriously," I say, "feel the leather and silver." I take her hand in mine and run it across the material. She oohs and ahhs dramatically. "Oh, yes, Killian, that leather feels so good!" She moans playfully. I know she's only joking, but the sound she makes has me imagining what she'll sound like when a man finally makes her come. And holy fuck, do I want to be that man.

I let go of her hand and press the power button, and it rumbles to life. I smile over at her and she groans. "I get it...It's powerful," she says dryly.

"Damn right it is."

As I back out, Giselle looks around, then asks, "Where's the radio?"

"There isn't one."

"Okay, stop," she demands, and I press the brakes. "I love Betty. She's sexy and beautiful and so very smart, but c'mon, Kill. We need a radio." She pouts. "We have like an hour drive to Serenity."

"Not in this car we don't. I'll get us there in fifteen minutes. And Betty doesn't need your fake praises. Soon enough you'll be singing them for real."

She laughs. "Ugh! Fine!"

I grin wide and pull my phone out. It's already programmed for Bluetooth, so all I have to do is press play and the music surrounds us. "No radio, but there is music." I give her a playful wink.

Once we get to her place, she argues she can take the subway but I'm not having it. Thankfully, she picks her battles and lets me win this one. Once she's showered and dressed in a new outfit, she gets back in the car and we begin our trip to Rye. We stop on the way to grab a couple croissants and Giselle gets another coffee. She groans when everyone stares at the car, but when a few guys ask if they can get a picture with it and me, she offers to take the pictures for them.

She fidgets as we drive through the city, messing with the music on my phone, but not saying a word. She's obviously nervous about meeting with her mom's doctors. I want to discuss her finding another option aside from working at A Touch of Class, but now isn't the time. Instead I go for a distraction. When we hit the interstate, I make it a point to speed up. Giselle's back hits the seat as the car surges forward. She leans over to check the speed, and when she sees it's already at one hundred miles per hour, she gasps.

"Holy shit! It's like we're flying." She laughs. She turns the music up louder and raises her hands in the air. Her head goes back as she belts out the lyrics. Not wanting to put her in danger—or get pulled over—when the car reaches one-twenty, I let my foot off the gas. It slowly descends until we're back to the speed limit. She continues to play the music loud, singing along to each of the songs. Her voice is horrible, and she sings completely off tune, yet I find myself wanting to take a detour, so she'll keep singing for several more hours. I like this version of the woman next to me. The playful, outgoing, doesn't-have-a-care-in-the-world Giselle is how she should always be.

"So?" I prompt as we pull up. "Is she still ugly and stupid?"

"No! I love her! She's so fast and smooth. When I win the lottery one day, I'm going to get me one." She grins playfully.

"See! I told you she would grow on you."

"Yeah, yeah." She laughs. "You win."

I hand my keys to the valet then walk around to open the door for Giselle. She tells me I don't have to join her, but when I give her a look that tells her to quit it, she simply nods.

After signing in, we're brought back to meet with her mom's doctors: Dr. Burns, who focuses on her mother's mental health, and Dr. Clay, who focuses on her physical health.

"After evaluating your mother for the last five days, my advisement is to admit her long term," Dr. Burns begins. "We've looked at her previous diagnoses, and while I've seen signs of depression, my thoughts are that there is more to it than that. Unfortunately, when it comes to diagnosing a patient, especially when dealing with medication, it's all trial and error. The brain doesn't send off a sure sign indicating the issue. It's not like cancer, for example. We can't do an MRI and have it find the mass."

Giselle listens intently, nodding as he speaks.

"If the patient isn't suicidal, we can have her see us as an outpatient."

"But my mom has tried to kill herself several times," Giselle says, finishing his sentence.

"Exactly. When we're working with someone as an outpatient, she would come in several times a week to determine what's working and what's not. Sometimes it's as little as finding the right medication and dose, while other times it's figuring out the diagnosis to begin treatment. In your mother's situation, it's best to have her under twenty-four-hour supervision. We have a team of highly-trained medical staff who can monitor her closely. That way if a medication isn't working, we will know right away. We can lower and raise the dosage and she'll be safe." Dr. Burns stops speaking and nods to Dr. Clay.

"Your mother has been evaluated completely, including extensive bloodwork, and physically she's healthy. That leads us to believe what's wrong with her is a chemical imbalance of some sort. If you decide to keep her here, she will receive additional bloodwork to continue to rule out any physical issues. With any medication, there's a risk to the body. We will monitor her closely."

"Do you have any questions?" Dr. Burns asks.

Giselle looks over at me and gives me a small smile. "Would you mind if I speak to the doctors alone for a moment?"

Not wanting to argue, I nod once and stand. "I'll be outside if you need me."

"Thank you."

I walk outside the door, but when I see the receptionist isn't at her desk, I close the door and place my ear up to it. Her voice is soft, and I can barely hear what she's saying, but then one of the doctors speak and his baritone voice is loud enough that I can hear what he's saying.

"She could see a therapist, but as I said, I don't recommend it. She's clearly suicidal, and if left alone we can't be sure she won't attempt it again, especially if she's on the wrong meds. If it's about money, we offer a private medically-needy loan. You can apply, and if you're approved, they will set up a payment plan."

The doctor stops talking, and Giselle starts. I can't hear what she's saying, but I don't need to. I've heard enough. I know what I need to do.

GISELLE LOOKS AROUND, and realizing we aren't headed toward Brooklyn Heights, asks, "Where are we going?" She's been quiet the entire drive back, and if it wasn't for her sniffling quietly every once in a while, I would've assumed she was sleeping.

When she walked outside an hour later from her meeting, I was sitting on the bench waiting for her. Under her eyes were puffy and her cheeks were stained pink. It was obvious she'd been crying. She told me they allowed her to visit her mom for a little while, which explained the tears. She mentioned her mom has forty-eight hours left in there and then she's going to have to make a decision.

"To get a late lunch," I tell her, answering her question. Then, before she can argue, I add, "And you already told me you took the day off, so I know you don't have to work." I shoot her a knowing smirk and she rolls her eyes.

I park my car in the garage, then get out and open Giselle's door for her.

"I thought you said we're going to lunch?" she asks.

"I said we're getting lunch...and we are. I'm going to have them deliver whatever we want to my place."

We take the elevator up, and once we're inside, I ask Giselle what she's in the mood for. She says she would love some soup and a sandwich, so I pull up the delivery app and order from the deli down the street. Once I've placed our order, I have her join me on the couch. Figuring she's had enough of talking for one day, I turn on the TV and click on Netflix.

"What do you want to watch?" I ask.

She eyes me curiously. "I don't know. I can't even remember the last time I watched TV. I've been wanting to watch Sons of Anarchy for a while." She shrugs. "I've been on a huge MC romance kick lately. It drives Olivia nuts." She laughs.

"MC romance?" I question.

"Motorcycle club romance. The hero is a member of a club. Olivia prefers sports romance, but I love to read about a sexy tatted up biker."

"I'm tatted up," I say with a smirk.

"True, but do you ride a motorcycle?" She grins, and for a split second I consider buying one just so I can know how it feels to have her thighs wrapped around me from behind.

"Whatever. So, SOA?" I confirm.

"Sure!"

I've seen the entire series, but I don't tell her that. When you travel a lot for work and spend a good amount of time in hotels, Netflix becomes your good friend. I click to start the first episode. A few minutes into the show and Giselle's head is on my shoulder as she snores softly. Not wanting the food delivery to wake her up, I gently pick her up and bring her into my room. She must be absolutely exhausted because she doesn't even stir as I set her on the bed and pull the covers out from under her. Once she's covered with my blankets, I quickly change into a pair of basketball shorts and a T-shirt to get more comfortable.

Closing the door behind me, I head back out to the living room and pause the show. Once the buzzer goes off indicating the food is here, I open the door, so he doesn't have to knock. I thank him and place the food into the fridge for later. Then I spend the next few hours playing Madden on the PlayStation while I wait for Giselle to wake up. I hear her cell phone go off a few times, so I dig through her purse and make sure it isn't her mom or sister. When I see it's neither one, I switch it to silent and put it back in her purse. A couple minutes later, Nick calls me.

"What's up?"

"Did everything with Giselle go okay last night?" he asks without even saying hello.

"Well, hello to you too. It did. How's Olivia?" I ask, changing the subject.

"I think she's hiding something from me. She woke up this morning and ran out the door with Celeste to go shopping."

I laugh. "Olivia hates shopping."

"Exactly. We were invited to go to some grand opening of a new restaurant, and she used the excuse that she needs to buy a new dress. Anyway, I have Reed with me for the day. Want to join us at the park?"

My bedroom door creaks open and out walks Giselle. She's still wearing her outfit from earlier: silky black shorts that are the perfect mix of professional and sexy, and a midnight blue top that dips just low enough to show off the perfect swells of her breasts. Her lids are still hooded from sleeping, but she looks refreshed. A nap seems to have done the trick. She comes over and sits down next to me. Her brows furrow slightly and her fleshy lips pucker. That's when I remember I'm on the phone with Nick.

"Umm...let me call you back in a few minutes." I hang up without waiting for him to answer and throw my phone to the side. My only thoughts are that I need to kiss this woman again.

Without warning, I lift Giselle onto my lap. Without giving her a chance to deny me, I grip the back of her head, her hair tangling in my fingers, and pull her in for a kiss. At first, she doesn't kiss me back, but when my tongue darts out, she shocks the shit out of me when she parts her soft lips and gives me access. We kiss for several minutes. I forgot what it's like to taste a woman. I focus on the way her lips brush softly against mine, and the way her tongue duals with my own. Kissing this woman could easily become an addiction.

Giselle's silky shorts are thin, and the more heated our kiss gets, the more I feel her hot cunt grind against my pelvis. Her fingers pull at the little bit of hair I have, and it spurs me on to take more from her. With one hand grabbing her ass, I use my other one to push aside her shorts and panties. They move easily. I hesitate for a second, wondering if Giselle is going to stop me, and when she doesn't, I push a single digit into her. And holy fuck, the woman is soaking wet. I can't help the groan that escapes me as her wet heat surrounds my finger. It's been too damn long since I felt the inside of a woman.

I say a quick prayer to the man above that I don't make a fool out of myself. Then I stifle a laugh...because let's be real here, God has more important prayers to answer than the one from a thirty-one-year-old man who's praying to remember how to give a woman an orgasm. The same man who might as well be a damn born-again virgin with no recent sexual experience.

Giselle moans into my mouth as she grinds down on my finger, trying to make herself come. I can't have that, though. When she comes, it will be because of me—not of her own doing.

Adding another finger to the mix, I fingerfuck her as deep as I can go while we continue to kiss. My thumb finds her clit and I massage it in slow circles, applying just enough pressure to make her squirm in pleasure. Giselle's breathing turns labored. Her cunt grinds down on my hand as my thumb finds a good rhythm. And then she's coming all over my fingers. Her thighs shake as her orgasm overtakes her, and her juices drip down and soak my shorts.

She ends our kiss, and I take a second to look at her. Her lips are puffy and pink from my beard. Her face is flushed, and her lids are half-closed. I can't help the grin that spreads across my face. It's been quite a few years since I've made a woman come, and Giselle looks like she's high from the orgasm I gave her.

She stares at me for a long moment, and when she doesn't say anything, I have to ask, "What are you thinking?"

She gives me a shy smile. "I'm thinking that felt amazing." She backs up slightly and her hand grips my hard cock. My eyes drop down to see the wet spot she left behind. "And I'm also thinking it's only fair I return the favor."

The last thing I want is for her to think she has to reciprocate out of obligation.

"You don't owe me anything." I lift her off me and set her on the couch. "I need to go change."

When she frowns at my words, I add, "Nick is taking Reed to the park. Why don't we take our sandwiches to the park to join them?" I don't want her to think I don't want her. I do. So fucking much. But only when she's sure I'm the guy she wants to get serious with, and not because she thinks I expect a tit for tat.

She gives me a confused look, but I ignore it as I stand and head into my room so I can change. When I come back out, she's put together—she must've used my guest bathroom—and checking her cell phone.

"You ready?" I ask.

"I actually need to get going," she says as she pulls her purse over her shoulder. "Thank you for taking me to see my mom today."

"Giselle, wait." I move in front of her so she can't run. "What happened a few minutes ago..." My eyes dart over to the couch.

"Was a mistake," she says, finishing my sentence for me. She pushes against my chest to move me out of her way and saunters out of my apartment, closing the door behind her before I can even argue. It takes me a few seconds to think about what just happened, but once I do, I run out my door and down the hallway to chase after her. Only, when I get to the elevator, she's already gone. I consider texting or calling her, but decide it's best if I give her some space.

FIFTEEN

GISELLE

"YOU SEEM like you're somewhere else," Andrew, my date for the evening, points out. We're finishing our dessert at a new French restaurant in the Upper East Side. The grand opening is tonight, and Andrew requested me to escort him to the event. It wasn't until right before he picked me up, I had a chance to read through the specifics and saw the line I was hoping wouldn't be there: nightcap.

"I'm okay," I tell him and then take another bite of my Gateau au Chocolat. I imagine it tastes delicious, but right now everything I put into my mouth tastes like cardboard.

The waiter comes over and asks if we would like anything else. Wanting to prolong the inevitable, I order a latte to go with my dessert. I feel Andrew's eyes on me, but I don't look at him. Instead, I focus on my dessert like it's the answer to all of life's biggest mysteries.

"Giselle?" I hear my name being called and my head shoots up. I would recognize that voice anywhere.

"Hey, I didn't know you would be here." Olivia's eyes dart back and forth between Andrew and me. Nick doesn't say a word, but his glare is enough to tell me he either knows about me escorting or he knows about Killian and me. And I know Killian wouldn't share my secret, which means Killian told him something happened between us.

"I'm Andrew Parker, Giselle's date." Andrew stands and extends his hand to shake Olivia's and then Nick's. "I would invite you to join us, but we're actually just finishing up. The food is delicious."

"I'm Olivia, Giselle's best friend and roommate, and this is my fiancé, Nick. It's nice to meet you." I can tell she wants to say more, ask how long we've been dating, but before she can, the waiter comes over and hands me my latte then hands Andrew the check.

No longer wanting to be here, I ask the waiter if I can get the coffee to go. I feel three sets of eyes on me, so I excuse myself to the restroom. "I'll meet you out front," I say to Andrew, then give Olivia a quick hug. "I'll see you later," I whisper before I scurry away from the table and down the hall, closing and locking the door to the women's restroom.

After going pee and washing my hands, I unlock the door and exit. I scour the room to make sure I won't run into Olivia and Nick again on my way to the front door. When I see the coast is clear, I hurry through the restaurant and out the door. I feel my phone vibrating in my purse, but I ignore it until I get inside the limo with Andrew.

Then I quickly check to make sure it's not my mom's doctors or my sister. When I see it's Olivia, I put the phone away. The ride to Andrew's place is quiet. Had we really been on a date, I'm sure he would have several questions for me, but we're not. I'm getting paid to go out with him. One of the main reasons men hire escorts is to keep things uncomplicated. That's why Killian hires them...

The thought of Killian has my stomach churning. Yesterday was a beyond shitty day. Finding out it's going to cost thousands of dollars to help my mom get better almost drove me into my own depression. The entire drive home my brain wouldn't stop trying to figure out how to handle everything. But when we got back to Killian's place and he helped me focus on something else by watching television with me, I was able to breathe again. And then when I fell asleep and woke up in his bed, my heart felt so full. I can't remember the last time someone took care of me the way he did. When he kissed me, everything around us faded, and for those few minutes while we made out and Killian pleasured me, I was able to just forget all of my problems and focus solely on him. But all too soon it ended. Because when I checked my phone and saw my schedule for tonight from Bianca, reality hit me directly in the face. I'm an escort, and right now more than ever I need the money my job brings in.

We arrive at Andrew's penthouse, and once we're inside, he doesn't waste any time. He pushes me up against the wall of the living room and his mouth goes straight to my neck. He sucks roughly on my skin, and I find myself pushing him away.

When he gives me a quizzical look, I say, "Please don't leave any marks." He nods once then focuses on unbuckling his belt. He undoes his pants and pushes them down to his ankles along with his briefs. He doesn't even notice I'm standing here, immobile. I watch as he grips his cock and my heart speeds up. I can't do this. I can't have sex with him. My stomach tightens and I push him out of the way. I don't know where the bathroom is, so I run to the closest sink I can find—the one in the kitchen—and throw up my entire dinner and dessert.

"Jesus!" Andrew says with a tone of disgust. I glance up and his pants are back around his waist. "You okay?" he asks, but the look on his face tells me he's not really asking because he cares, but instead because he's not sure what else to do.

"No...maybe it was something I ate." I feel like the worst person for blaming it on the food when there was absolutely nothing wrong with it. I rinse out my mouth and wash my hands.

"I'm sorry. I think it's best if I go. If you call Bianca, she will give you a credit." I glance over at the microwave clock. "It's still early...I can see if she has someone else available. I'll let her know it's my fault."

Andrew waves me off. "It's fine. I'll have my driver bring you home."

When I get home, Corrine and Olivia's dad, Stephen, are watching TV. They must be babysitting Reed. Olivia mentioned he doesn't want to sleep anywhere but here.

"Hey honey." Corrine stands and gives me a hug. "How are you?"

"I'm good. If you guys want to head home, I can keep an eye on Reed. I'm home for the night."

"Sounds good. Thank you," Stephen says. They both say good-bye, and once they're gone, I grab a quick shower to rinse off. When I get out, I check my cell phone to find a text from Killian: **I'm taking you to see your mom tomorrow. Be ready at nine.**

Olivia and Nick must not have had a chance to tell him they saw me on a date. Feeling guilty, I text him back: **That's okay. I need to handle this on my own, but thank you.**

When he doesn't respond, I put my phone to charge and head

out to the living room. Any time I watch Reed, I have a tough time going to sleep. I know parents have to sleep when they have kids, but I feel like I need to be awake until his own parents are back with him. I flip through Netflix and stop on Sons of Anarchy. I consider watching the rest of the episode I fell asleep during, but for some reason it feels wrong, like Killian should be here with me to watch it. *Well, in that case I'm never going to finish the series...*

Needing a distraction, I grab my laptop and work on a couple proposals I'm presenting to potential clients this week. One is for an office being completely remodeled, and the other is for a couple who are moving in together and want to merge their homes into one. I smile, remembering how cute they were when they explained they wanted to make sure their home felt like it was theirs instead of his or hers.

When an email pings through, I click on it and see it's the medical loan company I applied to yesterday. I was told I would know within twenty-four hours if I've been approved for the loan. I scroll through the email until I find their answer: **Denied**

Unsure of where to go from here, I set my laptop down and allow myself to cry. Of course, as I'm bawling my eyes out, Nick and Olivia walk through the door...and behind them is Killian.

"Giselle!" Olivia drops her purse and runs across the room to me. She throws her arms around me and hugs me tight. "What's wrong? Did your date end badly?"

My gaze flicks to Killian who's standing next to Nick. His jaw is tight, and his eyes are shooting daggers straight at me.

"No," I tell her. "My mom...umm..." I don't usually talk about my money troubles with Olivia because I hate for her to feel bad and offer me money. "She needs long term treatment."

"Oh, sweetie. I'm so sorry. But that's good, right? They will help her get better."

"Yes," I agree. "But...umm...I was denied the loan." Liquid drops of defeat fall down my face as I come to terms with what I knew the other day when the doctors told me the cost of the facility. I can't afford it. And I couldn't possibly borrow that kind of money from Olivia. It's more than I make in a year...hell, it's more than I make in two.

"Giselle..." Olivia's hands come up to my shoulders as she looks me in the eye.

"Please don't say it," I plead. She sighs in frustration but nods.

"Can we talk?" Killian cuts in. His words are formed as a question, but we both know he's not really giving me a choice.

"Sure," I say as I stand.

He heads down the hall toward my room. Before I follow him back, I stop and give Olivia a hug. "I love you. Thank you for not offering." She gives me a sad smile of understanding.

When I get to my room, Killian is standing with his back to me. He turns around with my phone in his hand.

"I wasn't snooping," he says. "It went off a few times and I glanced at it to make sure it wasn't an emergency." He hands me the phone, and I read the messages he saw. They're all from Bianca, and she's pissed:

This is the second date you've messed up! I'm taking it out of your pay.

You're going out with Andrew again tomorrow night. You WILL make it up to him.

I'll email you the information.

A simple OK to confirm you've received my messages will suffice.

"So, let me get this straight...not even twenty-four hours after I get you off, you're out with another man."

"I wasn't *out* with another man," I say. "I was working." I set my phone down and look at Killian. The hurt in his eyes is exactly why I told him I could only be friends with him. This is my fault. I shouldn't have let him kiss me. I should've stopped things when they got too heated. But it felt so good to be with a man who wasn't paying me to make it about him. Oh, no. Killian made sure it was all about me. Pleasuring me like it was his job. And if I'm honest, it wasn't just the physical part I craved. Killian has done a complete one-eighty. If he wasn't an athlete, and I wasn't an escort, I could see myself wanting more with him. Wanting to explore what could be between us.

Killian steps forward and takes my chin between his fingers. He lifts my face so I'm looking at him. And as if he can read my thoughts, he says, "I know you warned me we could only be friends, but I thought what happened between us yesterday changed things. Since I was in college and made my decision not to have casual sex, I haven't wanted to try again with someone until now. I assumed you felt the same way...That maybe you wanted to try too."

An involuntary whimper escapes my lips. I open my mouth to speak but the lump in my throat prevents the words from coming out. I swallow thickly and attempt to blink back the tears threatening to spill over.

"I'm sorry," I choke out. "In another life...if I wasn't...my mom..." I can't even form a damn sentence. I shake my head and the salty drops of devastation fall.

"It's okay," Killian says softly. Then he leans over and gives me a kiss on my forehead. His lips linger on my flesh as the tears continue to roll down my cheeks. And then he releases me and walks out my door.

SIXTEEN

GISELLE

"KILLIAN! OPEN THE DOOR!" I bang on his door with my fist. I was shocked when the security guard allowed me to go straight up, telling me I have permanent access. After I'm done with him, I can guarantee he won't be allowing me access. My mind goes back to this morning at Serenity, where I learned someone paid for my mom's treatment.

"Everything is completely covered for the next sixty days while your mother undergoes treatment at this facility. Should any other charges occur, we have the credit card on file."

After my jaw dropped in shock, I picked it back up and demanded to know how it was all paid for and whose credit card was on file. Because it sure as hell wasn't mine. And I'd be damned if Olivia went behind my back and paid for my mom's medical expenses. The woman in charge of the accounting department confirmed it was Killian. And are you ready for this? When I asked for him to be removed and to refund him his money, they told me it wasn't my decision! Because my mother approved it!

Needing answers, I asked to see my mom. I was then informed she isn't accepting visitors at this time, but she wrote me a letter. The nurse gave me said letter and told me once my mom is up for visitors, she'll contact me. I made the mistake of reading the letter on the subway while on my way home.

Giselle, my beautiful daughter,

I am sorry for everything I have put you and your sister through. I'm not sure how I will be feeling tomorrow or a week from now, but right now I am in a good place. I had the pleasure of meeting your friend Killian, and he made me aware of your struggles. I've put so much weight on your shoulders, even from a young age. You are strong and independent, and I know you would go through hell to help me get better. But he's offered to help, and I've accepted. He's assured me that when I'm better and have my life together, he'll accept my making payments to him. When the house sells please use the money to get yourself a place. It's your time to shine. Focus on your future while I focus on mine. My hope is when I get out of here, I will be healed. Maybe I'll even go back to teaching. Please don't be upset that I'm not accepting visitors at this time. I just can't stand the thought of you worrying or seeing me during my bad days. The next time I see you I want it to be on a good note. I love you. It's because of you I'm still alive and have this chance to get better. I'll be in touch soon. Please give Adrianna a hug and kiss from me. I love you both very much.

All my love,

Mom

So, here I am on Killian's doorstep. What am I hoping to accomplish? I'm not sure. But since I can't speak to my mom, he's next in line. I can't decide if I'm grateful or pissed off for what he did. Right now, it's a combination of both. I know my mom said she made the decision to allow him to help, but he knew what he was doing when he spoke to her! And God help him if he told her I'm a goddamn escort! He's going to pay for this. For taking the choice out of my hands. And then an idea hits me.

Just as I'm about to give up on Killian answering the door, it swings open. And standing on the other side is the man I'm looking for...in nothing but a towel slung low around his waist. His hair is dripping wet, and for a moment I'm frozen in place as I watch the tiny droplets of water run down his tattooed chest and over his delicious six pack of abs.

He clears his throat, and I force myself to look up. When my eyes meet his, he's smirking like a cocky fucking bastard. He knows exactly what he's doing. Well, two can play this game.

"Everything okay?" Killian asks in a concerned tone. "I was in the shower."

Wordlessly, I stroll past him and into his condo. I hear the door close behind him. When I turn around, he's standing less than a foot away from me with his arms crossed over his chest. I refuse to stare at his body, not wanting to get sidetracked. He might've started this damn game by going to my mom, but I'm going to win. I'm the ice queen when it comes to freezing out my emotions. I have slept with numerous men in the last several months and not once felt a single thing toward any of them. Not a single emotion. Not a single orgasm. Not a single ounce of pleasure. Nothing. And I can do it right now. Killian wants to treat me like a whore then I'll give him what he wants.

Stepping closer to him, I make sure my game face is on. The one that has men who are higher up than him falling to their knees and begging for me to pleasure them. His emotions are written all over his face: nervous, wary, cautious. He's unsure of how I'm going to handle what he's done. And he should be all of those things, because I'm not about to play fair.

"Everything okay?" he repeats.

My hand comes up to his neck and I pull his head down slightly until his mouth is only a breath away from mine. "Everything is perfect," I whisper against his lips before I kiss him softly. He sighs, letting his guard down. He thinks he's won this game. Only he has no idea that he was never even a worthy opponent. He never stood a chance against me. You don't date several multi-millionaires for months at a time and not learn a thing or two about how to play the game.

Rule number one: make him believe you've thrown in the white flag. I deepen our kiss for several seconds before I move my lips over to his cheek and across his jawline. I place kiss after kiss across his flesh, working my way down his neck. When he lets out a low groan, I know I have him exactly where I want him. He thinks I'm thanking him for what he's done for me—for my mom. He thinks, just like that, I'm going to let go of the fact that he went behind my back. He spent thousands of dollars I didn't ask him to spend. He thinks I'm going to forget he took my choices away. That I'll just accept I now owe him. Well, he better think again.

Rule number two: when he thinks he's won and his guard is down, get him off balance and bring him to his knees. With my hand gripping his neck, I use my other hand to release the towel covering his bottom half. I feel his hard length bob up and hit the front of my thigh. I wrap my fingers around his shaft and stroke him root to tip, making him even harder. He lets out a growl of pleasure, and I grin on the inside that I'm about to bring Killian Blake straight to the ground. Bending at my knees, I continue to stroke his cock as

I guide him toward my mouth. I know from experience, the second my lips are wrapped around his shaft it'll be game over. He said it's been years since he's been with a woman, yet it's only taken me less than a week for him to break every rule he's ever made.

Time to earn the money he gave my mom.

Bringing my mouth to his dick, I wrap my lips around the head and slowly take him all the way in. His shaft thickens as I wet his velvety flesh with my saliva. Using my hand to pump the part of his cock my mouth can't reach, I simultaneously suck and stroke him. I can taste the saltiness of his precum. Knowing he's close, I take his delicate balls into my hand and massage them gently. Killian lets out a guttural groan, telling me he's close. But then his hand grabs mine—the one stroking his cock.

"Wait," he says breathlessly. His grip is tight enough that it stops everything I'm doing. My eyes glance up at him, his dick still in my mouth, and his face is contorted in what looks like unbearable pain. "I can't do this." He shakes his head and pulls me into a standing position—his cock falling out of my mouth as I rise.

"You can," I murmur. "Let me make you feel good." My hand tries to grip his dick, but he stops me.

"I can't," he repeats. "You don't understand." He backs up and scrubs his face with his hands, trying to get himself together. He picks up the towel on the floor and wraps it around his waist. "When I found out Melanie had an abortion, I made a promise to myself." He gives me a pleading look to understand. He thinks he's going to hurt my feelings by rejecting me.

"The next woman I have sex with will be the woman I plan to spend my life with. I never want what happened to Melanie to happen again. If we're in it for the long haul, she will know I'm serious and won't run off and have an abortion."

My heart drops into my stomach at what I was just trying to do. Seduce a man who isn't sexually active because he lives in fear of letting down another woman. Jesus, if I'm not a fucking bitch.

Killian moves forward and I take a step back. He has no idea what my fucked-up intentions were. He doesn't have any idea what a horrible person I am. He's good. And I'm not. I need to walk away. Leave him alone. He deserves better than anything I'm capable of giving him. I might be broken, but Killian...he's not. He's just a little bent.

"Have you ever thought about seeing where Melanie is now?" I ask. Killian gives me a quizzical look, so I elaborate. "You've been punishing yourself over something that happened over ten years ago. Yes, it's true, you might not have handled it well, but you didn't demand she have an abortion. She chose to run. She chose to have an abortion."

Killian frowns but doesn't say anything, so I continue, "You both were so young. Maybe it's time you find her. See how she's doing. Has she moved on? Is she married with kids? Apologize to her and hear her out as well."

I walk past Killian to the front door. "You're a good guy, Kill. Stop punishing yourself. Get closure and then find a sweet girl to love the hell out of."

With a small smile, I open the door and walk out of his apartment. I barely make it halfway to the elevator when I hear his door open. "Giselle, wait," he demands.

I stop in my place, but don't turn around. I know what's coming.

"Don't leave, please. You're right. I should go see her and get closure. I'm sorry for rejecting you. I just...well...I..." He can't seem to word what he's trying to say, and it would almost be comical if our situation wasn't so fucked up. "Can you turn around and talk to me, please?" His voice is closer. His hand lands on my shoulder and he turns me around to face him. "Why did you come over? Did you see your mom today?"

"She wouldn't let me see her, but I know what you did," I tell him. "I came over here to seduce you. To get you to break your rules."

He cocks his head to the side. For a guy who has had his guard up for so long, you'd think he would be able to spot a manipulative woman from a mile away.

"You paid for my mom's medical expenses," I hiss. "So I came over here to pay you back."

His eyes widen in understanding. "You thought I would let you whore yourself out because I helped your mom?"

"Why not?" I throw my arms up in the air. "You gave my family thousands of dollars. It's not like I can afford to pay you back. But I am a whore, so I can at least offer you my services."

Killian flinches. "I told your mom I don't want you guys to pay me back. I did it so she would get better. I did it so you could quit escorting. It's the reason you keep pushing me away."

When I don't say anything, he adds, "You're going to quit, right?"

"No, I'm not going to quit!" I yell in frustration. I know it's not logical, but fuck! He took my options away. He can say I don't owe him, but I do. My mom does. He shouldn't have done what he did no matter how good his intentions were.

"Giselle," he says my name slowly, "please don't do this. I'm sorry for not talking to you first, but you wouldn't have agreed."

"Damn right, I wouldn't have. I don't want or need your help!" I turn on my heel, but Killian's next words stop me in my place.

"If you walk away, I'm going to tell Olivia. I'm not going to let you continue to sell your body when you have people in your life who are willing to help you. Stop being stubborn and accept our help...please."

I press the button to the elevator, which thankfully opens right away. When I get inside, he's still standing in the hallway, barefoot and in only a towel. His eyes are pleading, but I ignore them, glaring at him in a way that I hope conveys he better not say a word to my best friend.

After catching a cab, I head straight home. I'm walking in the door when my email pings. It's from Bianca. I click on my schedule and almost drop my phone when I see what's written: Killian Blake...every goddamned night this week.

"That motherfucker!" I shout, slamming the door behind me.

"Who?" Olivia asks, making me jump. Lost in myself, I didn't realize she was home. And then I spot Reed sitting in his highchair, eating. And I just said the F word in front of him.

"Shit...I mean shoot! I didn't mean to curse." I walk over to Reed and give him a kiss on top of his forehead. "Hey handsome," I coo, and he grins wide.

"Who were you cursing about?" Olivia asks again.

"It doesn't even matter." I wave her off. "I was just having a bad moment." My phone dings again and I consider throwing it off our balcony. I glance at it and see it's from Bianca confirming I received my schedule since I have a date tonight.

"I need to get going," I tell Olivia. "I just came home to change."

"Another date?" she asks.

"Yep," I say as I head down the hall to my room. I quickly change out of my jeans and into a more professional outfit. I'm going to have to go speak to Bianca regarding Killian. There's no way I'm going to spend every damn night with the man. And to top it off, if he's on the schedule, he's paying for my services! That only means he's spending more money on me.

As I'm reapplying my deodorant, I hear a man's voice and recognize it as Nick's. I didn't realize he was here.

"There's something you need to know about Giselle," he says, and my blood rushes downward. Motherfucker told Nick!

I hear Olivia say okay, and then Nick says, "Killian said he paid—"

"Don't you dare finish that sentence!" I yell, cutting him off. Just as the words come out and Nick and Olivia look at me, the front door opens and in walks Killian—without fucking knocking. "This is none of your business," I say to Nick. I give him a hard stare then turn my glare to the man who's blowing my world apart.

"Somebody, tell me what's going on, please," Olivia demands.

"Either you tell her, or I will," Killian says in a tone that tells me he will make good on his threat.

"I hate you!" I shout at him. And that's when I realize tears are raining down my face at lightning speed.

"No, you don't," he says back, "but if you continue this, you're going to hate yourself."

"I already do," I whisper before I run out the door.

SEVENTEEN

KILLIAN

I KNEW TELLING Nick would upset Giselle, but she left me no other choice. I can't just sit by while she continues to allow men to fuck her for a paycheck. I understand why she's doing it. I really do. I once thought Giselle was dependent on Olivia. I thought she was living with her because it's rent-free and she was taking advantage of her best friend. But I was wrong. Fuck, was I wrong.

When I went to the billing department at Serenity, where Giselle's mom, Sarah, is staying at, they told me they couldn't allow me to pay for anything without Giselle or her mom's consent. The doctor confirmed her mom is sane enough to make decisions. She has a chemical imbalance of some sort that affects her moods—they obviously aren't sure yet what exactly, hence her being there—but she's able to make decisions for herself. While Giselle signed for her mom to be committed, her mom actually signed for herself to be treated.

The doctor wasn't keen on me meeting with Sarah, but he gave her the choice, and thankfully she met with me. It was during our conversation I learned just how rough it's been for their family over the years. Sarah's depression affected her job, which ultimately led to her being fired and their family being dependent on Giselle's dad's income. It also affected her marriage as well as her relationship with her daughters. She wasn't able to be the mom they deserved, and because of her absence, Giselle stepped into the role. Sarah also confirmed what Giselle mentioned the other night: because their father walked out on his family, Giselle is not only paying for her own student loans but is also paying for her sister's college. And that's on top of covering all of the household bills and her mother's medical expenses.

The woman is working two full-time jobs and is still struggling to make ends meet. Something has to give. I didn't tell Sarah about Giselle's "career path," but I did make it clear Giselle needs some relief, and I'm here to help. I could see it in Sarah's eyes she didn't want to accept my help. She's been burnt by a man—her own husband—someone who promised for better or worse. But she agreed because she knew it was the right thing to do for her daughter.

"Killian, what's going on?" Olivia asks. Reed screeches to be let out of his high chair, and Nick picks him up.

"Giselle..." Fuck, now that I'm standing here, I feel like such an asshole for telling Nick Giselle's business. I just didn't know what else to do. The woman is beyond stubborn. I thought if I told Nick and he told Olivia, she could talk to Giselle. I clearly didn't think this through.

"Killian, tell me!" Olivia demands. "My best friend just ran out the door crying. Is she sick? What's going on?"

Remembering Giselle left, I say, "I'll let Nick tell you. I need to go find Giselle."

I run out the door and take the elevator down. I have no clue where Giselle even went, but I can't just sit here and do nothing. When I exit the front entrance, I hear her voice. She's sitting on a bench against the building and talking on the phone.

"I understand I need the money, but I have the right to pick who my clients are." She must be talking to her boss, and my guess is that it isn't the one at the design firm.

"Bianca, you don't understand..." She pauses to listen to whatever she's saying. "Okay, I understand. Goodbye." She presses end on the phone call, shoves her phone into her back pocket, and lets her head hit the back of the wall with a loud sigh. I want to be mad at her stubbornness, but if I'm honest, it's a damn turn on. Any other woman would've gladly taken my money. Not Giselle, though. She has a ton of baggage sitting on her shoulders and she's hell-bent on holding it all up herself.

I sit on the bench next to her, and she glances over at me. She doesn't even look mad anymore. She looks defeated. "So, does my best friend know I'm a whore?" Her voice is too calm, too even. She's definitely reached her breaking point.

"You're not a whore. You took a job to support your family, to pay for your baby sister's school."

"Maybe so, but it doesn't change the fact that I spread my legs for money." She looks down at her gloved hands, wringing them nervously. "Did you tell my mom when you spoke to her?" she whispers.

"No." I wouldn't do that to her. I want to help her, not humiliate her. Plus it would only hurt her mom to know what her daughter has resorted to, in order to pick up the slack in her absence. I only told Nick in hopes that Olivia would convince her to stop. I know Olivia wouldn't judge her. She doesn't have a judgmental bone in her body. Hell, she's even become good friends with Nick's ex-fiancée for God's sake.

She nods once. "It's not your job to take care of me and my family. That's my job, and I don't need or want your money, so you can stop wasting your money in an attempt to take care of me."

I thought it was obvious I didn't just hire her to take care of her, but I'm not going to assume anything. My assumptions are what caused me to take months to get to know the real Giselle.

"I didn't hire you to take care of you. I hired you because I enjoy spending time with you."

Her chest rises and falls with a soft laugh.

"I like you, Giselle, and I want to get to know you more. But I can't do that if you're being forced to be with other guys. You won't quit, so I fixed the problem."

"Apparently fixing problems is your thing," she says dryly. I'm about to tell her it's just money, but I stop myself. To someone like me, who earns millions of dollars a year, it's just money, but to someone in Giselle's position, there's nothing *just* about it. It's been ten years since I was picked up by the NFL, and it's easy to forget where I came from.

Giselle wraps her coat around herself and shivers. It's February in New York, and today, while it's a bit warmer, it's still in the high thirties. "So, what are we doing tonight?" she asks. "Whatever it is, can it be indoors?" She lifts the hood of her jacket up as small flecks of snow fall down around us, and I smile at how adorable she looks. Her cheeks and button nose are a beautiful shade of pink. She looks like one of those porcelain dolls my mom has from her childhood.

"You tell me." I stand. "What would you like to do?"

"You're the one paying." She shrugs. "It's your date." She

stands. "And to be honest, in all the years I've lived here, I've never really taken the time to experience New York. I was either taking care of my mom and sister or going to school. Then I moved to Paris for six years." She smiles at her mention of Paris. "And since I've been back, I've been working."

I love that she just told me all that. It doesn't seem like a lot, but even with her not thrilled with me, she's still opening up to me.

"There has to be one thing you enjoy doing in this city," I say.

"People watching." She laughs. "Adrianna and I would go to Washington State Park and people watch for hours." Her grin lights up her face.

"Then let's go people watch." I take her hand in mine.

"It's too cold!" She laughs some more.

"I have an idea." Still holding her hand, I pull her down the street to flag a cab. When I ran after her earlier, it was quicker to take a cab than my own car. Driving your own vehicle in New York is only done when necessary.

I pull up the place I'm going to take her to on my GPS and get the address, then I give it to the driver. About ten minutes later, we're getting out in front of Seward Park. Across the street is one of my favorite coffee shops. We enter the shop and Giselle eyes me quizzically.

"Sit down and I'll get us coffee." I point toward the tables that are lined up along the big, open window, and Giselle smiles.

The coffee shop is small, but the entire front is made up of one giant window, where you can drink your coffee and, as Giselle said, *people watch*. I don't sit in the coffee shop often, as I get recognized when I'm out, but I grab coffee from here a lot. Today, though, Giselle and I will people watch.

After I order two lattes and a couple pastries, I bring everything over to the table Giselle found. She's staring out the window with her chin in her hand. The happy look on her face has me wanting to purchase this fucking coffee shop so she can stare out the window like this for the rest of her life. But something tells me if I want to stay on her good side, that's not the way to do it.

I hand her a latte and a pastry, and she thanks me. When she takes a sip, her face lights up. "This is delicious." We stare out the window for several minutes, drinking our coffees and eating our pastries. When she lets out a cute giggle, I look around to see what has her laughing.

"What are you looking at?" I ask when I don't see anything out of the norm.

"I'm watching those kids over there." She points to a bench directly across the street. It's facing the park. There's a guy and a girl sitting next to each other. It's hard to tell how old they are, but from their side-profiles, they're at least in their teens. The guy's arm is resting on the back of the bench, but every few seconds he lifts it in an attempt to put his arm around her.

Giselle giggles again. "Guys act so tough, yet you place them in front of a pretty girl and they get scared and turn to mush." She gives me a playful side-eye, and that's when I notice that my arm is halfway over her chair. I laugh along with her. Then, gripping her shoulder, I pull her into my side.

"I'm manly enough to admit I might turn into mush around you, but I'm not scared." Giselle rolls her eyes, but as she turns back to watch the couple, I see a small smile splayed upon her lips.

We watch the couple for a few minutes, and the kid finally gets enough guts to slink his arm around the girl. She turns toward him, and you can see it from a mile away, he's going to go in for a kiss. Completely invested in this couple, Giselle leans in closer to the window. "It's like watching a love story play out," she murmurs. "Will he do it? Will he kiss her? Will she let him? Will she kiss him back?"

Giselle's grin widens as the kid leans in. His lips press against hers and she doesn't back away. "Whoop!" Giselle cheers like she's watching a football game and the receiver just scored a touchdown. When she glances around her, she remembers she's in a quiet coffee shop. She cringes slightly, but then goes back to watching the couple make out.

"Oh! Look!" She smacks my chest to get my attention, and I realize I've been watching her the past few minutes. "It's a horse drawn carriage!"

"It's like thirty-five degrees outside," I point out.

"So what! It's romantic, and they're bundled up in blankets." She sighs. "I should take a picture to show Olivia. It looks like Cinderella. She could do this for her wedding." She snaps a photo and sends it to her friend. "I wonder if he's going to propose, or maybe it's just a romantic evening out."

As I listen to her talk about how romantic it all is, it's clear that while she may be tough, she obviously has a soft spot in her that loves the idea of a romantic fairytale. She sighs in contentment as she watches the carriage go by, and I realize the key to her heart just may be through romance. And then it hits me that I want the key to her heart.

"Oh my god! Kill, look!" Giselle squeals, throwing her head back in laughter. The couple who were sitting on the park bench are now running and ducking behind the bench as several kids throw snowballs at them. With the bench being used as a shield, they gather snow and make their own snowballs to throw back.

"Let's join them!" I say, standing and grabbing Giselle's hand.

She looks at me in shock, then grins devilishly. "Okay!"

We run across the street, and the two of us start gathering up snow to make balls out of. The kids are still engaged in a snowball fight, and they don't see us coming. With a few icy cold balls in each of our hands, we step out into the line of fire. Giselle throws the first ball. It hits one of the kids in the arm and gets all of the kids' attention. They all turn to look at us.

"You want in?" the kid she hit, who can't be more than ten, yells. "Better watch out!" He grabs a snowball from his pile and throws it right at us. We both duck and it misses.

"You need to take some throwing lessons!" I shout before I throw a ball at him. It hits him directly in the chest, and his eyes widen in shock. The other kids start laughing, and everyone goes back to their snowball fight. Giselle and I run all over the park with the kids for who knows how long. We get hit several times, and we definitely get a lot of good hits in. When I notice Giselle's cheeks are a deep pink from the cold, and she's nearly out of breath from running, I take her hand in mine and raise our arms in defeat.

"We're out!" I say, waving the metaphorical white flag. The kids all laugh.

"Hey! Are you...aren't you Killian Blake?" one of the kids asks.

Giselle's eyes widen, afraid I'm worried about getting caught. I'm not, though. It's part of the job.

"I am," I admit.

"Holy shit!" another kid yells. "We just threw snowballs at Killian Blake."

This time Giselle laughs.

"Don't use that language around here," I admonish. There are tons of little kids running around. The kid has the decency to look sorry. "And you did. What's your name?"

"I'm Drake and this is my brother Dean." He points to the kid next to him. "That's my sister, Dana." He points to the girl who was making out with the boy earlier. They're standing next to each other and holding hands. "And that's her boyfriend, Mark." Drake scrunches up his nose in disgust.

"Nice to meet you." I shake their hands. "This is my friend, Giselle." I put my arm around Giselle, and she smiles softly at me.

"You have a good arm," I say to Drake, whose face lights up at my words. "You play ball?"

"I do! All of us do...well, not my sister." He shrugs. "I want to be a quarterback just like Nick Shaw...no offense."

"None taken," I tell him. "Nick's my best friend and a very talented quarterback."

"It sucks he's retiring," Drake states.

"Yeah, well, he wants to go back to school. He loves reading and writing," I say.

"That's cool, I guess." He shrugs.

"I can't believe you're here," Dean cuts in. "And my ball is at home. I can't even have you sign it." He shakes his head in regret. "Damn it." He glances at me. "I mean, darn it."

"How about this? I'll write down the email of my publicist. She's the lady who is in charge of my life. Have your parents email her, and she'll give you passes to the first home game next season, and I'll make sure to sign whatever you bring then."

"Are you fu—are you serious?" Drake yells. "Heck yes!" The kids all cheer. I ask a woman nearby for a pen and scrap piece of paper and write down Amber's email address. Using the kids' cell phones, Giselle takes a few pictures of me with them and then we say goodbye.

"That was very sweet of you," Giselle says as we walk toward Broadway to catch a cab.

"It's part of the job."

"No, catching a ball is part of your job. What you did back there isn't a requirement."

"Those kids are why I have a job. They watch the games and buy my jersey," I tell her honestly, then change the subject. "So, what's next?" I glance at my watch. It's still relatively early, and I'm not ready to say goodnight to Giselle yet. The past couple hours we've put aside all the drama from the outside world and have had a really good time.

She blows out a harsh breath. "I don't know...that snowball fight exhausted me." She grins playfully. "I can't remember the last time I used that many of my muscles at once."

"I think the last time I was part of a snowball fight was as a kid in North Carolina." I smile as I remember my childhood growing up.

"Is that where you're from?" she asks. We continue to walk

down the street, and since she hasn't mentioned wanting or needing to go home, I go with it.

"Yeah, I was born and raised in North Carolina. I received a scholarship to the University of North Carolina and that's where I met Nick. My parents still live there. I have one brother, Dylan, but he lives here in New York."

"I've met your brother," Giselle admits. "The game Nick was injured during, your brother and his wife were there. He seems nice."

"He is. He used to be a family attorney back in North Carolina, but didn't love it. So, he moved here and opened up his own firm focusing on sports law. Shortly after, he met his wife, Christina, who was a model. They got married and settled down and gave me my niece, Julia. She's an awesome kid."

We stop walking and I realize we're standing in front of my building. "Want to come up?" I ask. "We can order in..." Giselle flinches, but quickly covers it with a tight smile. "Or if you're tired, I can call you a cab."

"I am a bit tired," she admits. "I worked all day then had to take the trip up to see my mom's doctors, but I'm okay. We can go up to your place."

"You sure?" I ask just to make sure.

"Yeah." She smiles, but it isn't the same one she had earlier. I want that smile back on her face.

When we get up to my place, I tell Giselle she can have a seat in the living room. I pull out a few takeout menus from the drawer in the kitchen and grab us each a bottle of water. When I walk back into the living room, Giselle is sitting on the couch. She's removed her jacket and gloves. She's wearing a pair of black slacks and her pink top is see-through, but I think it's the way it's made. Her bra underneath is the same color pink. She's checking something on her phone, but when she hears me, she sets it to the side.

"If you don't see anything you like, we can order something else," I tell her, handing her the stack of menus and sitting next to her. She takes them from me and sets them aside.

"I'm not really hungry," she says. "I was thinking we could get right to the nightcap." She takes the bottom of my hoodie in her hands and lifts it up. I help her by lifting my arms and removing it from my body. She lifts my shirt next. This time I stop her.

"Giselle..." I say slowly. I don't want to offend her, but we've talked about this.

"What?" she asks sounding genuinely confused.

"I told you I don't want to be sexual with anyone until I'm in a serious relationship."

She frowns. "You requested a nightcap...I thought you changed your mind."

"I requested a what?" And then it hits me. The different options with A Touch of Class. A nightcap means coming back to the client's place for sex. When I called Bianca earlier today on my way to Giselle's place, I told her I wanted Giselle every day and night she's available for the foreseeable future. At first, she gave me shit saying she already has regular clients booked, but once I offered to pay double, she gave in. She must've marked me for a nightcap.

"Your boss must've included it by mistake," I tell her. "I wouldn't pay you to fuck me." As soon as the words are out of my mouth, I regret saying them. I didn't mean it like it came out.

"Oh," she says. "Well, make sure you get that fixed. It's a waste of money to pay for it and not get it." She laughs, but it sounds off.

She opens the top of her water bottle and takes a sip, then sets it down and laughs softly. "I understand you not wanting to have sex, but you do know you can't get a woman pregnant from oral, right?"

I let out a loud laugh that has her grinning, and it's the one I love to see on her face.

"Yeah, I know, but oral is a gateway to sex. When I first started my NFL career, I was young, and women would throw themselves at me. At first, I thought maybe they were doing it because they liked me. I'd meet a girl at a party and we would make out. Sometimes it would lead to more. Her giving me head or me going down on her. I would stop it there, though, not wanting to continue until I knew there could be a future with us. The girls would get pissed." I shake my head thinking about how many times a girl would accuse me of being gay.

"As I got older, I realized most women wanted me because I was a professional athlete with money in the bank. While many made it clear they would be more than happy to commit, they weren't what I was looking for. Because I didn't want to lead them on, or put myself in a position where I would have to explain why I wasn't going to have sex with them, I eventually stopped being with them in any capacity.

"I told myself I was going to wait until I found a woman I could see myself having a baby with, but it never happened. Every woman I came across I just couldn't imagine creating a family with." I shrug. "Look at Nick and Olivia. Sure, it worked out for them, but what if she didn't attend the football game? He would've never known he was a father. She would've had to raise their baby father-less. I guess I've just never been willing to risk it…" Until now, I find myself thinking but don't say out loud.

"That makes sense." She nods in understanding then stands. "But you did give me an orgasm." Her cheeks burn pink.

"I did," I agree, remembering how fucking good she felt as she came around my fingers and the fact that I wasn't the least bit concerned about where it would lead to.

"I should probably get going," she says. "I have to work tomorrow and…"

Before she can finish her sentence, I lean over and kiss her. Our lips curl against each other and we kiss for several minutes. She tastes like the vanilla latte she drank, and fuck if I don't want more. When we finally separate, I don't give her a chance to say whatever negative thing I'm sure is going to come out of her mouth.

"Stay the night with me." Her eyes go wide. "Not for sex. Let's have dinner, watch some crappy television, and when we're tired, we'll go to sleep."

"Why?" she asks.

"Because when you're around I don't feel so broken or lonely."

EIGHTEEN

KILLIAN'S HANDS massage my breasts as I moan in pleasure. His fingers tweak my nipples, and my back arches, needing more of his touch. "More, please," I beg. "Suck on my nipples, Kill," I plead. I'm so close to coming.

"You sure you want this?" Killian asks.

"Yes!" I demand. A little more and I'm going to explode. "Suck on my nipples, please!" I beg again.

He doesn't listen, though. He just continues what he's doing—massaging and pinching. My hands move to his head to force him to wrap those full lips around my nipples, only his head isn't anywhere near my breasts.

Then who's touching my breasts? Am I dreaming?

My eyes shoot open. My gaze goes to where Killian's face really is—between my legs. I glance around at my surroundings. I'm in Killian's room, in his bed. I look down and notice the hands that are on me aren't Killian's—they're mine! My hands are massaging my breasts. My fingers are pinching my nipples.

Killian's hands are holding onto the insides of my thighs as he licks and sucks on my clit. I don't even have time to ask him what is going on before I'm coming so hard my butt lifts off the bed.

"Jesus, woman," Killian murmurs, "that was so fucking hot." He sits up and lifts the bottom of his T-shirt to wipe his mouth, his perfect set of abs peeking out just enough to give me a tease.

I take a second to slow down my breathing and then ask, "Did you just make me come while I was sleeping?"

He gives me a quizzical look. "I'm pretty sure you begging for more indicated you were awake."

"I thought I was dreaming!" I pull my shirt down and sit against the headboard. I glance down and notice the boxers I borrowed from Killian last night are no longer on me but instead on the floor.

"Giselle, did you have more to drink last night other than the one glass of wine with dinner?" He stands and picks his boxers up from the floor and throws them to me.

"I thought you said you wouldn't pay to touch me!"

"No," he says, "I said I wouldn't pay to fuck you, and I wouldn't. However, it's eight in the morning. I paid for you from five p.m. until midnight, which means you're off the clock. Plus, you came on my tongue and fingers, not my dick."

"What happened to oral being the gateway to sex? This is the second time in a week you've made me come!"

"You woke up this morning begging for me to make you come. A man only has so much restraint." Killian tilts his head to the side. "Wait a second...when you were begging me, you were asleep?"

"I—" I clear my throat. "I think so..." I try to remember begging Killian to make me come but can't.

Killian smirks. "So that means that while you were sleeping, you were dreaming of me making you come?" His grin grows wider. "I haven't had sex in over ten years, yet I'm pleasing you while you're awake *and* in your dreams."

Cocky. Fucking. Bastard.

Grabbing his boxers, I slip them on and get out of bed to go pee. When I'm done, I change back into my clothes I left in the bathroom. I'll need to stop at home to shower and get dressed before I go into work. Shit! Work! It's already eight and I have a client meeting at ten.

I step out of the bathroom and Killian is changing his clothes. His shirt is off, and his back muscles are on display. My goodness, no man should be this good-looking...this perfect. He turns around and grants me a sexy lop-sided grin, and I just about melt into a pile of goo.

"You've made me come twice," I blurt out. Killian's smile grows bigger. "When are you going to let me reciprocate?"

His smile deflates slightly, but it's still there. "When you make the choice to want me." He shoots me a wink. "Now, let's get going, so you're not late to work. I have a meeting I need to get to and can't be late."

The entire drive to my place, I think about what Killian said. *When you make the choice to want me.* Last night, despite only hanging out with him because I was getting paid to, was a lot of fun. Until we got back to his place, I don't think I once thought about the fact that I was getting paid. It was also the first time I spent the night at a client's place, but the truth is, I didn't view Killian as a client. After he told me he didn't mean to request the nightcap, I could've gone home. Without a nightcap, a client only has until nine o'clock, unless he pays extra because of an event that will run later. I stayed because I wanted to.

Killian parks in front of my building and I get out, but before I close the door, I lean into the car, so I can look at him while I speak. "Just so you know, I've never spent the night with a client." His eyes widen in understanding. "Last night, when I spent the night, I made the choice to."

I close the door and head upstairs. I take a quick shower and get dressed for work. When I come out, Olivia is sitting on the couch reading a book to Reed.

"Morning," she says cautiously.

"Morning," I reply.

"Giselle." "Livi."

We laugh at having said each other's names at the same time. Reed has no idea why we're laughing, but he joins in, which only has us laughing harder.

"You go first," she says.

"I'm sorry for hiding so much from you." I open my arms and Olivia stands and gives me a hug. "I love you."

"I love you too," she says.

"I know things have been crazy, but I'm ready to talk."

"Good!" Olivia exclaims. "How about tonight? Nick and I have some news to share. We can go to dinner and afterward Nick can take Reed for the night while you and I talk."

"That sounds great." But then I remember I have to work. I'm about to tell her tonight won't work after all, when I remember it's Killian who's hired me. "Is Killian invited too?" I ask.

"We were planning to invite him...Is that okay?"

"It is." I smile, and Olivia gives me a questioning look. I'm sure while I'm at work she'll be writing down a list of questions to ask me tonight. The first one starting with what's going on with Killian.

"Great," she says. "I'll text you the time and location."

I give Reed a kiss goodbye and head out. It's already after nine o'clock. If I don't haul ass, I'm going to be late to my meeting. Figuring it will be quicker to take a cab—even though it's more expensive—I start to head toward where they all wait, when I see Killian's car still in the same spot with him in it. At least today he's being more practical by driving a Dodge Challenger. I wonder just how many cars this man has. I mean, we live in New York. You barely need one.

He lowers his window. "Let's go."

"You waited for me?"

"Yeah, I figured you could use a ride to work." He shoots me that damn panty-dropping wink. "Plus, that means I get you to myself for a little longer."

"I thought you had a meeting," I say.

"I do, now get in before we're both late to our meetings!" He laughs.

"Fine!"

We stop at a coffee shop on the way and Killian buys us both a coffee and a breakfast sandwich. We arrive at the building I work in with ten minutes to spare. I tell him he can just drop me off in front of the building, but he insists on finding a parking spot.

"Thank you," I tell him. "I totally would've been late."

"No problem. I told you I have a meeting as well."

"Oh!" I say, remembering Olivia's and my conversation. "Olivia and Nick want to have dinner tonight with us. They have an announcement to make."

"Sounds good," Killian replies. He turns off the car and gets out. We start heading toward the building. "Do you know what they're announcement is? Nick said she's been a bit off lately."

I roll my eyes. I probably shouldn't tell him, but he'll find out tonight anyway. "Olivia hasn't told me yet, but she's pregnant."

Killian stops in his place. "Really? Well, damn. She must not have told Nick yet, because he would've told me."

"I think she was living in denial for a little while." I laugh. "Good thing they're getting married in a few months."

Killian laughs as well. "They're going to need a bigger place for their growing football team." He presses the button for the elevator.

"I put my mom's house up for sale," I admit. "I told Olivia I'm moving out as soon as it sells." The elevator doors open and we get in. I press the button to the floor I need to go to.

The doors close and Killian corners me. "I'm sorry about all the shit I said to you...about you living off Olivia. I didn't know, Giselle. I really am fucking sorry." He runs his finger down the side of my face. It's such a simple yet intimate gesture.

"It's okay, you were right. I need to stand on my own two feet." I give him a small smile, so he knows I really don't hold a grudge over what he said.

"Stand on your own two feet?" He eyes me incredulously. "I don't even know how you stand at all with all that damn weight on your shoulders."

"I'm handling it," I tell him. "I'm hoping if I prove myself at work, I'll get a promotion sooner rather than later. And once I do, it will mean better pay and benefits." The elevator dings and the doors open. I check and it's my floor.

"And if you get it, are you going to quit your other job?" he asks as we step off the elevator.

"I would like to say yes, but I have to see how much I'll be making," I tell him honestly. "Even if I sell my mom's house, I'll still have to pay for another place to live, plus my sister's school and my student loans." I sigh. "Thank you for what you did for my mom. I don't like that you went behind my back, but the truth is, I don't know what I would've done. I got denied the loan." I open the door to my small office that my boss, Lydia, has given me and have a seat. Killian sits across from me.

"You're welcome," he says. I pull my laptop out of my bag and open it up. It makes the sound indicating it's starting up. I type my password in and pull up my calendar since it has all the details I need for my client who is due to arrive any minute. And that's when I notice Killian is sitting in my office. With me. I was so focused on our conversation, I didn't even think about the fact that he didn't just drop me off. He got out and followed me in.

"Umm...Kill, you're in my office," I say dumbly.

Of course he laughs. "I know. I told you I have a meeting."

"Okay...well, I do too. And..." I click on this morning's agenda. "Mr. Blake is due to arrive here any second." Killian nods, and I gasp.

Mr. Blake.

Killian Blake.

Killian is my ten o'clock appointment.

Motherfucker.

"Why are you on my calendar?" I hiss. "This is not the place to play these games."

"What games?" he says, sounding genuinely confused. "I made

an appointment with the receptionist yesterday. She told me you had a last-minute cancelation."

"Kill," I snap. Then I stand and walk over to the door to close it, so nobody hears our conversation.

"What?"

"This is my place of employment. I am trying to establish a career here." I don't understand why he's doing this. "This isn't A Touch of Class."

"I know...it's Fresh Designs." He nods once. "I've decided it's time to have my condo professionally decorated. I'm tired of the whole bachelor look."

"You're serious?" I ask.

"I am."

"You're just doing this to find another way to give me money... but I work under Lydia, Kill. I don't get paid commission."

"I'm not doing this to give you money." He grins. "Now, treat me like any other client. Where do we begin?"

I fall into my chair and take a deep breath. This man is encroaching himself in every part of my life. And if I'm honest with myself, I kind of like it.

"HOW DID you know I was pregnant and I didn't?" Olivia laughs.

"Maybe because I know you." I grin and give her a hug, but when I pull away, she's frowning. "What's wrong?"

"Nothing...it's just...you know me so well, yet I had no idea you were—" Olivia looks around and whispers "—working every night. I'm such a horrible friend." Tears pool in her lids and fall down, and I pull her in for another hug.

"Stop it. I kept it a secret from everyone. You couldn't have known."

"Known what?" Celeste asks.

Olivia's eyes go wide, and she gives me an apologetic look.

"That Giselle and I are dating," Killian says, pulling me into his arms. "We were hiding it for a while."

Celeste's face contorts into a look of disbelief. "Really? I thought you hated her almost as much as you hate me."

"I don't hate you," Killian says. "And I definitely don't hate Giselle." He grabs my face and kisses me hard, his tongue quickly delving into my mouth. When we break from our kiss, he gives me a wink and a smile, and butterflies attack my belly.

"Okay...on that strange note..." Celeste stands. "I need to get going. I'm heading to Paris tomorrow morning."

"You'll be back for Reed's baptism, though, right?" Olivia asks.

"Of course." She makes her way around the table, giving everyone—besides Killian—a kiss on their cheek.

"Don't you have something to say to her?" I nudge Killian.

"Hey Celeste, wait." Killian stands and approaches Celeste. "I just wanted to say I'm sorry for the shit I've said to you. You might be friends with Nick, but I never took the time to get to know you. Maybe we can change that."

Celeste gives him an incredulous look like she's waiting for the punchline. But when it doesn't come, she says, "Okay...well, thank you...yeah...." She gives me a soft smile before she turns to leave.

Nick and Olivia are both staring at Killian, stunned as he walks back over and sits next to me.

"You ready to go?" he whispers into my ear. We spent the day going over what he wants done to his condo. We went to lunch and to several stores so he could show me what his tastes are. His likes: whatever I like. His dislikes: whatever I don't like. When Olivia texted that we were meeting for dinner at six o'clock, and it was already five, Killian insisted on us driving together.

"Actually, I made plans for tonight," I tell him. His jaw visibly ticks.

"Tonight is my night with you," he comments.

"Until nine o'clock," I counter and stand. "Reed, come give your favorite aunt some loving." I pick up my sweet soon-to-be-godson and pepper kisses all over his face. He giggles and my heart melts.

"You ready?" Olivia asks me.

"Yep," I answer her. Then I give Nick a smile. "Congratulations, soon-to-be-daddy of two. Tag, your it."

He gives me a confused look.

"You weren't around when your fiancée was pregnant the first time. The cravings, the night sweats, the freaking out if she was gaining the right amount of weight. Waking me up in the middle of the night to go out and buy her orange juice because she read it will make the baby move more."

Nick laughs and Olivia groans.

"I can't wait for every damn minute of it," Nick says and gives Olivia a kiss. "I will gladly buy you orange juice at midnight, Brown-Eyes." Olivia grins at the nickname he's called her since the day they became reacquainted.

Then Nick pulls me into a hug. "In case I haven't told you enough, thank you for being there for her."

"You don't have to thank me. She's my best friend."

"You're more than that to her...to us...you're family," Nick points out.

"Thank you," I say, trying not to get choked up.

I start walking toward the exit when a hand grips my arm. I feel a hard body against my back, and then I smell the sweet yet masculine scent that is all Killian. "You made me think you were going out with another guy," he growls into my ear.

"You assumed that," I say.

He chuckles. "I want you in my bed tonight." My body stiffens at his words, and then he adds, "To sleep, Giselle. Just to sleep." I make sure not to react to what he's said, but inside, I'm not sure whether to smile that he enjoys my company enough to just want to simply spend time with me, or pout that deep down I was hoping he wanted to have sex with me. Because if he did, that would mean he wants me on a deeper level. One that allows him to be with me in a way that he hasn't been with anyone in over ten years. Yet, at the same time the thought of him wanting me scares the ever-loving shit out of me because I'm not in a place to want that. I can't want that.

"I can't," I say. "I'm hanging out with Olivia tonight."

"All right," he concedes. "But my bed will miss having you in it."

I release a giggle. "Your bed or you?"

"Me...definitely me."

Olivia and I end up riding back with Killian since we're going to Nick's place. He's staying at our place with Reed. I told Olivia we could hang out on the patio, but she said if we were there, Nick or Reed might interrupt us and she wants some time with me alone.

Once we're inside, we change into comfier clothes Olivia has here. I head out onto Nick's balcony with a thick down comforter for us to bundle up in, and Olivia follows, bringing me out a glass of wine and her a bottle of water.

"Okay, start from the beginning," she says, and I do. I tell her everything, beginning with my mom and her illness. I tell her about my paying for everything since my dad left us. And then I tell her about Killian being with me when my mom tried to commit suicide and how he went behind my back to help my mom get the treatment I couldn't afford.

"I've only known Killian for a short time," she says, "but I've never seen him so smitten before." She giggles. "Nick thought maybe he was gay but didn't want anyone to know."

My thoughts go back to this morning when I woke up to Killian expertly eating me out. The way he fingerfucked me like it was his job, one he took seriously. My cheeks heat up and I'm thankful we're sitting in the dark, so she can't see just how affected I am.

"Trust me, Killian is not gay."

Olivia giggles. "So, what are you going to do?"

"With what?"

"With your second job...you can't date Killian *and* escort."

"We're not dating."

Olivia gives me an *oh please* look.

We head back inside, and Olivia's phone goes off. She smiles and shows me the text. It's of Nick and Reed lying in bed together blowing her a kiss.

"You should go home," I tell her.

"What? No." She shakes her head.

"Yes. Go home and be with your boys. I'll call you a car, so you don't have to catch a cab."

"Wait, you aren't coming?" she asks. Then she slowly nods her head. "You're totally going to see Killian, aren't you?"

"Your car will be here in ten minutes," I say, not answering her question. A few minutes later, Olivia locks up Nick's place. I walk her down and wait until she's safely in the car. Then I head back up to Killian's place.

I knock once, and he opens the door, his eyes slowly raking down my body. "Are you here to invite me to your sleepover?" He smirks playfully. I glance down and groan when I see I'm still wearing Olivia's Victoria's Secret Pink hoodie and sweats.

"Olivia went home. I was wondering if...uh...if you're up for company?" I ask nervously, suddenly second-guessing my idea of inviting myself over.

But then Killian grants me a sexy lop-sided grin and says, "I'm always up for your company," and my nerves are instantly calmed.

"Sons of Anarchy?" I suggest.

"Sounds good."

We go straight to Killian's room. He folds his comforter down and throws me a pillow. We climb into bed, but neither of us turn the television on.

"Did everything go okay with Olivia?" he asks. A few strands of my hair fall out of my bun, and Killian reaches over and tucks them behind my ear.

"It went good. We're good."

"I'm glad."

"I guess I have you to thank." I scoot closer to Killian. "Ever since you came into my life, it feels like everything has been turned upside down...in a good way."

"I haven't really done anything..." he begins to say, but I stop him.

"You took me to see my mom the day my dad left, you were there the day she tried to kill herself. It was your phone that saved her life. You sat with me in the hospital, you paid for her treatment...you even hired me so I wouldn't have to have sex with other guys." I lay my head down on Killian's chest and my arm goes around his torso as I let out an exhausted yawn.

"When you can't look on the bright side, I will sit with you in the dark," Killian murmurs, and even though I can't see him, I know he's smiling.

"That's very sweet," I tell him, "but it's not from the book."

"Damn it." He laughs. "Google keeps failing me."

"Read. The. Book."

Those are the last words I say before I fall asleep in Killian's arms feeling safer and more content than I've ever felt in my life.

I WAKE up to an empty bed. When I open my eyes, I notice there's a note.

Good morning, beautiful,
Going to the gym with Nick. There's coffee waiting for you. I'll be back soon.
Xo Killian

After my heart picks up speed and the butterflies in my belly attack my insides, I roll over and grab my phone to check the time. It's eight a.m. on a Sunday and I have no plans. Before I get out of bed to make myself a cup of coffee, I click on my emails to see if there's anything new. There's one from Bianca, confirming the upcoming week's schedule. Of course my entire week consists of Killian. I smile at the thought of getting to spend my evenings with him. Whether I want to admit it or not, the man is growing on me.

I click out of it and send my sister a text, asking how she's doing and suggest we get together soon. Then I send one to my mom's doctor to ask if there are any updates and when he thinks she might be up for company.

I climb out of bed and use the bathroom. As I'm walking to the kitchen, the front door opens. "Home already?" I yell. "I hope you brought me breakfast." I'm only joking, but if he really did, brownie points for him.

"Uncle Killian," a tiny voice calls out. I stop in my tracks, looking down to make sure I'm decent. I woke up in the middle of the night, warm from Killian being wrapped around me, and took off my sweats, leaving me in only a shirt that barely covers my ass.

"I'm so sorry!" Killian's sister-in-law, Christina, says. "We didn't realize Kill wasn't here."

"Or that he would actually have a woman over," Dylan adds. Christina shoots him a glare, and I laugh through my embarrassment.

"It's—it's not like that...we're not."

"We're not what?"

My eyes dart over to Killian, who is standing in the doorway in a pair of basketball shorts with his shirt slung around his neck. His entire upper half is covered in sweat. When he notices I'm ogling him, he smirks.

"Your family is here." I say, tilting my head toward them. His eyes move to them and widen. When he sees his niece, he grabs his shirt from around his neck and puts it back on.

"Sorry, I thought Giselle was on the phone...or talking to herself."

Dylan and Christina laugh. I glare. "Isn't it a little chilly outside to be running around half-naked?"

"I could say the same for you." He chuckles. My cheeks heat up in embarrassment, and it only makes him laugh harder. Throwing his arm over my shoulders, he pulls me into his side and kisses my temple. "I was at the gym downstairs," he clarifies.

"Uncle Killian, you're so gross and sweaty!" his niece yells, her nose scrunched up in disgust.

Killian looks around at everyone standing in his condo then curses under his breath. "I'm watching Julia today, aren't I?"

"If you have plans, we can bring her with us," Dylan says, his gaze darting from me to Killian, who still has me in his hold.

"No!" Julia pouts. "We're going ice skating and to the zoo, right, Uncle Killian?"

"Right," he confirms. Then he looks over at me. "Join us."

"Yeah!" Julia exclaims. "Join us." She skips over to me and extends her hand. "I'm Julia Blake."

"Nice to meet you. I'm Giselle Winters." I shake her hand.

She grins wide then runs over to the TV, clicking it on and changing the channel. She's clearly been here before, which makes sense since she's Killian's niece.

"I need to go home. I don't have any clothes here," I tell Killian quietly, not wanting to have this conversation in front of other people, especially his family.

Killian, on the other hand, doesn't seem to care who's here. "Maybe you should keep some stuff here, so we don't have to drive across the bridge all the time to get your clothes."

My gaze bounces between him and his brother and wife. They look more shocked than I do. Killian doesn't notice. He removes his arm from around me and walks into the kitchen. He makes a cup of coffee then hands it to me—kissing my cheek as he does.

"I'm going to jump in the shower. Why don't you just grab another outfit of Olivia's? We can get some of your stuff to keep here later." Without waiting for my answer, he says to his brother and Christina, "You guys can go. I got Julia." Then he says to Julia, "Once I'm out of the shower, and Giselle is ready, we'll go."

NINETEEN

GISELLE

I'M SWIPING through my photo album on my phone, trying to find a particular couch I know I took a picture of. My finger stops on a photo of Killian and me at the zoo in front of the tiger exhibit last weekend with his niece. After I took a picture of Julia with Killian, she insisted on taking one of us. Unable to tell her no, I handed her my phone and stood next to Killian. He wrapped me up in his arms and kissed me on my cheek as Julia took the picture. She laughed and said to smile nice. So Killian did as she asked and smiled for the camera. I can't even remember the last time I enjoyed myself as much as I did that day. I swipe to the next photo of Killian devouring an ice cream. He didn't care how cold it was outside. He said when you go to the zoo, you have to eat ice cream. The next photo is one of him and Julia. My heart squeezes at how good he is with her. Had Melanie not have gotten an abortion, I know deep down in my heart, Killian would have done the right thing, and he would've been a damn good dad.

I keep scrolling through picture after picture of Killian's and my time together the last couple weeks. From the snow ball fight with the kids at the park, to our visit to the Belvedere castle and Shakespearian Theatre, to the Alice in Wonderland statues I never knew existed in Central Park until the other day when Killian took me to see them. The man has made it his life goal to show me a little bit of

New York every day, ever since I told him I've lived here most of my life but have never really seen it.

As I stare at each of the pictures, an idea begins to form for what I can get Killian for Valentine's Day. Grabbing my purse, I let the receptionist know I'm leaving for my lunch. I'm not sure if I'll be able to pull this off since *today* is Valentine's Day, but I have to try.

I find the store I'm looking for and explain to the associate what I would like done. An hour later and my gift for Killian is wrapped in pretty red and black wrapping paper.

At six o'clock on the dot, there's a knock on my office door. Killian is standing in the doorway, dressed to the nines in a three-piece suit that fits every inch of his body to perfection.

"You ready to go?" he asks.

"Yep!" Grabbing my jacket, I throw it on over my outfit. "You're all dressed up," I tell him when I get closer. "You look very handsome." I pat his crimson-colored tie. He gives me a chaste kiss on my lips—an intimate act that has become the norm between us.

"Thank you. The place we're going to for dinner has a dress code."

I glance down at my outfit. I'm not in jeans, but I'm not exactly dressed to go anywhere that requires a black tie, either. "Can we stop by my place on the way?" I ask.

"I have you covered." Killian pulls a box out from behind him that I didn't notice before. "Olivia gave me your size."

"You didn't have to do that," I tell him.

"I know, but I wanted to."

I take the box into the women's restroom and open it. Inside is a beautiful crimson-colored dress—that matches Killian's tie—and black heels. When I pull them out, I notice the dress is a well-known designer and the heels are donning the signature red soles. This outfit probably cost more than I make as an intern here in a month. And suddenly, the gift sitting inside my purse feels childish and stupid. What was I thinking? I should've bought him a watch or something. *Right, like I could actually afford one a guy like Killian would wear.*

When Killian and I woke up this morning, he had a dozen roses and a box of chocolates waiting for me. He had also run to the coffee shop and picked us up coffee and adorable heart-shaped donuts. When he dropped me off at work on his way to the gym, he told me he would be back at six o'clock to take me out to dinner.

Until he walked through the door, I thought I got him the perfect gift. I mean, what do you even get for the man who's paying you to date him and redecorate his home? The man you're slowly falling in love with but are afraid to tell him? Candy? Flowers? Sure, he got me both of those, but he can also afford to buy me anything he wants if he desires to do so. Killian is a professional athlete who makes millions of dollars a year. There isn't anything he can't afford to buy himself.

I put the dress and heels on and place the outfit I was wearing inside the box. I apply a light layer of lip gloss and then fix my hair the best I can. My mood has plummeted, but I remember Killian is paying me to go out with him, which makes this about him and not me. So, I plaster a smile on my face and head out of the bathroom.

"Jesus, Giselle. You look stunning," he murmurs as I enter the lobby where he's waiting for me. "Everything fits perfect." He lifts my chin with his fingers and gives me a soft kiss to my lips.

"Thank you," I tell him, forcing my smile to remain on my face. He gives me a concerned look but lets it go.

The ride to the restaurant is quiet. Killian has gone all out and rented a car and driver for the night. It reminds me of the first night when we went to the charity gala. Instead of enjoying Killian's company, the entire drive I'm stuck in my own thoughts and insecurities. I know he can tell something is wrong because he's holding my hand a little tighter than usual. He keeps glancing at me like he wants to say something, but he's not sure what to say. I need to snap out of this. It's not worth it to ruin tonight over a stupid outfit I can't afford, and a gift I've already decided Killian will never see. I've escorted tons of rich men. I never cared before. *That's because Killian is different*, I remind myself.

When we arrive at the restaurant, we're shown to our table immediately. I have a seat and Killian sits across from me. He orders us a bottle of wine. Once the waiter leaves, he turns toward me. "What's going on?" he asks, getting straight to the point.

"Nothing," I say, already knowing he's not going to accept my answer but not knowing what else to say.

"Talk to me, please."

I hate that I'm ruining our date. Killian deserves better than this. Knowing he'll need some type of explanation from me, I go with a half-truth. "I don't like that you spent a lot of money on me," I admit. "It's bad enough you're paying to take me out."

Killian frowns. "I'm not paying to take you out."

"Yes, you are. You're on the schedule for tonight. If you weren't, I would be on a date with another guy." Killian flinches at my words.

"I'm sorry," I add, "I didn't mean it like that. I just hate that you're wasting your money on me."

"Let's just enjoy our night, okay?" He takes my hand in his. "The reasons we're here together don't matter. The only thing that matters is that on Valentine's Day I'm out to dinner with the most beautiful woman in New York."

"Just New York, huh?" I joke.

Killian laughs. "I was trying to be romantic without sounding too over the top."

"Ah... okay, then you nailed it. Just the perfect amount of romantic."

The waiter brings us over our drinks. We order our food and then we're left alone again.

"I worked on some ideas for your condo today," I tell him. "Want to see?"

"I want to say no because we shouldn't be discussing work at dinner, but something tells me you're going to show me anyway."

"I am." I laugh, grabbing my purse, which is draped over the back of my chair, to pull out my phone. My purse strap gets stuck on the ear of the chair and then falls to the ground—several items falling out. Killian jumps into action, helping me pick up everything that rolled every which way. Luckily, we're seated in the back of the restaurant, away from other people.

"What's this?" Killian asks, holding up the wrapped gift.

"Nothing." I try to grab it from him, but he moves it out of my reach at the last second.

"Is it for me?" He grins like a little boy.

"It was, but I'm not giving it to you anymore." I try to reach for it again, but Killian takes it with him back to his seat.

"You bought me something for Valentine's Day?" His face is lit up like a damn Christmas tree as he shakes it like one does with their gifts on Christmas morning. Boy, is he about to be disappointed.

"It's nothing much," I tell him.

"I bought you something too." He pulls a small box out of his pocket and sets it on the table. Of course he bought me jewelry.

"You shouldn't have done that." I nod toward the imposing item now sitting on the table between us.

"Stop saying that. Open it."

Reluctantly, I pick up the box and open the lid. Inside is a white gold—maybe platinum—necklace. The chain itself is delicate. In the center of the necklace is a charm in the shape of a heart with a crack going down the middle, accented with tiny diamonds. It's beautiful, but I'm confused as to why he bought me a broken heart. I lift the necklace out of the box.

"Turn it over," Killian murmurs, so I do. And engraved on the back is a quote, that if I wasn't already sitting, would have me falling to my knees.

She made broken look beautiful and strong look invincible.

"Killian," I whisper, my throat clogged with heavy emotion.

"Everybody is broken, Giselle," he says, "but not everybody handles it with such strength and beauty." He stands and comes around behind me, taking the necklace from my hand and placing it around my neck.

Now that I've seen what he's given me, I'm especially terrified of him seeing my gift. I can't even imagine how much this cost him.

"Thank you," I say. "It's beautiful and perfect." I eye my gift in his hand. "Is there any way I can convince you not to open your gift?"

"What? Why?" Killian asks, confused.

"Well, for one, it probably cost less than the box this necklace came in." I laugh humorlessly through my tears.

"I don't give a fuck how much your gift cost," Killian says seriously. "You should know me better than that."

"No, I know. It's just that you spent so much money on me, and..." I let out a deep sigh of defeat. "Well, whatever. Just open it. Let's get this over with."

Killian eyes me curiously then proceeds to open his gift. He opens the flat box and inside is a book.

"It's a coffee table book." A lot of clients like to have one on their coffee table. It makes for a pretty center piece. They're usually of something they enjoy, like architecture or art. The one Killian is holding is of him—of us. I had several photos printed that we've taken on our phones over the last couple weeks. I also had Nick and Olivia send over some they had of him. There are some from the games he's played. One from the Super Bowl he won last year. They're all in dated order. The last image is of us. I wrote a note on that one: Thank you for being broken and lonely with me.

"Giselle," Killian whispers, "you weren't going to give me this? Why?"

"Well, because it only cost me like twenty bucks to make. I just had the photos printed. Like I said, it's a coffee table book. You leave it on the coffee table as decoration." I shrug. "You bought me this beautiful necklace and outfit. It really isn't comparable."

Killian's eyes meet mine, and if I'm not mistaken, they're a tad glossy. "I love...it. I love it. Thank you."

He reaches over and pulls me into a hug. "I'm going to use the restroom. I'll be right back." He sets the book down on the table and stands, walking in the direction toward the restrooms.

My phone pings with a new email. I still have it out because I never showed him the items I found for his condo. When I check it, I see it's from Bianca. I click on the schedule, and once again, it's filled with an entire week of Killian. My heart drops at the thought of him spending all this money on me. He might be able to afford it, but that doesn't mean he should have to. I glance toward the restrooms and notice Killian is still gone.

I dial Bianca's number. She answers on the first ring.

"Giselle, how can I help you?"

"We need to talk. I can't allow Killian to pay to see me anymore."

TWENTY

KILLIAN

I NEED A MOMENT TO BREATHE. To think. When I opened the gift Giselle gave me, I almost told her I loved her. I had to walk away before I did something that would push her away. I'm falling hard for this woman, but we aren't quite in sync yet. I'm sprinting down the field toward the end zone, waiting for her to throw me the ball. I'm completely open and ready, but she isn't. She doesn't trust us enough yet. She's scared of not making a complete pass, so instead she keeps throwing it out of bounds. That's okay, though, because I'm willing to wait until she trusts in us enough to make the play, and when she does, I'll be right here ready to catch whatever she throws. And I can assure you, it will most definitely be a fucking touchdown.

As I stand in the bathroom, rinsing my face off, my phone rings. It's Bianca, Giselle's boss. Confused as to why she would be calling, I answer the call.

"Killian, this is Bianca. I'm calling to let you know Giselle is no longer available to escort you. If you would like to see the women who are available, I can have my assistant send you over their profiles."

Shocked by this turn of events, it takes me a second before I respond. "Giselle is who I choose. We spoke about this."

"Giselle is no longer available to you effective immediately. I'm sorry for the inconvenience, but as I said, I can send over—"

I cut her off. "I don't want anyone else. If she isn't available to me, who is she available to?"

There's a slight pause, and then Bianca says, "I am not at liberty to disclose my employee's clients with you."

Without responding, I hang up.

This can't be fucking happening. For the last ten years I've focused on my career, my family, my friends. This is the first Valentine's Day where I've actually taken a woman out. I'm aware that, up until right now, I was technically paying for her to escort me places, but these last couple weeks haven't been about her job. They've been about us. She wasn't paid to spend her nights with me in my bed, tucked into my side. She wasn't paid to take her lunch break with me. She definitely wasn't paid to go with my niece and me skating and to the zoo. She's been doing all of those things because she wants to. Giselle has come to mean so much to me in such a short amount of time. She isn't just some woman I want to help or date. She's important to me. We have fun together. We laugh and joke and we have a lot in common.

I saw the gift she gave me. That wasn't from a woman who doesn't want to be around me. She wouldn't do this. She wouldn't refuse to see me anymore, only to see other men. *But she also isn't in a place to quit her job...*

Not wanting to cause a scene, I decide not to bring up Bianca's phone call while we're at dinner. We will definitely talk about this, but it will be later. I adjust my suit then head back out to our table. The food has arrived, but Giselle is waiting for me to eat. I lift my fork and knife to cut my steak, but then Giselle looks up at me and smiles sweetly, and my earlier decision flies straight out the window. My blood boils at the idea I was so inconsequential to her she could just walk away from us and smile at me like nothing has happened— like nothing has changed.

My utensils clatter against my plate, and Giselle gives me a concerned look. Did she really think I wouldn't care? Maybe she was hoping I wouldn't find out until after dinner. After I took her home. Does that mean she wasn't planning to spend the night? Bianca said effective immediately. This time tomorrow Giselle will be out with another man. She will accompany him to an event of some sort. He will parade her around on his arm like a trophy he's won. One he doesn't deserve. He'll treat her like an object. He won't pay attention to whether she's happy. Whether she's satisfied. He'll be undeserving of her, but still she'll give herself to him. My thoughts go back to her confession a couple weeks ago: *"I just want to feel connected to someone. I'm tired of feeling so alone."* If that's what she craves then why is she pushing me away?

"Was I not enough for you?" I snap before I can stop myself. Giselle's brows furrow together in confusion at my question.

"Excuse me?"

"Was. I. Not. Enough. For. You?" I repeat slower. "Was it because I wouldn't fuck you?"

"Killian," she hisses, looking around at the other patrons, "what are you talking about?"

"You know what I'm talking about, don't play stupid. I know you called Bianca and told her to take me off your schedule."

Giselle goes pale. "Can we please talk about this in private?" She glances around at the couples near us, clearly embarrassed. I feel like shit for calling her out right now, but fuck if with one phone call she didn't go and break my goddamn heart. The thought of her with other men tears me apart.

"Please," she whispers, and it's then I notice her eyes are glossed over as if she's about to cry. Why would she cry? She's the one who's ended us, not me.

"Fine." I stand, our meal disregarded. "Let's go." It isn't as if we're going to sit here and eat our food now anyway. Giselle stands as well, and the light hits the necklace I gave her. I want to turn the clock back to ten minutes ago, when I was still ignorant to the decision she made about us behind my back.

Grabbing the book she gave me, I stalk out of the restaurant with Giselle trailing behind. We're at a restaurant where I have an account on file, so the meal will be paid for. I text the driver, and a few minutes later he pulls around. Once we're in the car, I give him my address and then press the button for the privacy partition.

The second it's closed, Giselle turns to face me and says, "I did call Bianca." Several tears fly down her pink cheeks. Has she been crying since we were inside? I was so hellbent on not looking at her, I didn't notice her tears actually fell. "I told her I couldn't continue to let you pay for my services. That when you fall in love with a man..." She chokes on a sob. "When you fall in love with a man, you don't request payment from him." It takes a second for what she said to soak into my brain.

Fuck. Me.

She quit her job.

For me.

She's fallen in love with me.

Needing to touch her, to feel her against me, I grab her hips and pull her onto my lap. She squeals in surprise and wipes the tears from her eyes. "Giselle, baby, I just...I assumed you were tired of waiting for me to get my shit together. I can't even tell you how sorry I am. God, I am such a jackass."

Lifting her chin, I look into her beautiful, soulful eyes. The same ones I had once mistaken for being cold, but in actuality were broken and lonely—like me. "Please forgive me. I was a damn fool. A fool who was too blinded by his love for you to see that you were always mine."

"You love me too?" she whispers. A single tear escapes down her cheek and I use my thumb to wipe it away.

"I do. I love you, baby."

Her breath hitches and then our mouths crash against each other. Our lips molding, our tongues swirling. We kiss fervently as Giselle undoes my pants. I glide my hands up her creamy thighs to find she's wearing a silk thong, then palm the globes of her perfect ass. She lifts slightly and pulls my dick out of my boxers, stroking it a few times before she pushes the thin material to the side and guides me into her slick cunt. A throaty groan escapes as she begins to ride me with abandon. Our kiss not once stops, instead it gets harder, rougher. Her fingers tug on the strands of my hair as she grinds against me, pelvis to pelvis. Up and down. She feels so damn good.

Hot. Wet. Tight.

And then I'm coming.

Like a motherfucking virgin.

I break our kiss, embarrassed as fuck. My head drops to Giselle's chest. She's breathing heavily from doing all the work, yet she didn't even get off.

"That's not how I wanted this to go down," I mutter, and her body shakes with laughter. I look up at her and she's smiling down at me. I shake my head in frustration. "I wanted to make love to you, not fuck you in the backseat of a town car and blow my load in ten fucking seconds like a horny teenager."

Giselle giggles. Fucking giggles.

"Actually," she says, "it was me who was fucking you."

I groan and close my eyes. She giggles some more. "It's not funny. You didn't even get off." I go to lift her off me, but her thighs clench around mine. My now-flaccid dick is still inside her.

"Hey," she murmurs. When I don't open my eyes, I feel her cold palms against my cheeks. "Look at me, Kill." I do, and fuck if she isn't the most stunning woman I've ever met. Her hair is tousled, her lip gloss is smeared. Her cheeks are a light pink. She's fucking gorgeous.

"We have all night," she says. "Once we get back to your place and your dick recuperates, you can fuck me."

"I don't want to fuck you," I say, repeating my earlier words. "I want to make love to you."

TWENTY-ONE

GISELLE

"TAKE THAT DRESS OFF NOW," Killian demands when we enter his condo. I watch as he pulls at his tie until it comes loose, then he drops it to the floor along with his jacket. He unbuttons his shirt and drops it haphazardly, then kicks his shoes into the corner before he removes his pants and boxers. I follow him into the bathroom—enjoying the view of his tight, muscular ass—where he turns the water on in his spacious shower. He looks at me and frowns. "Giselle, clothes."

I giggle—because apparently a man telling me he loves me leads to me turning into a teenage girl—and unzip my dress. It falls to the marble floor and pools around my high-heeled feet. I step out of it and am left in a pink and black satin bra and panty set and my heels. I didn't plan on Killian seeing me in this, but when I woke up this morning and remembered it was Valentine's Day, I wore it to feel pretty. Now, based on the way Killian is looking at me, I'm very glad I did.

I unlatch my bra and let it fall to the ground. My nipples pebble from the slight chill in the air. Next, I hook the sides of my panties with my index fingers and slowly lower them down my legs until they reach my heels, then I step out of them, fully aware I'm putting on a show for Killian.

"Fuck me," he groans as he eye-fucks his way down my now-naked body while I stand in front of him in only the heels he bought me. He stalks over and lifts me up, placing me onto the counter. The granite is cool against my overheated body, and it causes me to shiver. His lips land on my neck. He peppers kisses downward, stopping along the way to suck and lick my overheated flesh. My fingers pull on his hair, demanding more. My heels wrap around his bare ass and pull him into me. His dick, once again hard, teases my clit. I pull him in closer and his dick enters me.

Killian groans, biting down on my shoulder. "Fuck me," I beg, and he does. His hips thrust powerfully as he fucks me harder than I've ever been fucked in my life. My head lulls back and hits the mirror as I moan in pleasure. His lips go to my breasts, sucking on my nipples. His dick is thick and long and hits my G-spot over and over again. And unlike last time, I come completely undone. My entire body shakes, my vaginal walls clench, and I orgasm around Killian's cock as his warm seed fills me.

"Jesus fucking Christ, woman!" he growls. "I can't control myself with you."

I laugh at his words. "Well, at least we're getting closer to the bed," I point out. "What's the saying? Third time's a charm?"

"Shower, now," he grunts, and I laugh some more.

"Yes, caveman."

He glares playfully then pulls out of me. When he backs up farther, his eyes go wide, and I follow his gaze downward to see what he's looking at. Fuck! We didn't use protection. Both times. I'm about to tell him I'm on birth control when he says, "That's the sexiest fucking thing I've ever seen in my life."

"What?" I look down, confused. I waxed recently, but surely he's seen a hairless pussy before.

"My seed dripping out of your cunt and running down the inside of your thigh."

His words have me wanting him back inside me, but I know he needs time to recuperate. "C'mon, dirty boy, I want to soap you up." I jump down and kick my heels off. The water is still on and the bathroom is now all fogged up. I step into the hot water and moan as it rains down on my body. Killian joins me, pulling my body against his and laying a hard kiss to my lips.

"Thank you," he murmurs. When I give him a puzzled look, he elaborates. "For quitting your job. For taking a chance on us. For opening your heart and letting me in. I will do everything in my power to make sure you never regret it."

A lump forms in my throat and my eyes become blurry through

my tears. I'm thankful we're in the shower so he can't tell I'm crying again. This man. He's quickly come to mean so damn much to me.

Pulling his head down, I kiss him softly. "You don't have to thank me, Kill," I whisper against his lips. "You loving me, broken and all, is everything."

MY EYES FLUTTER OPEN. The room is dark. It must still be nighttime. Why am I awake? Then I feel it...Killian's strong yet firm lips on my flesh.

Kiss behind my ear.

The front of his body is pressed against my back. We fell asleep naked with his dick nestled between my ass cheeks.

Kiss to my neck.

His rough hand makes its way down my arm and over my bare hip. I wiggle my ass to tease him and his cock twitches slightly.

Kiss on my shoulder.

He rolls me onto my back. Spreading my legs, he situates himself between my thighs. His fingers thread with mine, our hands landing on the pillow over my head. Then, he pushes ever so slowly into me. His wide girth stretching me oh so deliciously.

He doesn't thrust.

No.

He glides.

In and out of me.

Like my body was made for him.

His lips meet mine and he kisses me softly.

And for the first time, I know what it feels like for a man to make love to me.

TWENTY-TWO

GISELLE

"WOW! This dress is exquisite! You're going to be the most beautiful bride," Corrine, Olivia's stepmom, gushes as Olivia turns in a full circle.

"It's perfect," Olivia agrees. "I'm just glad there's room for growth and we're getting married soon, or I would have to buy a different dress."

"It would be worth it," Corrine says. "You're bringing another little miracle into this world."

"I know. I just can't wait to finally marry Nick and move into our new home." She smiles into the mirror and our eyes lock. Her lips turn down, and I hate that she's putting her future off because of me.

"You could move into the house now," I suggest. "It's practically move-in ready. You don't have to wait until your married." When she looks like she's going to argue, I add, "I could keep an eye on our place until it sells."

"I haven't put it up for sale." She frowns.

"Not yet, but you are, right?"

"Well..."

"Olivia, we've gone over this." I stand and turn her around so we're facing each other. "I love you. You're the best friend a woman could ever have. But it's time to put yourself first. It's only a matter of time until my mom's house sells. Move in with your fiancé and put your place up for sale."

"Okay." She nods but still looks unsure.

"It's not a request. I'm demanding you, as your best friend, to move in with Nick now."

"Okay." She smiles softly. And then her eyes glance down and spot my necklace. "This is beautiful. Who gave this to you?" She fingers the heart and flips it over to read the inscription. "Oh, Giselle."

"Killian gave it to me for Valentine's Day," I admit.

"You two are..."

"We are." I can't help the grin that lights up my face, and Olivia's smile widens as well.

"Oh my god! I'm going to need all the details."

I laugh. "Okay, but first, let's finish our fitting."

"Fine!" Olivia pouts playfully.

"I'm very happy for you, Giselle," Corrine says, pulling both of us into a hug. "I'm so glad you two have found love."

"Thank you."

After we finish at the bridal boutique, we head out to brunch. While we're there, my friend Tabitha texts me with some info I was waiting on. I excuse myself for a moment and make the call.

"Good afternoon, may I please speak to Benjamin Fields? My name is Giselle."

I'm put on a brief hold, and then a baritone voice appears over the line. "This is Benjamin Fields. How can I help you?"

I explain to him that Tabitha gave me his info and I'm looking for an evening job—one where I don't sell my body—or soul—for money. Because I hold several of the qualifications he's looking for, he agrees to meet with me tomorrow night.

After thanking him, we hang up and I see a text from Killian: **No wise fish would go anywhere without a porpoise.**

I let out a soft laugh at his, for once, correct Alice in Wonderland quote, then text him back: **Google finally got it right.**

Another text from him immediately comes through. It's a picture of a hardcovered copy of Alice's Adventures in Wonderland. I text him back a big smiley face. I love that he picked up the book simply because he knows I love it.

A few seconds later, his response comes through: **What time will you be done?**

It's been a little over a week since Valentine's Day and every night has been spent in his arms. He picks me up from work every day, and we either go to dinner or order in. Today is Saturday, so I'm off, and I know he was hoping to spend the day together. But then I remembered Olivia made an appointment for us to get fitted for our dresses for her wedding. Killian pouted as I left this morning, but I promised we would spend the rest of the weekend together. I'm not sure how I'm going to explain it to him if I get this job. It will mean once again working evenings.

I text him back I'll be done in a little while, and he responds that he'll be here to pick me up. For a man who's never been in a serious relationship, he sure makes it look like he's an expert.

After lunch, we step outside, and sure enough Killian is waiting on the sidewalk, only he's standing against the light post and not in his car. He smiles when he spots me. He stalks over, picking me up and twirling me around while kissing me like he didn't just see me this morning. It reminds me of the shit you see in those cheesy Hallmark movies. I crack up laughing when he puts me down, and Olivia and Corrine both swoon. I guess that's why you see stuff like that in those movies...

"Ladies," Killian says as he bends at the waist and bows. "Do you need a ride anywhere?"

Olivia giggles but shakes her head. "Nope, I drove. You two have fun, but not too much." She mock glares and then she and Corrine head to her car.

"Your place?" I ask.

Killian takes my hand in his. "Actually, I have a surprise for you." He opens the car door for me and I get in. He doesn't tell me where we're going but when we get onto the interstate, I have an idea. Forty minutes later we pull up to the facility my mother is staying at.

"She's accepting visitors?" I ask, hopeful.

"She is, and she would like to see you."

I throw my arms around him. "Thank you."

"Your sister is here too. We're going to meet with the doctors and go over her diagnosis, and then your sister and you will have some time with your mom."

We're greeted by the receptionist who walks us back to the office. Adrianna is already in there. "Addy!" I run into the room and give my sister a hug. It's been too long since we've seen each other. "Oh, Addy," I murmur, "I've missed you."

"I missed you more." She smiles brightly. "Thank you for making sure mom is getting the best care. I hate that I can't do anything..."

"Hey, stop," I say. "Your job is to go to school. I peeked at your grades the other day, and you're doing phenomenal."

"Thank you." She glances over at Killian and gives him a knowing smile. "It's nice to see you again." The one and only time they met was the day my dad left my mom. Now they're meeting for the second time to discuss my mother's mental health. *Can you say dysfunctional family?*

Adrianna extends her hand to shake his, and he takes it. While chatting with my sister the last couple weeks, I've mentioned Killian a few times, and while I haven't come out and said what we are to each other—hell, I'm not even sure we know—the grin my sister's currently sporting tells me she's drawn her own conclusion, which means she's imagining us married and with kids in the near future.

"Killian is actually the one who—" I begin to tell her he's the reason our mom is getting the help she needs, but Killian cuts me off.

"I'm the one who made sure your sister got to this appointment on time." I give him a confused look, but then it clicks. He doesn't want my sister to know I needed his help for our mom. And my heart expands at his selflessness.

The doctors come in and introduce themselves since it's their first time meeting Adrianna, and then in walks my mother.

"Mom!" Adrianna and I both jump up and give her a hug.

"Oh, girls, I'm so happy to see you both," our mom coos.

Killian pulls a chair up, so she can sit between Adrianna and me. "Killian, it's good to see you, again." She gives him a hug.

"You too, Mrs. Winters. You look good."

"Oh, thank you." My mom blushes, and I stifle my laugh. Killian seems to have that kind of effect on all the Winters women— even the one who's gay.

Dr. Burns begins, "We wanted your mom to be in this meeting because it is her health we're discussing. After the last few weeks of close evaluation, we have determined your mother was in fact misdiagnosed. It's actually something that is very common, especially since the symptoms are alike. Looking at her history, the different psychiatrists diagnosed her with MDD: Major Depressive Disorder. What we've determined is your mother actually has Bipolar Disorder. While the symptoms are similar, the medications are not."

Dr. Clay continues, "Oftentimes you might've thought your mother's medications were working. She would have good days, and you probably assumed it was because of the medications. But then when she would have bad days, you thought they weren't working, and so you did what most people do. You took her to a new doctor to get reevaluated."

My heart plummets in my chest as I listen to them. They're describing exactly what we went through, and what we did the last fifteen years.

"I see the look on your face," Dr. Clay says. "Don't do that. Don't feel like you've let her down. She doesn't feel that way. Do you, Sarah?"

Everyone turns to my mom. "If it weren't for my daughters, I wouldn't even be alive right now." Tears fill her lids. "Nobody could've known. I didn't even understand it myself. The highs, the lows. The depression. I hate that my daughters spent their childhood without the kind of mother they deserved."

"Oh, Mom, we love you. We just want you better," I tell her.

"And I appreciate that, but now that I'm able to see things more clearly, I need to take responsibility. I failed my family."

"Mrs. Winters," Dr. Clay says, "have you spoken to your counselor about your feelings regarding this matter?"

"I have," Mom says. "We're agreeing to disagree at the moment."

Dr. Clay laughs. "Okay, please make sure you continue to speak your thoughts. While accepting responsibility is a good thing, you weren't aware of what was wrong and didn't understand what was happening. I don't like you using the word failed."

Mom nods in understanding.

"So, what now?" Adrianna asks.

"Now that we have a firm grasp on your mother's situation, we continue to treat her. We're going to keep her here for at least another few weeks. Bipolar is treatable, but it's also about learning how to live with it. She will continue to see her counselor here and be monitored closely. Once she's discharged, in the beginning, she will need to see a counselor several times a week. She'll need to live a life free of as much stress as possible. We want her to work on figuring out how she can accomplish this. Bipolar isn't something that will just go away. It's something she will have to be aware of and manage every day.

My stomach knots at the thought of my mom having to deal with this forever. I was so sure her being here would mean she would be fixed. But from what they're saying, the only thing they can offer her are heavy duty Band-Aids. She's going to have to deal with this for the rest of her life.

"Mom, how are you feeling?" I ask her.

"I feel really good," she says with a confidence I don't think I've ever heard from her before. "I feel calm and less anxious. I'm beginning to feel like my body and my head are actually my own."

I reach over and place my hand on top of hers and squeeze it. She gives me a watery smile. And I vow once she gets out of here, I'm going to make sure she never loses her smile again. I'm going to sell the house and find us a place to live, and I'm going to make sure she takes her meds and sees a counselor. The last fifteen plus years were a rollercoaster between heaven and hell, and I will never let her get back on that ride again.

The doctors continue to explain the diagnosis and treatment plan some more, and when they're done, they let us know we can spend some time with our mom in the visiting room.

"Dr. Burns, can I ask you a question in private?" I ask as everyone stands.

"Sure," he says.

Everyone steps out of the room while we remain inside. "I was just wondering...Bipolar Disorder, is it...can it be genetic?"

The doctor gives me a quizzical look, so I elaborate. "My mom wasn't always like this. I can remember the good times from when I was little. There weren't many, but there were enough to think she wasn't born like this."

"Bipolar is a brain disorder which can develop any time," he begins. "Some people are born with the vulnerability to the disorder, which means they have a higher chance of eventually developing the disorder. In your mom's case that's probably what happened. She might've had the symptoms when she was younger, but nobody knew to pay attention to them."

"Can my sister and I have this...vulnerability?"

"Some studies have shown it can run in families, but just because your mom has it doesn't mean you will. It's important for you to pay attention to the symptoms we've discussed, and if you feel you're experiencing them, see a counselor immediately. Bipolar Disorder isn't a death sentence. You saw your mom today. She is doing well. The key is to monitor her and teach her how to live with the disorder. Many people with Bipolar live a normal life."

A normal life. My mind goes to all the years my father tried to love my mom but couldn't handle it. To the years my sister and I practically raised ourselves. Nothing was normal about any of that. I know it was before she got help, but who's to say once she gets out we'll ever have a *normal* relationship with our mom. The medications are working for now, but what happens when they don't? Yes, this facility is one of the best, but like the doctors said, it's all trial and error to find a way to manage the disorder.

"Thank you, Dr. Burns."

After spending some time with Mom, we all say our goodbyes. Adrianna heads back to Boston, and Killian and I head back to his place. While he's driving, I make the mistake of looking up my mom's condition. Of course there are a million and one horror stories—from patients having a higher chance of suffering from substance abuse, to a higher risk of suicide. So even if my mom's medication works and for the most part she's okay, there's still a chance of things going wrong. Just as I'm about to click on another page, my phone rings. It's the realtor.

"I have some good news," she tells me. "An offer has been put in for the house."

"Oh, thank God." My entire body relaxes.

"It was actually placed a few hours ago, but I had to type up the contract. It's a cash offer and they have agreed to your asking price."

"Really? They didn't even try to counter?" Weird...I'm asking for what the going rate of the homes in the area are, but still...

"All you need to do is have your dad sign the papers, and since you have the power-of-attorney for your mom, you'll need to sign them as well, and then we'll get the deal done."

Shit! My dad...I'm going to have to find him and get him to sign the damn papers.

"Giselle...that won't be a problem, will it?"

"No, I just need to find my dad..."

We hang up and Killian glances over at me. "Your mom's house?"

"It sold. A cash deal. This is perfect timing..." And then it hits me. The timing is too perfect. "I told Olivia today to move into her new house with Nick. You don't think she bought the house, do you?"

Killian's eyes flit back and forth between the road and me. "I don't think she would do that," he says.

"You're right. She knows how upset I would be. Now I just need to find my dad."

"I can have my brother search for him."

"Thank you."

"So what did you want to talk to the doctor about alone?" he asks.

"I asked him if Bipolar is genetic."

"And?"

"It can be, and I've made a decision." One that was cemented the minute I viewed all those posts online. When Killian doesn't say anything, I continue, "I don't want to have any children."

Killian glances over at me then back to the road. "Giselle, what you went through growing up was because your mother wasn't diagnosed properly. You heard the doctor. Your mother will live a normal life."

"There's that word again...*normal*...nothing was normal about what Addy and I went through. I can't imagine ever putting my children through that. The physical and emotional abuse. I won't do it. And who's to say this time will work?"

"Maybe take some time and think about it. It's not like you have to decide right now."

"There's nothing to think about. I won't put my family through that. The doctor said it can develop at any time."

"So, what? You just won't have a family? You won't get married?"

"It's one thing to get married. I'm not saying I'm going to not have a life. But had my parents not had kids when my mom got sick, they wouldn't have had to deal with us."

"I can't speak for your father, but I don't believe your mother would view it as *dealing* with you. She was so happy to finally feel good. You heard her when we were talking to her afterward. She's excited to start this next phase of her life with her daughters."

Killian pulls into the parking garage and parks in his spot, then he turns to me. "I feel like I'm finally living again, and you're the reason why. Please don't stop what's happening between us out of fear."

I take a second to assess his features. His messy chocolate-brown hair and deep mesmerizing green eyes. The way he smiles at me like I'm everything. He's the perfect mix of sexy and beautiful and perfect. And I know exactly what he means, because it wasn't until he entered my life, I felt like I was finally really living. I don't want to stop living...I just don't want my living to negatively affect those around me.

"I don't want to stop anything between us. But Killian, I have to ask, and I know it's too early to even mention children, but would you be okay with...I mean..." I take a deep breath. "I don't want to have kids. I know it sounds like overkill, but you weren't there when I was growing up. You didn't see what we went through because of my mother's illness. You didn't read the articles I read. I want to live my life and love you. But I don't want you to feel you have to stay with me out of obligation, if what happened to my mom, happens to me. My dad sucks, but I believe that a lot of the reason why he stayed with my mom all those years was because of my sister and me. I don't think it's a coincidence that he left once Addy went away to college. I don't ever want you to feel you *have* to be with me. And I don't ever want to put my children in the position Addy and I were put in. I'm not trying to blame my mom. I know she didn't know. But I do know. And it would be irresponsible of me to have kids knowing there's a chance that at some point I might not be able to be the mother they deserve. Are you okay with it just being the two of us?"

"Shit, baby, I know what you went through was rough, but I would never leave you. Whatever happens in life we will face it together. And you can't go by all the crap on the internet."

"It wasn't just crap. Many of those sites are credible. Did you know people with Bipolar run a higher risk of committing suicide? Of becoming addicted to drugs? Is that what you want to potentially expose our kids to? I found my mom on the floor half-dead. I would never wish that on another person."

Killian stares at me for a long moment. I don't even realize I'm holding my breath until he nods once. "I just want you, Giselle. Whatever it is you want or don't want I'm okay with. But I think you should speak to someone."

"Like a counselor?"

"Yeah, I can go with you if you want. I just think it would be a good idea to speak to someone about how you're feeling."

"Okay," I agree.

We get inside and Killian gives his brother a call. Not even twenty minutes later he calls back with an address for my dad.

"That was fast."

"My brother has connections." Killian winks playfully.

"Will you go with me to see him?"

"Of course. When?"

"Now? The address isn't too far from here. We can swing by and get the papers from the realtor and take them to him to sign and get notarized."

WE PULL up to an older yet still beautiful brownstone in Chelsea. I'm not a real estate expert, but if I had to guess, the place is worth a few million. "Are you sure this is the address?" I ask Killian.

He double checks the information his brother sent over. "Yeah."

We get out and walk up to the front door. I ring the doorbell and immediately hear the sound of children's laughter. The door swings open, and standing there is a young, gorgeous blond-haired woman of maybe thirty. Based on how she's dressed and the way she presents herself, it's obvious this woman has money. Two little boys who can't be any older than five peek out from behind her, giggling.

"I'm sorry. I think I have the wrong address. I'm looking for Craig Winters."

The woman smiles softly. "You have the right address." She turns her head back toward the inside of her home. "Craig, honey, someone is here for you." My stomach lurches at the term of endearment. Killian's hand finds mine. Something isn't right here.

My dad steps forward, and when he realizes it's me, his face pales. "Giselle..."

"Dad."

"Craig," the woman says, "why is she calling you 'Dad'?"

"Heather, give us a moment, please." My dad steps outside, shutting the door behind him.

"Is she...are they..." I can't even finish my sentence. I'm in shock. Killian's grip on my hand tightens.

"She is, and they are," my dad murmurs softly.

Oh my god! He has two kids by a woman who isn't my mom— his wife. "But you're still married to mom!"

"Heather and I aren't married. We're engaged, though. I was waiting for your mom to get out of the facility before giving her the papers."

"You knew she was in a facility?" I shout. "Those little boys aren't babies! And that woman doesn't even know you have a daughter!"

"Giselle, please let me explain."

"No! Fuck you, *Dad*!" I'm about to storm away when I remember the papers I need him to sign. I turn back around and push the contract into his chest. "The house sold. You need to sign these papers, and don't you dare even think for a second you're getting a penny. Did you take out the second loan on the mortgage to purchase this place?"

"No, Heather has her own money." I notice he doesn't explain what he did take the money out for. At this point, though, it doesn't matter. I just need him to sign these damn papers so I can deal with what he left behind.

"Just sign the papers," I tell him.

He nods once.

Knowing how upset I am, Killian goes with my dad to get the papers notarized while I wait in his car. When they return, my dad tries to speak to me, but I refuse. He made his choice, and clearly he's having no problem living with it.

"Do not bring those divorce papers to mom to sign," I say before he walks away. "Send them to me, and when she's healthy enough, I'll tell her the man she married is a lying, cheating, asshole."

Dad looks like he wants to say something, but I don't give him a chance. "Don't ever contact any of us again. As far as I'm concerned you're no longer part of our family...not that you've been for a long time." I roll up my window and wait for Killian to get in.

I try to tell him I'd like to be dropped off at my place, but in typical Killian-fashion, he ignores me completely. Once we're inside his place and changed into comfier clothes, he pulls me into his side on the couch.

"It feels like today has been the never-ending day." I laugh humorlessly.

He lifts me into his lap and kisses me tenderly. "How about I make you forget about today?"

"That sounds like a damn good idea to me."

Killian kisses me harder this time, his fingers reaching up and pinching my nipples. My fingers thread through the strands of his hair. We kiss for God knows how long, getting lost in each other. Eventually, he carries me into his room and lays me on the bed. We remove each other's clothes and then he spreads my legs and enters me slowly. He makes love to me several times, successfully making me forget the craziness of today.

TWENTY-THREE

KILLIAN

"DAMN, I don't want to pat my own back, but this sleeve is going to look fresh as hell when it's done. Shit, it already does." Jase turns the gun off and the buzzing sound immediately stops. He brings a hand-held mirror down to my arm so I can see the new work he's added. He's right. It looks damn good. What started out as a tattoo of my college team football helmet has turned into an entire collage of my career. From my NFL team logo to the numerals from the super bowl we won last year. Today, though, I had him add in something more personal. The quote on the back of the heart I gave Giselle on Valentine's Day has been artfully wrapped around my bicep and woven through several of my other tattoos. I know it's only been a couple weeks since we made this thing we have going on between us official, but I can feel it. She's it for me.

My phone rings, so I pull it out of my pocket while Jase rubs Vaseline across the new artwork. The caller ID shows it's my brother.

"Hey, bro, what's up?"

"I have news on Melanie." Damn, straight to the point. The other night while lying in bed, Giselle mentioned again that maybe I should find Melanie to get some closure. So, the following night when she said she had to work late and couldn't come over, I went over to my brother's place for dinner and told him everything. And like I knew he would, he agreed I needed closure and told me he would get Melanie's contact info.

"All right."

"She's living in North Carolina...Cedar Wood Acres."

"She's back living where we went to school?" It would make sense since she once told me she grew up there, but it's weird to imagine her back after she made it a point to run away from that very same place all those years ago. She even went as far as to drop out of school just to get away.

"Yep," Dylan confirms.

"Is she married? Have kids?"

"I didn't tell him to find anything out. I have a phone number and address. I'll text it to you. I think if you want to know about her it's best if you find out from her yourself."

"You're right," I agree. "I'll give her a call and see if she's up to meet with me. I can even visit Mom and Dad while I'm there."

"Good idea," he says. "Are you going alone?" He knows Giselle and I are dating. I didn't tell him about her old job as an escort, but he knows things are serious between us. I try to imagine flying to North Carolina by myself, but I can't picture it. I'd love to introduce her to my parents and show her where I grew up.

"I'm going to ask Giselle to go with me."

"All right, cool. Let me know if you need anything. Don't forget your niece's birthday is next weekend."

"I won't. I'll talk to you later."

We hang up and I text Giselle: **Dinner tonight? I can pick you up from work.**

She responds immediately: **Can't. I'm sorry. Working late. Rain check?**

Shoving my phone into my pocket, I head out to the main lobby of Forbidden Ink. This is the third time this week she's asked for a rain check because of work. My only thought is that maybe because of the lack of paycheck from A Touch of Class, she's asked for more hours at Fresh Designs. I hate to think she's struggling now to make ends meet because of me, but it makes sense. She needed that income and now it's gone.

"Sorry about that," I say to Jase. "My brother called. The addition looks amazing." I slide my card across the counter, and he takes it to ring me up.

"No worries." He hands me the receipt to fill out. "So...uh...have you seen Celeste lately?" My gaze leaves the receipt and lands on Jase. Why the hell is he asking about Celeste? And then I remember the night of Giselle's birthday and the awkward as fuck vibes Jase and Celeste gave off...

"Here and there...I think she said something about Paris." I shrug. He nods, trying to appear nonchalant but his eyes are darting all over the place like he's nervous.

"You don't like her, do you?" I'm well aware I sound like a gossipy teenage girl.

"Nah." He shakes his head emphatically and clears his throat.

"You sure?" I ask while I fill out the tip and sign my name.

"Yeah, man. The last time I saw her she left a bit pissed, and I was just wondering how she's doing. Forget I asked." He takes the receipt from me and hands me back my card.

And that's when I remember something. "You know Celeste..." Jase's face doesn't give anything away. "When I was in college, you came to the campus looking for her." It was a good ten years ago, but now that I'm thinking about it, it was clear that day he not only knew Celeste but was really upset.

"That was a long time ago," Jase says. "And to be honest, I don't think I ever knew her."

"She doesn't seem to let a lot of people in," I tell him. A few weeks ago I would've told him she's a gold-digging bitch and to run, but now, after seeing how wrong I was about Giselle, I'm done assuming the worst in every female. Giselle, Olivia, and Nick are good people and all three of them like and care about Celeste, so that has to mean something. "From what Nick's said over the years, Celeste's upbringing caused her to keep most people at arm's length. I don't know what happened between you two, but I wouldn't take it personal. Celeste's sole focus has always been on her career." I'm not putting her down, but being honest. The woman came from nothing and has made it her life mission to make herself into something, and she's done just that. If nothing else, Celeste Leblanc is determined.

Jase flinches but doesn't respond. He extends his hand and we shake. "Thanks for the heads up."

"Sure thing."

"Quinn isn't here right now, but give her a call when you're ready to set up your next appointment."

"Sounds good, man."

I head out and jump into my car. I check my phone and remember I never texted Giselle back. It's already after six. An idea hits me. She mentioned working late, but she needs to eat. She might be stuck in the office, but I can bring dinner to her. Stopping by the deli, I order us some soups and sandwiches, then drive over to Giselle's office. When I get to her floor, the place, for the most part, is empty.

"May I help you?" an older woman asks, stepping out of what I assume is her office.

"I'm looking for Giselle."

The woman's brows furrow slightly, then she must remember her manners because she smiles and introduces herself. "I'm Lydia, Giselle's boss."

"Nice to meet you. I'm Killian, her boyfriend." The title rolls off my tongue easily. We haven't discussed labels, but giving myself that title feels right.

Lydia looks confused but quickly composes herself. "It's nice to meet you as well," she says, but it's obvious Giselle hasn't mentioned me. "Unfortunately Giselle isn't here. Our office closes at six."

"Is it possible she stayed late to work?" I eye the hallway which leads to her office.

"Occasionally she does, but tonight she actually left a few minutes early, so no, it's not possible."

A sinking feeling hits me hard. I thank her and head back to the elevator. When I get back in my car, I text Giselle: **Where are you?**

A few minutes later, she texts back: **I told you I'm working.**

There's no way she lied to me, right? She wouldn't tell me she quit working for A Touch of Class and it not be true. Not wanting to play games, I go for the truth.

Me: I'm at your office and you're not here.

The bubbles indicating she's typing appear...then disappear. This happens several times before they disappear for good. A minute later my phone rings.

"You're at Fresh Designs?" she asks, sounding out of breath.

"Yes, and you're not."

"You came to check up on me?" Accusation drips in her words.

"I came to bring you dinner."

She sighs. "I'm not there."

"I know."

Another sigh.

"Giselle, talk to me, baby." Whatever it is we'll figure it out.

"Promise me you'll listen before you react." Jesus, fuck.

"Giselle..."

"A friend of mine who works at A Touch of Class mentioned a

popular nightclub recently opened, so for the hell of it I applied." I notice she doesn't name the club. "I didn't think I would get hired, but I did."

"And that's why you haven't been able to hang out..." The pieces are slowly coming together.

"Yes, because I've been working evenings."

"When did you get hired?"

"Umm...like two weeks ago." I do the math in my head. The day after we met with her mom and went to her dad's place, she mentioned she had an appointment. Several times since then she's canceled our plans. She must've been working and didn't tell me. Why wouldn't she tell me?

"Giselle, what club are you working at?" I close my eyes and wait for the blow. The one I know is coming.

"Assets," she whispers.

Fuck! The goddamned strip club. A high class one no less, but still a strip club.

"I'm not stripping," she rushes out.

"Then what are you doing there?" I try to keep my voice composed, but fuck, this woman is going to be the death of me.

"I'm waitressing and working the bar. I worked the bar throughout college..." We're both silent for a beat, and then Giselle adds, "Please don't be mad."

"I'm coming to get you."

"Kill, please. I searched all over New York for a job! You don't understand how hard it is to find a job that will pay me enough to cover my sister's school *and* my school loans. Sure, the house being sold helps, but I still need to find a place to live and rent isn't cheap. I have a masters in interior freaking design. I might as well not even have a college degree. The tips I make here are more than I make working at Fresh Designs."

I put my car in drive and peel out. "I get it, babe. I do. But you're not working there. I'll be there in ten minutes. You can come out willingly or I'll carry your ass out."

Giselle gasps. "You wouldn't."

"I would."

"There's no way my boss—"

"Benjamin Fields?" I laugh humorlessly. "Trust me, he won't do a damn thing about it."

"You know him?" she shrieks. "Of course you do! You're a goddamned NFL player. You know everybody!"

"Eight minutes, Giselle," I warn.

"Kill, please! I'm on break. I took it just to call you."

"And now you're clocking out. Seven minutes."

I click end on the call and throw my phone into the center console. Damn woman is testing my patience. I'm pissed as hell she'd get a job at a fucking strip club without telling me, but at the same time, it's what I love about her. She's hellbent on being independent, and she's determined to take care of her mom and sister. While I'm furious, I'm also pretty sure I just fell even more in love with her.

I pull up to the valet and park my car. "I'll only be a minute," I yell to the guy. When I get up to the front, the bouncer who scans in the VIP members immediately recognizes me. Assets is a newer club but already well-known. Several of my teammates have VIP memberships here.

"Killian, how are you?"

"Good. You?"

"Can't complain."

"I didn't know you were a VIP member." He types away on his iPad. Before I can correct him and explain why I'm here, out walks Giselle from the side door. Her hair is in a high, tight ponytail. Her makeup way overdone. She's wearing sweats and a hoodie, which means she changed out of whatever the uniform is. I expect her to be mad, furious even, but she's not. She's frowning and her eyes appear to be glassed over like she's about to cry.

"I'm not," I tell the bouncer. "I'm just here to pick up my girlfriend." I wrap my arm around Giselle's shoulders and kiss her cheek. "You ready?" I ask her, and she nods wordlessly.

The ride home is quiet, and once we're inside, Giselle excuses herself to shower. I consider joining her, but figure she needs some time to herself. I reheat the soups and place the sandwiches on plates. I pour us both something to drink then wait for her to get done. When she comes out, she's in my boxers and Henley. Her hair is in a messy bun and her face is makeup-free. She's back to looking fucking gorgeous.

She sits across from me at the table and thanks me for the food before she starts to eat. We eat in silence for a few minutes, and then she finally speaks. "I'm in debt with over a hundred thousand dollars in student loans. The interest accrues every month."

I set my spoon down to give her my full attention.

"My mom's house sold, but because of the second loan my dad took out on it, which was probably to help out his *other* family, I only got so much from the sale, and now I need to find a place to live. My mom is due to get out in a few weeks. She needs somewhere to go."

I nod in understanding.

"Right now, my sister has zero financial aid, which means I have to cover her tuition, room, board, books, and food card, plus her car insurance, which comes out to over sixty thousand dollars a year. And even once she applies for financial aid in the fall, it won't cover everything."

She continues, "You paid for my mom's care at the facility, but once she gets out, she will need to see a psychiatrist several times a week. And then there's her medications. Right now she has no insurance, and the quotes I've been given, due to her condition, are over ten thousand a year."

I do the math in my head, unsure how this woman hasn't collapsed from the weight she's been forced to carry.

"I make pennies at Fresh Designs. I'm busting my ass and Lydia keeps telling me that soon I'll be hired on as a regular employee with benefits, but even if or when that happens, it will only put a dent in the money I need to shell out."

Giselle stands and comes around to my side of the table. She climbs into my lap and straddles me. I back up slightly to give us room. "I love you," she tells me. "Tonight, when you called me your girlfriend to the bouncer, it felt like my heart leapt right out of my chest."

"You are my girlfriend," I tell her. "I love you, baby." I give her a kiss.

"Tell me a job where I can make enough to pay for everything I need to pay for." I don't need to think about it. I know there isn't one that doesn't require her to fuck someone or at the very least take her clothes off.

"The NFL," I joke. She glares, but there's a hint of a smile threatening to come out.

"Killian, I'm serious."

"I am too. I make enough money to pay for all of that. I get you want to be independent, but let me help you, please." There's no way she's going to agree, but I have to try.

She wraps her arms around my neck and hugs me tightly. Her face nuzzles into the crook of my neck, and her lips kiss my flesh softly. "I can't let you do that, Kill. I love you for offering, but we've barely even started dating."

"We'll figure it out, Giselle," I murmur. "But please don't work at Assets."

She lifts her head and eyes me. "Are you actually *asking* me not to work there and not demanding it?"

"I was mad, baby. Shocked. But we both know I can't force you not to work somewhere."

She nods and gives me a chaste kiss. "Thank you for not demanding it. I told Benjamin I made a mistake and quit." My body sags in relief.

"My brother found Melanie," I tell her, changing the subject. "She's in Cedar Wood Acres, North Carolina. It's only about twenty minutes from where we went to college. I grew up in the next town over."

"Are you going to go see her?"

"I am, and I was hoping you would come with me."

Her face lights up, telling me I made the right decision by asking her to join me. "I would love to."

"How about this weekend? I know it's last minute, but maybe you could take a day or two off work. We could take an early flight and make a long weekend out of it. I would love for you to meet my parents while we're there."

"I have a few personal days left I can use," she says. "Let's do it."

"And when we get back, we'll figure out your financial situation," I add.

She nods, but her smile loses its brightness. "Okay," she agrees.

TWENTY-FOUR

GISELLE

"THIS WAS MY LOCKER." Killian points to the half-rusted metal rectangle. His face lights up like it's a box that once held all of his hopes and dreams. "And this is where my coach told me I had a shot at playing in the NFL." He walks us over to a tiny office with a big smile. On our way here, he mentioned this is his first time showing a woman around where he went to school. I love that I get to be that woman. He knows so much about me, and I love every time I learn more about what makes Killian who he is.

After speaking with Lydia, who assured me she was okay with me taking a few personal days—after I promised to work remotely—we took an early flight out of JFK to Charlotte. We're going to check into our hotel this afternoon, and Killian has spoken to Melanie, who has agreed to meet him for dinner this evening. Tomorrow, the plan is to spend the day with his parents. But this morning, Killian is showing me some of his favorite spots, starting with the University of North Carolina. We've seen the football field, the cafeteria, and he even convinced the kid currently residing in his old dorm to let him show me around. Of course, once the kid recognized Killian as one of the wide receivers for the New York Brewers, he practically gave him the room. Right now, we're currently standing in a smelly locker room he's showing me around.

While I'd rather not be in here, where it's clear football players aren't aware of the benefits of deodorant, the prideful look on his face and the twinkle in his eye as he speaks makes it all worth it.

We spend the next hour catching up with his old coaches. They share some funny stories of Killian as a college football player. A few of the players are in the locker room for a Saturday practice, so Killian talks to them about working hard and making sure to take school seriously. I learn Killian has a business degree, and had he not made it into the NFL, he planned to get his MBA. When Killian tells them we need to get going, his old coaches make us promise not to be strangers.

"New York is where you were drafted to?" I ask as we walk out of the locker room and head to our rental car. North Carolina is so different from NYC. It's quiet, low-key, and people are actually friendly. It's hard to imagine Killian being happy here and then moving to New York.

"Yep, I've been there for ten years." He opens my door for me and I get in.

Once he's inside, I ask, "Do you think you will retire in New York?"

"Yeah," he says. "At this point in my career, if they made the decision to trade me, I would retire before I would move."

"Even if it meant not playing?" I ask, curiously.

"Most wide receivers retire by the age of thirty. I'm almost thirty-two. I've had a damn good career. I've even won a Super Bowl, something most can't say. Every year I play now is just a bonus." He glances over at me and his hand goes to my jean-clad thigh, squeezing it gently.

"Kind of ironic," I say, "you're at an age of retirement and I'm still trying to get a real job in my chosen profession." I laugh.

"You'll get there, Giselle. You're hard-working and motivated."

"I know, it just seems like we're at different points in our lives." I'm not sure why I say that. Even to my own ears I can hear doubt creeping in. The differences between us. Wondering how this is all going to work. Maybe it's knowing he's going to meet with Melanie today. Maybe I'm scared that once he sees her and gets his closure, he'll question why he's with me. He asked to be broken and lonely with me, but what happens once he's healed? When he's no longer broken? Will he still want me when he's fixed and whole and perfect while I'm still damaged?

"Look at the bright side, when we have kids, I can be a stay-at-home dad." He winks flirtatiously, and my stomach does some weird flip-flop thing at the thought of having kids with Killian, and then it sinks like a body in a lake being tied down by a heavy stone. My breaths turn labored, and then Killian's eyes land on me.

"Shit, Giselle. I'm sorry!" Killian realizes his slip. "It was meant as a joke. Fuck. It just came out."

"It's okay," I say, trying to calm my breathing. "But maybe that slip..." He's already healing, while I'm still broken. Soon I'll be lonely once again.

"No, don't you dare go there. I told you I'm okay with us not having kids, and I meant it." He scrubs his face in frustration. I know he feels bad for what he said, but that doesn't mean he didn't mean it. "I really am sorry," he says again.

"It's okay," I promise him, my tone betraying my words.

We arrive at The Ritz Carlton, where Killian has booked us the penthouse suite, even though I told him any old hotel will do. He said it's near his parents, which prevented me from continuing the argument. After we check in, he suggests we hang out and order lunch in, since he'll be leaving in a few hours to meet Melanie. When he originally made the plans with her, he asked if I would like to go. I told him I appreciated him wanting to include me but felt this is something he needs to do on his own. I'll be here when he gets back.

After we eat lunch, we settle on the couch. I wait for Killian to grab the remote, but he surprises me when he instead pulls out *Alice's Adventures in Wonderland* and insists on reading the next chapter to me. I'm shocked to learn he's already on chapter eleven: Who Stole the Tarts? Less than ten minutes into him reading, though, my eyes slowly shut, and I pass out in Killian's arms, dreaming of hearts instead of tarts being stolen.

TWENTY-FIVE

KILLIAN

I ARRIVE at the restaurant Melanie suggested and let the hostess know there'll be two people. It's a small hole-in-the-wall place that if it wasn't for how good it smells, I'd be a bit concerned. I'm sitting on the bench when Melanie walks in. She looks the same as she did twelve years ago, only a bit older. Her blond hair is a tad lighter and instead of her glasses, she must be wearing contacts. Her body has transformed from a teenager to a woman. She smiles shyly at me, and I pull her into a friendly hug.

"Killian," she murmurs into my ear, her voice thick with emotion. "I never thought I would see you again." She pulls back, her eyes filled with unshed tears.

"You mean you don't watch football?" I joke, and she laughs. The tears spill over and she quickly wipes them away.

"My husband does," she says with a soft smile.

The hostess comes over and lets us know our table is ready. We sit and each order a Coke.

"So, you're married?" I ask, not sure how to start a conversation I requested to have.

"I am. His name is Brian. We'll be married for six years in August..." She looks like she's about to say more, so I don't say anything. And then she adds, "And we have two daughters: Brenda and Bridgette."

"How old?" I ask, unsure of what else to say.

"They're actually twins." She laughs softly. "They just turned three."

"I'm happy for you, Mel," I tell her truthfully, because I am. Regardless of what happened, I'm glad she's found happiness.

The waiter delivers our drinks and we place our food order. Based on the menu, this place is known for their seafood, so I order the Salmon and Melanie orders a Mahi sandwich.

"Killian, I need to apologize to you," Melanie says once the waiter leaves.

"I'm the one who should be apologizing to you," I argue.

"Just let me go first, please," she requests, so I do. "When I found out I was pregnant, I was scared and I went to you in hopes of you comforting me, but I didn't even give you a chance. I had known I was pregnant for weeks. I had time to process and scream and cry and curse the world and everything else. I didn't even give you ten minutes to process."

A loud sob escapes her, and she covers her face with shaking hands. I'm not sure if I should comfort her or wait for her to speak again. I'm so far out of my comfort zone here. Grabbing a napkin, I hand it to her so she can wipe her face.

"Thank you." She smiles sadly. "I was a teenager and scared, and I should've given you more time, but instead I ran and had an abortion, and for that I am truly sorry." Her lips tremble as she cries. "Every day I have regretted my decision. I often wonder if it would've been a boy or a girl. If she would've had my eyes or if he would've been an athlete like you."

A flood of new tears gush down her ashen cheeks. "Every day that I look at my beautiful daughters, I ask God to forgive me for not giving our baby a chance in this world. I'm..." She chokes on a sob. "I'm so sorry." My heart aches over her words. She doesn't blame me. She's given me an out, but I don't want one.

"I shouldn't have pushed you away, Mel," I tell her. "I should've pulled you into my dorm and told you it would all be okay. Had I not pushed you away our baby would be here with us."

She shakes her head. "No, you did what anyone would do. You reacted out of shock. We were both so young. Just babies ourselves. I struggle every day with being thankful for my life because had I had our baby, I wouldn't have my two beautiful daughters." More tears race down her face. "I just hate myself for..." Killing our baby. She wants to say it, but she can't even get the words out.

"I know," I tell her, giving her an out. I don't need to hear the words. I've felt them every day for the last decade. While I've been being eaten up by guilt all these years, I can't even possibly fathom what this woman has been feeling, knowing she's the one who ultimately had to make that decision. It wasn't my body the baby was in. I didn't have a choice in the matter. I want to be mad at her for not choosing to keep our baby. I want to be mad at myself for not reacting the right way quicker. But she's right. We were just babies, and we both made decisions we have to live with. I thought coming here, I would tell her that the last ten years I haven't had sex so I could never put myself in that position again, that I wanted our baby and would've loved him or her, but I decide against it. She already feels guilty. She doesn't need more weight added to her load.

So, instead I say the only thing that's left to say, "I forgive you, Melanie, and I hope you can forgive me too."

Fresh tears escape her lids. "Thank you, Killian." She sniffles loudly. "And just so you know, I forgave you a long time ago."

I stand and give her a hug. "Don't ever feel bad for the beautiful family you have," I whisper. "One choice shouldn't dictate the rest of your life. You deserve to be happy."

I sit back down, and a few minutes later, our food is brought out. We eat, mostly in silence. When the waiter brings me the bill, I pay and walk Melanie out.

"Thank you for asking to meet up," she says when we get to her car. "I didn't realize how much I needed your forgiveness."

"Probably as much as I needed yours." I give her one last hug. "Have a good life, Mel."

"You too, Kill."

As I get in my car and think about everything we discussed, my mind goes to what Melanie said about struggling to be thankful for her family, knowing they came at the cost of our baby. It's time for both of us to move forward. We can't change what happened, and while I would give anything to have a chance to raise our baby, my mind goes to Giselle, and I have to wonder if maybe everything happens for a reason. If Giselle is my reason. When I wouldn't let any other woman into my heart or bed, I let her in. I didn't even ask if she was on birth control when we finally had sex. It just felt right with her. *It's because she's the one.* Even if she sticks with her decision to never want children, I know she's the woman I want to spend my life with. Just simply being with her is enough for me.

Instead of going back to the hotel, I take a detour into the city. There's somewhere I need to stop first. When I get back to the hotel,

Giselle is sleeping. Only this time she's lying in bed with her laptop still open, which tells me she woke up and later fell back asleep. My poor woman is working herself to death. I'm not sure how much longer she can keep going like this.

When I move the laptop from the bed to set it on the night-stand, it comes to life. On the screen are online classified ads. She was looking for another job. To the left of the website is a digital notepad with a list of the jobs she's found so far: maid services at a couple different hotels, a nighttime cleaning position for a law office. I scroll farther and see a few waitress positions at a few different diners. My eyes flit to Giselle, who is snuggled up in her blanket. She's dealing with this because of me. I know she wants to take on the world alone, but she can't do it all. And if it wasn't for her loving me, she wouldn't have to deal with this.

I'm sure she's going to give me shit for this later, but I'll deal with it when the time comes. Taking her laptop out to the main room, I search for her usernames and passwords. Once I find them, I forward them to my email then delete it in her sent mail. I close her laptop and set it on the counter. Then I pull up the email on my phone and get to work.

I'm just finishing up when I hear Giselle's feet padding out of the room. "You're back." She stops in front of the couch I'm sitting on and gives me a concerned smile.

"I am. I didn't want to wake you." I open my arms and she fills the void. Her arms wrap around my torso and her head lands on my chest. I inhale her sweet scent.

"I prefer waking up next to you," she murmurs.

"How would you feel about waking up next to me for the rest of your life?" I ask, and Giselle stills. Then she sits up, and I immedi-ately want her back against me.

"Killian..." She stares at me as I sit up and reach into my pocket. I pull out the ring box and get down on one knee. I hadn't planned on proposing tonight, but it feels like it's the right time.

Giselle's hands cover her mouth. "Killian..." she says again.

"I know some would say what's happening between us, this rela-tionship, is probably moving too fast." She nods slowly, and I laugh. "As you know, I'm a wide receiver. My job is to catch the ball." She laughs out loud, calming my nerves. "There's a phrase in football. Going Deep. Have you ever heard of it?"

She shakes her head no.

"It's when you run down the field for a long pass. You're serious. Committed. Unstoppable. I'm in this *deep* with you, Giselle. I'm serious. Committed. There's no stopping what I feel for you. I'm running down the field to catch the ball. I just need you to throw it."

I open the ring box and pluck the engagement ring from the felt that's holding it in place. After leaving Melanie, I went to a few jewelers in the area my mom recommended. After the third one, I found the ring I knew was meant for Giselle. A three-carat halo cut diamond on a simple platinum band.

"Will you throw the ball to me, baby?" I ask her, holding the ring up for her to see.

Tears leak from her eyes. I'm not sure if they're happy or sad tears. And then she says in a voice so quiet I can barely hear her, "You're healed."

"What?" I ask. I heard what she said, but I'm unsure what she means.

"Be broken and lonely with me." She repeats the words I said to her before. "You're no longer broken." She swipes a falling tear. "But Killian, I still am."

It takes me a second, but when I piece together what she's saying, it all clicks. She thinks by me meeting with Melanie, I've been healed.

"Giselle..." I set the box down on the table and take her hands in mine. "Yes, meeting with Melanie helped me find closure, but she didn't fix me. I'm still broken, baby, but I'm no longer lonely. Since the day you stepped into that limo, I haven't felt lonely. Nobody is perfect, Giselle. We're all broken, filled with imperfections, scars from the wounds life has inflicted on us. Being with you has shown me that it's not about trying to fix the broken, but finding the person you can be broken with. Be broken with me, baby. I can't play in this game alone. My arms and heart are open. The ball is in your hands. Will you throw it to me?"

Tears fall harder down her beautiful face as she begins to nod, slowly at first then quicker. Finally, she speaks. "Okay...Yes! I'll throw the ball to you. I mean, I have no clue how to throw a damn ball, but you've won a Super Bowl, so surely you can catch just about any pass I throw, right?"

I laugh loudly, loving that my woman just went along with my football analogy. Standing, I take her hand in mine and slide the ring onto her finger. I wasn't sure her size, so I called Olivia and she was spot on. Giselle eyes the ring for a second before she throws her arms around me and kisses me hard.

"Let's get married now," I suggest, shocking the hell out of both of us.

"Now?" she squeaks.

"Yeah, we can meet with my parents for breakfast and then take off somewhere to get married. Just the two of us. I don't want to wait. I want you to be my wife."

"Okay," she agrees, excitedly. "Let's do this!"

WE'RE LYING in bed after celebrating our engagement for the second time tonight—with me balls-deep in my gorgeous fiancée. Giselle is drawing letters and pictures across my torso and chest with her sexy thigh draped over the top of my legs and her head in the crook of my shoulder. We haven't discussed my dinner with Melanie yet, but we need to. I need to. I don't want to ruin the moment, but Giselle assumed by my meeting with Melanie everything is now perfect when in fact it's not.

"Melanie's married with twin daughters," I say, and Giselle's finger stills. "She apologized for having the abortion."

"I'm glad you two finally talked. It was long overdue," she murmurs.

"She felt the same way. She lives with a lot of guilt over the decision she made, and she said she doesn't blame me."

Giselle sighs softly. "I can't imagine having an abortion at any age is an easy thing to do, but as a teenager...it must've been absolutely traumatizing."

"Yeah," I agree. "She told me she should've given me more time to process..."

"If she would've, the baby would be here," Giselle states.

"Maybe...but we can't look at it like that. What's done is done. She's happily married with her two daughters, and I'm about to marry you. Everything is the way it should be."

Giselle nods into my chest. "I love you, Kill. If it meant you'd get to raise the baby you never had the chance to raise, I would give you up, but since that's not possible, I'm really glad all the situations out of our control lined up and gave me you."

TWENTY-SIX

GISELLE

"YOU SERIOUSLY GOT MARRIED WITHOUT ME?" Olivia yells into the phone. Killian is lying next to me under our umbrella by the pool. We're currently enjoying the sunshine as husband and wife at the Cozumel Palace in Mexico, where just a few short hours ago we said our 'I do's' in a tiny church with a priest, who barely spoke English, and two witnesses, who work for the church and didn't say anything but grinned with twinkles in their eyes. I'm not exactly sure *all* of what the priest said, but I know what Killian said:

"I, Killian Blake, promise to be your best friend, your lover, your protector, your partner. I will cherish you and love you and do every-thing in my power to make sure you're happy and never feel lonely. I promise to be broken with you every day for the rest of our lives."

It was in that moment it really hit me. I was marrying Killian, and everything he was promising to do, he had already been doing since the day I let him in. I might be broken, but every day spent with Killian has been far from lonely. I feel loved, cherished, and if I'm honest, a little less damaged when I'm with him. He loves and embraces every part of me: the good, the bad, and the ugly.

"Giselle!" Olivia shouts into phone, reminding me she's still on the phone, pissed off because like the chicken shit I am, I texted Olivia a picture of our wedding rings instead of calling her.

"I'm here, sorry...I was..."

"In newly-wed bliss?" she screeches. "When Killian asked for your ring size, I knew he was going to propose, but nowhere in our conversation did he mention eloping." Her tone has gone from mad to hurt.

"I'm sorry, Livi. It wasn't really planned. He proposed and I said yes, and then we decided not to wait."

"Yet, you went to breakfast with his parents..." She's got me there. When we told his parents we were engaged, they were thrilled. And then Killian told them we were planning to elope. I thought for sure his mom would be upset she wouldn't get to see her son get married, but I think she was so sure he would never get married, she was just happy to know it was actually happening. We agreed to go to dinner in a couple weeks to celebrate since they'll be flying in for the birth of Christina and Dylan's baby.

"Livi, I know you're upset, but you know I'm not into being the center of attention like that. Plus, my mom is still getting better and my sister is crazy busy with school. I have nobody from my family to even attend a wedding."

"I'm your family," Olivia whispers, and my heart breaks. Tears sting my eyes. When Killian notices, he flies out of his chair to my side. I put my hand up to stop him from taking the phone, but he reaches around and grabs it anyway.

"Olivia, this is Killian. I understand you're upset you weren't there for the wedding, but here's the thing. Everything Giselle has done has been about other people. She moved here for you. She takes care of her mom and sister. This wedding, this marriage, it was about us."

My heart squeezes at Killian's words. He couldn't have worded it better, and if I'm honest, I didn't even think about any of that. For the first time I wanted something for me and I went after it. I didn't think about anyone else but myself, and I'm not going to feel bad for that.

Olivia says something I can't hear and Killian grins. "Okay," he says. I hear Olivia reply, but I can't hear what she's saying. When she stops talking, Killian says, "You have my word."

He hands me back the phone and leans in to kiss me. "I love you, Mrs. Blake," he murmurs.

I put the phone back up to my ear, swooning so damn hard. "Hello." My voice is breathy, and Olivia notices.

"My God, you have it bad." She laughs. "I'm sorry for freaking out. Killian is right. This was about you two. You deserve to get married how and where you want. I love you, Giselle, and I'm so happy for you."

"Thank you." I'm shocked she's suddenly so okay with this.

"You're welcome. Plus, Killian told me I can throw you guys a party when you return," she says, triumphantly.

"Oh, well...actually, his parents are coming to New York in a few weeks and we're just going to go to dinner."

"Sounds fun! But I'm still throwing you a party! Enjoy your honeymoon! Bye!" She ends the call before I can argue.

AFTER SPENDING the day switching between the pool and the beach, Killian and I head up to our room. Although, 'room' doesn't do the place we're staying in justice. How Killian managed to pull everything together in such a short amount of time baffles me, but at the same time, it shouldn't surprise me. Money talks. While Killian is showering, I pull out my laptop to do some work. Killian doesn't know it yet, but when we return tomorrow night, his condo will be done. I left the key with Olivia so she could let the workers in. Working remotely isn't as easy as being there in person, but with technology, it makes it possible.

After confirming the painters have arrived and are working, I go through my emails. I notice one from Adrianna and click on it. It's a forwarded email from her school. Any time I pay the bill, it goes to her school email, so she forwards them to me to keep on record. It's a receipt indicating the remaining balance on her food card. It's enough to feed her until graduation. I click on the email and sign into her account. Why the hell is there so much money in there? Did she somehow get approved for some type of financial aid I didn't know about? I click through the account. Everything was paid, and her denial of financial aid hasn't changed. I click on next semester and there's a positive balance. This doesn't make sense. I pull up my bank account. If they took all that money from me by accident, my account must be in the negative! I do a double take when I see the amount of zeros in the balance of my checking account. Something is wrong here. Even with the sale of the house, I shouldn't have this much money. I scroll down and find the deposit. Killian Blake. *Motherfucker*.

I sign in to my student loans, and sure enough everything is paid off. My credit cards. Paid. I am one hundred percent debt free.

"Killian!" I scream across the massive suite, which is more like a small mansion than a hotel room. Instead of responding, he comes out of the bathroom, a worried look on his face. For a second, as he stands there in nothing but a towel hung low around his waist with beads of water clinging to his tanned, perfect body, I forget how pissed I am at what he did behind my back. My eyes fall to the brightly colored tattoos and land on one in particular. I stand and walk toward him to get a closer look. It's shinier than the others. Newer. How did I not notice this before?

He glances down and grins, knowing which one has gotten my attention. My fingers trace the same quote that is on the back of the heart he gave me. He had it tattooed on his body. The quote. The heart. It's permanent. Tears burn my eyes as I stare at the words. I want to be mad over the money, but I can't muster up the anger. My heart is just too damn full.

"When did you get this done?" I whisper.

"Right before we left for North Carolina."

Gently, I wipe the water off it so I can get a better look at it. "It's beautiful," I tell him. I lean in and kiss the broken heart, the one identical to mine. His skin is chilled from the cool air. I trail kisses along the words, which are woven through his other tattoos. Killian's hand grips the back of my head, his fingers threading roughly through my hair.

I continue peppering wet kisses across his chest and down the center of his torso. His hand stays in my hair, but he doesn't move a muscle. My eyes meet his as I bend down and undo his towel. When he realizes what I'm about to do, his pupils dilate. Even at only half-mast, his dick is beautiful. My fingers attempt to wrap around his shaft. It's thick and soft like velvet. I stroke it a few times and it thickens under my touch. Bringing my lips to the tip, I give it an open-mouthed kiss. He smells clean, a mixture of soap and Killian.

I suck on the tip and a bit of precum drips out. It's salty on my tongue and has me thirsty for more. Killian's grip on my hair tightens. My gaze goes up, and his eyes, which scream hunger and want, are locked with mine. Lifting his dick up slightly, I run my tongue along the thick vein on the underside of his shaft, my eyes never leaving his. When my tongue returns to the swollen head, more cum has leaked out. I lick it clean.

"Jesus, fuck," Killian groans. I take him completely into my mouth, not stopping until he hits the back of my throat. He growls out as he tries to stop himself from thrusting. I pull back slightly and then take him all the way into my mouth again. With every bob of my head, his dick grows thicker, more cum dripping out. His grunts and groans are getting louder, and in return, I feel myself dripping wet. I know he's getting close when I feel his dick swell, and I prepare myself to swallow him. But before that happens, my hair is pulled, and my mouth pops off his dick.

Killian lifts me from the ground and throws me onto the couch. He tears my clothes from my body, then spreads my legs and pushes into me. I'm drenched and he slides right in, bottoming the hell out. My back arches in pleasure, my butt lifts off the cushion, and I'm moved several inches up. One of his hands takes both of mine and pins them above my head, the other grips my throat to hold me in place. And then he begins to fuck me. I've never seen him like this. So overcome with emotion. With every thrust, my climax rises closer to the surface. My ankles lock around his bare ass. His thrusts get deeper, harder, rougher. His eyes never leave mine. My orgasm reaches the edge and spills over. I throw my head back, his grip on my throat tightening. My eyes close and I swear I see stars as I come harder than I ever have in my life.

Killian's thrusts turn savage, unrestrained, and then he's growling out his orgasm. His fingers leave my throat and I take in a deep breath, air quickly filling my lungs. His lips land on mine and he kisses me with such love, my heart feels like it's going to explode.

"I'm the luckiest fucking guy alive," he whispers against my mouth when the kiss ends. "I get to keep you and kiss you and make love to you for the rest of our lives." He kisses me again and then pulls out.

"You paid off all my debt and deposited a shit ton of money into my account," I tell him now that my head isn't fogged up.

His eyes go wide. "You're my wife." That's the only explanation he gives, because to him, me being his wife means he has the right to do what he did. I knew this would happen. It's who he is.

"Next time you talk to me first." I give him a stern look that has the corners of his lips twitching to break into a smile.

"Yes, ma'am," he agrees, clearly happy I didn't give him more shit. I wanted to. Believe me, I did. But I know what he did came from a good place. He loves me and wants to be, as Olivia would say, my prince charming. I've been doing this alone for so long, but I don't have to anymore. And knowing it's Killian by my side, I don't want to.

TWENTY-SEVEN

KILLIAN

THE ENTIRE DRIVE to the condo, Giselle has been quiet and kind of...fidgety. She keeps checking her phone, but when I ask her if everything is okay, she tells me everything is fine. The driver pulls into the parking garage and jumps out to help us with our bags. I grab our suitcases, which are significantly heavier than they were when we left, since we had to purchase beach attire when we arrived in Cozumel, and then Giselle insisted on buying several mementos from the touristy shops to remember our trip.

When we get to the door, she steps in front of it. "I need to go in first. Wait here." She plucks my key from my fingers, which is strange since she should have her own. A few minutes later, she calls out my name and I take that as my cue to enter. The condo has been completely redone. The walls, which were once a plain off-white are now a deeper shade of cream, with the back wall a dark coffee color. New art fills the walls. The furniture is the same, but a new leather recliner has been added to the mix. New pillows are in the corners of the couches. There's a new rug. And this is only the living room.

Giselle stands to the side as I walk through the condo. In the hallway, pictures of my friends and family line the walls in thick wooden frames. It's still masculine, yet it no longer feels cold. She's added warmth. My bedroom, office, the bathrooms, the kitchen.

Every room has been transformed. And it hits me, she did all of this while in a different state and country.

"What do you think?" she asks shyly when I walk back out to the living room.

"I think you need to start your own interior design firm."

She laughs and it sounds like a sweet melody. "I wouldn't go that far, but I'm glad you like it. I wanted your place to feel more like a home for you."

"You mean for us," I say, gripping her hips and pulling her into me. She comes willing, her arms encircling my neck. "We're married, which means you're moving in here. Now." Needing to feel her, I give her a soft kiss and she melts into my arms.

"Okay," she says, but then her body stiffens as if she's just remembered something. "What about my mom? She's getting out soon and I can't move her into here. There are only two rooms." She frowns. "I can't kick you out of your own office."

"We'll figure it out," I tell her. "We still have a few weeks."

IT'S BEEN ALMOST a week since Giselle and I became husband and wife. Nick and Olivia officially put their places on the market and moved into their new home, which is just outside the city. Giselle is living with me in the condo and has spent every day after work organizing our stuff. What she doesn't know is we won't be living here for long. I have a plan.

We're on our way to my brother's place for my niece's birthday party. Giselle asked me to stop at the bookstore, so she can run in and grab her a gift. I told her I bought her a gift card, but she just gave me a look and told me that's not from her.

"Got it!" she squeals as she jumps back into the vehicle. She holds up a wrapped square.

"A book?"

"Not just a book. *The* book. *Alice's Adventures in Wonderland*." I should've known. "I also got her the movie since you told me she loves watching movies with you." She holds up a matching wrapped gift, only smaller in size.

We arrive at the party, and it's already in full swing. Kids are running around everywhere. There's a bounce house, several games, a creepy-looking clown painting the kids' faces, a cotton candy machine going, and tables of food and drinks. It looks like a damn carnival came to town in my brother's backyard.

"Killian!" Christina waves us over when she spots us standing there, taking it all in. She waddles her now very-pregnant self over to us and throws her arms around Giselle. "Welcome to the family!" she gushes.

"Thank you," Giselle whispers, and my eyes dart over to her. Why does she sound like she's ready to cry? "You look great." She nods toward Christina's belly.

"Thank you! Only a few more weeks." She grins happily, unaware my wife looks like she's a second away from losing it.

"We're going to get some food, and then we'll find the birthday girl," I tell Christina. Taking Giselle's hand in mine, I walk us over to the corner where the food is. "You okay?" I ask her.

"Yeah, I've just never seen anything like this before." Her eyes glance around the backyard. "Were your birthdays like this?"

"No." I laugh. "I mean, sure, they were fun. Sometimes at the skating rink or a park, but nothing like this." Giselle nods absently.

"What about you?" I ask, wanting to know what's going through her head. She almost looks frightened by the extravagance of the party.

"Addy and I never had a birthday party. At least not one I can remember. My dad didn't want to overwhelm my mom. Sometimes we would go to dinner or he would bring home a cake, but that's it. I thought Olivia went all out for Reed's first birthday, but this party makes it look like hers was reserved." She laughs.

"Uncle Killian!" Julia squeals. I turn around and she flies into my arms. "You're here!"

"I am. Happy Birthday! How old are you now? Eighteen?"

"No!" She giggles. "You always say that! I'm five!"

I set her on her feet. "Well, you certainly look older than five." I shoot her a wink and she giggles some more.

"Come play with me in the bounce house." She tugs on my hand and I look back at Giselle, whose face is completely devoid of all emotion.

"In a few minutes," I begin to say, but Giselle cuts me off.

"Go play with your niece," she insists. "I'll get us some food."

"You sure?"

"Yeah." She nods and smiles, but it's forced. I want to ask her what's going on, but in front of everyone at a kid's birthday party isn't the right time or place, so instead I allow my niece to drag me to the bounce house. I spend the next few hours playing games, getting my face painted, and—against my brother's warning that I'm going to pop it—jumping in Julia's bounce house with her.

Giselle and I eat lunch, and after singing Happy Birthday, have cake. We watch Julia open dozens of presents. The entire time Giselle is here with me in body, but it's clear her head is somewhere else.

After wishing Julia Happy Birthday one last time and promising Christina and my brother we'll do dinner soon, we head home. Giselle is quiet, lost in herself. I try to think about what might've happened. Could all of this be simply because she's never had a birthday party? Her birthday just passed, so I make a mental note to throw her a party next year.

We get home and Giselle excuses herself to take a shower. When she gets out, she tells me she's going to head to bed. Normally, I would follow her, but something tells me she needs some time to sort out whatever is going on with her. So, I tell her I'm going to watch some television. She gives me a chaste kiss goodnight and heads into our room.

A few hours later, I join her and she's fast asleep. I pull her into my arms, and she snuggles up against me, right where she belongs.

TWENTY-EIGHT

Giselle

IT'S MONDAY MORNING, and I'm beyond exhausted—mentally and physically. Watching Killian with his niece yesterday was bittersweet. He says he's okay with us not having kids, but as I watched him, so clearly in his element at the party, I couldn't help but think, who the hell am I to keep this man from becoming a father? But then I would try to place us in Christina's and Dylan's shoes, and the picture wasn't the same. Because I'm my mother's daughter and there's a chance I could one day end up like her—bipolar, depressed, and as a result, emotionally and physically abusive.

After I went to bed last night, I called my sister and we talked for a while. I told her about Killian and me getting married, and she congratulated us. We talked about mom and our childhood. She told me she spoke to her girlfriend about it, and she refuses to allow our mother's condition to affect her life. She's determined to live life to the fullest. I wish I could adopt her outlook on the situation, but it's hard. Addy has no desire to have kids. She wants to travel and see the world. She's blissfully away at college, while I'm trying to figure out how to have my own life and take care of my mom when she gets out of Serenity.

I stretch my body out and find Killian's rolled over on his side and is watching me. I know he's concerned about my behavior yesterday and wants to ask me about it, but how do I tell the man I love, I'm scared he's going to miss out on life's greatest blessings like having children because of me? And I'm petrified he will one day resent me because of it.

Grabbing my cell phone, I check the time and realize I'm late. "Shit!" I hiss, jumping out of bed and running into the bathroom. "I'm late!" I yell to Killian. "How long were you staring at me while the clock was ticking away?" I run the brush quickly through my hair. He laughs a throaty laugh, and I hurl the brush at him. Of course, he catches it and laughs harder.

"I have a ten o'clock appointment!"

"I'll drive you," he says, joining me in the bathroom. We go about getting ready, brushing our teeth and washing our faces. We've only been living together for less than a week, yet it feels so much longer than that. I always thought when I moved in with a guy it would take some getting used to. Who puts their toothbrush where? Which side of the bed do we each sleep on? Do I cook and clean and he does the dishes? My parents were hardly role models for how married living should go. But with Killian, it all just fell into place so naturally. I'm not sure what it will be like once his football season starts, but at least we have some time before he's traveling again.

We rush out the door. On the way, he insists we go through a drive-thru for breakfast and coffee. When we arrive, he shuts the car off, and we head to my office. We're alone in the elevator on the way up. Killian cuts across the small area and cages me into the corner, his body flush against mine. He kisses me with such force and passion, my entire body shivers in pleasure.

"I'm here when you're ready to talk," he murmurs against my lips. My throat clogs with emotion. How did I, Giselle Winters, the woman who spent the last year selling her body for money, get so lucky to end up with a man like Killian Blake? I don't deserve him.

"Thank you," I murmur against his lips.

The elevator dings and we enter Fresh Designs. I take my messages from the receptionist and head back to my office. I unlock the door and have a seat behind my desk. Setting my coffee and breakfast down, I pull my laptop out of my bag. I open it up and press the power button to turn it on. Killian falls into the seat across from me, and I realize he's followed me in.

I can't help but laugh. This isn't the first time he's done this. Although, the last time he did it, it was because he had an appointment...Oh, Jesus. The screen comes to life, and I click on my schedule. Sure enough, my ten o'clock appointment is with Killian Blake.

I glare, and he laughs.

"What the hell are you doing?" I demand, humor seeping out of my words. "Your condo is done."

"*Our* condo is done," he corrects me. I roll my eyes. And then it hits me...

"Killian, we didn't sign a prenuptial agreement."

He gives me an odd look.

"You know...a document that protects the rich people from being screwed over by the poor people they married when shit goes south." It's kind of a joke, but it's still true. Killian doesn't take it that way, though.

"That's not funny, Giselle. I'm not having you sign a document that specifies what you get or don't get in case we divorce. We aren't divorcing, ever."

I open my mouth to argue, but he gives me a look that says he's not playing around. "Now, I'm here to hire your services."

"Okay." I laugh. "What would you like me to decorate now, Killian? Your locker room?"

"No, smartass. Our house."

"Killian, I seriously have a lot of shit to do today. As much as I love having you in my office, I need to get to work."

"And that includes decorating our place." He pulls a sheet of paper out of his pocket and pushes it across the desk. I take it and read over it. It's a house listing. The address looks familiar. Where have I seen it? It's a five-bedroom, four-bathroom house with a three-car garage. An indoor/outdoor pool, a huge backyard according to the images. When I see the name, I remember where I've seen this street name.

"This is Olivia and Nick's house?" I ask, confused.

"No, it's ours. It's two doors down from Nick and Olivia."

My eyes volley between the paper and Killian. "You purchased a house on the same street as Olivia?" Oh my god! This man!

"We did. I had you sign the papers in Cozumel. You just didn't realize it. Everything is ours. And the house has a mother-in-law suite in the back. Your mom will have her own place. Bedroom, bathroom, kitchen, and living room. She'll even have her own side-walk, so she doesn't have to walk through our house if she doesn't want to."

My jaw drops as I flip through the pages, reading all the details confirming what Killian said. He bought us a house...no, a goddamned mansion, two houses down from my best friend in Park Slope. I spring from my seat and fly into Killian's lap. He laughs as I straddle him and pepper kisses along his jaw, over his cheeks, his forehead, and lastly to his lips.

"Thank you," I murmur. "We don't need a house that big, but thank you. For the mother-in-law suite and moving me near Olivia. Thank you."

Killian kisses me tenderly. "You're welcome. I would've moved us directly next door, but the old lady living there refused to sell." He mock-glares, and I laugh. "Once you're done decorating it, we'll move in. Think you can have it done before your mom gets out?"

"Yes!" I wrap my arms around his neck and kiss him.

His phone starts ringing, and I remember we're in my office, so I climb off him. He pulls his phone out of his pocket and answers it.

"Hey bro, what's up?" He pauses then grins. "No shit? Yeah, we'll be right there. Do Christina's parents have Julia?" He listens to his brother. "All right, see you soon." He hangs up.

"Everything okay?" I ask him.

"Yeah, Christina went into labor this morning. They had to deliver the baby early, but he's perfect. Why don't we go visit them at the hospital then we can head over to the house so you can check it out?" He stands, ready to go.

"Umm... well..." I try to think of a reason I can't go, but the truth is, I have no reason. My appointment this morning is with Killian and he knows it.

He gives me a concerned look. "What's wrong?"

"Nothing. Sure, we can go by there on the way to the house. I just have an appointment this afternoon, so we can't stay too long."

"Okay." He smiles and takes my hand. "Grab your coffee and breakfast. You can eat on the way."

We arrive at the hospital, and after showing our identification, the receptionist gives us visitor passes and sends us up to the maternity ward. The door is open, so Killian knocks once and then we enter.

Dylan is sitting in the chair next to Christina's bed. She's holding their baby and they're both speaking to him. They look up, and Dylan stands and walks over to us. He gives me a hug and then Killian.

"Congratulations, bro," Killian says before walking over to Christina. He leans over the bed and gives her a kiss on her forehead. "He's beautiful," he tells her. "Looks just like his handsome uncle." He shoots me a playful wink, and my stomach plummets.

I stand frozen in place as I watch everything like an outsider. Killian sanitizes his hands, and Christina hands him the baby. He holds him in his arms like a pro as he walks over to show me him.

"His name is Kyle," his brother tells him.

"Hey there, Kyle," Killian coos. "How much does he weigh? Ten pounds?" he jokes.

Christina laughs. "Funny! Seven pounds, four ounces."

"Nice! Kid is going to be a linebacker." Killian grins. Dylan laughs.

"Well, don't hog him, Kill," Christina chides. "Let Giselle hold him." Killian looks up, and before I can get my facial expression under control, he sees the truth in my features. He flinches, suddenly realizing why I struggled to come here. He looks like he's trying to make up an excuse as to why I can't hold the baby. His gaze filled with apology. I look around and see Christina and Dylan watching us. Not wanting to seem rude or have to explain why I don't want to hold their baby, I walk over to the sink and wash my hands.

Killian whispers, "Are you sure?" and I nod.

He places the baby into my arms. He's so tiny. I lift him up to my nose to see if he smells like Reed did when he was born. He does. He smells like a tiny little miracle. My throat begins to close, and it becomes difficult to breathe. Tears blur my vision. Killian notices and steps forward, ready to take Kyle from me. Suddenly, I feel sick to my stomach. I hand him back the baby and dart to the bathroom, just making it to the toilet in time.

I throw up everything in my stomach as Killian holds my hair back for me. When there's finally nothing left to throw up, I stand and wash my mouth out in the sink then wash my hands and face. I glance in the mirror and see Killian watching me. Concerned. He's always concerned.

"I'm sorry."

He shakes his head. "No, I am. First the comment about being a stay-at-home dad, then taking you to Julia's birthday party, and now bringing you to see a baby. I know I've never been in a relationship before, but damn, I'm sucking at this." He chuckles humorlessly.

"Kill..."

"No, I couldn't figure out what was wrong yesterday at the party. I'm such an idiot."

"No, you're not. This is my problem, not yours. This is your family. Julia is your niece. Kyle is your nephew. Olivia and Nick have Reed and soon will have another baby. It's something I'm going to have to get used to...but you don't have to." I close my eyes and shake my head. When I feel Killian's hands on my hips, I open them back up. "Do you think maybe we rushed into things?" My eyes fill to the brim with tears.

"Baby, don't do this," Killian pleads.

"It's just..." I can't even get the words out. I don't want to say what I'm thinking. I'm being selfish being with Killian. He deserves more. To be with a woman who isn't as broken as I am. To become a father. I'm bringing nothing to this marriage, while he's bringing everything.

"Giselle, please," he begs. "Let's go take a look at the house, okay?"

I nod my agreement, not wanting to disappoint him.

He has me wait for him outside the room while he tells his brother and Christina I'm not feeling well. The ride to the house is quiet, both of us lost in our own thoughts. When we arrive, the home is beautiful, but I can't find it in me to get excited. I go through each room, taking measurements and making notes. Killian and I discuss what each room could be: a gym, office, reading room, guest room. But the entire time I keep thinking, if he were with someone else, the rooms would be labeled completely different: nursery, play room, library, game room.

When we're done, he drops me back off at the office, and for the first time since we've been together, when we say goodbye, we don't kiss. As I walk to the elevator I wonder if maybe it's a sign of what's to come.

TWENTY-NINE

GISELLE

EVERYONE IS STANDING in the church watching Reed get baptized. Nick and Olivia are all smiles as they watch their son squirm while the pastor says his speech. He dips his fingers into the holy water, then rubs it along Reed's forehead. Reed giggles and everyone laughs. Everyone is watching but Killian. Because the entire time I can feel his eyes on me. He's worried I'm going to lose it. When I agreed to be Reed's Godmother, it was before I learned my mother's condition could be hereditary. I considered telling Olivia I couldn't be who she needed me to be, but when I tried to make the words come out, I couldn't do it. I couldn't disappoint her. What are the chances something happens to them anyway? The Godparents only come into play if both parents die, right?

Killian and I step forward and repeat after the pastor, promising to guide Reed in his spiritual journey. The pastor sets him down and Reed toddles over to me, lifting his arms up for me to take him. So, I do.

"Gi Gi!" he squeals, and everyone laughs. His tiny hands land on my cheeks and he squishes my face, placing a big wet kiss on my lips. My eyes, of their own accord, meet Killian's. His facial expression is caught between smiling and frowning. Jesus, I'm so fucked up, and now I'm fucking up my husband too.

Like the toddler Reed is, he squirms to get down, and I set him on his feet. He runs over to his dad, and Nick picks him up. The ceremony ends, and Olivia announces everyone will be meeting at the restaurant down the street for lunch. Needing a moment, I excuse myself to use the restroom. I'm washing my hands when the door creaks open and in walks Killian. He locks the door behind him and stalks toward me.

I don't even get a word out before he's lifting me onto the sink and spreading my legs. His fingers enter me as our lips crash against each other. It's been almost a week since I've felt this connection with Killian. A week of sleeping together yet feeling like we're a million miles apart. Every night I can tell he wants to say something, but he's waiting for me. And I have no clue what to say.

He adds another finger and then another, pumping them in and out of me until I'm soaking wet. He pulls my top down and his lips wrap around my nipple. Licking and sucking on it. And then he's pulling my panties off my body and lifting me into the air. My back hits the hard wall, and he thrusts inside me. My arms wrap around his neck as my husband fucks me like a goddamn madman—punishing thrust after punishing thrust, not once slowing down or relenting. I find my release within minutes, Killian's following shortly after.

We're both breathing heavily, but he doesn't set me down. Instead, with his semi-hard cock still inside of me, his mouth smashes against mine with such force, I'm almost certain every emotion he feels is being projected into that one kiss.

"This has to stop," he demands.

"What?" I try to get down, but he won't release me. I feel his cum dripping out of me.

"Pushing me away. Thinking you know what's best for me. I want you, Giselle. Baby, no baby. I don't give a fuck. It's you and me. So whatever you're thinking, get it the hell out of your head. Got it?"

I nod in understanding.

Killian walks us back over to the sink and sets me down, spreading my thighs and using a wet paper towel to clean me up. I watch as he takes care of me. He always takes care of me.

"I want to take care of you," I blurt out. He gives me a quizzical look. "You always take care of me. I hate us being so uneven. You give me so much, and I give you nothing."

Killian shakes his head and sighs. "If I have to spend the rest of our life explaining to you just how much you give me, I will. You give me so much." He lifts my necklace. "Your heart." He kisses my temple. "Your mind." A playful smirk splays across his lips. "Your body." He grabs my panties from the corner of the counter and puts them back on me. "Our life together has only just begun," he tells me. "Neither of us are experts at this, so how about we just learn as we go, okay?"

"Okay," I agree.

Killian helps me off the sink and it's then I remember we're in a church. "Oh my god! We just had sex in a church!"

Killian throws his head back with a laugh. "It's a good thing we're married."

***

"GISELLE! SWEETIE, YOU LOOK SO GOOD."

I'm standing in the facility staring at my mother, only it doesn't feel like it's my mother. She's glowing. She's dressed in a pair of jeans and a fluffy sweater. Her hair is straightened. She looks beautiful.

"I look good? Mom, you look amazing!" I try to keep the shock out of my voice but even I can hear it. My mom laughs. *Laughs!* And it's not that crazy laugh she used to give us. It's melodic and genuine.

Killian and I are here to pick her up. The house is ready to move into and it will be our first night spending the night there. I was terrified of how it would go. That she wouldn't be ready. But she looks so healthy. Is it possible? Is she fixed?

"Where's Addy?" Mom asks.

"She's meeting us at the house," I tell her. "She's bringing her girlfriend, Kassie, with her for everyone to meet. But if you think it might be too much..."

"No." She smiles. "I'm so glad you both have someone." Tears prick her eyes, and I freak out.

"Mom, don't cry." My eyes dart around the room for the doctor, my heart picking up its pace. Damn it! She's going to lose it. "Excuse me, Dr. Burns!" I yell when I spot my mom's doctor. He gives me a concerned look and comes over.

"She's crying," I point out, and my mom laughs through her tears.

"Sarah, you're leaving today." Dr. Burns gives her a hug, ignoring the fact my mom is crying.

"She's crying," I say again.

"Giselle." Killian wraps his arms around me. "Your mom is crying because she's happy, baby," he whispers.

"But she's..."

"It's okay," my mom says, "Killian is right. I'm crying because I'm happy, but after everything I've put you through, I don't blame you for freaking out. I think it's going to take some time for everyone."

Dr. Burns nods in agreement. "We've found a therapist for your mother to see three times a week near you guys. Maybe you will consider going with her one day a week to talk things out."

"That would be great," my mom says with a smile. "Now, let's go home. My son-in-law told me all about this beautiful mother-in-law suite. I can't wait to see it."

The drive home is spent with all of us talking about everything that has been going on. Olivia being pregnant, Killian and my wedding and mini-honeymoon, my job and the possibility of getting a promotion soon. And then she brings up my dad.

"How is your father?"

Killian and I both go silent. She just got out. I can't tell her about my dad's other family.

"Giselle," she pushes, "I know."

My head whips around to her. "You know what?"

"About his other family. His other children."

"Should we maybe go back to the facility to discuss this?"

Mom laughs. "No, I've known for years. I'm sorry I never told you. He came to see me and told me you knew. I know you're angry with him, but I need you to know I forgive him. What I put him through..." She shakes her head. "My being sick isn't what he signed up for."

Killian clears his throat. "While I think it's great you forgive him, I beg to differ. He married you. When he said those vows, he signed up for better or worse. Those times were the worse."

Mom grins wide a watery grin then leans forward and whispers, "He's a keeper."

I get choked up. I try to keep the tears from falling but they spill over anyway. "Yeah, he is."

"You're right, Killian, we did make vows, and we did say for better or worse. But we fell out of love many years ago, and instead of letting him go, I held onto him. I was sick and depressed. Scared. He deserves to be happy. And I'm ready to move forward. So please don't be too hard on him. He tried. We tried. We didn't make it."

We arrive at the house and show her around. She loves the

mother-in-law suite I decorated. Shortly after, Addy arrives with Kassie, and then Nick, Olivia, and Reed come over with dinner. At some point in the meal, my eyes find Addy's and she gives me a soft smile. Words don't need to be spoken. This meal, this moment with our mother, was exactly what we prayed for, for so many years. And it's because of Killian it was even made possible.

THIRTY

Giselle

"SO WHEN ARE YOU DUE?" Celeste asks.

"Excuse me?" I glare at her.

We're standing in the bathroom of Assets. Celeste is reapplying her lipstick, and I'm washing my mouth from having just thrown up. When Olivia found out I briefly worked at a high-end strip club, she insisted we all go and check it out. She's never been to one, and apparently four months pregnant is the right time to experience half-naked women dancing on poles for the first time. Nick and Killian laughed, thinking she was joking. Olivia pouted. Nick, of course, gave in. So here we are.

"I don't know what you're talking about." I grab a paper towel and dry my face.

"Do you have the flu?" she questions.

"No!" I snap. "I think it's just nerves. It's my first time leaving my mom home alone. I've been working remotely from home since she got out." My mom has told me several times she's fine and I need to go about my everyday life, but I'm scared. The last time I came home, she was on the floor of the bathroom, a few minutes away from her death. Every time I attempt to leave, I imagine coming home and finding her too late. It's been over a month since she moved in and I'm still not ready to leave her yet.

"Yeah, okay." Celeste rakes her eyes down my body. "So, is it the nerves that are making you put on weight?"

"Not all of us pay a trainer to keep us in perfect model shape." I glare, and she shrugs.

"Whatever you say. Looks like I'll be throwing two baby showers instead of one." She winks and walks out of the bathroom just as Olivia walks in.

"You okay?" she asks.

"Yeah, Celeste is just being her usual bitch-self." My side cramps up and I rub it with my fingers. It's been doing this the last few hours. Maybe I am getting sick. I've heard the flu is going around...

"What did she say?" Olivia asks with a laugh.

"That I'm getting fat." The pain in my side strengthens, and I place my hands against the sink to steady myself.

Olivia now looks at me concerned. "You're hardly fat."

"What do you mean hardly?" I turn the water on again to splash my face. My eyes meet hers in the mirror

"Well..." She flinches. "I mean..."

I turn toward the full-length mirror and assess my body. I look the same...although, my pants were a tad harder to put on. I just chalked it up to Killian drying them by mistake.

"When are you due?"

Celeste's words send me running back to the toilet. There's nothing left to throw up, though, so instead, I spend the next five minutes dry-heaving. Olivia doesn't say a word. When I rinse out my mouth again, I catch her face in the mirror. She looks concerned.

"What?" I hiss. My stomach contracts—the pain radiating down my side.

"Is it possible?" Her gaze goes to my stomach.

"No, I'm on the pill."

Olivia scoffs. "Have you missed any? I only missed a few... and POOF—" her hands shoot open at the same time her eyes go wide "—came Reed, and now this baby." She covers her adorable protruding belly.

"No..." I shake my head. "No, no, no. That shit happens to you, not me. I take them every goddamned day..." Except a few nights I ended up sleeping at Killian's place but left my pills at mine... and then when we went to North Carolina and then Cozumel. Holy fucking shit! I am just as irresponsible as Olivia.

"Giselle," Olivia says, "are you okay?"

"Yeah, I'm just going to go pee. I'll be right out."

"Is it possible...that you're pregnant?"

"I don't know," I lie. "Please...just go tell Killian I'll be right out."

Olivia agrees and heads out of the bathroom. I wait a few seconds and then go out the back door. This seriously can't be happening. I'm so stupid. I thought I was invincible, like if the pills were there, I wouldn't get pregnant. There's a reason doctors tell you to take them at the same time every day and not to miss any.

I flag down a cab and give him my address. I need time to think. This is my fault. I should've been more careful. I've been throwing up on and off for weeks. I knew deep down there was a good chance I was pregnant. I just didn't want to deal with it. I saw how Melanie having an abortion affected Killian. Could I do that? Could I abort a tiny baby that we created? No, I couldn't. Which is why I chose to live in denial.

I feel that sharp pain on my side once again, and my hand goes to my belly. "Sir, I'm going to throw up. Can you please stop?" He pulls over, and I barely make it out of the cab when I start throwing up nothing but acid. My knees hit the cement, and I try to release whatever is making me feel sick and nauseous. My stomach cramps are now so unbearable, I can barely stand, so instead I remain on all fours.

"Ma'am, should I call you an ambulance?" the driver asks. I'm in so much pain, I can barely speak. It's like the wind has been knocked out of me. I'm dizzy and queasy. Maybe I have food poisoning. This can't be how morning sickness is. Something is wrong.

"Yes, please," I choke out. I stay doubled over as I wait for the ambulance to arrive. The pain is now so horrendous it's hard to see straight, hard to think. This isn't like any flu or food poisoning I've ever had. I'm losing my baby. I know it. I was afraid to admit I was pregnant. I considered, even if only briefly, not having this baby, and now I'm about to lose it.

When the pain gets so intense, my arms cave in, and I fall to the ground. Worried about my baby, I cushion my belly, and my shoulder hits the cement hard. I pull myself into the fetal position, praying the ambulance gets here soon. My eyes close. It hurts so much. I can hear the sirens. I try to open my eyes, but I can't. I hear the driver speaking to the medics.

"I-I'm pregnant," I try to tell them. "I'm pregnant."

"Okay, miss. We're taking you to New York General. We're just going to find your identification in your purse."

I think I nod, but I'm not sure. They lift me onto a gurney and push me into the ambulance. My eyes are squeezed shut as I try to block out the excruciating pain as they let me know what they're doing every step of the way. They place an oxygen mask over my face. I'm not sure when it's finally too much for me to handle, but at some point, I feel myself begin to black out. My last thought: a plea to God to not take my baby. The baby I was in denial of, the baby I want more than anything in this world but was too afraid to admit, until the idea of losing him became all too real. Isn't that how the saying goes? You don't realize how much you love someone until he's gone...

THIRTY-ONE

KILLIAN

"SHE'S NOT IN THE BATHROOM!" I shout. "I've checked every fucking stall. She's not there! Where is she?" Celeste and Olivia are both wearing nervous looks on their faces. Not scared like they're afraid something happened to my wife, but nervous like they know something I don't.

"Olivia, you have to give me something here. Did she leave? Did something happen?" Giselle has been off the last few days. She told me she was just stressed and tired, but it felt like something more.

Olivia glances between Nick and me. Then her eyes go to Celeste. "I-I don't know..."

"She's pregnant," Celeste blurts out. "She was throwing up and I pointed out she's pregnant. She probably got spooked or something and left."

"Celeste," Olivia hisses.

"What? I'm sorry but the guy is assuming the worst here. She wasn't kidnapped or anything. She's just pregnant."

Pregnant.

Giselle is pregnant.

And she ran.

That may not be the worst-case scenario to Celeste, but that's only because she doesn't know Giselle doesn't want to have kids. She's terrified at just the thought of becoming a mother. And then it hits me...She ran! Like Melanie ran. I pull my phone out and dial her number. It rings and rings and rings and then goes to voicemail.

"We have to find her," I say. "She..." I can't say the words out loud. That there's a real possibility of another woman, who's pregnant with my baby, and is about to...fuck! I can't even think the words. This can't be happening. Could I forgive Giselle if she does what I think she's about to do? Could we get past it?

Olivia's phone rings and she pulls it out of her back pocket. "Is it Giselle?" I ask.

"No, I don't recognize the number." She answers the call. "Hello?" Her eyes dart over to me. "Yes, I am." Her hand that's not holding the phone goes to her mouth in shock. "Okay...Okay, thank you."

She hangs up and tears pool in her eyes. A million scenarios run through my head of what could've happened, but there's only one thing in this moment I know for sure. I can forgive Giselle for anything as long as she's okay. I knew she didn't want to have kids. We didn't use protection. Yes, it's on both of us, but she's not over what happened with her mom. She's been afraid to leave her for weeks since we brought her home. She's alone and not in her right mind. Fuck! This can't be happening...not again.

"She's at New York General," Olivia says, snapping me out of my thoughts. "They couldn't tell me anything over the phone, but I'm her emergency contact. All the nurse could say is she's in surgery and should be out within the next hour and will need someone to bring her home once she's released."

My heart plummets. Giselle had surgery. There's no way she ran straight to the hospital to have an abortion. Something else has to be wrong. Without waiting for anyone else to follow, I start to run toward the entrance. We came in a cab tonight in case we both drank...which Giselle didn't. I hail a cab and Olivia, Nick, and Celeste jump in as well. After I tell the cab driver where to go, the drive is silent with worry.

We get to the hospital and I go straight to the front desk. "My name is Killian Blake. I am Giselle Blake's husband."

"Killian," Olivia says, "when the nurse called, she said Giselle Winters." Shit! We hadn't gotten around to getting her driver's license changed yet. We're still waiting on the documents to go through.

"Giselle Winters," I say. "I'm her husband."

"And you are?" the nurse asks Olivia.

"Olivia Harper."

"I have permission to speak to you. She's just coming out of surgery. She'll be moved into recovery, and once the doctor has checked on her, she'll be able to have visitors."

"Why is she in surgery?" I ask.

"She was brought in for appendicitis."

I let out a sigh of relief. She didn't run... maybe the throwing up wasn't that she was pregnant, but that her appendix was about to burst.

"Do you know if she's pregnant?" I ask.

The nurse's expression gives nothing away. "I don't have that kind of information. I'm sorry."

Everyone sits down to wait, but I head over to billing to make sure whatever my wife needs, she gets. I know she doesn't have insurance, and we haven't added her to my policy yet, but I'm going to make damn sure they understand she gets the best treatment.

After requesting a private room for her recovery, and giving the woman my credit card to charge everything to, I sit down to wait with the others. I remember Giselle's mom is at home and would want to know about her daughter, so I give her a call to let her know what I know. When she tells me she's on her way, I offer to go and get her, but she scoffs. "I've been hailing cabs since before you were born," she says before we hang up.

For the next couple hours we wait to hear something from the doctor. Sarah shows up and lets me know she called Adrianna, who is on her way, despite her mom suggesting she should wait until we hear from the doctor.

"Family of Giselle Winters," a nurse finally calls out, and we all stand. "I can only bring one of you back at a time until she's brought to her private room."

"Go ahead," I tell Sarah. As much as I want to see my wife, I know she's been waiting a long time to be able to be there for her daughter.

"Thank you," she says. Pulling me into a hug, she murmurs, "Thank you for loving my daughter."

THIRTY-TWO

GISELLE

I'M STARING at the ugly, dreary-looking pictures on the wall as I wait for Killian to walk through the door. I don't know what I'm going to say...what he's going to say. I don't know what he knows or doesn't know. I left without telling him and ended up having emergency surgery to remove my appendix. Instead of telling him something felt wrong, I chose to hide it and run. I put myself and our baby at risk. I can only imagine how mad he must be with me. Mentally, I'm preparing myself for the shit he's going to give me. And I deserve it. So, I'm shocked when, instead of Killian, in walks my mother.

"Oh, Giselle," she coos. She frames my face with her hands and gives me a kiss on my forehead. "I'm so glad you're okay." The tears, which were threatening, spill over. My entire life all I wanted was for my mom to be a mom, and here she is doing just that. My side is in pain, the drugs are barely helping because my options are limited due to being pregnant, but none of that matters, because right here in this moment, my mom is holding me.

"I-I'm pregnant," I blurt out.

My mom smiles. "Did you finally figure it out on your own or did the doctor tell you?"

I gasp. "You knew?"

"Well, I have been pregnant a couple of times." She winks.

"Did everyone know but me?" I laugh, but then remember Killian doesn't know...or maybe he does but didn't mention it.

"I think you always knew," Mom says, grabbing a chair and sitting next to my bed. She's right. In the back of my mind I knew something was off, but didn't want to have to face it.

"I think I did too," I admit.

"Is the baby okay?" Mom asks.

"The doctor said so far everything is good. They did an appendectomy. Luckily, I'm only ten weeks, so they were able to go in and do the surgery easily. They've ordered an ultrasound for the morning to check everything over, and I'll be here for the next few days."

Mom grabs my hand and squeezes it. "I know you were brought in here because of your appendix, but it seemed like maybe your husband didn't know where you were until Olivia got the call from the hospital. Were you running?"

I let out a sigh. "I was...I told Killian before we even got married, I didn't want to have kids." I hate having to admit this to my mom, that because of what she put us through, I didn't want to have my own children.

Realization dawns on my mom, causing her to frown. "Oh, sweetie." She pulls me in for a gentle hug, and I melt into her arms. I've missed my mom so much. Why couldn't the doctors have figured out what was wrong with her years ago? "Please don't do this to yourself or to your husband."

"You said it yourself. Dad couldn't handle you being sick. What if I become Bipolar? What will it do to Killian and our children?"

"That won't happen because we know what to look for. We will recognize the signs and get you the help you need. I wasted so many years unable to be the mom you girls deserved. The wife your father wanted. We won't allow that to happen to you."

"What if I get sick and Killian cheats on me like Dad did to you? He says he'll handle it, but what if he can't? What if he leaves me?" But even as I say the words, I know in my heart Killian would never do such a thing.

"You can't live with what ifs, sweetie," Mom says. "That man loves you so much."

"She's right, I do." I startle at the sound of Killian's voice as he walks into the room. "We were told only one person at a time, so I let your mom go first, but I couldn't wait any longer." He shrugs unapologetically. "So...where were you attempting to run to?"

"I'll leave you two to talk," my mom says, standing. She bends at the waist and kisses my forehead. "You've spent enough time being affected by my illness. It's time you start living, sweetie. It's time we all do." Then she whispers into my ear, so only I can hear, "I'll be back in the morning to check on you and my grandbaby."

Once she leaves, Killian sits in her place. He takes my hand in his and gives the inside of my wrist a soft kiss. "I was so worried," he murmurs. He kisses the center of my palm. "I was so mad when I found out you ran, but when Olivia got the call from the hospital…" He kisses the top of each of my knuckles. "Every worst-case scenario ran through my head, and my only thought was that you had to be okay." He looks me in the eyes. "I just found you. I can't lose you."

"I'm pregnant," I blurt out. He grins but quickly schools it, unsure how I feel. I hate that he can't just simply be happy. "I forgot my pills a few times, and I haven't gotten my period in the last two months…" That was my first red flag I might be pregnant, but I chose to ignore it.

"I'm ten weeks along. The doctor said as of right now the baby is okay, but they've scheduled an ultrasound for tomorrow."

"And how are you?" Killian asks.

"I'm okay. The doctor said I'll be here for a few days and then I need to take it easy for a few weeks once I'm discharged."

"And how do you want to handle the pregnancy?" Killian asks softly.

"What do you mean?"

"You have choices, Giselle. Abortion, adoption, or keeping the baby. I'm your husband, and I'll stand by your side no matter what you choose to do." I stare at this beautiful, selfless man who loves me so much. There was never a choice. I always wanted a baby with him. I was just too scared to admit it. Scared I would end up like my mom. Scared Killian would end up like my dad. But we aren't them. We're us. And it's time I start throwing that damn ball, so he has something to catch.

"I want to create a family with you, but I'm scared," I tell him honestly. My hand palms his cheek, and he moves closer.

"Then I'll be brave for the both of us," he vows, then gives me a passionate kiss that I feel all the way down to my bones.

"ARE YOU READY FOR YOUR ULTRASOUND?" the ultrasound tech asks, kicking the brakes out from under the bed and pushing it toward the door. I give Killian a look, and he smiles warmly at me. I know with him by my side, I'll be ready for anything that comes my way.

"Yes," I tell her, my eyes never leaving my husband who's holding the door open for the tech so she can push me to wherever they do the ultrasounds.

When we arrive, the room is pitch black, with only a single light coming from a computer monitor. The tech rolls me next to the monitor and presses down on the brakes.

"You can sit in that chair," she tells Killian. He thanks her and drags the chair next to me, taking my hand in his and giving the inside of my wrist a kiss.

While she types away on the computer, Killian moves a few wayward hairs out of my face and leans in to kiss my forehead.

"I'm nervous," I admit to him.

He smiles softly. "I love you. Whatever happens, we'll handle it together."

"I'm going to go ahead and put this paper across your lower half, so I can lift your gown," the tech says. Once she does so, she squeezes some warm blue goo onto my belly and begins to search for the baby. The room is quiet, and my heart begins to pick up speed. I wasn't awake when the doctor did the ultrasound after my surgery, so I've yet to hear my baby's heartbeat, and now there's a chance I might not ever.

Just as I finish my thought, a whooshing sound fills the silence, and the tech smiles. "That's the baby's heartbeat. One hundred and seventy. Good, strong heartbeat."

She explains that with me only being ten weeks along, there's not much to see. According to her, our baby is the size of a strawberry. I laugh absently at what she says, but the only thing I can really focus on is the continuous whooshing sound. Our baby has a heartbeat. He, or she, is alive in there.

I look over to Killian, and he has tears streaming down his face. Lifting my hand to his cheek, I wipe one of the tears and say, "When I used to read fairytales, I fancied that kind of thing never happened, and now here I am in the middle of one."

Killian's shoulders shake with laughter as his tears fall faster. "*Alice's Adventures in Wonderland.* Chapter four: The Rabbit Sends in a Little Bill."

"You really did read the book," I say back through my own laughter and tears.

EPILOGUE

Killian
Two months later

"WE COULD HAVE this if you want," I tell Giselle as we sway to the music on the dance floor. We're at Olivia and Nick's wedding reception, and Giselle has sighed and gushed over every detail. Apparently, a pregnant Giselle is an emotional Giselle. She seems to shed tears—happy and sad—over everything, from what to eat, to seeing a baby playing at the park, and it's absolutely adorable. She's been reading every book imaginable about what to expect when she has the baby, and she's even been seeing a therapist to discuss how she's feeling. She's facing her fears head on, and I'm so damn proud of her for that. She's eighteen weeks pregnant, and we found out a couple days ago we're having a girl. Olivia and Nick are having one as well, and the women are now hell-bent on them becoming best friends.

"I loved our wedding," Giselle murmurs. "I don't want what other people have. I want what we have." She kisses me softly then rests her head on my chest. It's well past midnight and almost everyone has retreated back to their rooms. Olivia and Nick are on their way to Florida for their honeymoon. Although, I'm not sure you can call it a honeymoon when they're bringing Reed and going to Disney.

I can tell Giselle is getting tired on her feet, but she insisted on one more dance before we head up to our room. We could've driven back to our house from the Hamptons, but I thought a weekend away would be nice, and plus, there's a surprise waiting for Giselle when we return in the morning.

"I need to use the restroom," she says. When she leans in, she whispers, "Meet me in the bathroom in three minutes." My dick twitches at her words, and I can't help my grin. My pregnant wife is always horny, which suits me just fine. I watch, as she saunters toward the bathroom, and begin to count down the seconds until I'm inside of her. While I'm waiting, my phone vibrates in my pocket, so I check to see who it is. It's from Sarah, and it's only one word: **Done**

***

GISELLE

I SCURRY across the dance floor toward the bathroom to make sure it's empty. I've been craving to have Killian inside me all night, and I can't wait another minute. I've already seen the Yacht Club's bathroom, and it's more extravagant than most homes!

When I open the bathroom door and step inside, there are three stalls. I need to make sure they're all empty. I'm not even three steps in when I hear grunting and moaning. I stop in place, shocked. Apparently, someone else had the same idea we did. Just as I'm about to turn around and give them their privacy, I hear, "Fuck, Celeste." My hand covers my mouth to silence my gasp. Is Celeste having sex in here? And with who? It couldn't be...

The door swings open, and in walks Killian. He locks the door and stalks toward me like a man on a mission. "Shh..." I put my finger up to my lips. "Someone is in here. We need to go." His brows go up, and he takes my hand to guide us out of the bathroom. But before the door opens, Celeste moans out, "Yes, right there!"

"Is that?" Killian whispers, and I stifle a giggle, nodding my head. We exit the bathroom quietly, and then I answer him, "Yeah, Celeste is totally having bathroom sex!"

"Goddamn." Killian laughs. "I guess I'll just have to wait until I get you up to our room to get between your thighs." He pulls me close and gives me a kiss.

KILLIAN

THE NEXT MORNING, after stopping for breakfast, we head home. Once we arrive, Giselle heads straight back to her mom's suite. She always does. The therapist they're seeing together says it'll take time before Giselle feels comfortable enough to not check on her mom. When it's late at night, she just peeks in, but when it's earlier, she'll hang out and they'll have coffee or tea together. They're finally getting the relationship they've longed for.

About twenty minutes later, she returns, and I hear her call my name when she doesn't find me in our room. I hear her feet padding down the hallway as she searches for me. When she finally gets to the last door on the left, she turns the knob and enters. "Killian!" Her hands come up to her mouth as she takes in the nursery.

"When did you do this?" She steps farther into the room and takes in all the Alice in Wonderland décor. When I got ahold of her Pinterest page, I hired her boss, Lydia, to decorate it. Giselle has been busy since she got her promotion, and I wanted her to enjoy the fruits of the labor instead of her having to do the labor herself.

"It's beautiful," she coos. Her hand glides over the mahogany wood crib and stops to feel the bedding. She eyes the walls which have been transformed into scenes from the book with floor-to-ceiling trees and animals having tea parties.

"It's exactly how I imagined it would look," she says, coming over to me when she's done checking it all out. "Thank you." She stands on her tippy-toes and gives me a kiss.

"I'd like to take the credit, but Lydia did all the hard work." I take her hand in mine and guide her to our room. Pulling my shirt off, I throw it onto the dresser.

Giselle comes up behind me and wraps her arms around my waist. I look down at her tiny fingers before I pull her around to face me. "Not just for the room, Kill," she says. "Thank you for loving me...broken and all."

I unzip then lift the yellow sundress Giselle is wearing over her head. Then take a moment to appreciate all of her new curves pregnancy has brought with it. I can't help it. Every time I get her naked, I have to stop and see if she's grown any more. I love watching our baby growing inside her. I place kisses along her neck and down her collar bone. She moans when my lips suck on her tender breasts. Picking her up carefully, I move her to the center of our bed. Hovering over her, I begin to worship my wife's body. Her breasts, her soft stomach, making my way down to her wet cunt. I give it a kiss before I make my way back up to her lips, giving her a hard kiss before I back up slightly, needing to look into her beautiful blue eyes.

"I already told you, babe. I'm in deep. There's nobody I'd rather be broken with than you."

ON THE SURFACE

IMPERFECT LOVE SERIES: BOOK THREE

We are all broken. That's how the light gets in. –Unknown

To the readers who see under the surface, through the fakeness, beyond the shattered, and love the broken characters. This book is for you.

ONE

Celeste

"TWO WEEKS until I'm finally Mrs. Shaw." Olivia squeals loud enough that the patrons sitting at the table next to us look over. Her hands clasp together in excitement as her eyes run along everyone at the table and land on her fiancé, Nicholas Shaw, who is known to most as the newly retired quarterback from the New York Brewers. To me, though, he's my childhood best friend. Despite our four-year age difference, I've spent the last two decades following Nick around while he's chased his dream of playing pro ball, and I've chased mine of becoming a model. There was even a short span of time when we almost got married—a stupid decision on both our parts, stemmed from a teenage pact in a moment of weakness.

Of course, that was all before he met Olivia, who swooped in with her sweet and adorable self and stole his heart—while simultaneously winning me over and becoming one of the few people I call a friend. She and Nick are expecting their second baby in September. Their son, Reed, is eighteen months old, and at home with his grandparents tonight.

In response to what Olivia says, Nick snakes his arm around her shoulders in a protective manner and pulls her into his side with a wide grin. His lips press against hers softly in a loving gesture, and I'm almost positive they've just given me a cavity from all the sweetness that's radiating off them.

"Which means a bachelorette party is in order!" Olivia's best friend, Giselle, states. She's also pregnant—due in November—and someone I consider a friend. Her husband, Killian Blake—who is a receiver for the Brewers—also wraps his arm around his wife and pulls her in for a kiss. Only theirs is more intense, more passionate. I can't help but watch as things between them become heated. It's one of those kisses where you want to look away to give them their privacy, but you can't stop watching. *Yep! I've definitely got a cavity, maybe two.* It isn't until Nick clears his throat that they come up for air. Giselle's face is bright red—not sure if it's out of embarrassment over their public display of affection, or if she's turned on—either way, she's completely captivated by her husband.

"Oh, I don't know." Olivia's nose scrunches up, and she shakes her head. "I'm half-baked." She points to her protruding belly. "And you're pregnant too." She eyes Giselle. "The only person who'll actually get to party is Celeste!" She laughs, shooting me a soft smile.

My gaze goes to my—and I use the term loosely—boyfriend, Chad Vacanti. Chad is forty-five years old and the VP for the investment banking firm he's a partner in. We met at a function we were both attending and hit it off. Shortly after, I left for the UK to promote my clothing line that went international. Apparently, he had some business over there as well and reached out. We spent several weeks together—when we weren't both working eighteen-hour days—and decided to keep things going when we returned. It's worked out well for both of us—giving us someone to attend functions with and get lost in after long days of work. He's a lot like me and knows the score, so there aren't any hurt feelings. Chad's nearly twenty years my senior, which is the way I prefer it. Older men tend to have their shit together and are far more mature than the guys my age.

"And it will stay that way," I say with conviction in response to Olivia's comment. Chad looks up from his phone as I finish saying the words, completely focused on work and having no clue what the conversation is about.

"What will stay what way?" he questions—apparently, he's somewhat good at multitasking—good to know he at least hears me when I speak.

"My getting pregnant." His eyes go wide in fear, completely misunderstanding. "That I *won't* be getting pregnant anytime soon," I clarify, and he lets out a harsh sigh of relief, as if having a baby with me would be the absolute worst thing in the world. It's not as if I would want to have kids with him—or with anyone for that matter—but Jesus, does he have to look so relieved?

Taking a bite of my shrimp salad, I try to ignore the four pairs of eyes staring at me—not including Chad's, as his are already back on his phone. It's no secret I'm the odd one out in our group of friends. Unlike Olivia and Giselle, who are both happily doing their part to add to the ever-growing human race, I have no desire to ever procreate. I have one goal in this life: to make something of myself. Which I happen to think I'm doing a damn good job at. I've learned over the years that independence is the key to a woman's success. While Chad is decent in bed and someone I can talk business with, he'll never be anything more than that. I don't need him—or any man for that matter. I push back the thoughts of the one guy I allowed myself to need and how that turned out...*with my heart broken and my future nearly destroyed.*

"I still say we need to throw a party!" Giselle insists. "We can do a combined bachelor and bachelorette party at an upscale club." She stops talking, so I look up, and she's giving Olivia the stink-eye. "And not at a strip club."

A loud laugh escapes me as I remember not too long ago when Olivia convinced Nick to take her to Assets, a high-end strip club. I thought he was going to kill me when I surprised her with a lap dance. The poor guy wasn't sure whether to be turned on or upset that his fiancée was thoroughly enjoying another woman grinding on her.

"No, not at a strip club," Olivia agrees. "But it would be fun for all of us to go out and have a good time before we get married." She looks at Nick, who of course nods in agreement. She could tell him she wants him to participate in a shit-eating contest and the guy would nod in agreement if it meant making her happy.

"Mind if I invite Jase?" Killian asks. It doesn't go unnoticed that his gaze quickly meets mine before he looks away. The hairs on the back of my neck stand at the mention of that name. *Jase Crawford.* The one who... I shake myself out of my thoughts, refusing to even finish that sentence. He doesn't deserve a place in my thoughts, in my head, in my... Nope, not going there. He's nothing more than a mistake from my past. A lesson learned the hard way.

"I saw him yesterday at the shop," Killian says, "while getting some work done. Seems like he doesn't get out much."

"Of course he's welcome to come!" Olivia says, speaking for Nick. "He's also invited to the wedding." Her hand comes up and rests on top of Nick's. "After we ran into him on Giselle's birthday, he and Nick have been keeping in touch again. Jax and Quinn are both invited as well." Jax and Quinn are Jase's brother and sister. They own a tattoo shop here in New York called Forbidden Ink. We went there the night of Giselle's birthday so she and Olivia could get their first tattoo. Olivia chickened out, but Giselle ended up getting a beautiful quote across her upper back just below her nape.

"How many people are coming?" I ask, trying to remain calm, even though the reality of having to see Jase at the wedding has me feeling anything but. "I thought you were keeping it small and intimate." Nick doesn't speak to his parents, which only leaves Olivia's family and their friends. She didn't want something huge, which could easily happen since Nick's a four-time Super Bowl champion and Olivia's dad is an NFL coach. And then there's her mom—who is no longer alive. She was a huge international supermodel—one I spent many years looking up to. So you can imagine how many people they're acquainted with.

"Only about a hundred and fifty people. We're still keeping it small." She gives me a questioning look. "Jase isn't in the wedding party if that's what you're worried about."

"I'm not," I say far too quickly. Everyone's gazes swing over to me—except Chad, who's still typing away on his phone. "I'm not," I repeat in a tone that makes it clear to drop whatever they're all thinking. It makes sense that Jase and his siblings are invited since Nick has been friends with them since high school.

"I like your new hair color," Olivia says, changing the subject. "It makes you look less...harsh."

"Less like an evil witch?" I wink, and she laughs. When Olivia and I first met, Nick referred to me as the evil witch in their story, and I've yet to live the nickname down. So I figure, if I can't beat them, I might as well join them. But she's right, the black hair gave me an edgier look, which is what the modeling agency I used to be signed with was going for. Since I'm no longer signed with anyone, and I'm free to do as I want with my hair, I dyed it back to my original color—a mahogany brown with hints of auburn mixed in.

"Yes! I mean you can totally pull off any color, obviously, but this color is really pretty."

"Thanks."

"Hey Chad," Giselle calls out from across the table. He looks up to see who said his name. "What do you think about Celeste's hair?"

Chad looks over at me in confusion. "It looks nice," he says with a shrug.

"What does?" she presses.

"Uh...the length?" he says, but it comes out more like a question. "Did you get it cut or something?"

"Actually, it's a different color," Giselle points out—with a big fake smile—before I can answer. It's no secret my friends aren't a fan of Chad's. Olivia is too sweet to say anything mean, but Giselle has no problem calling him out.

"Really?" he asks.

"Yep," I say, taking a bite of my food.

The rest of the meal is spent with everyone hammering out the details for the party, but my mind can't get off the fact that Jase and Nick are hanging out again. He's going to be invited to the party. And he's going to come to the wedding. I try to think of a reason to get out of going to either one, but I know I can't do that. Nick has been there for me my entire life. I'm not just going to ditch one of the biggest days of his life because of who will be in attendance. I refuse to be affected by this. Jase will just be another guest attending the wedding. Of course, since I'm in the wedding party as Olivia's bridesmaid, I'm going to have to walk down the aisle in front of everyone, including Jase. I've walked down a million runways at fashion shows—sometimes more than half-naked. I've been on dozens of billboards and in more commercials than I can count. Yet, the thought of having to walk down the aisle, knowing Jase will be there—most likely with a date—has me feeling sick to my stomach. He shouldn't make me feel like this. Not after all this time. Not after the way things ended.

When the bill is paid, everyone makes their way outside to say their goodbyes. Chad's driver comes around and we slide into the back of his town car. Since it's Saturday night, I'd usually go back to his place, but tonight I tell him I'm going home instead. He simply nods, not even questioning why I'm canceling our evening plans. He doesn't ask if anything is wrong. The entire drive he's on his phone. His arm never snakes around my shoulders like Nick's did to Olivia. His hand never touches mine like Olivia's did to Nick. And when his driver drops me off in front of my building, he doesn't kiss me the way Killian kissed Giselle.

After showering and changing into silky pajamas, I pour myself a glass of white wine to help calm my nerves before bed. Usually, this is when I go through my emails. I confirm my meetings and engagements with Margie, my assistant, for the upcoming week, since she doesn't work Sundays. I check my company's financials to make sure we're where we need to be. But tonight, I do none of that. Instead, I head outside onto my balcony, which overlooks Central

Park. With my condo being on the tenth floor, I'm able to just barely make out the people bustling about. Some are walking their dogs; others are strolling hand-in-hand. It's dark out, just after ten o'clock, but this is the city that never sleeps.

I take in a deep breath, then bring my lips up to my glass, swallowing a taste of the fruity wine. This is what I wanted. A sky-rise condo in Lennox Hills overlooking Central Park. And I finally got it. The day I signed the papers on this condo, I felt like I'd finally made it. I purchased it on my own, with my own credit and my own money. Yet, as I look out at the luscious trees that fill the park, it feels like every goal and dream I've ever made wasn't enough. I should feel complete, fulfilled. I should feel accomplished. But I don't. I feel empty.

After I finish my wine, I rinse the glass out then climb into bed. I lay here for several minutes, trying to figure out what's wrong with me. I barely even touched my cell phone tonight. *That's because you were too busy watching the sickeningly-sweet couples at the table.* Usually I don't pay attention to how the couples around me act with each other. I don't care whether Chad pays attention to me, or if he kisses me goodbye.

I snuggle into my blankets, trying my hardest not to remember a time when I wanted nothing more than to be one-half to a sickeningly-sweet couple. When my world, for just a brief moment, was filled with hand-holding and kissing and sweet words whispered to one another. I close my eyes, refusing to let the tears come, only my heart—and tear ducts—seem to have a mind of their own, and when the memories of him surface, the tears fall of their own accord.

TWO

CELESTE
The Past

"TELL ME EVERYTHING!" I bounce up and down on Nick's bed in his old room in his parents' house. He's home for my graduation, and I'm beyond excited to have my best friend back—even if it's only for a short time. He may only live a hundred miles away, and in the same state, but without me having my own vehicle, it might as well be a million miles away. This past year without Nick has been excruciatingly difficult. I've lost my best friend, the person I talk to and hang out with. He's now an uber-famous professional football player, and I'm just a high school senior.

"You know everything." He laughs. "We talk every day." He strips out of his sweatpants and shirt he wore for his drive over and into a pair of distressed jeans and a collared shirt.

"It's not the same," I whine. "You're living this amazing life, and I'm stuck here in Piermont without you." I pout. Up until this last year, Nick and I have always lived close enough that I could take the bus, or bum a ride from someone, to visit him. He even went to college locally at North Carolina University. Now, though, things have changed.

"I need details," I beg. "Tell me about the traveling, the money, the fame. I saw you on TMZ at a charity function in New York with Alessandra Starr!" I sigh. Alessandra Starr is an up-and-coming model. She was a lot like me—a nobody from a small town—trying to make a name for herself. She was at the right place at the right time, and boom! Now she's the face of several different companies, including MAC and Lancôme.

"She's not really my type," Nick admits, as if I care about who his type is. I want to know what it's like, not who he's in love with this week.

"Nicholas Shaw!" I shriek. "I don't care who you like or don't like. I want to know about New York... about the event! Did you meet a lot of famous people? When you travel, do you get to order room service? Did you go to any popular clubs? What's it like to see your name and picture plastered all over the magazines?"

Nick rolls his eyes and sits next to me on his bed. "You know I don't care about any of that. I'm doing what I love. Playing ball." It's my turn to roll my eyes. I shouldn't have expected Nick to understand. He was raised with money. To him, this is all just another day in the life of Nicholas Shaw. He might be my best friend—and our moms might be best friends—and we might've grown up only a few miles apart—on opposite sides of the train tracks—but we might as well be from two different planets.

"I have a surprise for you." He grins wide and stands, then walks over to his luggage. He pulls an envelope from it and hands it to me. Just as my fingers are about to grasp the paper, he pulls it back and laughs.

"Nick!" I growl. "Give it to me."

Chuckling, he hands the envelope to me, this time letting me take it from him.

I open it and read over the document once, twice, a third time. This can't be real. "Nick," I whisper, "what did you do?" Tears form in my eyes. The paper falls from my hands, and my arms wrap around his neck. "Is this for real?"

"It is." He laughs. "I had to do a photoshoot with Elite for Movado, and while I was there, I ended up having brunch with Alessandra and Brenna Myers.

I gasp. "Brenna Myers? As in *the* Brenna Myers...the VP of Elite?" Elite is one of the top modeling agencies in the world.

"Yep. I mentioned I have a friend who would give her left arm to get her foot in the door..."

"Please tell me you didn't make me sound desperate, Nick," I chide.

He laughs some more. "Give me some credit," he says. "Anyway, Elite has a summer internship program, and after showing her your photos, she opened up a spot for you."

"Ohmigod!!!" I squeal. "I can't believe it. This is really happening." I hug Nick again. "Thank you so much!" I grab the paper from the floor, where it fell, and read it again and again. This is actually happening. I'm going to graduate and get out of this hellhole. I'm going to New York!

"Wait," I say, thinking about the details. "Where am I going to live?" This is New York we're talking about. I doubt I can even afford a cardboard box there.

"While you're in the summer program, you'll be living in an apartment with the other girls. It'll all be paid for by Elite. Once it ends, if I need to help you, I will. Don't worry about that now, though," he says, reassuring me. "Just focus on your dreams."

I don't even realize I'm full-on crying until Nick swipes a falling tear with his thumb. "Celeste, I know this is what you want, but trust me when I say, being famous isn't all it's cracked up to be. Everybody is so damn fake." His voice is soft, non-judgmental. He's simply being honest—as honest as he can be as a man who's grown up with money, while I've grown up in a trailer park. "I thought once I was away from my parents it would be different," he adds. "The women are all fake. Alessandra...she's fake." Nick frowns in disappointment.

"I told you once, and I'll tell you again," I say, "the world revolves around money and status, and until you accept that, you're going to keep getting your heart broken and being disappointed." While Nick is looking for love—some non-existent soulmate to give his sappy heart to—I'm looking for a future.

"And I'll tell you once again, we'll have to agree to disagree." He pulls me into a side-hug and kisses my temple. "One day you're going to meet a guy who's going to knock you right off your feet, and you're going to finally understand that no amount of money can buy love."

"That sounds like it would hurt," I joke. "I'll leave the falling to you...on the football field." I shoot him a playful wink, and he laughs. "So, what's going on tonight?" I nod toward his outfit. He's obviously dressed up for a reason. Unless Nick is going somewhere, he's always in basketball shorts and a T-shirt.

"Party tonight. Some friends from high school are getting together for a reunion of sorts." He pulls on his shoes. "Wanna go?"

"Hmm, let's see here..." I tap my lower lip with my index finger, pretending to contemplate whether I want to go. This is the first time I'll get to meet Nick's high school friends. Because of our age difference, he'd never let me tag along to any of the parties he attended while he was in high school or college. "Rich, hot, older guys all in one place, or another night spent with my drunken mother...What do you think?"

Nick frowns. "How is Beatrice?"

"Same as she's been my entire life. Drunk and waiting on the love of her life to mend her broken heart."

His frown deepens. "You could be a little more understanding."

"Seriously?" I scoff. "Some biker guy knocks up my mother and takes off, promising to return, only to disappear. My mom chooses to pine after him for the next eighteen years, forcing me to live in a rusted metal can in a damn trailer park, barely working enough to pay our electric bill and rent, and I'm supposed to be understanding?"

My blood is now boiling, and my skin is heating up. My mother could've gotten us out of our shitty situation. She's best friends with Victoria, Nick's mom. She's been introduced to dozens of wealthy men. But instead, she refuses to leave our seven hundred square foot trailer, and continues to work at the same hole-in-the-wall diner, in hope that one day he'll come back like he promised. I've tried to look him up a couple times at the public library, but the only thing I know is that his last name is Leblanc—same as mine. Apparently, he once referred to me as baby Leblanc, and when my mom asked, he confirmed that was his last name.

According to my mom, he was a member of some biker gang and went by the name of Snake—*really classy, huh?* He met my mom while passing through town. They fell in love and spent the next few months planning their life together. My mom got pregnant, and supposedly Snake was just as excited as she was. He said he had some affairs to get in order, promising to return soon, only he never did—making my mother a single mom. And yes, in case you're wondering, Snake is actually written on my birth certificate. Who in their right mind falls in love with a man but never takes the time to learn his real name? My mother, that's who!

"I get it," Nick says, "but you've never been in love, so you don't understand."

"And you have?" I snort in disbelief.

"No, but I'm at least capable of it," Nick volleys back. "If I met the love of my life and she promised to return, I would wait for her. Your mom is heartbroken. She can't imagine loving anyone else but him. It's kind of romantic."

"Yeah, well, if that's how love works, you can have it," I hiss. "Her love for my *father* destroyed her, and I refuse to ever be destroyed by a man."

"No, you'd rather *do* the destroying," Nick smarts.

"What's that supposed to mean?" I snap. It's not often Nick and I argue, but when we do, it's usually over this very subject. We don't see eye-to-eye on love and never will.

"Never mind." Nick sighs. "Just try not to *destroy* any of my friends' hearts tonight. I prefer to keep them as friends."

"I can't help if they fall for me and get hurt." I turn on my heel, done with this conversation. "I need to run home and change my outfit. Drive me?"

"Sure."

We pull up to my place, and Nick parks his Audi along the road since my mom's piece of shit clunker is parked in the tiny driveway. She's sitting outside with a beer in one hand and a joint in the other, and our neighbor Dale—the nasty drug dealer I know she fucks on occasion when she's feeling extra lonely—is sitting next to her with his hand resting on her thigh.

"Want me to go in with you?" Nick offers. Anyone else and I wouldn't have even let him bring me here, but Nick has seen my home more times than I can count, so it's pointless to hide it from him. I'm not sure why our moms have remained friends over the years, but it's the one thing I'm grateful for. Their friendship was the only good part of my life growing up. Nick's mom has always treated me like I'm her own daughter—always including me in their trips and holidays.

"No." I shake my head. "I'll be quick. Plus, we might come out and find your car to be missing." I laugh humorlessly, and Nick rolls his eyes.

I jump out of the passenger seat and head up the sidewalk. My mom notices me and gives me a small smile. "Hey, pretty girl," she coos. I bend at the waist and give her a kiss on her forehead. I want to hate her for this life—and many days it feels like I do—but then she smiles and calls me *pretty girl* and my heart breaks for her. She fell in love and got her heart broken. If you want to know what a broken heart is capable of, spend a day with my mom. It looks just like this: a once beautiful, vibrant woman who was full of life, burnt into ash. With wrinkles around her lips from smoking, and dark circles under her eyes from never feeling rested or content, she's nothing more than the rubble left after the fire—which has ruined everything it's come in contact with—has finally gone out.

I've never personally experienced the former version of my mother, but I've heard about the woman she used to be. And oftentimes, when I was younger, I'd wish that one day I would get to experience that woman for myself. But now that I'm older, I know that once something's been burnt to ash, there is no coming back.

"What are you and Nick up to?" she asks, taking a hit of her joint and then passing it to Dale.

"Going to a party."

"That was nice of him to come in for your graduation. Victoria said she's going to host a gathering at her place for you afterward."

"Sounds good," I say, giving her a fake smile. "I'm going to go change."

Stepping into the trailer, beads of sweat instantly surface on my skin. I check the thermostat and it shows eighty-nine degrees. I try the light switch to see if the AC is broken or if the electric is out. The light doesn't come on. *Damn it, Mom!* She didn't pay the electric bill. I try the water and no such luck. She didn't pay that either. Looks like I'm going to have to dip into my savings to pay it. I have no clue what she's going to do once I leave for New York, but my hope is that once I hit it big, I'll be able to convince her to move with me, or at the very least, buy her a better place to live in. Although, if I'm honest, I know she won't allow either option to happen. That would mean moving out of this piece-of-shit place, and if she hasn't moved yet, I doubt she ever will.

After changing into a cute yet sexy burgundy tank dress that Nick's mom bought me for my eighteenth birthday last month, and sliding on a pair of cute wedges, I use a bottle of water to quickly brush my teeth, then head out.

When I step outside, the cool air sends goosebumps running up my arms. I give my mom a knowing look as I dab my forehead with a paper towel.

"Sorry," she whispers, her face filled with apology. She's said the word so many times over the years, it's been desensitized.

Once I'm back in Nick's car, he takes off to his friend Jared's house, which is in the same gated community Nick's parents live in. Apparently, Jared's parents are on a cruise and he has the house to himself. Most of Nick's friends are still in college. The only reason he's not is because he was drafted into the NFL at the end of his junior year and currently plays for Carolina. When we pull up, the street is already packed with expensive cars that line both sides of the road.

"How long do you give it until someone calls the cops?" I joke.

"Maybe another hour." Nick laughs. We get out and head up to the front door. Nick doesn't bother knocking since the music is thumping so loud no one would hear it anyway. It's only nine o'clock, but it's clear this party's been going on for some time.

When we enter, it's a typical rich kid party. Tons of expensive liquor everywhere. Guys dressed in Lacoste, and girls donning Louis Vuitton and Burberry. Nick might've gone all big brother on me over the years, but that didn't stop me from finding my way into parties elsewhere, especially once he left last year for the NFL and couldn't keep tabs on me. I follow Nick over to the large dining room table where several guys are playing poker. Chips are stacked high and hundred-dollar bills are being thrown around like they're singles at a strip club.

When one of the guys spots Nick, he yells out his name, and everyone at the table stands to give Nick attention. I mentally roll my eyes. Nick is right about one thing: rich people are fake. But you know what else they are? Rich! I'll gladly take a fake, wealthy man over a heartfelt, poor one. Love doesn't pay the bills. Love doesn't have connections. These guys...they're the future of America. They'll graduate from college and follow in their rich daddy's foot-steps, going on to work at Fortune 500 companies all over the world, and I'm going to snag one of them. Nick might've gotten me in the door with Elite, but that will only get me so far. Everyone knows money talks. My last name doesn't mean anything to anyone. But some of these guys...one mention of their name and I'll be heading straight to the top.

"How's it going?" Nick asks, greeting each of his friends, who are probably already thinking of how they can use their friendship with a famous quarterback to their advantage. Nick went into the NFL as a first-round draft pick as a backup quarterback. Due to an injury of the starting QB, he got a chance to show everyone what he's made of, and he soared. He took Carolina straight to the Super Bowl and won. Something that almost never happens with a first-year rookie.

"Jase!" Nick fist bumps his friend. "It's been too long, man."

His friend nods in agreement, but his eyes aren't on Nick—they're on me. And now, mine are on him. I take in his gelled ink-black hair, short enough not to be messy, but long enough I could run my fingers through it. His eyes, just as dark. Hard. Unforgiving. He's wearing a button-down white shirt with the sleeves rolled up to his elbows. I immediately spot several tattoos donning his muscular forearms. All shades of black and grey, no color. It's obvious, whoever this guy is, he isn't one of Nick's typical friends. He doesn't even try to suck up to Nick like the others do. My eyes continue their perusal down his front. He's lean, and if judging by the veins running down his forearms, he works out, but he's not a gym rat. He's wearing jeans that fit him just right and a pair of Nike's. Football player, maybe? The business majors usually wear Tom Ford or Brooks Brothers.

"And who's this?" Jase asks Nick with a knowing smirk. He's caught me checking him out.

"Just a friend of mine," Nick says dryly. When Jase clears his throat, indicating, not so subtly, he wants Nick to introduce us more thoroughly, Nick groans. "Celeste, this is Jase. We played ball together at Piermont Academy and at NCU. He was two years ahead of me." Hmm...so, he is a football player and a rich kid.

"Jase Crawford," Jase says, extending his hand. I give it willingly. "I'm pretty sure I've seen you on campus, but we've never formally met."

"Celeste is—" Nick begins, but I cut him off.

"...busy with school," I say, finishing Nick's sentence for him as I shake Jase's hand. There's no reason for Jase to know the *school* I'm busy with contains grades nine through twelve. I'm eighteen. That's all that matters.

Nick groans again, and I quickly shoot him a look that says if he groans one more damn time, I'll kill him.

"Nice." Jase grins, still holding my hand in his. "I graduated a couple years ago. Definitely don't miss the school work." Wealthy, educated, in shape, and hot as hell. I'm pretty sure I've just hit the jackpot.

"It's nice to meet you. How about you take a break from playing poker and get me a drink?" I bat my lashes, and Jase throws his head back with a laugh—one that has my insides melting like a pile of goo. What is wrong with me? I don't melt. I'm not that girl.

"All right," he says. "What would you like?" His lips curl up into a sexy smile.

"Something fruity would be great." My gaze stays glued to his mesmerizing mouth. His lips are full, and I try to imagine what it would feel like to kiss him.

"Got it." He lets go of my hand, and I miss it immediately. Jesus! Get a grip. He's just a guy. A rich guy who's hot and educated, but just a guy all the same. He went to Piermont Academy like Nick. He most likely comes from an influential family, and my goal is to see if he's someone I can use as a stepping stone to get me to where I want to go. Stick to the plan, Celeste!

When he walks away, Nick turns toward me. "Listen, Celeste, I know what you're thinking, but—"

"Nick, don't you dare cock-block me!" I say, cutting him off. "I swear to God, I will beat your ass," I hiss lowly, so no one can hear me.

Nick laughs. "One, you don't have a cock..."

"Fine! Vagina-block me," I cut in. "You know what I mean! Don't freaking block me!"

"Celeste, listen to me. Jase—"

"Jase!" I say a tad too loudly as I spot him walking back toward us. "That was quick." I take the drink he's holding out for me and take a sip. It's mostly liquor with a splash of...sprite? I choke down the burning sensation in my throat as I swallow. That...whatever it is...is definitely not fruity.

"Sorry." He cringes. "You took a sip before I could warn you. There wasn't anything fruity. The only thing close I could find was vodka and Sprite."

I let out a deep breath. "That's okay." I smile. "I love vodka." Nick laughs under his breath, knowing I'm lying through my teeth. I'm more of a rum girl...mixed into a fruity daiquiri.

"Celeste, can I talk to you for a minute?" Nick asks. My eyes swing over to him. I know he's protective of his friends, but he's never tried to block me like this, and I've gone on dates with a few of his college friends.

"Later, Nick," I say, trying to make it clear he needs to mind his own business.

He opens his mouth to speak again then closes it. Then his lips upturn into a wide smile and he says, "All right." He nods and laughs softly. "I'm going to play poker. You two enjoy yourselves." I'm not sure what made him suddenly change his disposition toward me going after Jase, but I'm not about to question it. Before Jase or I can say anything, one of the guys yells over at him to get his ass back to the poker table.

"Join me?" he asks. "You can be my good luck charm."

"Sure." I dramatically roll my eyes. "But you are aware every guy has at some point used that same line, right?"

Jase laughs. "I like you." Before he sits in his seat, he grabs another chair and pulls it next to him for me.

"All right, now that Nick is here, we can play a real game," some guy says, throwing some more cash onto the table.

Nick chuckles. "Shut up, Ross. I'm on a damn rookie contract! Your allowance from your mommy and daddy probably pays more." The guys all laugh.

"Just deal," Jase says dryly. His hand lands on my thigh, and he leans into me. "All good luck charms have to do something to create the good luck." Before I can ask him what he's referring to, his lips meet mine. The kiss is soft and sweet, only lasting a brief moment. Yet in that short time, my entire body shivers in pleasure, my heart picks up speed, and if I wasn't sitting, my legs probably would've given out on me.

Jase pulls back and grants me a boyish grin. "Even if I lose, I'm considering that kiss getting lucky." His smile widens, and I release a giggle I didn't know I had in me at his cheesy flirting.

"Real smooth!" My hand smacks his shoulder playfully, and he grabs it, entwining our fingers together and bringing it up to his lips for a quick kiss before settling our hands in his lap. Nick eyes me warily, but I ignore him as I try to push away the butterflies which are currently fluttering in my belly. Nick might be worried about me destroying Jase, but right now, I'm more concerned about being the one destroyed.

I sip on my drink as the guys play. I've watched Nick play poker a few times with his friends when he lived on campus, but I don't know enough about the game to know who's winning. Several guys say they're out. Then the ones remaining lay their cards down flat for everybody to see.

"Hell yeah!" Jase cheers. He swipes all the chips toward him then turns in his chair to face me. "It's official, you're my good luck charm." And without giving me any notice, he slants his mouth over mine. This time, the kiss is harder, more possessive, as if he's claiming me right here in front of everyone with this one kiss. Those fluttering butterflies are now attacking me as Jase's tongue pushes through my lips. He tastes of vodka and sprite, and it feels as if I could get drunk from this kiss alone. I can't help the small moan of pleasure that releases from my lips as his hand lands on my thigh and squeezes. But just like the last kiss, this one also ends much too quickly, leaving me breathless and turned on, wanting, for the first time, more from a guy.

One of the guys says he's done and another guy takes his place, and then the cards are dealt. Everyone places their bets. Jase's hand finds my thigh, once again, and he gives it a soft squeeze. My eyes find Nick's and he smirks. It's almost as if he knows I'm losing all my control to Jase. I don't know anything about him: does he have a trust fund? Where does his father work? Where does he work? What's his ten-year plan? But for some crazy reason, I don't seem to care about anything other than when his lips will find mine again.

Once again, I have no clue who's winning or losing, but it wouldn't matter because I can't focus. As Jase plays his hand of cards, his fingers run up and down my flesh, leaving a burning sensation in their wake. As his hand travels farther up, I clench my thighs together. He isn't going to do what I think he is...

He glances my way, asking for permission, and without even thinking twice I open my legs for him—*Jesus, when did I become so easy?* His fingers find my panties, but he doesn't move them to the side. Instead, he teases me from the outside. His one finger trails up and down my slit through the thin material, and I squirm in my seat. I know I'm wet, probably drenched. There's no way anybody can know what he's doing, or see my reaction, yet I feel like all eyes are on us.

I can't believe I'm letting him do this. I don't even know this guy. For all I know, he does this with every girl he meets. I'm well aware everyone our age hooks up at parties, but that's never been who I am. Easy girls don't end up married to powerful men. They end up their mistresses.

Feeling like things are moving too quickly, I reach down and take his hand in mine. If he's annoyed I stopped him, he doesn't show it. He just continues to play poker one-handed like that's completely normal.

Jase wins for the third time, and the guys all groan. He leans over and presses his lips to mine. "One more hand and then I'm done," he murmurs against my mouth. Before I back up, his tongue darts out and licks across my bottom lip. "Mmm...you taste good... sweet."

Less than ten minutes later, Jase wins. "I'm out," he announces as we stand. My eyes move to the front door, where I spot Killian Blake walking in. He glares my way, and I roll my eyes. Killian is Nick's *other* best friend. They met their freshman year of college. He's in his senior year at NCU and was recently drafted to the New York Brewers in the first round. To say we can't stand each other is a gross understatement. It's a good thing Jase is done playing poker and guiding me away from where Killian is walking toward. Had we stayed, I know, without a doubt, Killian would've made it a point to talk shit about me to Jase.

"So, you mentioned you recently graduated," I say to Jase, trying to get to know him as he pulls me toward the kitchen. Both of our cups are empty, so I'm assuming he's going to refill them.

"Yeah, I received my business degree." He takes my empty cup from me and sets it on the counter next to his. He drops a few ice cubes into both cups then pours some alcohol into them. Then he tops them off with a new can of sprite. "Cheers," he says, handing me my cup and taking a large drink from his own.

"Cheers," I say back. My sip is far smaller. Unlike Jase, who must be a good six feet tall, almost two hundred pounds, and clearly a seasoned drinker, my tiny one-hundred-and-ten-pound body can only handle so much alcohol before I'm drunk.

"Jase! Get your ass over here!" someone yells. "Drinking game!"

Jase laughs but shakes his head. "Nah, next time!"

"Now, bro," the guy demands. Jase gives me a look, silently asking if I mind. Not wanting to be the girl who takes him away from his friends, who he obviously came here tonight to see, I nod my okay.

"Fine, what game?" Jase yells over the music.

"Never have I ever!" a bleach-blonde girl shouts. I've seen her around NCU a few times, and I pray she doesn't ask me if I go there. "You in?" she asks me, not giving a shit about where I'm from.

"Sure." I hold up my drink.

Everyone goes around the room calling out things they've never done, and those who've done them have to drink:

Gotten wasted—most drink

Stolen their parent's car—a few drink

Went skinny-dipping—most drink

Smoked weed—almost everyone drinks

Had a three-some—only a couple drink

And then some girl yells through a fit of drunken laughter, "Had sex." I watch as everyone around me drinks and laughs at her because she's just announced that she's still a virgin. Until she joins in with everyone else and downs her drink. "Whoops! My bad!" She laughs harder.

Jase's eyes go to mine, and I realize I haven't taken a drink. I tip my cup back and take a large gulp. He smiles and raises his cup in a 'cheers' motion, so I do the same.

The questions continue for a little while longer, but when Jase notices that I've run out of alcohol, he excuses us from the game. We head out the back door and onto the patio. There are people out here, but not as many. With the door closed, the music is now muffled, allowing us to hear each other better. We walk down the dock and find an empty spot on the beach. In contrast to the warm weather we've been having lately, it's a bit chilly tonight, but luckily there's hardly any breeze. In an attempt to look good, I didn't think to bring a jacket.

Jase, the gentleman he is, shrugs out of his and drapes it across my shoulders. "Thank you." I smile over at him. "I was clearly going for sexy and not practical." My words are a tad slurred from the drinking I've been doing, and we both laugh.

"Well, you did sexy to perfection," he says, sitting down on the damp sand. I eye it, afraid my dress will get ruined or my butt will end up frozen. But before I can make the decision whether to sit, Jase pulls me into his lap. My dress rises, and I'm thankful we're in the dark because my panties are definitely on display. I'm straddling his thighs with my legs wrapped around him—the tips of my wedges are resting in the sand. Alarm bells should be going off in my head. This is all happening too fast. But all I can focus on is the way his strong hands grip my hips. The feel of his lips—strong yet soft—as they work their way down the side of my neck and over to my throat. My fingers run through his hair as he trails soft kisses down my throat. I relish in the delicious friction our bodies are creating as my butt grinds against his pelvis.

The sound of police sirens ring through the air, and Jase stops what he's doing, his eyes locking with mine. "I've had too much to drink to drive," he says. "Let me call my brother." With me still sitting on his lap, he pulls his phone out of his pocket and dials a number. "Jax, it's me. I need you to come get me from Jared's. The cops have been called." There's a pause. "I've been drinking." Another pause. "Thanks, bro. I'll meet you down by the south pier." He hangs up, and lifting me off him like I weigh nothing, stands me on my feet.

"I came with Nick," I point out. "He wouldn't leave without me."

"Call him and let him know that I'm dropping you off," Jase says, walking us down the beach toward the pier. I do as he says and call Nick. He answers on the first ring. When I tell him Jase is going to drop me off, he points out he's been drinking and insists on finding me. But when I tell him his brother is coming to get us, Nick concedes, but makes me promise to text him as soon as I'm home.

When Jase's brother shows up, Jase opens the door for me to get into the front seat. Once I'm in, he climbs into the back. "Quinn grabbed your car," Jax says. "She's meeting us back at home."

"Thanks, bro."

"I'm Jax," Jase's brother says, introducing himself.

"I'm Celeste. Thank you for getting us."

"No worries. Where am I taking you?"

Jase's hand lands on my shoulder, and he squeezes softly. Then his cool breath is at my ear. "Come home with me," he whispers. My body thrums at the thought of spending more time with Jase, of our night not coming to an end just yet. I've never spent the night with a guy before, and while it makes me somewhat nervous, I remember that Nick is friends with him, and he wouldn't have introduced us, or let Jase and his brother take me home, if he was worried something would happen to me. For a few seconds I weigh my options, but ultimately my need to spend more time with Jase wins out.

I nod once. "Okay."

"Just take us back to our place," Jase tells his brother.

We arrive at their apartment, and just as I suspected, it's in a nicer part of town. The apartment itself isn't huge, but it's clean and decorated beautifully. When we walk inside, a gorgeous woman is standing against the island, drinking a bottle of water. She's wearing a cute grey hoodie and matching tiny shorts that show off her thick, toned legs. At a second glance, I spot a few colorful tattoos peeking out from under her shorts. Her jet-black hair is down in waves, and her face is free of all makeup. She throws a set of keys at Jase. "You're welcome."

Jase gives her a simple chin lift. "Thanks." He puts his arm around my shoulders and pulls me into his side. "Celeste, this is my baby sister, Quinn."

"Baby?" She scoffs. "I'm a whole five years younger." She rolls her eyes.

"You're nineteen. A baby," Jase argues, and I stiffen. If she's a baby in his eyes, he would throw my ass out if he knew I'm only eighteen. Sure, I'm legal, but I'm a good six years younger than him.

"And yet, I'm the one playing the parent by picking up your vehicle because you're out partying." She snorts.

"Yeah, yeah, we're going to bed," Jase calls over his shoulder as he walks us away from the kitchen and down the hall. When we get to the last door on the right, he opens the door so I can walk through first, then closes it behind him.

Suddenly I'm nervous. I never imagined I would end up here with Jase—or any guy for that matter. I attend parties for the sole purpose of finding myself a wealthy guy to take me to dinner, to use as a contact. Men have never been anything more than a potential stepping stone to me. Until now. I knew what I was agreeing to when I said okay to coming back here. I know what the people our age do when they go back to each other's places, but it didn't hit me until this very moment that, for the first time, *I've* agreed to go back to a guy's place. And surprisingly, while I am nervous, I'm not scared, and I don't regret saying okay. "I better text Nick to let him know I'm here," I tell him.

"Okay." He shrugs. "I'm going to change." He pulls some clothes from his drawer and hands them to me. "So you're more comfortable."

"Thank you."

I pull my phone out of my bra, where I keep it when I have no pockets, and am about to text Nick to tell him where I am, when something stops me. It's not like Jase is going to murder me here. He lives with his brother and sister. He played high school and college ball with Nick. If I text Nick where I am, I'll never hear the end of it. So, instead, I text him that I made it home safely, and he, none the wiser, texts back that he'll see me tomorrow.

I change out of my dress and peel off my wedges, then I throw on the clothes Jase gave me—a shirt and boxers. The masculine, fresh scent of him hits my senses, and my only thought is *my god, he smells good.*

Not having a hair tie on me, but wanting to get my hair off my neck, I twist and pull it all up into a makeshift bun and tie it using my hair. While I wait for him to come out from his attached bathroom, I take a slow stroll around his room. It's a guy's room. Simple for the most part. Plain wood dresser, matching nightstands. A large king size bed with a simple black comforter. But the walls are another story. Each one is filled with beautiful hand-drawn art. Some are shades of black, white, and grey, and others are vivid colors that pop out as if the images are coming to life. One of his walls looks like it's been graffitied, but it's too pretty to call it that.

Jase comes back into the room as I'm staring at one of the pictures on his walls. It's a wolf that looks to be morphing into some kind of scary-looking skeleton. "This is...amazing," I tell him. "Did you draw all these?"

When he doesn't answer, I look over at him. He's leaning against the dresser, his hands in the pockets of his sweatpants, staring at me like he wants to devour me. "You look sexy as hell in my clothes," he says, his eyes dragging down my body. I swallow thickly at his statement. I'm so far out of my comfort zone here. With him now in a short-sleeved T-shirt, more of his tattoos are on display. They cover most of the skin on his arms. I wonder if he has any on his chest or his back. I bet he does.

Without saying another word, Jase stalks toward me and presses me against the wall. His hands find mine, and he pushes them over my head, my wrists making a thumping sound as they hit the wall. My mind goes foggy with lust as I get lost in this man's touch. His knee parts my thighs and grinds against my core, forcing a shudder of pleasure from me. Then his hands release mine, and he grips my hips, lifting me. My legs wrap around his waist as he carries me to the bed, dropping me onto the middle of the mattress. He climbs on top of me, his lips immediately finding mine. We kiss hard as his hand cups and massages my breast. I squirm under his touch. I've never felt like this before. This turned on. This reckless. All of my man-goals have flown out the window.

Without breaking our kiss, Jase pushes the boxers I'm wearing down my thighs along with my panties. Alarms of warning sound off, but they're too faint to pay attention to. My brain is too hazy. My judgement is too clouded. I want him. Bad. Jase's hand pushes my thighs apart and his fingers enter me. "Fuck, you're wet," he murmurs against my lips. I can't speak. I can't respond. All I can do is moan in pleasure as he fingers me. His thumb finds my clit and massages slow circles over the tight, swollen nub.

Ending our kiss, he dips his head down, and with his nose, pushes my shirt up, trailing kisses up my stomach. I pull my shirt the rest of the way over my head and throw it to the side. My bra is still on, but my nipples have pebbled through the thin material. He kisses then sucks on each one, leaving a wet spot where his mouth was.

"Your tits are fucking perfect," he murmurs as he lowers one of the cups and wraps his perfect lips around the hardened bud. And then he bites down—hard—and that's all it takes for my orgasm to rip through my body.

Before I can catch my breath, Jase is reaching back and pulling his shirt over his head. I only have a moment to appreciate the work of art that is his body before he pushes his sweatpants down, forcing my gaze to leave his tattoo-covered chest and go lower. Gripping his thick shaft in his hand, he strokes it once, twice, and then in one fluid motion, enters me.

I could've stopped him. But I didn't. The pain tears through me. Not wanting to scream, my mouth finds his shoulder, and I bite down. The act spurs him on, and he thrusts deeper into me, pushing through the barrier of my virginity. Then he stills as if he felt it.

"Celeste," he whispers. He's about to pull out. I can feel it. But before he does, I lock my ankles around his backside.

"Keep going," I plead. His head lifts, and his eyes meet mine. They're dark and filled with regret. "Please," I beg. His eyes squeeze shut as he wars with himself. It's too late now. He's already taken my virginity. "Please," I repeat. My hands come up to his head, and I tug on his hair, pulling his face toward mine. My lips fuse against his. Without opening his eyes, he kisses me back and thrusts into me again. This time, though, it's slower, gentler. He knows. One of his hands cradles the side of my head while the other comes down between us, landing on my clit.

Jase continues to fuck me, but I'm not sure if what he's doing can even be called fucking. It's more like he's making love to me, only it can't be called making love either. We barely know each other. You can't love someone you barely know. He works me up once again, and before I know it, I'm climaxing for a second time with Jase following right behind.

We both still as we catch our breath. Jase's head falls onto my chest, and I feel his thick lashes flutter against my over-sensitive flesh. He lets out a groan and shakes his head. I'm afraid to say anything. I should've told him I was a virgin. That's on me. He lifts off me as he pulls out, taking his warmth with him. His eyes go wide as he looks down. My gaze follows his, and that's when I see it. Blood covering his still semi-hard length, proving what he was probably hoping wasn't true.

He stands, and without saying a word, heads into his bathroom. I'm stuck, frozen in place, unsure what I should do now. I need to clean up. And that's when it hits me. We didn't use protection. I'm on birth control, but that's beside the point. I consider joining him in the bathroom, but wonder if that would be too intimate. Should I wait for him to get out and then haul my ass inside? Before I can figure out what to do, Jase exits the bathroom carrying a washcloth. He spreads my legs and wipes down my center—the cream-colored material turns crimson.

He tosses it into his hamper and grabs a new pair of boxers for himself. Then he picks the shirt I was wearing up off the floor and hands it to me. I thank him and shrug it on, barely making eye contact. I think he's going to hand me back my panties or his boxers, but he doesn't. Instead, he crawls into bed next to me and pulls me into his body until our fronts are almost flush against each other.

"You should've told me," he murmurs, pushing my hair out of my face.

"I'm sorry," I whisper back, feeling completely embarrassed.

"I should've used a condom. I know it's going to sound cliché as fuck, but I *always* use one. I don't know what the hell got into me." I flinch at his words, but try to hide it. I'd rather not think about all the other women he's been with.

"I'm on birth control," I admit softly.

We lay together in silence for a few minutes, and then Jase murmurs, "I've never felt anything like this. I've been with my fair share of women, but I've never felt this connection. I know we've only just met, but tell me you feel it too."

I nod in agreement. It's crazy to feel the way I do. To let this guy I barely know take my virginity. There's a good chance I'm going to regret it tomorrow, but right now, it feels right.

"Tell me something about you," he says, his lips curling into a beautiful, lazy smile. "But first, what's your last name?"

I laugh. We're obviously doing this all backwards. "My last name is Leblanc."

"And..."

"And I want to be a model," I admit. It's the only thing I can think of that won't scare him away. My age, where I go to school, where I live...it's all off limits.

Jase smirks. "You're definitely beautiful enough. What kind of model?" He takes my fingers in his hand and brings them to his lips for a kiss. "A hand model? Because you have seriously sexy fingers." He sucks my middle finger into his mouth erotically, and a soft moan escapes my lips. How can something as simple as him sucking on my finger turn me on?

"No," I croak, then clear my throat before I continue. "A real model." I gently pull my finger out from between his lips. "My dream is to be on billboards across New York. I want to walk the catwalks for high fashion designers during the New York, Paris, and Milan Fashion Weeks. I want to get a deal with Victoria's Secret or Tommy Hilfiger, or maybe Donna Karen or Chanel." I can't help the excitement I feel when I talk about my goals and dreams. Growing up, I used to toy with the idea of wanting to become a model. I would play dress up with Nick's mom's clothes when she wasn't home, and force Nick to watch me put on fashion shows.

When I got older, I would watch the various fashion shows on television when Mom remembered to pay the bill. But it was confirmed the first time Nick's mom brought Nick and me along with her for Fashion Week when I was twelve year's old. Nick's nanny got sick and canceled last minute, and his dad was out of town on business. Like always, my mom was in a drunken stupor, so Victoria ended up taking us with her to New York. She was able to find a replacement nanny for the rest of the week, but that first night we went with her, and it was that one night that changed my life. Up until that day, my dreams were puffs of clouds in the sky—beautiful to look up at, but unreachable. But as I watched the fashion show from the third row, it was as if I was floating in the air. I could taste it, smell it, feel it. For the first time, my dreams were within reach, and I knew I would do everything in my power to grab ahold of them.

"But I don't want to stop there," I continue when I see Jase's eyes are on me, that he's actually listening and waiting for me to explain. I can't remember the last time someone just listened to me. "It's common knowledge that a modeling career peaks by twenty-two and is over by twenty-seven, thirty, if the model is lucky. Modeling is my dream, my foot in the door, but I don't want that to be it. I want to start my own jewelry and makeup lines. Maybe even a clothing line. I love fashion," I exclaim.

"Why?" he asks thoughtfully.

"I love the way an outfit can give a woman confidence. The way makeup can make her feel beautiful. I love how a single necklace or bracelet can make her feel... more." I don't know how to explain it without telling him I was raised in a shitty trailer park, in an ugly, tiny trailer. I grew up being made fun of for wearing the Walmart clothes my mom would buy me secondhand from the thrift stores. The no-name brand shoes that she would pick up from the local consignment shops. Kids were mean, and I always felt so ugly.

That was until Nick's mom, Victoria, bought me a beautiful Marc Jacobs gown for the function we were attending. She took me to get my hair and makeup and nails done. Then she lent me a pair of pearl earrings and a matching necklace. That night, not only did nobody make fun of me, but I was complimented on several occasions on how beautiful I looked. I watched the models strut up and down the runway as everybody oohed and ahhed, and it was in that moment I knew I would do whatever it took to become a model. I want to travel the world, wear gorgeous, expensive clothes, get paid to put on makeup. I want to live in a penthouse that overlooks Central Park. I want a husband who's rich and takes care of me and thinks I'm beautiful.

Jase eyes me curiously and then says, "You don't need to do anything to make you beautiful. You already are." We've only just met, yet it's as if he has the ability to read the words I'm not saying.

Say the things I long for someone to say. Tears sting my eyes, and I force them away.

"What about you?" I ask, my throat clogged with emotion. "What do you want to be?"

"I want to open my own tattoo shop." His answer should be the equivalent of ice being thrown onto my overheated body. *A tattoo shop.* That's hardly a fortune 500 company. He's nothing like the wealthy husband I envisioned for myself. But for some reason, I don't care. Instead, his answer makes me smile. I can totally see it. The drawings all over his walls, the gorgeous ink covering his body. The dark aura that surrounds him. It all fits.

"Is that why you majored in business?"

He nods. "Yeah, Jax and I both have our licenses to tattoo, but he wasn't able to go to college. We didn't have the money." He frowns, appearing to be embarrassed. "I got a football scholarship to attend NCU and figured it would do us good for me to learn how to run a business." He grants me a soft smile. "Now we just have to save up."

"Didn't you go to Piermont Academy with Nick?" I ask, confused. He's clearly not from a family with money and that school is over fifty thousand a year alone just for the tuition.

"Yeah, another scholarship." He shrugs one shoulder. "My brother went to Piermont Public."

"Your sister?" She's only a year ahead of me, but I've never seen her at school.

"Piermont Academy on an academic scholarship. She's now attending The Art Institute. Between her financial aid, and Jax and me helping her, we're handling it okay." He flinches at his own words, telling me there's more to it than him and his brother handling it. Is it possible he comes from a home like mine? One where your parent doesn't handle shit? I want to open up to him, but if I do, he'll find out I'm not in college and that I'm younger than I led him to believe, and there's no way he won't push me away.

"Does she want to do tattoos like you and your brother?" Absentmindedly, my hand finds its way to Jase's scalp, and I thread my fingers through his thick hair. It's like I need to touch him in some way at all times. He must feel the same, because as we talk, his hand, the one that isn't trapped under me and gripping my hip, roams over my body.

"No, she's more about the traditional type of art. She loves photography, graphic design, sculpting." The way he speaks about his sister, it's obvious he's proud of her.

Jase's gaze drops to my mouth, and he dips his head down to snag my lower lip, pulling it roughly and sucking on my flesh. "We should get some sleep. I'm on the verge of wanting to take you again, and I imagine you're sore." Before I can respond, his lips find mine, deliciously contradicting his words. This kiss is soft and sweet, and when it ends, I sigh in need. Jase chuckles under his breath before rolling onto his back and pulling me into his side. No words are spoken. No promises of tomorrow. Instead, we remain in the present, falling asleep in each other's arms.

THREE

CELESTE
The Past

I WAKE up to the feeling of... well, I'm not quite sure what it is. Something is tickling my back. My eyes open, and it only takes a second to remember where I am. At Jase's place in his bed. I'm lying on my belly, only Jase is no longer my human pillow—albeit a firm one. The light glaring in through the blind slats have my eyes closing. My hand reaches out blindly for Jase, but his side of the bed is empty. That's when I feel it again. The tickling on my back. *Oh, God, please don't let it be a bug or an animal...* I'm about to turn over to see what it is, but a strong hand weighing down on my butt prevents me from moving.

"Don't move," Jase's husky voice says. "I'm almost done." Twisting my head without moving the rest of my body, I peek behind me and see the tickling is Jase drawing on my skin.

"Are you drawing on me?"

"I couldn't help it. Your body is flawless..." The hand that was on my butt, cups my cheek and then slides down the back of my thigh. "Like a blank canvas, just waiting for its story." Goosebumps prickle my skin at his words as I wonder if my story will include him.

"You were sleeping so soundly, and when I woke up to take a piss, I noticed my shirt had risen, exposing this sexy ass" —he trails

his hand back up my thigh and gives my backside a playful slap—
"and these perfect dimples." My head falls forward onto the pillow.
His cool lips graze my lower back as he gives the two dimples
located just above my ass a kiss.

"I had to mark you," he adds, and my eyes flit over to him again.
He's back to drawing on me while he talks. "You know, I've done
quite a few dimple piercings. Do you have any piercings?"

"No." I shake my head.

"Tattoos?"

"Nope. Piercings and tattoos are a no-no when you're trying to
become a model. Most high-class agencies frown upon that sort of
thing."

Jase grunts his displeasure, continuing to draw on my body.
"Nobody would know if you got one here," he states. His fingers
trail down to just above the crack of my ass. "Or here." He
continues his descent along the center of my ass. Then he spreads
my legs open and pushes a single finger into my pussy. "Nobody
should ever see these parts of your body. They're mine," he growls
lowly. "This body, and this pussy, is mine." He pulls his finger out of
me, and I immediately miss his touch.

"It's a little soon to be claiming me, don't you think?" I sass.

"Nope, you made it mine the moment you let me take your
virginity," he says matter-of-factly, and my cheeks flush at his
words.

"Don't move," he demands. He pushes off the bed, and a second
later, I hear the sound of a camera clicking. "Perfect."

I try to flip over, but his hands prevent me from doing so. Jase
spreads my thighs wider and pushes his fingers back inside me, my
body accepting the intrusion all too willingly.

"Jesus, woman, you're so wet," he groans. While he fingers me
with one hand, his other comes around and lifts my lower half
slightly off the bed, so I'm on my knees. He palms my breast and
plants sweet kisses down my spine until his lips are back where he
was drawing. He blows softly on my skin, sending chills up my
spine. Then his lips once again kiss each of my dimples. He makes
his way downward, and when his teeth sink into my butt cheek, I let
out a girly screech.

He laughs softly. "Sorry, I needed a taste," he admits, and I can't
help the grin that makes its way across my face in response.

He continues to fingerfuck me, and then his tongue hits my clit.
He sucks it into his mouth and then licks up my center, causing my
entire body to shudder in pleasure. With his tongue, and lips, and

fingers, Jase works me up until I'm calling out his name as I orgasm around him.

Then he flips me over onto my back and crawls up my body. My legs wrap around his waist as his hands cage me in. His lips angle against mine as he pushes into me. I'm still a tad sore, but those thoughts are overpowered by our kiss.

This kiss. It ignites something deep within me, heating my frozen walls and melting the ice away until there's nothing left to protect my heart and soul. They're visible and vulnerable, leaving Jase with full access to every exposed part of me. Our kiss becomes more heated. Like a wildfire that can't be contained. I've always been so careful—never to let anyone in. Yet, here I am, handing myself over to this man, knowing if I'm not careful, I'm going to get burned. The heat between us is all-consuming. I'm lost in everything that is Jase.

My hands hold on to his shoulders, my nails digging into his skin, as his thrusts turn frantic. His pelvis grinds against mine, rubbing my clit just right. We're both chasing our release. My climax builds, and builds, and builds, until I'm so high, I have nowhere to go but down. But with Jase in charge, I'm not afraid to fall. In fact, I welcome it. And with one last thrust, he pushes me off the edge, taking himself with me. Our lips find each other, swallowing our moans as we both lose ourselves in one another.

Once we've reached the bottom safely, Jase breaks our kiss and nuzzles his face into the crook of my neck. We stay like this for a long moment as we calm our beating hearts and labored breaths. When he lifts slightly, pulling out, I wince at the tenderness I feel between my legs, hoping I never stop feeling it, so I always remember the times Jase and I became one.

"Shit, I didn't use protection *again*," he admits, looking down. It's then I feel the liquid between my thighs *again*. I should be bothered that Jase and I have yet to use protection. I know this is a one-night stand. But for some crazy reason, being with Jase feels like so much more.

"It's okay," I blurt out, "I trust you."

Jase pulls my face into his for a hard kiss. "What are you doing to me?" he murmurs against my lips. "All my sanity flies out the window with you."

"Because you forgot to use a condom?" I ask, confused.

"I never bring women back here. Not to my apartment, not to meet my family, and definitely not into my bed."

"I should get cleaned up," I tell him shyly, not completely sure what to say in response to his admission. His words have my insides on fire, my heart thumping in my chest. But I just met him not even twelve hours ago. I don't have any other relationships to compare this to, but I can't imagine falling for someone this fast is the norm.

Jase backs up so I can climb off the bed. Following me into his bathroom, he insists we shower together. I've never showered with a man before, but Jase doesn't make me feel the slightest bit uncomfortable. The entire time we're in the shower, he makes it a point to touch me in some way. Whether it's soaping me up, or massaging the shampoo into my scalp, his hands are on me. And the more he touches me, gives me his undivided attention, the more I want to stay in our little bubble and never leave.

When we get out, he tells me he'll be right back. He returns with a pair of sweats and a hoodie. They're pink and similar to the outfit Quinn was wearing.

"Thank you. I'll wash them and then get them back to her." I pull my hair up into a messy bun then get dressed. I put my bra back on but go commando, not wanting to wear my day-old panties. I gather up my clothes from last night and fold them into a neat pile while Jase gets dressed. My heart tightens in my chest when I hear the clinking of his keys. This is it. Our night together is over. He's going to take me home, and then he'll continue his life while I continue mine. Tears prick my eyes, and I quickly lift my finger to wipe them away. I don't cry. Why am I crying now? Grow up, Celeste! This is what people our age do. We have one-night stands. We hook up and then go our separate ways. Don't act like an immature weirdo.

"I almost forgot to show you," Jase says, breaking me out of my crazy silent monologue. I take a deep breath and turn to face him. He's dressed in a plain white T-shirt that stretches across his broad chest and shoulders, and a loose pair of jeans. His one arm comes up so his fingers can run through his damp hair, and I spot a hint of his thick happy trail leading down to the Promised Land. I should've spent more time getting to know his body while I had him. I didn't even have a chance to taste him yet.

Jase clears his throat, and it's then I notice he's facing his phone toward me and sporting a knowing smirk. He totally caught me checking him out. I simply shrug. No point in denying it. I step closer to see what's on his screen and immediately recognize the one dimple on my lower back. And then my focus turns to the most beautiful artwork I've ever seen. A black and grey dandelion that looks like it's blowing in the wind comes up my hip with stray petals dancing in the wind. A smaller one next to it. Along the stem of the larger dandelion is a quote: *And from the chaos of her soul flowed beauty.*

"Jase," I whisper. How could he possibly write something that hits so close to home without even knowing me? Understand the chaos that I feel deep inside of me every day? The confusion that flows through me when I think about where I come from and where I want to go. The struggle to love myself but at the same time want more.

"My mom used to wish on dandelions," Jase says, his voice thick with emotion. "She would take Jax and me for walks in our neighborhood when we were little, and she would find every single one she could, blowing on them as she made wish after wish."

"What did she wish for?"

"I don't know." He shrugs a shoulder. "But my guess is success. She wanted to be an actress." He smiles warmly. "She was beautiful. At least from what I can remember." The corners of his mouth turn down slightly. "She was actually in a couple small shows, but then she met my dad. She fell in love and found herself pregnant with my brother. A year later came me." I notice he doesn't mention Quinn. "She didn't know it at the time, but my dad was already married. His wife couldn't have kids...or so they thought. A few years later, Quinn was born. My dad juggled his two families for a while, but eventually he got caught. When his wife found out about us, he proved my mom to be an unfit parent and got custody of us. My mom couldn't handle it—losing my dad and us. She had given up her dreams for him, only to learn he didn't feel the same way about her. She ended up committing suicide."

"Oh, Jase!" My arms wrap around his neck for a hug. "I'm so sorry."

"You remind me of her," Jase murmurs into my ear. "I saw that quote captioned under an image at an art gallery I visited once with my sister. I can't remember who said it, but the words always stuck with me. I don't doubt one day you will conquer the world, Dimples." He backs up and shoots me a playful wink to lighten the mood, but my heart is still with Jase's mom and her chaotic, beautiful soul.

"Where's your dad now?" I ask. He obviously accepted Quinn as his sister even though she has a different mom.

"He died of a heart attack when I was thirteen." Jase doesn't sound the least bit sad when he tells me this. "Quinn's mom thought she would get his life insurance, but it came out that he wasn't really married to her either. He was married to another woman, Tricia, and had two other kids with her. He had left her several years back but never got a divorce. She got everything in his will, leaving Quinn's mom broke. She lost her shit, and the minute Jax turned eighteen, he got a job and moved out. He petitioned the court and got custody of Quinn. I was already almost eighteen, so the judge approved for me to become emancipated."

"Wow," I say in awe of how well they handled everything.

"Yeah, talk about some crazy 60 Minutes meets Jerry Springer shit." Jase laughs humorlessly. "My dad was a fucking liar, and his lies destroyed not one but two women who loved him." He shakes his head with disgust. "I hope he's rotting in hell." His words hit me like a brick to a glass house. Jase's hard limit is lying, and I've lied to him several times since we met. No, I didn't actually say the words, but I might as well have. I should tell him the truth now. What do I have to lose? But if I walk away with things the way they are now, he won't think of me the way he thinks about his father. As a liar.

My eyes dart to his phone, the screen is still showing the fake tattoo he drew on me. "Can you send me that picture?" I ask. It's the only thing I will have left of our night together once I walk away.

"Sure." He grins. I give him my email address since my phone is one of those crappy prepaid ones, and he sends it over.

We walk out of his room and find Jax cooking in the kitchen with Quinn sitting on a stool watching him. "Morning," Jase announces. Jax and Quinn both glance our way. Quinn grants me a soft smile, and Jax waves the spatula in the air.

"Morning," they both say in unison.

"You hungry?" Jax asks.

"Starving!" I admit before I can stop myself. Jase is probably ready to send me packing, and I'm over here practically begging to stay and eat.

"Well, have a seat." Jax points to the empty stools.

"Oh, umm...I think Jase was about to take me home." I avoid looking at anyone in the room, instead choosing to focus on the pancake batter that's bubbling in the pan. It's embarrassing enough having to do the walk of shame...

The contrast between the coolness of Jase's lips on my ear, and his warm body pressed up against mine, sends a visible shiver straight down my spine. He must notice because he chuckles softly before he says, "You aren't going anywhere, Dimples. Sit." I do as he says, while trying to school my excitement over his somewhat public display of affection and sweet yet commanding words, but a grin stretches across my lips anyway.

Quinn laughs. "Such a gentleman," she jokes.

"Hush your mouth," Jase volleys back.

Jax serves us each a stack of delicious-smelling pancakes and eggs then has a seat as well.

"What's everyone up to today?" Quinn asks.

"I have a guy coming into the shop to get more of his sleeve done," Jax says.

"What about you guys?" Quinn turns her attention to Jase and me.

"Not sure yet," Jase answers her. The hand he's not using to eat squeezes my thigh. I assumed Jase was going to bring me home, yet he told me I'm not going anywhere. Did he just mean to stay for breakfast? We haven't discussed what happened between us last night, and for all I know this was just a one-night thing to him. At least that's what I keep telling myself when I justify why I haven't told him the truth about my age and where I go to school. Maybe he just plans to fill my belly with food before he sends me on my way.

"I'm heading to the beach to take pictures," Quinn says. "I have my final photography project due next week."

Jase swallows a mouthful of food, then turns to me. "Want to go?" The look he gives me is so hopeful. Before I can think about the ramifications of my answer, I'm nodding my head yes. He smiles an adorable lopsided grin. "Cool. We can go by your house to get your suit on the way."

Shit! This is exactly why I should've given this more thought before saying yes. I need to tell him the truth. He needs to know I'm only eighteen and in high school. That I live in a trailer park with my drunken mother, and my only way out is the summer internship in New York Nick surprised me with. Jase would understand. He comes from a broken home. And I am of legal age...

I open my mouth to tell Jase I need to talk to him, when Quinn says, "I have a spare." She shrugs. "It'll save time."

"You good with that?" Jase asks, taking another bite of his food.

"Yeah," I mutter with a plastered-on smile. *Later... I'll tell him later.*

Once we're done eating, and we've worked together to get the dishes done and the kitchen cleaned, we head out in Jase's Dodge Charger to the beach. It's such a man's car. Black on black with smooth leather interior. It's not flashy or expensive, but it's damn sexy. And it totally fits him.

When we arrive at the beach, Quinn takes off on her photography mission, and Jase and I head toward the ocean to find an empty spot to lay a blanket down near the water.

After stripping off Quinn's shirt and shorts, leaving me in only her bikini—which fits a tad loose on my body since she has more curves than I do—I turn my attention to Jase. He reaches back and pulls his shirt over his head, exposing his delicious tattoos, along with his firm chest and ripped abs. I never imagined falling for a guy like Jase. I always pictured a wealthy, put together businessman, dressed to the nines in a designer suit. Nowhere in my fantasies did it include a tattoo artist bad-boy. The term causes my heart to skip a beat. My mom fell for the tattooed bad-boy. She's not only broken-hearted but *broken. It's not the same,* I tell myself. Jase isn't really a bad-boy. He just looks like one. He's educated. He has a college degree, and he wants to open his own business.

Does it really even matter when this time next week I'll be in New York?

My heart sinks at the thought of leaving Jase. Can I do it? Can I walk away from him?

You don't have a choice, my inner self argues. It doesn't matter how fast and hard I'm falling for him. New York is my future. I can't give that up for a *man.* There will be plenty more men in New York.

"You okay?" Jase asks, forcing me out of my thoughts.

"Yeah," I say, and then quickly add, "tell me about your tattoos," in hope of distracting myself from my own thoughts. My mind and heart are warring with one another, and it's not a battle I'm ready to enter yet.

Jase looks down and runs a hand along the planes of his abs. "Which ones?" he asks. "I kind of have a lot." He laughs, and the melodic sound calms my nerves. No, he's not a bad-boy. He's a good guy wrapped in a bad-boy body.

He drops onto the blanket and lays next to me. His leg entangles with mine as he explains each one. They all mean something to him in some way. We spend the next several hours laughing and talking and kissing, completely lost in our own little world. We watch people come and go, and eat the lunch we packed. The water is warm, so we go swimming as well. Eventually Quinn makes her way back over to us, ready to go home. I have no clue how the entire day passed so quickly, but what I do know is I'm not ready to say goodbye to Jase yet.

So when he murmurs, "Come home with me" against my lips, I

agree without thought. On our drive back, Nick texts, asking where I am. I text him back that I have a couple things I need to do before graduation, immediately feeling guilty for lying. But I'm not ready for him to know about Jase yet. It's pointless for him to know about a man I can't have a future with. It's not like I'm going to stay. And on top of that, I lied to Jase. Sure, they're technically lies by omission, but a lie is still a lie. He doesn't even know I'm planning to leave soon.

Jase's hand squeezes mine, and my heart feels like it's going to thump right out of my chest. How did this happen? How did I manage to fall for someone this fast? This isn't who I am. I want to be mad at myself for being so stupid, but I can't muster up the negative energy. My heart feels too full...too happy. And suddenly I can almost empathize with my mom. Imagining how I'm going to feel when I leave next week nearly has my heart crumbling into pieces.

Grabbing our stuff, we head upstairs to their apartment. Jase unlocks the door and opens it wide for Quinn and me to walk through. I stop in my place when I see a woman sitting on the couch, fiddling with her cell phone. I glance around and don't see Jax anywhere. Does she live here as well?

She looks up, and it's as if she doesn't even notice Quinn or me in the room as she smiles at Jase. She's naturally beautiful with fiery red hair and emerald green eyes, but she looks exhausted—like she has the weight of the world sitting on her shoulders. Her eyes then dart to me, and she glares daggers my way. When her gaze goes back to Jase, her smile comes back. *Interesting...*

"Jase!" She jumps off the couch and flies into his arms. His eyes meet mine, and he shoots me, what looks like, a silent apology. The woman is dressed in black jeans that are clearly too tight on her, and a tiny blue tank top. A large tattoo peeks out from under her shirt on her lower back, disappearing under the top of her jeans. And a twinge of jealousy surfaces as I wonder if Jase was the one to give it to her.

"Amaya," he says, pulling away from her. "How are you?" His eyes trails down her body, not like he's checking her out, but more like he's making sure she's okay.

"I'm fine," she says a bit too upbeat. It reminds me of the way my mom speaks to Victoria to hide how drunk she is, or when she doesn't want her to know we're without electric or water. "Are you going to introduce me to your friend?" She nods my way. "Or is she Quinn's friend?" she adds, hope evident in her voice.

"She's with Jase," Quinn says matter-of-factly to the woman, and I bite down on my bottom lip to stifle a smile. Quinn just got major points for that in my book.

"This is Celeste," Jase says, then turns toward me. "This is my friend, Amaya."

"Best friend," Amaya corrects with a bit of snark in her tone.

"Nice to meet you," I say politely. "I'm going to shower the sand and ocean off me." I give Jase a soft smile, so he knows I'm trying to be nice and leave them to talk. She's obviously here for a reason.

"Bye!" Amaya waves at me like she's five years old.

Jase shoots her a cool glare, then mouths a *thank you* to me.

I LET OUT a soft sigh as the hot water rains down and massages my scalp. My eyes are closed so the shampoo doesn't burn them as the water rinses the suds and salt from my hair. I'm completely lost in myself, in my thoughts, so I don't hear Jase come in. When the shower door opens, and the cool air pricks my heated flesh, I let out a loud shriek. Jase laughs, but when his eyes land on my now pebbled nipples, his laughter stops, and the smile he was just sporting turns into pure hunger.

"Get in or get out! It's cold out there!" I yell, trying to sound mad. A laugh breaks through, though, giving me away.

Jase steps in and closes the door behind him, and that's when I notice he's naked—which makes sense since he's getting in the shower with me. His dick is semi-hard, and it bobs heavy between his thighs as he steps toward me. The shower is a decent size, but not huge, so he doesn't have far to go. Wordlessly, Jase picks me up and pushes me against the wall. The water continues to fall around us, but it doesn't deter him in the slightest. My legs wrap around his waist, and my fingers grip his shoulders. His mouth finds mine, and he devours me. His tongue pushes through my lips, and I taste everything that is Jase. His cock pokes against my ass, and I let out a moan, needing him to be inside me. The air around us grows thick with lust. Our bodies go from zero to one hundred in a split second, with a single touch. And a million thoughts hit me at once, like how is it so easy to get lost in this man? Is it like this for everyone in the beginning? Will it always feel this way with Jase? This explosive? Is this how it was for my mom?

My heart constricts as Jase pushes up into me, filling me completely. Our kiss turns rougher, more demanding. I can feel him everywhere. His fingers digging into my ass, his mouth devouring mine. His dick thrusting in and out of me. Every part of him is touching me. It's as if he's become an extension of me. He's gotten under my skin, and there's no getting him out.

The thought of leaving him has my throat tightening. Tears of devastation leak from my eyes. My arms wrap tightly around Jase's neck, needing to mold myself to him— to feel him even closer. I want to burrow myself just as deeply in him as he's done to me. My tears fall as Jase makes love to me against the shower wall. As reality hits that I can't leave this man. I am falling in love with him. I don't care if it's too soon, too fast. I can't help how my heart feels. I need to lay my cards down, put it all on the line—tell him the truth and see where it takes us. Maybe I can convince him to join me in New York. He could work at a shop there and eventually open his own place. Would his sister and brother be willing to move? Would he move without them? Am I crazy for even having these thoughts?

"Celeste," Jase moans, "stay with me, baby." His words push all my thoughts aside, so I can focus completely on being right here, in this moment, with Jase—on how good he feels inside me. His face nuzzles into the crook of my neck, and he bites down on my flesh as he comes deep inside me. Once he catches his breath, he lifts his head, pulls out of me, then sets me down on my feet.

"You didn't come," he says with a frown. It's not a question, he knows I didn't. We've only had sex a couple times, but every time he's made sure I find my release before him.

"I'm sorry," I whisper in embarrassment. I was so lost in myself, in him, I didn't even notice.

"What's going on?" He runs two fingers down the side of my cheek.

"Nothing." I shake my head. "Was everything okay with your friend?"

Jase's brows furrow. "Is that what's wrong? You have nothing to worry about. Amaya is only a friend."

"I know." I nod emphatically. I wait for Jase to further explain himself, but he doesn't.

"Hurry up and finish rinsing off," Jase says. "I owe you an orgasm." He shoots me an adorable wink before stepping out of the shower.

FOUR

C ELESTE
The Past

MY SKIN IS OVERLY WARM, and it feels like there's a two-hundred-pound weight on top of me. When I try to roll over but can't move, I tilt my head to the side and see Jase's body is wrapped around mine. His legs are entwined with mine, and his free hand is holding my breast. We fell asleep naked last night, after devouring a pizza while we attempted to watch a movie on Netflix, which only ended in us making out and eventually making love.

"Morning," Jase murmurs against my ear. His dick presses against my ass, and I let out a groan, which has him chuckling darkly. He pulls away from me, only to flip me over so he can hover above me. "What's on the agenda for today?" he asks. I love that he's assuming we're going to hang out.

"I don't know." I shrug my shoulders. "Do you have to work?"

"Nope." He shakes his head then dips it down to grab one of my nipples between his teeth. He tugs on it playfully, then looks up, releasing it. "I was thinking I would quit my job and spend the rest of my life with you in this bed." He waggles his eyebrows, and I giggle, rolling my eyes. "I'm just kidding," he says. "It's Sunday, so I have off, which means...if you don't have anything going on, I was thinking we could hang out." He smiles shyly, his cockiness and confidence dropping a couple notches.

"That sounds good to me," I tell him as I run my fingers through his hair and pull him to me. We kiss for several minutes before we finally get out of bed to get ready for the day. Jase surprises me with my clothes, as well as the outfit I borrowed from Quinn, neatly stacked. Apparently when he left the room to get our pizza from the delivery guy, he threw a load of laundry in the wash, and then Quinn threw them in the dryer. I get dressed and then head into the bathroom. Using Jase's toiletries, I brush my teeth and put on deodorant. When I come out, Jase is ready to go as well.

"Where are we going?" I ask as we head toward his car.

"I was thinking we could go downtown, maybe go see a movie." His eyes seek mine for approval.

"That sounds perfect."

Jase opens my door for me, and once I'm in, closes it, but not before ducking his head in and giving me a swoon-worthy kiss.

The drive to downtown is filled with comfortable silence with the music playing in the background. My phone buzzes in my hand, and when I check it, I see it's almost dead. There's also a text from Nick asking what we're up to today. I feel like the worst friend in the world when I text him back that I have more stuff I need to take care of and then promise that we'll hang out soon.

"Everything okay?" Jase asks, eyeing my phone.

"Yeah, it's almost dead. I'm turning it off."

He nods. "Quinn has exams this week. I can't remember... Does NCU too?" His gaze bounces from the road to me.

"I'm done with my exams." Technically, I'm telling him the truth. I finished my exams last week. Seniors get out a couple weeks earlier than everyone else as a senior privilege. The day before graduation, I have to attend the rehearsal, but other than that, I'm completely done with school. A few of my friends headed over to White Oak to spend the week camping and going water rafting, but that's not really my thing, so I didn't join them.

Jase pulls into the parking garage and finds a spot. Before I can open my door to get out, he jogs around and opens it for me. "A girl could seriously get used to this kind of treatment, Mr. Crawford," I joke.

"Good." He leans down for a kiss, then taking my hand in his, walks us over to where a bunch of booths are set up. "Looks like the farmer's market is here."

We spend the next couple hours checking out all of the home-made goods. We stop at one stand where there's an older couple who are selling fresh baked treats from their bakery. Jase buys us a giant cinnamon bun for us to share. We also stop at a couple fresh grocers and buy some delicious looking strawberries and blackberries to munch on while we walk around.

When we stop at a cute homemade jewelry booth, I spot the most beautiful dandelion necklace. It reminds me of the fake tattoo Jase drew on me yesterday morning and the story he told me about his mom. The necklace is silver, and dangling from it, in a clear, thin, circular glass, is a real dandelion. With its petals flailing out every which way, it looks like it's been frozen in time. Hanging from the charm is a tiny plaque that reads **wish** on one side, and **dream** on the other.

"This is beautiful," I tell the woman.

"Thank you. I find them and make them myself." She smiles softly. When I see the price, and know I can't afford it, I set it down and walk over to another area of the tent to check out her other pieces. When I look around to see where Jase is, I spot him talking to the woman.

"Thank you," he says to her.

"You're very welcome." She grins.

Once we're out of her tent, I ask him what he was thanking her for.

"This." He pulls a small bag out of his front pocket. "Turn around."

I do as he says, and a second later, I feel something cool touch my chest. When I glance down, I see the dandelion charm is there.

"Jase." I twirl around to face him.

"I saw you eyeing it." He shrugs nonchalantly. "You said yesterday that a necklace has the capabilities of making a woman feel more." His gaze lands on the necklace before he locks eyes with me. "It looks beautiful on you."

"Thank you." I wrap my arms around his neck and give him a hug. Tears threaten to fill my eyes, and emotion clogs my throat, but I will them both away, not wanting to scare Jase. It's not his fault that the girl he brought home has fallen for him this hard and fast.

I'm about to pull away when Jase grips my hips, and holding me close to him, says, "Never stop wishing and dreaming, Celeste." Then he kisses me softly. The kiss doesn't last long since we're standing in the middle of the sidewalk, but it's one of those moments, one of those kisses, that I know I will remember for the rest of my life.

With our fingers entwined, we continue to walk until we reach the end of the farmer's market and the beginning of the promenade.

The area contains a movie theater, a couple restaurants, some upscale stores, and a coffee shop.

We stop in front of the lit screen that displays the movies and show times. "You pick," he says. I decide on a romantic comedy— I've clearly lost my mind and have decided to just embrace it. After getting a large soda and popcorn for us to split, we head inside the theater. The movie either must suck or be on its way out because aside from one other couple who are sitting all the way in the front, the theater is completely empty.

We head straight to the top of the theater and sit in the corner. A few minutes later, the lights go out and the previews begin. Jase raises the armrest between us and tucks me into his side, his arm curling around the back of my neck. I have to stifle my giggle at how couple-y we must look. I've been on plenty of dates, but with the type of guys I usually give my time to, a date generally consists of an expensive dinner or a charity event. This is my first time at the movies with a guy.

The previews end and the movie begins, but I can't focus on it because Jase is running his fingers up and down my arm. Goose-bumps pebble my skin, and when I look up at him, he glances in my direction, granting me the sexiest smile. I don't know what comes over me but suddenly I have an insatiable need to be close to this man. Closer than is allowed in the middle of a public movie theater.

Pulling his face down to mine, I kiss Jase hard. My tongue pushes through his lips, and the kiss deepens. But it's not enough. I need more. As our kiss continues, I run my hand along the top of his jeans. The bulge in his pants is prominent and spurs me on. Undoing his button and zipper, I pull his dick out. Jase groans against my lips, and his hand, which has been massaging circles into my thigh, tries to stop me.

"Uh-uh," he whispers against my lips, noncommittedly.

"Yes," I murmur back. Breaking the kiss, I look around real quick just to make sure nobody is watching, before I bend at the waist and take Jase's entire shaft into my mouth.

"Fuck, Celeste," he moans quietly. His fingers run through my hair, but he doesn't make any move to push my head down. Instead, when I glance up, I notice his head is tilted back, and his eyes are closed. I bob up and down over his entire length, getting to know him on a much more personal level. My tongue runs along the underside of his hard shaft, and then I suck on the plump head. When I take him all the way down—well, as far as I can go—his dick begins to swell, and a bead of precum seeps out, hitting my tongue.

He must be about to come... I've never even given head, let alone swallowed a man's cum, but we're in the middle of a theater, and there's no way I'm spitting it out on the floor, so I squeeze my eyes closed as Jase moans out his orgasm, the hot seed spurting into the back of my throat. I do my best not to gag and choke, but it's hard. It's salty and warm and thick.

Once I'm sure he's finished, I lick him clean and then sit back up. Jase's eyes meet mine. They're glossed over and, even in the dark, I can see the lust and awe in them. He shakes his head and leans in to whisper into my ear, "My turn." My eyes go wide as he spreads my thighs to reciprocate.

FOR THE THIRD morning in a row, I wake up in Jase's bed to the sunlight seeping in through the blinds. *I'm going to need to purchase some curtains,* is my first thought. My second is that I'm going to be graduating this week, and once I leave, I'll never sleep in this bed again, so there's no need to purchase curtains. My stomach tightens at that horrible thought. I roll over to find Jase's side of the bed empty. *Jase's side of the bed...* Three nights with him and I'm already assigning us sides of the bed. I spot a piece of paper and pick it up to read it.

Dimples,

I had an early appointment. Feel free to stay as long as you want. If no one is home, just lock the door if you leave. There's a key under the mat in case you need it. I realized we never exchanged numbers. Here's mine. Text me yours.

Xo Jase

Directly under his name is his phone number. Grabbing my cell phone from atop the nightstand, I program it into my phone. I'm about to send Jase a text to give him mine, when a text comes in from Nick: **Where are you?**

Still not ready for him to know about Jase, I text him back that I'm getting things situated before graduation since I'll be leaving shortly after. I hate lying to Nick, but I'm afraid to tell him the truth, like if I tell him about Jase, it will make what we have that much more real, and with it will come the reality that I'm supposed to be leaving soon.

Another text comes through from Nick, telling me he wants to take me shopping for luggage and anything else I might need for my trip to New York. I want to tell him I can't make it. For one, shopping for luggage means I'm leaving, and right now, leaving is the last thing I want to think about. And two, the only thing I want to be doing is spending time with Jase. But I know Nick, and if I tell him I can't make it, when I've been so excited about New York, it will send up a huge red flag. So, I send him a reply thanking him and agree to meet up with him later, then get out of bed. My body feels relaxed and well-rested, despite having been up most of the night with Jase. *It must be from all those orgasms he gave me.*

I stretch my arms over my head and my stomach rumbles. We were too caught up in each other last night and completely forgot to eat dinner. And then an idea forms. Heading out into the living room to see if anyone is home, I find Quinn sitting on the couch, working on her computer.

"Morning."

She looks up from whatever she's working on. "Hey, morning."

"I was...umm...thinking about surprising Jase at work. Maybe bring him some breakfast. Do you think he would be okay with that?"

"I think he would." Quinn grins. "Need to borrow another outfit?" She nods toward me. I'm in another one of Jase's shirts and my panties.

"That would be great. Thank you."

After showering and getting dressed, Quinn gives me a ride to pick up some food. I also run into the store to grab a charger before my phone goes completely dead. When we arrive at the shop, I ask her if she's coming in, but she tells me she's around them enough and needs to get her project done for class so she can officially be done with the semester.

The sign above the door reads Get Inked. I've seen it many times in passing but never gave it a second glance. When I open the door, a bell jingles, indicating someone has entered. The guy standing behind the counter looks up and smiles. With inky black hair formed into a high mohawk, tattoos covering every inch of his visible skin, gages in his earlobes, and a hoop jutting out of his bottom lip, he reminds me of Travis Barker from Blink-182.

"Good morning," he rasps. "How can I help you?"

"I'm here to see Jase."

"Aren't they all?" He laughs with a quick roll of his eyes. It's meant as a joke, but my stomach plummets at his words. Jase is a beautiful man on the inside and out, so it doesn't surprise me that women are lined up to get their bodies permanently altered by him.

"He's booked up today." He pages through the calendar. "He

has an opening for Monday, next week." My throat clogs with emotion. Monday, next week, I'll be in New York, and Jase will be here. Will he have already moved on? Will I have been nothing more than a blip in his radar? My nose tingles and my eyes blur at the thought.

There's a throat clearing, and it's then I realize I'm just standing here, mourning the loss of Jase and me before we've even happened. I look up and see Jase standing next to the other guy.

"Dimples." Jase grins wide, and I shake my head at his nickname for me. "To what do I owe this pleasure?"

I lift the bag of food. "I brought you breakfast." I shrug, suddenly feeling stupid for showing up at his place of work. He's booked all day—probably with beautiful women, who will let him mark their skin, and afterward, they'll give him their number because they aren't going anywhere. They aren't planning to move over five hundred miles away.

"I'm starved," Jase says. "Come back with me. I just finished my appointment, and I have a few minutes before my next one." He saunters around the counter and takes my hand in his, leading me down a narrow hallway and into a small room that must be his workstation. It's filled with drawings similar to the ones on the walls in his room.

There's a burley guy standing in front of the mirror, checking out his newly tattooed shoulder. When he sees us come in, he nods once. "Looks great, man," he says to Jase. Not wanting to be in the way, I sit on the stool that's situated in the corner of the room.

Jase smiles at the guy. "Damn right, it does." He grabs some thin plastic, and after covering the art with some gooey looking stuff, lays the plastic over it, securing it with tape. "You know the drill. Keep it covered for a few hours. Once you remove the bandage, wash it with soap and apply more ointment. Pete will make your next appointment up front."

"Thanks." The guy fist bumps Jase before walking out.

Once he's gone, Jase closes the door behind him then stalks over to me. Grabbing the bag of food out of my hands, he drops it onto the counter, then spreads my legs wide, situating himself between them. He cages me into the corner, his hands landing on the wall on either side of my head. His lips come down and meet mine for a passionate kiss that has my toes curling and the apex of my thighs squeezing around him. With his face only a hairbreadth from mine, he murmurs, "I almost canceled my appointments this morning. Leaving you, laying in my bed, in nothing but my shirt...it almost killed me." His nose brushes against mine. "I was worried I might not see you again, Dimples."

"Why?" I ask, breathlessly.

"I was afraid once you woke up and the weekend was over, you would disappear." His lips brush against mine, then linger momentarily, as if he needs to touch me in some way to believe I'm really here. I swallow thickly. I need to tell him the truth. He needs to know I'm graduating from high school and leaving for New York in a few days. But today, all I want to do is spend the day with Jase. I want to watch him do what he loves. These few days may be all I get with him before he either hates me for lying or I graduate and move. Both of those possibilities leave me feeling sick to my stomach. I'm falling so fast, *too fast*, and my only hope is that Jase will be at the bottom, ready to catch me.

"I'm here," I say softly. "Could I...maybe hangout for a little while? I'll stay out of the way."

Jase's face lights up. "That would be great." With one last kiss, he backs up and takes the bag off the counter. He dishes out the food and grabs us both a cup of coffee. While we eat, we talk about his upcoming appointments. It's obvious from how animated he is, he loves his job.

Shortly after we're done eating, his next appointment comes back. He's an older gentleman named George, looking to get his late wife's name inked on his arm. He shares that they were married for forty years and she passed away six months ago from cancer. He explains what he would like, and after Jase draws up the image, and George approves it, Jase gets to work. The tattoo gun buzzes a low humming sound, but it's drowned out by George's voice. He shares memories of his life with his wife while she was alive. He talks about how they met and fell in love, and how he knew the moment he saw her that she was the one.

As he reminisces, I can't help the tears that fall. This is what I want. An entire life full of memories with Jase. A few days...a week...a month isn't enough. And then it hits me. This is what my mom wanted with my dad but never got. It's why she's chosen to live in the same trailer, in the same town, my entire life. She knows what it feels like to fall in love, and refuses to let go of that feeling, in hope that one day the man she loves might come back and love her in return again. And while I never understood it before, I now get it. Because if I can feel this strongly about Jase after only one weekend, I can't imagine how my mom felt after being with my dad for months.

An hour later, Jase wipes George's arm down and hands him a small mirror. Tears leak from his eyes as he nods slowly. "Thank you," he whispers. Jase runs through the same speech he did with his other client about caring for the tattoo. When he's done, George turns to me with a sad smile and says, "I see the way you two look at each other. It reminds me of the way my Melinda and I used to look at each other." And with a wink, he stands and walks out of the room.

The rest of the day continues much the same—although, thankfully, not as emotional. All types of people come in and out of the shop to get tattooed. Some have back stories, others just want something fun, or cool, or pretty. I can see why Jase is booked up. He treats each tattoo like it's going to be a masterpiece. It doesn't matter if it's a simple butterfly or a remembrance piece, he gives each person one hundred percent of him. He makes them feel as though what they're getting tattooed isn't just ink, but rather a piece of them, and through extension, a piece of him.

Lunchtime arrives, and Jase orders in for us. He breaks for lunch, and we spend the hour kissing, talking, eating, and laughing. I can't remember a time when I felt this content. When my phone buzzes, I check it and see it's Nick. It's already five o'clock, and he's asking where he should pick me up. I text him back to pick me up near the movie theater. It's only a couple blocks away, and he won't piece it together that I was here.

"Everything okay?" Jase asks. I look up and notice his latest client has left.

"Yeah, but I have to get going." I frown. "I promised Nick I would hang out with him."

"All right. Will I see you later?"

My heart skips a beat at his question. He wants to see me later. "Yeah." I nod. "I'm not sure how late I'll be, but you will definitely see me later."

"Good." He gives me a searing kiss goodbye, and I take off to meet Nick. He's waiting for me at the theater where we agreed, and thankfully doesn't ask any questions. We head straight to the mall, where he helps me pick out my first set of Louis Vuitton luggage—a gift from his family for my graduation—as well as some new outfits and toiletries I'll need to get me started once I'm over there.

Once we're done shopping, we head to dinner, and then afterward Nick drops me off at home. I quickly change my clothes and pack a bag. Since my mom isn't home, I leave a note that I'm spending the night at a friend's house, and then take a taxi over to

Jase's. When I arrive, he's already home from work and greets me at the door with a kiss.

The next few days continue the same way. During the day, while Jase is at work, I hang out with Nick—he keeps me company while I pack for New York, we have lunch with Killian on campus since he's finishing up the last of his finals, and I even join him at the gym, since he's insistent he gets some training in, even though he's in his off-season.

My nights are spent with Jase. We hang out with his brother and sister just long enough to not be rude—usually ordering in dinner—and then we excuse ourselves to bed, where we spend the rest of our night kissing and cuddling and making love.

Now it's the day of my graduation rehearsal and my time has run out. I've spent the entire morning with Jase in bed since his first appointment isn't until this afternoon. Just like every morning before he leaves for work, he leans down to kiss me and asks, "Will I see you later?" But unlike every morning when I tell him yes, I can't say that. Because tonight after my rehearsal, I have a family dinner with Nick's family and my mom, and then tomorrow morning is my graduation.

I open my mouth to explain all of this to him, but I can't do it. There's a good chance he's going to be pissed that I've lied. Tomorrow. I'm going to tell him tomorrow. Once I've officially graduated. We'll sit down and I'll be honest with him. *But then what?* I ask myself. He loves his job. He has an entire life here. He isn't going to follow me to New York. I shake the thoughts from my head. We'll figure it out.

"Celeste?" He says my name, getting my attention. "Will I see you later?" he repeats.

"No." I shake my head. "I have this family thing I have to do tonight and tomorrow. How about tomorrow night? I can come by after you get off work."

Jase looks like he wants to ask for details but instead nods. "Okay. Tomorrow night."

Pulling him down to my level, I wrap my arms around his neck and kiss him hard. I'm not sure why, but it feels like I need to somehow convey every feeling I have for him into this kiss. So when I tell him the truth tomorrow night, he'll be understanding.

Once our kiss ends, we say goodbye, and Jase leaves for work. After I shower and get dressed, I text Nick to see if he can drive me over to NCU to my rehearsal, since it will cost me a fortune to take a cab there. He, of course, says yes. Since the theater is too far of a walk, and I don't want to bug Quinn to drive me, I have him pick me up at the corner store around the block from Jase's place, using the excuse that I spent the night at a friend's place. I'm not sure if Nick buys it, but he at least doesn't question it. I'm not even a block away from Jase's apartment and my heart and body are already missing him.

WE ARRIVE at NCU and head straight over to the auditorium where the graduation is taking place. The teachers and administrators walk us through how everything will go tomorrow. When my row is called up, I walk across the stage, along with everyone else in my row. It's only the rehearsal, but for some reason it all hits me hard. Tomorrow I graduate, and then I'm supposed to get on a plane and fly five hundred miles away from Jase. This wasn't supposed to happen. I wasn't supposed to fall in love a damn week before leaving. Hell, I wasn't supposed to fall in love at all. I have a dream, a goal. I've had a vision of what my future is supposed to look like since I was a kid. And nowhere in that future, am I supposed to fall in love with Jase.

"What's going on?" Nick asks as he turns onto his parents' street.

"Nothing."

"Don't lie to me, please. I've known you your entire life. Something is going on with you. It's like you're lost or something..."

"Lost?"

"I don't know...I can't explain it. Something is off with you." He's not going to let this go, and he, of all people, deserves to know what's going on with me.

"I don't think I want to go to New York," I blurt out. Nick's head whips around to look at me. The car swerves a tad, but he quickly straightens it.

"What's going on? Are you scared? You know Killian will be in New York too. He's leaving right after his last exam."

"Killian hates me, and no, I'm not scared."

"Then what is it?" Nick parks the car but doesn't get out. "This is what you've wanted your entire life. Talk to me."

"I—I don't know what's going on with me." And that's the truth. Nick is right. I've wanted to be a model my entire life. I'm being given the opportunity of a lifetime. I can't just give that up for a guy I've only known for a week. But maybe once I talk to him, we can figure it out. Maybe he'll be willing to do the long-distance thing or be willing to move with me. I need to talk to him. I won't know anything until I tell Jase the truth.

"Celeste, you're going to be amazing. You always are. Every modeling ad you've been in over the years..."

"Those were nothing," I whisper. They were just local shoots for department stores. They put some money in the bank so I could help out my mom.

"Every play and musical," he continues. "Everything you do, you excel at. You're going to take New York and the modeling world by storm. Okay?" He smiles at me.

I nod once, unable to speak. It means the world to me that Nick believes in me. I can't let him down. He put himself on the line by asking for this opportunity for me. I have to go. This is my future.

"You've got this," he says with conviction. "And you know I'm always here for you, right? It doesn't matter if I'm hundreds of miles away. I'm here."

"Thank you." Nick pulls me into a hug, and the tears fall.

The minute we walk through the door, Victoria tells us that dinner is being served. We sit at the dinner table and make small talk while we all eat. When my mom is around Victoria, it's the only time she attempts to clean herself up and stay sober. She's dressed in a pair of jeans and a blue off-the-shoulder sweater. Her brown hair is brushed and straightened, and her makeup is done nicely. She also doesn't look like she's high or drunk. When my mom cleans up, she's beautiful.

"Are you excited for New York?" Victoria asks as she sips her coffee while we each have a slice of apple pie for dessert.

"New York?" my mom asks, confused.

"You didn't tell her?" Victoria chides. I was meaning to, but since I found out, I've either been with Jase or Nick every day. And when I stopped home, she wasn't there. It seems we just keep missing each other. "Nicholas got her an internship in New York with Elite Modeling. She's leaving in a few days."

My mom's eyes dart from Victoria to me. "Wow, so you're leaving." It's not a question. She knows I am. Only I'm not so sure anymore. Before this last week, I would've had zero doubts about getting on that plane and never looking back. It's crazy how quickly one's priorities can change.

"Yeah," I admit softly, "I'm leaving."

"Congratulations, pretty girl. I'm very happy for you." Mom gives me a rare, genuine smile, and it makes me feel worse for even considering not going. As much as I care about Jase, I have to go to New York. The only way I can one day take care of my mom, take care of myself, is by going.

"Thank you," I say, forcing a smile on my lips.

After a few moments of uncomfortable silence, Victoria excuses us from the table so we can go over the last-minute details for the celebration that will be taking place after my graduation tomorrow. Half the senior class is invited, even though I barely talk to any of them. They heard the party was being thrown by Nick Shaw's family and of course accepted the invite.

Nick's dad, Henry, waves us off. "Good, I need to speak to Nick about some contract stuff anyway." Henry Shaw is a well-known sports agent, who owns an agency here in North Carolina. He's also Nick's agent.

After Victoria and my mom have gone over everything twice, my mom gives Victoria a hug and thanks her. "This is very sweet of you."

"Of course!" Victoria grins. "You know Celeste is like a daughter to me." She gives me a hug. "We'll see you tomorrow."

"You haven't been home in a few days," my mom says as we make our way to the front door. Nick and his dad have stopped talking, and Nick is now giving me a curious look as he stands and walks over to say goodbye. Every day we've hung out, he's dropped me off at my house. "Will you be coming home tonight?" My mom never asks about when I'll be home. I think her knowing that I'm leaving in a few days has her suddenly wanting to spend time with me before I leave. It wasn't said, but I think we both know once I leave this town, the chances of my coming back are slim.

"Yes," I tell her, ignoring Nick's glare. "I'll ride with you."

The ten-minute drive home is quiet. When we pull up to the trailer, a couple bikers pass by, and my mom's head turns. She does it anytime a bike passes by. She's checking to make sure it's not my dad. She's been doing it my entire life.

"You were only with my dad for a couple months, right?"

She looks at me stunned. I never ask about him. "Yes, two and a half months." She smiles sadly. "But I knew I loved him the minute I met him."

"How did you know?"

"It was the way he smiled at me. Like, without even knowing me, I was already his entire world." A single tear rolls down her cheek. "I know it seems crazy, Celeste." More tears fall. "I tried to move on a few times…when you were younger. I just couldn't." She shakes her head. "My heart just can't let go of him."

"But what if he's moved on?"

"I don't believe it. He loved me with his entire heart. I don't know why he never came back, but I refuse to believe it's because he found someone else."

"I think…I've fallen in love," I admit out loud to my mom.

"Oh, sweetie," my mom coos. "What's his name? Can I meet him?"

"His name is Jase, and I don't know. I'm leaving in a few days to New York. It's like the worst timing ever. And on top of that, I lied to him…well, kind of lied. He thinks I'm in college and older than what I am." I leave out that he also has no clue that I live in a rundown trailer park on the other side of the tracks. "And he has no clue I'm leaving soon. I doubt he'll even forgive me for not being honest."

My mom takes my hand in hers, and my throat clogs with emotion. Over the years, I've dreamt of having boy talks with my mom, and of course, when we finally do, it's over a boy I'm going to have to walk away from, while also walking away from my mom.

"You need to talk to him, Celeste. Find him and tell him everything. If he loves you, he'll forgive you. He'll put all that shit aside and focus on what matters. If it's true love, you will find a way to be together. Every day I wish I would've spoken to Snake before he left. I wish I would've gotten more information, so I could look for him. Don't live with regrets."

"I hate that you're so heartbroken, Mom," I admit. "I want more for you. For you to fall in love, again, or for you to move on. Come to New York with me," I plead.

My mom gives me a soft smile. "I can't do that, pretty girl. New York is your dream. I need to stay right here. I have to believe one day Snake will return."

"It's been eighteen years," I point out.

"I know." She sighs. "I know I'm stupid to think that maybe one day he'll return, but I just can't stop hoping. Your heart can't help who it loves. I love Snake, and I can't just stop. Now, go find that boy and talk to him. You can take my car. Follow your heart, pretty girl."

"Okay, thank you." I lean over and give my mom a hug. I hate that she's been stuck in the same place for the last two decades. I hate that love did this to her. It's the reason I never wanted to fall in love, yet somehow it found me anyway. She's right. I need to talk to

Jase. I need to follow my heart. I can't end up like my mom—always wondering what if.

I pull up to Jase's apartment complex and park my mom's car. I run up the stairs and knock on the door. When nobody answers, I check the time on my phone. It's already after ten o'clock. Maybe they're sleeping. Remembering there's a key under the mat Jase told me I could use, I pluck it out and unlock the door. The apartment is quiet, and I wonder if maybe I should've called first.

My need to talk to him wins out, and I head down the hall to his room. I can hear the shower running from outside the door. A smile forms on my lips. I can join him and then talk to him. But when I open the door, joining him is the last thing on my mind. Because laying in his bed is Amaya. Her fiery red hair is fanned out across his pillow. And she's naked. My heart feels like it's just been ripped out of my chest. The bathroom door opens and out walks Jase in nothing but a towel around his waist—his full focus on Amaya. Because of the location of the doors, he can't see me standing here. He can't see my heart breaking into a million pieces.

I want to yell at him for leading me on, making me believe we were something more. I want to scream at him for fucking his best friend only hours after making love to me. I want to curse him for not loving me the way I've fallen in love with him. But I don't do any of it. I followed my heart and this is where it led me to. Reality. Smacking me right in the face. I was stupid to ever consider for a second I should choose a man over my future. That I should listen to my heart instead of my head.

I watch as Jase gently pulls the blanket over Amaya's naked body, and then pushes several wayward strands of hair out of her face. Unable to be here for another second, I back away from the door and run away as fast as my feet will carry me. I lock the door behind me and put the key back under the mat.

I go back to my house. My mom is already asleep, and I don't wake her up. Instead, I call for a taxi and write her an apology note. Because tomorrow when she wakes up, I won't be here. Not at my graduation, or at the celebration. I'll be in New York. But my heart, it will still be in pieces right outside Jase's bedroom door. Because like my mom said: You can't help who your heart loves. And my stupid heart loves a man who doesn't love me back.

FIVE

Celeste
The Present

"IF I GAIN MUCH MORE weight before this wedding, I'm going to have to buy a new dress." Olivia pats her growing belly and giggles. "I don't know how much more the seamstress can stretch the fabric." We've just finished having dinner and are heading over to the valet so they can bring Olivia's car around. Over the last several months, weekly lunches-slash-dinners have somehow become a thing. It was hard at first to accept Olivia's and Giselle's friendship. I've never been the kind of girl to have friends—aside from Nick—but these two women have grown on me, and now, I actually find myself looking forward to us meeting up.

"It's because you're having a girl," Giselle says. "They carry high, making you look fatter."

"Wait." I stop in the middle of the sidewalk. "You didn't tell me you're having a girl. So she finally cooperated?"

Olivia blushes. "Yes! She spread her legs during the ultrasound!" She giggles. "We actually just found out yesterday. We were planning to announce it at brunch this weekend."

"Congratulations!" I give Olivia a hug. "She's going to be the most spoiled little girl to ever walk this earth. How's Nick doing with the news?"

"He's freaking out," she says, handing the valet her slip.

"Having a boy is one thing. A girl is apparently a whole other story. He's already planning all the ways to keep her locked up once she becomes a teenager."

I laugh at that. "That doesn't surprise me. He's probably thinking of all the women he slept with in his younger years." I flinch the second the words leave my mouth, and Giselle cackles. I'm obviously still getting used to this whole friendship thing. "Shit! What I meant was...well...I mean..."

Olivia laughs, once again proving how understanding and sweet she is. "I know what you meant. And you aren't wrong."

"Do you also know what you're having?" I ask Giselle, giving her a *don't lie to me* look.

"I do!" she squeals. "We're also having a girl."

"Oh my God!" I give her a hug. "I'm going to need to make a baby clothing line just to spoil all these babies!"

The three of us are laughing when Olivia says, "Hey, isn't that Jase?" My eyes follow her line of vision, and sure enough, Jase is standing on the sidewalk hailing a cab.

My mind goes back to a few months ago when I ran into him on Giselle's birthday at the tattoo shop. I never imagined in a million years I would ever see him again, let alone in the same city I'm living in. It's been well over a decade since I last saw him. Since I saw Amaya in his bed and him in nothing but a towel. I wish I could say the years have been bad to him, but that would be a lie. Jase looks nearly the same as he did all those years ago. The main difference being, he now looks less like a boy and more like a man. He's filled out, his muscles now more defined. His skin dons several new tattoos, and his face looks harder. No less beautiful. Just more guarded.

I stood in the middle of the tattoo shop, frozen in place, while Quinn spoke to Killian, who she apparently knows because he gets all of his work done there. And then Jase spoke. He made eye contact with me and asked if I was going to get a tattoo... as if it completely escaped his mind that over ten years ago he stole my heart then destroyed it.

"Are you going to finally let me mark this flawless skin of yours?" His finger runs up my arm, and I visibly shiver at his touch. His voice, a bit deeper than it was all those years ago, but no less smooth and captivating. And then I remember how it was that same smooth voice that made me fall in love with him. Only to have him break my heart shortly after.

"Don't touch me," I snap, finally gaining my composure.

Giselle and Olivia ask if I'm okay, both concerned with the way I'm suddenly acting. Olivia even suggests they go somewhere else. Then Nick speaks up, introducing Olivia to Jase.

"Nice to meet you," Jase says. "I've heard a lot about you." All these years, Nick and Jase have been keeping in touch? Nick has never mentioned him once.

Nick explains they played high school and college ball together.

"Did you go to school with them?" Giselle asks me.

"No, I went to public school," I tell her, trying to get my shit together. My heart is beating quickly. It's hard to breathe. I can't believe I'm standing here with him right now. Is this his shop? Does he own Forbidden Ink? How ironic is it, that in the end, we ended up living in the same city?

"You met him at the party I took you to, right?" Nick asks, shaking me from my thoughts. "I forgot about that. Do you two... know each other?" His eyes volley between Jase and me. I never told Nick about Jase. When I didn't show up to my graduation, Nick called me and I told him I needed to go. I was ready to start my new life and didn't want to wait another second. My mom and Victoria were both upset, but eventually got over it. To this day, nobody knows why I left early.

"Yes, I did," I admit to Nick, "but I don't know him." Even to my own ears I sound like a woman scorned. I need to get myself composed. I am not that woman. Jase did me a favor that night. I should be thanking him. He reminded me that love is nothing more than a wasted emotion. Because of his indiscretion, I got off the plane in New York a hundred times more motivated to make something for myself. I would never become my mother: a brokenhearted woman pining over a man who clearly never loved her the way she loved him. I'm stronger and wiser because of Jase.

Quinn sneers. "Oh, that's rich! What's wrong? Is my brother not worthy of your memories? Did you block out everything that happened before you ran your stuck-up ass to New York? What are you even doing slumming it in East Village? It's a far ride from the Upper East Side."

"You know what—" I step into Quinn's face. She has no idea what really happened "—I don't need to take this shit from you. I didn't know you guys worked here, and if I had, trust me, I never would've come."

"Well, now you do know. And FYI, my brothers don't just work here... they own the place. Don't let the door hit you on the way out," Quinn says before turning her back on me. I consider outing her

brother. Telling her he's the reason I ran to New York, but I don't. For one, admitting he cheated on me will open up a can of worms that I'm not prepared to deal with. And two, I don't owe anybody an explanation.

As I'm about to leave, Jax appears, introducing himself to everyone. "Celeste, it's good to see you again," he says, giving me a kind smile. "Although, with those billboards of you all over New York, I feel like I see you every day." He winks playfully, and I can't help but smile back at him.

"Great, if we're all done with this reunion, how about we figure out who's getting inked?" Jase says, sounding annoyed. I want to snap at the cheating asshole. Because fuck him!

"I want the nice guy," Giselle says, pointing to Jax. "It's my birthday. Livi, you can take the cranky one." Everyone laughs, and Jase cracks a small smile. One that makes the butterflies in my belly flutter. Damn him for giving me butterflies. He's a cheater, I remind my heart and head.

"I might be the crankier one, but I'm still the better artist. Ain't that right, Dimples?" He looks my way, and I shoot daggers at him. How dare he use the nickname he gave me. He lost his right to use that name when he chose to fuck another woman.

"Bullshit!" Jax laughs. "I'm older, wiser, and a better artist."

"Nah." Jase cackles. "Just older." He gives me another look, and I know I need to get out of here. My body and heart aren't accepting what my head knows. Jase is bad for me. He's a lying, cheating, asshole.

"I really need to get going," I announce, turning for the door. I give Giselle a hug and wish her a Happy Birthday. Olivia tries to stop me, but I tell her I have an early morning meeting and promise we'll do lunch this week.

Then I give Jax a quick hug. I'm not sure why. I think maybe it's because he's the only person in his family not acting like I'm in the wrong. "It was nice to see you again," I tell him before I run out the door. Nick, of course, follows after me, demanding to know what's going on.

"I'm just upset that I didn't know Jase works here!"

Nick gives me a confused look. "You just said in there that you don't know him, so why would you even care where he works?" He's right. I know he is. I'm being ridiculous and throwing this way out of proportion. I know I am. But I can't help it. Every emotion, every painful feeling I've worked my ass off to bury is being dug up, and I can't stop it from happening. For every shov-

elful I throw back into the grave, two more are flying out and landing on my feet.

"We..." The need to confide in Nick is so strong, but I can't do it. It would mean admitting that I went against everything I believed in and fell in love. It would mean admitting that Jase broke my heart. I'm too worked up. I just need to get away from here. Thankfully a cab pulls up. "I need to go," I tell him, rushing to get into the cab and get away before he can call me out on my obvious lie.

Thinking back to that night in Forbidden Ink, a thought niggles in the back of my mind. I didn't put the pieces together before. I was too upset. But now, the way Jase is acting...it all makes sense. He has no idea that I know he cheated. I mean, how could he know? I left his apartment without making myself known. I switched out the ticket Nick had bought me as my graduation present and took the next flight out, never looking back. He probably thinks I left for New York without saying goodbye.

"It is Jase," Olivia says, answering her own question. And she's right, it is in fact Jase Crawford, standing on the edge of the sidewalk, waving his hand in the air as he tries to snag a cab. With the memory of what he did to me still fresh in my mind, I stalk over to him. It's about damn time he knows I'm aware of what he did to me all those years ago.

"Hey!" I scream over the blaring horns and people chattering about on the busy sidewalk. "Jase!" I yell to get his attention. He turns his head toward me, a slow smirk creeping up on his lips. My only thought is that I'm going to knock that damn smirk square off his face. This conversation is years overdue.

"Oh my God! Dad! It's Celeste Leblanc!" a tiny voice squeals. I look down, and for the first time, notice Jase is holding hands with a young girl. Because of his size, she was being blocked by his body. She grins wide, and letting go of Jase's hand, steps in front of me. "I am seriously your biggest fan!" Her emerald eyes glimmer with happiness. "Do you...do you know my dad?" She points back at Jase as I finally absorb her words.

Dad. She called Jase, *Dad.* He's her dad. I trail my eyes over her, taking in her features: fiery red hair. Green eyes. It's been over ten years since I've seen *her*, but I'll never forget what her eyes and hair looked like. The girl standing in front of me is Amaya's daughter. No, correction. She's Amaya *and* Jase's daughter. While she has her mother's eyes and hair, she's naturally tan like Jase. She's dressed in an adorable red crop top that shows just a hint of her belly and black skinny jeans with rips in the knees, and she's sporting a pair of...are those Burberry rain boots?

"Hello?" She tilts her head to the side. "You *are* Celeste Leblanc, right?"

My name out of her mouth has me snapping to attention. "Yes, I am Celeste." I muster up the best smile I can.

"Do you know my dad?" she repeats.

"I..." I will myself not to look at Jase. "I do know your dad."

"Ohmigod!" she squeals again, and I force myself not to flinch. Once in a while, I'll come across a college-aged woman asking for an autograph, but I've yet to have someone this young recognize me. My clothing, jewelry, and makeup lines are mainly geared toward women in their late twenties and older—the businesswomen and the wealthy who can afford the price tag that comes with my brand.

"I am *literally* your biggest fan." Her eyes sparkle, and for a second I forget who she's standing with. "When I grow up, I want to be just like you. I want to be a model and travel all over the world. I've watched every episode of America's Elite Model," she gushes. Last year I guest-starred on a television show where dozens of women competed to get a modeling contract with Elite—the same modeling company that gave me my start when I was eighteen. The winner was also given a spot in my clothing line launch a few months ago in Paris.

"Thank you." When I give her a closer look, I notice she's wearing makeup, and it's done beautifully. I wonder if her mom did her makeup, and my heart drops at the thought as I remember who she is—who she belongs to. I suddenly want to get as far away from here as humanly possible, but instead I take a deep breath. It's not her fault who her parents are.

"My name is Skyla." She extends her tiny hand to shake mine. She's petite yet tall—all legs—so I can't tell how old she is, but she acts more like a young adult than a child. If I had to guess, I would say she looks to be about twelve... maybe thirteen years old. I do the math in my head. Did Jase know he had a daughter and not tell me? I take her hand in mine, and it's then I notice my hands are shaking. "Could I...could I get your autograph?" she asks, suddenly shy.

"Sure," I say, taking my hand back. "Do you have something for me to write on?" She looks back at her dad, and my eyes lock once again with his. He's frozen in place. He probably never imagined the two separate parts of his past would one day collide. We were only together for a short time. I doubt he's even thought about me over the years. I was probably nothing more than a blip in his radar.

A week-long fuck. *Although, he did remember the nickname he gave me...*

Flustered, I begin to dig through my purse to find something to write with, or write on, when a hand taps my shoulder. I look over and Giselle is handing me a cocktail napkin. She smiles softly, and I silently thank her. When I look back at Skyla, she also has something in her hand.

"It's my sketch pad. I want to design clothes one day, like you. Will you sign it?" Oh, the irony of this situation. I take the book from her and open it up. The first page is a sketch of a gorgeous ballgown. The details are so intricate and perfect, it looks like something an artist would draw.

"Did you draw this?" I ask in awe, as I continue to flip through the pages of exquisite drawings, each one more beautiful than the last.

"I did." I glance back up at her and she's beaming with pride.

"They're amazing. Keep it up and one day everyone will be wearing your designs."

Skyla's smile brightens even more, if that's even possible. "Thank you." She hands me a pen.

I sign my name on the inside cover with a couple words of wisdom, then hand it back to her. She opens it up and reads what I wrote. When she makes eye contact with me, she frowns, and I worry maybe what I wrote wasn't the right thing. I've never signed something for a young girl before, so I simply wrote to always follow her dreams.

"Could you sign something for my mom as well?" she asks softly. "I wish she were here to meet you."

"Umm... sure," I say, trying, and failing, to keep my voice light. I can feel everyone's eyes on me, especially Jase's, but I don't chance looking anywhere but at Skyla. If I look at Jase, I might just lose it. He still doesn't know I saw him with Amaya. Using the napkin Giselle gave me, I sign my name.

"Can you make it out to Amaya? That's her name."

"Sure." I write her name on the top then hand it to her. When the napkin passes from my hand to hers, I make the mistake of looking at Jase. And I'm shocked to find that he's glaring at me. Glaring! Like I'm at fault here. What in the ever-loving fuck! He's damn lucky his daughter is standing here or I'd give him a piece of my mind.

"It was very nice to meet you," I tell Skyla, and with one last fake smile, I turn to walk away. Giselle and Olivia are both staring at me. I walk past them and can feel them on my heels. I don't even need to look back to know they're chomping at the bit to ask me questions. "Not now," I say as we walk back over to the restaurant.

Thankfully, the valet brings Olivia's car around and opens the door, forcing them to get in. I tell them I'll see them tomorrow and then take off. Only instead of taking a cab home, I decide to walk to clear my head. It's only a few blocks away. Tomorrow night is the bachelor-slash-bachelorette party. It was going to be hard enough to go knowing Jase might be there. But now that I know he's still with Amaya and they share a child, possibly one he had while he was hanging out with me—I'm strong, but I don't know if I'm strong enough to face that. Will Amaya be there? Nick and Olivia have never once mentioned her. I would've remembered her name being said. Maybe they're no longer together.

As soon as I get home, I change out of my work clothes and into a pair of pajamas. Then, after pouring myself a glass of wine, I head out onto my balcony. I want to text Nick and ask him about Jase and Amaya, but I know if I do, he'll come back at me with an entire slew of questions. So instead, I sit outside and drink my wine with the hope that once I'm drunk enough, I'll no longer think about Jase. And drunk I do get, but not even the insanely large amount of alcohol in my system can stop the thoughts of Jase.

THE CAB STOPS in front of Olivia's beautiful two-story home in Park Slope, complete with a white picket fence. I swipe my card, thank the cabbie, and get out. I glance around and take in my surroundings. I can't imagine ever not living in the city. Why live in New York if you can't experience the hustle and bustle of what makes New York, *New York?* But then again, I don't have children, nor will I ever. As I'm straightening the creases in my skirt, I spot Giselle and Killian walking down the street toward me. They live two houses down from Olivia and Nick. Giselle waves and gives me a knowing grin, telling me that she and Olivia are going to interrogate me the moment the three of us are in the same room. When I roll my eyes at her, Killian's lips curl into a half-smile. Ever since he and Giselle got together, he's been friendlier toward me, which is both strange and nice at the same time.

I wanted to meet them at the club where the party is being held, but Olivia insisted we meet here, have dinner, and then ride over together. I know this is just her way of cornering me about yesterday, but I have a hard time saying no to her. She's just too damn sweet. My suspicions are confirmed the minute we walk inside and Olivia starts in on me. "Okay, you've had enough space. I even gave you twenty-four hours, now spill."

"Yeah, the chemistry between you and Jase was so thick, I could barely breathe," Giselle adds.

"I think you're confusing chemistry for tension," I mutter.

"Oh no, there were sparks," Giselle says. "Sure, there was tension too, but the chemistry was definitely stronger."

"Did something happen between you two?" Olivia asks.

"Did something happen between who?" Nick questions. My eyes swing over to him. He's holding Reed in his arms, his head resting on his daddy's shoulder, his eyes barely open. Nick must be about to put him to bed before we leave. My mind goes to Jase. He's a dad. Does he live in the city, or in the suburbs? Does Amaya live with him? Does he make sure he's home every night to put his daughter to bed? I can't even remember a time when I was little that my mom put me to bed.

"We ran into Jase when we were leaving the restaurant yesterday," Olivia says. "He was with his daughter. She's apparently a fan of Celeste's."

"Oh, Skyla? She's a sweet kid," Nick says. "I can see that. From what Jase has said, she's really into fashion."

"You knew he has a daughter?" I snap, and instantly regret it, knowing my harsh tone is going to make Nick ask questions.

"Yeah..." Nick gives me a confused look. "I *am* friends with him."

"I know," I say dumbly. "I need a drink." As I'm about to head to the kitchen, Nick's hand lands on my shoulder.

"Celeste, what the heck is going on?" I open my mouth, about to say something—what, I have no idea—but Nick adds, "And don't you dare say nothing. First you lost it at Forbidden Ink, and now you're acting like I committed a sin by not telling you a guy you barely know has a daughter. I want the truth. Did something happen between you and Jase?"

When I divert my eyes, they land on Killian, who's glaring intently at me, like he's waiting to hear my answer as well. So much for him being nicer...

"It doesn't matter what happened. It was a mistake. One I'd rather not think about ever again." And without waiting for anyone to ask me what I mean, I stalk out of the room and into the kitchen. I pluck a bottle of white wine out of the fridge and pour myself a glass. Giselle walks in after me, pulls a bottle of Patron out of the freezer, and pours some into a shot glass.

"You might want this instead." She hands me the shot. When I eye her quizzically, she says, "Jase confirmed he'll be at the party tonight."

Just. Fucking. Great. I set the wine glass down and take the shot from Giselle. Tilting my head back, I throw back the entire shot, reveling in the burning trail the alcohol leaves behind as it goes down my throat.

I'M SITTING in the plush booth of the M Lounge, one of New York's most exclusive nightclubs, watching everyone I'm here with dance with someone else. Olivia and Nick are swaying to the music with their arms around each other. Giselle and Killian might as well be getting it on right there in the middle of the dance floor. My good friend, Mercedes—who is also a model—and her husband, Brandon —who plays for the New York Brewers—are grinding against one another. Several other friends of Nick and Olivia are dancing as well. All with someone in their arms. Me? I'm alone, sipping on a strawberry Mojito, while waiting for Chad to arrive. He's late. Again.

My eyes, of their own accord, find Jase and Jax, who are both leaning against the bar, each nursing a beer. We have a VIP area roped off with several booths to accommodate everyone who's here to help celebrate Olivia and Nick's upcoming nuptials—complete with our own waitress. While I'm sitting in one of the booths, sipping my drink, I notice that Jase hasn't once come near where I'm sitting since he initially showed up and said hello to everyone but me.

As I'm taking another sip of my drink, a cool pair of lips brush against my cheek. When I look over, I see Chad is here, still dressed to the nines in his three-piece suit he wore to work. It's not that I saw him leave for work this morning, it's just that he wears the same version of this suit every day. He sits next to me and grants me with a quick "Hello," before he pulls his phone out from his jacket pocket and starts typing on it. I eye him for a long minute, annoyed as hell that he's already back to business, but too exhausted to argue about it. Instead, I down the rest of my drink and look back out to the sea of people on the dance floor. Only this time another couple has been added to the mix. Jase is holding hands with a blond-haired skanky-looking woman as they make their way to the middle of the dance floor. She immediately turns her back on him and starts grinding her ass against his front. Her arms go up, raising her already short shirt to just below her tits. My eyes scan down her body. She might be dressed like trash, but there's no denying she's hot—in a two-bit stripper sort of way.

Before I can look away, Jase's eyes lock with mine, and for a brief second, it feels as if we're the only two people in the room. Only we aren't, and the woman rubbing all over him is proof. He doesn't smile, but he doesn't glare either. I can't quite pinpoint the look he's giving me. Is it apologetic? Regret? Maybe it's indifference. I'm not sure, but I have to force myself to look away before any of the emotions I've managed to keep hidden, surface.

"Dance with me," I murmur into Chad's ear. He glances up from his phone and eyes me speculatively. "Please."

He releases a frustrated sigh. "In a few minutes. I'm in the middle of an important chat with a client in China."

"No, now," I demand, fully aware I sound like a bratty teenager.

Chad's brows furrow as he takes me in. "Are you drunk, Celeste?"

"No," I snap. "I just want to dance with my boyfriend. Is that too much to ask?" I stick him with a hard glare.

He sets his phone down on the table, but I notice he's still in the group chat. "What's gotten into you lately?" he questions. "You're acting like a petulant child."

"Because I want the man I'm dating to pay attention to me?"

"You've never acted like this before," he accuses, his tone a mixture of confusion and annoyance. He stares at me for a long second before he says, "You've changed. What's going on with you?"

I scoff as if I have no idea what he's talking about. Even though he's right. I have changed. And I hate it. I don't want to feel this way. I want my company and success to make me feel complete. I want my beautiful high-rise condo to not feel so lonely. I want my wealthy, hard-working boyfriend to be enough. But I can't stop all of my emotions from breaking through. I've felt myself changing for a while now, but I ignored it. And then I saw Jase, and every raw emotion I've kept buried deep, surfaced without my permission.

"I can't do this anymore," I whisper.

"What?" He tilts his head to the side in confusion.

Unsure if his response is because he can't hear me over the music, or if he doesn't understand what I'm trying to say, I repeat myself, this time louder. "I can't do this anymore." Then I add, "I'm not happy."

This time his eyes widen, indicating he heard and understood me. "What is it you want, Celeste?" he asks, clearly aggravated. Chad is a businessman. When there's a problem, he fixes it. But he can't fix this. He can't fix us. He can't fix me.

"I want..." I glance out at all the couples still dancing. Olivia has her head thrown back in laughter as Nick whispers into her ear. Giselle's eyes are filled with a mixture of lust and love as Killian holds her close to him, his fingers digging into her ass possessively. Even Mercedes, who isn't much different from me, is smiling as her husband holds her tight. My eyes land on Jase, who now has his back to me. The woman he's dancing with has her arms around his neck and her face plastered against his chest.

"Celeste," Chad says, bringing my attention back to him. "What do you want? What will make you happy?"

"Love," I say softly, yet loud enough for him to hear. "I want to be in love." Tears prick my eyes as memories of Jase holding me in bed surface. Of the way he made love to me. The way he would hold my hand and kiss me. It might not have been love on his end, but it was on mine. And while I have no desire to ever be with that two-timing asshole again, I want to feel what I felt when I was with him. I want to feel the butterflies attacking my belly, and my heart-strings being tugged. I want someone to look at me the way Nick and Killian look at Olivia and Giselle. I want to be somebody's entire world.

Chad blinks slowly, his face completely devoid of all emotion. He knows there's no fixing this problem. Our relationship has never been about love, and Chad isn't capable of loving anything but his business. No words need to be spoken to know we're over.

SIX

*J*ASE

I'M STANDING in the middle of the dance floor while a woman, who I'm not the least bit attracted to, grinds and shakes her ass all over the front of my body, while I chant over and over again in my head not to look back and make eye contact with Celeste. The woman turns around and her arms snake around my neck. Her head falls to my chest and her thigh pushes through the middle of my legs as she attempts to rub her knee against my dick. I've had enough.

When she asked to dance, I had just witnessed—who looks to be —Celeste's white-collar, rich-as-shit boyfriend approach and kiss her. He was sporting a suit, one that screams wealth and power, but looks douchy-as-fuck when worn in a club. Needing to take my mind off them, I accepted this woman's proposition to dance, but now I'm regretting it. Because the longer I stand here and smell her cheap perfume, the more I crave the sweet scent of Celeste.

It's been over ten years, and I only had her for a week—one fucking week—but I can still remember how she smelled—a perfect mixture of her natural scent, that sweet, rose lotion she would rub all over her body, and me. I've been with several women over the years, but not one of them smells like Celeste did. And that makes me wonder, if I walked over to the booth and dragged her away from her boyfriend, would she still smell the same? Or would it be different because she's no longer with me? She's no longer in my bed, in my clothes. She's older now, more refined, but just as fucking gorgeous as she was back then. Maybe the smell I remember is only because she was with me. If I brought her home and forced her to stay in my bed all weekend, could I get her to smell like I remember, again?

Unable to take another second of my back toward her, I peel the woman's arms off me and back away, turning my body toward where Celeste is sitting...only she's no longer there—and neither is the guy she was with.

"I need a drink," I tell the woman. Her face lights up, taking my words as an invitation to join me. "Alone," I add. Her lips turn down into a frown, but I don't care. I'm too annoyed to care.

"You sure?" She flutters her fake eyelashes. "I can give—"

"I'm sure," I say, cutting her off, not giving a shit what she can *give* me.

I stalk off the dance floor and over to the bar where my brother, Jax, is still nursing his beer. I lift my finger and the bartender comes over. "Double shot of Johnnie Walker Black."

"You got it." She gives me a flirtatious wink before sauntering away to make my drink.

"Damn, what's with the hard shit?" Jax asks.

When I shake my head, he says, "It doesn't happen to have anything to do with that brown-haired, legs for days, bombshell I saw sitting across the room with her uptight boyfriend, does it?" My gaze flies over to Jax, and he's grinning ear-to-fucking-ear. "Guess so."

"How do you know he's her boyfriend?"

"I don't. I just wanted to see if I could get a rise out of you." Jax laughs. "When are you going to admit she's the one that got away?"

The bartender lays a napkin down in front of me then sets my shot on top. Before it even touches the paper, I snatch it out of her hand and throw it back. "She didn't get away," I snap, slamming the glass down. "She left. And she was nothing more than a fuck."

Jax's eyes go wide, but he isn't looking at me. He's looking just past me. When I turn to see who, or what, he's looking at, Celeste is standing there, frozen in place. I could be wrong, but I'm almost positive she has tears in her eyes. But before I can confirm it, she takes off back to the table, clearly having heard what I said. Although, I'm not sure why that upsets her. She chose to leave. And without even so much as a goddamn goodbye.

SEVEN

CELESTE

"SHE WAS NOTHING MORE THAN A FUCK." The words pound against my heart, shattering what little is left of it, piece by piece. I would've thought his words wouldn't be able to hurt me. Once the heart is broken, it shouldn't be able to break again. It's not as if it's been fixed or even repaired. It's been damaged for the last ten years, just hanging together enough to continue to beat—enough to keep me alive. But it's not in any shape to do any other type of job like hold love. At least I didn't think it was...until now. Because as I walk back to the table, tears burning my eyes, I realize that my broken heart *was* intact enough to still feel. I was just simply protecting what was left of it. But his words...they were like a hammer to crystal. My fragile heart didn't stand a chance against that force.

I always assumed he felt that way about me. If he felt more, he wouldn't have hooked up with Amaya while with me, right? But hearing the actual words come from his mouth, confirming what I always suspected, hurt worse than any assumption. *"She was nothing more than a fuck."*

When I get back to the table, Nick and Olivia are sitting in the booth with their limbs wrapped around one another—her adorable baby bump hitting the side of the table. They're smiling and laughing, and look completely in love. I need to get away. I can't ruin this night for them. Next week they're going to get married and they deserve, more than anyone I know, to be happy and not be brought down by me.

I'm about to grab my clutch and leave, figuring I can make an excuse through text, when Nick looks up and spots me. His brows furrow in confusion, then all too quickly, his eyelids form into thin slits, his entire face morphing into anger. I'm not sure what he sees, until my hand comes up to my cheek and I feel the wetness. I'm crying.

"What the hell happened?" he demands, which makes Olivia turn toward me as well. Her look isn't one of anger but sympathy. She's worried.

"Nothing," I say, reaching for my clutch. Nick eyes it and snatches it before I can.

"Celeste, don't fucking 'nothing' me," he growls. "What's wrong?"

"Nothing. Give me back my clutch."

"No, tell me what's wrong."

"Are you guys excited for your big day?" I ask, changing the subject like a crazy person. But I don't know what else to do. He has my clutch, and I can't tell him what's going on.

"Yes, you know we are. Don't try to change the subject." Nick glares.

"How are classes going?" I ask, moving onto another safe topic.

"He graduated!" Olivia squeals, then throws her hand over her mouth.

"Brown-Eyes," Nick groans, "you weren't supposed to tell anyone." He's trying to sound annoyed, but everyone knows, in Nick's eyes, Olivia walks on water.

"Sorry." She bats her lashes playfully.

"Hey, don't apologize!" I shoot daggers at Nick. "We're best friends and you don't even tell me you've graduated? Why wasn't I invited to the ceremony?" My feelings are seriously hurt right now. When Nick announced he was going back to school to get his degree in literature, I was one hundred percent supportive. Why would he hide that he graduated?

"Nobody was invited," he admits. "I didn't want to make a big deal out of it." He shrugs. "Besides, it's not like I saw *you* graduate." He sticks me with a pointed look.

"Yeah, well..." I take a deep breath, not wanting to remember why I didn't attend my graduation or party afterward. And then it hits me... Needing to move our conversation into safer waters, I blurt out, "I'm going to throw you a graduation party once you guys get back from your honeymoon."

"Oh, yay!" Olivia claps excitedly. "And we can also celebrate that—"

"No more changing the subject," Nick says, cutting her off. "What's going on?" It's clear in his voice he's not going to let this go, but I really don't want to have this conversation.

"Should we do it at a restaurant or your house?" I ask Olivia, ignoring his question.

Before she can answer, Nick says, "Stop. I'm not fucking kidding, Celeste. You don't cry. Ever."

"Give me back my clutch," I demand.

"After you tell me why you're upset enough to shed tears."

Unable to have this conversation sober, I down a shot that's sitting on the table. It burns like a bitch, but I more than welcome the discomfort. After I repeat this two more times, Nick pulls the tray out of my reach.

"You've had enough to drink," he chides. "Now tell me what's wrong."

I've never told anyone about Jase. No one. I left for New York without looking back and kept everything that happened between us to myself. But suddenly, as I look at Nick and Olivia looking at me, I feel like the weight is too much. I need to tell someone, and if I'm going to trust anyone to know my truth, it's them.

"I fell in love," I admit with a harsh breath as I fall into the chair across from them. Their eyes go wide, and Olivia moves from next to Nick over to me.

"With Chad?" Olivia asks, confused.

"No, we actually broke up tonight," I admit. "When I was eighteen. I fell in love...and then he broke my heart. And I—I just don't understand why I wasn't enough."

"Celeste," Olivia coos, reaching over and giving me a side hug. "You are enough. I don't know who this guy was, but fuck him." A burst of laughter escapes my lips at Olivia's choice of words. She isn't one to just curse on the regular. "I'm serious," she says, "and if he were here right now, I would tell him that myself."

I shift uncomfortably in my seat, and Nick eyes me curiously. He's probably putting the pieces together. Jase and me meeting ten years ago, me getting upset at the tattoo shop... It wouldn't take a rocket scientist to figure it out.

Giselle and Killian come over and sit next to Nick, both of them eyeing the situation, probably feeling the tension surrounding us. "What's going on?" Giselle asks, concerned.

Before I can stop Olivia from talking, she says, "Some dickhead broke Celeste's heart ten years ago, and I was just telling her that if I ever see him, I'll punch him in the arm for hurting her." She glares, and I stifle my laugh at how adorable she is. Olivia wouldn't hurt a fly.

"Ten years ago..." Killian muses. His head tilts to the side slightly and then his gaze goes over my shoulder. I don't need to look back to know who he's looking at. He knows who broke my heart. How? I have no clue. But he knows. I saw it in his eyes when we were at dinner and Jase got brought up.

"Yeah, when she was eighteen," Olivia adds.

"I need another drink," I tell no one. Reaching over, I snag a shot from the tray and down it in one gulp. Giselle's brows raise. She knows too. She's perceptive. She saw the way I reacted to Jase coming tonight.

"What was his name?" Nick asks. "The guy who broke your heart."

"It doesn't matter," I tell him, but my words come out in a slur since I'm now well on my way to being drunk. Both Killian and Giselle eye me speculatively, but I ignore them.

"Give me back my clutch," I say to Nick.

"Give me a name."

"Fine. Keep my clutch!" I huff. "I'm going to go dance." Standing slowly, so I don't wobble or trip, I turn on my heel and walk away, not waiting for anyone to respond. The music is pumping through the speakers and the crowd has filled in. I head straight for the middle, where I saw Jase and that skank earlier, and find a guy who isn't attached to dance with.

One song blurs into the next. I have no clue how long I've been dancing for, but the alcohol has officially made its way through my body. I'm drunk and sweaty. The guy I've been dancing with pulls me into his body and whispers, "You're fucking sexy. Let's go." I attempt to shake my head no, but because of how drunk I am, I'm not sure it actually moves.

"Yes," he insists, taking my hand and pulling me off the dance floor.

"Umm..." I begin, but my fuzzy brain works too slowly, and I can't think clearly. "My...my clutch is over there." I turn to find where everyone is sitting, but the room spins slightly, and I stumble on my own two feet. I squint my eyes to find the table, but everything is kind of blurry. The guy ignores me, pulling me along, not even slowing down when I stumble once again.

"I...I need to find my friends," I slur, trying to pull on his hand to stop him—with no success. His grip is too tight. I have no clue where we're going or where we even are, but suddenly my body flies backward and hits a hard...wall? No, that can't be right. From the force of being pulled back, my hand is yanked out of the guy's. When he notices, he looks back and his eyes go wide. I tilt my head to the side to see what's going on, and that's when I see him. Jase.

"What the fuck, dude," the guy hisses.

"She won't be going anywhere with you," Jase growls, and without even waiting for the guy to respond, he grabs my hand and pulls me in the opposite direction. I stumble slightly, but unlike the other guy, Jase notices, and instead of ignoring it, he stops walking and turns around, then lifts me into his arms, bridal style. If I were sober, I would yell at him to put me down. He's the last guy I want to carry me. The last person I want to touch me. But I'm drunk, and his warm body feels good, even comforting. So, I just go with it, wrapping my arms around his neck. The room is now spinning, so I close my eyes and nuzzle my face into his chest. Taking a deep breath, I inhale his scent. He still smells the same as he did all those years ago. All man and comfort and warmth. I should be pushing myself away from him instead of snuggling closer. Being this close to him is not going to bode well for my emotional or mental health once I'm sober. But drunk me doesn't seem to care. So, instead of freaking out, I release a long sigh and allow the vibration of his body to lull me to sleep.

EIGHT

*J*ASE

AS I CARRY Celeste through the club, toward the VIP section, so I can get her shit and take her home, anger is emanating through my veins at the fucking asshole who thought he would take advantage of a drunk girl, at Celeste for putting herself in that situation in the first place, at her friends for not keeping a closer eye on her, and most of all, at me. Because there's no doubt in my mind that she's drunk because of the lies I spoke to my brother. Because even after all these years, I'm still butt hurt over her walking away without even so much as a fucking goodbye, like what we shared, what she gave me, didn't mean shit to her. When the truth is, it meant every-fuckingthing to me.

The second her friends spot her in my arms, they jump up to come to the rescue—too late, I might add. Nick and Olivia start spitting out questions, and Celeste's model friend—I can't remember her name even though we were introduced earlier—Benz, Cadillac, or some shit like that—reaches for Celeste, as if she's going to carry her herself. With her still in my arms, I shake my head, not bothering to speak. It's too loud for anyone to hear me, and right now, I know if I do talk, shit will come out that I might regret later. I have one goal right now: to get whatever she came with and find out where she lives. My eyes lock with Nick's and he frowns. I'm not sure if it's at me, Celeste, the situation, or at himself, but right now it doesn't even matter.

"Is she okay?" Olivia asks. All I can do is shake my head. "She only had a few shots over here. I saw her dancing with that guy, but I don't think she had any more to drink."

"We can get her home," Nick offers. I shake my head again, still unable to speak without freaking the fuck out.

"Okay," Olivia says, "let me get her purse." She scurries around the table while everyone stays standing in place, unsure of what to do or say.

"She can come home with me," Mercedes—that's her name!—offers, and her husband nods in agreement. I simply shake my head again.

Olivia places her tiny purse on Celeste since my hands are currently full, then says, "I'll have Nick text you her address." She moves a few damp strands of hair from Celeste's face, but she doesn't even stir. She's out. "Can you please let us know when she's home safe? Maybe I should go too and stay with her." Olivia's eyes fill with tears. "I knew she was drinking, but I didn't know..."

"Hey," Nick says, "Celeste just doesn't drink...like ever." He gives me a hard stare. "She's a lightweight. We should've cut her off. She was upset, so I didn't stop her. She's okay," he says to Olivia. "Jase will get her home and make sure she's okay. Right, man?"

"Yeah," I grunt. "I'll let you know," I tell Olivia.

"Okay, thank you. I'll go by and see her in the morning."

With one last nod, I carry her out of the club. Even though she weighs no more than a buck twenty dripping wet, because of her being out cold, she's like dead weight in my arms. So I'm grateful when I spot a cab parked in front of the club, and I'm able to sit down with her still in my arms. She shifts slightly, and I take a breath I didn't know I was holding. Pulling out my phone, I find her address in a text from Nick. I relay it to the cab driver and he takes off. When we arrive, we're in front of a huge building directly in front of Central Park. I double check the address and throw a twenty at the driver, not needing change. I walk through the lobby and the concierge eyes me cautiously. Something I'm used to. It doesn't matter where I go, with the tattoos covering my body, I get noticed.

"I need to bring her up to her place," I tell him. "I imagine she has a key in her purse, but I can't grab it."

He nods once. "What's your name?" I give him all my information, glad Celeste lives somewhere safe, somewhere that cares about her well-being. Once I'm done, he scans his card, so the elevator opens, gives me Celeste's floor and number, and hands me a spare key to her place.

"Thank you."

Once I get us inside, I take her straight to her room. The doors are all open, so it's easy to spot which one is hers. I lay her in the middle of her big bed, which makes her appear even tinier than she is. Pulling off each of her heels, I drop them to the floor. She's dressed in a tight black dress, and I can't imagine it's comfortable, but I'm not about to take her clothes off. Instead, I pull the blankets out from under her and cover her. Celeste stirs, her eyes opening slightly.

"Stay, please," she slurs. "I don't want to be alone." Her eyes are already closed, and I doubt she'll even remember what she said, but I still stay. I use the excuse that I need to make sure she's okay before I go. I spot a chair in the corner of her room, but it's too far away to see her in the dark. So, I toe off my shoes and climb into the bed next to her. I watch her sleep for a few minutes before she stirs once more.

Her eyes flutter open once again. "Jase?" she croaks.

"Yeah, I'm here." I run my fingers through her hair and her eyes roll back slightly.

"What does she have?" she whispers.

"Huh?" I question, unsure of what she's talking about.

"I could've given you it," she slurs, "whatever you wanted." I have no clue what she's talking about, but now isn't the time to ask. She's drunk and barely conscious. I almost wonder if maybe she's mistaking me for her boyfriend, but she used my name, so she knows it's me...

"Shh...go to sleep, Dimples."

Her lips turn down into an adorable pout as she mumbles, "But I don't want this dream to end." I continue to play with her hair until her breathing evens out and I know she's back to sleep. Pulling my cell phone out, I send a text to Jax and Quinn to let them know where I am and that I'll be home before Skyla wakes up. And then for the next few hours I watch Celeste sleep and wonder what our life would be like had she not left me. I know it's probably crazy to assume we would still be together. We were young, and the odds were against us, but the way I felt about her back then...I have no doubt I wouldn't have tried with every part of me to keep her.

"DAD! YOU'RE HOME!" Skyla bounds toward the front door, her errant red curls bouncing along the way. She wraps her arms around my waist and gives me a hug. I thought as she got older, she would shy away from being a Daddy's girl, but she hasn't, and it warms my heart at the relationship we have. I've heard horror stories about girls in their teenage years, but so far, my daughter is proving to be the exception. "Where were you? It's not like you to be out all night." She smirks slyly. "Were you...out on a date?" She waggles her eyebrows playfully.

My little girl is growing up too damn fast and is becoming way too perceptive. My hope was to get home before she woke up, but when I sat down on Celeste's bed to watch over her, I ended up passing out. I woke up to my phone going off with a text from Quinn, letting me know Skyla was up and asking questions. After leaving a bottle of water and two Advil on Celeste's nightstand, I left her sleeping to come home. Since the day Skyla became mine, I've done everything in my power to provide a stable home for her, and that includes being home every morning when she wakes up and being the one to put her to bed every night. At thirteen years old, she technically doesn't need me to tuck her in, but I still want to be there.

"No, I wasn't out on a date. A friend of mine wasn't feeling well, so I was taking care of her," I tell her, trying not to lie too badly. Quinn comes from around the corner and gives me a curious look but doesn't say anything.

"If you're good, I'm going to head out," Quinn says. "Sky, your pancakes are ready." She shoots my daughter a wink, and Skyla heads straight to the kitchen to eat her breakfast, leaving Quinn and me alone.

"Jax already told me you took Celeste home," Quinn says, judgment evident in her tone. I love my sister to death, but she's as protective as they come. It doesn't matter that Jax and I are older than she is. "It's been what...ten years since she left you, Jase?"

"Eleven," I murmur, then flinch at the fact that I know exactly how long it's been. "I was just making sure a woman who drank too much got home safe," I say nonchalantly, but even to my own ears, I sound like I'm full of shit. "How did everything go here?" I ask, changing the subject.

"Good. We hung out and watched a movie. Skyla insisted we watch Pirates of the Caribbean, so..." She shrugs a shoulder.

"Yeah, I'm sure." I laugh. "More like, you begged, and my daughter took pity on you." Quinn is obsessed with the Pirates of the Caribbean movies. The woman has probably watched all of them a hundred times. She even has a tattoo of Jack Sparrow on her thigh. And since I'm the one who did it, I can tell you it looks damn good.

"Semantics." She rolls her eyes playfully, knowing it drives me nuts. Especially since my daughter does the same thing, having had picked up on it from her aunt years ago.

"I need to get home. Rick flew in this morning, and I want to make him breakfast." She winks, then grabs her purse off the couch as I playfully gag at her insinuation of what she really wants to do with him. Rick is her boyfriend of about six months. I'm not happy with how fast things are moving with them, but my sister is a big girl, and I have to let her make her own mistakes.

When we first moved to New York, Quinn, Jax, and I all lived together in a small apartment. But once the shop started to make decent money, we moved into a bigger home in Cobble Hill—a smaller, less busy neighborhood in Brooklyn. While Jax still lives here with Skyla and me, a few months ago, Quinn and her boyfriend decided to get their own place—an expensive high-rise condo in the Upper East Side. He's some type of corporate mogul who owns several businesses all over the world. It seems like he's gone more than he's home, but Quinn doesn't ever complain, so I keep my opinions to myself. Plus, while he's traveling, Quinn will often spend the night here with us, so that works out well for me, and Skyla loves spending time with her Aunt.

"Dad, your pancakes are getting cold," Skyla yells.

"Be right there!" I shout back. "Thanks for keeping an eye on her," I tell my sister.

"Any time...Oh!—" she stops in her place and turns around "—Rick has to fly out next weekend for a last-minute business deal, so he won't be able to attend the wedding with me after all." She frowns. "Would you mind if I tagged along with you?"

Olivia and Nick's wedding is at the Yacht Club in the Hamptons, and since they both insisted Skyla was more than welcome to join, I thought it would be a nice weekend getaway. It's the summer in New York, and the place we're staying at has a nice pool that Skyla will love to swim in.

"Of course. Jax is leaving Gage to run the place, so we can all drive over together." Gage is one of the tattooists that works for us. When the shop took off, Jax and I couldn't handle the place on our own any longer, so we hired two other artists—Gage and Willow. Quinn has also been helping us out while we look for a fulltime receptionist. She's building up her photography business, which means she's able to make her own hours.

After Quinn leaves, I join Skyla for breakfast. She pushes the butter and syrup my way, and when I look up, she's smiling nervously.

"What's up?" I ask, knowing my daughter. That smile means she wants to ask me for something.

"I was thinking, once school is out for the summer, we could go visit Mom. I really want to give her the signed paper Celeste gave me. I still can't believe I met her. She said she knew you... How do you know her? Why didn't you tell me? That's something super important, Dad. She's the best model in the industry...in the entire world."

I tune out her rambling, stuck on the words that she wants to go visit her mom. It's been a little over a year since the last time we went to visit Amaya. While I would never stop my daughter from visiting her mom, I hate going there. I hate Skyla seeing her mom in that state. Every time we go to visit her, she ends up afraid and upset, asking questions I don't have the answers to. In the past, because she was so young, once we were back home, she would forget how scared and upset she was and ask to visit her mom again. Now, though, she's getting older, and I'm not sure whether she'll be scared and upset or understand and be okay. It shouldn't be this way. No child should have to visit their mom in that condition. But it's out of my hands. I can't control the decisions her family makes. I'm just grateful that, for the most part, they leave Skyla and me alone.

"Dad..." I'm not sure how many times Skyla has said my name, but by the annoyed look on her face, it must've been a few times.

"Sorry, yeah, we can go visit your mom," I tell her, ignoring the second half of her question about how I know Celeste. I'm not ready to go there, especially not with my daughter. "I'm not sure when, but we'll go for sure this summer."

"Thanks!" Skyla jumps out of her seat and comes around the table to give me a hug.

NINE

*C*ELESTE

"THANK YOU, again, for coming with me." I squeeze Adam's hand and he smiles softly at me, knowing how much him being here truly means to me. I met Adam several years ago when he was just beginning his modeling career. We clicked immediately and a wonderful friendship blossomed. Over the years, Adam's and my friendship has turned into so much more. He's like a brother to me. When Chad and I broke up and I knew I was going to have to attend this wedding solo, Adam insisted he join me so I wouldn't be alone. His boyfriend, Felix, is one of the top photographers in the business and is away on a shoot, so it worked out perfect.

"You know I wouldn't be anywhere else." Adam leans over and gives me a kiss on my cheek. "Now, get your butt inside and get dressed. I can't wait to see you walk down the aisle." He shoots me a flirty wink and I laugh humorlessly.

"Take pictures. It will probably be the only time I ever walk down an aisle." I roll my eyes, trying to play my insecurities off, and Adam frowns.

"If I didn't know better, I would think the idea of you *not* getting married is what's upsetting you. Has my little ice queen thawed?" He gives me a quizzical look, but I don't answer him. Instead, I turn to head to the room where all the women in the wedding are getting ready.

"See you soon!" I call out over my shoulder.

"This conversation isn't over," Adam yells back through a laugh.

I'M DRESSED in a simple royal blue V-neck halter gown with a floor length charmeuse skirt that has a slit running up the side. It's tasteful and elegant. I must admit, Olivia did a fabulous job when she chose my dress. I've seen enough wedding designs to know most bridesmaids end up in something ugly because the bride is too afraid to be outdone. The other women in Olivia's wedding party are in something similar, each dress varying slightly. Olivia, of course, looks absolutely stunning in her wedding dress. It's a white strapless gown with a fitted bodice and a wide, full tulle skirt that shows off her adorable baby bump. She truly looks like a Disney Princess. Giselle and her stepmom, Corinne, dote on her while the hair and makeup team finish getting her ready. I use this time to slip out and visit Nick. I knock once on the door and Killian opens it.

"Celeste," he says politely with a curt nod. "You look beautiful." After I stare at him stunned for a second, I smile and thank him. I'm not sure I'll ever get over the shock of Killian being nice to me.

"I'll give you two a moment alone," Killian says before making himself scarce.

"Celeste," Nick says, giving me a hug and a kiss on my cheek. "You look gorgeous as always." He hands me a small box. "Thank you for doing this."

"Of course," I say back, taking in his fitted tuxedo. His tie is royal blue, matching the bridesmaids' dresses and the jewels in Olivia's princess tiara. As I stare at my best friend, I can't help but get choked up. While I'm extremely happy for him, I'm also sad. It wasn't too long ago that Nick and I were engaged, and I was planning our wedding. I know we never would've worked out, and I don't view Nick as anything more than a friend, but being with him kept what's left of my heart safe. I didn't run the risk of it being stomped on or broken any more. Now it feels as though the tiny slivers of my heart, which are still left intact, are out there for anyone to take and destroy.

"Thank you," he says softly.

I give him a confused look. "You already thanked me."

"Not for bringing Olivia my wedding gift." He shakes his head. "For being my best friend. For being you." His eyes gloss over with unshed tears. "You know I'm always going to be here for you no matter what, right?"

"I know." I nod. "I'm so happy that you found your one." Tears of my own surface and I blink several times, willing them away, so they don't ruin my makeup.

"You know it's time, right?" Nick says. "To find yourself someone to love."

"I don't think I can do it," I admit quietly. "I don't think I know how to."

"You do," he says with a small smile. "You just have to let go of all that hurt."

"How? How did you let go of it all?"

"I had no choice," he says, his smile widening. "I had to make room in my heart for Olivia and Reed."

"Yeah, well, my problem is a little different," I blurt out. My heart isn't just filled with hurt. It's damaged beyond repair. Nobody wants something that's been used and abused, when they can have something new and shiny and perfect.

"How?"

"It doesn't matter." I flick away a traitor tear and plaster on a smile. "Today is your big day. Don't let my problems bring you down." I shake the box he handed me. "I'll make sure Olivia gets this."

I turn to walk away, but Nick catches my wrist. "Was it Jase, Celeste? Did he break your heart?"

The tears I worked so hard not to let fall, do, as I nod my head once and whisper, "Yes."

Nick turns me around to face him, and with a deep frown, asks, "What happened?" I can see it in his features, hear it in his tone, he isn't going to take a brush-off. We're no longer in a crowded, loud club surrounded by our friends. It's just Nick and me, and my truth.

"I-I fell in love with him. It was stupid, really. It was only a few days, and I was young..." I try to downplay my feelings, but Nick's head tilts slightly, telling me he isn't buying it. "Anyway, I was going to give up the summer internship to stay with him." Nick's eyes widen at my words. "But when I went to talk to him about it, I caught him with another woman." I shrug.

"Fuck, Celeste." Nick pulls me into a hug. "Say the word and he's gone."

"No, it's okay," I tell him as we pull away. "It was a long time ago and clearly all the feelings were one-sided. What's done is done."

"Except it's not," Nick points out. "Whatever happened between you two has been lingering and festering for years. Maybe it's time you two talk and get some closure."

"You're right." And he is. I've spent too many years allowing my broken heart to steer my life. I meant what I said when I broke things off with Chad. I want to find love. In order to do that, I need to have a whole heart to give someone, and I can't do that as long as I allow mine to remain broken. Now, I just have to work up the courage to talk to Jase.

After giving Nick one last hug, I head back over to Olivia's room to give her Nick's gift. It's a beautiful necklace with a charm of an open book on it. On the back is their wedding date with an inscription that reads: *This isn't the epilogue... it's the first chapter of a new book.*

THE WEDDING WAS BEAUTIFUL, full of happy tears and laughter. Happy tears, when Olivia and Nick said their vows, promising to love each other as they continue to write their story. Laughter, when Reed insisted on joining them at the alter as they kissed.

Once they were pronounced husband and wife, we spent the next hour taking pictures, and then came the reception. So far— through the couple's first dance, the sit-down dinner, the toasts and speeches, and cutting of the cake—I've managed to successfully avoid Jase. Nick and Olivia have announced their departure, thanking everyone for joining them, and I've just taken a deep breath, feeling confident that I might make it through the wedding *and* reception without running into Jase. But apparently my confidence was premature, because I haven't even finished exhaling, when I spot a beautiful red-head, dressed in a pale pink shift dress, heading straight over to me. She locks eyes with me, grinning wide, and I know my luck has run out.

"Celeste!" Skyla screeches, and Adam gives me a curious look. "You're here! Wow! Your dress is gorgeous. Not quite as beautiful as your spring couture line, but still gorgeous, especially for a bridesmaid's dress. Have you seen some of the ones brides pick out? I swear they design them ugly on purpose, so they can't outdo the bride." She shivers dramatically, her nose scrunching up in disgust, and I giggle, having thought the same thing earlier. "It *is* possible to go simple *and* pretty without outshining the bride." When she stops speaking, her eyes find Adam and she smiles, as if she's just now noticing I'm not sitting alone.

"Hello," she says, lifting her chin a tad and extending her hand. "I'm Skyla." Adam takes her hand in his, and I notice her nails are done. They aren't fake, but they're long and neat, and she's sporting a french manicure.

"Skyla, this is my friend Adam. He's a model."

"I know." She nods. "I've seen you in ads for Ralph Lauren, Tom Ford, Gap, and for Celeste's clothing line," she says matter-of-factly. Adam's eyes light up, and I grin. Girl knows her stuff.

"I was," Adam says, extending his hand. "It's nice to meet you. Are you a model?"

"Not yet. Dad says I'm too young—" She rolls her eyes "—but I plan to be. I also want to design jewelry and makeup and clothes like Celeste does, but I'll have a children's and teen line as well. You have no idea how hard it is to find stylish clothes when you're a kid, and being a teenager isn't much better. Designers don't seem to understand that not all teens want to dress trashy."

Taking a closer look at Skyla's outfit, I notice the tiny gold tulle layers and the embellished gold sequin flowers on her dress. Then my gaze goes down to her matching pale pink ballet flats. I'm not sure who she's wearing, but I know her outfit isn't cheap. The girl seriously has good taste in fashion.

I can't help the laugh that escapes when I think about how ironic it is that Jase's daughter is the exact opposite of him. I can't even imagine how he deals with her. Then it hits me... he probably doesn't. It's probably all her mom—Amaya. And with that sobering thought, my laughter comes to an abrupt halt.

"I agree," Adam says to Skyla. "Class over trash any day."

When he shoots me a confused look, silently asking who this girl is, I say, "Skyla is *Jase's* daughter." It takes him a second, but I can tell when it all clicks. He's one of the few people who knows my entire story. "Is your dad here?" I ask Skyla. The last thing I need is to run into Jase...and his date.

"He's getting us another piece of cake. I wish my mom could be here. Red Velvet is her favorite."

"Why couldn't she be here?" I ask before I can stop my nosiness.

Her lips turn down into a frown. "She's sick." Then, as if she's just remembered something, her face lights back up. "My dad said I can give her the paper you signed. We're going to visit her this summer once school's out."

Her words swirl in my head, and it hits me that she said they're going to visit her this summer. They must not be together after all. If they were, they wouldn't be going to visit her. Well, serves him right. But then I feel bad because if they aren't together that means Skyla is part of a broken family, and I wouldn't wish that on any child.

"Will you be in Paris for Fashion Week?" Skyla asks.

"Leblanc will be participating, but I won't personally be there. I'm actually partaking in a new fashion show, right here in New York."

"Oh! The Global Fashion Extravaganza? I heard it's going to be amazing! That it could even possibly replace Fashion Week."

Adam laughs. "Well, look at you! All in the know. You should be interning at Leblanc." He gives me a knowing look, which I ignore.

"I'm still in school," Skyla says with a shrug.

"You're right," I tell her, "it is the Global Fashion Extravaganza, also known as GFE. We're hoping, not to replace Fashion Week, but give fashion four seasons instead of two. There's also a huge charity fashion show on the last day."

"I'm planning to live-stream it the entire week," Skyla says excitedly. I almost tell her I could get her tickets, but remember Jase is her father, and the last thing I want to do is weave my life in with his—even if his daughter is completely amazing.

"Skyla, there you are!" Quinn exclaims. She glances from her niece to me and glares. "You can't take off on your own."

"I'm not a child." Skyla scoffs. "I'm thirteen." Thirteen... I quickly do the math in my head, but it doesn't add up. That would mean Skyla was two years old when I met Jase. He had a daughter and didn't mention it? He introduced Amaya to me as his *friend*...so what were they? Friends with benefits? They had a daughter together but weren't together... *Just sleeping together apparently.*

"Celeste," Quinn says curtly, knocking me out of my thoughts.

"Quinn," I say back. Then to Skyla, I say, "I need to use the ladies' room before I leave, but it was wonderful to see you again. Enjoy your cake, sweet girl." I stand and bend at the waist to give Skyla an air kiss to each of her cheeks. She reciprocates, acting more like an adult than her actual age. And as I walk away, I can't help but wonder what it would be like if Skyla were mine and Jase's instead of Amaya's and his.

With that thought, I change course, suddenly in need of a stiff drink, ignoring the part deep inside of me that is wagging her finger and telling me that drinking is not the answer. My mother is proof of that.

When the bartender asks what I would like, I tell her I don't care. She grabs a metal shaker, pours a few different ingredients into it, then shakes it all up. Grabbing a tall shot glass, she pours the bright red concoction into it then grabs a strawberry, slipping it onto the rim. "One red-headed slut," she announces as she lays down a napkin in front of me and sets the drink on it. I bark out a loud laugh at the name. How fitting. I down the alcoholic beverage and ask for another.

Just as she's taking my empty glass, a good-looking gentleman approaches and says, "Make that two."

"But you don't even know what I'm drinking," I sass.

"If you're drinking it, I'm sure it's top shelf. I can't imagine you wasting your time on anything less."

The bartender repeats what she did before, only this time doubling the ingredients. When she sets our glasses in front of us, she once again says, "Two red-headed sluts." The gentleman laughs with a shake of his head. We both take a glass and, after clinking them against each other, throw our shots back.

"Real nice," I hear a voice hiss. When I turn around, I spot Jase. At one point he must've been in a suit, but now, his jacket is missing, and his powder blue button-down shirt is rolled up at the sleeves, exposing all of his sexy-as-sin tattoos. His hair is gelled neatly to the side, and peeking out of his collar are a few more intricate tattoos. He screams sex and bad boy and... cheater. "You are aware my daughter is a redhead as well," he points out.

"And you do know she isn't the slut I would be referring to had I actually picked the drink." I wave him off. The bartender, God love her, hands me another shot, which I down as quickly as the last two. "She picked the drink, not me, but I must say it is rather fitting."

I slam the glass down and walk away from Jase. I don't realize he's following me until I enter the ladies' room and hear the door close behind me. When I whirl around, Jase is standing there with his arms crossed over his chest, his muscular forearms on display.

"Jealousy doesn't look good on you," he says with a smirk.

"Fuck you."

"Tsk, tsk, that's not very ladylike, Celeste. What would all your admirers think if they heard you talking like trailer trash instead of the high-class woman everyone knows you as?" *They would probably think it makes more sense since that's where I came from...*

"For your information," I hiss, ignoring his question, "I'm not jealous."

"As you shouldn't be." Jase shrugs nonchalantly, but when he speaks, his words are anything but. "You have everything you could ever want, right? Money, fame, status. You achieved every dream you ever dreamt." He steps closer and I back up, my butt hitting the edge of the marble counter.

"Maybe you should focus on your perfect little family and not worry about what I have." I wait to see if he confirms or denies what I'm implying, but he does neither, giving nothing away.

Instead, he simply laughs, but it comes out all wrong. It doesn't sound melodic and carefree and beautiful like I remember it sounding all those years ago. No, this laugh is devoid of all humor and happiness. He places his hands on either side of my body, caging me in. "The perfect family?" He chuckles darkly. "You have no fucking idea what you're talking about." When the coolness of his breath hits my ear, I let out a shaky breath. It's been too long since I felt Jase's body against mine. He's so close. His groin rubs against my front, and I shiver in response. *Damn traitor body.*

"It's been eleven years, yet your body still responds to mine," he murmurs. Backing up slightly, his hazel eyes meeting my onyx ones. Then his eyes travel a few inches south, landing on my mouth. His tongue darts out slightly, wetting his lips. He's going to kiss me. I can feel it in my bones. I should stop him. Push him away. But I don't. And just as I predicted, seconds later his mouth crashes against mine. Our tongues meet and duel with one another. Jase's fingers dig into my sides as he lifts me onto the counter. My legs wrap around his waist as my fingers grip the back of his hair, pulling him closer to me.

As our kiss deepens, moans release from the both of us, echoing in the otherwise silent bathroom. His hands glide up my thighs, my dress bunching up at my waist. I release his hair, undoing his button and zipper. Using my heel, I push his pants and briefs down as Jase pulls my lace panties to the side, pushing his fingers into me. A loud sigh escapes my lips as my head goes back, hitting the mirror. His lips find my neck, and as he trails soft, wet kisses across my now-heated flesh, he pulls his fingers out of me, jerks me forward, and thrusts his entire hard length into me. He feels so good, but different...something about him is different. Is that...Is he...pierced?

"Fuck, Celeste," Jase growls, pushing my thoughts away as he fucks me hard and deep. His fingers are digging into my sides. It should hurt, but it only adds to the pleasure. I feel my orgasm building with every thrust of his hips, and then he hits my sweet spot.

"Yes, right there!" I scream. Jase listens, hitting it again and again. And before I know it, my entire body lets go, and I come harder than I ever have before. My body shakes as my orgasm continues to rip right through me. Jase nuzzles his face into my neck, his lips sucking on my perspired skin as he follows right behind. My eyes are closed, and I take a deep breath, enjoying the moment of pure bliss.

But then he stills, his now semi-soft dick still in me, and reality hits. I just let Jase fuck me...without a condom. I'm on the pill, but that's not really the point. I'm about to say something, when Jase speaks first.

"Fuck, this was a mistake." I might've been thinking the same thing, but fuck him for saying it first. I push him back and his dick slides out—the mess of what we just did drips out of me.

I can't help the maniacal laugh that escapes my lips as Jase stares at his cum dripping down the inside of my thigh. Reaching over, I grab a paper towel to wipe it up.

"That shouldn't have happened," Jase says. "I don't cheat." And with those words, I snap my head up to give him my full attention, my focus on cleaning up no longer a priority.

"Good to see you now have morals," I say, laughing even harder, "but you don't have to worry." I jump down off the sink and throw the paper towel into the garbage. "My boyfriend and I broke up last week."

"And the guy you're here with?"

"Just a friend."

I turn around slowly and lock eyes with Jase, realizing I just had sex—granted, it was hate sex, but still sex—with the man who cheated on me and broke my heart. And then his words sink in. He said he doesn't cheat. I assumed he was referring to me being in a relationship, but he could've been talking about himself as well. I don't even know if he's with anyone. Does he have a girlfriend? A fiancée? Oh my God, is he married? Suddenly, I feel cheap and dirty and want to take a long, hot shower to get Jase off my flesh.

"And what about you?" I whisper. "Are you...with someone?" If he could cheat on me, who's to say he wouldn't do it to someone else. We might be older, but there's a reason for the saying: once a cheater, always a cheater... "Are you with anyone?" Based on what his daughter said, I assumed he was single. But you know what they say about people who assume...especially with his track record. I quickly glance down at his left hand, relieved that there's at least no ring on his finger.

"What if I am?"

"Then it wouldn't surprise me that you have no problem fucking someone else." I shrug my shoulders with all the confidence I don't have, and walk out the door.

TEN

*J*ASE

"THEN IT WOULDN'T SURPRISE *me that you have no problem fucking someone else.*" I can't get Celeste's words out of my head. They don't make any sense. Why would she believe I would ever be okay having sex with someone while with someone else? I wanted to chase her down and ask her what she meant by that, but when I got outside, she was nowhere to be found. My daughter and Quinn were, though, and while Quinn kept giving me a knowing look like she could tell something went down, she couldn't voice her suspicions because of Skyla being with us. During the elevator ride up to our room, Skyla went on and on about how she ran into Celeste and met her model friend Adam. She didn't even notice that, while I was gone for a while, I didn't return with the cake I originally set out to get us.

After Skyla showered and went to bed, I grabbed a bottle of Johnnie that the resort keeps in stock to purchase and took it out onto the terrace with me before Quinn could start in on her interrogation. My thoughts couldn't escape what Celeste and I did—what she said afterward. Over the years, I've had my fair share of one-night stands. I've even been in a couple short-term relationships. But not once have I ever gone in raw. No glove, no love. Every man knows that rule. Sure, when we were together before, she was on birth control, but I don't know her situation now, and I definitely don't know who she's been with.

Yet, I didn't even think twice about going in without a rubber—just like all those years ago. From the moment I laid my eyes on Celeste at that party, it's as if she somehow bewitched me. I don't think logically or rationally when she's near me. My dick and my heart seem to be the only two organs that function when she's around.

The longer I drink, the more my mind replays the events from tonight. The way Celeste felt with her legs wrapped around me. The way she tugged on my hair, and the way her tight cunt clenched around my cock as I fucked her. I couldn't even tell you who initiated it—probably me—but I can tell you that, even though it's been eleven damn years since I've been with her, it felt as if no time had passed.

While her body is less girl and more woman, her soft, pouty lips haven't changed a bit. The way she kissed me, it was as if everything of mine was hers for the taking. She owned my body, heart, and soul all those years ago, and tonight, I realized she could easily take it all again. But the question is, could I let her? Would I even have a choice? First things first, I needed to find out why she left me all those years ago without even so much as a goodbye. The way she's acted every time I've run into her, it's as if I'm in the wrong, which makes no sense. She's the one who lied about her age, and where she went to school, and about her damn modeling gig in New York. Hell, she's the one who got on a plane and left me.

I should be the one that's pissed—and I am. But at the same time, all those damn feelings I had are coming back in full swing. No woman has ever affected me the way Celeste does. With a single look, a simple touch, she knocks me off my game. Over the years, I thought Skyla being so into modeling was God's way of laughing at me, mocking me. Of all the things my daughter could be into, of course she has to be into fashion—sketching, drawing, designing, modeling. She loves it all. And for most kids, that would mean observing the latest trends from afar. But for Skyla, because her grandparents are ridiculously wealthy, it means she's able to enjoy the luxuries of name brand clothes up close and personal. Some days, my daughter puts on outfits that cost more than the monthly payment on the mortgage for the townhouse we live in, which is something I try not to think about. Because, despite me not wanting my child to wear shit like Burberry and Ralph Lauren, Amaya's parents, Monica and Phil, asked that I accept the gifts they send her every month. It was one of their stipulations when I told them I wanted to move to New York. Most grandparents would ask to visit every so often, or to receive phone calls, but not them. Their way of showing love is through materialistic possessions. While I didn't agree with it—still don't—it meant getting to leave with my daughter without them putting up a fight. I've learned over the years to pick my battles with them.

Their other stipulation was for Skyla to attend private school. Since there was no way I could ever afford to send her to one myself, and I'm man enough to admit that, I agreed. Being a father comes first, and if that means allowing her grandparents to pay for her schooling, then so be it. Skyla loves her school, and I love that she's getting a top-notch education. There's even an art club she's part of there. Several days after school she also attends a STEM program for kids, which allows her to learn technology through fashion design. My daughter has a bright future ahead of her.

"You drunk yet?" Quinn asks, stepping out onto the terrace.

"Not enough," I murmur, taking another swig.

"I saw Celeste storm out of the bathroom..." When I don't acknowledge her words, she adds, "And you storm out right afterward."

I nod in affirmation, but still don't speak. What is there to say? Quinn was there the day I found out that the girl I could see a future with had lied to me then skipped town. She was there the day I saw Celeste on the stupid modeling show and threw my phone at the screen, shattering it. And she was there the day my daughter announced Celeste was her role model and wanted to be just like her. And I had no choice but to smile and nod and agree that Celeste is beautiful and talented. Which she was—is—but it still hurt like hell admitting out loud.

One week was all I had with her. She shouldn't have been anything more than a blip on my fucking radar. I've been with dozens of women since her, and I couldn't tell you half their names. But Celeste, if I close my eyes and focus hard enough, I could tell you everything about her. The way she smelled like the beach and roses. The way she moaned softly every time she came because she was young and embarrassed, but it felt too good for her to hold it in. I could tell you how soft her skin was and point out where every freckle she has is located because I spent hours learning every inch of her body while she slept—and while she was awake. I could tell you the adorable way she scrunched her nose up when she wasn't sure of something. The way she blushed when I said something crass—which I did just to see her cheeks flush pink.

So while she shouldn't have been anything more than some chick I fucked a few times—okay, several times—she was more than that. Through my daughter, I watched Celeste's career explode. From her modeling, to the startup of her company. I watched her grow and blossom into an amazing woman who chased her dreams and held onto them like they were her lifeline. I watched her become engaged to Nick...and then I watched it end. All while assuming she probably wouldn't even recognize me if she saw me in person. Until she walked into my shop and did, in fact, recognize me. And in that moment, I thought maybe she would apologize for leaving, or at the very least, explain. But she did neither. She snapped at me and acted like I was the bad guy. And then after hugging my brother, who she barely fucking knew, she walked out the door once again.

"Jase, are you going to tell me what happened?" Quinn asks. When I raise a brow, she rolls her eyes. "I didn't mean those details. I meant what's going on with the two of you. I know she's always been the one who got away..." What the hell is up with my siblings referring to her as that?

"She didn't get away. She ran," I say, repeating the same words I said to my brother at the club. After taking another swig of my drink, I add, "And I don't want to talk about it. There's nothing to say." I stand, and without another word, head into my bedroom and close the door behind me.

WANT to know why parents don't get drunk as often once they have kids? It's not because they're more responsible or mature. No, it's because the next day, when those kids wake up at seven in the fucking morning, demanding breakfast and to go to the pool, there is nobody to save your hungover ass because you're the damn parent. Which means, even with a pounding headache that won't go away, you have no choice but to drag yourself out of bed, take a shower, order room service, and pray she doesn't pick today to talk too much or ask too many questions.

"Dad, come in the pool with me!" Skyla screams way too loudly. I've taken several aspirin, but nothing is helping the throbbing pain that feels as if my head was smashed into a cement wall instead of me drinking a bottle of Johnnie last night.

"Alright, alright." Taking my shirt off, I throw it onto the chair, kick my sandals off my feet, then head over to the steps to slowly work my way into the pool. With my aviators on, the sun is slightly dulled. When my feet touch the water, I thank whatever pool God is up there for the pool being warm.

"Yes!" Skyla screeches, and I do my best not to flinch at her voice. It's not my daughter's fault that her father thought it would be a good idea after she went to bed to get stupid drunk in an attempt to temporarily forget the woman he fucked bare in the bathroom at their friends' wedding reception.

"Celeste!" Skyla yells, and my head whips around so fast it feels like a million nails were just hammered into my skull. "Over here!" When I finally spot where Skyla is looking, I see Celeste standing next to a lounge chair in a tiny-as-fuck black and white string bikini. She's bending over as she pushes her shorts down her tanned, toned legs, and her tits, the same ones I was kissing all over last night, are on display. She stands back up, and it's then I notice her flat stomach is donning a belly-button ring, which is glittering in the sunlight. Her hair is pulled up into a messy bun and she's smiling at Skyla hesitantly, trying to decide whether to come over or run away since I'm standing right next to my daughter.

"Celeste, come in!" my daughter yells. "It's warm in here." Celeste's eyes land on mine, but she can't make out my expression because of my shades. She places her shorts on the edge of the lounge chair and kicks off her flip-flops. She's obviously stalling, and I'm secretly enjoying her feeling of uneasiness. She doesn't want to say no, but she also doesn't want to come anywhere near me. But then when my daughter adds in a "please" in her cute-as-fuck innocent voice, I know she's got her. And I grin, despite myself, because I know all too well how hard it is to say no to her when she uses that voice.

"Okay," Celeste says with a nod. After she applies sunscreen to her front, she hands the bottle to her friend, who applies it to her back. And it takes everything in me not to stalk out of the pool, rip the bottle out of his hands, and demand he not touch her. *Friend, my ass...*

I watch as Celeste fixes her hair into a low ponytail and grabs a huge, floppy black hat from her bag, tugging it on so it shades her entire face. The hat is so big, it should look ridiculous, but on her, it looks fucking adorable. A complete contrast to her barely there skimpy bikini. She glides through the water and stops in front of my daughter, making it a point not to look my way.

"Hey, Skyla! Did you enjoy your cake last night?" She smiles so wide, it lights up her entire face.

Skyla frowns and looks at me. "Dad, you never brought me cake." She pouts.

"Sorry, I didn't see any more." I shrug. Thankfully, Skyla doesn't question it because the last thing I want to do is dig myself into a deeper hole. Technically, I'm not lying. I never made it over to the cake to see if there was any more. I hate lying to my daughter, even if it's something as little as a piece of cake. I was lied to by my dad growing up, and I swore I would never be anything like that man. Even if it hurts, I will always tell Skyla the truth.

Celeste's lips twitch, and I know she's thinking about why I never made it to see if there was any more cake. But thankfully she doesn't call me out on it. Instead, she keeps her attention on Skyla. "Are you having fun in the pool?"

"We just got here. Dad woke up with a bad headache and took forever to get out of bed." Skyla rolls her eyes dramatically, and Celeste's lips twitch again. "He said we can only stay for a little while and then we have to go home. I have school tomorrow." Skyla groans.

"Well, school is important," Celeste replies.

"I guess so. I just want to be a model and design clothes. I don't know why I have to go to school for that." Her nose scrunches up in annoyance.

I'm about to give my standard Dad speech—the one I give every time Skyla says this—but Celeste speaks first. "Skyla, school really is important," she says seriously. "It's where you'll learn how to do the math you need to design your clothes. Would you want to wear a shirt that has one arm longer than the other?" Her eyes go wide, and Skyla giggles with a shake of her head.

"No!" Skyla exclaims.

"It's also where you'll learn how to use a computer. You need to know how to use programs like PowerPoint and Excel for meetings, and that's just the beginning."

"What about geography?" Skyla counters like the teenager she is. "Why do I need to know that?"

I stifle a laugh, almost positive my daughter has stumped her, when Celeste says, "Where's Milan?"

"Where Fashion Week is held."

"True, but *where* is Milan?"

"Isn't it a country?"

"Wrong," Celeste says. "It's in Italy. I just got back from there last month. If I didn't know my countries, how would I be able to sell my clothes and jewelry and makeup all over the world." She raises a brow, and Skyla's shoulders slump in defeat.

"I get it," she mutters. "I am in the STEM program," she adds.

"What's that?" Celeste asks.

"I'm learning how to use science and technology to design clothes. I can draw them on the computer."

"Wow!" Celeste exclaims. "That's amazing. It was so hard for me to learn how to use the programs. Sometimes I still have trouble." She frowns, but I can tell it's exaggerated for my daughter's benefit. "I didn't go to college, but I wish I would've. I could've learned so much more. Instead, I needed a lot of people to help me."

"I can help you!" Skyla beams. "I'm practically a genius on the computer."

Celeste smiles warmly. "I would love that." The grin I've been sporting suddenly disappears as I take in the huge smile on Skyla's face. The conversation went from hypothetically designing clothes one day to Skyla helping Celeste. It's not Celeste's fault. I don't even think she realizes what she implied, but that won't stop my daughter from taking it that way.

"Hey Sky..." I start to say, knowing I need to nip this conversation in the bud quickly. But I know I'm too late when Skyla ignores me and asks, "When?" and Celeste's eyes bug out in realization of where the conversation has led to.

"Umm..." she sputters, and for the first time, her gaze goes to me, silently begging for my help.

"Sky, Celeste is really busy," I say. Celeste's brows furrow and her head tilts to the side slightly. I didn't mean it in a bad way, but she's clearly taking it as such. I'm just trying to get her out of the hole she unknowingly dug herself into.

"Oh," Skyla whispers, disappointment dripping in those two letters. She nods once and my heart plummets. I should've figured out sooner where this was leading to, so I could've put a stop to it.

"Actually," Celeste says with defiance clear in her tone, "I'm not that busy at all. I would love for you to come and help me." She plasters on a smile, but I can see through it. It's all false bravado. The woman is so far out of her element right now, but fuck if she isn't trying. And her trying is only making her that much fucking hotter. Because the fact is, she doesn't have to try. Skyla is nothing to Celeste.

"Celeste," I begin, about to tell her she doesn't have to do this, but before I can get the words out, Skyla cuts me off. *What is with these damn women and ignoring me as if I'm not standing right here?*

"Really? That would be awesome! Oh! Since you aren't busy, can you come to my career day next week? It's the last day of school." *Oh, Jesus...*

"Sky," I groan. "Leave her alone, please." I glance over at Celeste, who is now chewing on her bottom lip nervously. My guess is she jumped the gun when she invited Skyla to help her, out of spite, and now she's realizing all that she's agreeing to. The thing about kids is if you give them an inch, nine times out of ten, they'll take a fucking mile.

"Can you?" Skyla repeats.

"Umm...I think so..." Celeste nods once. "I would have to check my calendar, but I think it would be okay..." She bites down on her lip again.

"Yes! Dad did you hear that? Celeste is coming to my career day!" Skyla closes the gap between her and Celeste and pulls her into a hug. Wrapping her arms around my daughter, Celeste's eyes close briefly, and when she opens them, I'm almost certain her eyes are glossed over with unshed tears. But she turns her face away from me quickly, so I can't confirm. *Why would she be about to cry? Does she really hate me that much?*

"Sky, she said she'll try." The last thing I want is for my daughter to get her hopes up and then to be let down. She's been let down enough in her life.

Their hug ends and Celeste says, "I'm going to give your dad my business card so he can text me the info."

Skyla nods and claps her hands together in pure bliss.

ELEVEN

CELESTE

"I'VE BEEN WAITING for over a week for the proofs from the photoshoot, so I can approve the winter mockups, and my email still has nothing from you!" I yell into the speaker at Vince, my photo editor who works with Adam's boyfriend, Felix. He remains silent on the phone—I'm sure shocked as to why I'm snapping at him, when technically the proofs aren't due until the end of the day today, and he's never once, in all the time he's worked for me, been late.

When I stop yelling to breathe, Margie takes my cell phone off the desk and presses the button to take him off speaker. "Please excuse Celeste. She's currently having an out-of-body experience. Aliens, dressed in Gucci and Marchesa, have taken over. We'll be on the lookout for your email later. Ciao." She hangs up and gives me her attention, her head tilting slightly to the side while I glare at her, annoyed at her making jokes while I feel so annoyed and agitated I'm about to rip my skin from my own body.

"This sudden little outburst doesn't have anything to do with a handsome, tattooed, muscular man and his sweet daughter, does it?" She smirks knowingly, and I let out a growl.

"Adam!" I yell at the top of my lungs, knowing he's somewhere close. He was scheduled for a photoshoot today and we're supposed to have lunch when he's done. "Stop talking behind my back!"

I hear a light-hearted chuckle but no response. My phone rings and Margie looks to see who's calling, then hands it to me. "It's Victoria Shaw."

I answer it, praying nothing has happened to my mom. Ever since Nick and I called off our engagement last year, and he disowned his parents after they tried to ruin his relationship with Olivia, Victoria and I have been somewhat on the outs. It was as if a line was crossed, and I chose to side with Nick and Olivia. She was in the wrong, but refuses to see it. Therefore, she hasn't once called me unless it's regarding my mom.

"Victoria," I say, putting the phone back on speaker. I do it out of habit so Margie can take notes.

"Celeste," she says, her voice formal, "I'm calling because I thought you should know your mother has lost her job." My heart plummets into my stomach. Even though I pay all of my mom's bills, she continues to work at the diner for one reason...

"The diner closed," she adds. "She's been sitting outside of it every day..." She doesn't need to finish her sentence for me to know why—in case Snake shows up.

I let out a long sigh, unsure of how to handle this situation.

"Celeste." When Victoria says my name, I remember we're still on the phone.

"Thank you for calling. I'll figure something out." We hang up, and that's when I notice Adam has joined us in the office.

"Your mom needs help," he says, stating the obvious.

"She doesn't want help," I counter. "She wants a man, who, if I wasn't alive as proof, wouldn't even believe exists."

"When's the last time you searched for him?" Margie asks. She, too, is aware of my mother's entire situation.

"I haven't."

"What do you mean, you haven't?" Adam gives me a shocked look. "You have more than enough money to hire a private investigator." When I don't say anything, he searches my face for several seconds before he adds, "You're afraid."

I drop my eyes to the floor, not wanting to be further analyzed. "I'm not afraid..." But even to my own ears, I can hear the lack of conviction.

"Yes, you are," he argues. "You're afraid of what you might find. That maybe he's not really your dad, or he's dead. He might be some asshole who isn't everything your mom has made him out to be." I flinch at his words, but he doesn't stop there. "Or worse, you're afraid that you'll find him alive and that would mean he left because he didn't want your mom...or you." I don't bother to argue. He's hit the nail on the head.

"Celeste," Adam says, putting his hands on my shoulders. "You need to find out what happened to him. Your mom needs closure, and so do you." He raises a brow. "Are you seriously going to let her die never knowing what happened because you have daddy issues?"

"You're right," I admit, my voice choked up from the guilt I'm now feeling. It was easy to pretend the situation doesn't exist when my mom lives over five hundred miles away and doesn't bring it up during the rare times we speak. But now that Adam has opened the closet, spilling out all of the skeletons, I can't just stick them back inside and pretend they don't exist. "I'll look into finding a PI."

"Felix's best friend from college is one. I'll give him a call."

"Thank you." I give Adam a hug. I don't have a lot of friends, but the few I do have are nothing short of amazing.

"So what time is career day?" he asks, and I groan. Margie, of course, laughs. When I don't answer right away, Adam gives me a look of disappointment. "You're not going to let that girl down, are you?"

"You don't understand..."

"That you're in love with her father?" he cuts in.

"No!" *What is up with him calling me out on all my shit today?*

"Yes!" Adam argues.

"What?" Margie squeals in shock.

"Oh, yes, girl." Adam pulls Margie onto the couch. "She totally banged him in the women's bathroom at the wedding reception." Margie giggles. Damn traitor. You can't even pay for loyalty anymore.

When she spots me glaring, she stops abruptly. "You're going, right?"

"Yes, of course." I pull up the single text message Jase sent me late last night. It's the address to Skyla's school, along with the time I need to arrive. He might've waited until the last minute to let me know the details of the event, but luckily, I didn't wait to get things ready. Skyla only mentioned me having to speak, but I wanted to do something extra to make it memorable for her, so when I returned to my office the next day, I got to work putting together a surprise I think she's going to love.

Every day, I've checked my phone, waiting to get the details from Jase, and day after day, when nothing came in, I started to wonder if maybe Skyla changed her mind about the invitation, and it pissed me off that Jase couldn't even take a second to let me know.

Yesterday I considered calling Nick to get Jase's number to ask him, or looking up his address so I could at least mail the surprise to Skyla, so she could give them to her classmates if she wanted to. Then, last night, as I was deciding what to do, Jase's text finally came through. Annoyed that he waited until the last possible second, I didn't even bother to respond. It was immature, but on the other hand, so was him waiting that long. I just hope Skyla doesn't think my lack of response means I'm not coming. Surely, if Jase thought that, he would've texted again to ask. Right?

Glancing at the current time on my phone, I tell Adam to call us a car, then have Margie help me grab the box of goodies. Today is about Skyla, not Jase, and if he thinks texting me at the last minute is going to ruffle my feathers, he better think again. I'm Celeste-fucking-Leblanc, and I'm about to show Jase he's messed with the wrong woman. I didn't get to where I am today by letting people screw with me.

TWELVE

*J*ASE

MY ALARM GOES OFF, reminding me that I need to head over to Skyla's school for Career Day. Originally, I was supposed to be the one speaking on behalf of her. That was until she invited Celeste. Now Celeste is the one representing my daughter. One might take offense that his daughter would rather have a woman she barely knows, speak, instead of her own dad, but I'm not offended in the slightest. Skyla has never shown any interest in tattoos. Her entire life, since she was barely old enough to pick out her own clothes, has been about fashion. I know how important today is for her. While she may not know Celeste personally, my daughter has grown up following her career and worshipping the runway she struts down.

So, no, I'm not offended, but I am worried. Because last night when I finally got the guts to text Celeste the address and time of Career Day, along with an apology for waiting until the last minute, she didn't text me back. Not even a simple OK. I have no idea if she'll even be there today. Several times, I've considered texting her to ask, but pride is a funny thing. But now, as I shut down my station and head out the door, I wish I would've. I could have prepared Skyla properly.

Since Skyla's school is located in Lower Manhattan, I snag a cab. I rarely drive my own car in the city, especially since Skyla rides the bus to school, and it's quicker for me to ride the subway or grab a cab to work. Mostly it just stays parked in the driveway, unless I take it for a drive out of the city, like when we went to the wedding in the Hamptons. I really should consider getting rid of it, but I love my car and I'm not ready to part with it yet.

After checking in with the front office to get my visitor pass, and getting a mixture of odd looks, from lust—the secretary, who I'm sure is imagining what it would be like to fuck a "bad-boy with tattoos"—to disgust—the Headmaster, who is scrunching up her nose, that a parent, even dressed in a white button-down dress shirt and black slacks, looks like I do—I make my way to the auditorium where career day is being held.

I step in quietly, since there's a parent currently at the front discussing his career as a bankruptcy attorney, while lecturing the kids on not putting themselves in a situation where they accumulate too much debt. I spot my daughter immediately, her head moving from side-to-side as she looks around for someone. When our eyes lock, I know right away it's not me she's looking for, it's Celeste, and judging by the pitiful frown she's sporting, Celeste isn't here yet. Fuck! Maybe she didn't get my text. Maybe I texted the wrong number. I pull up the message and pull the card out of my pocket. They match. I copy and paste the message and click send again, watching intently for the bubbles to pop up, indicating she's texting back. Nothing.

A few minutes later, Skyla's name is called, and she stands to introduce the person she's brought. She speaks softly into the microphone. "My name is Skyla Crawford, and the person I brought with me is..." She stops speaking and her lips curl into a bright smile. "The person I brought with me is Celeste Leblanc. She's not only one of the highest paid models in the industry, but she also owns her own company, Leblanc, Incorporated, which includes several fashion lines from jewelry, to her most recent, clothing. My dream is to be just like her when I grow up."

I glance around to find Celeste. My daughter wouldn't have announced her if she wasn't here. And that's when I spot her. She's dressed in a form-fitting navy blue and white pin-striped suit with heels that clack along the marble floor as she sways her ass up to the podium with all the confidence in the world. When she gets to the front, she gives Skyla those stupid air kisses to each cheek like all the famous people do, then addresses the audience.

Skyla remains standing next to Celeste as she discusses her career. She laughs and smiles, and of course is completely fucking captivating. With her on stage, I'm able to admire just how damn beautiful Celeste is. Her auburn hair is down in waves and her makeup is barely there. She holds her head up with confidence, and not for a single second, does she ever show one ounce of fear or nervousness. And even though to this day, my heart tightens over the loss of this woman, I can't help but grin, because she did it. She achieved the goals and dreams she made. And while I thought for the longest time that my daughter looking up to her was a curse, I have to admit that if she's going to worship someone, I'm glad it's Celeste. She's strong, independent, and hard-working. She's everything Skyla's mother wasn't and everything I want my daughter to be.

"...and now to conclude my presentation, my assistants will be passing out friendship bracelets I've designed for today. They are inspired by my new friendship with Skyla and a preview to my upcoming jewelry collection, which will be launching this winter. Each box contains a bracelet with an inspirational quote written on it for you to give to a friend who inspires you."

A man—the one I recognize from the wedding—and a woman begin to pass out tiny gold-colored boxes to each person in the room. When the guy goes to hand me mine, I shake my head. He nods once then shoots me an exaggerated wink before moving on to the next person. *Did he just flirt with me?*

"THANK YOU SO MUCH FOR COMING!" Skyla throws her arms around Celeste. Career day has ended, and since it's the last day of school, we were told that we can take our kids home with us now if we choose to. Of course Skyla wants me to. Now we're standing in the parking lot with Celeste, saying our goodbyes.

"You're welcome," Celeste says. "It was my honor."

Skyla nods in response, her cheeks turning a light pink, which is an indication she's embarrassed. Why is she embarrassed? "I was wondering..." she begins, her voice a tad bit wobbly. *She's not embarrassed; she's nervous.* "I was wondering if you would wear my friendship bracelet."

"Only on one condition," Celeste tells her. "You wear mine." She pulls a box out of her purse and opens it, handing it to Skyla. Skyla takes the silver bracelet in her hands and reads the quote: "You are amazing. Remember that." Then she turns the charm over and glances up. "Dad, look." She shows me the charm. "It's a dandelion. Just like the one you have a picture of in the shop. Like the ones grandma used to wish upon."

My eyes meet Celeste's, and for the first time, I can see her confidence waver.

"Put it on me, please," Skyla requests, and I do.

"It's beautiful," I tell my daughter.

"Thank you," she tells Celeste. "Do you want me to put yours on for you?"

"Please." Celeste holds her wrist out and Skyla locks the clasp.

"Thank you for coming today," Skyla says again. "It's the last day of school. Every year, on the last day, Dad and I go to the FIT museum and then to dinner. Would you like to join us?"

Celeste's eyes go wide. I should reprimand my daughter for inviting someone out without asking me first, but for some reason, I'm not ready to let Celeste go yet, and if having dinner with her and my daughter gives me more time with her, I'll go with it.

"Please," Skyla adds, and I don't even have to look at her to know she's giving Celeste her signature pleading look she always gives to my sister and brother when she wants to get her way because she knows they don't stand a chance against it. I, on the other hand, have a special dad forcefield, that shoots up the minute her lower lip juts out, to protect myself, and wallet, from that look.

"Sure." Celeste nods. "I would love to."

"Yay!" Skyla exclaims. Because it was the last day of school, she doesn't have a backpack or anything. After Celeste introduces us to her assistant, Margie, and me to her friend, Adam, since apparently my daughter already knows him, I call for a car service to pick us up. Because we're at Skyla's school, there's no way to snag a cab. We could walk to the subway, but I doubt Celeste will want to walk that far in her heels. It's a bit of a hike.

When we arrive at the museum, Skyla grabs Celeste's hand and starts to drag her around to each exhibit. Celeste doesn't complain once, instead she gives Skyla her complete attention the entire time. They ooh and ahh over everything, while I follow them around, joining in occasionally. We spend the next few hours there, until Skyla begins to slow down and complain she's hungry. Then we head a couple blocks over, on foot, to Jake's Burger Joint. It's Skyla's favorite place to eat, and it has a decent arcade she used to like to play games in when she was younger.

While we sit at the table, eating our food and sipping on our milkshakes, Skyla keeps the conversation flowing. But then she spots a couple friends from school, leaving Celeste and me at the table alone while she goes to hang out with them.

After a few minutes of awkward silence, Celeste says, "So...any summer plans now that Skyla is out of school?" *Great, cue the awkward, forced conversation.*

"I still work, so she goes to a couple different camps, hangs out at the shop, or stays with Quinn, but we are planning a trip to North Carolina." I cringe the second the words are out of my mouth, hoping she doesn't ask what for. She knows I don't have any family there. My only family are my brother and sister and they both live here in New York.

"Skyla mentioned that...going to visit Amaya, right?" Her tone has changed from awkward and soft to...cold?

"Yeah."

"Well, make sure you tell her hello from me." I look up in time to see her roll her eyes as she says the last word. *Great! Another woman in my life who relays her emotions by rolling her eyes up into her head.* She only met Amaya once during the time we spent together, so I'm not sure why the mention of Skyla's mom has her attitude changing. I don't usually tell people about Amaya's situation, but decide I should tell Celeste, in case it gets brought up by Skyla in front of her.

"Amaya does live in North Carolina," I start, but Celeste cuts me off.

"I don't really wish to hear about her. I was just trying to be polite." She takes a sip of her lemonade and it hits me...Celeste thinks I was—or am—with Amaya. And she's jealous.

"We're not together."

"I didn't ask if you were," she quips.

"No, but your tone indicated you were thinking it."

"No, it didn't. Obviously, you're not together still, or she would be living in New York." She looks everywhere but at me as she speaks. "I still don't want to hear about her."

"She's in a coma," I tell her bluntly.

The hand holding her cup stills and she sets it down. "Excuse me?"

"She's in a coma. When Skyla was four years old, Amaya was found unconscious. They were able to revive her, but she slipped into a coma."

Celeste's hands go to her mouth, and her eyes widen in shock. "I'm so sorry. I didn't know. She asked for an autograph for her...I assumed..."

"Every year we go to North Carolina to visit her. When Skyla was younger, the nurses would say that her mom could hear her when she talks, so every time we go, she talks to her mom like she's still alive...well, I guess technically she is, but..." I let out a frustrated sigh. The whole situation is just so damn fucked up.

"Wow, Jase." I look up and see tears in Celeste's eyes. "I'm so, so sorry."

"You were just rolling your eyes over the mention of her...now you're crying..." I sound like a dick, calling her out on it, but I don't need her false sympathy.

"Excuse me for having emotions." She huffs. "No, I didn't particularly like the woman I found in bed with the guy I thought I was in love with, but I wouldn't wish that on anyone... not even my biggest enemy."

"In bed?" What the fuck is she talking about? There's no way Amaya and Celeste ever ran in the same circles, let alone slept with the same guy. For one, Celeste lost her virginity to me...and then left for New York. And two, Amaya was several years older. "Who do you know that slept with Amaya?"

Celeste hits me with a hard glare that has me backing up slightly. "Are you serious right now?" she sneers.

"I didn't even know you two knew the same people."

"We knew the same *person*," she snips.

"Who? Me?" I ask, confused as fuck. And then it's like a light-bulb comes on. She thinks I slept with Amaya because I'm Skyla's dad. But why is she so mad about that? Skyla was born years before I even met Celeste.

"I didn't sleep with Amaya."

Celeste rolls her eyes. "So, Skyla was what? Created out of immaculate conception?"

I glance around to make sure Skyla isn't near us, then I lean in and whisper, "Skyla isn't biologically mine. But she doesn't know, so please don't repeat that." I've never admitted that to anyone but my siblings, but for some reason, I feel the need to defend myself to Celeste.

"You still slept with her." She glares.

I open my mouth to argue, when Skyla comes running over. "Look at this adorable stuffed bear I won."

"Wow, it is adorable," Celeste says as she stands. "I have to get going."

"So soon?" Skyla pouts.

"Skyla," I warn. "Celeste has given you all afternoon. You know she has a company to run."

"I know," Skyla murmurs. "Thank you for coming. Do you think I could visit your work one day this summer?"

Celeste nods. "Absolutely. Your dad has my cell phone number. Have him text me and we'll set something up."

"I have my own," Skyla says, pulling her iPhone out that her grandparents bought for her so they could reach her without having to deal with me. Celeste laughs as she rattles off her number to Skyla.

"Text me and we'll figure it out." She winks and then gives Skyla a hug before walking away.

Skyla and I spend the next half-hour in the arcade playing Pacman before we head home. When we step inside, we find Jax sitting on the couch watching television. Skyla gives him a quick hug and shows him her friendship bracelet before taking off to her room.

"Shop closed?" I ask, sitting next to him.

"Nah, Willow and Gage both have clients. Gage is going to close up. My last appointment had to reschedule, so I came home." He pauses the show he's watching and turns to face me. "How was career day? I take it by the way Sky was talking, Celeste showed up."

"Yeah." I nod absently, unable to get Celeste's accusation out of my head.

"So, what's up?"

"Celeste and I were talking, and things got a little heated. She mentioned Amaya... I don't even remember all that was said now. But what's got my head reeling is that for some reason Celeste is under the impression that Amaya and I slept together."

Jax snorts. "You and Amaya? Where the hell would she get that from?"

"I don't know." I scrub my hands over my face. This is going to drive me nuts until we finish our conversation. "Hey, would you mind watching Sky for me?"

"Sure."

Not having the slightest clue as to where Celeste might be, I decide it's best to take my own vehicle. About halfway to her house, I figure showing up unannounced probably won't go over well with her, so I give her a call. She answers on the third ring.

"Hello?" Her voice is timid, unsure as to why I'm calling.

"Hey, it's Jase," I say stupidly. She obviously knows it's me.

"Yeah, I know. Is everything okay with Skyla?"

"Yeah, but I need to talk to you."

"Now?"

"Yeah, are you at home? I can come by."

There's a sound of papers shuffling. "I'm about to leave the office. I can meet you there."

"See you in a few," I say before I hang up.

After finding a parking spot, I pay the meter, then head inside Celeste's building. The doorman must recognize me from when I brought Celeste home because he says, "Sorry, but she's not home."

"I know. We're meeting here," I tell him as the door opens and Celeste saunters inside.

"Mr. Walters, how are you?" She gives her doorman a sincere smile.

"I'm good, Miss Leblanc." He tips his hat to her.

Celeste walks straight to the elevator and the doors open. We both step inside, neither of us saying a word. When we arrive on her floor, I follow her to her door and then inside.

"Coffee?" she offers.

"No thanks."

"Wine?"

"I'm good."

"Cognac?" She holds up a bottle of brandy.

"How about a beer?" I counter, and she scrunches her nose up.

"I'm just kidding," I say through a laugh. I knew she wouldn't have any beer. Celeste rolls her eyes.

"Thank you for coming today," I tell her, sounding like my daughter. I think between Skyla and me, we've now thanked Celeste at least ten times.

She pours herself a glass of white wine and takes a sip. When the glass leaves her mouth, her tongue swipes across her fleshy bottom lip, tasting the wine. It makes me want to swipe my own tongue along her lips to taste what she's tasting.

"I didn't do it for you," she says, taking another sip.

"I know, but I'm still thankful." We're both standing in her living room, facing each other. She hasn't offered me a seat, and I'm pretty sure she's not going to.

"You asked to come by... So, how can I help you?" I guess we're getting straight to it.

"What you said at dinner, about me sleeping with Amaya. I never slept with her."

Celeste scoffs. "It's been over ten years, Jase. There's no reason to lie. I saw you."

"You saw me in bed with Amaya?" I ask slowly. There's no way. It never happened.

"Well..." She shifts from one foot to the other. "I didn't see you *in* bed with her. You were coming out of the shower and she was naked in your bed." What the fuck is she talking about? Has she lost her damn mind?

"And when was this?"

"The day before..." She swallows thickly. "I came to see you. I came over to talk to you, and when I opened the door, I saw Amaya in your bed. She was naked, and you were in a towel, stepping out of the bathroom. Your hair was wet like you just got out of the shower." And suddenly it all comes back.

"So, let me get this straight. You saw Amaya in my bed, and because she was naked and I was in a towel, you *assumed* I had fucked her?"

Celeste releases an exasperated sigh. "Yes, it was obvious."

"Wow." I shake my head slowly. "You must've had zero faith in me. You saw the first thing that might've *looked* like I was cheating, and you ran." I step closer to Celeste. My body is on fire. All these years and she just *assumed* I cheated on her. She didn't even have the decency to confront me. She was right fucking there. She could've spoken up. Yelled, screamed. And I would've explained. Instead, she ran.

"I meant so little to you that you didn't even stop for a single fucking second. You saw what you wanted to see so you could leave without feeling guilty." All the puzzle pieces finally fit together. All these years I wondered why she left without saying goodbye. Now I know.

"Guilty for what?" She sets her glass of wine down and puts one hand on her hip.

"For playing me like a fool, for one. For lying to me about your age and where you went to school. For not telling me you had a fucking internship waiting on you in New York!"

Celeste gasps in shock. "How did you know?"

THE PAST

. . .

I HAVEN'T HEARD from Celeste in two days. She was supposed to come by last night, but she never showed up. I thought maybe I misunderstood her, but when she didn't show up tonight either, I knew something was up. I went to text her and realized I never got her number. So, I emailed her, only it bounced back. It didn't bounce when I sent her the image of the tattoo, which means the account has only recently been deleted.

Unsure of where to go from here, I call Nick to get her info, but he doesn't answer. Without leaving a message, I hang up and jump in my car to head over to NCU. While I'm scouring the huge campus that is almost empty since exams are pretty much over and everyone is leaving for the summer, I spot Killian juggling a couple of boxes.

"Hey, man!" he yells from a distance. "How's it going?"

"Good." I grab one of the boxes from him, so they don't fall. "Finally done?"

"Don't you fucking know it. This is the last of my stuff. I'm heading out to New York tonight. Just dropping this shit off at my parents' place before I take off." Killian was picked up by the New York Brewers as a first-round draft pick.

"Congratulations. You deserve it."

"Thanks." We start to walk together in, what I'm assuming is, the direction of his vehicle. "So what are you doing on campus?" he asks.

"I'm looking for a girl...actually you might know her." Killian and Nick are good friends, so it would make sense he also knows Celeste. "Her name is Celeste. She's friends with Nick."

Killian stops in place. "Yeah, I know her. But why are *you* looking for her?"

"We hung out." I shrug. "Forgot to get her number."

For a good thirty seconds, Killian gives me a hard stare, and then he says, "She's no longer here. She moved to New York a couple days ago."

What. The. Fuck. "You sure?" I was just with her a couple days ago.

"Yeah, she actually left earlier than planned. She was supposed to be at her graduation, but didn't show up. Nick said she skipped it and left for New York early. He got her an internship at some modeling agency."

"She graduated from college?" Why wouldn't she tell me she was graduating. We hung out for days, talking and getting to know each other. Her graduating from college seems like something she would've mentioned.

"Umm...no..." Killian looks at me confused. "Celeste is eighteen. She graduated from high school." Jesus fucking Christ. I try to think back to our conversations. There's no way I would've missed her telling me she was a fucking senior in high school. Holy fuck, she's younger than my little sister. I just spent the last week fucking someone six years younger than me.

"You okay?" Killian asks, but I'm in too much shock to answer him. "Look, I don't know what happened between you two, but it's probably for the best if you don't find her. Celeste...well, there's no nice way to put this, so I'll just say it. She's a gold-digging bitch." He shrugs, and I have half a mind to punch him in the face for calling her that. "I'm not saying it to be mean, but it's the truth. Unless you have money, she isn't wasting her time on you. If you want, I can get her number from Nick..."

"No, that's okay," I choke out, flabbergasted by these turn of events. It's like I didn't even know Celeste. I spent the week falling for a woman who was playing me for a fool. But why? She had to know I have no money, yet she still acted like she was falling for me just as hard. She gave me her virginity, spent the week in my bed. We hung out with my family, went to the movies. She even came to see me at the shop several times. None of it makes any sense. But it really doesn't matter because she left. She got on a plane and flew over five hundred miles away without so much as a goodbye.

THIRTEEN

CELESTE

"DID you really think you would leave, and I wouldn't go looking for you?" Jase asks. "You disappeared. I was scared out of my fucking mind that something happened to you. Then I ran into Killian and learned that the girl I was falling in love with was nothing more than a liar and a coward." Jase takes another step toward me. "What was I to you, Celeste?" My name comes out as a sneer. "Something to pass your time with while you waited to graduate and go to New York? An experiment? You wanted to see how the other side lives..."

"You know nothing about me!" I shout, unable to hear another word out of his mouth. "The other side? I *am* the other side! I lived in a two-bedroom piece-of-shit trailer that more times than not didn't have any working electric or water!" I throw my hands up in frustration. My hand hits my wine glass and it topples to the ground, shattering into pieces as it hits the hardwood floor. I flinch but leave it alone. I'll deal with it later.

Lowering my voice several octaves, I admit, "I was embarrassed to tell you where I lived. I didn't want you to know I was trailer trash."

"But you knew I wasn't rich," Jase says. "I told you my story."

"I know, but you also told me you hated your father for lying, so I was afraid to tell you the truth."

"So instead you just continued to lie?"

"No." I shake my head. "I never lied. I omitted the truth." Jase opens his mouth to argue, but I put up my hand to stop him. "I know that's still lying, but I'm just pointing out that I never actually gave you my age or where I lived or where I went to school. You assumed it, and I allowed you to. I knew it was wrong, and I was going to tell you the truth. But the night I came over to, I saw Amaya in your bed, naked, and I ran away."

Jase takes one last step toward me, bridging the gap between us. Lifting my chin with his thumb, he forces me to look him in the eyes. "I never slept with Amaya." He doesn't blink or speak for a long moment, giving me time to absorb what he's saying. "She came over drunk and high and threw up all over me before she passed out. I got her out of her soiled clothes and laid her in my bed so I could get out of my filthy clothes and shower. Once I got out, I dressed her in one of my shirts and let her sleep it off."

Oh my God. Oh. My. God. All these years I assumed he slept with her, assumed he cheated on me. That he wanted her and not me. I close my eyes, embarrassed over how stupid I was.

"Celeste," he murmurs, and I open my eyes. "I didn't sleep with her," he repeats. "You were all I wanted."

I nod slowly. He wanted me and I left. Tears burn my lids. All these years wasted because I assumed. I should've talked to him, but I didn't. His words from earlier fill my head.

"You saw what you wanted to see so you could leave without feeling guilty."

Maybe he's right. Maybe I saw what I wanted to see so I could take the coward's way out and leave. I could've walked in and yelled at him. I could've asked questions, demanded an explanation. But instead I got on the first flight out and left. I was so terrified that he would tell me he couldn't go to New York, or worse, that he didn't want me to stay. I was so scared he would break things off, I ended what was going on between us on my terms.

"I think you're right," I whisper, and Jase gives me a quizzical look. "I think I saw what I wanted to see so I wouldn't have to put my heart on the line."

"What do you mean?"

"That night I was coming over to tell you about New York. I was going to ask you to go with me." A huge lump fills my throat.

"You were going to ask me to go?" Jase's eyes lock with mine.

"Or..." I swallow thickly. "I was going to tell you that I wasn't going to go." The tears burning behind my lids, spill over and slide down my cheeks.

"Dimples." My nickname leaves Jase's mouth like a prayer. "I never would've let you go." He brings his hand up to the side of my cheek and my face tilts slightly into it, my eyes closing, as I lose myself in his touch and in his words. I don't know if he means he wouldn't have let me go to New York, or if he wouldn't have let *me* go, but either way, his words are my breaking point.

With my own hand, I cover Jase's—the one still holding my face—and lean in to kiss him. Our lips touch, softly at first. I'm scared he's going to push me away. But when I feel his tongue run along the fleshy part of my lip, my confidence soars and I throw myself completely into the kiss.

Jase removes our hands from my face and pushes me back against the wall. Only breaking our kiss long enough for our shirts to come off, we strip out of our clothes as if they're on fire, until we're both completely naked. Then picking me up, Jase walks us through my condo, our kiss not once faltering. My fingers tug on his hair, not wanting our kiss to ever end. I know when we've made it to my room because Jase drops me onto my mattress. His lips remain seared to mine as he crawls up my body. Gathering my hair, he fists my locks tightly, tilting my chin up. He kisses me long and hard, with reverence, before tilting my head to the side so he can move downward. His soft yet masculine lips rain kisses down my neck.

Needing to feel him, I reach for his dick to stroke it, and that's when I feel something foreign. Something metal... I knew I felt something when we had sex the night of Olivia and Nick's wedding, but I was too far gone to give it much thought.

"Jase," I murmur against his lips, "did you have this the night we..."

"The night I fucked you on the sink in the bathroom?" He chuckles, his lips suckling on the soft spot just below my ear. "Yeah." He kisses along my collarbone, sending chills of pleasure down my spine.

Needing to explore, I push his chest back lightly. He pouts slightly, but it quickly turns into a grin as my hand wraps around his shaft and I stroke his hard length. Folding at the waist, I kiss the tip of his dick before slowly taking him all the way in my mouth. I count the number of barbells as my lips touch each one. Four in all. They're cold to the touch, and I make it a point to give each one special attention, running the tip of my tongue along each one.

I feel Jase lean forward, his tight abs brushing against the top of my head as he reaches for my backside. He massages circles along my butt and then gives one side a stinging slap.

"Jesus, woman," he grunts. "That ass. This mouth..." He grips my hair once again, pulling me off his cock and pushing me onto my back. His mouth crashes down on mine, and his tongue parts my lips—exploring, stroking, tasting, and worshipping. With his free hand, he lifts my leg up high, resting it above his forearm, and then sinks inside me. The feel of Jase filling me up is like being lost and then finally finding my way home. I feel full, complete, whole. If possible, even with all the years we were apart, the connection between us has intensified. With deep yet frenzied strokes, he works my body over.

His fingers release my hair so he can lean on both hands to go even deeper, and I pull his face down to mine, not wanting to lose any part of our connection. Our tongues move frantically against each other. My nails scrape lightly along his back, my orgasm starting to build. My fingers slide across his damp skin. We're both working up a sweat. Jase's thrusts get harder, rougher, more demanding.

"Jesus, you feel so good," he murmurs against my lips. "Fuck." His head drops to my chest, and his lips wrap around my hardened nipple. When his teeth clamp down, my climax rips through my body. My walls clench around his dick, and I can feel the barbells massaging my insides as Jase finds his own release.

He moves his arm, and my leg drops down onto the bed, but he doesn't pull out. Instead, he spends the next several minutes nuzzling my neck. Kissing my fevered skin. Licking my nipples. His dick throbs, reminding me he's still inside me. I've never felt so completely worshipped in my life. When he finally pulls out, he lowers his body until his face is up close and personal with my pussy.

"Jase," I groan. We're no longer in the heat of our passion. I don't want him hanging out down there...

"Shh..." He gives the hood of my pussy an open-mouthed kiss. "I need to get fully reacquainted with your perfect cunt."

"Jase." I moan, as he pushes his fingers into me. They make a slurping sound, reminding me that we just had sex without a condom. "What are you doing?"

His answer is to grab the backs of my thighs and flip me over. Before I can lay my head down against the cotton sheets, he entwines my hair around his fist and pulls me up onto my knees, tilting my head to give him access to my neck. He enters me from behind, his other hand gripping the curve of my hip, his lips sucking on the sensitive spot below my ear. Unlike last time, which was rough and frenzied, this time he makes love to me nice and slow.

With my body already sensitive, I feel my orgasm surfacing once again. He releases my hair and pushes down on my back. My ass pops out farther and he sinks himself into me deeper. My cheek presses against the sheets and my eyes close as I get lost in all that is Jase.

AS MY EYES FLUTTER OPEN, the tickling sensation I feel causes my heart to expand. I breathe out a soft sigh as I allow myself to remember the last time I woke up to Jase drawing across my skin. The last time I thought it was a bug crawling on me, but now I know it's the feeling of the pen running along my flesh.

The tickling stops, and then I feel Jase's warm lips press a kiss to each of the dimples just above my ass. "Morning, Dimples," he murmurs, the sound of his voice like a soft velvet blanket I want to grab ahold of and cuddle with.

"Morning." I roll over and come face-to-face with Jase. His hazel eyes are playful, and his day-old stubble has me wanting to rub my cheek along his. His lips press to mine for a chaste kiss before he backs up and sits upright.

"I need to head home. My brother is keeping an eye on Skyla, but he needs to head into the shop. He has an early appointment." He runs his fingers down the side of my cheek in such a loving way, my body shudders. Jase notices and smirks. "I love how responsive your body is to me." I bring myself into a sitting position, and he kisses me again before standing to get dressed. I can't help the pout my lips make at the thought of leaving this bedroom, but I know he's a man with responsibilities. Especially since he's a single dad.

"What made you move to New York?" I ask curiously. I never would've imagined him moving here.

"Quinn originally wanted to work in a museum. She got picked for an internship at the MET."

"So you all moved here?" I knew they were close, but wow.

"I had recently gotten custody of Sky and felt we all needed a fresh start. She was almost five and ready to start school, so I figured it was a good time to move."

I quickly do the math in my head. "You've been living here for the last eight years." It's a huge city, and it's not like we mingle in the same circles, but I can't believe he came here only a couple years after me, and this entire time I never knew it.

Jase nods. "Of course, Quinn didn't end up loving the position and quit shortly after." He rolls his eyes, but I know behind his mock annoyance, there's a sibling bond he can't hide. "She realized she loved photography, so she took a job working under some well-known photographer, and after a few years, branched out on her own. She mostly takes family portraits and shoots weddings and stuff, but she loves what she does."

"I thought she works at the shop with you guys."

"She does part-time, but only until we get around to finding someone permanent."

Jase pulls his boxer briefs up, tucking his beautiful dick inside, and I frown. He, of course, sees and laughs. "Don't give me that look, or I'll never be able to leave."

"Is that supposed to be a threat?" I ask, half playful-half serious.

Jase laughs again. "Woman, you're going to be the death of me."

I giggle at his playfulness. "I was so shocked when I walked into that tattoo shop and learned it was yours. I mean, I always knew you would open up your own shop, but I never thought it would be right here in New York."

"Yeah," he agrees, "getting custody of Sky changed everything. Our dream took a little longer than we originally planned. We worked at another shop for a few years while we continued to save, and then about four years ago, we finally took the plunge and opened Forbidden Ink."

He pulls up his jeans, zippering and buttoning them.

"It's a beautiful shop."

"Thanks." The corners of his sexy mouth curve into a boyish grin. "I love it there. It's like home away from home. I love that Sky can be there and we can make our own hours. There's nothing like working for yourself." He gives me a lopsided grin. "I'm sure you can understand that."

"I do," I admit. "It gives me a sense of control I never had growing up."

Jase comes over and sits on the edge of the bed, his fingers finding the curve of my hip. I'm briefly distracted by the view of his taut muscles and rock-solid abs on display, but quickly shake myself out of my haze and remember the subject we were originally discussing.

"If you didn't sleep with Amaya, how did you end up as Skyla's father?" I wanted to ask him this last night, but instead ended up jumping his bones. Jase opens his mouth to speak, but I put up my finger to stop him. Reaching down, I grab his shirt off the floor and hand it to him. "Put it on, or I won't be able to focus on anything you say."

He throws his head back in the most beautiful laugh but does as I say. "Amaya came to me when she found out she was pregnant. She had no idea who the dad was. She had been partying a lot and it could've been several guys. She asked me to help keep her sober. She wanted to do right by her baby.

"So I moved her in with me and helped her the best I could throughout her pregnancy. Unfortunately, her staying sober only lasted a few months after Skyla was born. She was colicky and Amaya just didn't have that maternal gene."

I swallow thickly. I know all about lacking that gene. I can't even imagine if I ever got pregnant, what I would do with a baby. Sure, financially I can afford one, but money can't parent. It can't nurture and love and protect. Nick's mom was rich and lacked every maternal gene. My mother was poor and wasn't any better.

"So you took care of her?" It wouldn't surprise me. Jase's heart is so damn big. I only knew him for a short time but could feel how deeply he cared for those around him.

"No." He frowns. "We got into a fight over her choosing drugs and alcohol over her daughter. I came home from school one day to find she had taken off with Sky. I'm not sure what happened to her during those next two and a half years. I tried to find her but had no luck." His eyes gloss over with emotion, and my heart squeezes for him and Skyla.

"She came back when Sky was three years old." Jase is quiet for a moment, then adds, "It was actually the day you met her. She asked around and found out where we had moved to." He shakes his head. "She told me she was back and apologized for taking off. She said things would be different. She wanted to get herself cleaned up."

He takes a deep breath then continues. "The night you saw her in my bed, she had come over high and drunk. She had Sky with her. Quinn took care of Sky, feeding her and giving her a bath, while I tried to take care of Amaya. After she threw up and passed out, I laid her in my bed and watched over her to make sure she was okay. When she woke up, she begged me to be with her. Told me she needed me in order to stay sober. I told her that I could only be friends with her, but I offered to take her and Sky back in. I hated that she had her daughter around all those druggies she hung out with. She left upset, taking Sky with her. She said if I didn't want her in that way then she would find someone who did."

"That poor baby," I whisper.

Jase nods in agreement. "I begged her to let me keep Sky, but she refused. About a week later I got a call from Child Protective Services. Amaya was in the hospital in a coma after overdosing. The guy who called it in handed Sky over saying she wasn't his. Apparently, Amaya had put my name on the birth certificate as the father."

I hear myself gasp at his admission. "So, you what? Showed up and claimed her?"

Jase nods once. "I felt so damn guilty, Celeste. I thought if I wouldn't have pushed her away, maybe she wouldn't have overdosed."

"You can't think like that. She had serious issues. Unfortunately, more than likely, something along those lines would've happened eventually."

"I know," Jase says solemnly. "I've, for the most part, come to terms with it all over the years."

"Is that why you took Skyla? Out of guilt?" I ask, not trying to judge him, but trying to understand.

"No. Amaya's parents are rich as fuck, but they're older and flat out said they couldn't handle raising another child. Hell, they barely raised Amaya. They said they were going to hire a full-time nanny, but I couldn't let that happen. They chose their freedom, Amaya chose drugs... Sky needed someone to choose her." He shrugs like it's no big deal, when it is in fact a very big deal. He took on a three-year-old who wasn't biologically his. He loved her and nurtured her, providing a home for her.

"Monica and Phil, Amaya's parents, didn't even put up a fight. A couple years later, when I told them I was planning to move to New York, they just asked that they be allowed to financially provide for Sky, including her education." Now it all makes sense. The expensive clothes, the private school, the iPhone. "I could've argued, but it was a small price to pay to get full custody of her and be able to move. They could've fought me, and with the money they have, they would've won."

"What you did is so selfless, Jase." I climb into his lap, wrapping my legs around his waist. "Moving for your sister, taking on a little girl who wasn't biologically yours. I don't know anybody who would've done such a thing...well, except Nick. He has a big heart."

Jase's brows dip down. "Then you're associating yourself with the wrong people. Speaking of Nick..." He lets his words linger, but the way his brows shoot up tells me he's asking about our engagement.

"It was all fake," I admit. "We made a stupid pact that, if we didn't find love by the time Nick turned thirty, he would give up on love and marry me."

Jase's lips turn down. "You were going to marry him without being in love with him?"

Hesitantly, I nod. "We made the pact before I met you...before I fell for you. And then after I saw you and Amaya...well, after I *thought* I saw you and Amaya, I was done with love."

"Celeste." Jase sighs. "You were so young. You're telling me, you didn't once find love in the last eleven years? I've seen you dating."

"So, you've been keeping tabs on me?" I joke to lighten the mood.

"Damn right, I have," he admits with conviction. "I was so pissed you left, but I was also so damn proud of your success. I watched you grow and blossom into this beautiful, successful businesswoman. I just figured along the way you would've found love too."

"I wasn't looking for it. I didn't want it. To be honest, in a lot of ways, you're the reason I'm where I am today. When I got on that plane, I was driven and determined to succeed on my own. And since you, I've only dated guys I knew my heart would be safe with."

"Why?" Jase asks, his voice free of judgment. "That doesn't sound anything like the woman I fell for all those years ago."

"Actually, the woman you met never planned to fall in love. The only guy I wanted was one who could help me climb up the proverbial ladder. Someone with a daddy in a fortune 500 company who would take over one day. Until I met you, I only saw myself with a rich guy who would take care of me."

"Why?"

"Well," I begin, "you now know I grew up in a trailer with my mom."

I avert my eyes out of embarrassment, but Jase tips my chin with his thumb so I have no choice but to look at him. "Don't do that," he says. "Don't hide."

I nod once and then tell him the story of my mom and dad.

Aside from the few people I'm close to, Jase is the first person I've ever told. When I'm done, he asks, "So, have you found him?"

"I haven't called the PI yet," I admit sheepishly.

"Call him. You're a lot stronger than you give yourself credit for. No more hiding behind your fears. You're not alone anymore. I've got your back. Okay?"

"Okay," I agree.

Gripping the back of my head, Jase pulls me in for a kiss, then asks, "What kind of guy do you see yourself with now?"

"Huh?" I ask, confused.

"You said when you were younger, you wanted a rich man to take care of you...until you met me. What kind of man do you want now?"

"One who will love me," I admit softly.

"LET ME GET THIS STRAIGHT," Giselle says, taking a sip of her coffee. "You hooked up with Jase when you were eighteen, but then thought he was also sleeping with Amaya, who is Skyla's baby momma, but he wasn't."

I nod once, and Olivia shouts, "Can you please verbally speak? I'm on Facetime, in case you forgot." I roll my eyes, and Giselle giggles. Olivia is currently at Disney on her honeymoon, but insisted on not missing our weekly get together, so we're using my laptop to Facetime with her from the coffee shop Giselle and I are sitting in. We usually do lunch or dinner, but I was only able to meet early this morning, so coffee and pastries it is.

"Sorry," I say through my laughter. "Yes, I was with Jase when I was eighteen."

"I can't believe this!" Olivia chides. "I feel like I never really knew you." She pouts, and sitting back, rubs her belly.

"Oh, stop, nobody knew about Jase and me."

"So, are you guys back together now?" Giselle asks.

"I-I don't know." I shrug. "We didn't talk about it." After I told him I wanted a man who would love me, his phone rang, reminding us he needed to get home to his daughter.

"Because you were too busy having s-e-x." I laugh at Olivia spelling the word. Reed repeated one word he shouldn't have, and now the woman spells everything she doesn't want him to repeat.

"Jesus, Liv," I hear Nick say from the background. "I don't want to hear about Celeste fucking..." The lady sitting at the table next to us glances over, and I lower the volume a tad while Giselle laughs.

"Nick!" Olivia shouts, turning around to, I'm sure, glare at him.

"Sorry." He groans. "I don't want to hear about her f-u-c-k-ing Jase." I can't help the laugh that escapes. These two are fucking nuts.

"Thank you." She sighs then turns around. "We'll be discussing this further once I'm back."

"Oh!" Giselle clasps her hands together. "Speaking of which. Do you remember that yacht rental I won at the fundraiser?" Olivia and I both nod. A few months ago, Olivia and Nick threw a fundraising event to announce their expansion of Nick's charity, Touchdown for Reading, into Touchdown for Reading and the Arts. Killian, thinking he was hilarious, bid on the yacht rental in Giselle's name, and won.

"Well, since it's nice out, we've made a reservation to do a day trip the second weekend of July. We have no clue when we'll find the time to go once Killian's football season begins, on top of us having this little girl—" She pats her growing baby bump "—right in the middle of the season."

"Oh, yes! That will be so much fun," Olivia says. "I'll have my parents watch Reed."

"And you should totally invite Jase." Giselle waggles her eyebrows.

"Agreed!" Olivia adds.

"Yeah, yeah. It's time to say goodbye. See you when you get home. Give Reed a kiss from me."

"Bye!" Giselle waves at the screen.

"Bye!" Olivia smiles. I press the end button and she disappears.

Once I close the screen, Giselle leans in, and with a big grin, says, "Okay, now that Olivia and Nick are gone, I want all the juicy details. He looks like a bad boy with all those tats. Please tell me he fucks like one." She lifts one brow.

"I'm not kissing and telling," I say, "but I have two words for you: pierced dick."

"WHAT CAN you tell me about the gentleman you're interested in locating?" It's Saturday evening and I'm working from home. Adam texted me a few minutes ago, asking if I've contacted the PI yet, which I hadn't, so I figured I should call him now before I chicken out.

"Unfortunately, the only info I have on him is that he went by the name Snake, his last name is Leblanc, and he met my mom in Piermont when he was having dinner at the diner she worked at," I tell Duncan, the PI Adam referred me to.

"Okay, well that's a start. Why don't you email me all the details you have, including the dates they were together and any description of him you know of. Ask your mom if she can recall any specific tattoos."

"I'm not telling my mom. I don't want to get her hopes up. If you're able to locate him, I will then decide what to do with the information."

"Gotcha." He gives me his email and lets me know that once I send him all the info I can think of, he'll start immediately. I thank him for his help and then we hang up.

As I'm setting my phone on the coffee table, it rings, Jase's name popping up on the screen. We haven't spoken since we parted ways the other morning, aside from a good morning and good night text.

"Hello," I say, answering the phone. I have to admit, I was getting worried that maybe Jase regretted what happened between us. Neither of us are the same people we were all those years ago. While I'm still—if not more—attracted to him, I'm not stupid enough to believe we can just pick up where we left off. We're in a different city, both running businesses. Jase is a dad! I swore I would never have kids. I don't know where we stand, and I'm starting to wish I would've asked him when he was here the other day, but at the same time, I don't think I'm ready to put a label on us. It's all just too new, yet not. Ugh! It's so confusing.

"How are you?" Jase asks, his voice smooth like the finest silk. I don't realize it, until I release a harsh breath, that I was holding my breath. The way he speaks doesn't sound like a man who regrets being with me.

"I'm good," I say nonchalantly. "You?"

"Aside from missing a certain brown-haired woman like crazy, I'm okay." And there goes my heart.

"Oh, yeah?" I squeak out like a school girl with a crush. Damn it! How does Jase always manage to turn me into such a girly-girl?

"Yeah," he says, his voice husky. "My sister is having a sleepover with Sky at her place tonight, so I was thinking you could come by the shop and hang out and then I could show you my place."

"What about Jax?" He mentioned before that, while Quinn

moved out and lives with her boyfriend, Jax still lives with him and Skyla.

"He's having a sleepover too...with some chick he tattooed earlier...at her place." He coughs out a laugh. "So, what do you say?"

"Should I, umm..." I clear my throat, suddenly nervous. "Should I pack a bag?"

"Hell, yes, you should," he growls, and I let out an annoying giggle.

"Okay, I'll see you soon."

FOURTEEN

*J*ASE

FOR THE LAST TEN YEARS, my life has been about my daughter and our future. I have spent hours upon hours learning how to navigate being a single father to a little girl with a sad past, while also trying to grow a business. When I first got her, she was malnourished and mute. She didn't talk or smile for almost a year. The day she smiled at me for the first time, I swear I cried for an hour straight. And then when she finally spoke, I fucking lost it. Over the years, my focus has been on building a thriving relationship with Skyla, and later, it shifted to building a thriving business that would provide for Skyla.

Because of that, no-strings type of sex became my go-to. On the nights my sister or brother would watch my daughter, I would meet up with different women. Some, I hung out with a few times to see where things might go, others, it was nothing more than a one-time thing. But there was never a single woman I met that I could imagine bringing home to meet my family, to meet my daughter. Skyla had been through enough in her first three years to last a lifetime. When I wasn't working, I was taking her to the doctors, including several children psychologists. And then once she was finally on the right path and blossoming like the beautiful flower she is, I wasn't about to risk any set-backs. So I made it a point to keep my family life and my private life separate.

But now, for the first time, I can see those two parts that I worked so hard to keep from touching, merging together and becoming one. The house, the family, the marriage. Spending my days doing what I love, my evenings with my family around the dinner table or on the couch watching a movie, taking family trips to amusement parks, and my nights...I can see them vividly. In bed, getting lost in one woman—Celeste. The problem is, I'm almost positive, if I told her any of that, she would most likely run for the hills...or the runway. Sure, she said she's looking for a man to love her, and at the time, those were the best damn words I could've been told. Until I started to think about how different our lives are.

Celeste's life is glamorous and consists of traveling to different countries and designing clothes for the rich and famous, while mine is spent tattooing and parenting. We're complete opposites in every way, but she's who I want, and without spooking her, I need to show her we can work. It's why it took me a couple days to work up the courage to call her. I wanted to give her time in case she decided one night was all she wanted. In case she was caught up in the moment and didn't mean what she said about wanting to be loved. Or maybe she meant it, but didn't mean by me specifically. Or maybe she meant me at the time, but didn't think about what it would entail to be with a guy like me. Yeah, I'm fully aware that I'm overthinking the hell out of her simple five words, but I can't help it. It feels like I've been given a second chance, only everything has changed. We're no longer the carefree individuals we once were, lying in bed, wrapped around one another, with only the *thought* of our dreams and futures ahead of us. Now, we're *actually* living them.

So, with all that said, I planned to give Celeste more time, but then my sister asked to take Skyla, and I couldn't wait any longer to call her. When I asked her if she wanted to come over, I listened for any hesitation, but didn't hear any. She did sound nervous, though, which tells me I need to take things slow.

"All right, Gilbert. Take a look and let me know what you think?" I hand him the mirror so he can look at the tattoo I just finished.

"Damn, man, it looks fucking dope." He grins. "It's done, huh?"

"It is." I nod, satisfied with my work. It's a huge, intricate tattoo that covers his entire back, made up of different pieces that all interconnect into one large canvas. It's taken several sessions to complete.

"Thank you." He pulls a wad of cash out of his pocket and

shakes my hand, slipping me several bills. "I'll give you a call when I'm ready to start my sleeve."

"Sounds good." I apply the ointment to the newly inked area and cover it with cellophane. "You know the drill. Take care of it so it heals well."

"You got it." We walk down the hall toward the front. I'm the last one here this evening—Willow and Gage both finished up earlier, so I offered to close up shop. After we shake hands, I open the door for him to exit, then pull out my phone to text Celeste. I don't want to lock the door until she gets here. There's movement from the left that has me whipping my head around, and that's when I see her leaning against the pool table. She's donning a simple beige dress that's clearly business attire, yet it's still cut low enough to hint at how perfect and perky her breasts are, and still short enough to show off her tanned, sexy legs which are currently crossed at her ankles. She's wearing matching heels that are tall enough to be considered weapons. But the only thing they make me think of in this moment is how they would feel digging into my back as I fuck her on that pool table.

"You really shouldn't leave the door unlocked this late at night." She tsks. "Anyone can wander in without you knowing."

"I left it unlocked for you," I say, locking the door and then walking over to her. "You ever play pool?" I ask, nodding to the table she's leaning against.

"No." She shakes her head. "Is this the part where you offer to teach me how to play?" She smiles coyly.

"Do you want to learn how to play?"

She laughs. "I can only imagine how many times you've used that pick-up line on a woman." She runs her hands along the blood red fabric. "I bet you've taught *many* women how to play, haven't you?" She smirks playfully, but I can see it in her eyes, the hidden insecurity. She's asking, without asking, if I've been with a lot of women.

Gripping her hips, I set her on top of the pool table and spread her creamy thighs, so I'm standing between them. Her dress rises, showing off more of her skin. "I've never used that line before, and I've never been with a woman in here." I'm not going to beat around the bush. I'm a thirty-five-year-old man, and I don't want to play games with Celeste.

Pulling her face towards mine, I give her a hard kiss. It's only been a couple days, but fuck if I haven't missed the hell out of her. The longer we kiss, the deeper it goes. My hands skate along

Celeste's thighs as hers tug on my hair, pulling me closer. I can feel her heat pressed against my crotch. She's grinding against me, trying to get herself off.

Breaking our kiss, I push her legs farther apart and drop to my knees, so my face is parallel to her pussy. Running my hands up her thighs, I find her panties and tug them down her legs. She lifts, pushing her dress up to her waist and exposing her bare cunt. It's glistening with want, and just the thought of tasting her has my dick hardening in my jeans. I lean in and take my first lick right up her slit. Celeste's body shivers and goosebumps pop up across her skin.

"Jase," she murmurs softly, "what if...what if someone sees us?" Her question would be one of concern, if her tone didn't come across like the thought of someone watching us turned her on.

I glance up at her and notice her cheeks and neck are slightly pink. Her chest is rising and falling like she's out of breath. "What?" I ask, confused. Nobody is in here but us. I made sure of it.

"Out there." She nods. When I glance back, I see a couple walking by. It appears as if they're looking into the shop, but really, they're only looking at their reflection.

"It's a one-way mirrored window. We can see out, but they can't see in."

"Oh," she says, her voice breathless, confirming my suspicions.

"Does the thought of them watching us turn you on, Dimples?" I push my fingers into her tight center, and she's dripping fucking wet. I don't need for her to answer. It obviously does.

"I-I don't know." Her cheeks turn a brighter shade of pink.

"Oh, you know," I murmur, adding another finger to the mix. "I think it turns you the fuck on to think about someone watching me as I fuck this tight cunt." Celeste gasps and her muscles constrict. Apparently dirty talk also turns her on. While fingering her, I spread her lips with my other hand and take another lick of her sweet pussy. When I get to the top of her clit, I bite down on the swollen nub.

"You know what I think?"

"What?" she asks, the word stretching out through a soft moan.

"I think you should get this pussy pierced." I flick my tongue over her clit and her entire body shakes with pleasure. "And nobody would ever know," I add, remembering that her excuse for not being able to get a tattoo was because she wanted to be a model.

"I don't know if—" Her words are cut off with a loud moan when I lean back in and suck her clit into my mouth, my teeth scraping along the sensitive flesh, and my tongue darting out to lap up her juices. I continue to fuck her with my fingers while my mouth devours her. Her fingers pull on my hair to the point of pain, telling me what I'm doing feels good. Another few licks of my tongue and pumps of my fingers, and she's coming hard. Her juices flow down my chin and onto the pool table like a beautiful fucking waterfall. When I glance up, her head is thrown back and her back is arched as she rides out her orgasm.

After a few seconds of watching her, I pull my fingers out and yank her toward me. She comes willingly—her entire body limp from her orgasm—and I grab the back of her head, bringing her lips to mine. When she releases a low groan into my mouth, I know she's tasted herself on me. Reluctantly breaking our kiss, I back up and grab her panties, placing each heeled foot into a hole and pulling them up her legs.

When she gives me a confused look, I lift her off the table and set her down. "We have my place to ourselves. I'm not fucking you here. I need to take my time with you." I kiss her pouty lips once more and then walk over to the wall to flick off the lights so we can head out.

"This is really cool," she says, eyeing the wall I painted years ago when we first bought the place. It's the name of our shop, Forbidden Ink, graffitied, and to the right is a large gloved hand holding a tattoo gun. It's painted 3D to look lifelike. "Did you draw it?"

"Yeah." I nod, admiring the image.

"You're so talented," she says with awe in her voice.

"Talented enough to tattoo you?" I shoot her a wink and she rolls her eyes.

"Not a chance." She scoffs. "I have a reputation to uphold." She grabs a bag from the corner and hands it to me to carry. It must be her overnight bag. "Now, if you would've asked me earlier, while your tongue was down there..." She waggles her brows playfully. "I probably would've agreed to let you do whatever you wanted to my body."

"Good to know."

I swing the door open so Celeste can walk out first, but when she walks by, she purposely rubs her hand along my still-hard dick. Gripping her wrist, I pull her back into me, swiping her hair to the side, so I can place a kiss to her neck. I don't know what it is about this woman, but I'm fucking addicted. I can't even go five damn minutes without needing to touch her in some way.

"Jase," she says through a moan. "We'll never make it to your place if you keep that up."

After setting the alarm and locking up, we start walking down the sidewalk. I hit the unlock button on my key fob and my headlights flicker on and off.

"Is this your car?" Celeste asks as I pop open the trunk and toss her bag inside.

"It is." I slam the trunk closed then walk over to open the door for her.

"It looks like one of those cars in that Fast and Furious movie." She eyes the car further.

"You've seen those movies?"

"Nick made me watch one once." She slides into the car, and I close the door once she's all the way in. She puts on her seatbelt, and I start the car. When the V8 engine rumbles to life, Celeste's brows rise, impressed.

"It's a 1967 Chevy Camaro Z28," I tell her, even though she probably has no clue what any of that means.

"It's sexy." She runs her hand along the dashboard as I pull out into the heavy city traffic to head home. "I've never been in a car like this before. It's very...manly." Her hand leaves the dash and lands in my lap.

"That's because you date those rich twats," I point out. "They prefer town cars and limos."

She rubs the top of my pants, awakening my dick from its slumber. "True," she agrees. "But I prefer a car like this."

"Celeste," I warn, "We'll be at my place in twenty minutes."

"I'm not sure I can wait that long." She unlocks her seatbelt and edges closer to me. Her lips find my ear, and she licks the lobe before kissing down my neck—the entire time, she's stroking my cock through my pants.

And then her hand dips into my jeans, under my boxers, and she squeezes my dick. A car pulls out in front of me, and I slam on my brakes. "Jesus, woman, you're going to get us into an accident."

"You're the one driving." She giggles into my ear. Her fingers grip my shaft, stroking me root to tip, and her mouth trails kisses along my jaw.

"Oh! I forgot to tell you. Giselle invited us to go on a yacht they're renting. Want to go?" She's talking to me like she doesn't have her hands all over me. Meanwhile, I can barely think straight.

"Yeah, whatever you want." I let out another groan. Fuck! We're stuck in traffic. Damn New York!

Unable to handle another second of her touch without being able to reciprocate, I make a sharp right turn onto a side street. The alley is empty, but even if it was full of people, I wouldn't give a fuck. After unbuckling my seatbelt, I push my pants and boxers down, and my dick springs free. Leaning over, I grab her hips and pull her on top of me, her legs landing on either side of my seat. Wanting to be inside her, and annoyed that her panties are in the way, I rip the thin material off her body and pull her down onto my hard length until I'm so deep inside her, I bottom the fuck out in her tight cunt. She releases a loud moan, and then with her arms wrapped around my neck, raises her body slightly and then lowers herself onto me once again.

She grinds herself against me, her clit rubbing friction against my pelvis. "Oh my God, Jase." Her eyes roll upward into the back of her head. I was prepared to take charge, to fuck her until we both came, but instead I sit back and watch as my woman rides me. As she explores, like it's her first time finding her own release, and fuck if it isn't the hottest thing I've ever experienced.

"I've never...Jesus...This feels so good." Her words come out breathless. She's close. So fucking close. "Oh...Oh...Jase!" Her walls tighten like a goddamn vice grip as she comes all over my dick right before I come deep inside her.

"TURN AROUND SO I can clean your back." Celeste smirks, knowing the last thing I want to do is clean her. When we got to my place, I attempted to give her the full tour, but once we arrived at my bathroom, she insisted, as she stripped down out of her clothes, she could see the rest of my place later. Without waiting for me to agree, she turned on the shower and got in. So, I did what any self-less host would do, and joined her.

I've just spent the last ten minutes cleaning her front, which included sucking her pink, pebbled nipples, kissing my way down her flat stomach, and licking her clit until she came all over my tongue. Now, I'm just trying to wash her, but for some reason, she thinks I'm kidding.

"I'm serious," I insist.

"Uh huh," she says coyly. "That's what you said about my front."

"Well, unless you're okay with some backdoor action—" I

waggle my eyebrows playfully, and Celeste's eyes widen "—I promise I'm just going to wash your sexy back."

"I've never done anything like that before," she admits, taking this conversation in an unexpected, but completely welcome, direction. I was just messing with her, but hell, if she wants to discuss anal, I'm down. "Does it hurt?"

"Not if it's done right," I tell her honestly.

She bites down on her bottom lip and then says softly, "Does it feel good?"

"It can definitely feel good."

She nods once slowly, and then shocking the shit out of me, turns around, and with her back to me, says, "I think I want to find out." And fucking hell, she doesn't have to tell me twice.

Taking a step into her space, I tell her to put her hands on the wall, and she complies, placing her tiny hands flat against the tile. "Spread your legs," I say next, and she does. Opening the shower door quickly, I lean over and open the cabinet to grab the baby oil, then close the door.

"Celeste, baby, I'm not going to fuck your ass tonight."

"Why not?" she asks, sounding disappointed. What's that saying? *Lady in the streets, but a freak in the sheets?* Yep, I think that about sums up my woman. First, she likes the idea of being watched. Then she rides me in my car in an alley, and now she wants to know what it's like to be fucked in the ass. I'm pretty sure I'm the luckiest damn man in the world.

"Remember when you lost your virginity to me? How tight you were?"

"Uh huh."

"Well, your ass is just as tight, and on top of that, I'm pierced." I pour the oil onto the top of her ass, then set the bottle down on the ledge. Spreading her ass cheeks, I rub it along her crack. "Tonight, we're going to start small. Tell me if anything I do hurts, okay?"

"Okay." She whimpers as I slowly push my finger into her puckered hole, one knuckle at a time. With my other hand, I come around to her front and tweak her nipple. Celeste moans in pleasure, and her ass pushes back, forcing my finger to go all the way in.

"How does that feel, baby?" I ask, pushing my finger in and out of her tight hole.

"Like...I need more."

Chuckling softly, I pull my finger out then push two back in. "Oh...Oh my God, Jase." She groans, pushing her ass back. "Can you...add another?"

"I don't want it to hurt, babe." I move my hand that was pinching her nipples down to her pussy and start massaging circles against her clit.

"Okay, but can you maybe...go deep?" she says breathily. I do as she says, picking up the speed and fingerfucking her ass deeper.

"How does it feel now?"

"Oh, fuck, so good." Her ass is now meeting my fingers thrust for thrust. I watch as my fingers glide in and out of her tight asshole. I'm not even doing anything at this point. It's all her. She's fucking my fingers, working herself higher and higher. I glance up in time to see one of her hands leave the wall and go to her nipple, taking over what I was doing.

"Jase, I'm...I'm so close." She moans loudly. I apply some more pressure to her clit and then she detonates. Her clit throbs, her hole tightens, and her legs shake as she orgasms.

Needing to be inside her, I pull my fingers out and push into her warm cunt. Her walls are still contracting as I grip her hips and fuck her from behind. I feel it as her orgasm rolls into another. I thrust into her a few more times before I can't take it anymore and release my seed deep inside her.

It's never felt like this, ever. Being with her, in her. It's fucking perfect. *She's* fucking perfect.

"Jase." Celeste giggles as I pull out of her.

"Yeah?"

"My body feels like Jell-O."

Laughing, I turn her around and help her wash up. Then, after wrapping a towel around her body, I pick her up and carry her into my room.

"I think I really like butt stuff," Celeste says with a playful smile as I set her on the bed.

"I think I *really* like doing butt stuff to you."

"DAD, I'M HOME!" Skyla's voice rings out through the townhouse. It's two stories with the living room, dining room, kitchen, and half-bath downstairs, and the three bedrooms and two more bathrooms upstairs. I'm currently laying in my bed, but even one floor up, I can hear my daughter yelling for me as her feet stomp up the stairs.

"Dad!" she shouts, as if I'm down the street, even though she's almost to my room. I glance over at the clock and see it's already ten in the morning. I'm usually an early-riser, but I didn't get to bed until almost four in the morning because Celeste couldn't keep her hands—holy shit! Celeste is here. In my room. In my bed. I sit up, my gaze flying over to the naked woman who's lying next me with only a thin sheet covering the swell of her ass. The sound of Skyla's feet pad down the hallway, and I fly out of bed to stop her before she plows into my room.

Thankful I fell asleep in my boxers, I rush to the door to lock it, but I'm a second too late. The door swings open, smacking me in the forehead, and Skyla enters the room before I can stop her.

"Oh no! Dad, are you okay?" Her tiny hands reach up to check my forehead.

"Yeah, I'm good," I say, trying to push her out the door. She hasn't noticed Celeste yet. "Let's go get you breakfast. Is your aunt here?" I press my hand to her back, guiding her out of my room when Celeste, completely oblivious to what's going on, calls out my name. Her voice is raspy from sleep, and if my daughter wasn't currently standing in my room, it would have me wanting to sink balls deep inside her so I could hear her call out my name in that same voice over and over again. But my daughter is in fact in my room and now aware of Celeste laying in my bed.

"Celeste, you're here!" Skyla squeals, too excited that her role model is in her home to put the pieces together as to *why* she's here in my bed. My eyes swing over to Celeste, who flips over, shocked, and shoots up into a sitting position, her bare breasts on display. And fuck if they aren't perfect... *Jesus!* Now is *not* the time to be thinking about her bare breasts.

"You're missing your clothes," Skyla points out, the corner of her mouth quirked up into a knowing grin.

"Oh, shit!" Celeste gasps when she realizes my daughter is here and staring at her naked. She pulls the sheet up to cover herself and then stumbles out of bed, running straight into the bathroom.

"Yo, bro!" Quinn calls out. "What's for breakfast?" She enters the room and looks from Skyla to me. "Were you still in bed?" She eyes me in my boxers and scrunches her nose up in sibling disgust. "Get dressed. I'm hungry."

"Dad was in bed with Celeste and she was naked!" Skyla exclaims through a fit of giggles. Quinn's eyes go wide, her gaze darting around the room in search of the aforementioned woman.

"Skyla, why don't we head over to City Donuts?" Quinn suggests, and I've never been so thankful for my sister's quick thinking.

"But Celeste is here." Skyla pouts. "I didn't even get to say hi." Only my daughter would be more concerned about seeing Celeste than finding her naked in my bed.

"She's in the shower," I tell her. "By the time you get back with the donuts, I'm sure she'll be out, and then you can see her."

"Fine." She huffs. "Can you go ask her what kind of donuts she wants?"

"Surprise her," I say, trying to remain calm, when I'm really freaking the hell out on the inside. I've always been careful so that my daughter would never witness anything like this. And she's not a baby anymore, so I imagine she's put the pieces together on her own as to why Celeste was naked in my bed. But now what? Do I talk to her about it? Try to deny it? Admit to it? I have no idea how the mind of a thirteen-year-old even works. Is sex on her brain? Fuck! The thought of having to have a sex talk with my daughter makes me feel sick. This is why I'm so careful, why I never bring women home. But for some reason, when I'm around Celeste, all reasoning seems to fly out the window, leaving me to think with the wrong damn head.

"Okay," Skyla agrees then skips out of the room past my sister, who gives me an apologetic look.

"I'm sorry," Quinn says.

"For what?" I shrug, pissed off at myself.

"I should've called. You've never..." She nods toward the bathroom door. "I didn't even think about it."

"I should've warned you. It's my fault."

"So, Celeste, huh?" She raises one brow.

"Aunt Quinn, c'mon!" Skyla yells from downstairs.

"We'll continue this conversation later," Quinn threatens before she shuts my door behind her.

"You can come out now," I say once I hear the front door slam shut. Celeste steps out of the bathroom, the sheet still wrapped around her like an oversized towel, and I can't help but pull her into my arms.

Her head falls against my chest. "I can't believe that just happened." She groans.

"It's okay," I say, not wanting her to feel bad. None of this is her fault. "It happens."

"How many times has it happened?" She looks up at me with a scowl on her face.

"Well, never, but I'm sure other kids have walked in on their parents in the bedroom."

Celeste's eyes bug out, and she backs out of my arms. "But I'm *not* her parent," she states matter-of-factly. I'm not sure what's going on with her. While I may know Celeste on a very sexual level, there's still a lot I have to learn. I've never seen this look in her eyes before.

"Celeste, what's going on?" I step closer to her, but she backs up again. "Talk to me."

"Nothing." She shakes her head, but she's full of shit. Her face is full of emotion I've never seen on her before. "I need to get going." She snatches her overnight bag from the floor and goes straight for the bathroom. I follow her inside, but she doesn't pay me any mind as she drops the sheet to the ground and then quickly dresses. She brushes her hair and then teeth, not saying a word the entire time. I don't know what to say. She's obviously upset, but it feels like it's about more than Skyla walking in on us.

"Talk to me," I repeat.

She gathers up her stuff, shoves it all into her bag, throws the sheet back onto the bed, thrusts her bag over her shoulder, then heads out of my room and down the stairs.

"Celeste," I call after her, trailing behind.

"Nothing is wrong," she insists. "I just have a lot going on. I need to get my team and line ready for GFE next week. I'm usually working hundred-hour weeks at this point, but I've been..." She doesn't finish her sentence, but I know what she was about to say. She's been distracted by me. She didn't get to where she is by luck or accident. She's busted her ass.

She comes to a stop in front of the door and turns around to face me. "There's a lot riding on this show," she says. "If it's a success, it can singlehandedly revitalize the fashion industry."

"That's the new one, right? Like Fashion Week but different... Skyla mentioned how excited she is for it. She always watches them live or on YouTube."

Celeste smiles at that. "Yeah, it's a new show." She leans in and gives me a kiss on my cheek. "I'll see you later, okay?"

"All right." I'm not sure what else to say. Whatever has her freaking out, she's obviously not ready to talk about.

She opens the door, and we're met with a smiling Skyla and a frowning Quinn.

"Where are you going?" Quinn asks. "Skyla brought you donuts."

Skyla spots the bag in Celeste's hands and her smile dims. "You're not leaving, are you?" she whispers.

"Celeste has to get to work," I explain. "Fashion Week," I add, using her excuse.

"But...it's Sunday." Skyla pouts. "Please just stay for donuts."

"Sky..." I start to say, but Celeste nods once. "Okay."

"Are you sure?" I ask her.

"Yeah, she's right. It's Sunday...and there's donuts."

"Sky, go inside and pour us all a glass of milk, please." She and Quinn head inside, and I shut the door behind them. "Tell me what happened in there. Did I do something?"

Celeste sighs. "It's not you..." She seems to be warring with herself, and since I don't know why, I have no clue what to say. While I wait for her to explain, my eyes scan down her body. She's dressed in a pair of tight blue jeans with an off-the-shoulder maroon shirt. She's standing tall in a pair of black heels. The ones with the red soles that everyone knows cost thousands of dollars. Hell, they probably cost more than the mortgage payment on this house. I suppress a deprecating laugh at the thought. Even dressed 'casual,' the woman screams power and wealth. I glance down at myself, in a pair of basketball shorts and a white T-shirt, my tattoos covering my arms and even portions of my legs. In the bedroom, when the clothes and lights are off, it feels so right, but as soon as we're dressed, and it's daylight, I'm reminded of how different we are.

And that's when it hits me. Why Celeste freaked out. Skyla walking in on us reminded her that I'm a single dad, while she's a single, kid-less woman. I live in a townhouse, and she lives in a high-rise condo overlooking Central Park. I drive a '67 Camaro, while the guys she's used to dating ride in limos or have car services.

"Jase," Celeste says. "Why are you looking at me like that?"

"Finish what you were going to say. It's not you, it's me, right?"

"No...yes...I don't know." She drops her bag and brings her hands up to her face. I step forward, needing to pull her into my arms. Every time I touch her, I feel that much more connected to her. And as I feel her pulling away, I feel the need to pull her back in. "Skyla walking in on us was just a shock. I guess I freaked out."

"I'm a dad, Celeste. That's not going to change." She moves her hands from her face and looks into my eyes. "I know how different our worlds are. You're this gorgeous and rich businesswoman and huge model. Hell, my daughter is a damn fan of yours. And I'm just me...a tattooist struggling to make ends meet."

"Don't do that," Celeste chides. "Don't belittle yourself. You're an amazing, hands-on, single dad who owns his own tattoo shop and works his ass off to provide for his daughter."

"Well, when you put it like that..." I grin playfully.

"When Nick and I were engaged, he found out he was going to be a dad."

"Yeah, he told me a little bit about how it all played out. One-night-stand, they went their separate ways, and then she saw him playing..."

"Yeah, but when he found out, I freaked out on him. I told him I didn't want to be a mom...ever." I still at her words. "My childhood, Jase." She shakes her head. "My mom was heartbroken and always high or drunk. We could barely keep the electric and water running."

"Your situation's changed," I point out.

"Yes, financially it has. But..." Celeste's eyes tear up, and she looks toward the sky, trying to will them away for several long seconds before she finally speaks. "Skyla already had one shit mother. The last thing she needs is another. She deserves nothing less than the best."

There are so many things I could say to her right now. I could tell her she already has one up on half the parents in this world just by knowing and recognizing what makes a parent shitty. That the fact she unknowingly put my daughter first—even though she wouldn't make a shit mother—by simply saying what she did, speaks volumes.

After my mom died, and Jax and I were forced to be raised by Quinn's mom and my dad, I learned what it was like to be raised by parents who don't give a shit about anyone but themselves. Then I saw the shitty choices Amaya made for herself and her daughter, and how badly they affected Skyla. And it's because I've seen the difference in good and bad parenting, I've made it my goal in life to be a good father to Skyla, but that doesn't make me perfect. With every decision I make, all I can do is hope and pray I'm doing what's right for my daughter.

Celeste has only been around Skyla a couple times, and she's already done more for my daughter than her own mother ever did. More than what Quinn's mom ever did for her. The truth is, Celeste would make a damn good mom, and I want nothing more than to tell her that, so she knows just how amazing she is.

But I don't say any of what I was just thinking because that's not what she needs to hear. It's too soon for her. She's scared and freaking out. So I tell her what she needs to hear in this moment to talk her off the ledge. Because I can't let her go. I plan to keep this woman, and while she may come across strong and powerful, independent and confident, there's a piece of Celeste deep down that is vulnerable as fuck, questioning every decision she makes, scared of falling back down to where she came from.

"You're not her mom, Celeste," I tell her. "You're just you. Someone she can debate Gucci or Prada with." I give her a small, playful smirk, hoping to lighten the mood. "I'm her only parent. I'm her dad."

Her shoulders visibly sag, confirming this is what she needed to hear.

"You hang out with Olivia, right?" She nods. "But you aren't Reed's mom." Another nod. "I'm not asking you to parent Sky in any way. We've only just reconnected. All I'm asking is for you to give us a chance. Hang out and get to know each other."

She nods once again, but this time she smiles. "I can do that."

"But do you *want* to do that?"

Her smile grows bigger. "I do."

"Okay then. Let's go inside and have breakfast."

"All right, but for the record," she says in a serious tone. "Prada...it's always Prada. That's not even up for debate."

FIFTEEN

Celeste

SHUTTING DOWN MY LAPTOP, I press my finger against my phone screen for the millionth time to check and see if Jase has texted me back to confirm our dinner plans for tonight. I haven't seen him since Sunday. I ended up having to take the red-eye to California to handle some modeling issues for the shoot for my upcoming winter line. Margie was over there handling it, but when she called to let me know several of my models appeared to be on drugs, I knew I had to fly out and handle it myself.

And I'm glad I did. After threatening to have them drug tested, they admitted to using. I fired them on the spot, canceling their contract, and told them if they ever wanted to model again in this industry, they would need to go to rehab. From there, I had to find new models available last minute and get all the clothes resized and fitted. It was an utter disaster, but once it was all handled, the shoot turned out beautiful—thanks to Felix, who handled it all like the pro he is.

It's now Thursday, and I'm back at home, and aside from a few texts, Jase and I have barely spoken. I told him all that was going on, but I know that most people can't really understand what it's like to run a business, especially one as time-consuming and demanding as mine. I should hire more people, delegate more, but it's my baby, and for so long it's all I've had. But now, as I check my phone for the millionth and one time, I'm wishing I did more delegating, so I wouldn't have had to go four days without seeing Jase.

My phone dings and I unlock it to check the message. It's from Jase: **I'm slammed at work**

My gut twists and the insecurities that I wasn't even aware I had flare up like a bad rash. Does he mean that or is he blowing me off? As I'm trying to think of how to respond, another text comes through: **Sorry, I hit send by mistake. I'm slammed at work. Sky wasn't feeling well, so Quinn had to bring her home. I miss you like crazy. Raincheck?**

"What's that smile for?" Margie asks, appearing out of thin air.

"Jase. I thought maybe he didn't want to see me, but he's just busy at work."

"Something you can relate all too well to." She winks.

"Yeah," I agree, "and not everyone has an amazing assistant like you." As soon as the words leave my mouth, an idea hits.

"Hey Margie, I'm going to head out. Can you lock up for me?"

"Absolutely."

Snagging a cab, I give the driver the address to Forbidden Ink, and fifteen minutes later, we arrive. When I walk through the door, I find several people hanging out in the waiting area. Some are playing pool; others are sitting on the couch looking through the design books. But nobody is sitting at the front counter. Then the phone rings and I hear Jax yell, "Someone get that!"

Walking around the desk, I grab the cordless phone and answer, "Forbidden Ink. How may I help you?"

"Yeah, I need to schedule an appointment," a guy says over the line. Sitting down on the stool behind the counter, I start searching for a calendar.

"Sure, just give me one minute, please." I press the hold button so I can find this damn calendar. There has to be one here somewhere. You can't possibly schedule four tattooists without having it written down somewhere.

"What are you doing behind the counter?" a deep voice asks, making me jump. I look up and into the prettiest blue eyes I've ever seen, which are a huge contrast to his harsh, spiky black hair and tatted up tanned skin. Based on his question, he must work here.

"I'm looking for your schedule. A guy is on the phone wanting to setup an appointment. Any chance you know where it is?"

"And you are?" he prompts. Shit! I didn't introduce myself.

"I'm Celeste." I extend my hand to shake his. "A friend of Jase's."

The guy looks me over then smirks. "Celeste, huh? The model, right? I've heard a lot about you."

"Hopefully all good," I joke, and he laughs.

"Yeah, definitely all good. I'm Gage." He lets go of my hand. "Did Jase ask you to come in and help out?"

"Actually, he doesn't know I'm here." I shrug. "He canceled our plans and I figured he could use the help." I chew on my bottom lip, hoping I haven't crossed the line.

Gage smirks and nods. "That's really cool of you." He reaches into the drawer and pulls out four small books. "These are how we schedule. Jase likes to keep it simple." He rolls his eyes.

"How long do I block off for each appointment?"

"It varies depending on the size of the tattoo. For now, just block off three-hour time slots and highlight the appointments you make in yellow so we can go back and double check them. Ask them what they're looking to get, and jot it down. It will help us, so we know what to expect. If they want something custom designed, you schedule a consultation and that's only thirty minutes."

"Got it," I say, repeating all of what he just said over in my head. Three hours, write down what they want, half-hour consultations.

"Oh, and if it's a piercing, let them know we only do walk-ins. They usually only take about twenty minutes."

"Okay." I nod my head once in understanding. The phone beeps, indicating there's another call coming in while the other line is on hold.

"You sure you got it?"

"Yep! You go draw and I'll handle this," I say with a wink.

Gage chuckles. "Alright, you want me to let Jase know you're here?"

"Actually, how about we just keep it between us? I'm sure eventually he'll come out and find me."

"Ha!" He laughs harder. "Okay, you got it."

When he walks away, I answer the phone and put the caller on hold. Then I go back to the other line and schedule the appointment. Once I hang up, taking the phone with me in case it rings, I walk around the room and take down everyone's information. There are several walk-ins, but Gage didn't tell me how to handle them, so I treat them all like appointments and schedule them in.

The place is busy and time flies. I turn off the main ringer, so the guys and Willow aren't bothered while they're working. Instead, it only rings on the phone I'm using. At some point, Willow comes out, and I introduce myself. She's really sweet and thanks me for helping out. I learn she handles most of the walk-ins and piercings, and when one comes in to let her know. Jase and Jax are completely booked with appointments, and Gage has a mixture of both walk-ins and appointments.

It's seven o'clock when a pretty brunette walks in and requests Jase. She's dressed in tiny cutoff jean shorts and a barely there tank top. She has several tattoos covering her arms and legs, as well as one peeking out from the front of her top over her breast. Looking at his book, I see he's booked solid for the next week. "I'm sorry but he's booked. I can get you in with Willow or Gage in about an hour." I take a look at Jax's book. "Or Jax has availability tomorrow at five."

"Okay, well, could I just go back and see him real quick?" She winks dramatically, and it takes everything in me not to smack her or throw up all over her.

"He's with someone right now," I say politely, remembering my manners. "I can let him know you're here, though. What's your name?"

"I'm actually hoping to surprise him." She blows a bubble and it pops. I do my best not to cringe.

"Okay...You're more than welcome to wait." I point to the couch. "He should be done in the next hour."

"Thanks," she says before she saunters over to the couch and plops down, pulling out her cell phone.

For the next hour, I stay busy—ignoring the skank still waiting for Jase—scheduling some more people and organizing the desk. Margie would seriously be so proud of me right now. I also place several ads into the online classifieds for a receptionist, putting my number and email so Jase won't be bombarded with calls and emails. Once I weed out the duds, I'll give him the info of all the serious applicants.

When Willow and Gage both finish up with their last appointments for the day, they thank me for taking over, and confirm their appointments for tomorrow, before they head out—leaving only Jax and Jase still with clients, and little miss skank still waiting on the couch.

When the clock hits eight and it's officially closing time, I consider whether I should go back and tell Jase or just kick her out. Figuring I should be the bigger person, I walk over to the door to lock it, in case anyone tries to come in, before I head back to let Jase know someone is here to see him. But before I make it to the door, miss skank stands and starts heading toward the back.

"Umm...excuse me," I say with a fake smile plastered on my face. "You can't go back there."

"Oh, well, I thought you were leaving." She shrugs. "And who are you? The Jase police?" She scoffs.

JASE

TODAY HAS BEEN a day from hell. There's no other way to describe it. First, Quinn overbooked me by accident, so I've been rushing all day to try to get ahead. Then one of my morning regulars showed up late, and at that point I knew I was screwed, so I had to cancel one of my afternoon appointments. But he didn't answer and, of course, showed up. Skyla was hanging out here with Quinn, when she, for the first time, started her period and started complaining of cramps and begging to go home. Luckily, Quinn was here to help her deal with her woman problems. But because that involved them going home, it left the shop with no one to answer the phones or greet anyone. Of course, both Jax and I had sleeves we were working on, which meant we were holed up for hours with no breaks.

I was supposed to finished by six, but didn't turn my gun off until just after eight. After applying the ointment, I walked my client out through the backdoor since he parked his bike behind the shop. Then I headed to the front to lock up. As I walked down the hall, I noticed Gage and Willow had both left, and Jax was still in with his client. I also realized the phone hadn't rang in hours.

As I walked farther down the hall, I heard two women talking. Maybe Willow is still here? But then I recognized one of the voices as Celeste's.

"You can't go back there."

Who the hell is she talking to? And why does she sound like she's pissed?

"Oh, well, I thought you were leaving," another voice says, "and who are you? The Jase police?"

I don't recognize the other voice, but when I get to the front, I recognize the person the voice belongs to. Missy. A longtime client who has wanted to get at my dick since the first time she stepped foot in here.

With Celeste's back to me, she doesn't see me as she pops her hip out and brings her hand down to her side. Damn, she looks hot in those tight jeans and those fuck-me heels. The shirt she's wearing leaves her back exposed and makes me want to bend her over the pool table and trail kisses down her spine.

"Actually, skank," Celeste hisses, and I stop in my tracks, waiting to hear the rest. "I'm the woman who's fucking Jase, so how about you turn your trashy ass around and call him tomorrow to make an appointment." I can't see her glare from behind, but I can hear the possessiveness in her voice, and holy fucking shit, I've never been so turned on in my life.

"Fuck you, bitch!" Missy screeches. "There's no way Jase is fucking you. He doesn't fuck women at the tattoo shop."

Celeste laughs. Not a ha ha kind of laugh, but a maniacal, my woman might be crazy, sort of laugh. When she finally stops, she says, "That may be true. We haven't fucked here." Her shoulders rise and fall. "But he did eat my pussy out over on the pool table."

Damn, my woman is scrappy as fuck! Figuring I better stop this before it turns into a full-blown cat fight, I step forward to make my presence known. Missy notices me first, her face lighting up. She obviously has no idea I just heard their entire conversation. "Jase!" she screeches, causing Celeste to turn around. Unlike Missy who looks delighted to see me, Celeste looks pissed as hell.

"Jase," she says, her voice devoid of all emotion.

As a man, I have two options: I can be nice to Missy, since she's a loyal customer, and explain to Celeste that sometimes bitches are just crazy. She might be understanding, or she might get upset and take off. I'll have to grovel for a couple days, but eventually she'll get over it. Or I can cut ties with Missy right here and now and end the night deep inside my woman. It's been four days and nights since I've felt the inside of Celeste's warm pussy. Which option do you think I'm going with?

Damn right.

"Missy, you gotta go," I say, getting straight to the point.

"But...but..." she stutters, while Celeste grins my way.

"One, you don't call my woman names, and two, you know damn well I've made it clear nothing will happen between us. Now you're going to have to find another shop to get your work done at." Taking Celeste's hand in mine, I walk over to the door, unlock it, and open it for Missy. "Bye," I tell her, leaving no room for discussion.

When she's gone, I close the door and pull Celeste into my arms, planting a kiss to her soft, plump lips that I've missed like hell.

"How much of that did you hear?" Celeste mumbles against my mouth.

"Enough to know better than to ever give you a reason to be jealous." I kiss her harder this time, pushing my tongue into her mouth so I can taste her. Fuck, I've missed this. Missed her.

"What are you doing here?" I ask once the kiss ends.

"I've been here since five o'clock," she admits sheepishly.

"What? Why didn't you let me know?"

"I didn't want to bug you while you were working. I've been answering the phones and scheduling appointments. I met Willow and Gage. They're really nice. Oh! And I put ads in the classifieds to hopefully find you a permanent receptionist." I stare at Celeste for several seconds, absorbing everything she just told me. I texted her that I was too swamped to get dinner, so she showed up here and spent her evening answering phones and scheduling clients. A woman who pays other people to assist her, sat here all night and helped me.

When I don't say anything, too in awe of the woman I'm falling for all over again, she says, "I should probably get going. I have an early morning meeting tomorrow and you're scheduled to come in at nine for a touch up."

"We don't even open that early," I say, finally finding my voice. "We don't open until noon during the week. Ten on the weekends."

"Oh." Celeste frowns. "I didn't know that. My office opens at nine, most do, so I just assumed you guys opened at nine as well...I can call him to reschedule," she says, stepping out of my arms.

Needing to feel her, I pull her back to me. "No, it's okay. I'll be here at nine. Thank you for everything."

"Are you sure? Because I can—"

With a quick shake of my head, I slant my mouth over hers. Her fingers tangle in my hair as my hands grab her ass, picking her up and pressing her back against the glass door. We kiss for several minutes, until Jax clears his throat, reminding us we aren't alone.

"Come home with me," I say once we break the kiss.

"I don't want to take you away from Skyla. You said she isn't feeling well." My heart swells at her statement. She may think she doesn't have it in her to be a good mom, but she has no idea just how selfless and caring she really is.

"She started her period. I was thinking we could pick up some chocolate and rent a movie to watch with her. Then once she's in bed, I can spend the rest of the night relearning every inch of your body. Four days without being inside you is too long."

"You're such a good dad." Celeste smiles softly. "And that sounds perfect."

After stopping by the store to pick up Skyla's favorite chocolate —as well as tampons, pads, bubble bath, and a bunch of other shit Celeste insisted my daughter might need to make her feel more comfortable—we swing by the deli to pick up dinner, then we head home. Skyla is ecstatic to see Celeste walk through the door with me. We spend the rest of the evening eating, watching movies, and Skyla even puts on a fashion show for us when Celeste asks to see the new clothes Skyla bought recently. When it's well after midnight, Skyla says goodnight and heads to bed. Quinn went home a couple hours ago. That leaves just Celeste and me sitting on the couch together in the living room.

"I should probably head home," she says, pulling out her cell phone to call for a car. I pluck it out of her hand and place it on the table. Picking her up bridal style, she squeals in shock, and I kiss her lips to muffle the sound.

"The only place you should head to is my room," I tell her, carrying her upstairs. Once we're inside, I shut and lock the door and then drop her onto my bed.

I climb up her body, my legs on either side of hers. "Stay the night. I wasn't kidding when I said I missed you like crazy. I need to be inside you ASAP." Dropping my head down to hers, I give her a kiss. "Please."

"Only on one condition. You make sure I'm up and gone before Skyla wakes up."

When I give her a confused look, she adds, "She deserves more than a woman who her dad is screwing, coming and going out of her home."

My eyes trace over Celeste's features: her beautiful onyx eyes. They're so dark, you could get lost in them. Her button nose that has just a small spatter of freckles that stay hidden with her makeup, but at night, when she wipes it all off, I get to see and kiss. Her plump, fleshy lips that have me addicted to not only her kisses but the words that come out of her mouth. Celeste is the entire package. Sexy and classy, independent and mature. She's caring and thought-ful. Tonight, when I thanked her for buying all that stuff for my daughter because she started her period, she just shrugged it off like it was no big deal. And here, right now, in my room, her only concern is that Sky doesn't get hurt or confused by whatever is happening between us. Celeste doesn't see it, but I do. She doesn't see the selfless, nurturing person she is. I want to explain all this to her, but I know she would fight it. She would come up with excuses or tell me I'm wrong.

So instead, I agree to make sure she's gone before Skyla wakes up, and then I spend the rest of the night trying to show her through my actions how appreciative I am of the way she puts Sky first, and hope like hell that one day Celeste will see herself the way I see her.

SIXTEEN

Celeste

"BRENNA, IT'S BEEN TOO LONG." I give Brenna Myers, the VP of Elite Modeling, an air kiss to each cheek. With the Global Fashion Extravaganza happening this week, everyone who is a part of the fashion world is in town.

"It has." She grins. "I saw the preview of your fall line. It's absolutely stunning. I imagine you will have more than your fair share of buyers knocking at your door after your show."

"Thank you." I can't help the smile that appears. Brenna was the first person to take a chance on me in this industry when I was eighteen. And when I won America's Elite Model and told her my goals, she didn't laugh. Instead she said, "If you want it bad enough, you will make it happen." Almost eleven years later, and I made it happen.

"Brenna! There you are!" Randy cuts in. "I'm so sorry. Celeste, how are you, dear?" He gives me a quick air kiss. Randy is the new VP for Calvin Klein, focusing on the children's and teen lines, and hasn't learned how to breathe yet. Fashion shows can be very stressful when you're just starting out. I remember my first one. Everything that could go wrong, did. But over time, I created a team of people I can trust, and now everything runs smooth—for the most part.

"Randy, everything is set," Brenna tells him slowly. "Breathe, darling." She laughs.

"We had several of the children and teenagers come down with the flu," he tells me. "It's like one of them got it and it spread like wildfire. Never create a children's or teen's line, trust me," he whispers. "It's more trouble than it's worth." I know he's only saying that because he's freaking out. I've looked at the numbers for a potential children's and teen line, and the profit would be well worth the trouble. You would be surprised at how much parents spend to make their kid's look good. And unlike adults, kid's grow, which means constantly having to purchase larger sizes, new lines. My thoughts go to Skyla and how adorable she dresses. When I hung out with her and Jase, she showed me all of her clothes, putting on a fashion show. She knows every designer and all the latest trends. She reminds me so much of me at her age, only I didn't have the money to actually purchase the clothes. Instead, I would buy a new fashion magazine every month and cut out all of the outfits and glue them into a book I made.

"And I told you I would handle it," Brenna tells Randy, and an idea pops into my head.

"Hey Brenna, do you by any chance have room in any of the lineups for one more teen?" Brenna gives me a curious look. "A friend of mine has a daughter who wants to be a model..."

Her eyebrows go up. I'm sure she's heard this line a million times. It's part of being in this business. Everyone who has a kid thinks he or she is model worthy, everyone who likes fashion is a potential designer. And of course, everyone with a camera thinks they have what it takes to be a photographer. But when I watched Skyla put on that mini fashion show for me, I knew instantly, she definitely has what it takes.

"I know, I know," I say with a laugh. "But I've seen her walk and she's got it. She's not part of this world, but it would make her life, and maybe it could get her foot in the door." When she doesn't say anything, I add, "It would be a personal favor to me."

Brenna nods. I've never asked for a favor. I've learned over the years, you don't want to owe anyone in this industry because they *will* collect. But Skyla is worth it. Plus, it really would be great exposure for her.

"Okay," she agrees. "She can walk for Randy." Randy opens his mouth to argue. "He is desperate." He closes his mouth. "On one condition." I wait for her to tell me. "If she's worthy of the runway, you have her sign with me."

"Deal." There's nobody I would trust more than Brenna.

Excited to share the news with Skyla, I finish up the details for tonight and head out. Margie is shocked when I tell her I'm leaving, but I know she can handle it.

"Celeste!" Skyla yells when she spots me walking into Forbidden Ink. She sets the pool stick against the wall and comes over. I can't help the way my thighs clench at the memory of Jase eating me out on the pool table not too long ago.

"I wiped it down," Jase whispers, as if he knows exactly what I was just thinking.

I jump at his words. "I didn't see you there," I admit.

"I can see that." He's about to pull me in for a kiss when we both remember Skyla is standing here. While we've been spending a lot of time together lately, we haven't really discussed what to say to her. That would mean labeling us. After my freak out last week over Skyla finding us in bed together, I told Jase the other night, I didn't want to be there when Skyla woke up. I tested the waters by saying that I didn't want her to see some woman he's sleeping with coming in and out of the house. I held my breath, hoping he would correct me, but he didn't. Instead, he agreed. I know that's for the best. I'm not stepmom material. But I can still admit—not out loud—somewhere deep in me, I was hoping Jase would tell me I was. But he didn't.

"You guys can kiss," Skyla states with a silly smirk on her face. "I know you're dating." She giggles. "I have had boyfriends..."

Jase growls at her last statement. "What boyfriends?"

"Chill, Dad," Skyla says with an eyeroll.

Jase glares at his daughter, but decides to let it go. "So, to what do we owe the pleasure of you coming all the way down to the East Village?" he says, shifting his focus to me.

"Up," I clarify.

"Huh?"

"I came up because I was in Tribeca at Spring Studio."

"For GFE!" Skyla screeches, excitedly.

"Yep, and I have some news." I waggle my eyebrows at Skyla.

"You got me a ticket?"

"Nope." I frown.

"Oh." Her mouth curls down into a pout.

"I didn't get you a ticket because models don't need one." It takes her a second to understand what I'm saying, but once she does, she screams so loud, I'm pretty sure the entire block heard her.

"Are you serious?" She runs over and throws her arms around

me, then looks up. "Please don't let this be a joke. It would be a very mean joke."

"It's not a joke. You're going to be walking for Ralph Lauren's teen line."

"Oh my God!" she screams again. Then she looks up at me again, this time with tears in her eyes, and says, "Thank you," and my heart feels like it's just been removed from my chest and handed to her. How could those two words and that look make me feel like this?

"You're welcome, pretty girl." I don't even realize the words are out of my mouth until I've said them. I've just called her the nickname my mom always called me. The one name that made me feel like I was more than just Celeste, the trailer trash on the wrong side of the tracks.

"When is it?" she asks.

"It's actually tonight. I was thinking we could spend the day together. Get manis and pedis. Get your hair done..."

"Really?" Skyla smiles. "Can I, Dad?"

She looks over at her dad, who is currently staring at me with a slight frown marring his features. Why is he upset? And then it hits me. Skyla is asking her dad for permission. Because he's her dad. And she needs permission. Oh my God! I'm so stupid.

"Oh, no," I say out loud. Jase's frown deepens and his brows furrow together.

"Sky, go get all your stuff together," Jase says, and she takes off down the hall.

"I messed up, didn't I? I should've asked you first. I'm so sorry."

"Whoa, calm down." Jase's lips form into a soft, comforting smile. "Sure, you probably should've asked me first, but you didn't mess up." He grabs my hips and pulls me toward him, until our bodies are flush against one another, and then kisses me. The kiss is slow and gentle and has me melting into a pile of mush.

"Then why did you look upset?" I ask him once we separate.

"I'm not upset."

"You were frowning."

"I guess I was a bit confused that you went from freaking out the other day over being in Skyla's life, to wanting to spend the day alone with her. You seemed like you were okay the other night hanging out with all of us, but I just want to make sure *you're* okay with all of this. With spending the day with Sky on your own." I bite down on the inside of my cheek while I contemplate what he just said. He's right. I have been hot and cold. It's no wonder he didn't jump at correcting me or putting a label on us the other night.

"I guess I have been all over the place lately," I admit sheepishly. "I was just so excited to share my love of fashion with someone else who loves it, I didn't even think about it." And it's not like I'm parenting her or anything. She has Jase for that. What harm can I do in one day? Plus, she'll be busy getting ready for tonight.

"I'm ready!" Skyla comes running out with her purse slung over her shoulder.

"You sure you're okay with this?" Jase murmurs low enough so that Skyla can't hear.

"Yeah, it will be fun." I give him a kiss on his cheek.

"Can my dad come?" Skyla asks.

"Of course. I'll send you some tickets in case your brother and sister want to go as well."

"I'LL JUST BE A MINUTE!" I yell across my condo to Skyla. Spending the day with her has been nothing short of amazing. She's so mature for her age, and we've had a great time. It's everything I always wanted with my mom but never got to experience. We got manis and pedis at the spa, then went to my favorite Bistro for lunch. I took her to get her hair done, even though once we arrive at the show, they'll do it how they want. We were on our way there when Margie called and asked me for the designer credit files for tonight. Apparently, she can't find the electronic copy on the cloud, but luckily, I keep all files on my home computer as well.

"Can I look at your jewelry?" Skyla asks.

"Go for it!" I find the files, send them to Margie, and then head into my bathroom so I can freshen up before we go. My outfit for tonight is at the studio.

"See anything you like?" I ask when I come out and find Skyla combing through my jewelry box.

"This." She holds up the dandelion necklace Jase gave me years ago. I almost threw it away the day I thought he slept with Amaya, but something stopped me. Instead, I put it in my jewelry box and never looked at it again.

"It's just like the one at my dad's shop...like the one on the bracelets you made for my career day."

I remember she mentioned that before—that Jase has a painting of a dandelion at the shop, but I didn't see it when I was there. "I haven't seen it."

"It's in his workstation," she says. *Hmm...looks like I'm going to have to make it a point to check out Jase's room at the shop.*

"He also has a tattoo of one on his ribcage," she adds, eyeing the necklace with a soft smile. *Interesting... guess I'll also have to make it a point to check out his body more thoroughly as well.*

"Your dad gave me that necklace," I admit. "A long time ago, when we were... friends."

"You mean boyfriend and girlfriend?" she asks, moving a hand up to her hip. "I'm not a baby, you know. I'm thirteen. I hate that my family acts like I'm still little." I stifle my laugh because to her thirteen is old, but to someone who is about to be thirty, thirteen is still in fact a baby. But I won't tell her that.

"Anyway," I say with a smile. "He gave me this necklace and told me to follow my dreams."

"It's beautiful," Skyla murmurs.

"Why don't you wear it tonight? You can't wear it on the runway since it's not Ralph Lauren, but you can wear it before and after."

"Wow, okay, thanks." She nods and lifts up her hair so I can put it on her.

"Hey Celeste," Skyla says when I finish clasping the lock on.

"Yeah?"

"Thank you." She turns around and gives me a hug, and the way she holds me tight makes me think she might be thanking me for more than just allowing her to wear my necklace. But I can't go there...

"You're welcome, pretty girl."

We arrive at Springs Studio and Skyla stays with me through the afternoon. Just like Fashion Week, GFE is running all week, at several venues, and all day, well into the evening. My fall line is being showcased today and then Skyla will be walking this evening. She stays with me the entire time, asking questions and commenting on the line. Several times Margie gives me an impressed look at how much Skyla knows about the industry at only thirteen years old.

Once the show is wrapped up, we head over to where Skyla will be getting ready, so I can introduce her to everyone she needs to know. Most girls would be nervous, but not Skyla. She's bubbly and outgoing and excited. She's polite to everyone she meets. Jase texts me when he, Quinn, and Jax have arrived and are seated. I couldn't get them in the front since that's only for the press, designers, and the who's who of fashion, but they do have decent seats. Skyla is taken from hair and makeup to wardrobe, and then is walked through what she'll be doing. I stay with her the entire time, not letting her out of my sight. Her dad is trusting me to take care of her, and I don't take that responsibility lightly.

When Ralph Lauren gets announced, all the kids and teens line up. Skyla has made a few friends, so I give her some space and tell her I'll be here when she's done. There are months and months of prep that go into getting everything ready for these shows, and oftentimes I'm too busy to actually enjoy what's happening around me, but today, with Skyla a part of it, I'm actually stopping and taking the time to watch and enjoy the show.

Skyla—dressed in an adorable tile-print mini-skirt with a matching top, leggings, and black leather boots—walks out onto the runway doing exactly as she was told and practiced. The cameras flash as she hits the end and then turns around to walk back. I look out and find Jase watching his daughter, a large grin splayed upon his face. He looks every bit the proud father. And my heart has never felt so full.

"I want her," Brenna murmurs into my ear. "She's going to be the next you."

I laugh softly. "No, she's going to be so much more." And then I turn to find Skyla. She's stepping back behind the scenes and her eyes lock with mine. Her smile is so wide, so pure, I want to bottle it up and save it.

"That was...amazing!" She squeals. "Thank you!"

"You were amazing," I tell her. "And being here, watching you has inspired me to consider creating my own children's and teen lines."

"Can I help you?" She clasps her hands together.

"Of course!"

JASE: **Hey gorgeous...**
  Jase: I have a big favor to ask of you
  Jase: Like huge
  Jase: Gigantic
  Jase: A word bigger than gigantic
  Jase: I'll make it worth your while ;)
I've just finished holding a meeting with my team—to go over the details of the buyers who have contacted Leblanc after seeing

the show—and have found two seconds to look at my phone. This week has been insanely crazy in an amazing way. There is nothing more magical, or exhausting, than putting on a fashion show. It's been a few years since I've stopped modeling and have attended the shows strictly as a designer, but the butterflies still appear with every show, and I hope they never go away. They remind me that my dreams have come true. That everything I've worked hard for is finally in my hands. But as I stare at Jase's texts, and my heart speeds up, I'm reminded that there's more to life than career goals. It's why I broke things off with Chad. Because I want more. I haven't seen Jase since Skyla's big debut into the modeling world, but we've talked every night on the phone, even if it's at four in the morning when I finally collapse into bed. For the first time, I'm looking forward to the craziness dying down. In the past, I lived for every fashion show, for the long days and even longer nights, but now it feels like it's only keeping me away from where I really want to be, which is with Jase and Skyla.

Me: anything

I've only just hit send when my phone rings. "Hello?"

"I was worried I scared you off with my hundred text messages," Jase says with a strained laugh.

"Sorry, it's been insane around here."

"Everything okay?"

"Oh yeah, great actually. We've already surpassed the number of buyers for the fall line than what we originally projected."

"That's amazing! Congratulations," Jase exclaims.

"Thank you." Then I remember the point of this call. "Is everything okay on your end? I saw all your texts."

"Yes, actually everything is great here as well. Have you ever heard of Max Harper?"

"The rapper?" I ask, confused.

"Yeah. I guess he has some reality show, and the producer called and said Max wants to come in for a tattoo. Apparently, Killian recommended me at some event."

"Wow! That's awesome. Are they going to film it?"

"Yeah, it will be incredible publicity for the shop."

"What do you need from me? Want me to dress you?" I joke. "I think I have a nice suit that would look rather dapper on you."

Jase laughs. "Nah, I got my wardrobe covered."

"So you're going with your usual jeans and a white T- shirt?"

He laughs again. "Am I that predictable?"

"Yeah, but I think we got off subject. What's the huge, gigantic favor you need from me so badly that you're willing to make it worth my while?"

"Right. Quinn is attending some last-minute function with her boyfriend and she was supposed to keep an eye on Sky. The producer said they don't want a kid on the show, and even if they did allow her to be on it, I don't really want her here at the shop. I imagine guys will be cursing and talking about things I don't want my thirteen-year-old daughter to hear. So I was wondering if you could watch her." I smile inside at how good of a dad Jase is. The guy is going to be on television and his biggest concern is making sure his daughter is taken care of and isn't exposed to anything that might affect her in a negative way.

"Of course, I can. When?"

Jase is silent for a second before he says, "Now?"

"Ahhh…" I laugh, now understanding why this is such a huge favor. "Where is she?"

"At home. Quinn had to leave to get ready. She's okay being left alone. I'm just not sure how long I'm going to be. Quinn offered to bring Sky to the charity gala, but I don't want to put her out. She's not even sure if she could get her a seat and—"

"Jase, breathe." I laugh. "I'll head over there now."

He releases a soft breath. "Thank you."

"You're welcome."

SEVENTEEN

*J*ASE

"LOOK, man, you don't need to thank me. That's what friends are for. Besides, your work speaks for itself," Killian says. I'm on my way home from the shop. The episode has been recorded, and Max Harper has been permanently tattooed with a custom piece, designed and inked by me. It's crazy. He posted one image, tagging the shop on Instagram, and we all spent hours making appointments —including the new receptionist, Evan, that Celeste found for me. The guy will be apprenticing with us at the shop while working in the front. It works out perfect.

Shocked over the fact that all of us are now booked well into September and the episode hasn't even aired yet, I called Killian, wanting to thank him again for recommending Forbidden Ink.

"Did everything go okay?" he asks.

"Everything went smoothly. Luckily, the tattoo he wanted wasn't too bad." I laugh. "I've seen some ugly as hell tattoos shown on those shows. The episode will be airing next month, and this will without a doubt be a game changer for the shop. You can't pay for this type of advertisement."

"Yeah, I've seen some, and not even the best artist can make them look good. I'm glad it all worked out."

"It did, so thanks."

Killian chuckles into the phone. "No problem. What are you up to tonight?"

"I actually just pulled up to my house," I say, putting my car in park and stepping out. "Celeste watched Sky for me."

"Celeste, huh?" Killian laughs. "Giselle told me a little about your past. I never would've guessed you and Celeste would've had a past...or a present." I know he doesn't mean it as a dig. It's merely an observation, but his words remind me once again how different Celeste and I are.

"Yeah, I guess she doesn't usually date guys like me," I say, leaning against the side of the car.

"Nah, I didn't mean it like that," Killian says, trying to backpedal. "She just usually... shit, okay, it's exactly what I meant." We both laugh.

"I get it. We're complete opposites. I know it doesn't make any sense. But trust me when I tell you there's so much more to her than what she lets people see."

"Yeah," he agrees. "That's what Nick has always said, and my wife is good friends with her. I guess I don't really know her all that well. But if there's one thing I've learned this past year, it's not to judge a book by its cover."

After talking for a few more minutes, we end the call with Killian telling me he's found a new piece he wants tatted, and that he'll be calling me tomorrow to schedule.

When I unlock the door and step inside my house, I hear the sound of laughter coming from the kitchen. I throw my keys into the key bowl and head that way to check it out. I was going to pick up dinner, but when I texted Celeste, she told me she and Skyla were taking care of it.

"I'm home," I say as I step around the corner.

"Jase!" Celeste laughs.

"Dad!" Skyla giggles.

I glance around at the destroyed kitchen, confused as to what the hell happened in here. There is what looks like flour everywhere. On the counters. All over the floor. It looks like it snowed in my kitchen. Celeste's hair is tinted white, and so are Skyla's clothes. They're both standing on opposite sides of the kitchen and holding balls of something gooey in their hands.

"What happened?"

Celeste laughs again then steps toward me. "Try this. Tell me what you think." She holds her fingers up, which are holding what looks like cookie dough, and brings them to my lips. "Open," she says playfully, so I do. She places a small bite of dough into my mouth, and Skyla's giggles get louder.

"Is it good?" Celeste asks. I chew the bite and swallow. It's a tad bit salty.

"Delicious," I say, and she grins.

"Ha!" She looks at Sky

"Try mine, Dad." Sky hands me a piece of dough. I chew and swallow.

"How does mine taste?" It tastes like there's way too much vanilla.

"Delicious," I tell her.

"So, whose is better?" Sky asks. Oh, shit... I didn't see that coming.

"They're both delicious."

Celeste cackles devilishly. "I think he needs to try some more," she tells Sky, who grins mischievously.

"I agree," Sky adds. "I think he needs to *experience* the dough to make a decision."

"Agree," Celeste says.

I watch as both of them walk over to where they were standing when I came in, unsure what they mean by *experiencing* the dough. But less than a minute later, I find out exactly what they mean when Skyla balls up a piece of the dough and throws it at me. The sticky dough smacks me in the face, and the girls crack up laughing.

"Hey!" I yell. "That's not cool."

"Oh no!" Celeste says, feigning concern. "Did the dough stick to you?" She cackles, and it sounds scary as fuck. "It's probably because it doesn't have enough flour. Here, let me help you." She takes a handful of flour and walks toward me. And before I can stop her, she dumps it over my head.

Now the mess in the kitchen makes perfect sense. Sky laughs so hard, she snorts.

"So, it's like that, huh?" I ask no one in particular. "All right..." I walk over to where the dough is sitting in the bowl, and grab it. "Game on!"

Celeste's eyes go wide, and she ducks, thinking I'm going to throw the dough at her. But instead, I take a large dollop in my hand, bridge the gap between us, and smoosh it all over her mouth.

Sky is now laughing so hard, she's bent over, holding onto her stomach. But when she sees me eye her, she stops and grabs a handful of dough. "Don't come any closer or I will be forced to use this on you." She raises her fist, and I laugh. And then I cut across the kitchen, and grabbing her by the waist, throw her over my shoulder.

"Dad!" She squeals. "Put me down." Taking some flour in my hand, I turn her right-side up and dump it over her head, at the same time Celeste dumps more over mine.

We spend the next however long throwing dough and flour at each other. I don't even want to think about the mess I'm going to have to clean up.

When the doorbell chimes, Celeste raises her hands in surrender. "I'm waving the white flag!" She giggles. "That's dinner."

"You ordered?"

"Well..." She traps her bottom lip between her teeth, nervously, then releases it. "I tried to cook."

"But it burnt," Sky adds with a shrug.

"Yeah," Celeste agrees.

"You two go get cleaned up, and I'll pay for the food."

"I can get it," Celeste insists. "It's my fault that dinner got ruined."

"I got it, babe," I tell her with a kiss, forgetting my daughter is in the room.

"I knew you two were a couple!" Sky yells as she runs up the stairs. "Friends my butt!"

After we finish eating dinner and clean up the mess in the kitchen—though, flour will probably be found in every nook and cranny for the foreseeable future—Sky asks if we can all watch a movie together. I look at Celeste, unsure if she has anywhere she needs to be, and she says she would love to.

Sky and Celeste pick out the movie while I make the popcorn, and then the three of us pile onto the couch to watch the movie. Jax comes home halfway through it, but says he's heading back out and not to wait up. When the movie ends, both Sky and Celeste are passed out. I lift them off me then carry Sky to bed. It's not often I get to carry my daughter to bed, so I try to engrave the moment into my memory for the times when she's rebelling against me and telling me she wants nothing to do with me.

Once she's tucked in, I head back down for Celeste. I should probably wake her up and ask if she wants to go home or stay, but she's out. So instead, I carry her up to my room and lay her in my bed. Apparently burning food and having food fights is exhausting. I laugh to myself as I recall the look of embarrassment on her face as she explained how she misread the directions for the roast. Then when she and Skyla tried to make cookies, they ended up spilling and eating more than actually got placed onto the cookie sheet.

In Celeste's eyes, she failed. There was no roast for dinner or cookies for dessert. The kitchen was a mess that we had to clean up. She apologized several times.

But in my eyes, she succeeded, and I told her just that. She made my daughter smile and laugh. She bonded with her—created memories that will last a lifetime. When I told her that, she just blushed and shrugged like I knew she would, and then apologized again, confirming just how guarded Celeste really is. With her fancy makeup and designer clothes, she appears strong from up in her high-rise expensive condo. As if she's on top of the world. But hidden behind her makeup and clothes, behind the walls she's built up to protect herself, is a vulnerable, insecure woman who just wants to be loved. And that's exactly what I'm going to do. I'm going to love her.

"DAMN, I can't believe how busy we are," Jax says, falling onto the couch next to me in the breakroom we have set up in the back of the shop. It has a couple of couches, a fridge, a sink, and a bathroom. Nothing fancy, but somewhere we can go between clients. It also has a door that leads out to the back alley, where those who smoke, can, since we don't like anyone smoking in the front. "Thank God for Celeste finding us Evan." He drops his head back against the wall and sighs in exhaustion.

"I know," I tell him. "We would've been screwed." My cell phone rings, and like the nosy-ass he is, Jax looks over to see who's calling.

"Tell Celeste I said hello," he says as I stand and walk away to speak to her without an audience.

"Hey, Dimples, how's it going?"

"Not good, Jase."

"What's wrong?" I close the office door behind me. With all four of us working today, there's several different songs going at once along with everyone bullshitting over the music.

"A few years ago, when I first launched my fashion line, I joined up with a couple other designers to start a charity called I Heart the Arts. It raises money to help the art programs in schools and clubs. This year we're going to be showcasing several models using body art to help raise money."

"That sounds like a good cause," I tell her, surprised and proud of this new fact I've just learned about Celeste.

"Yeah, it is. But the artists we hired for the show just canceled on us, so now I have twenty models with no art, and a show that's supposed to start in eight hours."

"What do you need from me?"

"Artists. I was wondering if maybe you knew anyone...well a few someones. Like maybe there's some network all artists are a part of. I know you're a tattoo artist, but maybe you all run in the same circles. I don't know." She sighs. "It's a paid job."

"I'm in, and I'm sure Jax and Gage and Willow will be too. And I can bring Evan. He's still apprenticing but he can draw."

"Oh," she says breathlessly. "I didn't mean you..."

"Am I not good enough?" I laugh. "I am an artist."

"No! I know you are. But you're super busy. You were just saying you're booked until like next year. I can't ask you to shut down for me."

"You're not asking. Text me the location and we'll be there soon."

"Yeah?" she asks with hope in her voice.

"Yeah."

"Thank you, Jase! I love you." The phone goes silent, and I pull it from my ear to see if Celeste is still there, or if she hung up. "What I meant was..." she starts to say, but she can't think of a way to justify or fix what she just said, which means she meant the words.

"What you mean is you love me," I tell her boldly, praying I don't spook her, but needing to tell her how I feel, "and I love you too."

There's another bout of silence and then Celeste whispers, "You do?"

"I do. See you soon, Dimples."

We hang up, and with the biggest fucking grin on my face, I call everyone into the office to ask them if they're willing to help. Of course they say they are. After telling everyone waiting that we have an emergency and need to close up shop, we start calling all of our clients who were supposed to come in today and reschedule them. After locking up the shop, we head over to Spring Studios where the show is being held. On the way, I call Quinn to let her know I'm not sure what time I'll be home, and she lets me know Rick has gone out of town for business, so she can keep an eye on Skyla without issue.

From the moment we arrive, everyone is in a frenzy. I wasn't sure what was needed to be done, but luckily Celeste has all of the supplies. All she needs from us is our talent. We spend the next several hours painting body art on each of the models. They are completely naked, but with the art painted on, it looks as if they're fully clothed. Celeste has specific outfits that need to be drawn on, and several designers, who are part of the show, oversee everything we're doing. Some of the names even have my eyes going wide. These aren't lowly up-and-coming designers. These are bigtime. And it hits me that the woman I'm dating is bigtime. She's a famous supermodel who has taken the fashion world by storm. I can still remember the teenage Celeste, who laid in my bed and shared her dreams with me. At the time, I didn't know all that was against her—that the hand she'd been dealt was even shittier than mine. She might've been Nick's best friend, but she wasn't raised with a silver spoon in her mouth like he was. She's fought for everything she has.

As I finish up the last model and stand to stretch my legs, the show begins. I hear Celeste's voice come over the microphone, and without getting in anyone's way, I peek out of the curtain. She's standing at the end of the catwalk speaking to the hundreds of people who are surrounding the stage about the charity and how all the proceeds will be spent. She's dressed in some sexy-as-fuck crème-colored tight dress that shows off her pert ass. Her sky-high fuck-me heels make her toned legs look like perfection. When she thanks everyone and turns around to walk back, our gazes clash. As she walks toward me, with her chin up and eyes bright with pride, she gives me a gorgeous smile that, I'm man enough to admit, takes my fucking breath away. And it's in this moment, I know that while our worlds may not fit perfectly, I will do whatever it takes to make sure they orbit close enough to keep her near me. Even if it means I have to jump into hers.

EIGHTEEN

Celeste

"I CAN'T BELIEVE you did this!" Olivia throws her arms around my neck for a hug, her pregnant belly hitting my front. "I...I...just thank you." She sobs.

Patting her on the back, I say, "You're welcome," while I search for Nick in hope of him saving me. When she finally releases me, her tears have dried up. But then she looks around, taking in her surroundings, and starts to cry again.

We're standing under an air-conditioned white tent I rented that overlooks the East River. It's Fourth of July, so there will be fireworks later, which is why I picked this particular park, but it's also a party to celebrate Nick's graduation and Giselle and Olivia's upcoming births. There are several tents set up throughout the area. A couple for people to sit and relax under, one where food is being catered, another where there's a bar set up, and one more for desserts and presents. Since Olivia and Giselle are both having girls, pink streamers, balloons, and other decorations are strung up all over the area.

"Celeste," Nick says, walking up, "this is too much." He gives me a hug and a kiss on the cheek. Reed, their eighteen-month-old son, toddles over with a balloon in his hand and Skyla running behind him.

"Ba-oon," he squeals. "Ba-oon! Da-da, ba-oon." Nick laughs and picks his son up.

"He let go of two of them," Skyla says with a laugh, "so I tied that one to his wrist."

"Good thinking," I tell her with a wink as Killian, Giselle, and Giselle's mom, Sarah, walk up to join us.

"Celeste!" Giselle squeals. "This is all amazing! When you told me you were throwing Nick a party, you didn't tell me it was also a baby shower." She points to the tent that's holding the three-tier Disney Princess cake. "That cake is incredible! Have you seen it, Livi?"

"No, not yet, we just got here," Olivia says.

"Come here, I have to show you." Giselle gives me a hug. "Thank you."

"You're welcome. If you're hungry, there's food over there." I point to one of the tents. "And there's a full bar set up in that one."

Giselle, Olivia, and Sarah head over to the tent to see the cake as Jase comes walking up with Jax, Quinn, and her boyfriend, Rick, who is staring down at his phone.

"Hey, Dimples," Jase says, giving me a soft kiss on my lips. "Everything turned out great." Jase and Skyla came here early this morning to help me set up, then left to take showers and get ready. Since I needed to go to my place to get ready, which is in the opposite direction, we agreed to meet back here.

"Thank you," I tell him. "There's tons of food and drinks. Please help yourself," I say to everyone.

"I'm starved," Quinn says to Rick. "Join me?"

"Sure," Rick says with a small smile, but doesn't look up from his phone. He reminds me a lot of the men I used to date. I try to think about all the times I've hung out with Jase. Maybe it's because his job isn't as demanding, but I can't think of a single time where he's been with me and didn't give me one hundred percent of his attention.

Gripping the curves of my hips, Jase pulls me in front of him and wraps his arms around my front, nuzzling his face into my neck. His two-day stubble tickles my skin, and I laugh, pushing him away. "You need to shave!" I joke.

"No, I don't," he growls into my ear. "I know you like my beard." He's not wrong. I love running my hands up and down his stubble.

"Hey, Dad, I'm going to get something to eat. Wanna go with me?" Skyla asks Jase.

"Sure, sweetie, let's go," he says, then turns to me. "You hungry?"

"I'll meet you guys over there in a minute. I just want to make sure the bounce house gets set up." The vender I ordered from was running late and is finishing up now. There aren't a lot of kids here, but Skyla thought it would be fun for Reed to play in, so I ordered one.

"All right." He gives me a kiss on my cheek then heads over to the food tent with Skyla. Since Reed has become her shadow, he follows, and Nick follows him—leaving Killian, Jax, and me standing here.

Killian steps closer to me. "You did good," he says. "Thank you."

"You're welcome."

"So, you and Jase, huh?" he asks.

"Yeah." I nod slowly.

"That's good. I'm happy for you guys."

"Thank you?" I squeak out, unsure of how to respond to Killian's overload of niceness, and a bit stunned that we've somehow apparently moved on to discuss my love life.

He laughs, and Jax joins in. "Ah, man, just be glad you don't have to live with Jase." He shakes his head. "It's disgusting to watch on a daily basis how in love they are."

"Oh, shut up!" I smack Jax's arm playfully, and he chuckles.

"Who would've thought, little miss 'I'm marrying a fortune 500 guy' would fall in love with a tattooist from Piermont." Killian laughs, hip bumping me. Had he said that a few months ago, I would've taken it the wrong way and gotten pissed, but I can see it in his face, he's just playing around—and he's not all wrong. When we were younger, that's exactly what I planned to do.

"So, what's next?" Killian asks. "A wedding? Babies?" He laughs harder, thinking he's so hilarious, and of course, Jax laughs right along with him. "I can see it now... Little Celestes and Jases dressed in Gap and Nike, running around with fake tattoos all over their arms."

"My kids wouldn't be dressed in Gap or Nike." I scrunch my nose up in mock disgust. "More like Dior and Dolce & Gabbana." Killian and Jax both crack up laughing.

"I'm just messing with you," Killian says. "You gotta admit, though. It's crazy how far we've come from the teenagers we once were, hanging out in the dorm room, refusing to fall in love while Nick ragged on us."

I laugh, remembering exactly what he means. Nick was the only one out of the three of us I ever imagined falling in love. Hell, when I was younger, I didn't even believe in love. Or maybe I did, but was too scared to admit it. "Yeah, sometimes it feels like it was another lifetime."

"Agreed." He nods once. "I better go check on my baby mama," Killian says with a smile, excusing himself. As I watch him walk away, my mind swirls with everything that was just said. I know he was only joking, but at the same time, what he said has truth to it. When two people are in a relationship, marriage and babies are what comes next, right? Does Jase want to have more kids? I just assumed since he already has a teenager, he wouldn't want to start all over again. What if I was wrong, though, and he wants to have more children? Give Skyla a brother or sister...

"You okay?" Jax asks. "You look like you've seen a ghost or something."

"Yeah...No...I'm okay," I choke out. "I'm going to go make sure everything is taken care of for the bounce house," I say, needing to escape for a moment before I have a panic attack.

"All right," Jax says, looking concerned.

After I make sure the party rental company is paid and let them know when to pick up the bounce house, I take a walk along the river, trying to calm my nerves over what Killian said. Everything with Jase and me feels like it's all happening so fast, yet slow at the same time. I think a lot of the reason for that is because of what we had all those years ago—it was so easy to slip back into where we left off. We've settled into the type of comfort a couple who've been together for a long time settle into, but we somehow skipped over the *getting to know you* part—like whether Jase wants more kids one day.

"Hey," a baritone voice calls out from behind me. When I turn around, Jase is walking up to me. "Jax mentioned you seemed off. Everything all right?"

He stops a few feet in front of me, and I stare at him for a few seconds, taking him in. His black hair, that's usually neatly gelled, is messy, as if he was running his fingers through it, his perfect lips are turned up into a slight nervous smile, and his signature white T-shirt is stretched taut across his chest, with his hands stuffed into his pockets. I should ask him right here and now if he wants more kids, but I can't bring myself to do it. Because if he says he does, I know I'll have to break things off with him. And if he says he doesn't, I will always wonder if he's lying, putting my needs first.

Instead, I take the couple feet toward him and wrap my arms

around his neck. His arms encircle my waist as I run my tongue across his lower lip, then his top one, teasing him. He groans, pulls me closer to him, and kisses me hard. His tongue massages mine, and I lift his shirt, sliding my palms over his abs. His skin is hot, and I crave his warmth. His hands glide down my back, landing on my ass. He lifts me into his arms, then carefully brings us both down to the grass. Hovering above me, with his arms on either side of my head, Jase and I make out like horny teenagers, his body grinding against mine, until we hear Skyla calling out our names. Quickly rolling off me, Jase stays lying down, his arm propping himself up, while I sit up and adjust my clothes.

"I've been looking everywhere for you guys," Skyla says. "Can we do cake and presents?"

"Sorry," I say, giving her a smile, while praying she didn't see her dad practically dry humping me in the grass. Jase stands first, and reaches down to help me up. "Yeah, we can do cake and presents." I stand and wipe the grass off my backside.

"Cool! You can go back to making out now." She winks and runs back over to where everyone is. With my hand in Jase's, we follow behind her. I think maybe Jase forgot about what he asked me when he walked over, until he leans in and whispers, "I know you were upset about something, and while that distraction was nice, I will ask you again later, and you will answer me."

The rest of the evening runs smoothly, and luckily, we're so busy with our friends and family that Jase doesn't find the time to ask me again what's wrong. We do cake, watch while Olivia and Giselle open their baby gifts, and Nick announces that he's been signed by a publishing company for the romance novel he wrote, based on Olivia and his love story.

At nine o'clock, we all make our way down by the river to watch the fireworks. Jase holds me in his arms while the bright colors shoot off, creating beautiful designs. And while I should be enjoying this moment, a small piece of me is wondering if every memory we're creating is only another weight being added to the reality that's going to drop right on top of us and knock us out of this fantasy we're currently living in.

NINETEEN

CELESTE

"IT'S SO BEAUTIFUL OUT HERE!" I spread my arms out wide so I can feel the cool breeze against the front of my body. I'm currently standing on the front deck of a seventy-five-foot luxury yacht as we enter the Atlantic Ocean. Killian and Giselle, Nick and Olivia, and Jax and some woman—Kirsten—he met at a bar the other night are all on board as well. I'm not sure where everyone else is, but what I do know is that Jase is currently standing directly behind me, with his arms wrapped around my naked torso and his chin resting on my shoulder. I can feel his bulge pressing into my ass, and it has me wanting to find one of the empty rooms on this boat and put it to good use.

"Not as beautiful as you are," Jase murmurs into my ear. I can't help the giggle that escapes my lips, remembering the last time he spouted a cheesy-ass line to me, ended with me losing my virginity to him.

"Smooth," I say through my laughter.

"It's the truth. The second you took off your bathing suit cover and turned around, my dick went hard." His hands glide down my sides and land on my nearly bare ass. "Please tell me you only wear this tiny fucking bikini in private," he says, squeezing a handful of each cheek. "Your sexy ass is hanging out for all the world to see."

"It's the style," I say by way of explanation. "They're called Brazilian bottoms."

"Well, I'm not sure I like everyone getting to see what's mine," he growls, and the sound of his voice has my thighs clenching.

"Okay, caveman," I say with a grin plastered on my face. I've never had a guy get jealous or possessive before, and it's definitely a turn on. Schooling my features, I turn around, so my back is pressed against the railing and my chest is pressed against Jase's. "Next, are you going to tell me you want me to quit my job and spend my days barefoot and pregnant in the kitchen?" When Jase's eyes light up, clearly more than okay with that image, I laugh nervously at my slip up. It's a typical cliché joke that everyone makes, but my making it can lead to a conversation about babies, and that's the last thing I want to discuss with Jase. It's been almost two weeks since the Fourth of July. I told myself that if he brought up my being upset, I would be honest, but luckily, he hasn't, so I'm pretty sure I'm in the clear.

"Down boy!" I say to hide my uneasiness. Then, standing on my tiptoes, I pull him in for a kiss, knowing if the talk of babies is on his mind now, it will distract him.

"Get a room," Nick yells just as the kiss is getting more heated, causing us to pull apart, both of us breathing hard with want.

"I think we should listen," I say in a whisper, and Jase's eyes go wide in shock that I would say such a thing. Before he can argue, I walk around him and head toward the stairs which lead down to the rooms. "I need to use the restroom," I announce without making eye contact with anyone. I've only just stepped off the stairs and into the cabin when I feel Jase's hands on my body. He shoves me into an open door and slams it shut behind us.

"That bathing suit is a fucking tease, woman," he murmurs as he lifts me onto what looks like a table of some sort and shoves my legs apart. He removes my bottoms and kneels down, set on eating me out. My back and head hit the wall with a thump as he spreads my lips and suckles my clit with his talented mouth. My hands go to my breasts, and I pull at the hardened peaks, losing myself to the pleasure.

When I've come so hard that I about see stars, Jase lifts me off the table and turns me around, so my back is to him. With my ass in the air, and my breasts mashed against the hardwood surface, Jase enters me in one fluid motion. Gripping my hair, he pulls my head back so he can suck on the side of my neck. His lips trail downward, kissing my shoulder, as he continues to fuck me, hard and deep. It doesn't take long until my legs are shaking and I'm screaming his name as we both come completely undone.

When he stills, his hard-length still deep inside me, he places another kiss to my shoulder and murmurs, "One day I'm going to tattoo this flawless body." I let out a content sigh. "I'm going to mark you permanently," he growls. "Make you mine." His voice is so matter-of-fact, it sends heat through my entire body.

He pulls out of me, and I miss the contact immediately. Turning around, I wrap my arms around him, not wanting our connection to end. He lifts me, and with my legs wrapped around him, carries me to the bathroom to get cleaned up. With me sitting on the luxurious marble countertop, Jase gently opens my legs and cleans me up—and my heart picks up speed at how sweet he is.

My thoughts go back to what he said a moment ago: *make you mine.* I've never wanted to be anybody's before. I've wanted to be wealthy and successful, have a nice home, a comfortable life. And I wanted to find a man who would help ensure that I would have all of that. But until Jase, I never wanted to actually *be* somebody's. Belong to him. Be his everything. Now I can't imagine anything I want more. And with that thought, I say a prayer that one day, when we have the conversation we need to have, our futures align.

AFTER SPENDING the rest of the day on the yacht, hanging out and relaxing with everyone else, we head back to Jase's place. He said he's cooking Skyla's favorite—chicken fettucine alfredo—and asked me to join them for dinner. Jax says he'll be home right after he drops Kirsten off. It was obvious she wanted to be invited back, but Jax either didn't catch on, or didn't care, because he made it clear he was dropping her off first.

When we arrive at Jase's house, we're greeted by a very excited Skyla and a glaring Quinn. I'm not sure why Quinn still has such an issue with me, but at some point, we should probably discuss it.

"Dad! Celeste!" Skyla hugs her father and then me. "Did you guys have fun?"

"We did," Jase says, giving his daughter a kiss on her forehead before excusing himself to go start dinner.

"Aunt Quinn showed me a picture of a yacht, like the one you guys were on. I wanted to go today, but Dad said no," Skyla says as we walk into the living room. "It's so beautiful!"

"They are," I agree. "Today was just for adults," I tell her, sitting down on the couch, "but we can go on one if you want."

Skyla sits next to me, her eyes as wide as saucers. "Really?" She pulls out her phone and shows me the image of a yacht a little smaller than the one we went on today. "One like this?"

"Sure." I smile at her. "You can invite some of your friends if you want, too. And we can even have the captain anchor, so we can go swimming."

"That would be so much fun," Skyla exclaims. "Aunt Quinn, do you want to go?" She turns her attention over to Quinn, who is leaning against the wall like she's not sure if she wants to join us—well, more like join me—and is shooting daggers my way.

"Sky, why don't you go wash your hands, so you can help your dad start dinner?" she says, not answering the question.

"Okay." Skyla shrugs and then takes off upstairs.

Once she's out of earshot, Quinn says, "You aren't her parent. You shouldn't make plans with Skyla without asking Jase." I frown at her words. She's right, I'm not Skyla's parent, but I didn't think it would be an issue.

"You're right. I'll ask Jase in the future."

"And what about the fact that renting a yacht will cost thousands of dollars?" Quinn continues. "You don't think that's a bit excessive? She's thirteen years old and needs to learn that she can't just have whatever she wants."

"Maybe." I raise a shoulder, not understanding why my wanting to make Skyla happy is such an issue. Her grandparents spoil her with materialistic possessions. "But if it's what will make her happy, then who cares?"

My phone rings with an incoming call, so I pull it out of the pocket of my bathing suit coverup and click the side button to silence it since it's my mom. Not having had spoken to her in a while, I'm about to excuse myself to call her back, when Quinn says, "You might be some rich and famous model or whatever"—she flicks her hand in the air—"and Sky may look up to you, but Jase wants more for his daughter."

Ouch! Okay, then. "What's your problem, Quinn?" I stand and walk toward her.

"You," she says simply.

"Well, that much is obvious." I roll my eyes. "But what about me is exactly your problem?" Other than a few times of hanging out during the week Jase and I spent together all those years ago, we barely know each other.

"For starters, my brother cares a lot about you, yet you were able to walk away from him without so much as a goodbye." I open my mouth to argue why I did just that, but she continues, "And how about the fact that you only date wealthy, white-collared business-men." Her brows raise, daring me to argue.

"Isn't your boyfriend wealthy?" Rick Thompson owns several investment firms all over the world.

"Yes, but unlike you, I don't have a type, and my brother defi-nitely isn't your type. So what are you doing with him? Getting your fix of the 'bad boy.'" She actually uses air quotes. "And once you've had enough, you'll what...leave him again?"

"For your information—" I step closer to Quinn, so I don't have to raise my voice "—Jase knows why I left. Not that I have to justify myself to you, but it was a horrible misunderstanding. I regret that I didn't speak to him before I left, but I can't take it back now. And while, yes, the wealthy, white-collared businessman *was* my go-to type, it was only because I wasn't looking for love."

"And now you are?" she volleys.

"Yes," I say with a nod, "I am, and I love your brother."

"And I love you, too," Jase says, pulling me into his side. I don't even know when he joined us. "Quinn, I know you mean well, but please give Celeste another chance. What happened back then was a shitty misunderstanding, and Celeste and I have both moved forward. I would appreciate if you would do the same."

"Fine," Quinn says, "but do you really think it's wise that Celeste is offering to take Sky on yachts? She's going to think that's normal."

"And her wearing Burberry boots and Coach glasses is?" Jase says, defending me and pointing out exactly what I was just think-ing. "Not everything is black and white, sis."

"That's different," she argues. "You don't have a choice. It's the only way Amaya's parents will leave you alone."

"We always have a choice," he says, "and you're right, it is differ-ent. My thirteen-year-old walks around in outfits that sometimes cost as much as the mortgage on this house." He chuckles softly with a shake of his head. "And it's because her grandparents choose money over love. They're doing the same thing to my daughter that they did to theirs. They're trying to buy her love. But as her dad, it's my job to teach her the difference. And I don't, for a second, think Celeste offered to take Skyla out on a yacht as a way to buy her love." My heart swoons at Jase's words. He didn't even hear our conversation yet he's giving me the benefit of the doubt.

"And," he adds with a sexy smirk, "I would like nothing more than for Sky to end up just like Celeste." Oh! He did hear our conversation. "Yes, she's rich, but that's only because she's strong and determined and motivated." Hot tears well up in my eyes at his words as he continues. "There are a million models out there *almost* as gorgeous as Celeste." He winks at me playfully. "But not all of them are as successful. Not all of them work as hard to pave their own future. Celeste isn't just some model. She's a smart and savvy businesswoman, and I fully support my daughter looking up to her."

Unable to take another second of hearing Jase talk about me, I pull his face down to mine and kiss him hard, hoping to convey every emotion I feel right now. When our kiss ends, I say in a whisper, "I love you. Thank you."

"Just speaking the truth, Dimples."

My phone begins to ring again. I pull it out and see it's Victoria this time, and my stomach knots. What if something is wrong with my mom? "I need to take this," I tell him. Then to Quinn I say, "I really do care about your brother and Skyla. I hope you can give me a chance." She nods once but doesn't say anything, so I press answer on my phone and walk outside to take the call.

"Victoria, how are you?" I say politely.

"I'm calling because of your mother," she says, getting straight to the point.

"Is everything okay?"

"No, she's been admitted into the hospital for alcohol poisoning. Someone found her passed out in front of the diner." Victoria had told me my mom was still going there daily in case Snake showed up, but I didn't know she was drinking while there. This has gotten out of hand. I need to give my mom answers once and for all. I should've done it sooner, but Adam was right. I was too scared. I'm not sure what would be worse: to find out he's alive and living his life, which would mean he just didn't want us, or to find out he's dead and all this time my mom has been waiting on a man that will never show up.

"I think you need to come back. She needs help, Celeste, and she won't let me help her."

"Okay," I tell her, "I'll be there as soon as I can." We hang up and I go inside. The aroma from the dinner Jase is cooking wafts into my nose and my stomach rumbles.

"Smells delicious," I tell him when I enter the kitchen. "Can I do anything to help?"

"Nope." He gives me a kiss on the tip of my nose. "Sky is setting the table and the fettucine is almost ready."

"Okay, I'll get the drinks," I offer.

Once the table is set, and the drinks are poured, Jase spoons heaps of pasta and chicken onto all of our plates, just as Jax walks through the door and joins us at the table.

"Rick will be gone all week," Quinn says to Jase as we eat our food. "So, if you need any help with Sky this week, I'll be available."

"Jase mentioned you have a photography business," I say, trying to make an effort.

"I do, but it's slow-building," she admits. "I started it about five years ago, but it's hard to get my name out there."

"What kind of photos do you take?"

"Mostly family portraits. I don't have an office. I shoot on location, like at Central or Bryant Park." I remember that earlier when Giselle, Olivia, and I were talking, Olivia mentioned she wanted to get professional pregnancy photos done. Giselle said she did too.

"My friends, Giselle and Olivia, want to get pregnancy photos done. Is that something you do?"

"Yeah." Quinn nods. "But you don't have to—"

"Don't do that," I say, cutting her off, knowing exactly what she was about to say. "You're running a business. When someone offers to bring you in business, even if you think it's out of pity, you take it." I shoot her a wink, and she laughs, and it feels like maybe she and I will be okay after all.

"Actually," Jase says slowly, "Sky and I are going to be flying down to North Carolina to visit her mom."

"Oh, yay!" Skyla exclaims. "I can bring her the signed paper Celeste gave me."

"I was wondering if maybe...if you don't have too much going on...if you would want to join us," Jase says softly.

"I was actually planning to fly down myself," I say. "My mom isn't doing so well, and I need to go check on her."

"Oh, what's wrong with her?" Jase asks with a look of concern.

Not wanting to get into it with Skyla at the table, I simply say, "She's just not feeling well, and I haven't seen her in a while." I don't mention that I actually haven't seen her in over ten years— since I left. I refused to return, and she refused to leave.

"All right, then how about we look at flights when we're done eating?" Jase suggests. "We can book a room, and while you're visiting your mom, we can visit Amaya."

"Sounds good," I tell him, taking a bite of my food. "And can we just make it official that you're the cook in this relationship? This is so delicious!"

TWENTY

Celeste

"SKY, PLEASE HURRY UP!" Jase yells across the hotel suite to his daughter. We arrived in Piermont late last night. After checking in, we were all so exhausted from flying, we crashed into our beds the second after we changed our clothes.

Now it's morning, and Jase is taking Skyla to go see Amaya while I go visit my mom. She's already been discharged from the hospital and is back home. While I haven't spoken to her, knowing she would just downplay it or lie to me, I spoke to the doctor at the hospital to make sure she was okay. I also put a call in to Duncan, my PI, hoping he might have some answers for me, but I haven't heard back yet.

"Coming," Skyla yells back. A few seconds later, she steps out of the bathroom looking adorable and fashionable. She's wearing pigtail french braids I did in her hair earlier, and is dressed in a cute jean skirt and a flowery flowy top. To complete her outfit, she's sporting silver glitter Kate Spade high-tops. Every time I see her dressed, the desire to create a children and teen's fashion line increases. Skyla and I have been working on several designs together, and I'm getting excited. I spoke with my partners and they're completely onboard.

"I'm going to head out too," I tell Jase.

"You're not going with us?" Skyla frowns.

"You knew Celeste was going to see her mom," Jase tells her.

"I know, but I thought you could go with us first and then go see your mom," she says with the saddest look on her face. "Please."

Powerless to say no to her, I nod. "Okay, yeah, I can do that."

"No, you can't," Jase argues. "Sky, we'll see Celeste later. She needs to go see her mom." He wraps his arms around my waist and kisses my cheek. "It's okay to tell her no," he whispers.

"I know," I tell him, "but I don't like to see her sad, and it really is okay. I can go...unless... you don't want me to." I didn't even consider he might not want me there.

"Of course I do," he states seriously. "I just don't want you to feel obligated."

"Well, I don't mind." I give him a quick kiss. "I can go see my mom afterward."

"We can go with you...if you want," Jase offers, but I shake my head.

"I appreciate that, but I have no idea the condition she'll be in, and I don't want to chance exposing Skyla to whatever state she may be in."

"When's the last time you saw your mom?"

I swallow thickly. "Eleven years," I whisper. My eyes dart to the picture on the wall, not wanting to look Jase in the eyes.

"Celeste, look at me," he says. "You never returned? Not once?" His tone is one hundred percent full of concern and curiosity, not an ounce of judgment in his words, but that doesn't stop me from feeling shame. What daughter doesn't visit her mom once in eleven years?

"No," I admit softly, "and she wouldn't visit me. I-I pay all her bills, but I haven't seen her since I left when I was eighteen."

Jase nods once. "Monica and Phil asked if they can take Sky to dinner. I'll tell them they can take her, and then I'll go with you. You're not doing this on your own."

"You don't have to do that."

"I can see it in your eyes, Dimples. You're scared. I'm here. You don't have to do this alone."

WE ARRIVE at the long-term care facility and, after signing in, head up to the third floor where Amaya is. When we get to the room number the receptionist said she's in, Jase stops and folds slightly at the waist so he's at Skyla's level. "Remember what I told you.

Because your mom is still in a coma, there's a good chance she's not going to look like the same person you've seen in the pictures Grandma and Grandpa have shown you."

"I know," she says with a nod. "I remember from last time." Jase sighs like he wants to say something more, or maybe take her away from here, but instead he simply nods back.

Not wanting to interfere in this moment, I attempt to stay back while Jase opens the door and walks inside with Skyla, but she notices, and taking my hand in hers, says, "Can you please come with me? I want you to meet her."

"Sure," I say, then walk inside with her. The room is a harsh white and smells like a mixture of bleach and antiseptic. There's a single bed in the middle of the room and only the sounds of the monitors fill the silence. It takes everything in me to stifle my gasp when my eyes land on Amaya laying still in the bed. She looks nothing like the woman I met all those years ago. Her face is pale and gaunt. There's no meat on her, which you would think would be the opposite since she's unable to exercise. Her hair is down and straight, as if it was recently brushed, but it's greasy looking, like it rarely gets washed.

Skyla's steps falter and the grip she has on my hand tightens. She's scared, and I don't blame her. Amaya doesn't look scary per se. She looks sick. Knowing Skyla wants me to meet her mom, I step forward, guiding us to the side of her mom's bed. We stand together in silence for a few minutes, and when I'm sure Skyla and Jase aren't going to speak, I do.

"Hey, Amaya," I begin. Skyla's hand squeezes mine. "I'm not sure if you remember me. We only met once."

"You met my mom?" Skyla asks. I look down at her, confused. Then I play back what I just said. Shit!

"I did once," I admit. "When we were really young. She was hanging out with your dad when I went over to his place to visit him." I'm not sure if I've said the right thing, but it's too late now.

Skyla nods once, but doesn't say anything.

"Why don't you show her what you brought her?" I suggest.

"She looks so different from what I remember," Skyla says, assessing her mom.

"It's probably because you're getting older," I tell her. "When we're little, we don't see things the same way we do once we're older."

"Do you think she can hear me?" she asks, sounding way

younger than her thirteen years. "The nurses said before that she can, but now I'm not sure if they're right."

I have no clue if Amaya can hear or not, and I can't lie to her. "I'm not sure, but a lot of people believe that when someone is in a coma they can hear what their friends and family say to them, so it's worth a shot." I did hear that once on a show.

"Okay," she says, then steps forward and begins to tell her mom about me—who I am, what I do for a living, how we met, etcetera. My eyes find Jase's and our gazes lock. He mouths a 'thank you' to me.

We spend the next half hour talking to Amaya—until her parents show up. They walk in and greet us, introducing themselves to me, but not once acknowledging their daughter. Skyla says bye to Amaya, leaving the signed paper on the nightstand next to her bed, and we all leave. Monica and Phil tell Jase they're going to take Skyla to eat and do some shopping, and will call him when they're done so he can pick her up.

After giving Skyla a hug goodbye, we get back into our rental car and head toward my childhood home. Jase is driving, so I have to guide the way. When we cross over the train tracks, my heart plummets into my stomach, weighing down on my insides like a lead weight. I'm holding Jase's hand, but I let go, feeling my palm getting sweaty. My heart gallops in my chest, and it gets harder to breathe.

"Hey," Jase says, darting his eyes to me. "It's going to be okay. I'm here with you. We'll get through it together."

"I know." I point to the upcoming stop sign. "Turn left there."

"What you did for Sky," he says, making the left turn, "the way you took charge and made her less afraid. Thank you."

"Why has she been in a coma for so long? Is there a chance of her waking up?"

Jase exhales a harsh breath. "Is there a chance? Yeah, but it's small. So damn small." He shakes his head. "Six months after Amaya was found, the doctors told her parents they had the option to pull the plug, but they were so riddled with guilt, feeling like they failed her, they refused. I think in some weird way, they think they're finally being good parents by keeping her alive."

"Wow, that's so sad," I tell him. "Turn right here." I point to the stop sign. "It's the fourth trailer on the left."

"It is sad," he agrees as he turns onto the street I grew up on. "Unfortunately, since they're her parents, they get to make that call. Once the doctors said there's only a fifteen percent chance she'll ever wake up, they had to move her to the long-term facility. I don't even think they ever visit her. It's just the idea that she's alive and they're taking care of her that makes them feel less like failures."

"I can't imagine having to make that decision," I say truthfully. "Having to decide whether someone lives or dies."

"This one?" Jase asks, pointing to my childhood home, if you can even call it that. *A home.* The trailer itself isn't bad looking. While it's older, it doesn't look as such. I pay a window cleaning company to come out every six months to clean the windows and pressure clean the exterior, a lawn service to mow the lawn, and a housecleaner—despite my mother's protest—to clean the inside once a week. But no amount of cleaning can make this place *feel* like home.

"Yeah," I whisper. He parks in the driveway behind my mother's newer Audi that I bought for her a couple years ago. She, of course, argued, but eventually gave in since her car needed to be fixed and I refused to pay for it. Allowing me to purchase her a car was the only way she could get to work and home every day since the bus service stops before her shift at the diner ends—or I guess did end, since the diner is now shut down.

We get out of the car and head up the sidewalk. Not sure of the condition my mother's in, I stop Jase and say, "Would you mind waiting out here?" I point to the table and chairs. "I just don't want to make her feel uncomfortable if she's not dressed," I add.

Jase nods his understanding. "Sure, I'll be right here."

"Thank you." I give him a chaste kiss, then step up the three small steps and take a deep breath, nervous of what I'll find in there. The door is unlocked, like always, so I walk right in. Everything is the way it was when I left eleven years ago. From the shit-colored brown couch, to the cheap pressboard cabinets my mother painted an ugly mustard yellow. She purchased this trailer when she found out she was pregnant with me. Snake helped her find the place and even paid for it. It's why she won't leave. She's afraid if she moves, he won't be able to find her.

"Mom," I call out to let her know I'm here.

"In my room," she croaks. I enter her room and find her lying in bed with her sheets pulled up to her chin. The room is pitch black, save for a tiny sliver of light seeping in through the slats of the blinds. I can't assess her features. It's too dark. Flipping the switch, a soft yellow glow lights up the room, but my mom doesn't open her eyes. Her hair is still the same color, but now there's gray mixed in. Her face is free of all makeup, and tiny crow's feet have been added to the corners of her eyes and mouth. But, despite all that—

and the years she's spent smoking and drinking—my mom is still beautiful.

"Mom," I say again, and this time her eyes open.

"Celeste," she whispers. "You're here." She sits up and smiles sadly. I'm not sure what to do or say, until she opens her arms wide, and then I cut across the tiny room and fill them. I hug her tight, ignoring the smell of cigarettes that bleeds from her pores. "Oh, pretty girl," she murmurs, "I've missed you so much." I'm too choked up to speak, so I just nod my head into her hair in agreement.

We hug for I don't know how long, and only separate when the sound of my phone ringing breaks through the silence. I pull it out of my purse. It's Duncan. Not wanting to answer the call in front of my mom, I press the button on the side to silence the call, then drop it back into my purse.

"I'm so sorry I stayed away for so long. I should've come home to visit."

"No, don't you dare apologize," she says. "You did it. You became everything I knew you would be." Tears fill her eyes, and when she blinks, they fall. "Please don't tell me Victoria called you."

"She did, and of course I came, Mom. Alcohol poisoning, dehydration." I don't bother to mention the fact that she's spending her days at the diner. It's pointless. If after almost thirty years she's still refusing to give up waiting for Snake, she's not going to now. I need to find out what the PI found out first.

"It's the anniversary of the day he told me he loved me." She sniffles. "The day he left."

"Oh, Mom." I pull her into my arms again. "I'm so sorry." I almost tell her I'm going to have answers soon, but stop myself.

There's a soft knock on the front door, and I remember Jase is waiting outside. "My boyfriend came with me," I tell my mom. "If you're not up for company, we can leave. We're in town for a few days. Maybe we can go to dinner or something."

My mom smiles. "I would love to meet him. Chad, right?"

I clear my throat. "Actually, Chad and I broke up. His name is Jase."

"How about tomorrow? We can do lunch," she suggests. "It will give me time to get myself together."

"Okay. I'll call you and let you know the name of the place. Do you need anything? I can run to the store for you."

"No, pretty girl, I'm okay. I'll see you tomorrow." She leans over and kisses my cheek. "I love you, Celeste."

"I love you too, Mom."

When I walk outside, Jase is standing by the door. "Everything okay? I didn't want to bug you guys, but I wanted to make sure she's all right."

"She's okay. We're going to meet for lunch tomorrow. She wants to meet you, but doesn't want you to see her like that."

"That's understandable," he says. "Sky will be with her grandparents for a few more hours. What do you say we head back to the hotel and spend the rest of the day with me inside you?" He waggles his eyebrows, and I throw my head back with a laugh.

"You're so crude."

"And you love it."

TWENTY-ONE

CELESTE

"ISN'T IT SO PRETTY?" Skyla flips her sketchpad over so I can see the dress she's drawing.

"It's beautiful," I tell her honestly.

While Jase watches a baseball game downstairs at the bar, Skyla and I are sitting outside on the balcony of our suite—I'm drinking a glass of wine, and she's drawing in her sketchpad. She returned from dinner with her grandparents a little while ago and put on a fashion show with all of her new clothes. The girl has exquisite taste, that's for sure.

Afterward, Jase asked if I minded if he met up with a few of his friends downstairs at the bar to watch the game. It's been a while since he's seen them, so they all wanted to catch up. He invited Skyla and me to join, but neither of us wanted to go—plus, none of the other guys were bringing their significant others. So I told him Skyla and I would hang out up here and insisted he go.

"We should make a swimwear line too," Skyla says while drawing the beginning lines of a swimsuit. Her tongue sticks out just a bit, her teeth biting down on it, something she always does when she's concentrating. "When I went shopping today, there were so many ugly bathing suits." She scrunches her nose up in disgust. "So many ruffles and hearts." She mock-shivers.

"There's nothing wrong with ruffles or hearts," I tell her. "You just have to know where to put them, and always remember less is more." I shoot her a playful wink and she giggles. "Speaking of bathing suits..." I glance down at the lit-up pool. "Why don't we go swimming?"

"Really?" She stops drawing to look up at me, her adorable face lighting up in excitement. "I've never been swimming in the dark!"

"Yes, really, and it's called night swimming. Let's go put our suits on and we can go down for a little while."

There are a few people at the pool, but because it's already almost ten o'clock at night, they're all adults and keep to themselves. One couple is making out in the corner of the deep end and look like they're halfway to going *all* the way. So I suggest we check out the shallow end, which luckily, since the pool is shaped like a kidney, is around the corner. The last thing I want to do tonight is have the sex talk with Skyla.

We spend the next hour or so swimming laps and talking about fashion. She tells me about a boy who she likes and is looking forward to seeing when school starts up again. When the jacuzzi empties, we turn it on and relax in the bubbles for a little while. I can tell when Skyla is getting tired because she yawns several times and rubs her eyes. She may act like she's older a lot of the time, but she's still barely a teenager.

After we rinse off and change into our pajamas, she asks if we can watch an episode of Elite Model on her iPad. Snuggling into her bed with her, I pull it up on YouTube. Not even ten minutes into it, her eyes are fluttering closed. I click pause on the show and her eyes open a little at the silence before closing again.

Climbing out of her bed, I stand and lean over to kiss her forehead. "Good night, pretty girl," I say softly. I turn to walk out, when Skyla murmurs sleepily, "G'night, Mom, love you."

My heart stills then picks up speed. *She didn't mean to say that,* I tell myself. She saw her mom this morning and the word just slipped out. But as I walk to my room, I can't get the three-letter word out of my head. Maybe she didn't mean to say it, but what if she did? And if she didn't mean to, who's to say that one day she won't say it on purpose? Every girl deserves to have a mother. One who loves and protects her. Skyla was cheated out of having a mom, and she deserves better than to have me as a poor substitute. I'm just learning how to love Jase. I can't be responsible for both of their hearts. I can't fail them both.

What was I thinking? That's the problem...I wasn't! My heart and body have been dictating my decisions. My thoughts go back to the conversation I had with Killian. *"What's next? Marriage? Babies?"* I should've pulled the brakes on all of this the minute I found out Jase was a dad. We never should've even begun. Instead, I chose to live in denial, refusing to give thought to what our future would look like. How could I be so irresponsible? I run a multi-million-dollar corporation for God's sake! I make huge decisions every day, yet I went into this thing with Jase without even giving it a second thought. I can't be someone's mom. I can't be responsible for the welfare of another person. My heart cracks at the thought of letting Skyla down in any way. And that's what will eventually happen. I will let her down. And with that sobering thought, I know what I need to do. Sure, we'll all be hurt on some level, but it won't be nearly as bad as it will be if I stay. With every day that goes by, we all get in deeper, and the deeper we get, the more it will eventually hurt.

Climbing into bed, I face the wall and pull the covers up to my chin. My eyes burn with unshed tears, but I refuse to allow them to fall. I'm doing this to myself. I'm making the right decision. I don't deserve to cry.

I hear when Jase gets back. When he joins me in bed, he tries to pull me close. I can smell the alcohol on his breath. I can feel his erection pressing against my butt. But I don't move. I pretend like I'm asleep, and a few minutes later, he's snoring softly.

Carefully, I roll away from Jase and off the bed, so as not to wake him up, then quietly pack my luggage. I don't bother getting dressed. I don't want to risk waking anyone up.

I'm about to exit the room, when the guilt of leaving yet again without a goodbye hits me. I find a pen and paper in the desk drawer and scribble out a note.

Jase,

I couldn't leave without saying goodbye. It's better to break our hearts now than later. I'm sorry. Please don't call or text me. It will only make this harder.

xo Celeste

"NOT THAT I'M not happy to see you, but I thought we were meeting for lunch." My mom is standing over me with her hands on her hips, her head tilted to the side in confusion.

"I broke up with Jase."

"Oh no, why?" Mom joins me on the couch and pushes my

messy hair out of my eyes, just like she used to do when I was little, during the rare moments she was nurturing.

"Because Skyla called me Mom when I was kissing her good-night," I tell her honestly.

"And who is Skyla?"

"Jase's daughter."

"And her calling you Mom is a bad thing, why?" She gives me a perplexed look, needing me to explain the issue. But how do I explain to her that my issue of not wanting to be a mom stems from my own mother. Before I can come up with a way to say what I'm feeling, my phone vibrates. Picking it up from the coffee table, I see it's Duncan again.

"I need to take this," I tell my mom, pulling the sheet she must have covered me with off and standing. "Hello," I say as I step outside.

"Celeste, it's Duncan, how are you?"

"I'm...okay. I saw you called yesterday, but I wasn't able to answer." Still in my pajamas, I walk a little ways down the sidewalk to make sure my mom can't overhear.

"That's okay. I didn't want to leave a message. I found your guy." My steps falter. Duncan continues, "Snake aka Fredrick Leblanc was killed in a motorcycle accident on July eighteenth, nineteen eighty-nine on State Road seventeen." I gasp as I recall what the date is today. July twentieth...which means July eighteenth was two days ago. He died the day he left my mom. "He was hit by a semi who had been driving for too long and fell asleep at the wheel. His mother was his emergency contact and she identified his body. The funeral was held three days later at Holy Cross cemetery in Atlanta, Georgia where he was born and raised."

"He died the day he left," I murmur mostly to myself. All these years of her wishing and hoping and dreaming, and the entire time there was no hope.

"I have some more information that I was able to find, but I know you wanted to know what happened. I'll email it all to you, and if you have any questions, please call me."

"Thank you," I say before I hang up.

When I get back inside, my mom is walking out of the bathroom in her robe with her hair wrapped in a towel. "I was thinking we could still go to..." She sees the tears falling down my cheeks and her words trail off. "What's wrong?"

I cover my mouth with my hand as my tears turn into a loud sob. I'm not mourning the loss of the father I've never known, but the loss of the mother I never had. The mother who spent my entire life waiting for a man who was dead within hours of driving away. I should've looked him up sooner. I might not have been able to afford it at first, but the last several years I could've.

"Celeste, talk to me." She pulls me down onto the couch. "You're scaring me."

"I found him," I choke out through a loud sob. "I found my father." My mother's eyes widen, and her teeth bite down nervously on her bottom lip. "He died, Mom." More tears glide down my cheeks. "I'm so sorry."

"When?" she asks, her voice wobbly.

"The day he left here. He was hit by a semi who fell asleep at the wheel."

She nods a few times slowly, the rims around her eyes turning red. "You found him," she says.

"I hired a PI," I admit. "I should've done it sooner. I'm so sorry."

"Oh, Celeste," she murmurs, "I knew there was a chance something happened to him. I could've asked you to find him. I think I was just too afraid of what I might find." Her fears mirrored mine.

"I was too," I tell her truthfully.

"I only had him for a couple of months," she says softly. "Only a couple short months. But I loved him so much." She looks at me, her eyes assessing my features like she's just now seeing me for the first time. "Oh, Celeste." She weeps. "I was so focused on wishing he would return to spend our life together, I forgot to live *my* life. I'm so sorry." Her hands come up to her mouth, and she shakes her head. Gut-wrenching sobs wrack her entire body as she stares at me.

She stands and walks toward the kitchen, then stops and twirls in a circle. Her eyes find mine. "What did I do?" she whispers. "What have I done?" She spreads her arms out. "This shitty trailer. My shitty job." She sniffles. "All I had from my love with Snake was you, and instead of taking care of you, I abandoned you."

I want to argue, tell her that's not true, but we both know it is. She may have been here every day in body, but in mind, in heart, she was gone.

"It's not too late," I tell her. "You can still start your life over."

A fresh flood of tears gush down her cheeks as she walks back over to me. She kneels in front of me and cups my face with her hands. "Start over?" She cries. "I missed it all! We were living under the same roof, but I missed everything. Every milestone in your life. I was here yet never present. Now you're thirty years old. I don't want to start over, Celeste. I want to go back in time." Her lips tremble as she cries. "You must hate me."

"No, Mom." I reach up, and removing her hands from my cheeks, entwine our fingers. "I don't hate you."

"It's why you never came back," she mumbles. "I didn't give you a home worth coming back to."

"Mom." I choke on the word, unsure of what to say. She's right, but I'm not about to kick her while she's down. She might've been a shitty mom, but I still love her.

"How do I fix this?" she pleads. "Tell me it's not too late."

"Move to New York with me," I blurt out. "Move into my condo with me and we can get to know each other. I can help you start over...please."

More tears fall down her face as she nods. "Okay, on one condition," she tells me. I nod once, and she continues. "You stop running from love, and you don't use me to hide from it anymore." Her tone is pleading. "I messed up...bad. But I can't sit by and watch you miss out on love and life because of what I did to you. You deserve it all, pretty girl."

"I-I'm not..."

"Yes, you are." She looks me dead in the eyes. "The scariest part of finally getting what you want is the fear of losing it. When you have nothing, there's nothing to lose, but once you do, once you've gotten what you've dreamed of, you now have everything to lose."

"I don't think I could handle losing them, Mom," I admit.

"I would give anything to have more time with Snake. Don't you dare waste a second being without the people you love because you're scared. I might've failed you while you were growing up, but I still know you. The last ten years, I've watched you from afar work your way up the fashion ladder. And I know damn well that you didn't get to where you are by being afraid. It's time to be brave, pretty girl. It's time for you to live and love."

TWENTY-TWO

*J*ASE

THREE DAYS ago I woke up and reached for Celeste, only to find the sheets empty and cold. I don't know how, but I knew she was gone before I even got out of bed. Before I saw her luggage and clothes and toiletries were gone. Before I found her note. It was as if she left and took a piece of me with her. My heart no longer whole. Ignoring her request not to call or text, I did both. Several times. Until her phone went straight to voicemail, indicating it had been turned off.

Then Skyla woke up and asked where Celeste was. Maybe it was my refusing to admit we were over, or maybe it was that I wanted to prolong my daughter's heart being shattered into a million pieces the way mine was. But I lied. I told her there was an issue with work and she had to fly back.

We spent most of the day with me showing her around my old stomping grounds and then the rest of it at the pool. The next morning we packed up our stuff, had breakfast, and then headed to the airport to go home. As I was pressing the button to turn my phone off before we entered airport security, my phone lit up with a call from Monica, Amaya's mom.

"She passed away early this morning," she said. "She developed an infection and they couldn't stop it. The funeral will be held the day after tomorrow."

Without explaining anything to Skyla, I went back to the rental car company and rented the car again. Then, on the way back to the hotel, I called them and booked a room for three more nights. Once we were in our new room, I went out onto the balcony and called my brother and Quinn. They both wanted to fly out immediately, but when Jax checked the flights, there wasn't one available for a couple days, so they decided it would be best to drive down.

A couple hours after we hung up, Jax called back to let me know he spoke with Killian, who was in the shop with a teammate who was getting some work done. After speaking to his coach, Stephen Harper, Olivia's dad, he offered to fly them here on their team's plane. I asked him to thank Killian for me, and told him I would see them when they arrived.

About an hour later, Jax called again to ask why Nick wanted to know if Celeste was flying down with them—you know, because she was back in New York, but everyone in my family thought she was with me. I had to tell him she broke things off and left, which made it feel real and made me realize I needed to tell Skyla, right after I told her that her mother died.

I made it through telling her that Amaya passed away, but she was so upset and confused about her feelings, I didn't have the heart to tell her Celeste and I were over as well.

Now, it's the day of the funeral. I'm dressed in a black suit I had to purchase at the mall, and Skyla is dressed in a black dress her grandmother brought over. Sky has asked for Celeste too many times to count. She doesn't understand why she isn't here. When you love someone, you're there for them. Quinn and Rick are sitting in the main room of my hotel room while my brother finishes getting ready in his room. Quinn is doing Sky's hair for her. I know she wants to say something about Celeste leaving, but she's at least considerate enough to wait until after the funeral.

"All right, your hair is done," Quinn tells Skyla, who gives her a small smile.

"Thank you, Aunt Quinn," she says softly. Skyla mentioned last night that she feels bad she hasn't cried over her mom. I told her that's completely normal. Everyone handles their grief in different ways.

There's a knock on the door, and for a split second I wish it were Celeste on the other side, and that thought makes me realize how easily I would be willing to forgive her. I know she's just scared. I don't know why or what happened, but I know she didn't run because she doesn't love me or Sky. The problem is, it's not just me this time around. Now it's my daughter too, and I have to protect her from being hurt, even if that means letting Celeste go.

I open the door and it's Jax, dressed in his suit. "Ready to go?" he asks.

"Yep." We all pile into the SUV they rented when they got here and head to the funeral.

The first part of the service is at Saint Catherine's church where Amaya's family are members. The priest will speak and then we'll drive over to their family plot for the burial. Because of Skyla being family, we sit in the front row for the service, next to Monica and Phil. My family sits behind us. It isn't until the service ends, and we're asked to stand and make our way to the burial, that I see *her*. She's standing, like everyone else, in the back, and next to her is her mother. I never saw her that day we went to check on her, but today, standing next to Celeste, she looks good. Like a slightly older version of her daughter. Both with wavy brown hair, olive skin, and slim yet toned bodies. Both wearing black dresses. Celeste's eyes meet mine and her lips curl slightly into a nervous smile.

Of course, my daughter spots her and insists on going to her. Celeste's eyes widen when she realizes Skyla is heading her way, telling me, while she wanted to be here for us, she wasn't sure if she was going to make her presence known. "Celeste, you're here," Sky says softly.

"I am. I'm so sorry for your loss." Celeste points to her mom, who is standing next to her with a sympathetic smile on her lips. "This is my mom, Beatrice. Mom, this is Skyla and her dad, Jase."

"Nice to meet you," I say politely.

"How are you?" Celeste asks Skyla. I feel my siblings come up behind us, and without even looking to confirm, I can feel the anger radiating off Quinn as she glares at Celeste.

"Quinn, chill," I murmur, not wanting a scene to be made right here in the church.

"I'm okay," Skyla says to Celeste. "But...my mom died, and...I haven't cried." Skyla looks down in shame.

"Oh, hey," Celeste murmurs, pulling my daughter into her arms. "It's okay. Not everyone cries when they're sad."

"Do you?" Skyla asks.

"Sometimes, but other times I just get quiet, or I work a lot. Some of my best work was done while I was sad. And sometimes when I'm really sad, I feel like I can't cry. My throat burns and my stomach hurts, but the tears just won't come."

"That's how I feel," Skyla says. "My stomach hurts." My heart hurts for my daughter. No kid her age should ever have to bury their mother, but Skyla's situation is even worse because the only Amaya she's ever known has been the one laying in a coma in a hospital. She has no good memories, no photos of the two of them smiling. She's trying to mourn for a woman she never really knew.

"We better get going," I tell Sky. "Everyone has already left for the cemetery."

"Okay," she says, then gives Celeste a hug. "Will you come with me?"

"Umm...well..." Celeste bites down on her bottom lip, unsure of what to say. If she's waiting for me to tell her to join us, she'll be waiting forever.

"The burial is really just for family," I tell Sky. Then, without giving Celeste a second glance, I take my daughter's hand and walk out of the church.

TWENTY-THREE

Celeste

"ARE YOU OKAY?" my mom asks once we get into our car. The entire flight I was quiet, using my laptop as a shield to keep my mom from asking me any questions. It worked because even though she gave me a couple sympathetic glances, she didn't press me to talk. Now, though, the laptop is gone, my shield removed, and she's ready to talk.

"I made a mistake," I blurt out, then close my eyes. I don't want to discuss this with my mom. She's too fragile, too delicate. Having this conversation would mean telling her that in a lot of ways I blame my childhood for the way I am, and I don't want to make her feel bad.

"Going to the funeral was not a mistake," she says, misunderstanding what I meant.

"No, running away."

We're both silent for the rest of the ride. When we pull up, Mr. Walters, the concierge in my building, helps us with our bags and to the elevator. The silence continues until we're inside. I'm about to head to my room to get settled when my mom's hand lands on my wrist to stop me.

"We never finished our conversation the other day, Celeste. When you showed up at the trailer and told me you ran because Skyla called you Mom."

Taking a deep breath, I shrug, unsure what to say. The last thing I want to do is hurt my mom's feelings. She guides me over to the couch and sits down, patting the cushion for me to join.

"When I found out I was pregnant with you, I was beyond ecstatic." I try to school my features not to look shocked, but I must do a shitty job because she laughs humorlessly and says, "I know, you would never know it."

"No, Mom...it's not that."

"Don't you dare make excuses for me." She gives me a pointed look. "The entire time I was pregnant, after Snake left, I stayed positive. I focused on making the trailer a home. I decorated the nursery with pink." She shakes her head like she's remembering that time in her life. "When you were born, reality hit," she says with a frown. "The money Snake left me ran out and I had to keep working at the diner. I was running on empty with a broken heart. Month after month, the chance of him returning, dwindled. Back then there wasn't the internet like there is today. It was harder to find someone, especially since I only knew so much. Victoria helped me out by allowing you to hang out with Nick and his nanny, but I felt like I was drowning. My heart shattered more and more every day, and instead of holding onto the one person in the world who loved me, I pushed you away. I saw the black of his eyes in yours, the straightness of your hair. Your button nose was identical to his."

Mom swipes away a falling tear. "I'm not making excuses, only trying to explain how it all got so out of control. Every day you went to Nick's home, you saw the wealth and luxurious lifestyle."

"They're far from perfect," I tell her. It took a long time for me to learn and understand that, but once I did, I knew I didn't want to be anything like Nick's parents.

"I know, but if I would've been giving you the love and attention you needed and deserved, you wouldn't have grasped onto thinking what they had was the way to live...to love. I felt it, Celeste. I felt love so deep in my bones, it had the ability to rock me to the core. And when I lost it, I was so wrapped up in my heartbreak, so afraid to love again, I didn't open myself up to let you in. You needed me, and I failed you. The truth is, had I shown you what love was, it wouldn't have mattered if we had electric or water. It wouldn't have mattered that I drove a shitty car, or that we lived in a rust-filled shitty trailer. Because real love is so overpowering and all-consuming it knows no bounds and overrides any hardships."

The tears that were burning my lids, fall. I know exactly what she means because it's the way I feel about Jase and Skyla.

"I love you." My mom pulls me into her arms, and my head rests on her shoulder. "You don't see it, but you would make an amazing mom because for your entire life, you've taken care of me. Even when you ran away, you never stopped caring for me. I gave up on life and love and lost myself, but you never once gave up on me."

"I should've visited," I tell her through my tears. "I should've come and got you sooner."

"No." She shakes her head. "You had to find yourself first, and you have through the love you found in Jase and Skyla. Now, go get your family back, pretty girl."

MY INITIAL THOUGHT was to go see Jase first. I have a lot I need to say to him. But then after I thought about it, I decided I needed to see Skyla first. She will always come first and that starts with talking to her before I go to see Jase.

Knowing that Jase is at work—I called earlier—I call Quinn to see if Skyla is with her.

"I don't think it's a good idea for you to see her," Quinn says. "She's been through a lot."

"I understand, but I would just like to speak to her. You were upset that I left all those years ago without a goodbye, but now I'm here and trying to talk to her. Please."

"You're saying goodbye?"

"No, I'm not." Even if Jase and I don't end up together, I'm going to make sure Skyla and I continue our relationship, if she'll forgive me.

"Fine, but just so you know, she doesn't know you ran. Jase told her you had a work emergency." Oh my heart. Of course he did. Because even when I'm failing at life, he's right there to save me.

"Okay. Can I come over now?"

"We're at my place. I'll text you the address."

I ARRIVE at Quinn's condo, which is in the Upper Eastside. After security lets me through, I take the elevator to the penthouse. When I step off, I notice it's the only door on the floor. I knock once and Quinn opens the door.

"She's in the guestroom, drawing."

"Did you...tell Jase?"

"No, you can tell him yourself."

"Thank you."

The bedroom door is open, but I still knock once. Skyla turns in her chair and smiles big. "Celeste!" She runs over to give me a hug. I take a second to breathe in her scent, to lose myself for just a moment in her love. This girl is literally the best part of Jase, and if I'm honest, the best part of me. I might not be her mother, but I want her to be mine in every way that matters. We separate and she sits down on the edge of the bed.

"Dad said you've been busy with work." She looks at me for confirmation, and I know I can't lie to her. She deserves the truth.

"Actually, that's what I wanted to talk to you about." I sit next to her. "I left that day at the hotel because I was scared."

Skyla's brows furrow. "Of what?"

"Of how much I love you and your dad."

She gives me a look of confusion. "Did I do something wrong? Did Dad?"

"No, pretty girl," I tell her, pressing my palm against the side of her cheek. "You did everything perfect. I was scared that I wouldn't love you the right way. That I would let you down. Hurt you. I know I'm not your mom, but I want to be in your life. I want to love you and be your friend."

Skyla nods once, and I hope she understands what I'm trying to say. I've never tried to have an adult type of conversation with a thirteen-year-old. But then she says, "What if I wanted you to be my mom? Would you...maybe want to?"

I want to tell her yes, that I would love nothing more, but I haven't spoken to Jase yet. Sure, he's texted me every day to tell me he loves me, but I don't want to assume that means he'll forgive me, and we'll end up together.

"I messed up with your dad," I tell her honestly. "I hurt his heart when I left."

"I knew he was sad, but I didn't know why."

"I plan to apologize to him, and if we end up together, I would love nothing more than for you to be my daughter. And even if your dad and I don't end up together, I want you to know I'm always going to be here for you. Even if it's only as a friend. I love you so much, Skyla. I already see you like family and that's never going to change."

"Dad will forgive you," she says with a smile. "He loves you."

I smile back, but don't say anything. I hope she's right. I would give anything to be thirteen again and view the world and love with such innocence.

"When you guys get married, can I help design your dress?" she asks, and I laugh.

"I wouldn't have it any other way."

After hanging out with Skyla for a little while, drawing and sketching more items for the fashion line we're planning to create, I say goodbye to her with the promise that I'll see her again soon. Then I put a call into Forbidden Ink to make an appointment so I can see Jase.

Evan tells me he'll have to move some clients around, but promises me he'll make sure it's taken care of. After going home to check on my mom—who tells me she spent the afternoon finding a place where she can attend AA meetings and looking at colleges, since she wants to go to school—she's thinking about studying to be a nurse—I get changed and then head over to East Village. When the cab pulls up, the place is dark. The shop is closed, but Evan convinced Jase to stay late. He also assured me that nobody would be there but Jase—he would make sure of it.

Opening the door that Evan told me would be unlocked, I step inside and lock the door behind me. The bell chimes and Jase walks out. When he sees it's me, he says, "We're closed."

"The door was unlocked," I say, walking toward him.

"I have a late appointment."

Walking past him, I head back to his room.

"Did you not hear me?" he asks, walking behind me. "We're closed. I'm only here for—"

"An appointment," I say, finishing his sentence. "I know. I'm your appointment."

Jase's eyes go wide, but he quickly covers it up. "Great, then I can head home. My daughter is waiting for me."

"Did you not hear me?" I ask, pulling out my phone and pulling up an image. "I have an appointment." I turn the phone around so he can see the image. "I want this."

Jase stares at the picture for several seconds, not saying a word. When he does, his voice is gravelly. "You still have it."

"I sent it to every email I've ever owned, put it in the cloud and every other online storage, to make sure I would never lose it."

"Why?"

"Because even thinking you slept with Amaya, I still loved you. I was young and immature, and I'm not even sure I knew what it meant to be in love back then, but still, in my own eighteen-year-old way, I knew I loved you. I loved who I was with you. And every day when I woke up, I would look at this image and remind myself what you said to me, to never stop wishing and dreaming."

I step toward Jase, but he steps back. It's his turn to be scared, and I need to understand that. "I love you, Jase. I love you and your daughter, and I love what we have together. You're the only person I've ever loved. You see me, beneath the makeup and the clothes and the fake smiles. You see the real me."

"You ran."

"I did," I admit, owning up to what I did. "Skyla called me Mom and I got scared. I was so afraid of screwing up, of failing her and you. I didn't think I was capable of loving Skyla like she deserved."

"And now?"

"Now, I see that I'm the perfect person to love her because I know what it feels like to not be loved like she deserves."

"A tattoo is permanent," he says, nodding to the image on my screen.

"Everything about us is," I tell him matter-of-factly. "We wasted so many years apart. I don't want to waste another second. Love me, Jase, and let me love you and Skyla."

Wordlessly, Jase cuts across the room and picks me up. The phone almost falls out of my hand, but he catches it and tosses it onto the counter before dropping me onto the chair where his clients lay down to get inked. He slants his mouth over mine and captures my lips. He sucks on my tongue, then licks the seam of my lips before working his way down my neck and over my collarbone. My shirt is lifted over my head and my bra is unclasped. Then he's lifting my ass up so he can push the skirt and thong I'm wearing down my legs.

While kissing all over my body, he slides his fingers into me, just enough to gather my juices, then slides them back out, circling his fingers over my clit. When I let out a needy moan, he chuckles softly—the vibration hitting my throat and sending chills down my spine—then he does it again, slowly building me up but never letting me come down.

"I can't take it anymore." I groan when he dips his fingers into me once again. "I need you. Now. Right fucking now. Please." Jase chuckles at my craziness, but I'm too turned on to care. All I want is for him to grant me my release.

"Soon," he murmurs as he pulls a nipple into his mouth and sucks on it, his fingers still teasing and taunting. And it hits me that he's punishing me. I ran away, left him hurting. I didn't answer my texts or calls. I left him hanging. And now he's trying to punish me by leaving me hanging as well.

"No, now." I pull his face back and look him dead in the eyes. "Either you make me come, preferably on your cock, or I'm going to do it myself." I push his chest back so I can touch myself. I know it won't take much, just a couple flicks to my clit and I'll be soaring.

Jase releases a loud growl, grabs my legs and pushes them apart, and then pushes into me. It's been over a week since we've been together, and at first, the fit is tight. But holy hell, does it feel good. His mouth finds mine and he kisses me hard, rough. He nips my bottom lip, then bites down on my earlobe. His fingers are digging into the insides of my thighs as he fucks me like a crazed man who can't get enough.

I'm so close to coming, I can feel it, but it's not enough. I need to touch myself, but I'm afraid of what he'll do—that he might stop fucking me. As if he can hear my thoughts, he grunts into my ear, "Go ahead, Dimples, touch yourself. Make yourself come all over my cock." And with his permission, I do just that, with Jase finding his release right behind me.

TWENTY-FOUR

*J*ASE

SHE CAME BACK...UNLIKE eleven years ago, she actually came back. She might've run scared, afraid of how strong our love and connection were, but this time, she turned her ass around and came back to face her fears. I could've pushed her away, made her prove herself. But that's not what you do when you love someone. You open your arms and heart and love the person, cracks and all. Every day I woke up and forced myself not to chase her. I texted her once a day, telling her I loved her, but ultimately, I knew she needed to find her own way back. I didn't know the reason she ran, but now knowing that it was because Skyla called her Mom, I can understand where she's coming from. Being a parent isn't something to be taken lightly, and Celeste's upbringing was as flawed as it comes. But the moment she told me she was the perfect person to love my daughter, I knew she was ready. Because for the first time, Celeste let her guard down. She allowed me to see who she really is. She's always shown me who she was, but until today, she's never done it on purpose. Until today, she's never made the conscious decision to show me what's beneath the surface: her heart.

"Are you sure you want to do this?" I pull on my gloves and open the different colored inks I'm going to need.

"Yes," she says, her voice sounding raspy. I glance over at her and see she's staring at me. My shirt is still off, so I reach down to pick it up, but she leans over and puts her hand on mine. "Can you leave it off?" She blushes a beautiful shade of pink. "It will give me something to focus on."

I chuckle. "It's being done on the back of your hip. You won't see me."

"Fine, hold on." She sits up and snaps a picture of me with her phone camera. "I'll just stare at this."

I laugh and nod. "Okay, Dimples." I prep the area I'll be tattooing, then lower the seat some more so she's more comfortable. It's not a big tattoo, so I'll get it done in one sitting if she isn't in too much pain...which reminds me. I grab a packet of Tylenol from my drawer and hand them to her with a bottle of water.

"Take these to help with the pain." She swallows them without questioning me then lays back down. "You're not going to be able to lay on your back for a few days," I tell her.

"We'll just have to have sex doggy-style," she says with a laugh.

"Woman, don't talk about sex right now. I need to focus." I grab the gun and turn it on. I dip the tip into the black ink and am about to begin when Celeste moves to look at me.

"Don't you have to draw it first? It's been like eleven years since you drew it."

"One, you can't move while I'm tattooing." I give her a serious look. "And two, it's my design. One I looked at many times over the years." Her brows rise at my admission. "Do you trust me?"

"I do."

EPILOGUE

Celeste

Four Years later

I WAKE up to the feeling of something tickling along my back, and without even opening my eyes, I know my husband is drawing on me. It's been three years since we got married and he, for the second time, inked my body—a small piece of his wedding vows that he recited to me at the alter: *you are every one of my dreams and wishes come true.* After we returned from our month-long honeymoon, where I got to show Jase and Skyla my world—literally and figuratively—including all of the clothing shops I've opened in Milan, Paris, and Italy, I made an appointment. He tattooed it along my right shoulder blade freehanded.

"Good morning," I say, my voice hoarse from sleep. I got in late last night and it feels like I've only slept for a couple hours. "Can I turn over?"

"Not...yet..." he says back. He's quiet for several seconds, and then I feel the tickling stop and the camera on his phone click. "Okay, roll over and spread those sexy thighs, Dimples."

I can't help the giggle that escapes me as I do what he says, noticing it's already almost seven in the morning. "You better make it quick," I tell him as he pulls my panties down and climbs up my body. His mouth presses against mine, and I can taste the mint on his breath. "How long have you been up?" I murmur against his lips, running my fingers through his messy hair.

"Long enough to brush my teeth and draw your next tattoo." With one hand above my head, he glides his other hand downward, his fingers landing on my sensitive nub. He nips at my bottom lip at the same time his fingers massage my clit, and I squirm slightly, letting out a soft moan. It's been too many days since I felt his hands on me.

"Well, if my calculations are correct—" I kiss the side of Jase's neck "—we have about twelve minutes before our door will get trampled through." Reaching down, I wrap my hand around his cock and stroke it up and down, getting it rock hard. I love the coldness of his cock piercing under my touch. I shiver slightly at the thought of it inside me, stroking my insides. Taking his face in my hands, I pull him up, so his dick rubs against my clit as he pushes into me, filling me completely.

"Fuck," he grunts, slowly thrusting in and out of me at a leisurely pace, like we don't have three kids under our roof that can wake up and interrupt us at any time. Bringing my hand down, I take over massaging my clit, working myself up. Time is of the essence.

"Don't fucking touch yourself," Jase growls, knocking my hand away. "That's my fucking job."

"Jase...time," I murmur breathlessly as he thrusts deeper into me.

"We have all the time in the world, baby," he murmurs, placing open-mouthed kisses along my jaw and neck.

"Did you give away the kids?" I joke.

"Dimples, no talking about the kids while I'm fucking you," he hisses. Lifting my thigh, he wraps it over his forearm to go deeper, hitting the special spot in me that's going to have me exploding in no time.

"Okay." I exhale a soft moan, focusing on my impending orgasm building higher and higher, and not on the door, that if unlocked, is going to fly open any minute.

"Come on, baby." Jase growls, his thrusts getting rougher. His mouth crashes down on mine, and my body comes undone with Jase following right behind, spilling his warm seed into me. I try not to think about whether this will be the time we make a baby. I don't want to get my hopes up.

He's barely rolled off me and onto his back, when I sit up and run to our bathroom to get cleaned up. I can hear him chuckling from our bed. His laughter gets closer as I pull my night shirt off my body and turn the hot water to the shower on.

"What's so funny?" I ask, stepping into the shower. The door is barely closed before Jase pulls it back open to join me. "Jase!" I shriek. "Have you forgotten about our kids?" I laugh.

He grabs the soap and begins to wash me down. "Relax, woman," he chides. "I locked them in their rooms."

I know he's only joking, but I still gasp. "That's not funny! Do you have any idea the mess we're going to walk out to? I doubt Skyla is awake yet. She's immune to them."

Jase laughs harder. "But it was so worth it to have morning sex with my wife." With his hands holding my cheeks, he kisses me hard before he lets go, so he can squirt shampoo into his hands. "I missed you," he murmurs.

"I missed you more," I say, turning around, knowing he's going to wash my hair.

When he's done, he trails his hands down the sides of my body and over my ass. Feeling extra horny this morning, I push back against his hands and wiggle my butt slightly.

Jase takes that as his cue to spread my checks and run his finger down my crack. He pushes his finger into my tight hole, and my hands hit the shower wall, my head falling forward.

"That feels so good." I moan as he adds another finger. With the water raining down on us, he works me up until my body is ready for him. After adding some baby oil to the mix, he slowly pushes his pierced dick, inch by inch, into my ass, until he's all the way in. While grabbing my breasts and tweaking my nipples, my husband fucks my ass until we're both coming for a second time this morning.

"I hate it when you're gone," he murmurs after he pulls out. "But I love it when you come home all needy for my cock."

"I'm always needy for your cock." I laugh.

We spend the next few minutes cleaning up and rinsing off. I quickly shave my legs, while Jase gives me a recap of everything I missed while I was gone.

"I need to do my hair and makeup," I tell him as we get out of the shower. "The caterers, party planner, and setup crew will be here soon. Can you show them to the back, please, if I'm not out yet?"

"Sure thing, babe." Jase gives my butt a playful smack and then walks out.

As I get ready, I think about how excited I am for the party today. I visualize where all the tents will go. Where everyone will sit. Where all the kids will play. Three months after Jase and I got married, I found out I was pregnant, and we started looking for a bigger house, one where we can grow our family. Jax decided to stay in the townhouse, moving his girlfriend, Willow, in with him, and my mom is still living in my condo. The second I saw this house with its massive backyard and pool, I knew it was the one. I could see the kids running around and playing on a swing set. I could picture Skyla swimming in the pool during the summer, hanging out with her friends here. I always told myself there was no point of living in the suburbs when living in New York, but the minute I heard my babies' heartbeats, I knew I wanted a place they would feel at home. A few weeks later, we moved in, and I can't imagine ever living anywhere else. At the time, Jase thought a six-bedroom, seven bath house was excessive, but now he's grateful for all the rooms.

Once I've finished getting ready, I head out of our room and down the hall, praying the place isn't too much of a disaster. You would never imagine the amount of destruction two two-year-olds can cause in such a short amount of time. When I see all the rooms are empty, I head downstairs, thinking to myself that it's way too quiet. *Where is everyone?*

When I get to the kitchen, I see Skyla sitting at the breakfast nook eating homemade waffles while looking at her cell phone. I walk up behind her and give her a kiss on her cheek. "Happy eighteenth Birthday, pretty girl."

She looks up and sets her phone down, giving me a huge smile. "Thanks, Mom." That word will never get old coming from her mouth.

"I would've made you breakfast." I point to her food.

"That's okay. Grandma made them." She waggles her eyebrows. Turns out my mother is an amazing cook—who knew. And instead of going to nursing school, she ended up going to culinary school, and now runs a very popular restaurant near Hell's Kitchen. I've offered to give her the money to open her own restaurant, but she insists she loves it there.

"My mom's here?" I look around.

"She's outside with the hellions." She laughs.

"Must you call them that?" I try to say sternly, but end up laughing as well. Because she isn't wrong. She just gives me a knowing look.

"How was the show?" I ask, changing the subject. I place a K-cup into my Keurig and press start.

"So good. I can't believe I walked for Versace, and in Milan!"

"I wish I could've been there." Not wanting her to turn out like most of the teen models, I make it a point to accompany her everywhere she goes. Unfortunately, I couldn't be in two places at once and couldn't be there. But thankfully, Margie and Adam were both there and hovered over her like mama hens.

"I know," she says, taking a bite of her food. "Oh! Did you see the shoot proofs for the upcoming line?"

"Umm...yeah." I give her a *duh* look. "You were gorgeous," I say, grabbing a mug from the cabinet, while inhaling the blessed scent of the coffee percolating. "Are you excited for your party?" I can't believe she's officially eighteen and in a couple months will be graduating from high school. While her modeling career had the potential to blow up, her father and I made the decision to keep her in school. We wanted her to stay young for as long as possible. We're hoping she'll make the decision to go to college, but she's mentioned wanting to model fulltime once she graduates. I was hoping, on the other hand, she might want to come to work with me one day. Leblanc's children's and teen's clothing lines took off, and because a lot of the designs came from Skyla, I had my attorney create a contract and trust for her, where she receives a percentage of all the profits the two lines bring in. We haven't discussed it yet, but between her earnings through Leblanc and as a model, Skyla is already a very wealthy young woman.

"Yes," she says, cutting me from my thoughts. "And today is doubly amazing because I have the best news!" she exclaims.

"What is it?"

"I want to tell you and Dad at the same time." The corners of her mouth curl into a huge grin.

"Tell me first, and I'll decide if he should know," I joke. "The last time you said that, you introduced us to your college-aged boyfriend and your dad almost had a heart attack."

Skyla giggles devilishly. "That was funny."

"No, it really wasn't," I say, trying to hide my laughter at the memory of Jase growling and threatening the kid's life when he walked through our door, covered in piercings and tattoos. Jase told him he looked like he belonged in an orange jumpsuit, and I about died laughing—especially since the kid looked so much like Jase, it was scary. Luckily, her relationship with that kid was short-lived, and a week later she moved on to someone closer to her age and with less metal in his face.

"Well, this news won't give him a heart attack, I promise," she says, standing and bringing her plate to the sink. I add some cream and sugar to my coffee while she rinses her dish, then we walk together outside to go find everyone.

When we step outside, I notice Angela, the party planner is here, giving orders. The tents are being set up just like I pictured, and the caterers are getting everything prepared. Skyla and I continue past the pool and jacuzzi, to the backyard.

I spot them before they see me, and I take a moment to watch the beautiful scene in front of me—my entire world. Jase is holding onto our two-year-old daughter's hand, while she slides down the slide of the massive treehouse-slash-swing set Jase had custom designed and built, while he holds our *other* two-year-old daughter on his hip. My mom is waiting at the bottom of the slide and catches Melina when she reaches the bottom, dramatically dropping to the ground on her back and lifting her in the air.

Mariah laughs and claps the entire time, completely content to be in her daddy's arms.

When Melina spots me, she squeals and wiggles to get down. My mom sets her onto her feet, and she immediately runs in my direction.

"Momma! Momma!" she yells. Setting my mug down on the table, I drop to my knees and pull my little hellion—as Skyla likes to call them—into my arms.

"Good morning, sweet girl," I murmur, giving the top of her head a kiss. I inhale her sweet scent, a smell I will miss like crazy when she gets older and no longer smells like a baby. I know I have baby fever, but I can't help it. Jase and I have been trying to conceive again for the last year with no such luck, and I'm starting to get worried it won't happen.

Mariah hears her sister and pushes against Jase's chest to let her down.

"I missed you, Momma!" she squeals as she throws herself into my arms.

"I missed you both so much," I whisper through my happy tears.

Since I gave birth to our twin daughters, I've made it a point to only travel when necessary. I had an issue at one of the stores in Miami and have been gone for three days. Even with Facetiming them every day and night, it was too much. I cried to Jase every night and told him the next time I go, I'm taking them with me. He laughed and told me I was crazy.

"Before people start arriving, there's something I need to tell you both," Skyla says.

"If you're dating another guy like—" Jase begins, but I cut him off.

"Tell us," I say nervously. While Skyla knows I would love for her to join me at Leblanc, I told myself I wouldn't push. I mentioned it once and never again. I want her to follow her own dreams, wherever they may take her. Sure, if she chooses to model fulltime, I'm going to miss her like crazy, but it's all part of your kid growing up.

"I was accepted into FIT, and I have decided to go. While I love modeling, I want to learn about the business side of the industry and intern at Leblanc." Skyla traps her bottom lip between her teeth. "So, what do you think?" She holds the letter out for us to see, and I walk over and take it from her.

Skyla Leblanc-Crawford, the letter begins. I smile at her last name. The day I married Jase, I took his last name, keeping mine as well because of my company and reputation. The following month, I legally adopted Skyla and was shocked when she insisted on taking my name as well. *"Leblanc is part of you, and I'm part of you now,"* she said. I swear I cried for an hour straight. I read through her letter of acceptance into the college of her dreams, my heart swelling at how proud I am of her.

"Well, this is no longer just a birthday party," I say through my tears. "This is now a celebratory party. I am so proud of you." I pull Skyla into my arms for a hug.

"You're okay with me officially interning for you?" she asks.

"Nothing would make me happier," I tell her honestly.

"Congratulations, Sky," Jase says, yanking Skyla out of my arms and into his. "You're going to stay living at home, though, right? FIT is expensive."

"Jase," I chide, smacking him in the arm.

"I was thinking we could look into the dorms or maybe an apartment near campus, so I can do the whole college thing. Would that be okay?"

"Of course it is," I tell her. "We are so proud of you."

I grab my coffee from the table and take a sip. The coffee hasn't finished going down my throat when a wave of nausea hits me full force. Dropping my mug into the grass, I run toward the house to throw up, but don't make it in time. Instead I end up vomiting all over the hedges that surround our back patio.

Jase is right behind me, holding my hair back, until I finish. When I turn around, he's sporting a huge grin on his face. At first, I'm annoyed that my husband thinks it's funny I just threw up, but then my mind plays catch up, and I'm grinning just as hard. We don't have to say the words. I'm pregnant.

IT'S ALMOST five o'clock and Skyla's party is starting to wind down. The only guests left are a few of her friends she's lounging by the pool with, as well as a couple of our friends. Jase and I are sitting at the table under the tent watching Melina and Mariah run around and chase Reed, Olivia and Nick's six-year-old son.

"If history repeats itself," Nick says, "my poor son is going to have not one, but two of your daughters following him around for years." He shoots me a playful wink, and I laugh. I'm so thankful for our friendship, but also really glad he met Olivia. Had he not, who knows if we both would've found true love.

"It's not just my daughters," I point out, watching Killian and Giselle's four-year-old daughter, Alice, chase Reed up the stairs of the treehouse.

"Poor kid," Olivia says. Francesca, her four-year-old daughter, lays against her mom's chest, sleeping soundly with her thumb in her mouth. "One of us needs to have a boy to attempt to even this all out."

"Maybe we will," Jase whispers into my ear, so only I can hear.

Quinn's gaze meets mine, and she smiles softly, but it's forced and a little sad. I would like to say that over the years she and I have gotten closer, but the truth is, we haven't. Not that she hasn't gotten nicer, because she has. She's accepted me into their family with open arms. But I worry about her. She married Rick a few years ago, but I don't think they're happy. She used to talk all the time about wanting to create a family of her own, but after a couple years of them trying with no success, she stopped mentioning it. I've watched the bright light that used to surround Quinn, dim little by little. I watched her put on some weight—not that she isn't still gorgeous, because she very much is—and slowly hide more and more of her body.

I feel so helpless, unsure of how to help her get that light back. When I've tried in the past to bring it up to her, she always pushes me away, so lately I've stopped bringing it up. The last thing I want is to push her completely away—she barely comes around as it is—especially when I have a feeling that one day she'll need us. No judgement. And when she's ready to talk, I'll be here.

"Did Nick tell you?" Olivia says, breaking me out of my

thoughts. "He signed with the publisher on his third romance novel." She beams proudly.

"Congratulations!" I tell Nick. "Look out Nicholas Sparks, there's a new Nick in town." Everyone laughs.

"I've decided to retire," Killian says. "Giselle and I are expecting again, and I would like to be home more with this baby." Everyone congratulates them, and Jase gives me a look. There's a good chance Giselle and I will be having our babies close to the same time. I don't want to get my hopes up, but I've been feeling queasy all day.

"Oh my God!" Olivia exclaims. "You didn't tell me you were pregnant."

"We just hit twelve weeks. We were waiting."

"You know I don't count!" She laughs. "We're expecting too! I'm eight weeks."

Giselle laughs with her. "And you're giving me crap? You didn't tell me either!"

As everyone is congratulating them, I notice Quinn sneak away. Concerned, I tell Jase I'll be right back. Jax, who's been sitting off to the side with Willow snuggled in his lap, watching the kids play, notices her leave as well. He looks like he's about to lift Willow off him to get up and check on his sister, so I give him a small nod to let him know I'm going.

On my way inside, Skyla calls out my name.

"Yeah?"

She gets up and comes running over to me. Her arms wrap around my neck and she hugs me tightly. "Thank you for everything," she murmurs into my ear.

"I'm glad you had a good time."

"I did, but not just for the party. For loving me and being here for me. Growing up, I never thought I would have a mom. Mine was... well, you know...and my dad was always enough. But..." She backs up slightly and her eyes are glossed over. "I'm just so thankful to have you," she says through a sob.

"You never have to thank me, pretty girl. You're my daughter, my world."

After we hug once more, I head inside to find Quinn. She's sitting on the edge of the tub in my bathroom. "You okay?" I ask, noticing her cheeks are stained pink from her tears.

"I think I'm pregnant," she whispers.

"And that's a bad thing..." I tread carefully, afraid if I'm too forceful, she'll feel backed into a corner and attack like a defensive feline. I need her to know I'm here for her.

She just shrugs, and I can see it in her face, in her posture, she's broken, defeated...maybe even scared.

"Well, there's only one way to find out." I pull out the box from under the sink and hand her a test.

"You keep tests on hand?"

"We've been trying for the last year," I admit. "We thought it would be as easy as it was last time, but it hasn't been."

"I'm sorry, Celeste. Here I am, unsure if I'm happy or sad that I'm most likely pregnant, and you're wishing for a baby."

"Everyone has their own stories," I tell her. "Take it, and I'll be right here with you."

I step out of the room while she pees, and once she lets me know she's done, I go back in. A few minutes later, the word **pregnant** lights up the screen, and I give her a hug. "Jase and I will be here for you no matter what."

"Thank you." She kisses my cheek. "I think I'm going to head home."

I want to beg her to talk to me, tell me what's going on. Is Rick hurting her? Is he emotionally abusive? What has happened that she's only a shell of the woman she used to be? But I don't. Instead I give her a small smile and say, "Okay. If you need anything, call me." And I pray that she will. I also decide it's time to talk to Jase about his sister. I should've done it sooner.

Quinn leaves, and I'm left alone in the bathroom. I eye the test, wanting to do one but afraid of the disappointment I'll feel if it says I'm not.

"Celeste," Jase says, making himself known. He sees Quinn's test and his face lights up. "You're pregnant?"

"No." I quickly shake my head. "I mean, I might be, but that test was Quinn's."

"Oh," he says flatly. It's no secret that Quinn's brothers aren't a fan of her husband. "Is she okay?"

"Truthfully," I tell him. "I don't think she is. I think maybe we need to get her alone and speak to her."

"You think that fucker's hurting her?"

"I don't know...but she never comes around anymore."

"I know," he says, choking up. Jase and Jax both love their sister so much. "She doesn't even visit the shop anymore."

"It's time we speak to Jax and figure this out. I have a feeling Quinn's going to need us."

Jase pulls me into his arms and kisses my forehead. "We'll talk to Jax tomorrow. I love you."

"Love you more."

"Want to take a test?" he asks, nodding toward the box with two more tests inside.

"I'm scared," I admit. "I shouldn't be. I have three amazing, healthy kids. I have a husband who loves me. A career I love. My mom is my best friend. I am so blessed. I shouldn't want more."

Jase looks down at me. "First of all, you never have to be scared, Dimples. I'm right here." He kisses the tip of my nose. "Second of all, there's nothing wrong with wanting more."

"What if us not being able to get pregnant is fate's way of saying fuck you to me?"

Jase chuckles softly.

"I'm serious," I say, "I never wanted to have kids and now that I want a house full of them, we can't get pregnant."

"I'm pretty sure me knocking you up with twins shows fate isn't out to get you."

"I think if I'm not pregnant this time, we should stop trying."

"If that's what you want, then that's what we'll do." He hands me a pregnancy test.

After I go pee and dip the test into the urine, I set it on the sink then walk away. Three minutes later, Jase stands and looks at it. He turns to face me, his features giving nothing away.

"Well?" I ask. "Tell me."

"It's a good thing you insisted we buy this ridiculously huge house because in nine months, we're going to be needing another one of the rooms."

I jump into Jase's arms, and he holds me tight, kissing me like I'm his entire world. "Thank you, Jase," I whisper against his lips.

"For what?"

"For seeing what's below the surface. For seeing the beauty in my chaos. For seeing *me*."

THROUGH HIS EYES

IMPERFECT LOVE SERIES: BOOK FOUR

*To all the women who have never been told...
you are enough.*

ONE

Quinn

SITTING ON MY TERRACE, in a comfy lounge chair I purchased when Rick first bought us this place, I hold a glass of red wine in my hand—one that I have yet to take a sip of. I want to. I look forward to my nightly glass of wine. I buy my favorite brand in bulk and have it delivered to the condo. But for the last several weeks, I haven't been able to drink it. I still pour it and bring it out here like I've been doing every night for the last four years.

Only once I go back inside, I pour the crimson liquid down the sink and rinse the glass out. I think, somewhere deep in my subconscious, I believe if I continue to pour it every night, eventually I'll be able to drink it. I've put it in my head, if I pretend like my life isn't about to change—well, technically, *already* has changed—then it won't. As if I can will my life to go back to what it was only a few short months ago. And that says a lot since I hated my life the way it was.

Drinking my nightly wine isn't just about drinking, though. It's about finding comfort in my nightly routine. It makes me feel like I have the tiniest semblance of control in a situation that, in reality, is completely out of my control. I can handle my current life. I know what to expect. It's routine and dependable. Rinse. Wash. Repeat. Now, though, not being able to drink wine means my routine is about to be shaken up, and I'm scared of what the future holds. It's easier to fight the monster you know than to take on the one you've never seen.

As I stare down at the hustle and bustle of the city, from the forty-seventh floor, I try to focus on what's in front of me and not what's inside of me. The problem is, from this high up, and this late at night, there's not really much of a view to focus on. Down below, I spot several flashes of lights from the cabs and bikes that make their way to their destinations. Tiny dots of people litter the sidewalks, but they're too small for me to see their features. I wonder how many of them are couples, holding hands and kissing, in love. My heart knots at the thought, and without thinking, I bring the wine to my lips. The liquid has only barely wet my tongue before I'm spitting it back into the glass and setting it down.

My eyes glide upward. The sky is clear tonight, so it should be filled with beautiful stars twinkling above. But with the bright lights that make up New York City, it's difficult to spot a single star. What I would give to be back in Piermont, in my old apartment in North Carolina I shared with my brothers, staring up at the sky and counting the hundreds of stars that wink down at me.

My cell phone vibrates on the table. When I see it's my sister-in-law, Celeste, I hit ignore. I've been pushing everyone away for years. I know I have. But I don't know what to do, how to handle the situation I've found myself in. Once upon a time, I dreamt of being right here, in this moment: married to the love of my life, living in the most beautiful city in the world, in a gorgeous home. Pregnant with my husband's baby. Looking toward our future. How ironic is it, when my dreams finally come true, nothing is the way it's supposed to be.

I'm married, but my husband doesn't love me—and if I'm honest, I don't love him either. How do you love a man who hates every part of you? It's hard, trust me, I've tried. Over and over again. And through trying, I've lost a large piece of myself I'm not sure I'll ever be able to find. When I look into the mirror, I'm not even sure who I see anymore, and that scares the crap out of me, because I wasn't always this way. I was strong and determined and full of life, and now... I'm not. I'm weak, and I hate that I know it, yet choose not to do anything about it. It makes me feel even weaker.

I might live in a beautiful city, but it's one I no longer get to experience because I'm stuck in this suffocating ivory tower, going through the motions but not actually living. Where I live is beautiful. The furniture, the paintings, everything expensive and top of the line, but it's not a home. It's simply a dwelling. A place to eat and sleep. And I can't imagine what it will feel like to raise a baby here.

Rick and I tried for years to get pregnant. He wanted a baby with his last name, and I wanted someone to love. After four years of trying, at thirty-four years old, I didn't think it would happen. I brought up the idea of using in vitro fertilization a couple years back, but my husband scoffed at me and told me he's not defective, and only defective people need to use IVF. Then, he proceeded to tell me I was probably the defective one, and if that were the case, he didn't want a baby with me anyway. I swallow thickly at the memory of crying myself to sleep that night. My eyes burn, and I close them tight, willing the tears to vaporize. Rick doesn't deserve any more of my tears. I know that. But, still, they come. Because I'm weak.

Glancing at the time on my cell phone, I see it's almost ten o'clock. Rick should be home soon. I'm planning to tell him about the baby tonight. I'm not naïve enough to believe a baby will repair our marriage, but I don't know what else to do. It's not as if things can get worse. My thoughts go back to when I was a little girl. Of my father and mother yelling and screaming at each other. Of my mother hitting him and calling him names. Of the way she turned her hatred onto me when he died from a heart attack, and she found out the extent of his cheating. I was only eight years old, but I can still remember the way my brothers tried to protect me. I know they would protect me now, if they knew, if I let them in.

I pick up my glass of wine, and once again, have to stop myself from downing the entire glass. Closing my lids, I try to imagine how my baby's life will look. I refuse to let him, or her, grow up like I did. Scared to talk out of turn, frightened of what mood my mother would be in when I got home from school. Terrified, the nasty words she spoke about me were true.

It wasn't until my eldest brother, Jax, turned eighteen and gained guardianship of me, I was finally able to breathe. At the same time, my other older brother Jase became emancipated. From the time I was eleven years old, I grew up in a loving home. I was given everything I could want or need. They treated me like a princess, and when I grew up, all I wanted was to meet a man who would treat me like his queen. Boy, was I naïve. Fairytales are overrated if you ask me.

Maybe the problem was that every girl wants a Prince Charming, and I got a king. One who rules with an iron fist to keep his castle in order. He's well-respected by everyone and answers to no one. Maybe what I should've looked for instead, was a sweet prince, one who would find my glass slipper, or show me a beautiful library. He would kiss me awake to save me from the evil witch, or take me away from the horrendous stepmother. Maybe the problem was that, because my brothers told me I deserved the world, when I wished upon those shooting stars, I aimed too high. You know what they say: *be careful what you wish for because you just might get it.* Well, I wished and wished and wished, and I got it...and now I have no damn clue what to do with it.

Glancing over at my phone, I notice five more minutes have passed. It's time to go inside. I need to clean the kitchen and put Rick's dinner out for him. He texted me earlier he would be home at ten. After rinsing out my wine glass, I take his dinner out of the warmer and place it on the table for him along with some silverware and the scotch he always has with his dinner. Then I head into the bathroom to freshen up. Using a makeup wipe, I swipe under my eyes, so the black is no longer smeared, and I no longer look like a racoon. When I reach into my drawer to grab a night shirt, I spot the lingerie I bought while out shopping with Celeste a while back. I was hoping to spice up my marriage, only when I put it on, Rick told me I looked like a trashy hooker and demanded I take it off. I'm not even sure why I kept it.

Instead of grabbing my cotton shirt, I pull out the silk, beige negligée Rick bought me for our honeymoon, from out of the bottom of the drawer. It's on the shorter side, touching just above the top of my knees, and is thin, showing all of my curves Rick used to love but now despises. Taking a deep breath, I throw it on. It's probably a stupid idea, but I'm desperate—for affection, for attention, for any sign my marriage isn't completely over. Maybe the sight of this negligée will remind him of a time when he actually found me attractive, and he'll go back to being the man I first met. The man I gave my heart to. The man I wanted so desperately to have a family with.

When I hear the door alarm chime, indicating Rick is home, I rush out to greet him. He's toeing off his expensive loafers and shrugging out of his suit jacket, when I make my presence known. He looks up, and I hold my breath, praying his reaction will be receptive. That he'll once again look at me like I'm his entire world. He'll take me into his arms and lay me down on the bed and make love to me. I'll tell him about the baby, and he'll spend the rest of the night worshipping my body.

I'll be the respected queen to my king.

For a brief moment, he stares at me. His gaze rakes down my body, and I think maybe today will be different. But then his face contorts into his usual look of disgust, and I know whatever he's about to say won't be good. So I do what I have learned to do over the years—put up my broken and fragile wall and pray his harsh words aren't strong enough this time to completely demolish it.

"You would think with all the time on your hands, you would make an effort to lose weight," he quips. "What else do you do all day?" He shoots me an accusatory look that makes me want to tell him to go fuck himself. And that makes me a bit proud that I still have even a single ounce of strength left in me to consider saying it. Even though it does no good when I don't actually have any intention of acting on it. Been there, done that. Not stupid enough to ever do it again.

Instead, I stay stuck in my place as if my feet are glued to the ground beneath me—my voice refusing to speak the words I so badly want to say. I'm well aware I don't do shit all day because he gives me a hard time every time I leave—always pointing out a woman's place is in the home.

After the first few times of Rick putting me down, I started to go to the gym in our building, only he showed up and caused a scene when he saw me talking to one of the men who worked out there. It didn't matter that he was only showing me how to properly use one of the machines. He forbade me to ever return, telling me I could workout at home. Months went by, and he kept pointing out I was putting on weight. He then began to put me down during sex, making comments about everything I ate, and pointing out the type of woman he *does* find attractive. At that point, I met with a nutritionist, who mentioned stress can cause weight gain. It doesn't help I'm an emotional eater, and dealing with my husband can be emotionally stressful. I try to eat healthy, but it doesn't matter because I'm not what he wants, and I never will be.

Whenever I would go to Forbidden Ink, my brothers' tattoo shop, to hang out, he would give me a hard time, saying it's not appropriate. When I would try to hang out with my sister-in-law, Celeste, and my niece Skyla, he would come up with a list of items that needed to be done. I still make it a point to see them when Rick goes away, but the more unhappy I become, the more my family notices, and the less I bring myself around them, not wanting to have to explain my entire life is a lie and in shambles.

Setting his jacket on the table, Rick steps closer and takes the silky fabric of the negligée between his fingers. "Delicate items like these are meant for women who take care of their bodies, not for women who let their bodies go to shit. Take it off. *Now.* You don't deserve to wear something so exquisite when you clearly don't appreciate it."

Knowing better than to respond, I nod once and turn on my heel. I knew this was going to happen, so why would I willingly put myself in this situation? Maybe I just needed to hear it one last time. For him to confirm where we stand.

"Wait," he says, and I turn around, my heart filling with false hope. "Put my shoes and jacket away," he commands, his voice devoid of all emotion.

I nod again, walking over to grab his jacket, and then reaching down to grab his shoes. When I stand upright, I feel his hand on my wrist. I look up into his cold, blue eyes. The same eyes I once found warmth in. "How do you think it makes me feel as your husband, to have to see the way you've let yourself go? I'm the one who has to see you naked...touch you... How can you expect me to want you when you don't care about your own body?"

"I'm sorry," I murmur softly, unsure of what else to say. The truth of the matter is, I've only gained about twenty-five pounds since we've gotten together, but it's enough my husband no longer views me as attractive. I've always been on the thicker side: wide hips, thick thighs, big breasts. I was never the most popular or the prettiest, but I was okay with who I was. Until Rick made sure to point out every flaw. Every imperfection. Day after day he broke me piece by piece. I don't know how I even let it go on this long.

But I finally did reach my breaking point and made the decision to leave—to go to my brothers and tell them everything. I formulated a plan to move out and file for divorce. I knew Rick would give me shit, but it couldn't be any worse than living under his roof. But fate is a fickle bitch and the day I was going to meet with my brothers, I realized I missed my period. I waited and waited, but it never came. Now, three months later and I still haven't gotten it. I've yet to take a test, but I know what the results will say. I'm pregnant by a man who hates me.

Rick's brows dip down at my apology—in confusion or frustration, I'm not sure—and I wonder, maybe, if I'd worked out harder, dieted more seriously, my husband would want and love me. It's too late now, though. Pregnant women only get fatter. I've already started to put weight on, and my body is already changing. My clothes are becoming tighter. What will he think of me once I'm fully showing? Will he despise our baby for doing this to my body, like he despises me for letting myself go? No, he's wanted an *heir* for too long. I refuse to believe he won't love our child. *But does he even know how to love?*

My thoughts and feelings are scattered all over the place. I'm a mess of hormones. Getting pregnant was what I wanted for so long, but now that it's happened, I can't help but wish it wouldn't have. I feel a tremendous amount of guilt for even thinking that, but the last thing I want is to bring a baby into this unloving home. I was raised in one for years before Jax saved me, and I wouldn't wish that on anyone, especially my own child. Even if Rick, by some crazy chance, loves our child the way a father should love his baby, he, or she, will still grow up watching him treat me like shit—the same way I watched my parents treat each other. Will my child resent me for being weak, or will he, or she, view me the same way Rick does? The thought has me wanting to throw up.

As I scurry back to the room, I try to recall when Rick changed. You hear about it in books and movies. They talk about it on those shows like Dr. Phil or Oprah. The woman who lives in the abusive household. How does she not notice? Why doesn't she leave? She must be blind, deaf, and dumb not to see the signs. All I can say is, until you are standing where I am, you won't understand. Words can hit as hard as fists. Without even realizing I was standing in the ring, being thrown into a fight I wasn't ready for, I had already been knocked to the ground. Did I get up? Of course. But when you get knocked down so many times, eventually you realize it's better to just tap out. I'm aware it makes me sound weak. But in my defense, the fight isn't even close to being fair. I never really stood a chance.

I can still remember the days when Rick would kiss me lovingly. The way he would hold me in his arms and tell me how much I meant to him. I can't pinpoint the moment when things changed. When we went from having sex every day, to a few days a week, down to once a week, and eventually it turned into once a month. When our weekly date nights turned into me leaving dinner out for him. And our weekend getaways turned into Rick going away by himself while I stayed home alone.

I kept telling myself we were just in a rut. His job is stressful. His father puts a lot of pressure on his shoulders. But at some point, I realized it was me. In my husband's eyes, I was no longer beauti-ful. No longer attractive. I didn't make him smile or laugh anymore. I didn't turn him on. He saw me as a burden, a nuisance. I was no longer his queen who was meant to stand by his side. Instead, I became a prisoner he kept holed up in this condo, waiting in the background to be at his disposal. I once was building a successful photography company, but he demanded I stay home. He said it would be an embarrassment for his wife to be working. We were trying to have a baby, and he told me he wanted me to be a stay-at-home mom just like his mother was. If I were working, people would think he couldn't take care of what was his. He cared more about the outward appearance than what was actually happening in our home.

I place Rick's shoes neatly on his shoe rack, then grab a hanger to hang up his jacket. As I'm shaking out the material to ensure there are no wrinkles, I catch a whiff of perfume. Bringing my nostrils to the lapels, I inhale deeply and confirm it. His jacket smells like a woman. My stomach roils in disgust. My hands begin to tremble in fury. My husband is having an affair. I am now *officially* the cliché.

The thought of him cheating on me sparks something inside me. I've given up everything for this man. Meanwhile, he's out screwing another woman. I don't doubt she's gorgeous. She's probably a size one with perky breasts, silky blond hair, and has flawless skin with zero tattoos—pretty much the exact opposite of my black, lifeless hair, dull black eyes, and tattoo-covered overweight body.

Peering out of the room, I see he's sitting at the dining room table, eating his dinner and texting on his phone. And a plan surfaces. Changing into a pair of sweats and a tee, I go pee and then lie down in bed, closing my eyes and pretending to fall asleep. As I wait for Rick to finish eating, I think about the woman's scent on his jacket. This isn't the first time I've smelled woman's perfume on his clothes, but I chose to remain in denial, making excuses—he was probably standing too close to his secretary, or he had lunch with his mom. I didn't want to admit my husband was having an affair. But deep down I always knew. It's only now, that I'm pregnant and carrying an innocent precious baby in me, I'm finally opening my eyes and looking around me.

A little while later, Rick enters our room without saying a word. I hear the bathroom door shut, and I jump out of bed. He takes a shower every night when he gets home, after dinner, and he always brings his cell phone into the bathroom with him. Because of the bathroom being so big, he can't see me enter, but the door creaks, and he calls out, "Quinn?"

"Sorry," I say, "I need to go pee. I'll be right out." When I don't hear him respond, I peek around the corner and see him standing in the shower under the water.

Cheater. Asshole. Home-wrecker.

Snatching his phone out of his pants that he has folded on the vanity, I type in his passcode and pull up his messages. I click on the first one: Sylvia. The name sounds familiar. I think she's his secretary. Just as I'm about to click out and go to the next one, I spot their most recent thread.

Sylvia: I miss you already.

Rick: I'll take you out tomorrow night. Send me a picture.

Sylvia: <insert topless image>

Of course he's cheating on me with his damn secretary. Because my entire story wasn't cliché enough, it had to add the young, hot blond with huge, fake breasts. I skim through a couple more texts before I get nervous of being caught. I'm not sure why I even care. Our marriage is obviously over, but something in me screams that I need to tread lightly. It's no longer just me. I now have my baby I need to protect. Screenshotting the messages, I text them to my phone and then send Sylvia's contact information to myself as well. I quickly scroll through Rick's other messages and find several other women he's been messaging with. I send all their info to myself, then delete all the evidence I was ever on his phone. Exiting out of his apps, I lock his screen and put his phone back where he left it, tiptoeing out of the bathroom and climbing back into bed. Putting my phone on silent, I store it in my nightstand drawer, so he won't see it, just in case.

When he gets out of the shower, he walks over to the dresser with a towel wrapped around his waist. I take a second to check him out. He's not fat like I am...he's skinny. Not toned or muscular, but thin and lanky. His skin is tanned, not a tattoo in sight. His brown hair is wet and combed over, and his face is clean-shaven. He's a good-looking guy, but he isn't like *Wow*. His looks aren't what attracted me to him, though. It was his charm and self-confidence. He was so sure of himself, sure of his place in the world, and even though I came across like I was just as strong and confident, I felt lost. I thought when he found me, I would feel like I finally belonged, and I did...until he decided I was no longer what he wanted, and he left me alone once again. Now I'm more lost than I was before, and my only hope is I somehow find my way on my own.

"What are your plans this weekend?" he asks, not looking at me as he drops his towel and pulls his boxers up his legs.

"Celeste is throwing Sky a birthday party at their place. She's turning eighteen." Skyla is my niece—Jase and Celeste's daughter. When she was younger, before Jase and Celeste got together, we were close. Helping Jase to raise her is what made me realize I wanted my own family. I wanted someone to love and to love me back. I wanted to feel wanted and needed. Once Jase and Celeste got together, Skyla and Celeste hit it off straight away. They're like two peas in a pod. I'm glad Skyla has a full-time mother-figure in her life, but I can't help but wish we had the bond they share. Maybe one day I'll have the kind of relationship they have, with my son or daughter.

"I have to work, so I won't be able to go." I don't know why he's letting me know this. He never comes to any of my family functions anymore.

"Okay, will I see you at home afterward?"

He stills in his place for a split-second, and if I wasn't looking for it, I wouldn't have noticed. But now my eyes are wide open, and I'm definitely looking. "Probably not," he says. "I have a late meeting." He clears his throat then continues. "I might not make it home. I'll probably just stay at the office."

Liar. Cheater. Asshole.

"But tomorrow is the weekend," I push. I never push. I never question. I just accept. And I hate I've become that woman who just accepts. "Why would you spend the night when it will be Sunday? You don't work on Sunday. I was thinking we could go to the farmer's market like we used to. Pick up some fresh fruits and vegetables." When we first got together, we used to go to the farmer's market every Sunday. We would check out each booth, hand in hand, laughing and talking about our week. Even when he was busy, he would make sure he left Sundays open for us.

"Maybe next weekend," he says, his eyes meeting mine through his reflection in the mirror. "This meeting is too important." And it's in this moment I know without a doubt my husband cheating on me isn't something new. His flat tone and blank expression are identical to the ones he's been giving me for too long. Of course, I couldn't have dug my head out of the sand before I got pregnant by my lying, cheating husband. And of course, after years of trying, and failing, we were successful the one time he came home sloppy drunk and actually wanted me—only to wake up the next morning and not even remember it.

He pulls his shirt over his head and says, "I have work to do. Goodnight," then leaves the room as quickly as he came.

TWO

Quinn

I'M SITTING in the backyard of my brother and Celeste's home, at Skyla's birthday party, watching everyone's kids run around and play. The laughter that fills the air should have my heart swelling with love, but instead, it fills me with dread. I was going to tell Rick this morning I'm pregnant, but when I woke up, he was already gone. No note, no kiss goodbye, not even a text message. Some would say I'm crazy for telling him I'm pregnant. I should run as far away from him as possible, but I know better.

This isn't some romance novel. I'm not going to escape and find myself some perfect single guy next door to fall in love with while I attempt to rebuild my shell of a life. This is real life, and in my reality, I have to deal with the cards I've been dealt. If I don't play nice, I know Rick will have no problem taking our baby away from me. He has more money than God, and I've seen the cruel and ruthless way he does business. There's a reason the companies he and his father run are so successful. My husband is a smart, conniving, businessman who never holds back. The last thing I need is for him to do what my father did to Jase and Jax's mom—prove me to be an unfit mom and take my baby from me.

I'm going to have to play nice. Let Rick take the lead. He's apparently busy screwing his way through New York, and as long as I continue to turn a blind eye, he will continue to do so while I raise our baby. His money will pay for everything materialistic our child needs, while my love will provide everything he, or she, emotionally needs. *That is if I can somehow keep him from putting me down in front of our child...* I will not allow my baby to suffer like I did. I won't argue with Rick. I won't fight against him. I won't let my baby become a pawn in this horrible game I'm being forced to play. I'll do my best to be the wife he wants me to be, so I can give my baby a stable and loving home.

I listen as Celeste and Jase's friends laugh and joke with one another. At one point, their friend Killian announces he and his wife, Giselle, are expecting their second baby. Everyone congratulates them, and then Olivia, another friend of Celeste's, announces she and her husband, Nick, are also expecting. It will be their third, and they are beyond ecstatic. Not able to take another second of being surrounded by all these happy couples—knowing my husband is somewhere most likely fucking his secretary—I duck out quietly and head inside. I'm not ready to go home yet, but I also don't want to be around people, so I slip into Celeste and Jase's bedroom, so I can use their bathroom without running into anyone.

I go pee, wash my hands, and then find myself sitting on the edge of the tub, unsure of where to go from here. What if I did run? What if I took whatever cash I could find and bought an old, used car to drive away from here? Would he search for me? Hell, he doesn't even like me. I don't understand why he even wants to keep me. He doesn't know I'm pregnant. If I ran away now, would he even think twice about me? I could send him divorce papers from wherever I end up and hope he signs them. I could raise my baby in a loving home by myself. But what if he comes after me? What if one day while I'm walking down the street, taking the baby for a walk, he finds me? He would take my baby. I know he would. He would make me regret leaving, every single day for the rest of my life.

I'm not even aware I'm crying, until a soft voice interrupts my thoughts. "You okay?" I look up and see Celeste standing in front of me.

"I think I'm pregnant," I admit nervously.

"And that's a bad thing..." she says carefully. I hate that she treats me like I'm fragile, but it's my fault. Both my brothers are happy and in love, and I want what they have. I want to be in love, and being around them every day has become harder and harder. So I've just stopped coming around. It's easier this way.

Not knowing what to say to Celeste, I just shrug.

"Well, there's only one way to find out." She pulls a box of pregnancy tests out from under the counter.

"You keep tests on hand?" I ask, shocked.

"We've been trying for the last year," she admits. As she rips the test open, she tells me how difficult it's been for them. The first time they got pregnant, it happened rather quickly, and they had twin daughters, Mariah and Melina, who are now two years old.

She hands me a disposable cup to pee in, and I blurt out, "I'm sorry, Celeste. Here I am, unsure if I'm happy or sad that I'm most likely pregnant, and you're wishing for a baby."

"Everyone has their own stories," she says with a soft smile. "Take it, and I'll be right here with you."

A few minutes later, the test confirms what I already knew. I'm pregnant. Celeste, as if she knows exactly what I need in this moment, pulls me into a hug. "Jase and I will be here for you no matter what." Not wanting to lose it right here in her bathroom, I thank her and tell her I'm going to head home.

"Okay. If you need anything, call me."

When I get to my car—a Porsche Cayenne Rick bought me for my birthday a couple years ago—I lay my head against the steering wheel and let every emotion out I've been holding in. As my chest racks with gut-wrenching sobs, I allow myself to mourn over the loss of myself, my future, the loving family I long for. With every tear that falls, I'm one step closer to accepting my fate. And when all my tears have released, and I'm incapable of shedding another drop of salty liquid, I turn my car on and drive home.

⁂

THE SOUND of my phone continuously vibrating against the top of my nightstand wakes me from a restless sleep. I contemplated leaving Rick more than a hundred times last night. Packing up my stuff and taking off. But in order to do that, I need to plan, and by the time I figure it all out, I'll already be showing, and he'll know I'm pregnant.

Reaching over, I grab the phone and press answer without even looking at who's calling. "Good evening, I'm calling from New York General Hospital. May I please speak to Quinn Thompson?" *New York General?*

"This is she," I say, sitting up slightly. Pulling the phone from my ear, I quickly check the time: two a.m.

"For security purposes, can you please confirm your current physical address and date of birth?" she asks.

After I rattle off my home address and date of birth, she thanks me and says, "You are listed as Richard Thompson's next of kin. We need you to come in, please."

My heart pounds against my ribcage and my breathing becomes labored—out of fear or hope, I haven't determined. "Did something happen to my husband?"

"Unfortunately, we can't give any information over the phone. We're going to need you to come in."

"Okay," I say, robotically standing and finding clothes to put on. I'm about to head to the hospital when Celeste's earlier words come back to me: *"Jase and I will be here for you, no matter what...If you need anything, call me."* I don't know how, but something tells me I'm going to need my family.

Not wanting to wake up Celeste and Jase since they have two little ones, I dial my brother Jax's number. He answers on the first ring, his voice groggy from sleep.

"I need you," I whisper.

Twenty minutes later, he picks me up and we head over to the hospital. When I get to the front desk, I give the receptionist my husband's name, and she gives me directions on where to go. As we step around the corner, I spot her. Blond hair, petite body, perky, young breasts. Sylvia, my husband's secretary-slash-mistress is sitting on the couch of the waiting room, bawling her eyes out. I've seen her a few times when I visit Rick at work, but he's never formally introduced us. I only knew she was his secretary by her name because she always answers the phone when I call.

Averting my gaze, I walk straight over to the desk I was told to go to and give them Rick's name. The woman types on the keyboard for several seconds before her eyes meet mine and she gives me a look of sympathy mixed with sadness. "The police have requested to speak with you." She stands and walks me over to the two men in uniform. Both are standing in the corner, near the coffee machine, but only one is drinking a cup of coffee.

"This is Richard Thompson's wife," she says, and both men's eyes widen.

When neither of them says anything, Jax loses his patience. "Can someone please tell us what the hell is going on?"

"Yes, sir," the cop, who was just drinking the coffee, says. "We received a call tonight about a man who was held at gunpoint." My body begins to tremble as I take in the words he's saying.

Pulling me into his side, Jax asks, "What happened?"

"A homeless man, under the influence and armed with a stolen weapon, approached your husband when he was getting into his vehicle. According to the witness—"

"What witness?" I ask, already knowing the answer, but needing to hear him say it.

The cop without the coffee, frowns. "The woman who was walking with your husband to his vehicle."

"Who?" I push. My hands fist at my sides in frustration.

"We're not at liberty to say, as the case is still under investigation," the cop with the coffee says, but his eyes dart over to where Sylvia is sitting. I nod once to thank him, and he grants me a sad smile.

"I'm sorry, ma'am," the cop without the coffee says. "According to the witness, your husband was asked for his wallet when they were coming out of the restaurant. Unaware the man had a gun, he told him no, and when he turned his back to get into his vehicle, he was shot from behind. The man took off, and the woman called nine-one-one. He was brought in, but didn't make it through surgery."

Jax's arm around me tightens, and when I look over, his gaze is flitting from the officers to Sylvia. He's putting the pieces together.

Liar. Cheater. Asshole.

"Did you catch the man who shot him?" I ask.

"We did. We found him shooting up on the corner. He wasn't even trying to hide. He's been arrested, and is being held, while we complete the investigation, but we wanted to be here to tell you what happened ourselves."

"Thank you," I tell the cops, fully aware my voice isn't even cracking. This is the part where I'm supposed to cry. Even though my marriage was in shambles, and my husband hated me and was cheating on me, I should still feel something. Anything. I was with him for just over four years—married for almost three of them. Surely, that has to amount to at least a tear. But standing here, in the hallway of the hospital, I can't conjure up a single damn drop of moisture. Maybe it really is possible to run out of tears...

And then I hear sobs coming from behind me. I look back over at Sylvia. Her tiny body is shaking uncontrollably. *That should be me*, I tell myself. I should be the one crying like my life is over. I'm pregnant, and my husband is dead.

Before I can think about what I'm doing, I'm standing in front of

Sylvia. She looks up, her perfect, flawless face, streaked with her makeup.

"You realize you're crying over a married man who you were having an affair with, right?" I say, my voice flat, devoid of all emotion. I hear several gasps, but I don't look anywhere but at Sylvia.

She wipes the snot from her nose and takes several deep breaths before she finally speaks. "You might've trapped him in a loveless marriage, but Rick loved me. He was trying to find a way to divorce you because he didn't love you. He didn't want you," she says, her voice getting louder with each word she speaks.

"Is that what he told you?" I ask, stifling the manic laugh I feel bubbling up inside of me. "That's a lie. He could've divorced me at any time he wanted. *Nothing* was keeping us together."

"He was afraid you would take all his money," she hisses. "He worked so hard and he knew you would try to take it all...because you're trash!"

"We have a prenup," I inform her, and her eyes go wide in shock. Yep, looks like he's been lying to you, too. "Did he mention he was sleeping with several other women besides you?"

Sylvia glares and stands. "You're lying. You are a lying, fat, needy bitch," she spits.

"Hey!" Jax booms, ready to defend his littler sister's honor, but I hold my hand up to stop him. I should be mad at this woman, but I'm not. Every time a man cheats on a woman, the mistress gets blamed. She's called a home-wrecker, told she's destroyed their marriage. But the thing is, if a marriage is solid, there's no wrecking a home. There's no destroying a marriage. This woman was lied to, just like I was. Just like all the other women I'm sure were lied to. Sure, she knew Rick was married, but he's the one who made the vows, not her. And I can see it in her eyes, she loves my husband.

The only thing I feel is pity towards her.

Pulling out my phone, I select the screenshots I saved and send them to her. "Rick Thompson was a lying, cheating, selfish bastard," I tell her. "I've sent you the proof he was sleeping with at least three other women aside from us that I know of. I wish you the best."

As I turn to walk away, Sylvia says, "Aside from us? That's how I know you're lying. Your husband wasn't sleeping with you. He could barely stand to look at you, let along fuck you." I consider pointing out that I'm pregnant just to spite her, but decide against it. It's none of her business.

"That's enough!" Jax roars. "Let's go, Quinn." Wrapping his

arm around my shoulders, he walks me out of the hospital. When I ask him to please take me home, he refuses and brings me back to the townhouse in Cobble Hill, the one I was living in with him and Jase before I fell for Rick's charm and agreed to move in with him. Since then, Jase and Skyla have moved out and in with Celeste, and Willow, my brother's girlfriend, has moved in. When we get back to his place, Willow makes me a hot cup of tea, while Jax holds me until I fall asleep. I have no idea what I would do without my family.

THREE

Quinn

I CONSIDERED GOING to the funeral, if for no other reason than to gain some closure. Jax insisted he and Willow would go with me so I wouldn't be forced to face Rick's parents on my own. The morning of, he came out of his room dressed in a suit, with his hair gelled neatly, and Willow came out looking gorgeous in a tight yet modest black dress. Jax drove over to the condo, and I picked out a black dress and heels, then showered and got dressed. But on the way, I told them I couldn't do it. I couldn't walk into that church and put on a fake front, playing the part of the heartbroken, mourning widow.

Especially after calling Rick's parents to tell them what happened, only to learn Sylvia was over and had already told them. Jacquelyn, Rick's mom, went on to say she and Sylvia would handle the funeral. That she knows what her son would want, and Sylvia, the amazing secretary she is, would help organize everything. While I should've been offended my husband's mistress was helping to plan his funeral, instead, I felt relief.

Kenneth, Rick's father, called me to let me know when and where the funeral would be held, and also to let me know the following day would be the reading of the will. While the thought of taking a single penny from my cheating husband made me sick, I now have a baby on the way, and I'll be damned if he, or she, will go without because of my stubbornness.

So, here I sit, in a chair in my father-in-law's office across from my mother-in-law, waiting for their attorney to begin the reading of the will. Jax, of course, offered to go with me, but I told him this was something I needed to do on my own. It's time I start standing on my own two feet again.

"Docs anybody need anything? Water? Coffee?" I glance over and see Sylvia standing in the doorway. She's wearing a loose, almost see-through flowy blouse matched with a conservative pencil skirt. Her blond hair is neatly pulled back into a harsh bun, and her makeup is done to perfection. As she strides across the room, her tiny ass sways, and I briefly wonder, if I completely starve myself, could I ever be as small as she is? I can't even picture it.

When I don't answer her, Jacquelyn says, "Quinn, don't be rude. Sylvia is asking you a question."

"Excuse me?" I snap, wishing now I would've let Jax accompany me.

"She asked you if you wanted something to drink. The polite response would be yes, please or no, thank you." A very unladylike snort comes from me, and Jacquelyn's eyes widen. In all the years I've been with Rick, I've never shown any kind of disrespect to his parents. Without having any of my own, I was hoping to develop a relationship with Rick's. Unfortunately, I learned fairly quickly the only people crueler and colder than Rick, are his parents.

"Let me get this straight," I say. "You want me to be polite to the woman who was fucking my husband for the last several months, maybe even years. The woman, who was with him the night he died because instead of being with his wife at a family get together, he was taking his mistress out to dinner with the plan to fuck her afterward." Jaquelyn gasps, Sylvia sniffles, and Kenneth glares. And I take a deep, cleansing breath because holy shit, it felt good to speak my mind and stand up for myself.

"Oh, you didn't know? That your son was a lying, cheating, piece of shit? And spoiler alert." I take a moment to look at each of them before I continue. "She wasn't the only one. There were several."

"How dare you!" Jacquelyn yells. "My son is dead! Don't you dare spread lies about him. You will not tarnish his reputation." Of course her only concern is his reputation.

Before I can respond, the family attorney walks in. Needing to keep up their appearances, Jacquelyn and Kenneth both compose themselves and greet Mr. Levine. Sylvia asks if he would like anything, and when he says no, she scurries out.

The will is read. Due to the prenuptial agreement I signed, and the fact we were only married for three years, everything that is related to the company goes to his father since they are partners. Rick left me the condo, since he paid it off and put my name on the deed as a wedding gift. The Porsche is also mine, as well as whatever is in our joint checking account where he used to deposit my "allowance" as he liked to call it. His sole bank accounts apparently go to his father, as it states in the will, to be used for the business. I am the sole beneficiary of the life insurance policy he took out on himself after we were married, though, so there's that. Mr. Levine hands me all the paperwork, and when I look at it, I see the policy is worth a million dollars. Outwardly, I don't show any emotion, but inwardly, I'm breathing a sigh of relief I'll have the means to take care of my baby.

After thanking him, and without saying goodbye to my in-laws, because good fucking riddance, I walk out of the door and out of the building for the last time. Of course, Jax is waiting outside for me.

"You okay?" he asks, walking with me.

"I will be," I tell him truthfully. When we get to my car, he takes my keys from me so he can drive.

"What's next?"

"I was thinking I would put the condo up for sale. I don't want to live there anymore," I admit, instinctually placing a hand over my belly. I can't imagine raising my baby in the same home where Rick would tear me down and belittle me on a daily basis. I need a fresh start. I can't change the past, nor would I want to, since it gave me the precious baby in my belly, but I can sure as hell control my future.

Jax notices my hand and asks, "Is it true?" He nods toward my belly. "Are you pregnant?"

"Did Celeste tell you?"

"No, she wouldn't say anything, but Jase hinted at it."

"Yeah, I am, which is why I want to move. I need a fresh start."

"You know, there's a perfectly decent-size townhouse with two out of the three rooms available." He smiles softly at me, and for the first time in a long time, my heart feels content. "And I heard it's a great place to raise a baby until you're ready to get back on your feet again." He's referring to Jase raising Skyla there until she was thirteen and they moved out to start their life with Celeste.

"Are you sure?" I ask. "I don't want to impose on you and

Willow." Jax and Willow have been together for almost as long as Rick and me, but I've never once heard them discuss having babies or getting married. I can't imagine a couple with no kids would want their home to be overtaken by a single mom and her baby.

Jax grins. "I'm more than sure. It was actually Willow's idea."

"Can I ask you a question?" I don't want to get in their business, but I've always wondered... He nods once. "Is there a reason Willow and you haven't gotten married or had any kids?"

Jax's smile drops, and I worry I've overstepped. I've always had a close relationship with my brothers—sharing a home with them for the first thirty years of my life will do that. But over the last four years, since I got together with Rick and my life slowly began to spiral out of control, our relationship has deteriorated. Now, I fear, I may never be able to repair the damage that's been done.

"I don't usually like to share someone else's story, but Willow already told me if the time ever came when I was in a situation where I needed to explain, I could." He scrubs his hands over his face before he looks back at me. "Willow was diagnosed with endometrial cancer at a young age. It required a full hysterectomy."

I gasp at his words. Poor Willow. I was over here feeling sorry for myself for getting pregnant by my asshole, cheating husband, meanwhile, she can never have a baby of her own. "I'm so sorry, Jax." I lay my hand on his arm. "Are you..." I feel bad even asking this, but I have to. He's my brother. "Are you okay with not having kids?"

Jax smiles and nods. "I am. I love Willow. I offered to adopt with her a few times, but she's said no every time. I think by getting cancer so young, it made her realize how short life can be. So instead of dwelling on what she can't have, she focuses on what she does have. And we're blessed with all our nieces from Jase and Celeste, and soon we'll have one from you. Who knows? Maybe you'll be the one to finally give everyone a damn nephew." We both laugh, and it feels good. It feels right.

"Seriously, though," he says with hearts in his eyes, "Willow is my other half. She's all I need to spend the rest of my life a happy man." I swoon over his admittance. Why couldn't I have found a guy more like my brothers?

"Well, if you guys are sure, then I'm there. But if, at any time, you guys want your privacy back, please just tell me. I'm not broke," I tell him. "I received money in Rick's will that will take care of my baby and me."

"Good," Jax says, "it's the least the asshole could do after what he put you through."

After we pack up a suitcase of my clothes, Jax tells me he'll have a moving company handle the rest. I let him know I don't want any of the furniture and it can be sold with the place. Anything that's Rick's, his parents can have, and whatever they don't take, can be donated to charity. He says he'll handle it all.

When we pull up to the townhouse, I spot Celeste's SUV in the driveway, and Jax says, "Celeste thought it was a nice day for a family barbeque. If you're not up for it..."

"No." I shake my head. "That actually sounds pretty damn perfect."

We walk inside, and I'm immediately greeted by Celeste, Jase, Willow, and Skyla. Everyone takes turns hugging me, and Willow even welcomes me home. Then, my two adorable nieces, in their little black pigtails and frilly matching dresses, come running over.

"Card for Auntie Quinn," Melina says, handing me a scribbled on, folded piece of paper.

"Love you," Mariah adds.

Bending down to their level, I scoop them both up into a hug, taking a moment to breathe them in and get lost in their innocence. In a few months I'm going to have one of my own. My own baby to love and spoil. The thought brings me to tears.

"Skyla, would you mind taking the girls out back to play for a few minutes?" Jase suggests, confusing my happy tears for sad ones.

"It's okay," I tell him. "I'm okay." I wait until the three girls are out of the room before I continue. "I was just thinking in a few months I'm going to be a mom." My sobs get harder as I admit the truth to my family for the first time. "He was so mean, and I was so weak." I shake my head. "He would call me names and tell me I'm fat and should lose weight. And instead of leaving, I joined the gym. But then he accused me of cheating and forced me to quit." Tears fly down my face as I rush to get everything out.

"And he wouldn't let me work. I told you guys I didn't want to continue my photography business, but I was lying. He wouldn't let me. He gave me an allowance. A fucking allowance." I choke on my sobs. It feels almost cathartic to finally tell my family everything. "He would only have sex with me when he was drunk. He was cheating on me with God knows how many women." I bury my face in my hands, completely embarrassed, but Willow pulls them away.

"Don't do that," she demands. "Don't you hide. You have nothing to be embarrassed of."

"I'm okay," I repeat my earlier words. "Even though my husband was a horrible, despicable person, before he died, he gave me the most precious gift." I cover my belly with my hands. "I was scared to admit I was pregnant. Terrified what my life would look like raising a baby with him. I thought about running away and never looking back. But he's dead." I smile because I'm finally free. "And I'm going to love my baby with everything in me. I'm going to be the best damn mother I can be."

Celeste and Willow both smile back, Jase looks like if Rick were still alive, he would find him and murder him, and Jax looks at me with brotherly love.

"So, where do you go from here?" Celeste asks. "What can we do?"

"First things first, I'm changing my last name back to Crawford, and then I'm going to take it one day at a time. It's time I finally find myself."

"And we'll be here for you every step of the way," Jase says, "just like you were there for me while I was trying to figure out how to raise Sky, how to navigate being a single dad." Jase pulls me into his arms for a hug. "We're family, Quinn. Let us be there for you, please."

FOUR

QUINN
  Five Years Later

"BUT MOM," Kinsley whines, "I don't want to go to the tattoo shop. It's not fair." I look in the rearview mirror at my frowning five-year-old daughter. She still has leftover tears in her eyes, and a red nose from all the crying that ensued about twenty minutes ago in the front office of her school as she threw herself onto the ground in a breakdown of epic proportions. During which time, I was forced to pick her up and carry her to the car, all while she screamed and cried and told me I was the worst mom ever.

As I drive to Forbidden Ink, the tattoo shop my brothers own, I remember my daughter isn't always like this. She's generally a very sweet and adaptable child. But today, she's mad at me. Because in the chaos and insanity of dealing with two engagement parties, a wedding, and a pregnancy photoshoot, all this week, I forgot Kinsley needed to be at school early for a field trip. The entire kindergarten class was going to the science museum and my little girl was counting down the days. Literally. With a red pen on our calendar that's pinned to the wall in our kitchen. She lives for the science museum, is obsessed with everything science related.

When we got to the school, late, we were told she would have to remain in the office all day because her teacher isn't there. I suggested taking her to the science museum and dropping her off, but was told, legally they can't allow that. Which left me no choice but to take my very pissed off and disappointed child to the tattoo shop, so Willow and my brothers can keep an eye on her while I drive across the city to the pregnancy shoot I'm already late for.

"I'm sorry, Kinsley," I say, for what feels like the millionth time. There's no worse feeling than that of a mother who's let her child down. "I'll make it up to you. This weekend, you and me, science museum all day. We'll get there before it opens and stay until they kick us out."

She lets out a frustrated huff, crossing her tiny little arms over her chest, and glares my way. It's during moments like these, when her features are put on display, I'm reminded of how much she looks like her father. I'm not about to blame the genetic card for her attitude. She doesn't have an ounce of malice or cruelty in her body. But with her shockingly bright azure eyes, light brown hair, and willowy body, Kinsley Crawford might've resided in my belly for nine months, and share the same last name as me, but she, one hundred percent, looks like her father—well, aside for our skin type. My poor girl inherited my pale complexion that alerts everyone, whether we want it to or not, of every emotion we're feeling.

"It's not the same," she murmurs softly, and my heart breaks at her letdown, defeated tone, which is a thousand times worse than the pissed off tone.

"I know," I tell her, turning off the car. I get out and open her door while she unclicks her seatbelt and jumps down out of my new SUV. After having the Cayenne for eight years, it finally was ready for retirement, so I traded it in and got the same model, only newer. My brothers laughed at me, saying I'm so predictable. It's not my fault, though. I'm not good with change. I know the SUV is good and reliable, so why chance buying something else? I'll be forty years old in less than six months. It's a little too late to take a walk on the wild side now.

We walk into the shop, and since it's only nine in the morning, they're not open yet. I haven't been here in quite a few months, but it still looks the same as it has since they opened the place over fifteen years ago. Graffitied walls, black leather comfy couches, a pool table on one side, and a front counter on the other. In the middle is the hallway that leads to each of the six rooms. When Jax and Jase first opened this place, it was just them. Now, every room is filled with a tattooist.

Forbidden Ink is one of the most well-known places to get tattooed. It probably has something to do with their best friends being retired NFL players, and Jase's wife, Celeste, being an international supermodel, who owns her own clothing line. But the truth is, even with all of that publicity, a business will only flourish if it provides quality service and product, and my brothers, along with their employees, are the best of the best when it comes to tattooing. People drive from all over just to get inked by them. Hell, I have several tattoos, and I would never let anyone but them ink me.

"Who are you?" Kinsley asks, grabbing my attention. When I look to see who she's talking to, I spot a guy standing at the front counter, who I've never seen before. He must be the new guy Jax mentioned he hired. The first thing I notice is his silver barbell brow ring. Moving my eyes downward, they land on his neatly trimmed mustache and thick, bristly beard. It's well-groomed, but still long enough that if he were to go down on me, he would leave rug burn behind on the inside of my thighs.

With a grey beanie on his head, I can't see the color of his hair, but I imagine it's the same golden copper color of his facial hair. He's wearing a white T-shirt that stretches across his chest, showing off all of his ink that covers his arms. I spot the Forbidden Ink signature logo in the corner. When I take a closer look, I notice he has sea-foam green eyes, and under all that facial hair is a baby face. He can't be any older than mid-twenties. And with that thought, my cheeks heat up, remembering I was just imagining his face between my legs. Which is kind of crazy in itself because I can't even remember the last time I thought about a man in that way, let alone him doing those types of things to me.

Without meaning to, my eyes lock with his, and I know without looking in a mirror, my entire face and neck is now flushed pink—thanks to my pale complexion I was *just* talking about. He smirks knowingly, and if it's even possible, I'm positive my flesh is now scorching hot. Jesus, he's fucking gorgeous...*and young*, I tell myself. Too damn young.

"I'm Lachlan," he says with a tinge of an accent that sounds like it might be Irish. He smiles warmly at my daughter before he looks back over at me—his smile turning from warm to arrogant. He totally knows I was checking him out. "We're not open yet," he tells me, "but I would be more than happy to help you in any way I can." His gaze trails down my body, and even dressed in a modest pair of dress pants, a loose blouse, and professional pumps, I feel completely exposed. I stare at him for a long second, waiting for the look of disgust to come now that he's gotten a closer look at me. And then I mentally slap myself for thinking like that.

Every time I think the wounds Rick caused have finally healed, these self-conscious, self-deprecating thoughts resurface. I should push them away, bury them right next to Rick, six feet under. I know I should. I've spent the last five years finding myself. Finding my strength, my voice, my sass—as my brothers call it. But one look from a good-looking guy and I shrink back into my old self. Worried I won't be enough. Scared he's not going to like what he sees. That he'll take a good look at me and be disappointed or let down or repulsed.

So, even though it makes me sick to feel like this—weak and insecure—I wait with bated breath for him to realize he's checking out an overweight, almost forty, single mom. But it doesn't happen. Instead, he cocks his head to the side and licks his lips like he wants to make me his next meal. His muscular arms flex slightly as he crosses them over his chest, and the side of his mouth pulls into a cocky grin. "Please tell me you're inked under all those clothes and my day will be made," he says.

My body ignites at his words, making me feel things I haven't allowed myself to feel in years. I haven't wanted anyone to see what's under my clothes since Rick, but with the way he's looking at me, and talking to me, my hormones are taking over and telling me to strip down right here and show him what he wants to see.

"My mommy has lots of tattoos," Kinsley says, reminding me there's a five-year-old in the room who's listening to every word he's saying.

And with that realization, I'm able to regain my voice. "What's underneath my clothes in none of your business," I state matter-of-factly, cringing on the inside because if he did, in fact, actually see what's under my clothes, he'd probably stop looking at me like he wants to devour me. "I'm here to see Jax," I say, grabbing Kinsley's hand and pulling her behind me down the hallway.

"Whoa! Wait!" he yells after me. "We're really not open yet, and Jax is appointment-only." I see him in my peripheral vision rushing to catch up to me, but I don't stop. I don't have time for this. I don't have time to play whatever games he's trying to play.

"I don't need an appointment."

"We have a *no kids in the back* rule," he informs me, chasing after me. When we get to the back office, I swing the door open to find Willow in Jax's lap, and the two of them making out like horny teenagers. *Jesus! It's not even noon yet.*

Kinsley giggles, and I quickly shut the door.

"I'm going to have to ask you to come back up to the front," Lachlan says with a scowl. I roll my eyes—a childish habit I've been unable to break over the years—as the office door opens and out walks Jax and Willow. Both dressed similarly in a black Forbidden Ink shirt and jeans—only Willow's shirt is lower, showing off her tattooed cleavage, and her jeans are a lot tighter.

"Uncle Jax," Kinsley yells, throwing herself into her uncle's arms, while a fresh set of tears fill her eyes. While I know my daughter is genuinely upset over missing her field trip, I'm also way too aware at how well she's learned to play her aunt and uncle over the years.

Jax, of course, buys her tears and picks her up. "What's the matter, K?" he asks, even though he already knows. I explained it all to him on my way here when I asked if they could please watch Kinsley for a couple hours. Speaking of which...I pull my phone out of my pocket to check the time. Shit! I am so late.

"Mommy made me late, and I missed going to the science museum," she cries, like it's literally the end of the world. Willow's brows furrow in sympathy as she rubs Kinsley's back. My heart swells as I watch my brother and his girlfriend love on my daughter. One of my biggest fears was that she wouldn't grow up in a loving household, so it makes my world feel complete to know my daughter is surrounded by so many people who love her and would do anything to make sure she's taken care of and happy. Even if it means buying into her dramatics.

"I'm sorry, K," Jax says. "I know it's not the same, but Willow and I are looking forward to hanging out with you today."

"It's not the same," my way too honest daughter says with a pout, causing Willow and Lachlan to laugh under their breath.

And then Lachlan glances my way. "Sorry. I didn't know you were Jax's sister." He shrugs unapologetically, then extends his hand. "It's nice to meet you, Quinn."

"No worries," I tell him, quickly shaking his hand, while trying like hell not to stare at his sexy mouth. "Kinsley, I'll be back in a couple hours," I tell my daughter, who's now refusing to acknowledge me. Apparently, we've left Upset Avenue and have ventured back onto Pissed Off Avenue. At least she's no longer yelling at me and saying I'm the bane of her existence.

"I love you," I tell her, giving her a kiss on her cheek. As I walk away, I try not to look back. For one, my heart is breaking over how upset my daughter is, and from the fact I caused it. And two, I have a strange feeling Lachlan is staring at my ass. I make it halfway down the hallway before I give in and steal a glance back over my shoulder. And sure enough, my daughter is back to crying on her uncle's shoulder, and Lachlan is, in fact, staring at my ass.

FIVE

LACHLAN

HOLY MOTHER OF MILFS. As I watch Quinn breeze by me out the door, with her shiny black hair and matching onyx eyes, I only have two questions: Who the hell is that woman? And how do I make her mine? When Jax and Jase mentioned they had a younger sister, my brain created one of those filters—you know, the ones that take the animal body and place a human head on it, and everyone posts it on their social media like it's not at all fucking creepy. Only in my filter, it took Jax's body, and put Jase's head on it. Okay, maybe I'm not making much sense right now. But bear with me. My world has just been rocked by a sassy woman in high heels.

My point, I'm doing a piss-poor job at making, is I never imagined the Crawford brothers' sister would be so goddamn beautiful. In my twenty-seven years of existence, I've never been so turned on and thrown off by a woman. She's a walking fucking contradiction. Even in that uppity professional attire she was wearing, I could still make out the perfect swells of her tits and those luscious fucking curves. And Jesus, those thick hips...and that ass. I could imagine taking her from behind and leaving fingerprint marks from gripping her flesh. And what I'd do to that ass...spank it...fuck it...both at the same time.

When she pursed those fuckable lips in a shitty attempt at

glaring at me, the first thought that came to my mind was how I wanted to bite them and then lick them. I wanted to kiss her fleshy lips until they were red and puffy. Which led me to my second thought. The visual of her on her knees, with me watching as she wraps those same plump lips around my dick. I wonder if she's ever been with a man who has a Prince Albert piercing. I sure as hell would love to show her the benefits of fucking a guy with one.

And *that* visual has me imagining what she looks like naked... again. Although her clothes covered most of her skin, I still managed to catch a glimpse of a tattoo peeking out along her collarbone, and fuck if it didn't have me wanting to beg her to strip down so I could see all the other tattoos she has inked on her body. And for a brief second, the way she looked at me looking at her, I think she might've agreed.

Her brothers are covered in tats, so if I had to guess, I would say she probably has quite a few. And as a man who spends his days inking people, I'm now wondering who Quinn has let ink her. Was it just her brothers and Willow? Or has she let Evan and Gage permanently mark her? And that thought has me feeling a ridiculous amount of unjustifiable jealousy toward them—that they were allowed to touch her when I haven't yet. Holy shit! What's wrong with me? I'm standing in the hallway of my workplace working myself up over a woman I literally met less than ten minutes ago. Pissed off at two guys I work with because they *might've* inked her.

When I hear a throat clear, I snap out of my craziness. I look over and see Willow and Jax both staring at me. Willow is smiling, and Jax is glaring. "I'm going to go get my station ready," I mumble, needing to get the fuck away from the both of them, and also needing to adjust the semi in my pants I'm now sporting.

The next couple hours fly by, with only a minimal amount of fantasizing about Quinn. I tattoo some dates on a retired Navy officer and a butterfly on a girl who is getting a tattoo for her eighteenth birthday. Because I'm new to this shop and haven't been here long enough to establish a clientele yet like the others, I generally get the walk-ins and piercings.

At ten thirty, Willow knocks on my door. When I turn in my chair, my eyes go to the cute little girl peeking out from behind Willow's leg. "Hey, Lach," Willow says, "my client got here early, and Quinn is running late. Would it be okay if Kinsley hangs out in here with you for a little while? Everyone else has someone in their room."

"Sure," I tell her. Even though I'm an only child, I come from a huge family with tons of cousins who have all had no problem adding to the world's population. I love spending time with their kids. I view it as practice for one day when I meet the woman I'll want to spend my life with and we start a family.

"Thanks," she says to me. Then to Kinsley, she says, "I'll be right next door. If you need anything, just ask Lachlan and he'll get it for you. Okay?" Kinsley nods once then enters my room. I've seen her laughing and talking to everyone else, so I'm assuming she's only shy around me because she doesn't know me.

"You having fun with your aunt and uncle?" I ask in an attempt to break the ice. Kinsley climbs up into my tattoo chair and shrugs, and that's when I remember she's here because her mom was late to drop her off for her field trip. I think she said it was the science museum. "Sucks you missed your field trip."

"That's a swear word," she says. "I'll give you a warning, but next time I get a dollar." She's dead serious, not even a hint of a smile on her face. It takes me a second to put together what she said, but once I do, I bark out a laugh.

"All right... So, what's your favorite part of the science museum?"

This gets me a small smile. "All of it," she says softly. "The bodies and dinosaurs and space and music and...and...water and animals and all of it." Her smile grows with each word she speaks, and by the time she stops to take a breather, her face is lit up like a Christmas tree, reminding me of the way her mother's skin flushed pink in embarrassment earlier. They don't have the same hair or eye color, but both of their skin is that shade you see on dolls, almost a translucent porcelain, and their smiles are identical, just a tiny bit crooked with a hint of mischief.

"I'm sorry you missed it," I tell her. We're both quiet for a long beat, and I'm not sure what to do with her. Being in a tattoo shop kind of limits what I can do to entertain a small child.

I glance around my room, trying to find something that might interest her. When I spot my markers, an idea forms. "Want me to give you a tattoo?" I flash her a playful grin, holding up my markers so she knows I don't mean a real one. And just like her damn mother, her eyes roll to the top of her head.

"My mom told me never to get a tattoo by anyone except my uncles and Aunt Willow because they know what they're doing." She shakes her head to emphasize her point. "Just because you can pick up a pen, doesn't mean you can draw."

"What?" I ask. I mean I heard her, but how old is this little girl? Twenty? "I work at the same shop as your uncles and Aunt Willow," I say, unsure why I'm trying to convince this mini version of Quinn that I'm not just another guy with a pen in his hand.

"Yeah... but how do I know you can draw? They're my family, and I can't really draw that great, and my mom can't draw at all." Her eyes go wide, and I laugh.

"Check these out," I say, grabbing my portfolio and placing it in her lap. She spends the next few minutes flipping through the pages before she finally reaches the end and closes the book.

"So?" I prompt.

"I guess you're good." She eyes me with cautious eyes...just like her fucking mother.

"You *guess* I'm good?" I scoff. "Listen here Mini-Q, I'm damn good."

"What's a Mini-Q? Wait! You owe me a dollar." She puts her hand out, and it takes me a second before I catch on that I just said the word damn. Pulling out my wallet, I flip through my bills until I find a dollar, then hand it to her. I can't even imagine how much she's made over the years from her uncles and Willow. Those three curse like drunken sailors.

"Where does the money go?" I question. "Into a swear jar or something?" My cousin Milstead uses one with her kids because her husband has a horrible habit of cursing in front of the kids, and when it gets filled to the top, they use the money to do something fun.

"Nope, right into my pocket," she says, folding the bill and shoving it into her pocket as she answers me. "We tried a jar once, but I caught Uncle Jax 'borrowing' from it."

I laugh at the way she actually uses air quotes when she says the word borrowing. She's obviously been hanging out with too many adults.

"So what happens when you curse?"

"I don't," she says, deadpan.

"What if you did?" I press.

She thinks about this for a moment. "I guess whoever catches me gets to keep the money."

"Nice. So am I good enough to tattoo you or not?"

"I suppose so." She shrugs a shoulder.

"Great!" I smile at the thought at having won her over. Hopefully it will be just as easy to win her mother over. "So, what do you want? A butterfly? A pretty heart? How about a unicorn?"

Her nose scrunches up in disgust, and she gags. "Mommy says a unicorn dies every time one is tattooed above a woman's ass."

I laugh hard, loving that Quinn would say something like that. I seriously need to get to know this woman. Then it hits me she just cursed. "Hey Mini-Q, you owe me a dollar."

"I wasn't cursing," she says, her tiny brows furrowed. "I was telling you what Mommy says."

"You still cursed." I tsk. "Dollar."

"Fine." She huffs, pulling the dollar out of her pocket and dropping it into my hand.

"Thank you," I say with an overzealous grin.

"Why do you keep calling me Mini-Q?" she asks, one of her brows raised. "My name is Kinsley Elizabeth Crawford, but Uncle Jax is lazy and calls me K."

"Because you look and act like a mini version of your mom... Quinn," I say, emphasizing the Q. "Get it? Mini-Q?"

She tilts her head to the side and glares, proving my point.

"Now, what tattoo do you want?"

"Mommy read me a book about the planets last night. Can you tattoo them on me?"

"Sure!" I pull my phone out and google planets. It only takes me a second to find a cool image. "What colors?"

"The colors the planets are," she says, dragging her sleeve up. "Are you sure you know what you're doing?"

"Yes," I say with laugh. "Alright, colors matching the planets. Got it."

When I take her tiny arm in my hand, she says, "Wait, you have to prep me first."

Stifling my laugh, I nod. "You're right. Sorry." This little girl is too fucking much.

She lets out a loud sigh. "I really hope you're good. My uncles and Willow never forget to prep me."

Twenty minutes later, I finish Kinsley's tattoo, pretend to rub ointment on it, and cover it with plastic.

"Thank you." She jumps down to check it out in the mirror, even though it's on her arm so she could just look down. "It's really pretty," she says. "You should take a picture and add it to your book."

"You're welcome." Pulling out my phone, I snap a picture of her arm. "There, I'll get it printed and added today."

Just as I'm finishing capping up my markers, Quinn enters the room. Her eyes go straight to her daughter, as if I'm not even in the room. "Wow, Kinsley! What a cool tattoo." She takes her daughter's arm in her hands and admires it.

"It's all the planets," Kinsley states matter-of-factly.

"I can see that. Who tattooed it?" she asks.

"Lachlan," Kinsley tells her. Quinn's gaze bounces over to me, finally acknowledging I'm in the room.

"Really?" Quinn asks. "I thought only your uncles and Willow were allowed to give you tattoos."

Feeling the need to gloat that I've won her mini-version over, I say, "She trusts me."

Quinn lets out a loud snort, then quickly covers her nose like she can't believe she just did that.

"I'm going to go show Auntie Willow my tattoo," Kinsley says, running out of the room. "Bye, Lachlan!"

Quinn looks from me to the door like she's either willing her daughter to come back, or scared to be in the same room as me. Both leave me grinning. I make her nervous.

"Snort all you want, but it's the truth." I step toward her, encroaching on her space. "I'm a trustworthy guy."

"I bet you are," she says with a bit of a laugh. "I better go..." She waves her hand in the air, not even bothering to finish her sentence.

"Wait," I say, sliding in front of her to block her only way out. "Since I'm such a trustworthy guy, how about you let me take you out sometime?"

"No," she says flatly, not even taking a second to consider it.

"No? Just like that? Why not?"

"Umm..." She places her purple-painted fingertip to her chin and pretends to think for a second before she says, "For starters, I'm old enough to be your mother."

I laugh at that. Sure, she's a few years older than me, but she's definitely not old enough to be my mom.

"What are you, like..." I'm about to say a number and then remember women hate when people guess their age. What if I guess too old and offend her? She obviously thinks she's way older than me.

"Go ahead," she presses. "Say the number."

"Thirty...one." I was thinking thirty-three, so I went two years lower to be on the safe side.

She stares at me for a brief moment and then throws her head back in laughter. "Wow, thank you. I don't know if you're just bullshitting me to make me feel better, but thank you. You seriously made my day."

"How close was I?" I'm assuming I went too low since she's happy I thought she's younger.

"You were off by eight years." I quickly do the math in my head. She's thirty-nine years old. Well, damn, I never would've guessed that. But that's not going to deter me. Age is just a number and all that jazz.

"And you?" she asks with a knowing smirk.

"Thirty-seven," I tell her, lying out my ass.

She laughs, knowing I'm full of shit. "Try again."

"Fine...minus ten."

I wait for her to do her own math, and once she does, her eyes bug out. "You're twenty-seven? Jesus." Her cheeks tint a light shade of pink, an indication I've already learned means she's embarrassed.

"What's going through your head?" I ask, taking another step forward.

"Nothing." She shakes her head.

"Yes, you were definitely thinking something." I run the backs of my fingers along the side of her neck. "You're all flushed. It happened earlier too. Whatever you're thinking has got you embarrassed."

"No," she squeaks.

"Yes," I argue. "Tell me, Q, what were you thinking?"

"One, my name is Quinn, not Q, and I was thinking, you're so young, I could probably get arrested just for talking to you." Her cheeks flush darker.

"What you mean is, you could probably get arrested for thinking about all the things you want to do to me." When her cheeks and neck get even warmer, I know I'm right.

"Doesn't matter," she states. "I was right. I *am* old enough to be your mother."

"My mom is forty-seven, so, no."

"Where are you from?" she asks, changing the subject and giving me whiplash.

"Here."

"You have a small accent. Are you Irish?"

"Ya," I say, putting emphasis on my half-ass accent. "But I was born and raised here. The accent only comes out because my family all have it and I visit Ireland often."

"Thought so," she says, a smile tugging on the corners of her lips. "I watch Sons of Anarchy and you sound like the Irish dude.

Anyway, your mom is only eight years older than me, and I'm twelve years older than you. I'm closer in age to your mom than you."

"I don't care," I tell her honestly. "My mom always told me when I met the woman I want to spend my life with, I'll just know. I'm not saying it's you, but at the same time, I'm not saying it isn't. I want to get to know you. You intrigue me, and I'm not about to let something as stupid as an age difference deter me."

Her jaw drops open, and for a second I think I've stunned her silent. Probably for the best so she won't argue. She blinks once, twice, shakes her head slightly, and then speaks. "Well, you should. Besides, I imagine a good-looking guy like yourself has plenty of young, gorgeous women to choose from." The way she inadvertently puts herself down by referring to other women as gorgeous, as if she's not in that category, rubs me the wrong way. I don't care how fucking old she is, she's sexy as hell.

"That's neither here nor there," I tell her, trying to keep the annoyance out of my tone. "I'm staring at a gorgeous woman right now who I want to get to know."

"My answer is no," she says, pushing my shoulder slightly so I'll move out of her way. I consider not moving, but know it will only piss her off if I don't.

Following her to the back, I say bye to Kinsley, who thanks me again for her tattoo. Quinn says hi to Jase, who wasn't in yet when she dropped her daughter off earlier, and tells Willow and Jax she'll see them at home later.

When Quinn and Kinsley are both out the door, Jax and Willow step on either side of me. I can feel both of them staring at me and know they're going to say something. So, rather than prolong the inevitable by walking away, I wait.

"My sister is not someone you mess with," Jax finally says. "She's been through a lot, and if you fuck with her, I *will* choose her, regardless of our friendship, or the fact you work here. She's family."

Meeting his gaze, I look him in the eye, so he knows I understand what he's just said. "I would hope you would always choose your sister over me," I tell him, "but all I want is to get to know her. I'm not trying to mess with her in any way." He nods once, then walks away back to the office, leaving just Willow.

"Your turn," I tell her, and she grins.

"Good luck," is all she says. And with a pat on my shoulder, she joins her boyfriend in the office.

"Thanks!" I call out after her, knowing damn well I'm going to need all the luck I can get on my side. Something tells me Quinn isn't your average woman, and getting her to agree to go out with me won't be as easy as it usually is for me. But that's okay because something else tells me she's worth the challenge.

SIX

QUINN

MY MIND IS a whirlwind of mixed emotions the rest of the week, which thankfully goes more smoothly than Monday. Every time I recall the way Lachlan looked at me like he wanted to devour me right there in his workplace, I'm at a loss. Or the way he point blank told me he thinks I'm gorgeous and wants to get to know me. Surely, a guy as young and hot as he is, has a line of equally young and hot women at his disposal. Even after I told him my age, it didn't seem to discourage him in the slightest.

Maybe it's because I was dressed professionally, covering the majority of my skin. I make it a point to buy work clothes that hide the rolls and imperfections as much as possible, but even the most expensive, flattering outfits can only do so much. He couldn't see the cellulite on my thighs that turned Rick off, or the newly formed stretch-marks on my stomach that came with being pregnant. I cringe, thinking about how Rick would've reacted to my stretch-marks. He would've blamed me for gaining too much weight during my pregnancy. Damn it! I hate that even after five years, I still allow that asshole to make an appearance in my thoughts. He doesn't deserve any place in my life, alive or dead.

The last few years I've made a conscious effort to eat healthy, and I work out at the gym a few times a week—when time permits. I'm proud to say I've lost the majority of the baby weight I put on.

I'd like to say my hard work has nothing to do with my dead husband's last words to me, but I would be lying if I didn't admit that more often than not, I hear him telling me how I've let my body go, and use it as motivation to workout harder. That being said, I'm still not skinny. My hips are still too wide, and my ass is too big. I hope one day to be at a size I can be proud of, but today is not that day...and tomorrow isn't looking good either.

Which is why I'm so confused as to why Lachlan was so insistent about taking me out. Maybe he saw it as a challenge. I told him no, and most men hate that word. Hell, most people do. But then I think about the way Kinsley droned on about him the entire way home and for several days afterward. How nice and funny he was. When he cursed, he paid her a dollar, she said. When I asked her where the dollar was, her cheeks flushed and she admitted she cursed, and then blamed me because she was only repeating what I always said. My daughter is a lot like me...well, the me before Rick. She's sassy and smart and takes nobody's shit, while at the same time, she wears her heart on her sleeve and trusts too easily. The last two are both a blessing and a curse.

It's now Sunday morning and I have nothing booked for today. Kinsley and I are on our way to the park to practice soccer and then we're planning to go to the science museum afterward. It's her first time playing a recreational sport and she's nervous, so she asked to practice first instead of getting to the museum for opening. She loves kicking the ball around at school, but it's different once you're playing an actual game—at least I imagine it is. I wasn't exactly one to play sports. I was more of a sit-in-the-stands-and-photograph-the-people-playing kind of girl.

"Can we invite Uncle Jax to play?" Kinsley asks as we walk down the sidewalk toward the neighborhood park. "No offense, but you're not very good, Mom." I stifle my laugh, shooting her a mock glare, and she shrugs. Damn kid is too honest. "Sorry, but it's true."

"I texted him and Aunt Willow earlier." They had already left for the shop before we were up. "Uncle Jax said if they get done with inventory and ordering early enough, they'll meet us."

When we get to the park, we head straight to the soccer field. There are a few other families playing as well, so we find an empty spot in the corner to kick the ball back and forth.

"Go stand at that end!" Kinsley exclaims. "I'll kick it to you, and you kick it back, okay?"

"Sure!" I yell with as much fake enthusiasm as I can muster.

About thirty minutes later, as I'm chasing down the soccer ball for what feels like the millionth time, I hear Kinsley yell, "They're here!" I breathe out a sigh of relief. Jax being here means I get to sit down on a blanket in the grass and watch, and take some pictures.

"Hey, Lachlan!" Kinsley squeals excitedly, and I find myself spinning around in shock to confirm he's here. And sure enough, dressed in another white T-shirt—this time with some band logo across the front, black jeans that are molded to his thighs perfectly, and a pair of Vans that match the color of the logo on his shirt, is Lachlan freaking Bryson (I may have stalked him on social media and learned his last name). He's sporting a beanie similar to the one he was wearing the other day, but this one is black.

As I watch him approach us, with his clear as the sky cocky smirk splayed across his perfect lips, and all of his various tattoos on display, my breath hitches. I felt it the other day, the unexplainable attraction to him, but I chalked it up to it all being in my head. I'm a single mom who hasn't gotten laid in over five years. My vibrator gets more action than Bruce Willis...you know, because he does action movies. Okay, maybe that was a bad analogy. But my point is, I'm having to charge that thing quite often. But now, standing here staring at the way Lachlan is looking at me once again, I can't deny it. The sparks are there, threatening to turn into an all-out fire.

Someone call 911 because I need a firefighter to put out these flames. There's only one outcome when you're dealing with a fire—someone's going to get burned. And I don't doubt for a second, that someone will be me.

What the heck is he even doing here?

When I finally peel my eyes off of him, I notice my brother and Willow are also heading toward us. He must've been at the shop and decided to join them. But why? I'm sure he has better things to do on his day off than hang out with a single mom and her daughter.

"Hey, Mini-Q," he calls out, and my eyes, of their own accord, roll upward into my head. Kinsley told me all about his nickname for her. Apparently because she's a little me. I would love to know if he considers that a good or bad thing. *Well, he did say he's intrigued by me and wants to get to know me...*

When the three of them reach us, Kinsley grabs the soccer ball and drags Jax down the field. Of course, Willow follows. Lachlan, though, remains standing in front of me. "Hey," he says, giving me a nonchalant chin lift.

"Hey," I parrot. Reaching down, I grab a bottle of water from the small cooler I brought with me and down half the bottle. When

I lower the bottle from my lips, I see Lachlan is once again staring at me.

"What?" I ask, glancing down at myself. Today, I'm dressed for the occasion in a pair of grey Victoria's Secret boyfriend style sweatpants and a matching hoodie.

"I'm just wondering when I'll get to see you without all that clothing covering your body." He nods toward my outfit with a glare, as if it's personally offending him.

"Sorry." I scoff. "But I'm not exactly in the habit of leaving my house in my birthday suit, so I'm pretty sure any time you see me, I'll be in clothes."

"I get that," he says with a hint of a smile, "but right now, all I have to go by is my imagination...and it's been running fucking wild." Jesus! This man sure has a way with words.

"Well, I can assure you," I volley back, "whatever images your *wild* imagination has conjured up is probably better than the real thing. Trust me when I tell you, you do *not* want to see all that is hidden under here. Stick to your imagination." I meant it as a joke, kind of. Okay, more like a warning, but Lachlan doesn't laugh, nor does he heed my warning. Instead, he frowns and steps closer to me.

"I highly doubt that," he says, his tone serious, "but I wasn't referring to your *body*. I was referring to your tattoos. Both times I've seen you, you've had them covered up." Oh...well, shit. He is a tattoo artist, so it makes sense he would be curious about what my tattoos look like. "But, I will admit," he continues, "I have *also* fantasized on more than one occasion since we've met, what you would look like splayed out across my bed, naked, and spread open for me." The way he grins, tells me he's being crass on purpose to get a rise out of me.

"Well, like I said," I say, trying, and failing, not to get flustered, "stick to the fantasy. The reality will be a severe let down." I laugh humorlessly, and Lachlan's frown deepens.

"Why do you do that?"

"What?"

"Talk about yourself in such a self-deprecating manner. Both times we've spoken, you've put yourself down." When my eyes fall to the ground, embarrassed, Lachlan lifts my chin, so I'm forced to look at him. "You're an extremely beautiful woman, Quinn."

"Whatever," I mutter, unsure how else to respond. "What are you doing here?" I take a step back so he's no longer touching me.

Lachlan gives me a look I can't decipher because I don't know him well enough. If I had to guess, I would say he's considering arguing with me, but he must think better of it because he says, "Jax mentioned coming here to play soccer with Kinsley, so I asked if I could join."

"Why?"

"Why not?" He gives me a perplexed look. "She's a cool kid, and I grew up playing soccer."

"Okay, well, I just hope you're not doing it as a way to get me to change my mind about going out with you...because..."

Lachlan chuckles. "Yeah, I know, it's not going to happen." Then he mutters something that sounds like "such a contradiction" under his breath. But before I can ask him what he means by that, he's already running over to join Jax, Kinsley, and Willow.

<hr>

DESPITE THE ROCKY START, the morning spent with Lachlan and my family is enjoyable. I watch while Lachlan shows Kinsley tons of moves, and join in so we can play a game of two-on-two—Willow offers to referee. Kinsley is on cloud nine with all the attention Lachlan gives her. She laughs and talks animatedly with him. She even insists on being on the same team as him. At one point, Jax jokes he should've just sent Lachlan here.

"He's just someone new," I explain, not wanting him to feel bad.

"I know." He grins, not the least bit upset. "Lachlan is a good guy, and Kinsley is a good judge of character." I allow his statement to swirl around in my head for a few seconds before I push it to the side.

When Kinsley is finally worn out, we say bye to Jax and Willow. I always feel bad with how much time they spend with Kinsley and me. They never complain, but I know they love their time alone as well. On Sundays, which is their only sure day off, I try to keep Kinsley out of the house so they can have time to themselves. Now that Kinsley is in school full-time, I've been thinking more and more about the two of us getting our own place. I've looked at a few places online, but it kind of scares me. I've never lived on my own before. It's something I know I need to do, though. For me and my daughter.

"Mommy and I always get a hot dog at the park for lunch," Kinsley tells Lachlan, who is sitting on the blanket, drinking a bottle of water. "Wanna go?"

"Oh, Kins," I say, "I'm sure Lachlan has other plans." Like my brother and Willow, I think Sunday is his only day off as well.

"Actually, I don't," he says. "A hot dog sounds perfect."

"Yay!" Kinsley yells. "Oh! Can you go to the science museum with us too? I can show you all the planets you drew on me. Please." I stifle my laugh at the way she flutters her eyelashes and exaggerates every letter in the word please, just like she always does to her uncles to get her way.

"That sounds like fun," Lachlan says, not even bothering to speak to me first.

"Lachlan, can I talk to you over here for a moment?" I drag him off the blanket and away from where Kinsley can hear us.

"What's up?" he asks, knowing full well what the hell is *up*.

"What's up is you just agreed to pretty much spend the rest of the day with us."

"Yeah...I know," he says, the corners of his mouth turning up into a lazy smile.

"I know you don't have kids, but when you're approached by a child, you don't just say yes without speaking to the parent first."

Lachlan chuckles. "I may not have my own, but there are a lot of kids in my family and I spend a lot of time with them."

"Okay, then you should know this."

"I know it." He nods. "But I also know if I were to ask, you would say no." He grins, and damn it, if it doesn't do something to my insides. Why can't he have an ugly smile?

"So, you're using my daughter to get to me?" My voice comes out harsher than intended, and Lachlan's playful grin instantly diminishes.

"Now you're twisting shit," he says. "I asked you out, and you said no, despite the fact I *know* you felt something between us." He raises his pierced brow, daring me to argue. "I wanted to get to know you, and the last time I checked, your daughter is a part of you, which means I want to get to know her as well. And at this moment, out of the two of you, she's the only one willing to give me a chance." His shoulders sag in defeat, and I suddenly feel like a mega bitch. He's right. I did feel something—I do—but I'm too damn scared to act on it. "I wouldn't use anyone," he continues, "especially a child, but you don't know that because you don't know me."

He walks away, leaving me standing here in shock, confused as to how we went from playing soccer to arguing. But I know how we got here. Through my insecurities and hang-ups. Instead of giving Lachlan a clean slate like everyone deserves, I've already placed him in the same category as Rick, simply because he's a man—and that isn't fair to him. I'd like to think I've come a long way in the last several years, but at the same time, I still have a lot further to go.

I watch him bend down to my daughter's level and talk to her. I'm not sure what he's saying until I see her tiny brows furrow and her head shake.

Speed walking over to them, I catch the end of whatever he's saying. "...can't wait to see what you want me to draw the next time you visit the shop."

"Okay," she says, her voice soft.

"See ya later, Mini-Q," he tells her before he turns to me. Without meeting my eyes, he says, "Have a good day, Quinn," then takes off toward the park's exit. Lachlan using my full name shouldn't bother me. It's what I told him to use. But for some reason, it does. It makes me want to drag him back and tell him to call me Q.

"I really wanted him to go," Kinsley says, and although, I don't admit it out loud, I feel the same way.

I watch as his body gets smaller and smaller, the farther away he gets, and then something in me snaps. As if the thought of him disappearing altogether is unfathomable. "Wait!" I yell, grabbing Kinsley's hand and running to catch up with him. When he doesn't slow down, I repeat myself. "Wait! Lachlan!" I shout. This time, his steps falter, and he turns around. Out of breath, and mentally telling myself I really should get serious about going to the gym more often, I finally reach him.

"We would...um..." I take a deep breath, nervous to actually speak the words I want to say. *It's just a hot dog and a museum*, I tell myself, but somehow, I know it's more than that. And while I'm not sure exactly what more means, it scares the hell out of me. "We would really like it if you would join us." I let out a loud exhale, waiting for Lachlan to respond. Afraid he's going to dismiss me.

"You sure?" he asks, his face showing no emotion.

"Yeah, I'm sure."

"All right," he says, a small grin teasing his lips. "Let's go."

"Yay!" Kinsley squeals.

SEVEN

LACHLAN

I CAN'T HELP the grin I'm sporting as I pay for the hot dogs and drinks. When Quinn pulled me aside, I knew I overstepped. I gambled and lost. So, I said my peace and then walked away. It sucked, but I wasn't about to force myself on the woman, no matter how much I want her. I know firsthand you can't make someone want you. You might feel the sparks, but if the other person doesn't, you have no leg to stand on. I knew she felt the sparks between us, but for whatever reason, she was trying with everything in her not to acknowledge them. Until I walked away and heard her calling after me.

I barely know the woman, but I could see it in the way she nervously spoke, the unsureness in her tone, it took a lot for her to chase me down and ask me to join her and her daughter. For a second, I considered giving her a hard time, but then I looked into her eyes and saw fear. Afraid of being vulnerable, afraid of putting herself out there and open to rejection. So instead, I asked if she was sure, offering her an out, and when she said she was, I considered that a huge step in the right direction.

"You don't have to get me one," Quinn says. "I'm not really hungry." I tilt my head slightly, not liking what she's saying. It shouldn't surprise me, though, since she's made quite a few comments pertaining to her figure.

"Yeah, you are," I say, holding up three fingers to the guy and handing him a twenty-dollar bill. When he hands me the food and drinks, I hand them out. Both girls say thank you and open their wrappers to take a bite.

"Eww, Lachlan," Kinsley says, watching me add every condiment available to the top of my dog.

"Have you ever tried all these together?" I ask her. She shakes her head. "Then you don't get to judge." She rolls her eyes as she takes a bite of her plain hot dog.

We walk down the sidewalk, eating and listening to Kinsley talk. She keeps the conversation flowing, telling us all about the mean boy in her class who bugs her, how she's excited for her first soccer game next Saturday, and all the exhibits she wants to visit once we get to the museum. When we stop by their house so they can quickly change, I look up the museum to find the easiest subway route. But when I mention it to Quinn, she says, "That's okay. We can just take my car. It'll be quicker."

Not many people drive in New York. I own a vehicle because I lived in Boston for a few years, but I keep it parked at my parents' place since I don't drive it often here. Not only does Quinn have a vehicle, she has a fucking Porsche SUV. From what I've heard, she has a photography business she's building. I'm not trying to get up in her business, but I'm definitely curious to know how much photographers make. Clearly, I'm in the wrong profession. But you know what they say: you don't become a tattoo artist for the money; you become one because of your love of the art.

The ride there doesn't take too long. When Kinsley falls asleep on the way, Quinn says, "She's reenergizing her batteries," with a laugh that makes the corners of her eyes crinkle. It's the first playful thing I've heard from her, and it has me wanting to make her laugh more often.

We spend the afternoon at the science museum, being dragged by Kinsley from exhibit to exhibit. Quinn was right. Her batteries are fully charged, and she's on a mission to see every single thing available. The only reason we leave is because the museum announces that it's closing. Kinsley pouts, and Quinn tells her they'll return again soon.

I offer to take the subway home, so she doesn't have to cross back over the bridge, but she insists on dropping me off. I live in a decent apartment, walking distance to the shop. It has two bedrooms and two baths, and I share it with my best friend and cousin, Declan, who is currently over in Ireland visiting his sister who just had a baby. He'll be back in a couple weeks.

"That's me," I say, pointing to the brick building. "Thank you for letting me crash your day."

Quinn smiles softly. It's not much, but I can tell I'm wearing her down slowly. "You live here?" she asks. I can tell she's curious how I can afford such a nice place when I ink people for a living.

"Yeah, I share the place with my cousin." I shrug, not bothering to mention I own it outright and he barely pays rent.

"Oh, well, thank you for joining us."

"I have a soccer game Saturday!" Kinsley says. "You have to come."

Quinn closes her eyes and shakes her head. "I would tell you that you don't have to come, but at this point, I feel like a broken record." She laughs. "It's at the same park we practiced at today. Nine o'clock. If you can't make it...or have to work..."

"You'll understand," I say, finishing her sentence for her.

"Yeah."

"Can you step outside for a second?" Quinn gives me a confused look, but opens her door and steps out anyway.

"Bye, Mini-Q," I say to Kinsley. "I'll try to make it Saturday." I don't want to say I'll be there and not show up. It's still six days away, so anything can happen. She waves goodbye, and I get out of the SUV and walk around to Quinn's side.

"What's up?"

"I didn't want to ask you in front of Kinsley..."

"Oh, wow, a man who listens." She grins playfully. "Thank you."

"Yeah." I chuckle softly. "Anyway, I was wondering if I could take you out one day this week." Quinn's smile drops, telling me I'm about to be rejected once again. "Or not," I add to lighten the mood.

"I really enjoyed hanging out with you," she says, "but I'm a single mom to a five-year-old."

Running my hand over my beard, I tug on the end, something I tend to do when I'm nervous or frustrated—right now I'm the latter. "I'm aware of all of that," I tell her. "I just spent the last nine hours with you and her."

"No, I know." She groans. "What I meant was...my life is crazy and chaotic on a good day. Take the day you met me for example. I was late, forgot my daughter had a field trip, my sitter was out of town and my back up was sick with the flu. I needed to leave my daughter with my brother and his girlfriend at their tattoo shop, so I could go to the photoshoot, which I was late to. And after I picked up Kinsley, I found out it was the last day to sign her up for soccer." Her eyes go wide dramatically, reminding me of Kinsley. These two are clearly two peas in a pod. "Can you imagine if I would've missed *that* deadline?" I laugh, but don't say anything, letting her finish what she needs to say.

"I raced all over town, signing her up and taking her to get shin guards and a soccer ball."

"You're a good mom," I tell her. I'm not sure why, but I just felt like she needed to know that.

"Thank you," she says warmly. "But part of being a good mom is putting my daughter first."

"That excuse sucks," I say honestly.

"Maybe, but it's only part of it."

"What's the other part?"

"I'm almost forty, and you're twenty-seven. You're a single guy with no kids, no strings. I'm a single mom with a child who has an eight o'clock bedtime."

"So what?" This woman has every excuse in the book, and if I thought they were being slung at me because she really doesn't like me, I would give up. But my gut is telling me they're being used as a shield because she's scared.

"What did you do last Saturday night?" she asks.

"Played poker at Gage's place."

"Exactly. You know what I did? I watched The Little Mermaid for the hundredth time, baked cookies, then after putting my daughter to bed, spent the rest of the evening cleaning up, taking a bath, and working on some edits before falling asleep only two pages into the book I'm reading."

"Jax and Willow were there too," I point out.

"They're kid-less," she says, "just like you."

I look at her, at a loss of what to say. I feel her slipping through my fingers before I've even gotten her. Figuring this is my last chance, I say what's on my mind. "Look, Q, I like you. I want to take you out. I get you have all these reasons why you don't think it would work between us, and in your head they very well may be relevant. But I don't see why any of those reasons you mentioned should prevent me from taking a beautiful, hard-working, woman out—kid or no kid."

When her eyes drop to the ground, I lift her chin. I hate when she feels like she can't look at me. "I think you like me too," I tell her. "But I also think you're scared." When she nibbles on her lower lip, I know I've hit the nail on the head. "So, here's what I'm going to do." I reach around her and pull her phone out of her back pocket. When I swipe up, it opens, indicating she doesn't have a passcode on her phone. "I'm going to put my number in your phone. If, or hopefully when, you want to get to know me, text or call me. We can take things slow, I promise. I just want to get to know you."

I type my number into her contacts list then hand her back her phone. "I hope to hear from you." Leaning over, I give her a chaste kiss on her cheek before I wave to Kinsley one last time and then head up to my place. The ball is in her court now. I just have to hope she thinks I'm worth stepping out of her comfort zone for.

EIGHT

QUINN

IT'S FRIDAY NIGHT, and for the first time in I don't know how long, not only do I not have any shoots booked, but I'm completely caught up on all my edits, and I'm off all weekend. And for the first time in what feels like forever, I'm kid-less. As I sit on the couch, with my Phish Food ice cream in one hand, I flip through the channels on the TV, hoping to find something to watch that doesn't involve princesses or talking dogs. On the coffee table is my phone, taunting me, the same way it's been taunting me the last five days since Lachlan input his number into my contacts list. I've typed out enough messages to have an entire one-sided conversation, but I haven't built up the courage to actually hit send on a single one.

The truth is, I don't have a lot of dating experience. Growing up, my two older, tattoo-covered, football playing brothers were several years ahead of me, yet made sure everyone knew who they were, so the boys tended to stay away. We lived in a small town. It wasn't until my senior year of high school I convinced Tommy Pines to take my virginity the night of prom. I know, how cliché. He was boring, to say the least. A book nerd of sorts, and because of that, he didn't know who my brothers were. A month later, he left to some crazy, smart college, and I started at the Art Institute. I dated on and off over the years, slept with a few guys, but never felt that spark you read about in those super mushy romance novels.

And if I'm honest, I'm not sure I ever *really* felt them with Rick. I think I was lost and felt lonely. I know I shouldn't have felt that way when I have two brothers who love me like crazy. But it's not the same thing. They were so career oriented. They knew what they wanted and were making it happen, while I was floundering around. First, I thought I wanted to work in a museum, so they picked up their entire life and moved to New York with me. Only a few months later, I realized I hated it, so I quit.

I did learn, though, my true passion was photography, and that's how I came to start my own photography business. The problem was I had no idea what I was doing or how difficult it would be to try to build a business in New York. Every day I felt like I was failing while my brothers were succeeding. So when I met Rick, and he promised me the world, I took the easy way out by latching onto him.

At first, he was charming and said all the right things. He made me feel like an equal. But all too soon, his attitude changed, and I learned too late my husband was a snake. He had me in a trance, mesmerized, and before I knew what was coming, he bit his poisonous fangs deep into my flesh, and I was fucked.

I never want to be in that situation again. The problem is, how do I ever move forward if I'm too afraid to give another man a chance? In theory, the solution is easy. Open myself up and let Lachlan in. The reality, isn't so black and white. I can't afford to make those mistakes again. Especially now that I have Kinsley. If I'm wrong about Lachlan, I won't be the only one hurt. It's clear my daughter already cares about him.

So that leaves me at a crossroad. Do I text him or not? The sexually deprived woman in me wants to text him and beg him to fuck me. I can just imagine the stamina that man has. When he was sweating on the soccer field, he lifted his shirt up, and I caught a glimpse of his six-pack of abs. He works out for sure.

But the responsible, single mother, whose heart has been shattered into a million pieces by my husband is yelling at me to run, and run fast. No good can come from this—well, aside from some potentially mind-blowing sex. But then he'd need to see me naked... which is why, while I won't admit it out loud, I've worked out at the gym every day this week. After seeing how fit Lachlan is, I can't imagine what he would think if he saw me naked.

Sighing heavily, I stare at my ice cream-covered spoon, recognizing I'm stress eating again. I haven't felt this out of out of sorts in a long time. Putting the lid back on, I take it back into the kitchen.

Damn Ben and Jerry and their delicious ice cream. Throwing the container back into the freezer, I slam the door shut. Sulking like... well, my five-year-old, I'm walking back to the living room, when the front door swings open and in walks Willow and Jax...and Lachlan.

Willow and Jax don't notice me standing here as they yell something about going out while running upstairs to change, but Lachlan does. With the front door still partially open, his gaze is glued on me. He's dressed in his usual T-shirt, jeans, and Vans, but added to the mix is a black leather jacket. Of course he's wearing a damn leather jacket. Because he wasn't already hot enough without it. I also notice he's not wearing a beanie, and I was right—his hair, messy and all over the place, is the same ginger color as his facial hair. It makes me want to run my fingers through it to see if it's as soft as it looks.

While imagining running my fingers through his hair, my gaze lands on his bright green eyes which are widened almost comically, and I snap out of whatever lust-induced coma I'm currently in, looking around to see what has him in such shock. But when I follow his line of vision, it takes me to...well, me. And it's then I wish the floor would crack open and swallow me whole. Because as I was standing here checking out Lachlan, I forgot I'm dressed in the shortest, tightest, pair of boy shorts, and a tiny cotton camisole. Yep, you heard me right. I'm standing here in my goddamn underwear! In my defense, I ran out of clothes, and they're currently in the washer and dryer. Not that it will do me any good right this second.

As if this moment couldn't get any worse, I hear my brother and Willow descending the stairs, talking and laughing. My own brother is about to see me in my freaking underwear. Great! As if Lachlan can read my mind, his eyes briefly go to the stairs and then he's pulling me by the curve of my hip behind him and against the wall to shield me from embarrassment. His hand stays holding on to my flesh as Willow and Jax enter the living room.

"What the hell is going on?" Jax asks, confused as to why his friend is hiding his sister behind him. Lachlan's so tall, that when I try to look over him, I fail, and instead have to look around him. He backs up slightly, and I'm sandwiched between his body and the wall. Without realizing what I'm doing, I slide my hands up his strong, muscular back to keep my balance, so I can peek around him. In response, his fingers tighten on my hip, and a soft moan escapes my lips before I can stop it.

"I'm...uh...not dressed," I say with a bit of an awkward laugh, fully aware I also sound slightly turned on and breathless. Remember those sparks I mentioned I've never felt? Well, holy fucking hell, I feel them with Lachlan, right now, between my legs. Willow cackles, and Jax fake-gags. Lachlan groans, and the way his body vibrates, sends heat flooding through mine. "Can one of you please grab me the throw blanket from the couch?"

Thankfully, Willow snaps into action and hands me the blanket, which I wrap around my shoulders to cover my body up. Lachlan moves forward and turns to face me. I'm so embarrassed, I can't even look him in the eyes. Nobody since Rick has seen me in such a vulnerable position.

"Where's Kinsley?" Jax asks, breaking the awkward silence.

"Sleepover at Celeste's with Olivia's and Giselle's daughters." Olivia and Giselle are two of my sister-in-law's best friends. Between the three of them, they have eight girls. It's a running joke how Olivia and her husband, Nick, are the only ones with a son, Reed. When I got pregnant with Kinsley, the three of them were all pregnant at the same time. We took bets on who would be the one to have the second boy, but all four of us ending up having daughters. When Celeste mentioned having Kinsley over, she asked me to join, but there was no way I was passing up a night to myself.

"You should join us," Willow suggests, but I'm already shaking my head.

"Oh, no. I'm too old and tired to keep up with you party animals," I joke.

"Yeah, yeah." Willow laughs. "Well, don't wait up." She winks dramatically and pulls Jax behind her.

"Night, sis!" Jax yells, following his girlfriend out the door, and leaving Lachlan and me alone.

"You better get going before they leave you behind." I nod toward the door with a small laugh.

"You never texted me," Lachlan says, changing the subject.

"I thought about it," I admit, which has him smiling, and in turn, has me smiling.

"And what did you think about texting me?"

"I don't know." I shrug a shoulder, refusing to tell him about the fifty different texts I thought about sending.

"I was thinking I could stay here...keep you company," he says, his eyes wandering down my blanket-covered body. Worried that at any moment I might drop said blanket, I tighten the corners around me. The blanket knocks my loose bun out and several stands of hair fall into my eyes. With my hands full of the fabric, and not wanting to chance dropping the blanket, I attempt to blow the hair out of my face. Lachlan laughs and, stepping forward, tucks the wayward strands of hair behind my ear. The simple touch of his fingers brushing my flesh shouldn't affect me the way it does.

"So, what do you say?" he asks. "You up for company?"

I shoot him an incredulous look. "Trust me, you don't want to miss going out with your friends and possibly getting laid, just to lounge on the couch and watch a cheesy rom-com with me."

"Don't tell me what I want," he says, his tone serious. "I wouldn't have suggested us hanging out if I didn't want to."

"Hey Lach!" Jax yells from outside. "Quit hitting on my sister and let's go!"

I roll my eyes, and Lachlan coughs out a laugh. As I look at him, I already know I'm going to give in. I've been fighting it since the first day I met him, but my resolve has been slowly weakening each time I'm around him and he says and does all the right things—then again, so did Rick in the beginning. I push that thought from my mind. Rick doesn't belong here with Lachlan and me. I'm so tired of allowing him, even dead, to rule my thoughts and decisions. It's my life!

Lachlan must mistake my silence for no because his smile drops, and he says in a defeated, very unlike Lachlan, tone, "All right, well, have a good night." He shoots me a half-smile and is walking away before I even know what's happening.

"Wait!" I say, running to stop him. This seems to be becoming our thing: he asks, I say no, and then I chase him. Only this time I wasn't going to say no. "Sorry, I was in my own head. If you want to stay and hang out, that's fine." Lachlan raises a single brow, and I cringe at how rude that sounded. "That came out wrong. I just meant if you really would rather hang out here instead of going out, you're more than welcome to join me."

The corner of his mouth quirks up into a sexy smirk, and he nods once. "I'll let Jax know I'm staying here while you go get dressed." His eyes light up mischievously, then he adds, "Or you can stay just how you are." He bites down on his bottom lip before turning to go outside. *What I would give to have him biting down on my bottom lip.*

When he's out the door, my body sags in relief. Holy hell, he is so freaking intense. Running up the stairs, I scour my room for a single clean article of clothing, but can't find anything. Damn it! I really shouldn't let my laundry pile up until I have nothing left.

Uncertain of what the hell to do, I stand in my closet willing for something to appear. I have a couple dresses, but how stupid would I look walking down there dressed like I'm ready to go to church or work?

Hearing the door shut, I know Lachlan is downstairs waiting for me. I open each of my drawers again, knowing I won't find anything. *My goodness, I seriously have a lot of laundry to do.*

Just then, I hear the dryer buzz, and thank the laundry gods above. Now I just need to get to the dryer, which is downstairs in the laundry room. Tiptoeing down the stairs, I pray Lachlan is in the kitchen, the only room you can't see the stairs from. Of course he's sitting on the couch and looks over at me as I descend.

"Decided to keep what you have on?" he says with a smirk. "I approve."

"No." I roll my eyes—I really need to break this habit. "I'm out of clothes, but I heard the dryer go off."

"Well, don't feel like you have to get dressed on my account."

"I'll be right back," I mumble, running off to the laundry room. Thankfully, there's a dry pair of sweats and a hoodie in there. I throw them on then head back into the living room with the blanket in my hands.

"So, what are we watching?" Lachlan asks as I sit down on the other side of the couch. When he notices, he shakes his head but doesn't say anything.

I flip through the channels but can't find anything to watch. "How can we have like two hundred channels and not a single movie is on?" I pout. "I told you, you should've gone out."

Lachlan edges across the couch toward me, and I stand. If I let him get too close, there'll be no turning back. "I need to rotate my laundry," I blurt out awkwardly.

Once I'm in the laundry room, I open the dryer and start folding and hanging up Kinsley's and my clothes. If I thought doing laundry would be an excuse to give Lachlan and me some distance, I was wrong. He, of course, joins me, and catching on quickly, starts handing me the pants and shirts hangers whenever I need one.

"I'm going to run these upstairs," I say, having no idea how to handle having this guy in my home, being sweet and helpful. I'm so completely out of my element with him, it's embarrassing. I haven't the slightest clue why he's even still here, when he could be out with his friends, getting his party on.

"I'll help you," he offers, grabbing the clothes that are hung up, while I grab the ones that are folded. All three bedrooms are upstairs. We stop by my room first, and I'm surprised when Lachlan doesn't comment on how girly my room is. It's Skyla's old room, and she was all about the pink. When I moved in, I was too lazy to change the wall color.

When we get to Kinsley's room, though, he laughs. Her walls are half-black, made of chalkboard paint, and half bright green, with science posters covering them. "This is awesome." He sets her clothes down on the bed and walks around, checking out her room while I put her clothes into their proper drawers. When I open her closet to hang up her clothes, Lachlan is right behind me.

"Oh, man, she has all the classics," he says, referring to her large stack of board games. He reaches over me and pulls one out. "Wanna play?" When I turn to look at him, I can see the evil glint in his eye. He's up to something.

"You want to play Candyland?" I'm not buying it for a second.

"My cousin Declan and I are the only boys in the family, and we're also the oldest. When we were younger, and our parents would make us play these boring games with his sisters and our other cousins, we would change up the rules to make it more fun." He grins wickedly. "Because they were younger, they didn't know we were making them up." He cackles, and I can't help the smile I'm currently sporting. Lachlan is so damn adorable and playful.

"Like how?" I ask, wanting to know more.

"Well, take this game for instance." He holds up the board game. "We would tell them if they landed on red, they had to give us a piece of their candy." He's smiling so hard, even his eyes are twinkling. "If they landed on blue, they would have to do one of our chores." He laughs, and the sound hits straight between the apex of my legs. Everything about Lachlan is sexy, even his laugh.

"That's so mean!" I say, but find myself laughing along with him.

"Yeah." He shrugs. "But that's part of growing up, right? I bet your brothers used to do shit like that to you."

"Nope," I tell him honestly. "They're a good six and seven years older than me and they treated me like a princess. They never would have done anything like that."

"Well, then you missed an important rite of passage," Lachlan says, his tone serious, which has me laughing harder.

"What a shame," I reply, sarcasm dripping from every word.

He looks down at the box that's holding the game, then up at me. "Let's play."

"I'm not falling for your chores rule," I joke.

"New rules."

"No way!" I can't remember the last time I laughed so hard. "I can just imagine the shit you'd have me doing."

"C'mon, it will be fun! Live a little," he taunts, and even though I don't doubt whatever rules he's about to make up will be dirty and leave me embarrassed, I suddenly want to play. He's right, it's time to live a little, have some fun. And then an idea forms. If I'm going to play his games, I need to even the playing field.

"I get to make up the rules."

"We both do," he volleys.

"Fine."

NINE

LACHLAN

WHEN JAX MENTIONED GOING out tonight, I checked my phone, hoping maybe Quinn would finally send me a text since it's the weekend, but when nothing was there, I agreed. After shutting down our stations for the night, he mentioned he and Willow needed to go home to change first, and that's when I formed my plan. All I needed for it to work was for Quinn to be home. Granted, I assumed her daughter would be there. I figured I would convince her to let me hang out with them, maybe watch a movie or play a game. I'm not picky. Getting Quinn to open up hasn't been easy, so I'll take whatever I can get. If it wasn't for the way I've caught her looking at me on several occasions, I wouldn't believe I even stand a chance at this point. Most people would wonder why the hell I'm even bothering. Quinn was right. It would be easy for me to find a woman to hook up with, but that's not the kind of guy I am. People assume because of the tattoos and piercings and the job description, I'm some bad boy looking for my next fuck. But that couldn't be any further from the truth. And if it was, my mom would tan my ass.

When we arrived at their place, Quinn's car was in the driveaway, so I knew she was home. I walked through the front door, expecting to see her and Kinsley hanging out, so imagine my surprise when instead, I saw Quinn in nothing more than a tiny pair of black and white polka dotted underwear and a white tank top, so thin, I could see her perky nipples poking straight through the material. I couldn't take my eyes off her. I knew she was hot, but damn! My imagination didn't even begin to do her justice. I've been with a few women over the years, but compared to Quinn, they all look like little girls. Her thick hips, heavy tits, and shapely thighs are all damn woman, and I've never been so turned on in my life. And if that wasn't enough, I was finally able to get a glimpse of her tattoos. And I was right...fuck, was I right. They cover parts of her upper arms, a little bit of her chest and collarbone, and span across her legs. I was too in shock at seeing her half-naked, I didn't get a chance to really check them out, but I'm going to. I could see it in her eyes when I mentioned making up the rules—she knows what's coming, and if she didn't want it to, she would've refused to play.

I set the game on the dining room table and open the lid. Pulling out the gameboard, I open it up and place it in the middle of us while Quinn organizes the cards into a neat stack and places them on the board. We pick out our colored gingerbread pawns—she picks purple, and I pick yellow—and then she excuses herself for a moment.

When she comes back, she's holding a skinny blue bottle that has blue and pink puffs on the front. "Is that cotton candy flavored vodka?" I ask, giving it a closer look.

"I figured it was fitting." She glances down at the board game with a small smirk, and I'm grinning on the inside because she's finally letting loose. "I was thinking for the candy spots, we have to take a shot."

"I like it." Maybe if she gets some alcohol in her, I can get her to open up more. "Okay, so the rules," I say, sitting down in the chair. "We each pick two colors."

"I go first." She sits at the square dining room table, diagonal from me. "I want pink and purple."

"Such a girl," I joke. "I'll take blue and red."

"Such a boy," she mocks.

"Yeah, yeah. Name your rules."

"If someone lands on pink, they have to answer a truth."

"So, I can ask you any question I want, and you have to be honest?" I clarify.

"You too," she says.

"Got it."

"The purple spot..." She thinks for a minute, her perfectly manicured finger tapping on her chin. "You have to explain one of your tattoos."

"And you have to show it to me," I add.

"Fine." She rolls her eyes as she twists the cap off the bottle and pours us each a shot.

"My turn," I tell her. "If you land on blue, you have to let the other person kiss you."

Her eyes widen even though she knew this was coming. "Where?"

"Anywhere the kisser decides."

"Fine." She huffs, giving in a lot easier than I expected. "And the red?"

I lick my lips and smirk, looking her dead in the eyes. "You have to take off an article of clothing." I doubt she's going to agree to this rule, but I have to try. I have a backup rule in mind just in case.

She chokes out a cough mixed with a shocked laugh, then grabs her shot glass, throwing back the liquid and slamming it down onto the table. "Okay."

"Okay?" I ask, just to be sure.

"Yep." She fills her shot glass back up. "I need to use the bathroom before we start."

While she's gone, I check my phone for any texts or calls. My mom is in Ireland with my dad for an extended vacation until my cousin's wedding, which is in December. With me being their only child, she usually calls or texts me on a daily basis. I'm looking down at my phone when I hear Quinn coming back down the stairs. When I glance up, something about her looks different, but I can't put my finger on it. And that's when I notice she's wearing socks. *Why is she wearing socks?*

And then it hits me. "You fucking cheater!" I bark out a laugh, and she cracks up. "How many articles of clothing did you put on? Ten shirts and twenty pairs of underwear?"

"No!" She cackles, sitting back down. "My toes were cold." She's so fucking adorable, I can't even be mad. She totally played me at my own game.

"You go first," I tell her. She picks up a card and it's pink.

"A truth," she says, moving her gingerbread to pink.

I consider starting off easy—asking her a simple question like what her favorite color is, but with my truths limited, and knowing how guarded Quinn is, I decide not to waste them. There's one question I've been wondering since I met her...

"Where's Kinsley's dad?"

Quinn's eyes widen slightly, and she frowns. "Starting off with a bang, huh?" She laughs softly.

"Go big or go home," I say to lighten the mood, and it works because the corners of her lips curl into a smile.

"Richard Thompson, Kinsley's father, is dead." Fuck... I wasn't expecting that. She grabs her freshly filled shot and gulps it down.

"Shit, Q, I'm so sorry." I bring my hand up to her arm and squeeze lightly. "I didn't know," I add, feeling like an ass. "How long has he been gone?"

"Since before Kinsley was born. He never even knew I was pregnant," she says with a shake of her head. "We were married for three years, together for a little over four. He was shot in the back by a druggie who wanted his wallet, when he refused to give it to him." Jesus, I can't even fathom how Quinn handled all that, especially while pregnant.

Being as she doesn't have to tell me anything more, I'm shocked when she continues. "He was getting into his car from dinner."

A thought hits me that has my stomach roiling. "Were you... were you with him?"

She laughs, but it sounds off. *Why the hell is she laughing?* "Oh no," she says with a sad smile. "One of his many mistresses was. I was at home trying to figure out how to tell the man who despised me I was *finally* pregnant with our child."

It takes me a second to string all of her words together. Her husband, the man who was supposed to love and protect and be there for her, was out fucking around on her while she was home alone and pregnant. If he weren't already dead, I would kill him my fucking self. Then another part of what she said hits me.

"What do you mean he despised you?"

She exhales a deep breath. "I can't believe I just said all that. I've never told anyone...not really. Only my family knows the basics. It must be the liquid courage," she muses, taking another shot. This time I join her.

"Quinn, if you don't want to talk about it, you don't have to," I say, giving her an out.

"I do," she says slowly. "For some reason, you make it really easy to talk to. But not now... If it's okay, I'd really like to play some more Candyland." She smiles softly at me, and my heart speeds up. I'm so fucked when it comes to this woman.

"Okay, it's my turn." I pick up a card, and it's red, so I move to the first red square.

Quinn laughs. "Your rule, and you're the first to strip! Take it off, Lach, now!" She laughs harder, waggling her eyebrows playfully. I know it's the alcohol helping her break out of her shell, but I'm loving this version of Quinn. I imagine that at one time, before her dickhead husband, she was like this all the time.

Reaching back, I lift and pull my shirt off my body. When she yells, "Yeah, take it off," I playfully throw it at her, and it smacks her in the face. She giggles loudly, and I want to bottle that shit up for later.

"Wow." Her eyes light up as she assesses my half-naked body. "You work out a lot, huh?" Her gaze drags down my chest and over my abs. I've never really cared what a female thought of my body. I work out because I enjoy it, and I want the art on my body to have a decent canvas. But right now, with the way she's eyeing me, makes me damn glad I do work out.

"A few times a week. I have a gym in my building."

She groans. "I have a gym membership, but I rarely go. I really need to change that."

"You're perfect the way you are," I tell her. She rolls her eyes as if what I'm saying is bullshit. We're going to have to work on that. If I have to tell her every day she's fucking perfect, until she finally believes me, I will.

"What does that tattoo mean?" She leans over, and the tip of her fingernail hits the top of my ribcage. Goose bumps dot my flesh at her touch. When I glance down, I see the tattoo she's pointing at is the one I had done after my grandfather passed away.

"When my grandfather was alive, we would go fishing every weekend on the dock behind his house." I point at the wooden dock with the fishing pole hanging off the edge. "We would sit and talk for hours. Rarely ever caught a fish, but they were some of my best memories with him."

"That's really sweet. I don't have any grandparents," she admits sadly. "My dad's family disowned him when they found out he was cheating on his wife, and my mom's parents passed away when I was little." Damn, so not only did her husband cheat, but so did her father. It's no wonder she has a hard time opening up.

"I'm sorry," I tell her. Then to lighten the mood, I say, "You asked about my tattoo..." When she gives me a confused look, I add, "I didn't pick up a purple card. Now I get to ask you about one."

"Gah! Fine!" She holds out her left arm, which is covered completely by her hoodie, and lifts up her sleeve, exposing a small tattoo on her wrist. "This was my very first tattoo. Jase tattooed it on me when I was sixteen." At a closer glance, I see it's a small anchor with a rope wrapped around it. "Jase, Jax, and I all have the same one."

"You guys are close, huh?"

"Yeah, until they met their significant others, we were all each other had. They're my best friends."

Quinn picks up a card. It's yellow, so nothing happens except her moving. I pick up orange, so I move. Quinn goes again, picking up a blue card. The second she flips the color over, her teeth bite down on her bottom lip. She's nervous. And suddenly I'm regretting my rule. Because while I want to kiss Quinn, I want her to want me to kiss her.

"You know what? I was just kidding about that rule." I force out a laugh to emphasize my point.

When she looks at me, her brows are drawn together. "You don't want to kiss me?" she asks softly, hurt evident in her tone. She continues to nibble on her bottom lip, and my heart drops into my stomach. Was it her husband who made her this insecure? She said he despised her, cheated on her with several woman. Is he the reason she's so self-deprecating when she refers to herself? Why she thinks it's crazy that I would want her?

Standing, I step the two feet to where she's sitting, then crouch down so I'm eye level with her. She looks down at me as I cup her soft cheek with my callused hand and bring her face down to mine. My lips first land on the corner of her mouth, and I can feel it, she's not breathing. She's waiting anxiously to see what's going to happen. I wonder if I'm the first guy to kiss her since her husband.

"Breathe," I whisper against her lips, just before I claim her mouth. Our lips crash against each other, then part. Our tongues stroking and teasing. Our mouths moving in perfect rhythm. I can taste the sweet vodka on her tongue. I suck on it, needing more.

More of her taste.

More of her touch.

More of her body.

Just. Fucking. More.

Oh, sweet, Quinn. I'm going to make you mine.

Quinn moans into my mouth, and her hands find their way to my chest. I think she's going to push me away, but instead, I'm shocked when her nails dig lightly into my chest. Not wanting to take it too far, and knowing I very well will if we keep going, I pull back gently. Needing her to know how much I want her, though, I go back in for one last chaste kiss.

When I sit back down, I give Quinn a look I hope conveys how much I want her. Her cheeks and neck are flushed, and her breathing is labored. She's turned the hell on. And the thought has me wanting to thump my fist against my chest like a fucking caveman. I did that to her.

"Your turn," she squeaks out.

I pick up a card. It's an image of gumdrops or some shit, so I down the sweet as hell shot. When I set it back down, Quinn fills it back up. She goes next, and it's red. She laughs, then slowly unzips her hoodie. When a white shirt appears, I laugh along with her.

"You're killing me." I groan. "I'm sitting here, shirtless, meanwhile you have God knows how many layers on you."

"Trust me. Seeing what's under here—" she waves a hand over her front "—*would* kill you."

I can't help rolling my eyes, and she giggles. "Are Kinsley and I rubbing off on you? I think you roll your eyes as much as we do."

"Why do you always put yourself down?" I ask, even though it's not her turn to answer a truth.

She looks stunned at my question, but doesn't deny it. "I-I don't know," she says with a frown.

"Yes, you do. You said your husband despised you. Did he call you names, Quinn?"

She considers my question for a moment before she nods once. "Yes," she answers softly.

"Did he think you were fat?" Another nod. This guy is so fucking lucky he's already buried six feet underground.

I stand abruptly, and the chair knocks back slightly, making a loud scraping sound against the wood floor. Quinn's eyes widen curiously, and if I'm not wrong, maybe a little in fear, which only makes me that much more pissed. Fear of a man doesn't happen on its own. A violent man causes a woman to fear.

Lifting Quinn into my arms, I carry her over to the couch. Her legs tighten around my waist, and I do everything in my power to ignore the warmth I feel between her legs.

"What are you doing?" she asks, breathlessly.

"Showing you something." I need her to see what I see. I need to wipe away every negative and nasty thought her disgusting fucking prick of a husband put into her head. Fuck him for thinking it's okay to make a woman feel like she isn't beautiful, isn't worthy of affection and attention. That because her hips are wide and her ass is plump, she's any less perfect than anyone else.

Setting her gently onto the couch, I kneel between her open thighs and press my mouth to hers, needing to feel her soft lips against mine once again. Her lips part slightly, and I dart my tongue out and into her mouth, tasting the sweetness mixed with Quinn.

"Your lips are perfect," I murmur. Even with my mouth so close to hers, I keep my eyes open, and she does as well. I need her to not only hear my words, but see the truth in them. "They're soft and full, and if I could, I would spend hours kissing them."

She averts her gaze, embarrassed. "Don't do that," I say. "Look at me, please." When she does, I smile. With one hand holding myself over her, I use the other one to trail a finger down her neck to her throbbing pulse point. My lips move from her mouth to that spot. I place a soft kiss to her flesh, my lips lingering for a second as I suckle gently on her skin.

"I love the feel of your skin." I run my nose along her flesh, breathing in her sweet scent.

"I'm pale and translucent."

"It's flawless and shows every emotion," I argue, reluctantly lifting my head, when what I really want to do is bury my face into the crook of her neck. "Take your shirt off for me?" I request. I don't doubt that right now, with her thighs clenching around mine, she wouldn't let me take her clothes off, but I need *her* to do it. It has to be her. Her decision. Her facing her own fears of letting a man see her body.

Her mouth twists into a nervous frown, but then she nods and lifts her shirt off, leaving her in only a black cotton bra and sweat-pants—and those socks she put on for the game. I trail kisses down her neck and over to her collarbone. There's a small quote: *this too shall pass.* When I lick my way slowly across the words, she inhales sharply.

"I don't like this quote," I tell her honestly. It means something bad happened. I can imagine her sitting in the tattoo chair, getting it inked onto her body to remind herself that one day things will get better. "Did you get this after your husband died or while you were married to him?"

She swallows thickly and her eyes gloss over. "While," she says, and I nod once in understanding.

"Your collarbone is so fucking sexy," I tell her, leaning down to give it a kiss. "So delicate." I trail my fingers across her chest, to the other side that doesn't have any ink on it. "One day you're going to let me ink you right here, and it's going to be something good. Some-thing that makes you smile."

Quinn bites down on her bottom lip and sniffles once. "Don't cry," I tell her softly. Her eyes flutter shut, so I lift up and give each of her lids a soft kiss.

"I really love your eyes," I tell her when she opens them back up.

"They're just black," she says dismissively with a small laugh.

"No." I shake my head in disagreement. "They remind me of the night sky...dark and mysterious...the possibilities are endless. They're just waiting for the bright stars to shine and reflect in them."

"Lachlan..." Quinn whimpers, but I ignore her. She needs to hear my truths.

Moving downward, I place an open-mouthed kiss to each of the swells of her perfect breasts. "I really, really like your tits," I tell her with a wolfish grin. She laughs, shaking her head.

I slide my body down the couch until my face is parallel with her stomach. Her hands fly downward to cover her flesh, so I take her hands in mine and pin them to her sides.

"Lachlan, I don't want to do this anymore," she pleads, tears suddenly racing down the sides of her face. My heart constricts at the thought of her being so insecure and self-conscious, the idea of me looking at her naked body brings her to fucking tears.

Lifting back up onto my knees, I kiss where the tears are landing. "Because you're uncomfortable with me seeing you, or because you think you're fat?"

"I'm uncomfortable with you seeing me *because* I'm fat," she admits.

Cupping her face in my hand, I kiss her softly before I pull back and say, "I'm not going to push you tonight because I think just you taking your shirt off and letting me see you like this was a lot for you, but this isn't over, Q. I don't think you're fat. I think your fucking gorgeous, and one day, you're going to be comfortable enough to let me see all of you. And when that day comes, I'm going to worship every single inch of your body until you're screaming my name. Got it?"

With a sniffle, she nods, but I need to hear the words.

"Say the words, baby."

"Got it."

TEN

QUINN

WHEN LACHLAN CLIMBS off of me, I stay lying on the couch, watching as he bends and grabs my shirt. His words are on replay in my head. The way he described my eyes and lips and breasts. Nobody has ever described me in that way. And when I freaked out over him seeing my stomach, he responded with such patience. I looked closely to see if he was mad or frustrated, but all I could find was compassion and want and understanding.

Sitting up, I reach out to take the shirt from him, but instead, he takes my hand in his and pulls me into a standing position, then puts the shirt on me himself. Once I'm back to being covered, I grab the bottle of vodka and pour myself a much-needed shot.

"Bring the bottle and glasses over here," Lachlan says, so I do. Once I set them down on the end table, he picks me up and sits back down on the couch, situating me across his lap, bridal style, with my legs stretched out in front of me. I lay my head back against the arm of the couch and he leans over and kisses me, starting with my neck, then moving to my cheek, the corner of my mouth, and finally my lips, his beard scratching my chin briefly before he pulls back.

"No more Candyland?" I ask.

Lachlan's eyes shine with laughter, but he shakes his head. "No," he murmurs. "I think we're past needing a card to tell us what to do." He tucks a wayward hair behind my ear. "It's your turn. Pick a color."

"No way. I just went. You pick a color."

"Fine. Pink. Ask me anything."

"Hmm..." I think about what I want to know about Lachlan. "When was the last time you were in a relationship, and how long did it last?"

His smile dampens, and his hands encircle my waist. I can feel his fingers clasp together, holding me to him. "That's two questions," he says, kissing the tip of my nose. "Her name is Shea. We dated for about three years on and off, finally ended things about six months ago."

"Is that why you moved here?"

"Kind of," he says. "I grew up in New York. My dad is Irish-American and was on vacation in Ireland when he met my mom. They fell in love and she moved to New York to be with him. They run his family business here. That's why I don't really have the accent. Growing up, we would visit often, but New York is our home. While I was on vacation in Ireland, I was hanging out with everyone, my friends and cousins, and Shea and I ended up hooking up. She's been around for years, but I never really noticed her before." He shrugs. "We did the long-distance thing for a couple years, and then one day she showed up. I was living and working in Boston at the time. I had gone to college there and ended up staying, even though it drove my mom nuts for me to be so far. It was at the same time my dad had a minor stroke and needed my help running his business."

"Oh no." I frame the sides of his bristly-haired face in my hands. "I'm so sorry. Is he okay now?"

"He is," he says with a smile. "But at the time, he needed to take a break, so I moved down here so I could help out. I still tattooed part-time, but I mostly focused on running the family business. I have a degree in business management, so that came in handy, I guess."

"That's really selfless of you," I tell him. "My brothers moved here for me too. I still feel bad about it because I didn't end up liking the job, so the move was kind of pointless."

"Hardly," Lachlan says. "Have you not seen their shop? It's one of the top tattoo shops on the east coast."

"Yeah, I guess you're right." Maybe moving here happened for a reason. Jase did get back in touch with Celeste because of the move, and Jax wouldn't have ever met Willow had we not moved here. And both couples are hopelessly in love...

"So, you moved back and what happened?"

"Shea moved with me to New York, but she wasn't really happy here."

"Was she happy in Boston?"

"No." He shakes his head. "She missed Ireland but wanted to be with me and knew my life was here. Once our relationship went from long distance to every day, I realized she wasn't who I wanted to spend my life with. We had different wants... different dreams. Eventually we broke up and she moved back to Ireland."

"Are you still working for your dad?"

"No, Dad is back to work now. That's why I took the job at your brothers' shop. I met Jax at an inkers convention and we hit it off. By the end of the weekend he had offered me a job."

"You must be really good," I say, remembering how Kinsley let him draw on her.

"Well, Kinsley did let me ink her," he says, voicing my thoughts. "Plus, my best friend and cousin, Declan, lives here, and so do my parents, so I decided to stay. Declan and I share the place you dropped me off at, but he's in Ireland right now. One of his sisters just had a baby, so he's visiting, but should be back in a few weeks."

"I've seen Ireland on Sons of Anarchy. It's really pretty."

Lachlan laughs. "I doubt the show does it any justice, but yes, it is beautiful. I think I got off track." He scratches the side of his beard, which reminds me of the first time I saw him and thought about that same beard between my legs. My neck and cheeks heat up, and Lachlan smirks. Thankfully, he doesn't ask what I'm thinking about.

"Your turn," he says.

"I pick the picture card," I say with a giggle that tells me the alcohol has worked its way through my body. Lachlan chuckles, pouring me a shot and handing it to me. Once I throw it back, I say, "Okay, your turn."

"I pick red," he says mischievously. Without waiting for him to prompt me, I sit up and press my lips to the tattoo of the Irish flag on his chest. It's one of my favorites of his I've seen so far. It's 4D and looks like the flag is in his skin with his flesh being ripped open. When I let my lips linger, Lachlan groans. Blaming it on the alcohol flowing through me, I move my lips to his other pectoral muscle and kiss the tattoo there. This one is of a four-leaf clover with the leaves in the shape of hearts.

"Quinn," Lachlan rasps. "I'm trying to be good here, but you putting your mouth on me isn't making it easy."

"I can't help it," I murmur, trailing my lips up his chest, to his collarbone, and ending at his neck. "You taste so good."

Lachlan tilts his head to the side to give me access, and I kiss along his pulse point and up to his ear, sucking on the bottom of his earlobe. Then I trail more kisses over his scratchy beard and to his cheek. "I pick blue," I murmur, my mouth only a hairbreadth from his. His lips brush against mine teasingly, and when mine part on a sigh, his tongue delves into my mouth. I suck on it, craving the taste of Lachlan. As our kiss deepens, I find myself turning in his lap so I'm straddling him. My arms wrap around his neck, and my fingers thread through his soft, messy hair. We kiss for several minutes, and not once does Lachlan attempt to touch me in any way. His hands stay situated behind my back, holding me to him. I don't doubt for a second he's doing this so I'm in control. So I feel comfortable. And ironically, the idea of him allowing me to go at my own pace has me wanting him that much more.

Just as I break our kiss and trail my lips down his bearded jaw and back over to his neck, a cell phone rings out loudly. Remembering Kinsley was supposed to call me before going to bed, I reach over to the end table and grab it, fully aware I'm still on Lachlan's lap.

"One second," I tell him, then answer the phone. "Hey Kins, how's it going?"

"I'm having so much fun, Mommy! We played the Wii and I'm a really good fake dancer! And then Uncle Jase made a big fire and cooked us all s'mores. They were so yummy! I asked Auntie Celeste if I can bring one home for you, but she said they would be bad tomorrow." As I laugh at my daughter's enthusiasm, I glance at Lachlan and see he's also listening with a big smile splayed across his face.

"I'm so glad you're having fun, sweetie. I'll be there in the morning to get you so you can go to soccer."

"Okay! And can you please ask Lachlan if he's going to come? He said he'll try." When she mentions Lachlan's name, his grin widens, and he winks at me. When I roll my eyes dramatically, his hands go to my sides, and he tickles me.

"Ahh!" I squeal before I can stop myself. Kinsley asks if I'm okay. "Yes, I...stepped on something by mistake. I love you, and I'll see you tomorrow."

"Okay, love you too. See you tomorrow. Don't forget to call Lachlan, okay?"

"Okay, Kins. Night."

"Night."

We hang up, and I drop my phone onto the table and then smack Lachlan in the chest. "Not cool! You can't tickle me when I'm on the phone."

"How was I supposed to know you would be that ticklish?" He laughs, then attempts to tickle me again. This time I see it coming and try to climb off his lap to get away, but Lachlan is stronger and holds me to him, not allowing me to get up. "I think your daughter likes me almost as much as her mom does," he says with a wink.

Gripping the back of my hair, he pulls my face into his for a quick kiss. "So?" he asks.

"So, what?"

"Aren't you going to ask me to go to her game tomorrow?"

"That's not what she asked me to do," I point out. "She asked me to ask if you're going."

"Okay, so ask." His hands move from my hair down to my waist, gripping the curves of my hips, and distracting me.

"Q," he prompts.

"Are you going to Kinsley's game?"

"That depends."

"On?"

"If her mom wants me there." His hands move down to my ass, and he gives my butt cheeks a squeeze that has me jumping in shock and laughing at the same time.

Wrapping my arms back around his neck, I lay my head down on his shoulder. His beard tickles my face as I kiss the side of his neck. "It feels like everything is happening so fast," I murmur, closing my eyes and relaxing farther into his lap. The amount of alcohol I've drank is definitely catching up to me. I feel warm and tingly all over.

"Maybe so," he says, running his fingers through my hair and pushing it to the side so it's out of my face. "But maybe when it's right, it doesn't matter how fast things move."

I nod into his shoulder in agreement, but not entirely sure if I really do agree. Things moved fast with Rick, but it definitely wasn't right. I think for a moment, trying to decide if I should voice my thoughts or just let it go. I'm so comfortable in Lachlan's arms, I don't want to say anything that will ruin the moment. His fingers move from my hair to my back, trailing lines up and down, forcing my body to become even more relaxed by his touch.

"When I was with Rick, it all happened so fast, but it wasn't right," I admit softly. "How will I know if it's right this time?"

Lachlan's fingers still momentarily and then start up again. "I wish I could say you will just know," he says, placing a kiss to my temple. "But the truth is, you never know. I was with someone for three years before I finally admitted to myself, she wasn't the one for me. There are no guarantees, Quinn, but I've only hung out with you a few times and I can feel the difference. The way my heart beats when you look at me and touch me. The way I missed you all week while I was waiting to hear from you. I could go days without hearing from Shea, and I wouldn't feel half of what I felt while checking my phone every twenty minutes, all week long, hoping to see a text from you."

Releasing a content sigh at his words, my eyes flutter closed. "I'm scared," I confess. "I think I'm falling for you."

"You don't have to be scared. I'll be right here waiting to catch you."

"I really like you holding me," I admit through a yawn, snuggling my body closer to his.

"I really like holding you," he says back. My eyes try to fight sleep, but the moment he nuzzles his face against mine, I'm a goner.

WHEN I OPEN MY EYES, it takes me a second to recall the details of last night. Folding the laundry, which led to playing Candyland with Lachlan and me drinking for the first time in years. The last thing I remember was sitting in his lap on the couch, so when I look around and see I'm lying in my bed, I'm a bit confused. Twisting my head to the side, I notice Lachlan is here and in bed with me. While I'm on one side of the bed under my blankets, he's on the other side with only a thin sheet covering his bottom half. He's asleep and shirtless, and I use the moment to admire how beautiful he is. He could've taken advantage of my inebriated state last night—and I would've let him—but he didn't.

As I watch his chest rise and fall, I think about everything we talked about last night. I learned a lot about him, and I'm surprised by how much I shared. Even during all the years I spent with Rick, I never felt this comfortable with him. We never just...talked. I really like talking to Lachlan...and kissing him. I *really* liked kissing him.

The way he used his tongue...I can just imagine what that tongue is capable of.

"What are you thinking about that has your flesh heating up like you're standing close to a fire?" Lachlan rasps, his voice scratchy from sleep. He turns over to his side, and his lips curl into a sleepy smile.

"N-nothing," I stammer, taken aback by how much Lachlan's presence affects me. His voice. His smile. Separately, they have the ability to take my breath away. But together...holy hell, together, I feel like I've just jumped off a plane and am soaring through the sky without a parachute. "I'm going to make coffee. Do you want any?"

Lachlan, grabs the curve of my hip before I can get away, and pulls me into him until our bodies are flush against each other. "What were you thinking about, Quinn?" he asks again.

I consider lying to him but go for the truth. "I was thinking about how much I enjoyed last night."

"Oh yeah?" He grants me the most adorable yet sexy grin. "What about it?" He kisses the tip of my nose.

"Playing Candyland."

"What else?" He kisses my cheek.

"Kissing you," I whisper, and he glances back to me. "I was thinking about how skilled you are with your tongue," I admit, shocking myself. What the hell is this man doing to me? "And how I wonder what else your tongue is capable of." I can feel my skin heating up like a freshly lit stove, but Lachlan doesn't comment on it. Instead, he flips me onto my back and climbs up my body, placing kisses along my jaw and down my collarbone.

Without him having to ask, I pull my shirt over my head to give him better access. *Who is this woman?* As he kisses the swells of my breasts, I hold my breath, waiting for him to move downward to my stomach. With one kiss to the center of my belly button, he keeps heading down until he's lying on his stomach between my legs. He stills for a second and looks up at me, silently asking for permission to remove my pants. Alarm bells go off in my head that this is too soon, but then I remember what he said: *when it's right, it doesn't matter how fast things move.*

Plus, I really do want to know what his tongue is capable of.

With a single nod, I lift my butt off the bed, and he pulls my sweatpants off my legs, leaving only the boy shorts I'm wearing. Embarrassed to have him down there, I lay my head back and cover my eyes with my arm, but I should've known Lachlan wouldn't let that fly.

"Eyes open," he demands softly. "I want you to watch me make you come." I can't help how nervous yet excited I am. I've only had one guy attempt to go down on me before, but nothing really came of it. We were young and he wasn't very experienced.

Lachlan loops his fingers around the sides of my panties and tugs them down, leaving me completely exposed. With the blinds shut, it's not too bright in here, but there's definitely enough light shining through that I'm able to watch him without issue, which means he can see all of me: every stretch-mark, every flaw, every imperfection. The thought has me wanting to put my clothes back on and run away.

As if Lachlan can sense the vulnerability in my thoughts, he says, "You look absolutely fucking stunning, lying in this bed with your legs spread open and ready for me." His words have such a calming effect on me. My shoulders slump, my body relaxes. "Good girl," he murmurs just before he spreads me open and begins to lick up my center. Not able to see what he's doing, I prop myself up on my elbow for a better look, just in time to see Lachlan's tongue dart out and lick my clit, eliciting a moan from me as my pelvis pops up in shock at how mind blowing it feels.

He eyes me curiously, so I answer his silent question. "This is... kind of my first time," I admit, sheepishly. My answer must be one he likes because he grins like a Cheshire cat before dipping his face back down and licking up my slit again. I continue to watch as Lachlan licks and sucks and nibbles my clit, working me up into a frenzy. I've made myself come many times over the years, but my vibrator sure as hell isn't capable of these functions.

When I feel my orgasm reaching the precipice, I throw my head back against the pillow, close my eyes, and allow myself to just feel what Lachlan is doing to me. And with one more flick to my clit, I'm coming so hard my toes curl into my sheets and my pelvis lifts from the bed.

"Oh. My. God," I scream as Lachlan continues to suck and lap up my juices that are flowing down my center, until I've completely come down from my high.

When I open my eyes, he's lying next to me on his side with the goofiest grin on his face. I try to recall a single time Rick smiled like that at me after sex, but I can't, and it's in this moment, I finally accept Lachlan is not Rick. He's not going to put me down or call me names. He's not going to blame me if I don't orgasm fast enough, or tell me I'm broken. For some crazy reason, Lachlan wants me.

And while I have no clue where this will go or how long we'll last, I'm done fighting it.

And with that conclusion, I blurt out the first thing that comes to mind. "Thank you." Lachlan throws his head back with a laugh, and I groan inside. I just thanked him for eating me out. Fabulous.

"You're welcome," he says through his laughter. "I don't think I've ever been thanked for going down on anyone before." He gives my cheek a kiss before he stands. "I don't have any clothes here, so I'm going to run home to shower and change, and then I'll meet you at the soccer game." Grabbing his shirt from the nightstand, he pulls it on over his head, and I mentally pout.

"What's wrong?" he asks. Shit! I must've been actually pouting.

"I was just wishing you could stay shirtless forever," I say, shocking myself at how honest and open I've become. Lachlan is bringing the old Quinn out in me, and I must admit, I've really missed her.

"I will if you do," Lachlan says with a grin, nodding toward me. How did I forget I'm still naked? Grabbing the blanket, I wrap it around my shoulders and get out of bed.

"I'll see you at nine," I say before I head into the bathroom.

Once I'm showered and dressed, I head downstairs to grab some coffee before I head out. Willow and Jax are both sitting at the table, in their Forbidden Ink shirts, drinking coffee and talking.

"Morning," I say, passing by them, going straight to the kitchen.

"Morning," Willow chirps, but Jax doesn't say anything. After I've made myself a cup of much needed coffee, I walk back out to the dining room to find them whispering in hushed tones.

"Everything okay?"

"Yeah," Willow says, at the same time Jax says, "I saw Lachlan leave...this morning."

"Oh, yeah, he spent the night." I sit at the table with them and take a sip of my coffee.

"Well fucking aware," Jax murmurs.

"What's that supposed to mean?" I ask, confused.

"Nothing." He shrugs, taking a sip of his coffee.

"No, tell me," I push, not liking my brother's attitude. This is the first guy I've allowed in my bed in years, and we didn't even have sex!

"Fine, what I meant was...in the future, try to keep it down." His nose scrunches up and his body visibly shivers. It takes me a second, but once I understand what he means, I flush with heat.

"Oh my God!"

"Hey! That's exactly what you were screaming earlier," Willow says with a giggle that has Jax hitting her with a hard glare. "Sorry, not funny?" She laughs some more.

"You don't think maybe you guys are moving a little too fast?" Jax accuses. "You only met him like two weeks ago."

"You are aware I'm a grown woman, right? I'll be forty in a few months."

"I just don't want to see you rush into anything," Jax says in his brotherly tone. "He's young, Quinn."

"I'm ten years younger than you," Willow says with a frown.

"You're supposed to be on my side," Jax hisses, and I laugh.

"I appreciate you looking out for me, but I've thought a lot about this for the last couple weeks, since the day I met Lachlan and he asked me out, and I want to see where things go with him." And then I add, "And I'm going to find a place for Kinsley and me."

"What?" Jax glowers. "Why?"

"Because it's time. We were only supposed to stay here until I got back on my feet. Thanks to the money I received from Rick's death, even if my photography business wasn't doing well, which it is, I can afford my own place."

"We'll miss you," Willow says, "but we understand." She pats my hand with hers and stands. "Come on, grouch," she says to Jax, who is now pouting like a child.

"Are you guys coming to Kinsley's soccer game?"

"Of course." Jax huffs. "And since you're taking her from us, I'm going to have to make more room in my calendar to see her."

"You know I'm going to find a place close by. Don't act like that," I tell him. "I'm not taking Kinsley away from you. I'm giving you guys some privacy, while trying to finally become independent. Wherever we move won't be far, and you know you can take her anytime."

"I'm sorry," he says, "I know you're right, but that doesn't mean I have to like it."

ELEVEN

LACHLAN

WHEN I GET to the soccer field, I locate Quinn right away, and then I notice, sitting with her are both her brothers and their significant others. And surrounding them are a shit ton of little girls running around. Unsure of how Quinn feels about public displays of affection, when I get over to them, I go straight for Kinsley, who is standing near them but kind of off to the side.

"You ready for your game?" I ask, kneeling down next to her.

"You came!" she exclaims, throwing her tiny arms around me. "I'm really nervous," she admits softly, reminding me of her mother.

"That's okay. It happens to the best of us," I tell her. "But don't worry, once you're out there, the nerves will go away and you'll kick ass." I'm well aware I've just cursed, but I'm hoping it will distract her.

She lifts her head from my shoulder and backs up. "You owe me a dollar."

"Damn it," I say, reaching into my pocket.

"Now two!" She laughs, bouncing on the balls of her feet in anticipation. I hand her the two dollars, and she runs them over to her mom, her nerves gone for the moment. "Can you hold these, please?"

"Sure," Quinn tells her daughter.

Everyone wishes Kinsley good luck and then she runs out onto the field.

"Hey," I say, having a seat next to Quinn on the blanket.

"Hey," she says back. When all the other adults around us go quiet, Quinn says, "What?" with an exasperated huff.

"You could at least introduce us to your friend," Celeste says with a knowing smirk, as if she hasn't met me several times when she's come by the shop to visit her husband, and sometimes to even help out.

"Umm...what are you guys looking at? You already know Lachlan," Quinn says, sounding annoyed.

"Well, yeah," Willow says, "But not as your..." She looks over to me. "What exactly are you?" She quirks her head to the side, and I bust out laughing.

"He's my...friend," Quinn answers, at the same time, I say, "I'm her boyfriend."

Everybody laughs as Quinn's eyes bug out of her head. "Baby," I whisper, leaning into her so only she can hear me. "What I was doing to your pussy with my tongue only a few short hours ago definitely makes us more than friends."

Quinn gasps, her sexy neck turning that beautiful shade of pink I love, and Celeste chokes on the water she's drinking. Oops...at least, I didn't think anyone could hear me. Oh well.

"Did I mention I'm moving out of the townhouse?" Quinn says to no one in particular, in an attempt to change the subject. Celeste gasps, and Jase curses under his breath.

"And in with Lachlan?" Celeste clarifies.

"What? No!" Quinn says, realizing her comment was vague and made everyone jump to conclusions. "I'm moving on my own, with Kinsley."

Jase's shoulders drop in relief, and I chuckle. "Damn, would it be so bad if she was moving in with me?" I joke, and Jase and Jax both glare my way, which only has me laughing harder.

"We'll be talking later," Jase says, pointing a finger in my direction. Quinn's eyes widen in shock, maybe fear, but once I lean over and squeeze her thigh, she calms.

We spend the next hour watching Kinsley play soccer. None of the kids are really good, but I guess you can't expect them to be at five years old. One kid makes a goal, and another blocks one. Kinsley runs back and forth, kicking the ball a few times. A kid from the other team kicks a goal, and another one attempts one, but it gets blocked. When the game is over, the kids crowd around the coach who tells them they did a good job and passes out drinks and snacks for them.

I'm watching Kinsley open her drink and snack, when I hear Quinn yell, "Oh no!" She jumps up from her seat on the ground and rushes over to Kinsley. Concerned something has happened to her, I follow her over.

"Kins, sweetie, you have to remember," Quinn says, her voice laced with worry.

"I'm sorry. I only forgot for a second," Kinsley tells her with an adorable pout.

"What's wrong?" I ask, coming up next to Quinn.

"Kinsley is allergic to raw fruit." Quinn holds up the juice box. "It doesn't contain a lot of natural fruit, but I'd rather not take the chance. When she was a baby, I gave her fresh peaches and her lips puffed up. I rushed her right to the emergency room, but by the time we arrived, she had rashes all over her and was having trouble breathing. I'd never been so scared in my life. After running tests, they said she has OAS, meaning she's allergic to certain types of fruit."

"So she can't eat any fruit?" I ask. I had no idea a kid could be allergic to stuff like that.

"If it's cooked, she can, but not raw," Quinn clarifies. "She has an emergency Epi-pen I keep in my purse, and one at school, in case she eats something by mistake that causes an allergic reaction."

"Too bad you're not allergic to vegetables," I joke, giving Kinsley a playful wink.

She laughs. "I'm allergic to carrots!"

"Only raw," Quinn adds with a laugh. "It's mostly fruits, but she is also allergic to carrots."

After everyone tells Kinsley how amazing she played, she thanks everyone for coming and hugs a couple of her cousins. I let Jase and Jax know I'll see them at the shop later since I only work a half day on Saturdays.

Once everyone has left, and it's only the three of us, I pull Quinn into my side and whisper, "Can I take you ladies to lunch?" so Kinsley can't hear. A slow smile creeps up on her lips and she nods. Inside, I'm fist bumping myself. Every time she says yes, it feels like another victory in my book, another step to completely winning her over.

We head over to a café nearby to eat lunch. Kinsley spends the entire meal going over her game play by play, asking us what we thought and what she thinks she can do better next time. Afterward,

Quinn offers to drop me off at the shop, since she and Kinsley are going to go meet with a friend of hers who is a realtor to show them some houses.

When I step into the shop, both Jase—who rarely ever works on the weekends—and Jax are waiting for me. "Back office," Jase grunts. Willow, who is pretending to dust the front desk or some shit, looks up and mouths *Good luck.*

"Make it quick," I tell them, "I have an appointment at noon."

"What are your intentions with our sister?" Jax asks, getting straight to the point once we're seated.

"To get to know her."

"You're aware she's almost forty, right?" Jase adds.

"So, what? She's too old to date? To fall in love? You planning on making her live the rest of her life alone?" I quip. When they both look at me like I have a third eye, I say, "Look, I like Quinn and Mini-Q, and I have every intention—"

"Wait, who's Mini-Q?" Jase asks, cutting me off.

"Kinsley." I smile. "You know? Because she's a mini version of her mother." I picture them both at lunch earlier, and how they rolled their eyes at the same time when I cracked a cheesy joke, and the way both their eyes lit up over the sundae I surprised Kinsley with for playing a good game. One has black and the other blue, yet when they smile, they sparkle similarly.

"True." Jase nods in agreement. "Okay, go on."

"I like them both, and I want to get to know them. I can't promise I won't ever hurt Quinn because I don't know what the future holds, but I can tell you right now, I would never do anything to intentionally hurt either of them. She told me about that fucker, Rick, and—"

"She told you about him?" Jax asks, shocked.

"Yeah...and if he were still alive, I would fucking kill him with my bare hands." Jase and Jax both grin.

"All right," Jase says, "I like you, and it's obvious you like our sister, but if you hurt her..."

"I know," I tell him, not needing him to finish his sentence. If I hurt her, I better be ready to find another job. But the fact is, if I hurt that woman in any way, I would never stay where she would have to see me. The last thing I want is for Quinn or her daughter to ever be hurt or sad in any way, let alone me being the cause of it.

TWELVE

QUINN

I'M SITTING on my couch with my phone in my hand, trying to decide what to do. After we left from having lunch with Lachlan, the plan was to meet with my friend Jenn, who is a realtor. I took photos of her wedding a few years back, and we hit it off. Unfortunately, she texted and apologized, asking if we could please reschedule for tomorrow due to a last minute emergency. I texted her back I understood and told her tomorrow would be fine.

Then Kinsley begged me to spend the night again with her cousins. When I called Celeste, she told me she invited her over and forgot to mention it. Apparently, they're going to the movies to see some new Disney flick. I offered to join, but Celeste told me to enjoy another night to myself.

I've thought about texting Lachlan to see what he's up to, but I don't want to appear too clingy. It's not like we're dating, and even if we were, I imagine couples his age aren't attached at the hip twenty-four seven. Although, he did refer to himself as my boyfriend to my family, so there's that...

Putting my phone away, I grab my iPad and pull up the book I'm currently reading. I'm not even through the current page when the front door swings open—much like it did last night—and in walk Jax and Willow.

"Hey!" Willow says, stopping in front of me. "Kinsley asleep?"

"She's actually sleeping over at Celeste and Jase's again."

"Wow! Two nights in a row with no Kinsley. What are you going to do with yourself?" she jokes. "You should come out with us." Instantly, my head is shaking of its own accord, but Willow raises her hand to stop me. "It's been over ten years since you've been out. I remember when I first started at Forbidden Ink... before Rick. You used to be the life of the damn party."

"That was a long time ago." *I was still in my twenties...Practically a lifetime ago.*

"So what?" She waves her hand dismissively. "Put on a sexy dress and some heels, and come out with us."

"I was actually thinking of texting Lachlan," I admit.

"Well, then you can surprise him because he's going to be there," Jax says, coming back down the stairs in a fresh outfit. "His cousin Declan surprised him by flying back in today from Ireland, and we all decided to go out to welcome him home."

"You know his cousin?"

"Yeah," Jax says. "He hangs out with everyone."

"I don't know..." What if he gets annoyed that I showed up there without letting him know? What if he's out with someone else? The thought makes my stomach sink. Just because we're getting to know each other, and he gave me the best orgasm of my life this morning doesn't mean I can just show up and stake a claim on him.

"Stop overthinking this," Willow says. "C'mon, let's get dressed. You can put on a little makeup and brush your hair." She laughs at her own joke as she grabs my hands and pulls me up.

"I should at least text him, so he knows I'm coming," I insist.

"Okay, so text him. Let's go!"

An hour later, dressed in a black off the shoulder dress and black heels with makeup on my face, and my hair curled into loose waves, I walk into Assets, an upscale night club in the Upper East Side. I texted Lachlan to let him know I was coming, but he never texted me back. I'm assuming he couldn't hear his phone over the bass of the speakers in this place.

Following Jax and Willow through the throng of people, I glance around the club for Lachlan, seriously hoping I didn't make the wrong decision in coming here. Any time I would offer to accompany Rick on his trips or to his business dinners, he would get a huge attitude, telling me I was too clingy, and if he wanted me to go, he would ask. I know now that a lot of the reason for his reaction was because he was cheating on me, but I still can't help but question everything I do now. Lachlan is young and carefree. The last thing he probably wants is an older woman dampening his fun.

"Stop overthinking this," Willow repeats as we approach a table that is filled with people. Immediately, I spot Evan and Gage, who work at the tattoo shop. From working there as their receptionist on and off for years, I've become good friends with both of them. Since I don't know who the other men and women are, and I don't see Lachlan anywhere, I head over to Gage, who smiles when he spots me walking over.

"Well, look who it is!" he shouts. "Am I seeing shit, or is it really Quinn Crawford in a dress, at a club?" He stands and embraces me in a hug.

"Yeah, yeah!" I laugh, and it feels good. I forgot what it was like to go out, without my daughter, and act like someone other than a mom. "How about you come with me to get a drink?" I might as well get a little bit of alcohol in my system to help me let loose.

"Gage!" a petite, brown-haired woman squeals, sidling up next to him and putting her arm around his waist—clearly staking a claim. "Who's this?" She bats her mascara-covered lashes, and I stifle a laugh. I'm probably a good fifteen years older than her. She must know I'm hardly competition.

"I'm Quinn," I say politely, "Jax's sister." I nod toward my brother who is leaning over and taking a shot from the center of Willow's chest. *Gross!*

"Cool!" she exclaims. "I'm Courtney, Gage's girlfriend." Realizing I had no idea Gage has a girlfriend, I suddenly feel like a horrible person. Even after Rick died, I didn't really make a huge effort to stay in touch with the people I used to be close to. Sure, I see Gage when I visit the shop—which isn't really often because I'm always working or taking care of Kinsley—but I haven't taken the time to find out how his life is going, what he's been up to. I was so relieved to be out from under Rick's hold, yet I never took the time to put the pieces of myself back together again like I promised myself I would do. I'm functioning, I'm mothering, I'm working, but I'm not actually living.

"It's nice to meet you," I tell her. I'm about to excuse myself to get a drink when Evan comes over and gives me a hug.

"It's been awhile, woman!" he yells over the music.

"I know," I agree, pulling back.

"Aren't you going to introduce me?" an Irish accented voice says. When I look over, I spot a guy, similar in features to Lachlan—same green eyes and ginger hair, but a much shorter beard. He's also a bit shorter than Lachlan, but not by much. His accent is a tad bit more pronounced than Lachlan's, but still nowhere near as heavy as the Irish people in Sons of Anarchy.

"Declan, this is Quinn, Jax's sister." Declan's eyes widen fractionally, and I briefly wonder if Lachlan has mentioned me.

"Nice to meet you," he says, just as a woman comes over and puts her hand on his forearm. She looks almost identical to him, only more feminine. "This is my sister, Riley. She's in town, visiting."

"Hey, I'm Quinn." I give her a small wave.

Another female comes over on the other side of Declan and gives his cheek a kiss. "Hey, baby, I was looking for you."

"Sorry, I came over to meet Jax's sister, Quinn." He tilts his head my way. "This is Venessa." When he doesn't give her a label, she frowns but doesn't say anything.

I give her a five-finger wave as well. "I'm going to go grab a drink from the bar. Does anyone want anything?"

Everyone who's paying attention shakes their head, so I head over to the bar by myself. I'm halfway to it, when I spot Lachlan standing over in the corner of the bar with a young, blond woman. He's leaning against the side of the bar, and she's standing extremely close to him. Her hand is resting on his forearm, but he's not touching her. I can only see their profiles, but they look to be in the middle of an intense conversation.

My first instinct is to run and hide and that really pisses me off because that's what the Quinn post-Rick would do, and I don't want to be that woman anymore. At the same time, I don't want to be the young Quinn who would've confronted him right here, making a scene. So instead, I do what I think the thirty-nine-year-old Quinn should do. I continue my walk over to the bar and order a drink. I'm generally a whisky kind of girl, so when the bartender asks what I would like, I tell him just to give me a double of whatever they have local, on the rocks.

After he hands me my drink, and I hand him my card, I take a sip. The whiskey goes down smooth, and I wonder which one it is.

"Excuse me?" I yell to the bartender before he walks away after dropping off my card and receipt. "Can you tell me who makes this?" I point to my glass.

"Bryson," he shouts back.

Bryson? Where do I know that name from? I glance over at Lachlan, who is still in the same spot, still talking to the same woman, and it hits me. That's his last name. Hmm. Could it be?

"Thank you." I write down a tip, sign the paper, and take my drink back over to the table. Declan, Riley, and...what was her name? Oh! Venessa...are sitting at the table, but everyone else is on the dance floor. I decide I'm going to enjoy my drink and then head home—that way it won't feel like Lachlan has chased me away, and I can call it a win.

"What are you drinking?" Declan asks when I sit across from him and Venessa and next to Riley.

"Whiskey." I smile and take a sip. "Bryson Rye," I add. Declan's eyes widen, confirming my suspicions. Someone in Lachlan's family owns a distillery. I want to ask him about it, but I would rather learn about Lachlan and his family from Lachlan himself.

"Quinn?" I recognize the voice without even having to look at him, and if I'm honest, I'm scared to look. If I see that girl attached to his side, I know it's going to hurt like hell. Not that I didn't see this coming from a mile away, but with all the convincing he's been doing, I guess a part of me started to believe what he was selling. Stupid me.

"That's me," I say, taking another sip before turning to look at Lachlan. "In the flesh." When our eyes meet, I see the girl he was talking to is standing next to him, shooting daggers my way.

"What are you doing here?" he asks, and the walls I've kept erected for the last several years, the same ones I now realize I've lowered to let Lachlan in, fly back up. This is exactly why I haven't dated, why I've chosen to focus on raising my daughter. Because no matter how much I want to leave Rick in the past, he's still very much in the present. Haunting and taunting me from the dead. Controlling my thoughts and actions and feelings.

"I..." I take a deep breath, reminding myself that Lachlan isn't Rick, and I'm no longer in a position to allow any man to make me feel weak. I'm allowed to be here. I'm a grown woman, and this is a public place. Sure, I came here with the hope of seeing Lachlan, but my brother and Willow and Gage and Evan are also here. I don't *have* to be here for him.

"Where's Kinsley?" Lachlan asks before I can answer his first question.

"She's at my brother's for the night." My eyes flicker from Lachlan to the woman standing by his side. Her hand brushes up against his arm, in an attempt to get his attention, and it makes me realize one thing: Despite every reason why I shouldn't be, I'm already falling hard for him. The question is, will he really be there to catch me like he said he would be?

THIRTEEN

LACHLAN

I CAN'T TAKE my eyes off of Quinn. The few times I've seen her, she's either been dressed professionally or dressed down—in sweats or jeans. She rocks both like a beautiful boss. But right now, even though she's sitting at the table, I can tell she's in a dress. One of her shoulders is exposed, showing the thin black lacy strap of her bra. I know it's her bra because it's the same one she was wearing last night. She's also wearing makeup. Not that she needs it, but the bit of color around her eyes make them appear mysterious. And her hair...it's no longer in her signature messy bun thing she's always sporting. It's down in waves. My gaze momentarily drops to her legs, which are half under the table, one crossed over the other. She's wearing tall as fuck heels. Jesus, she's fucking sexy.

When my eyes meet hers, I notice her pouty lips are glossy and...frowning. Why is she frowning? Just as I'm about to ask what's wrong, a hand touches my forearm and it all clicks. Shea is here, and Quinn must've seen us. Fuck!

"Lachlan, are you going to introduce us?" Shea asks, and Quinn's frown deepens.

"I was actually just leaving," Quinn says, downing the last of whatever she's drinking. "Have a good night." When she stands, I'm able to see her entire body. Her black dress covers all the important parts, yet shows off every single gorgeous curve. The top half is loose, but the farther down you go, the tighter the dress gets. As she saunters past me, my gaze falls to her backside. The woman can definitely fill out a dress like no other.

"Lach!" Declan yells, snapping his fingers in front of my face, and snapping me out of my thoughts. "She just walked away."

"Fuck!" I yell. I was so busy fantasizing about her, I blanked out. I start to chase after her when Shea grabs my arm and holds me back.

"You're not seriously going after that *woman*, are you?" Her face contorts into a look of disgust, and I can spot her jealousy from a mile away. She came to the states in hope of getting back together, and she was pissed to learn I've moved on. Even if I hadn't met Quinn recently, I wouldn't be willing to give Shea and me another chance, but knowing there is another woman, pisses her off.

"Hell yeah, I am," I say, pulling my arm out of her grasp and running after Quinn. I'm searching everywhere for her, when I spot her talking to her brother and Willow at the bar. Jogging over, I stop in front of them. Quinn's back is to me, so she doesn't see me coming, but Jax and Willow do, and both are glaring.

Not wanting to startle Quinn, I call out her name, and she turns around. "Can we talk, please?" I plead, but I can see it in her face, she's not going to give me the time of day. If I want her to listen, I need to act quick and talk fast. "What you saw wasn't what it looked like." When she flinches at my words, I internally groan. I sound like every guy who's ever been caught cheating, and Quinn has been cheated on. Damn it!

"That came out wrong." I place my palms up in a placating manner. "That woman you saw is my ex, Shea." Quinn's eyes widen slightly, but she does a good job at staying emotionless. "She showed up here without me knowing. Her best friend is Declan's sister, my cousin, Riley. I was already here when they arrived, and she cornered me at the bar, asking to get back together. I told her no. I even told her about you."

"You don't have to explain anything to me," she says so softly I can barely hear her over the loud thumping of the dance music. "We aren't together or even dating. Hell, I don't even know *what* we are. You can talk to whoever you want." She keeps her voice devoid of any emotion, but I can see the hurt in her eyes. I promised to never hurt her intentionally, and while this isn't intentional, she's still hurting because of me. Because of my drama. Drama she doesn't need to deal with.

"I disagree," I tell her. "Everything that happened with us last night and this morning means we are definitely something." Her eyes flit from me to her brother. I forgot he and Willow were even standing there. My sole focus is fixing this shit with Quinn. I'm not about to lose her before I've even gotten her, and especially not over my fucking ex.

"We'll let you two talk," Willow says, pulling Jax away.

Stepping closer to Quinn, I say, "We might not have officially placed a label on us yet, but that doesn't mean nothing is going on. I don't just go around eating women out. I told Willow I'm your boyfriend because that's what I want to be." I take another step toward her and grip the curve of her hip. "You're the only woman I'm talking to." I brush my lips across hers, tasting the fruit-flavored lip gloss she's wearing. "You're the only woman I'm kissing." I lean into her and nip the bottom of her earlobe, eliciting a shiver out of her. I love the way she reacts to me. "You're the only woman I want, Q." She exhales deeply. "Don't leave, please." I bring my face back up to hers. "You're standing here in this club, looking sexy as fuck in that black dress and those heels. Dance with me."

She takes a long moment to answer, but just as I'm beginning to lose hope, she nods once. "Promise me one thing."

"Anything." And that's the truth. I've only known this woman for a short time, but I would do anything for her.

"If you ever decide you don't want me anymore, or you want someone else, please let me go." She bites down on her bottom lip, and her eyes go glossy. She didn't ask me not to cheat on her. She didn't ask me to tell her if I do. She asked me to let her go. Because her fuck-nut of an ex strung her along while he cheated on her. She felt trapped when all she wanted was to be set free.

"It's never going to happen—"

"Lachlan, please," she cuts me off, begging, and fuck if I don't want to slam my fist into something right now.

"But," I say emphasizing the word to make it clear I wasn't done, "if I ever do, I promise to let you go." The words taste sour on my tongue, but I know she needs to hear them. And when her shoulders visibly sag in relief, it's confirmed. "Now will you please dance with me?"

Her eyes dart behind me, and I look back to see what—or who—she's looking at. I spot Shea standing by the table staring at us with her arms crossed over her chest.

"Ignore her. Come dance with me." Taking her hand in mine, I guide her out of sight of the table and over to an empty-ish area. The club is crowded as hell. It's a popular place, and it's Saturday night, but here in the corner, it's not *as* crowded.

Pulling her into my arms, I glide my hands down her curvy sides and land on her ass. Fuck, I love her ass. Quinn's hands link together behind my neck as she begins to grind her front against mine. Needing to taste her again, I bring my mouth to hers, tasting the lip gloss again, but when my tongue delves between her parted lips, I can taste the whiskey on her breath, and I know it's my family's. It has a very distinct taste to it, and the thought that she was drinking my family's whiskey has me wanting to take her right here and now. She moans softly into my mouth, finally kissing me back. My tongue sweeps past her teeth once again, finding hers. Tasting. Teasing. Our tongues find a rhythm as our kiss deepens.

Needing to be even closer to her, my thigh pushes her legs farther apart, and I run my knee along the apex of her thighs, against her heat. "Oh, God," she groans into my mouth. I continue rubbing my knee forward and backward. Teasing. Tormenting.

"Lach," she moans, and I know she's coming. Her legs shake, and if I wasn't holding her, she would probably collapse. Our kiss breaks, and her head lands on my shoulder, her teeth biting down gently as she comes undone right here on the dance floor. And fuck if it isn't the hottest thing I've ever witnessed.

"I've made you come twice now," I whisper into her ear. "You're most definitely mine." She doesn't say anything, but I can feel her nod into my shoulder. "Let's get you home." Another nod.

After Quinn uses the restroom, we head back over to the table to let everyone know we're leaving. I feel bad it's Declan's first night back and I'm bailing on him, but there's no way I'm asking Quinn to hang out with Shea. But when Declan gives me a slight head nod, I know he gets it.

"I'll see you back at home later," I tell him.

"I'll get Shea and Riley set up in a hotel," he tells me.

"Thanks, man."

I snag a cab, and even though Quinn insists she can get home on her own, I ride with her back to her place. When we arrive at her house, I ask the driver to wait a second, so I can get out and walk her to her door.

"Thank you for the dance," I tell her with a grin that makes her laugh. Pushing her up against the door, I lean in and nip her bottom lip. She giggles, and her hands, which are as soft as her lips, touch my cheeks.

"Thank *you* for the dance," she murmurs before deepening the kiss.

Wanting to be a gentleman, and still trying to take shit slow, I reluctantly pull back, breaking the kiss. "Call me."

She nods in understanding. "Okay."

FOURTEEN

Quinn

IT'S SATURDAY NIGHT, and Kinsley is in bed. She was feeling a bit under the weather and conked out early, giving me some time to finally work on my edits. This week has been literally one failure after the next. After the horrible-turned-amazing evening with Lachlan at the club, I met with Jenna Sunday morning. When we sat down and went over my finances, I learned that even with Rick's money, I can't afford a home where my siblings live. Well, I could, but it would mean having to use the money from my savings, and since I don't make enough to afford the house with my income, I would eventually run out. I had no idea Cobble Hill was so expensive. In order to buy, or even rent, I'll have to be willing to move to another area, and that will mean Kinsley switching schools. I thanked Jenna for taking the time to go over it all with me. I know a lot of realtors would just want the commission. I told her I would think about it, and she offered to send me over several listings that are in my price range.

The rest of the day was spent visiting several of those listings, to which Kinsley whined and cried that she loves her school and would die if she had to leave it. Yes, she actually said she would die. When we got home, she told Jax, who assured her she wouldn't have to switch schools. Which caused Jax and me to get into our first fight ever when I told him he had no right to tell her that.

My week did get a bit better when Celeste called in need of a last-minute photographer when hers canceled due to a family emergency. I spent the day with Celeste and Skyla—who co-owns Celeste's company, Leblanc, Inc. It's made up of several mini-companies which focus on clothing, makeup, and jewelry. I was thrilled to learn how much I would make from doing the shoot, and it made me see that I might need to branch out to more than just weddings and family shoots. While I love doing them, I need to think about providing for my daughter, and weddings and engagement shoots just don't bring in enough. When I brought it up to Celeste, she told me she would hire me in a heartbeat, and that the only reason she never suggested it was because she didn't think I wanted to go in that direction. She's already scheduled me for several upcoming shoots.

Thursday took a nosedive when my daughter's teacher called to let me know that Kinsley punched a boy in the stomach and would have to go home until Monday. I learned he's been picking on her, and she had enough. I explained we don't put our hands on anyone, and Kinsley said she understood. I also let her teacher know of the situation. When I told Kinsley there would be no electronics or soccer this weekend because of the choice she made, she cried and went straight to her room. Sometimes being a mom is hard.

Friday, I photographed a wedding, and Ember watched Kinsley. She's a college student at NYU and has been babysitting Kinsley for the last couple years. And that leads me to tonight. I'm in my comfy cotton pajamas, exhausted as all hell, and determined to get these edits done, so I can look at some more of the listings Jenna sent over. When the doorbell rings, I set my laptop down and walk over to the front door to answer it, and standing there, looking sexy as all hell in his Forbidden Ink T-shirt and jeans, is Lachlan.

And no, he wasn't mentioned in any of my recollection of the week. Why? Because when I texted him Sunday night, asking if he could talk, he texted me back: **No**. I was a bit thrown by his clipped response, but didn't want to assume anything, so I texted him back: **Later?** And when he responded with another **No,** I took the hint.

I thought about asking him why, but I was too upset. And if I'm honest, I was afraid he would tell me it's because of his ex, Shea. He had promised to let me go if he decided to be with someone else, so maybe that was his way of doing so. On the other hand, he could've texted a bit more explanation. But if he doesn't want to talk to me, then I'm not going to beg. I spent years begging Rick to love and want me, and the only thing it did was make me look pathetic and give him more power. So instead, I responded with two letters of my own: **OK**

"Hey," he says, giving me a nervous half-smile.

"Hey," I say back. "What's up?"

"Can I come in?"

"Sure." I open the door for him, even though I don't want him here. He steps into the house and walks straight to the living room.

"Is Kinsley here?"

"She's upstairs sleeping."

"Okay, so, I just wanted to say..." He digs his hands into his pockets, and his arms stretch out, the muscles flexing. It reminds me of last Saturday, when we had finished eating and Kinsley asked if she could feed the ducks some bread. She said her feet hurt from playing soccer, so Lachlan picked her up and placed her on his shoulders. She giggled and kicked, and he carried her like she weighed nothing.

My gaze goes from his muscles to his eyes and see he's staring at me with his brows raised. Shit! While I was drooling over his arm-porn, did I miss what he said to me?

"Can you...umm..." I clear my throat. "Can you repeat what you said?"

"I said, even though things didn't work out with us, I want you to know I really did like you. I think you're beautiful, and I hope, despite what we did last weekend, we can still be friends."

"You could've just texted that," I say, not understanding why he felt the need to come here. But maybe *this* is his way of letting me go. He still could've done it through text, though.

"I would've, if I had your number." He gives me a confused look. "I asked Jase for it, but he told me if you wanted me to have it, you would've given it to me, so I figured I would just come over and say what I needed to say in person."

This doesn't make any sense. "I texted you my number Saturday night when I was on my way to the club...and Sunday." Grabbing my cell off the coffee table, I pull our message thread up and show him. "You never responded to my text Saturday night, and you made it clear on Sunday you didn't want to talk."

"Quinn," Lachlan says slowly, taking the phone from my hand. "I didn't text you that. I never got a single message from you." He clicks around on my phone, then I hear it ringing. A few seconds later, someone answers.

"Hello." We both look at each other, confused.

"Who's this?" Lachlan asks.

The person on the other line giggles, clearly a child, and then there's shuffling. "Hello?" an older voice comes on the line. "Who's this?"

"My name is Lachlan. Who answered your phone?"

"I'm sorry, do I know you?" the woman asks.

"No, I think I called the wrong number," he says before he hangs up. I look over his shoulder as he pulls up his name on my contact list and curses under his breath. "I gave you the wrong number." He backspaces the last digit which was a nine and inputs a six. He hits call, and less than a second later, his phone is ringing in his pocket.

"I thought you changed your mind about us," he says, handing me back my phone.

"I thought the same thing," I admit. "When you...well, the fake you...responded like that, I thought maybe you didn't want me anymore. I thought about asking you why, but..." I take a deep breath, preparing myself to give him more truth. "I used to beg Rick to be with me. To stop putting me down and to love me." Tears fill my eyes before I can stop them. "I thought maybe after everything... and with Shea being back..." I release a harsh sigh.

"Fuck, Q." Lachlan pulls me into his arms, and for the first time in a week, I finally relax. "I didn't know." Stepping back, he picks me up and carries me over to the couch, setting me down into his lap. "Shea is staying at a hotel. I haven't spoken to, or seen, her since the club. What did I tell you Saturday night?"

"I know what you said," I say, willing the tears to stop, "but I figured maybe once you stepped back, you realized you didn't want me after all. People can change their minds. I mean, she's really freaking pretty and skinny and all girly, and I'm, well, I'm..." I wince as I say the words, not able to even finish my sentence. Even though I've been thinking them, saying them out loud makes me sound so ridiculously jealous and insecure.

"Finish your sentence," Lachlan demands.

"You know what I'm saying."

"I want to hear the words," he pushes. "Say them. Finish the damn sentence."

"Fine! I'm fat. Shea is skinny, and I'm fat! Why would you want me, when you could have her?"

Lachlan takes a calming breath, and then says, while looking me in the eyes, "This has to stop. I hate what that fucker did to you, and I'm sure it was worse than what you've said. But I'm not him, and you aren't overweight or ugly. I'm not saying there's anything wrong with an overweight woman, but you are so far from fat, it's ridiculous."

He cups my cheeks with his hands. "You. Are. Gorgeous. No more comparing yourself to my ex. She doesn't exist in what we have going on here. Got it?"

Before I can verbally answer him, Lachlan presses his lips to mine, and I sigh into his mouth, completely content at being in his arms and kissing him.

When the kiss ends, Lachlan glances over at the laptop and leans over to grab it. "Did you take these pictures?" On the screen are photos of a newlywed couple standing in the garden where they were married. She's dressed in an elegant, white gown, and he's in a tux. The image is of them laughing together.

"I took it without them realizing," I tell him. "She had just tripped in the grass over her high heel and he caught her."

"It's a really good picture," Lachlan says, clicking from image to image. "It's like you can feel every emotion through their expressions." He stops at one where the husband is looking at his wife, but she's looking down at her dress, fixing it.

"It's easy when two people are in love."

"Still, it takes someone who knows what they're doing to capture it."

"It's like you and tattoos," I point out. "You take an idea, sometimes a crappy drawing, and turn it into a masterpiece."

Lachlan grins. "You know..." He sets the laptop back down and twists me around so I'm straddling his lap. "Your daughter trusted me enough to tattoo her." He waggles his eyebrows.

"One, she's five, so she trusts easier. She hasn't experienced real life yet. And two, I haven't gotten a tattoo done since..." My throat clogs with emotion when I think of the last tattoo I got. When I came home and *he* saw it, and lost it on me. I don't even realize I've turned my face away from Lachlan in shame until his cool fingers are gently touching my chin, and he's bringing my face back up to look at him.

"Since you were with him." Lachlan finishes my sentence for me. "Fuck him, Quinn." He brushes his thumb down my cheek and then across my bottom lip. "Fuck. Him. You're a beautiful woman who should be covered in art if that's what you want. And one day, you're going to trust me enough to let me ink *my* art on your body."

Lachlan reaches around behind my head, grips my hair, and covers my mouth with his. My body melts into his touch, and if I were listening to my hormones, I would not only let him ink me, but let him do whatever the hell he wants to do to me. But I've learned the hard way I need to be smarter than that. I need to listen to my heart, but also my head. My body might trust Lachlan, but my head and heart aren't completely there yet.

The kiss is slow and gentle. His strong calloused hands cup my jaw, and his tongue massages mine. I lift his shirt, sliding my palms over the ridges of his abs. His skin is hot, and I crave his warmth. When I let out a soft moan, it seems to spur him on. His hands leave my face, and we break our kiss just long enough to pull each other's shirts over our heads.

His lips find my neck at the same time my fingers thread through his hair. He trails soft, open-mouthed kisses down my neck and chest. Then he pulls the cups of my bra down, one and then the other, exposing my erect, pink nipples. Wrapping his beautiful lips around one, he sucks it into his mouth, and the sensation zaps straight to the apex between my legs. My thighs clench, and my butt grinds down, revealing the large bulge in his pants.

Lachlan's lips move to my other breast, sucking and licking my nipple. I haven't the slightest clue how it is that he's sucking on my breast, yet it feels like my pussy is on fire. When I grind down again, needing relief, he bites down on my nipple and I yelp, which reminds me we're sitting in my living room, where my brother and Willow can walk in at any time, or my daughter can come out of her room and find us.

"Lach," I try to say through a moan. When he bites down on my other nipple, sending waves of pleasure straight to my core, I grab his face and push him back. "We can't do this out here."

He looks around as if just now realizing where we are. Picking me up, he takes me upstairs to my room, closing the door behind us. Laying me on the center of the bed, he tugs my pants and under-wear down my thighs, and then gripping my ankles, pulls me to the edge of the bed, so my legs are dangling down.

My brain goes mushy, my only thought being how much I want and need this man.

Bending over me, Lachlan's lips softly caress mine before he travels south, placing kisses along the center of my chest, one to each breast, my belly, and finally the hood of my pussy. He leans in and inhales deeply. My breathing becomes embarrassingly labored, my chest rising and falling quickly. I'm in shock that he just smelled me...there! *Who does that?*

Spreading me wide, Lachlan stares at my pussy for a long minute. "Fuck, Q, you smell so good, and you're so damn wet." He swipes his finger down my center and brings it to his lips, wrapping his mouth around the glistening wet digit, and licking it clean. And I about come on the spot. *Who is this man?*

A whimper escapes my lips, and Lachlan grins, staring back down at me. "You taste delicious." He swipes his finger back down and licks it again. "So perfect," he murmurs.

"Lachlan," I groan, unsure what I'm even wanting to say.

"What's wrong?" His brows furrow. "Do you want to know what you taste like?" When I gasp in shock, his mouth tips into a half-smile that has my insides heating up. How can one look, a simple touch, affect me in such a big way? He runs his middle finger down my center once again, this time slowly, then brings it to my mouth. "Open," he commands, and I do. My lips wrap around his long digit, and I suck on my own arousal. My eyes stay glued to his, and his are glued to my mouth. When I pull back, he licks his lips. "Perfect, right?" It's a tad tangy and not all that sweet—not really a taste I would personally find delicious—but if he thinks it tastes good, more power to him.

He backs up slightly without waiting for a response, places my legs on top of his shoulders, and then his hot mouth begins to lick me so skillfully, with so much precision, I'm squirming in pleasure, silently begging for my release within seconds. His fingers push inside me, massaging my insides intimately, and then I'm coming. Bright lights behind my lids burst through the dark as my body comes completely undone.

When I open my eyes, Lachlan is wiping his mouth and beard with the back of his hand, a satisfied grin splayed upon his lips like he's the one who was just pleasured. And then it hits me he's now made me come three times without even asking or suggesting to be pleasured back. And that thought has me wanting to satisfy him the same way he's satisfied me.

Sitting up, I turn my body around so I'm on my stomach and my head is in the direct line of his crotch. Lachlan, the intelligent guy he is, catches on quickly, and his eyes go wide. "Quinn," he whispers as I pull him closer to me.

"My turn," I murmur, unbuttoning and unzipping his pants.

"Okay, but there's something you need to know."

"Not now," I say, on a mission to please him. Pushing his jeans and boxers down, his dick, hard as a steel pole, springs free and hits his stomach. It's thick and smooth, neatly trimmed, with only a single vein running along the underside. I've only been with a few guys, so I don't have a lot to compare it to, but it's perfect. And then a small sliver of metal catches my eye, and I gasp.

"You're...you're..."

"Pierced."

"Holy shit," I breathe, entranced by what I'm seeing. "Can I touch it?"

FIFTEEN

LACHLAN

"CAN I TOUCH IT?" she whispers, and I have to will myself not to come from her words alone. This woman, she has no idea how fucking beautiful and sexy and goddamn motherfucking perfect she is. The way she tastes and smells. The sound she makes when she comes all over my fingers and tongue. I can't get enough of her. Sure, I'm a guy who's attracted to a woman, so of course I want nothing more than to sink into her hot, tight cunt. But at the same time, I'm completely content to just make her come. Every time I give her attention, she soaks it up like she's dying of thirst. She eats up every compliment like she's starved. And all I want to do is nourish the fuck out of her by bringing her pleasure and giving her the happiness she deserves.

"Yeah, you can touch it," I tell her, taking a small step forward. She's lying on her belly, her elbows holding her up with her plump ass and smooth back on display. Her bra is still on, but her tits are spilling out of it, exposing her pink nipples. Her legs are cross-legged, dangling in the air. If I wouldn't look like such a perv, I would pull my phone out and snap a picture of her, so I never forget how she looks right now. So goddamn beautiful, and all. Fucking. Woman. How she can even begin to compare herself to Shea is fucking stupid. Yeah, Shea is skinny and blond, and she's definitely easy on the eyes, but she isn't even in the same league as Quinn.

Tightening her fingers around my shaft, Quinn runs her sexy mouth across my Prince Albert piercing. A smidge of precum drips out and lightly coats her lips. I watch as her curious tongue darts out to taste it just before she parts her lips and gives the head of my dick a soft kiss. I groan, and she smiles a shy smile. Gently closing her mouth around my piercing, she tugs on it playfully, glancing up at me from under her thick lashes. Her tongue darts out and licks my slit, and I nearly come on the spot. Watching her explore my body is a fucking turn on. Not just because she's touching me, but because I can see it in her eyes as she becomes more comfortable with herself, with me.

"I want to suck you," she says, "but..." She sighs softly, and her eyes fill with liquid. What the hell just happened?

"Hey." I pull her up so she's kneeling on the bed. "What's going on?" My eyes dart back and forth between hers.

"I don't want to bring *him* up..." Her gaze drops down, and she doesn't even have to finish for me to know this is about that piece-of-shit.

"Tell me," I insist. "We can't get past it if I don't know."

"He said I wasn't good at it. I think..." She inhales then exhales. "I think maybe he cheated on me because I wasn't good at satisfying him." She bites down on her bottom lip, and it takes everything in me not to punch the drywall in. What *man* makes a woman feel like she isn't perfect? Makes her feel as though she can't do anything right? Single-handedly takes her confidence and self-esteem and destroys it? A piece-of-shit asshole who needs to bring his woman down, in order to make himself feel better, that's who.

"Quinn," I start, but she cuts me off.

"Could you just maybe...if I do something you don't like...can you tell me, please?" she pleads. And I can hear the words she doesn't speak. *So you don't resort to cheating on me.*

"Look at me," I implore, needing her to understand how serious I am. "I will never cheat on you. Ever."

"You can't possibly..."

"No!" I boom, and regret it when she winces. "I'm sorry," I say softer, gliding my hands down the smooth flesh of her hips and pulling her into me until she's so close, my dick is nestled between her legs. "There is not a single, tiny, minute possibility of me ever cheating on you. You are mine, and I am yours. And as long as you keep letting me come around, you are it for me. I don't care what you say or do. I don't give a shit how badly you piss me off, or if you push me away a million times. I will never touch or look at another woman besides you. Got it?"

"Got it," she says with a nod.

"Now, listen carefully," I say, grabbing two fistfuls of her ass and rocking my hips against her heat. "You simply *choosing* to wrap your perfect lips around my dick makes me the luckiest fucking bastard in the world. Everything you do once you're down there is merely a bonus." I shoot her a playful wink and her cheeks tinge that beautiful shade of pink I love.

"Okay." She concedes with another nod. "Sorry..." She winces. "I just totally killed the mood, didn't I?"

"You didn't kill anything, baby." I have Quinn kneeling on her bed, with her heavy tits hanging out of her bra, and her entire lower half bare and rubbing against my hard dick. "Feel this." I grind my dick against her. "It's hard as granite. That's what you do to me." I press my lips to hers briefly, then tell her to lie down. "I want to make you come again."

"No." She shakes her head. "You already did it three times. It's my turn."

"This isn't a game, Quinn. We're not keeping score."

"I know, but I want to."

"Keep score?" I tease.

"No." She giggles. "Make you come." She pushes me back slightly, then climbs off the bed, dropping to her knees. And without any warning, she damn near takes my entire dick down her throat. She gags softly, and the sound almost has me shooting my load straight down her throat. She pulls up briefly then sucks me back down. And with renewed confidence, my girl sucks my dick like she's out to win a fucking award for Best Head Ever Given.

When my balls begin to tighten, and my dick starts to swell, I know I'm close. Not wanting to come down her throat—for her sake, not mine—I entangle her hair in my fingers and pull her mouth off my dick. Her lips come off with a pop, and a bit of saliva drips down her chin. The sight has me losing my mind, and before I can stop myself or warn her, my cum is shooting out and covering her luscious tits.

She watches with fascination, and once I'm done, she leans forward and licks the head clean. "You taste better than I do," she says with a wink, and I know without a shadow of a fucking doubt, I'm keeping this woman for eternity.

Once we're both cleaned up, we go back downstairs to watch

TV. Quinn is snuggled into my side with her head on my chest when the front door opens and in walks Jax and Willow. Willow smiles, and Jax grimaces. I laugh at how cranky he is over me dating his sister. I know he supports us being together, but he refuses to show it. When Quinn doesn't acknowledge them, I glance down and see her eyes are closed and she's sleeping.

"Night," Willow whispers.

"Keep it down," Jax adds.

I finish the episode we're watching of Gilmore Girls—yeah, yeah, I know...not very manly, but in my defense, I needed to know if Rory and Dean end up hooking up even though he's married. Spoiler alert: they do—and I'm about to carry Quinn up to bed, when I hear a child cry out. Remembering Kinsley is here, I wake Quinn up.

"Kinsley's crying," I tell her, already standing to go to her. She quickly shakes off her sleep and flies up the stairs behind me. When we get to her room, I let Quinn go in first.

"Oh, Kins!" Quinn rushes to her side.

"I threw up everywhere," Kinsley cries.

"Shh...it's okay," Quinn tells her. She places her hand on her forehead, then turns to me. "Can you grab me the thermometer? It's in the top drawer."

"Yeah." I rush out of the Kinsley's room and into Quinn's. She has two nightstands and a dresser. She didn't specify which top drawer, so I open her dresser drawers first but don't find anything aside from some shirts and her pajamas. I move to the nightstand on the side of the bed she sleeps on and open the top drawer, finding nothing but her underwear in there. I'm about to close it, when I spot something. Grabbing it out of the drawer, I examine it for a moment. It's rose gold and has a power button, but when I press it, it doesn't turn on. It has a thick handle and a silicone top to it. It almost looks like something a doctor uses to check your ears.

"Lachlan!" Quinn yells out.

"Coming!" Uncertain if this is it, I check her other nightstand just to be sure, and when I only find a couple baby photos of Kinsley in the drawer, I figure this must be it.

"Hey, is everything okay?" Willow asks, stepping out of her room.

"Kinsley isn't feeling well," I tell her, walking toward Kinsley's room. "Quinn is in there with her."

"Oh, no! Let us know if she needs anything."

"Will do."

When I get inside Kinsley's room, Quinn is removing her soiled clothes. "Here ya go." I hand her the thermometer. "I couldn't get it to turn on." I shrug. "Thermometers have gotten a whole lot techier since I was a kid."

Quinn laughs and turns to grab it. When she spots it in my hand, she jumps to her feet, her entire face glowing red. "Oh my God!" she shrieks. "That's...that's not a thermometer." She snatches it from my hand. "I said the top drawer in the kitchen, not my bedroom!"

"Umm..." I say, having no idea why she's freaking out right now. "You didn't specify, actually. I just assumed." And then it hits me. Why is she blushing like I just walked in on her?

"What is that thing?" I ask, trying to get another look at it.

"Can you just go grab the thermometer, please? I'm going to get Kinsley bathed, and I need to change her sheets."

"Okay, want me to put that back?" I nod toward the *not*-thermometer.

"No!" she screeches. "I will."

Doing as she says, I find the correct thermometer, and while I can now recognize it as the actual thermometer, the item I grabbed is very similar in size and shape. The only major differences are the color and there's a screen on this one. After I give Quinn the correct thermometer, I grab Kinsley's soiled clothes and sheets and bring them down to the washer and turn it on. Then, I find the linen closet and locate some fresh sheets so I can make her bed. By the time I'm done, Kinsley and Quinn are coming back into her room.

"How you feeling?" I ask Kinsley who tries, and fails, to smile.

"I don't feel so well," she admits. "Can I go back to sleep, Mommy?"

"Are you sure you don't want to sleep in my bed?" Quinn asks.

"You know I like my own bed." Kinsley pouts.

"I know," Quinn tells her. "Here's the trash can in case you wake up again, and if you need me, just call out and I'll come running."

"Okay." Kinsley lies down and Quinn gives her a kiss on her cheek. "Will I able to go to school Monday?"

"Probably not," Quinn says with a frown. "But we'll see."

"Fine." Kinsley huffs and rolls over.

"Night, Mini-Q," I say. She rolls back over and gives me a small smile.

"Night, Lach."

When we step out of her room, Quinn walks next door to her room, and I follow. "Thank you for changing her bed," she says, grabbing her shirt and pulling it over her head. "I just need to change real quick. I don't know if any throw up got on me, but just in case." She sticks her tongue out and scrunches her nose.

"Not a fan?" I laugh.

"I hate throw up. Blood, I can handle just fine. But throw up." She mock shivers, then pulls a new shirt over her head. "I can't handle it, like at all."

"I should probably get going," I tell her, and she nods.

"Okay." She cuts across the room and encircles her arms around my neck. "Seriously, thank you." She presses her mouth to mine. "Where did you put the sheets? I need to throw them in the washer."

"Already in there," I say, giving her another kiss.

"Mmm." She moans. "A man who does well under pressure, changes puked-on sheets without being asked, *and* puts them in the washer. I feel like I've won the lottery." She giggles, and the sound goes straight to my chest.

"Speaking of which, what was that thermometer-looking thing I gave you by mistake?" When her cheeks stain pink again, my mind goes straight to the gutter. "Wait a second!" I laugh, removing her arms from around my neck and walking over to the nightstand.

"It's not in there!" she exclaims. "I left it in the bathroom."

"Was that... a vibrator?"

"Lachlan, stop!" she screeches, and I laugh harder.

"I've seen vibrators before and none of them looked like that. That was like some high-tech shit."

"It's a clitoral stimulator," she says matter-of-factly. When my lips upturn into a grin, she huffs. "When you're a single mom, and your pussy may as well be a graveyard, you have to bring in the big guns."

"A graveyard?" I ask, slightly turned on that she just said *pussy*.

"You know...because it hasn't gotten any action in so long, it might as well be dead."

I bark out a laugh at that, shaking my head. "You're fucking nuts." Then I think of something. "Have you used it since we started..." I waggle my eyebrows.

"No," she says pointedly.

"Damn right, you haven't. Because that techy shit can't compare to the orgasms I give you."

Quinn laughs. "That techy *shit* can make me come in under a minute." She raises her brows.

"Challenge accepted." I pick her up by her ass and throw her onto the bed., peeling off her pants and underwear. Once she's completely bare to me, I give her a smirk. "Start counting now."

———

"LACHLAN...LACHLAN, you have to wake up," Quinn whispers. I glance around the room, taking in my surroundings. I'm at her place, in her room, in her bed. We must've fallen asleep. Grabbing my phone from the nightstand, I check the time. It's five in the morning.

"We fell asleep," she says softly. "You have to go before Kinsley wakes up."

Nodding in understanding, I give her a kiss on her cheek, then roll out of bed, throwing on my shirt and jeans, then slipping on my shoes.

"I'll walk you out," she offers, but I shake my head.

"No, go back to sleep." I lean over the bed and give her a kiss to her forehead. "Want to do something later?"

Her face lights up with a bright smile. "Yeah." But then she frowns. "Actually, no. Kinsley will most likely wake up still sick."

"How about I go home, shower and change, and then come back with breakfast? We can rent some movies and make it a lazy day so she can rest."

"That sounds perfect," she says, pulling me back down to her for a kiss.

A couple hours later, I return with breakfast from a deli nearby. Kinsley and Quinn are both up, and Kinsley is lying on the couch, looking like someone told her that her favorite puppy has been killed.

"You okay, Mini-Q?"

"I feel blah," she says. "Mommy said you're going to watch movies with me. Can I pick it out?"

"Of course."

"Okay." She grants me a bright smile that's identical to her mother's. "I want to watch Mary Poppins." I have no clue who Mary Poppins is, but I tell her that sounds great. After Quinn gets the food sorted and we eat, we spend the entire rest of the day watching movie after movie together. In between, the girls share their likes and dislikes. They tell me about the trips they've taken and want to take. I share with them a little bit about my family and friends. About my time in Boston. We have lunch and dinner together.

It's such a simple kind of day. We didn't really do anything, yet at the same time, it's also absolutely perfect. A day I hope to repeat many more times in the future.

I'VE JUST FINISHED a two-hour-long session and am stretching my arms over my head, when Jax walks through my door. "Hey man, got a minute?"

"What's up?" I stand and walk to the back to get a drink.

"I wanted to talk to you for a second."

Glancing at my phone, I see it's a quarter to five. I don't have any more clients scheduled, so unless someone walks in, in the next fifteen minutes, I'm done for the day. It's Saturday, so I'm off tomorrow, and looking forward to hanging out with Quinn and Kinsley.

This last week I've been hanging out at Quinn's place every second I'm not working or sleeping. I never spend the night, but we have dinner together if I'm off early enough, or dessert, if I get there after dinner. After Kinsley goes to bed, we hang out on the couch, talking, and eventually make our way to Quinn's room, where we make out like teenagers, but never take things further. I've learned Quinn is submissive by nature until I coax her and make her feel comfortable enough to take charge, then she spreads her wings and flies. I know it's because of her ex. He probably got off on clipping Quinn's wings instead of letting her fly high. I can tell she's waiting for me to take things to the next level sexually, but I'm not going to do so until I know she trusts me—trusts what we have. So, every night after I've made sure she's satisfied, I kiss her goodnight and go home.

Thankfully, Shea has returned back to Ireland with Riley, so I don't have to worry about Quinn bumping into her, or Shea causing any problems.

I sit on the couch and shoot a text to Quinn to see if she wants me to pick up take out on my way over. Now that Kinsley is feeling better, I'm thinking we can order pizza or something. We've been eating healthy while she's been sick, mostly soup and foods she won't throw up. She was home from school through Thursday with the sitter, but went back to school yesterday, and was back to her usual self in time for her soccer game this morning. Her mom only let her play half the time, which bummed Mini-Q, but her scoring a goal during her time made up for it.

Jax sits next to me. "Willow and I have decided to move out of the townhouse." My head snaps up. They're moving? Is Quinn moving too?

"Quinn's staying," he says, answering my thoughts. "She's been looking for a place, but she can't afford anything in Kinsley's school zone."

"She hasn't mentioned anything to me about moving." We've talked about her work, mine, Kinsley, a lot about her past, but thinking about it, we don't ever discuss the future.

"She probably didn't want to say anything until she found a place. We bought the townhouse during the recession and fixed it up. It's now paid off, thanks to Quinn who insisted on paying it off when she sold her ex's condo and moved back in with us. She's been through enough. It doesn't make sense for her to have to find another place and switch Kinsley to a new school that might not be in a good area, when Willow and I can live anywhere." Jax shrugs like it's no big deal, and it makes me wonder something.

"Why didn't you guys get Quinn away from that asshole?" My question isn't meant to come out as an accusation, but even to my own ears, I hear the blame dripping from my words.

Jax sighs, scrubbing his hands over his face. "I know she was with him for four years, but it feels like it all happened so fast." He exhales harshly. "One minute she was dating him and the next she was living with him. He was rarely home, and when he was gone, she would come over. She would never complain or say anything bad about him. Her smile never faltered." He looks at me dead in the eyes. "I didn't see it, and I hate myself every day for it. I thought she was just busy doing her own thing. I should've looked deeper, asked more questions. It wasn't until her wedding when I knew something was wrong."

"What happened at her wedding?"

"Quinn is several years younger than us. She got her first tattoo at sixteen. I shouldn't have let her, but..." He shrugs, and I nod. We're tattoo artists. "She walked down the aisle in this hideous, frumpy-looking dress, man. It was white and expensive, but it wasn't Quinn. It covered every tattoo on her body." He curses under his breath. "She was proud of her tattoos before she met him. She used to wear clothes that showed them off. I used to yell at her all the time to put on more clothes." He laughs. "But she wouldn't listen. She lived in cut-off jean shorts and tiny shirts. An older brother's nightmare. When Celeste asked her why her dress covered them all up, she said she's older now and they look immature and trashy. She should've been beaming at her wedding, but she looked awkward and nervous."

"She's not proud of them now," I tell him. "Her tattoos...You know she's only gotten one tattoo since she's been with him? And it says, 'this too shall pass.'"

"Yeah, Gage tattooed that one. I don't think she wanted us to know, but Gage was worried about her. They used to be good friends. She wouldn't discuss anything with us. When she gave up her photography business to stay home, I could tell she was devastated, but she made excuses, saying it was for the best because they planned to start a family, and she wanted to be home with their kids. Looking back, that's all those four years with him were...one excuse after the next."

"I've never hated someone so much in my life," I admit. "Every time she questions herself or gets nervous. Every time she makes a comment about being fat or ugly. I want him to rise from the dead, so I can slowly murder him all over again."

"Yeah, well, I'm just glad he died before finding out about Kinsley. I can't even imagine what would've happened if she had to raise a baby with him. She said she thought about running, but the guy was loaded. He would've found her and fucked her over."

"Hey!" Willow exclaims, joining Jax on the couch. "What're you guys talking about?"

"Us moving this weekend." Jax throws his arm over Willow's shoulders and pulls her into his side. "We found a nice two-bedroom condo and are renting to buy." Jax tells me. "We want to make sure it's what we want before we commit."

"Nice, need any help moving?"

"That's actually why I wanted to talk to you. Quinn is going to throw a fit when she learns we're moving, so we aren't going to tell her."

"So, you're what? Going to move out while she's gone?" I wince, imagining how pissed Quinn is going to be when she comes home and finds all their stuff gone.

"I know it sounds bad, but trust me, it's the only way. Otherwise, she'll try to move out first," Jax says.

"And let me guess...you want to use me as a distraction to keep her busy tomorrow while you move your stuff out."

"Bingo," Willow chimes in. "You guys are practically inseparable anyway."

"Fine, but when this shit creeps down, you better let her know, you made me." Jax and Willow both laugh.

When Quinn shoots me a message, saying Kinsley wants to get a pumpkin to decorate, an idea forms. "I think I can actually give you tonight and tomorrow," I tell them. "I'll text you in a little bit and let you know for sure."

SIXTEEN

QUINN

"ARE you going to tell us where we're going?" I ask Lachlan for the fourth time in twenty minutes, well aware I sound like my five-year-old, but too nosey and nervous to care. When Lachlan texted and asked if I trusted him enough to let him take us away, I didn't even have to think about it. I trust Lachlan with everything in me. And I loved that he was including my daughter. So, I packed Kinsley and me a bag, texted Jax to let him know we wouldn't be home tonight so he wouldn't worry, and waited for Lachlan to go home and get his stuff and then come to my house. He insisted on driving so I could relax, and I didn't argue.

"Nope," he says for the fourth time. "You'll see when we get there."

"Mommy," Kinsley says, looking up from her coloring book. "Can Lachlan come to my birthday party?"

"Your birthday is coming up?" Lachlan asks.

"Yep!" Kinsley squeals. "I was born on Halloween!"

"When's her birthday party?" he asks, his eyes darting from the road to me.

"Next Sunday," I tell him. "We always do it the weekend before Halloween, so it doesn't interfere with trick-or-treating."

"How long have you known about it?"

I'm not sure where he's going with this... "Invitations went out a few weeks ago."

"You haven't once mentioned it."

"It's not really a big deal." I shrug. "It's usually just her friends from school and family."

He nods once. "Got it."

When he goes quiet, I think about how I worded what I said. "I didn't mean it like that. I just didn't think you would be interested in going to a child's birthday party. I'm sure there are tons of adult parties going on with it being the weekend before Halloween." Lachlan's jaw ticks, and the act brings back memories of when Rick would get mad at me.

"Lachlan," I say softly, trying to keep my composure. "Can you tell me what's wrong, please?" This is when Rick would yell at me, blame me, and call me names. Mentally, I prepare myself for it, so I'm shocked when Lachlan takes my hand in his and brings it up to his lips, giving each of my knuckles a kiss. We don't show a lot of affection in front of Kinsley, but a few days ago when she asked if Lachlan was my boyfriend, we told her he was, and she seemed okay with it. I have no clue how this is all supposed to work, so I'm just going with my gut and taking it one day at a time.

"We'll talk later," he says.

"But..." I need to know what I did, so I can make it better.

"Not now," he insists, his eyes darting back to Kinsley. "I promise we'll talk later." He gives me a comforting smile that calms my nerves.

The rest of the drive is spent with Kinsley telling Lachlan all about her upcoming party, who's going, what the theme is, and what she's going to be for Halloween. He listens intently to every word she says, and responds as if whatever she's talking about is the most important thing he's ever heard. A little over an hour later, we're pulling up to what I assume is our destination. The sign reads: Westchester Bed and Breakfast.

We drive down a dirt road, and when we turn the bend, the most gorgeous cottage comes into view. It's two stories tall with a beautiful wrap around porch on the bottom floor, complete with bench swings. Lachlan parks the SUV and then goes around to the back to get our stuff out.

"We're sleeping here?" I ask dumbly.

"Yep. Grab Kinsley, and I'll grab the stuff."

The second we walk in, Lachlan's name is called, and a young, petite, blond-haired woman comes scurrying out from behind the counter to greet him. "Ay, my sweet boy," the woman says in a similar accent to Lachlan's, only much, much heavier. "It's been too long. How's your ma? Your da?" She hugs him tightly then backs up. "I feel like I haven't seen them in forever."

"They're good. They decided to stay in Galway through the holidays," he tells her. Then he turns to me and Kinsley. "This is my girlfriend, Quinn, and her daughter, Kinsley. Ladies, this is my cousin Kiara. She owns this place with her husband, Kevin."

"It's nice to meet you." I extend my hand to shake hers, a little shocked I'm meeting someone in Lachlan's family and a lot giddy that she's so sweet.

"Kinsley, here, wants to get a pumpkin," Lachlan tells her.

"Yes!" Kinsley hops up and down. "Can we?"

"Well, Lachlan has brought you here during the perfect weekend," Kiara says, bending slightly so she's closer to Kinsley's level. "Tomorrow is the annual fall festival. There will be bounce houses, face painting, fresh popcorn, hay rides, and...there will be thousands of pumpkins to choose from."

Kinsley's eyes light up. "Thank you, Lachlan!" She runs over to him and hugs his waist. "I want to get a pumpkin so big!" She stretches her arms out wide as far as they can go, and Lachlan laughs.

"Whatever you want," he says, but when I shake my head, he adds, "as long as your mom says it's okay." His last comment has me laughing and Kinsley pouting.

"Let's get you guys settled in." Kiara walks back behind the desk and grabs a couple of keys from the hanging board. I love how old-school this place is. I love New York, but I also miss all the country comfort you find in North Carolina. "Quinn and Kinsley, you're in room 201, and Lachlan, I've put you right next to them in 202. They're on the second floor." She hands us our keys. "Here's an activity guide for tomorrow. Breakfast is served from six to eight, and lunch from eleven to one, but I imagine you will be at the festival during that time. If you need anything, just dial zero."

"Thank you," I tell her, taking my key at the same time Lachlan takes his.

To me, she says, "Kevin isn't here right now. He's running around, getting everything ready for tomorrow. It's an all weekend event. But please find us tomorrow, so I can introduce you." Then to Lachlan, she says, "I know he would love to see you."

"Sounds good," he tells her at the same time I nod.

Lachlan takes our suitcases up the stairs, and we follow him.

When we get to my room, I unlock the door and let Kinsley run in. When I see it's not a single room, but a suite with a living room, and two bedrooms, I say to Lachlan, "We could've shared a room."

"If you don't feel Kinsley is ready to see me wake up in her home, she's not ready to share a hotel room." He kisses my forehead. "I'll hang out like I always do and then head over to my room to go to sleep." *Oh, this man...*

Kinsley picks her room, and since we haven't had dinner, we venture out to get something to eat. The entire town is as adorable as the B & B is, reminding me of Gilmore Girls. When we get back, Kinsley takes a bath and puts on her pajamas. She's excited to have a TV in her room and asks if she can lie down and watch a movie. I can tell by her yawn, she'll be out within minutes.

"Would you mind hanging out while I shower real quick?" I ask Lachlan. He gives me a mischievous look, and I almost ask him to join me, but my self-doubt rears its ugly head, and I chicken out. We haven't even had sex yet. I think Lachlan is trying to take things slow for my sake, but a small part of me wonders if maybe he isn't as attracted to me as I am to him. I immediately chide myself for thinking like that. I've been working on being more positive lately and thinking like that is not a step in the right direction. I know Lachlan is attracted to me. I can see it in his eyes, in the way he kisses me and loves on my body. And if that's not enough, he makes it a point to tell me every day how beautiful I am.

"Sure," he says, eyeing me up and down. "I'll be right here." He kicks his Vans off and sits on my bed, leaning back against the headboard.

My intent is to shower quickly, but once the hot water is raining down on me, I take my time, washing my body and hair and shaving my legs. When I get out, I wrap the plush towel around my body. After brushing my hair and teeth, I'm about to drop my towel to get dressed when I realize I didn't bring a change of clothes in here with me. Taking a deep breath, I step out into my room.

When Lachlan's eyes leave his cell phone and land on me, his brows rise, and if I'm not mistaken his pupils might even dilate slightly. "I forgot my pajamas," I tell him, going straight to my luggage. After sifting through it twice, it's apparent I completely forgot to pack my pajamas. Damn it!

"Everything okay?" Lachlan asks.

"I forgot to pack something to sleep in." I pout. I only brought one outfit for tomorrow, and the clothes I wore today aren't exactly comfortable to sleep in. "Any chance you brought an extra shirt I could sleep in?"

"Sure," he says, but the devilish grin on his face contradicts his words. And when he stays seated, but leans forward and removes his shirt, I know why.

"I meant a clean shirt!" I say with a laugh.

"Beggars can't be choosers," he volleys back, extending his hand that's holding his shirt.

When I reach out to grab it, he doesn't let go. Instead, he yanks on the material, tugging me toward the side of the bed. When I'm within his reach, he leans over and lifts me, plopping me down onto his lap so my legs are straddling either side of him. I laugh as I look into his gorgeous, flirty, emerald eyes.

"Mmmm..." He reaches around and grabs my towel-clad butt, pulling me closer to him. "I like this." He fingers the knot holding my towel together. With one pull, he could expose me completely. Sitting this close to him, I want to nuzzle my face into his neck, but I also really want to talk to him, so I decide to go with the latter.

"Can we talk?"

He looks up, meeting my gaze, and nods. "Yeah."

"In the car, you seemed really upset..."

Threading his fingers through my damp hair, he grips the back of my head and our mouths meet for a brief moment. In return, my arms snake around his neck and my fingers weave through his messy hair. The kiss lasts long enough for me to taste his cool, sweet breath, but ends far too quickly, leaving me wanting more. "I know it's going to take time," he begins, "but I can't help feeling like every time we take one step forward, you take two back."

When I attempt to pull my hands away, Lachlan's fingers wrap around my forearms, holding me in place. "No." He shakes his head, so I keep my arms around his neck. "I need you to stay with me, Quinn. I need you right next to me every step of the way."

I swallow thickly. "I hate this," I admit. "I hate the way I feel around you... and about you."

When his brows furrow in confusion, I explain. "You're twelve years younger than me, Lach. You're a single, good-looking guy with a good career. You could have your pick of any woman you want." I'm fully aware I'm back to being negative, but he needs to understand where I'm coming from. How different our lives are. "I just...I don't understand why you're sticking around. Why you would even want to go to my daughter's kiddie birthday party when you can be out living your adult life. Going drinking and dancing at the club." I inhale and exhale slowly, waiting for Lachlan to respond.

For a few seconds, he rakes his gaze over my face, as if he's trying to memorize my features. I begin to worry that maybe I've pushed him too far with my honesty and negativity. I worry what he's going to say in response to my question—my accusation.

But then he brings my face to his and whispers, "Because I'm falling in love with you," and my entire world feels like it's spinning. *He's falling in love with me...*

"What can I even give you?" I blurt out. "I have nothing to give."

"All I want and need is you."

SEVENTEEN

LACHLAN

THE SECOND I tell her what I'm feeling, I regret saying the words. Not because I don't mean them. I do. I am one hundred percent falling in love with Quinn Crawford and her little girl. No, I regret them because I told myself I would take things slow, so she feels safe and secure. I swore I wouldn't throw caution to the wind. And confessing my love for her isn't exactly driving cautiously—foot tapping lightly on the brake while keeping at a slow and steady speed. It's more like pressing the gas pedal all the way to the floor and gunning it, ignoring the rising RPMs, and saying fuck it, with the windows down as I fly around the bends without once slowing down. It's risky as hell, and can easily send her running scared.

So I'm shocked as shit when Quinn responds to everything I've just laid out for her by attacking me. Her mouth crashes against mine, and her tongue delves between my lips. Her hands tug on the strands of my hair, and her hot cunt grinds against the bulge that's quickly thickening in my pants.

My hands, of their own accord, pull her towel apart and yank it from her luscious body, leaving her completely naked and vulnerable. When she doesn't try to cover herself up like she usually does, I smile on the inside. One step forward...

"I need you," she murmurs against my lips, her words sending warmth through my veins and setting my body on fire. Flipping her onto her back, my hands land on either side of her head, my arms caging her in. I kiss all over her body, worshipping every perfect inch of her: her face, her neck, her delicious tits, her delicate collarbone. Frantically, she undoes my pants, and I push them down, along with my boxers. Our mouths fuse together as I bury myself to the hilt in her slick, hot cunt. It's never felt like this before. This perfect, this real, this fucking raw. This woman is it for me. I can feel it in every fiber of my being. She and her daughter are all I need in this life to be happy.

A small whimper escapes Quinn's lips, and I swallow it down as I deepen our kiss, massaging and sucking on her tongue, tasting and devouring her.

Mine. She's all fucking mine.

"Lachlan," she whispers, letting me know she's close. My piercing is making sure of it. Her hips rise to meet mine, thrust for thrust, and I lose myself in this woman. *My* woman.

Breaking our kiss, I find the crook of her neck, trailing kisses downward and over her collarbone, licking and suckling on her skin. I don't want this to end. I want to stay buried deep inside her for the rest of my life.

Too soon, though, her fingernails dig into my back, and her walls clench around my dick. Her legs, which are wrapped around my waist, shake as she comes completely undone, taking me with her.

When we've both somewhat come down from our high, I reluctantly pull out of her. "Take another shower with me," I whisper, not wanting to let her go yet. She nods in agreement.

Once the water is hot enough, we both step into the massive shower that comfortably fits us both. There are two shower heads, so we're both standing under the water. I watch Quinn for a moment consider how to hide her body. Her hands come up, and she's not sure where to put them, but when I smile her way, she relaxes, and I feel like we've just taken another step forward together. While we wash each other's bodies, we talk and kiss and laugh.

So simple. So fucking perfect.

When we get out and dry off, I give her my shirt to wear. When it drops over her head, the front is taut against her heavy tits, and her nipples poke through the thin material. The bottom goes to just below her underwear, and when she walks around the bed to get in, I can see the bottom of her ass cheeks peeking out. She looks fucking incredible. And all mine.

"We should probably have the obligatory safe sex conversation," she says, lying on her side. I'm so distracted by her in my clothes, her thick thighs bare and begging to be felt up, it takes me a second to put together what she's just said. But once I do, I bark out a loud laugh at the formality in her words. She sounds like my mom... And that makes me laugh even harder because she is a mom.

"I know you're older than me..." I give her a wink, so she knows I'm joking. "But my parents already gave me the sex talk when I was a wee lad."

She smirks, but doesn't laugh. And of course she rolls her eyes. "And did they explain to you what happens when two people have sex and don't use protection?"

"Yeah...they make a baby...or catch crabs." I grimace at that last part. My parents really did have the talk with me, and my dad really did mention catching crabs. I was scared for months I would have sex and some girl would be covered in red-clawed sea critters waiting to pinch my balls off.

"Oh, good," she continues, "so you do know the risks. Well, just so you know, I haven't had sex in over five years, unless you count my vibrator or dildo, neither of which can spread venereal diseases, so I'm clean." My brows rise at her mention of a dildo. I didn't see that in her drawer...

She keeps going, so I don't have time to conjure up the image of her lying, spread eagle on her bed, fucking herself with a dildo. I stow the thought away for later, though. "And since it took me nearly four years to get pregnant, we're most-likely okay, but in the future, we should probably use protection. I'm old, but I haven't hit menopause yet."

I'm almost positive there was a joke and maybe even some sarcasm mixed in with what she just said, but since I'm not exactly sure which parts are which, and I think overall she's being serious right now, I don't crack a joke. What I do, however, is imagine how sexy she would look with her belly swollen with my child. How beautiful she would look rocking our baby to sleep. Jesus effing Christ, we've only been doing this thing for a few weeks. I shouldn't be okay with her falling pregnant, let alone fantasizing about it.

And holy hell, would my mom kill me if I knocked up a woman out of wedlock. But I can't help it. I don't care if it's been a few days, weeks, or months. I know what I want, and it's to spend my life with this woman. I want us to be a family. Maybe I should suggest we get married. Then we wouldn't have to use protection, and if she ends up pregnant, it would be all good.

When I look at her, looking at me, I notice her brows are furrowed, and her lips pursed together into a thin line. Is she scared of getting pregnant by me? I know she's in her late thirties, but a lot of couples have kids later on in years. Oh, shit! Maybe she's worried I'm not clean.

"I'm clean," I assure her. "I haven't been with anyone in months, and I was checked." I don't comment on being okay with her getting pregnant or that I just thought about making her my wife. She might run for the hills.

"I can make an appointment with my doctor to get on birth control."

"All right," I say, trying not to sound too disappointed. "Until then, I'll make a better effort to use condoms." I edge closer to her and hitch her top thigh above mine. "Even though I really, really enjoyed the feeling of my dick inside you raw."

"Lachlan!" She slaps my chest playfully, her face and neck heating up.

"What? It's the truth." My hand moves between her legs, and I rub my fingers up and down her pussy over her underwear. "I could feel everything. How slick and warm you were." Fuck, I can't get enough of this woman. I slip my fingers inside and flick her already swollen clit. She lifts her leg slightly to give me better access, and when I push two fingers inside, I find her soaking fucking wet.

"I know you liked it too," I tell her. "The way you could feel my piercing rubbing and coaxing that orgasm right out of you." I add a third finger, pushing them in and out of her tight cunt, and Quinn's breathing becomes labored. "It won't feel like that with a condom, you know."

Grabbing her by her hips, I pull myself up into a half-sitting, half-lying position, bringing her with me, so she's straddling my thighs. I yank my dick out of my boxers and pump it a few times while Quinn watches with hooded eyes. "You know you want me inside of you with nothing between us." I continue to stroke my dick, but this time, I push the material of her panties to the side and rub my head up and down her center, massaging her clit with my piercing.

Quinn moans softly, grinding herself against my shaft and hand. And before I can taunt her anymore, she's rising and guiding herself over my dick, filling herself completely with me. Her hands go to my shoulders, and I watch in wonderment as she rides me, circling her hips and rocking back and forth, finding the spot she needs to get off. With one hand still on her hip, my other lifts her shirt over her head, exposing her body. As she fucks me, her tits bounce up and down in rhythm, taunting and teasing me to touch them. I capture one with my mouth, biting down on the hardened peak.

"Oh, fuck," Quinn groans, pushing herself up then sinking all the way back down. Her moans get louder the closer she gets to finding her climax. Leaning my head back against the headboard, I watch her continue to ride my cock, completely okay with being naked on top of me, exuding the kind of self-confidence that only a few short weeks ago was nowhere to be found. She's not worried about her weight or her looks, whether or not she's perfect. She's not concerned with our age difference or anything else. It's just the two of us, lost in the moment. *Three steps forward...*

"Come on, baby," I murmur. She's so close, but she's not quite there yet. Wanting her to get off before I do, I push my thumb against her clit. She's soaking wet, which makes it that much easier to take her over the edge. With only a few swipes of my thumb, Quinn is coming all over my cock, taking me along with her.

When she finally stills, her head lulls forward onto my shoulder. I can feel her body shaking with laughter. "That's the exact *opposite* of what was supposed to happen," she says through her laughter.

"Really? Because it was exactly what I was hoping would happen."

Mine. All fucking mine.

THERE'S a knock on the door, and my eyes pop open, trying to remember where I am. I'm at the B & B, but when I glance over, I spot Quinn lying next to me. Shit! We fell asleep in her room, and I never went back to mine. As I'm scrambling out of bed, throwing my jeans on, the door opens and Kinsley steps into the room.

"Is Mommy asleep? I'm hungry." Her hair is up in a loose messy bun just like her mother wears, and she's half asleep. She also doesn't appear to be at all concerned I'm in her mom's room.

"She is," I whisper, grabbing my shirt off the floor and throwing it on since Quinn never put it back on last night. "How about we let her sleep in, and I'll take you downstairs to get breakfast?"

"Okay." A smile tugs at her lips. "Can we bring her back food?"

"Of course. Go get dressed."

Once Kinsley is dressed, and I leave Quinn a note letting her know where we are, we head downstairs to eat. My cousin Kiara and her husband, Kevin, are walking around and talking to the guests. When they spot us, they come over to say hi.

"And who is this little girl?" Kevin asks to Kinsley, who I notice is hiding slightly behind me.

"This is Kinsley; Kinsley, this is my cousin's husband, Kevin."

"Nice to meet you," he says. Kinsley smiles shyly, but remains quiet. "The food is along that back wall. Take as much as you'd like and grab any open table."

"Sounds good, man. Thanks." I clasp him on the shoulder then head over to the buffet with Kinsley. "Can you make your own plate, or do you want me to make one for you?"

"I can do it." She rolls her eyes. I hand her a plate, and she goes to town piling an assortment of foods onto her plate. Once there's no sign of a plate left, we find a table and start to eat.

"What are you looking forward to doing the most?" I ask her to make conversation.

She shoves a bite-size waffle into her mouth, and once she's swallowed, says, "Finding a pumpkin and decorating it. I hope there's a hay maze too! I saw one on a show and it looks fun. I also want to get my face painted."

I take a bite of my fruit-filled pastry and groan at how delicious it tastes. The peaches are fresh and sweet, and the pastry is flaky and baked to perfection. Kiara has always been an exceptional baker. When she lived in Ireland, she owned a small bakery that did very well. As I'm taking another bite, I look over at Kinsley, who is about to take a bite of the same pastry I'm eating. I don't even know how I remember, but the next thing I know I'm screaming for her to put the food down. She drops the pastry onto her plate, but she's already taken a bite.

"Shit!" I yell, not caring that I'm causing a scene. "Spit it out." I'm out of my chair and over to her with a napkin, trying to wipe the food out of her mouth. Kinsley is now in tears, and I'm terrified she's having an allergic reaction.

"Someone call nine-one-one," I yell.

"Lachlan!" I look over and see Quinn running over to us. "What's wrong?" she asks me. Then to Kinsley, she says, "Why are you crying?"

"She ate a pastry. It has peaches in it. I'm trying to get it out of her mouth." My heart is pounding so hard, it feels like it's about to thump right out of my chest. Am I having a heart attack?

"What's wrong?" Kiara comes over and asks.

"Kinsley is allergic to fruit," I tell her, "and she took a bite of the pastry. It has fruit in it. Call nine-one-one. She can die."

I glance around, confused as to why everyone is remaining so calm when there's a little girl whose throat could be closing right now.

"Lachlan, it's okay," Quinn says. "She's okay."

When I look back over to Kinsley, she still has tears in her eyes, but she's not hyperventilating or having trouble breathing. "She was crying," I point out.

"Because you scared me," Kinsley says with her brows knitted together. "I didn't know it had fruit in it," she tells her mom.

"It's baked," Quinn says, picking up the fruit I removed from Kinsley's mouth. "She's only allergic to raw fruits."

"Oh," I breathe, suddenly feeling really damn stupid because I knew that. "I-I'm sorry. I..." I look over to Kinsley. "I don't know what I would do if something happened to you, Mini-Q." The ache in my chest is still there in full force. If something would've happened to Kinsley, I don't think I would survive it. I've already grown to love that little girl as if she's my own.

Quinn takes my hands in hers and leans on her tiptoes to give me a soft kiss. "You have nothing to be sorry about," she murmurs against my lips. "Thank you."

"For what?" I just caused her daughter to cry and demanded people call for help for no reason.

"For caring about my daughter enough to remember about her allergy. When I walked in and saw how scared you were..." A single tear slides down her face. "I was terrified something happened to my daughter. But there you were, taking charge, doing exactly what I would've been doing. Thank you."

She steps back and sits down at the table next to Kinsley. "Lachlan didn't mean to scare you, sweetie. He was worried the fruit would make you sick."

Kinsley nods in understanding. "It's okay. But can I eat it? It's really good."

Everyone laughs, and Quinn nods back. "Yes, you can eat it." She glances up at Kiara and Kevin, who are standing next to the table. "Sorry about all that. Kinsley is allergic to raw fruits."

"We're just glad she's okay," Kiara says. "One of the guests did call nine-one-one, but she's called them back to let them know it was a misunderstanding. All the pastries that have fruit inside have been baked with the fruit in them." She turns her attention to Kinsley. "Are you ready for a fun day at the festival?"

"Yep!" Kinsley exclaims, already over what happened. I sit back down, but I can't eat or speak or think. I'm still freaking the fuck out. I have no clue how Quinn manages to let Kinsley out of her sight for even a second.

As if she can hear the chaos in my head, Quinn looks over to me and smiles softly. "Are you okay?"

"I don't know how you do it."

"Do what?"

"Parent."

Quinn chuckles. "One minute, one hour, one day at a time."

"I would put her in a bubble and never let her out," I admit half-jokingly, which has Quinn throwing her head back in laughter.

"You'll make a wonderful father one day," she says, patting my arm.

Thankfully, the rest of the day goes more smoothly than breakfast. We pick out a couple of pumpkins and decorate them, get lost in the hay maze, where I'm able to sneak a few kisses with Quinn. Kinsley gets her face painted like a princess, and fills her belly with every kind of junk food imaginable. All too soon, it's time to head home. Kinsley sleeps the entire drive to my place, where Quinn gets out and kisses me goodbye before getting behind the wheel to head home. I text Jax to give him a heads up, and he lets me know everything of theirs is out and the house is ready for the girls.

Quinn calls me a little while later to let me know Jax and Willow moved out. She cries over how generous and kind they are and curses me—jokingly—for knowing about their plan the entire time. When Kinsley calls for her to tuck her into bed, we say goodnight.

Later that night, as I'm lying in bed, I wish I were with Quinn and Kinsley. Declan is over at his girlfriend's place, so my house is quiet. I want to be on the couch with Quinn cuddling into my side, in bed with her, stealing all the blankets. I want to wake up and have breakfast with the two of them. The more time I spend with them, the more I miss them when I'm not with them. I fall asleep trying to think of a way to make Quinn—and Kinsley—mine, sooner rather than later.

EIGHTEEN

Quinn

"I CAN'T BELIEVE after all these years we still can't keep a receptionist around longer than a couple months." I laugh as Jase complains of another temp not working out at Forbidden Ink.

"The only one who stuck around was Evan." Celeste cackles. "And that's only because I hired him."

"Yeah, because he's a tattooist!" Jase laughs, wrapping his arm around his wife.

We're sitting in the backyard of my townhouse under a tent that's been erected for Kinsley's birthday party. There are several kids from her class, as well as all of her cousins, running around and playing. There's a bounce house and a blowup slide, along with a new swing set. Earlier, they hit the piñata shaped as a Troll that Jax tied to a tree, and fought over the candy like they were participating in the Hunger Games. Now it's time for cake, but I can't seem to locate Kinsley—or Lachlan—anywhere. A little while ago, she asked to show him her new swing set, but I don't see them over in that area anymore.

"Any chance you can work at the shop in the afternoons this week?" Jase begs. "Skyla and Celeste both switched on and off last week. We have a few people coming in to interview this week."

"Of course," I tell him. "The only thing I have this week are the shoots Monday and Tuesday for Leblanc, and a wedding shoot Friday."

"You're a lifesaver," Jase says, leaning over and giving me a kiss on my cheek.

"You know I love the shop."

"Plus, it now has Lachlan there." Willow waggles her eyebrows playfully.

"You and Lachlan?" Olivia gasps. "Isn't he a bit...young?" At her words, my face feels like it's being set on fire. While my family knows about Lachlan and me, and have seemed to accept it, Celeste's friends, Olivia and Giselle, didn't know. I know it's stupid to keep us a secret, but I'm still getting used to the age difference myself, and when you look at us, you can clearly tell there is one.

"So, what?" Giselle says, defending me. "Let the woman get her groove back."

"I'm not judging!" Olivia frowns and throws a chip at Giselle, then turns to me. "I was just shocked, that's all. I think the last guy I saw you with was Rick and he was older and...well, a lot different looking." Nobody besides my family knows anything about what Rick put me through, but hearing his name and having him be compared to Lachlan makes me want to throw up. Although, she is right. Rick was a good five years older than me, and obviously without a single piercing or tattoo.

"Lachlan is nothing like Rick." Jase grunts. "Thank fucking God."

Celeste puts her hand on his arm to calm him and says, "How are things going with you and Lachlan? When I was at the shop last week, he couldn't stop talking about you." She smiles softly. "He seems very taken with you."

"They must be doing good because Lachlan hasn't been home in weeks," Declan pipes up with a chuckle. Everyone's eyes swing to me, and I stand, suddenly feeling the need to flee. This entire conversation is just too much.

"He's gone before Kinsley wakes up," I say by way of explanation, not wanting to be judged.

"Hey, you don't have to explain yourself," Giselle says. "You do you, girl. Lachlan is definitely a looker." She waggles her eyebrows and her husband, Killian, growls. Everyone laughs.

"Yeah, and I bet he's stellar in bed!" Skyla cackles. "I read in Cosmo, a man is in his prime from twenty-six to thirty-four."

"Hey!" Jase and Jax both yell in unison. "Don't be talking about men and when they're in their prime!" Jase adds. "You're too young for that crap."

"Dad, I'm almost twenty-three." Skyla laughs. "But sure, we can pretend I'm not having sex." She rolls her eyes, and Celeste and I both cover our laugh with a cough. That girl will be giving Jase a run for his money as long as he's alive—and probably even once he's dead.

"I'm going to go find the birthday girl so we can do cake," I tell everyone, heading over to find Lachlan and Kinsley. When I spot them both in the bounce house, Lachlan is sitting against the side of the knitted wall, and Kinsley is bouncing up and down in the middle. I'm about to yell for them when Kinsley drops to her knees, her usual happy face, frowning.

"Do you have a mom and a dad?" she asks Lachlan. Curious as to where this is going, I step to the side, so I can hear them, but they can't see me. Kinsley has been told her dad died before she was born, but she never brings it up.

"I do," he tells her.

"Where are they?"

"They live here, but they're in Ireland right now, visiting family. It's where I'm from."

"What's Ireland?" She tilts her curious head to the side.

"It's a country in another part of the world."

"My dad is dead," she says matter-of-factly. "When someone dies, they never come back. Ever." Her eyes are wide, and her head is nodding slowly.

"That sucks," Lachlan says, even though I know he doesn't give a shit that Rick is dead. He's stated on several occasions that if he wasn't, he would gladly kill him.

"My friend Fiona's dad died too."

"I'm sorry. Death sucks."

"Yeah, he had..." She puts her tiny finger to her chin and taps it a few times. "He had cancer. I don't know what that is, but Fiona said it made him die."

"Cancer sucks for sure," Lachlan says.

"Yeah, but Fiona's mommy married another guy and now he's her new daddy." Oh shit! I step into view, but I'm too late when Kinsley adds, "Can you marry my mommy and be my new daddy?"

"Hey guys!" I squeak out. "It's time for cake!" Lachlan and Kinsley both turn toward me, and I wince at how awkward I sound. Lachlan gives me a curious look, telling me he knows I heard what she asked.

"Okay!" Kinsley cheers, jumping out of the bounce house and running toward the picnic table with her cake on it.

"You heard."

"Yeah, sorry about that."

Lachlan climbs out of the bounce house and walks over to me. "You have a very observant and smart daughter. You have nothing to be sorry for. It would be my honor if one day you made me your husband and Kinsley viewed me as her father."

"Lach... We've only been..." My breathing picks up slightly. His admission has me at a loss for words. I don't know what to think or feel.

"I'm not saying now. I'm just saying that if one day it happened, I would be the luckiest fucking man in the world." He slants his mouth over mine, kissing me with such passion, I feel it all the way down to my toes. "I wasn't lying when I said I was falling in love with you."

* * *

"I'D LIKE to get my belly button pierced," the bubbly, bleach-blond bimbo asks, twirling her hair around her finger.

"And I'd like to get my clit pierced," her equally bleach-blond bimbo friend adds with a giggle.

I've only been helping out at Forbidden Ink for a few hours and I'm already the hell over it. One thing I've learned is that because Lachlan is the newest hire, he handles the majority of the walk-ins, which includes the piercing—which are usually women. I already knew this rule, but I didn't think about the fact that at the moment *he's* the new guy.

So far today, he's pierced a woman's nipples and the hood of her pussy, tattooed a chick's hip bone, where she insisted on taking her pants off, leaving her in her barely there panties. Two of the women have left me their number to give to Lachlan, and one asked for his number right in front of me. He didn't give it to her, mentioning he had a girlfriend, but it still had me bristling. This is a freaking workplace for crying out loud!

I glance down at the schedule for today and see Jax has an opening at the same time Lachlan does. "Sure, just have a seat and someone will be with you shortly."

Stomping back to Jax's room, I knock once, and he announces to come in. "How's it going?"

"Why must you guys pierce private parts?"

"Because we're a tattoo and *piercing* shop," he says with a confused look. A few seconds later, though, his lips tip up into a knowing smirk.

But before he can call me out, I say, "Well, you have two women who need to get *pierced.*"

Jax laughs. "I don't pierce."

"You *can.*"

"But I don't," he volleys back, his smirk never faltering.

"Just because you're a part owner doesn't make you exempt from doing the gritty work once in a while," I snap. "Everyone else is busy."

"Everything okay in here?" Lachlan asks, and my back straightens. Oh, jeez, Jax, please don't embarrass me...

"Yeah, everything is good." Jax's smirk turns into a full-blown grin. "My sister was just asking me to do a couple of walk-in piercings."

"I can do them, man," Lachlan offers. "I'm wide open."

"Really?" Jax laughs. "Quinn, here, said everyone else was busy." Damn him! What happened to the brother who treated me like a princess?!

"Quinn," Lachlan says, giving me a perplexed look. "I am open, right?"

"Yeah." I clear my throat. "Sorry, I forgot," I say dumbly. After glaring at my brother, who just cackles louder, I stomp out of the room past Lachlan.

"Hey, wait!" Lachlan grabs ahold of my arm. "What's going on?" He guides me into his room and closes the door, sitting down on his stool and pulling me into his arms. My body immediately relaxes, and I'm able to finally think clearly.

"I'm jealous," I admit.

"Of what...who?" He looks confused, but not mad. He never gets mad. Every time a weakness of mine plows through, he handles it with such patience. He may be several years younger than me, but he never acts like it.

"Of the women you're piercing and tattooing." I huff. "I swear you see more vagina and boobs than a gynecologist!"

Lachlan bites down on his bottom lip to stifle his laugh. "You know you're the only woman I want." He pulls my head down to his level and kisses me.

"Why do you put up with me?" I groan, fully aware I'm acting like a crazy person. "I'm such a hot mess."

"Because you're *my* hot mess," Lachlan says with the most

adorable boyish grin. "Speaking of which, I talked to Jax. He and Willow are taking Kinsley Saturday night. I'm finally taking you out on a proper date."

"Really?" I beam. "Where?"

"It's a surprise."

When I pout, he laughs softly. "How about I do those piercings you mentioned and then we pick up some takeout and head home to relieve the sitter?" *Home...*the word coming out of his mouth sounds so right.

"That sounds really good."

After the blond bimbos leave, I head back to Lachlan's room. He's cleaning up his station, so I hop onto the tattoo chair and lie back while he finishes up. "I hope that chick's clit gets infected," I say half-jokingly, and Lachlan chuckles.

"You're so adorable." He throws several empty containers of ink into the trash.

"And that stupid girl who got those stupid seahorses on her hips. I hope when she gets pregnant and fat, they expand into killer whales."

Lachlan just laughs harder. "When are you going to let me tattoo you?" he asks, leaning over and kissing me. His lips are soft yet demanding, so damn perfect. My fingers tug on his strands of hair, trying to pull him on top of me. He chuckles into my mouth, but doesn't obey. "Not here, babe," he says, pulling back.

"See? You're already denying me. It's because you saw like fifteen pussies today, isn't it?" I pout, and Lachlan snorts in laughter. "It's not funny. You never say no to me."

"You want me to fuck you right here with your brothers in the other room?" His hand glides up my thigh and under the bottom of my shorts and panties, landing right on the hood of my pussy. "Fine," he murmurs, leaning over and slamming the door. Subconsciously, I know this is a very bad idea, but my hormones and jealously have taken over, and I just want to feel Lachlan inside of me.

He pulls my shorts and underwear down and then yanks my body so I'm sideways on the chair. He unbuckles his pants and pulls his dick out, stroking it a few times to get it hard.

"Flip over, baby," he commands. I do as he says, flipping onto my stomach and spreading my legs so my ass is in the air and I'm open for him. "Jesus," he growls. "This ass." He slaps my ass cheek and then pushes into me from behind.

Entwining his fingers into my hair, he yanks my head back and drives into me before he pulls back out. "Fuck, you're so tight. We're going to have to make this quick," he groans. "Rub your clit, baby." I bring my hand down to my clit and do as he says as he sinks back inside of me oh so slowly.

"Fuck me harder, please," I beg, needing more. And with another hard smack to my ass, Lachlan starts to fuck me deep and fast. His piercing is nudging and stroking my insides, and it feels so freaking good. His lips find my shoulder, and he bites down hard. All too quickly, my orgasm slams into me. My legs shake, and my head lands on the edge of the cool leather seat. I ride out every wave of my orgasm as Lachlan finds his own release.

With his dick still inside me, he leans forward and whispers into my ear, "You're mine, and I'm yours, and whatever the fuck you need from me to understand that, I'll *always* give you. Even if it means I have to fuck the jealousy right out of you."

NINETEEN

QUINN

I'VE CHANGED my outfit no less than a dozen times. Since Lachlan refused to tell me where we're going or what we're doing, I have no clue how to dress. I haven't been on a real date in years—since a year after Kinsley was born and I attempted to date, only to quickly realize I wasn't anywhere near ready.

It's the first week of November, and a small cold front has come through, so I decide on a pair of dark blue ripped skinny jeans, a mauve off the shoulder sweater, and a pair of black heels. I figure with the heels, I can at least look a little dressed up if we're going somewhere nice. After straightening my hair, I grab my purse and head downstairs. It's so weird living here without Jax and Willow, but I also love having my own place. I would feel bad about them leaving if they weren't now living in a super gorgeous condo only a few blocks away from their shop.

There's a knock on the door, and since Kinsley left a little while ago with Willow and Jax, it has to be Lachlan. After applying a smidge of lip gloss, I swing the door open to find the most stunning man standing on my front stoop. His hair is messy as usual, but his beard has been trimmed so it's short and neat, exposing a bit of his chiseled jaw. He's dressed in a white button-down shirt with his sleeves rolled up, showing off the intricate tattoos that cover his forearms, and jeans that mold to his muscular thighs. And in place of his signature Vans, he's sporting wheat-colored boots.

When he clears his throat, my eyes swing back up to meet his sea-foam green eyes, and that's when I notice he's holding a gorgeous bouquet of white, pink, and purple flowers. My heart thumps rapidly against my ribcage as I take in the man in front of me—the man I was hellbent on not giving a chance to in the beginning because of something as stupid as our age difference. Who has turned out to be everything good in my life, giving me the confidence I never thought I would find again. Reminding me every day of how beautiful I am. Loving my daughter as if she's his own. And I know in this moment, I have hopelessly and irrevocably fallen in love with Lachlan Bryson.

"You look absolutely stunning," he says, his eyes remaining locked with mine. "These are for you." He hands me the flowers. "They're Gillyflowers," he says, and if I'm not mistaken, he looks almost embarrassed. "The florist said they mean happy life."

"You asked what the flowers meant?" I bring them up to my nose and inhale the fresh scent of them. I've never been given flowers before.

"Yeah, well, there were a lot of options." He shrugs. "And I've never bought flowers before."

"They're beautiful. Let me put them down and then we can go."

After putting the bouquet of flowers into a vase I find under the sink, I lock my door, and we head down the driveaway. "We can take my car," I offer. Lachlan shakes his head, and that's when I notice there's a metallic blue BMW parked in the driveaway. "Is that your vehicle?" I don't know a lot about cars, but it looks to be on the expensive side.

"Yeah, I haven't really driven it since moving back to New York," he admits, opening the door for me so I can get in. The inside is gorgeous, all black leather and new-age electronics. I know he makes a decent living working at Forbidden Ink, but I'm not sure how he could possibly afford a vehicle like this and live in such an expensive condo. Suddenly, I feel like there's still a lot I don't know about Lachlan.

We drive for about twenty minutes, until we arrive in downtown Brooklyn. Lachlan parks and we walk over to a restaurant called O'Connor's. From the outside, it looks like one of the typical hole-in-the-wall restaurants that New York is littered with, but once we step inside, I'm amazed by the extravagance of the place. Elegant wood-panel walls, finished with crown-molding and high-vaulted ceilings are the first things I notice as we approach the hostess. When I glance around, I see an expansive bar off to the side. The back wall is mirrored glass, and the bar top is black shiny marble.

"Lachlan!" The woman manning the hostess stand comes around and gives Lachlan a hug. "It's been a while. Does Declan know you're here?"

"Yeah, he made a reservation for me," he tells her. I didn't even know Declan works here. Actually, I don't really know much about him or any of Lachlan's family. I know Lachlan's parents are in Ireland, and I think someone in his family might own a distillery. I know one of his cousins owns the B & B, but other than that, I don't know anything else.

"Perfect! Follow me to your table." She takes us to a small table in the back, away from the other tables. "Your waiter will be right with you." She hands us each a menu.

Once she's out of hearing range, I set my menu down and look at Lachlan. "You know, I was just thinking that you know my family and friends, but I feel like I don't know a whole lot about you."

"That's actually what tonight is about," he admits. "With my parents out of the country, I realized I haven't shared a lot about myself with you, so tonight our date will double as a crash course in everything Bryson." He winks playfully. "Starting with my best friend and cousin, Declan O'Connor."

"Hey, man!" Declan comes into view and clasps his hand on Lachlan's shoulder. "Quinn." He nods with a smile. "Welcome to O'Connor's."

"Wait!" I exclaim, putting the pieces together. "You own this place?"

"That I do." He grins. "Every Irish family needs at least one pub."

I can't help the laugh that escapes past my lips. "This is hardly a pub." It's an upscale restaurant. I peeked at the prices on the menu, and they're no joke.

"Eh, semantics," Declan jokes, before bidding us a good dinner and excusing himself, just as the waiter comes over to take our drink order. Lachlan orders a water, so I do the same.

"Where I'm taking you next has alcohol," Lachlan explains.

"And where's that?" I have a feeling I know, but I want him to tell me.

"Not falling for that." He laughs.

"So, Declan owns a pub, and your cousin Kiara owns a B & B.

Any other family members own any restaurants or hotels in the area?"

"Nope, although, my aunt and uncle own a corner store in Galway."

"Is Galway where you're from?"

"It's where my parents were raised."

When I grin, Lachlan asks, "What?"

"It's like that song by Ed Sheeran...Galway Girl."

Lachlan laughs. "I'm a guy."

"Yeah, but I bet you dated tons of Galway girls." I waggle my eyebrows, and he shakes his head.

When the waiter returns with our drinks, we order our food. I get the scallops, and Lachlan gets the steak. We spend the rest of the meal with Lachlan telling me about his aunts and uncles and all of his cousins.

"Declan and I are leaving the weekend after Thanksgiving for our cousin Emily's wedding," he says, taking a bite of food.

"That will be fun. In Ireland?"

"Yeah."

"How long will you be gone for?" I take a sip of my water, trying to ignore the sinking feeling in my stomach at the memory of every time Rick would let me know he was leaving. Lachlan isn't Rick, though, and I have to remember that.

"I told your brothers I'll be gone for five days: Thursday through Monday." He sets his fork down. "And I was hoping you would join me." My heart skips a beat at his words. He's inviting me to go to Ireland with him. To meet his entire family.

"Wow... Five days in Ireland sounds like a dream, but I have Kinsley." Just the fact he invited me means the world to me. I want to explain that to him, but I don't want to bring up Rick and taint the moment.

"You can bring her," he says, as if it's a given, and my heart constricts at how amazing he is.

"That's so sweet of you, but she has school."

"She'd only miss a few days." He shrugs. "Just think about it, please. I would really love for you guys to meet the rest of my family."

"Okay, I'll think about it."

After we finish dinner and say bye to Declan, Lachlan drives us to the next stop on our date. When we arrive, the parking lot leading up to a beautiful two-story brick and mortar house is empty. I look for a sign but can't find one. I must've missed it when I was looking at the video Jax sent me of Kinsley playing the Wii.

Taking my hand in his, Lachlan guides us past a large yard and up the wooden steps. He unlocks the door, and switches on the light. As I take in my surroundings, I'm not sure exactly what I'm looking at. I expected to see the inside of a home, but it's definitely not that. The two stories are completely open with mahogany wood walls and matching floors. There are several barrels turned sideways in the middle of the room, and when I walk to the wood railing and look down, I spot a... distillery?

"Is this where whiskey is made?" I glance at a barrel and read the logo branded on the side: Bryson Distillery. I was right! His family does own one. How cool!

"Yeah, gin too." He grins. "Come, take a look." He walks over to one of the barrels and shakes it back and forth. That's when I notice the barrel isn't like a normal barrel. It has a glass bottom so you can see the liquid sloshing around. Lachlan points to a small hole in the wood. "Put your nose up to it."

I do as he says and the aroma of the whiskey hits me hard. "Mmm...that smells good." I beam up at him. "I drank your whiskey at Assets," I admit. "It was delicious. I can't believe you guys make this!"

"I know. When I kissed you, I could taste it on your tongue." He grins devilishly. "C'mon, let me show you around. I had Salazar close the place early so I could give you a private tour." He winks and threads his fingers through mine.

"Who owns this place?"

"My family."

"I know that." I smack his arm playfully. "But I mean, your parents? Or extended family?"

"My parents and I own it."

We take the stairs down to the first floor and Lachlan explains each piece of equipment and how the process of making whiskey and gin works. He's so charismatic about it all, I have to wonder why he's tattooing instead of working here when he said he owns the place with his parents. I save my question for later, though. Right now, I'm enjoying getting the full tour. When we make it back upstairs, we walk through a shop that sells all their drinks as well as some other goodies such as shot glasses and magnets.

"Is your whiskey and gin in a lot of stores?" I ask curiously.

"We're in most stores, bars, and restaurants on the East Coast," Lachlan says with pride. "When my dad moved here from Ireland to expand, his dad wasn't thrilled. He didn't believe he could make a living selling whiskey and gin in the United States, but my dad was determined. My mom said he would go from business to business offering free bottles for them to try. Over the years the business grew bigger and bigger, and now we're one of the largest distilleries in the east."

"That's amazing." Lachlan opens the door for me, and we enter an open area with an expansive lacquered wood top bar and several matching tables and chairs. He steps behind the bar, so I follow him.

"Hop up." He grips the curves of my hips and lifts me onto the top of the bar. He separates my thighs and leans in to kiss me. When his lips start to move gently against mine, I sigh into his mouth. Reveling in his touch and his warmth. I can't remember a time before Lachlan came into my life when I felt so completely content. Now, I feel that way all the time.

"Whiskey or gin?" he asks, pulling back and taking his warmth with him.

"Usually I would say whiskey, but I'm curious about the gin."

"All right, one Red-Headed Ginger coming right up." He grants me a panty-melting, lopsided grin that has me cracking up with laughter. I watch as he pours the different ingredients into a metal cup, adds the ice, and then shakes it all together. He pours it all into a Collins glass when he's done, and hands it to me.

I take a sip of the red-tinted drink, immediately tasting orange and lemon. It's the perfect mixture of sweet and sour. "This is delicious," I tell him, taking another sip.

"Let me have a taste," he says, but when I try to hand him the glass, he sets it aside and pulls me closer to the edge so he's standing between my legs, his stomach right up against my center. And then his mouth is on mine. He kisses me like he's dying and I'm his lifeline. With every brush of our lips, I'm bringing him back to life. And he has no idea that he's doing the same to me. I'm finally living, and it's all because of Lachlan. "You're right," he murmurs against my lips, "it does taste good."

And then he's unbuttoning and unzipping my jeans. I lift up slightly, and he yanks them down my legs. My heels fall off, making a clacking sound against the tiled ground. "Let's see if you taste as sweet as the drink," he whispers, spreading my legs so I'm completely open and on display for him to do as he pleases. A few weeks ago, I would've shied away from something like this, begged him to close my legs, but now I welcome everything Lachlan does to me because I know when he looks at me, he sees me as beautiful, regardless of all of my flaws.

I close my eyes, waiting to feel his warm breath on me, so I'm shocked when, instead, I feel something cold and wet hit my center. When I look down, I see a piece of ice between Lachlan's lips. His head moves up and down, the freezing cold ice running along my slit and landing on my clit. When he swirls it around my already swollen nub, my body nearly convulses.

"Lachlan," I moan, having no clue what I'm even calling his name out for.

"What do you need, baby?" he purrs, pushing the melting ice into me. When I squirm, he chuckles softly. "Hold still." And then his tongue is hitting my clit, and he's lapping and licking me like I'm a popsicle on a hot day that needs to be devoured before it melts completely. With every swipe of his cold tongue, I'm pushed closer to the edge, and then I'm falling. My legs are shaking, and I'm writhing against him as warmth spreads throughout my entire body.

Before I've even come down from my orgasmic bliss, Lachlan is lifting me off the bar top and setting me on my feet. I faintly hear his pants unzip before he knocks my legs apart and thrusts deep into me. And then, once again, I'm coming completely undone as I lose myself to Lachlan Bryson. And I know in this moment, as he fucks me into oblivion, there is no turning back.

Fuck our age difference.

Fuck my being overweight.

Fuck Rick.

Fuck the rest of the world.

The only thing I can think about is spending the rest of my life being well and truly fucked by this perfect man.

"WHEN'S YOUR BIRTHDAY?" I ask Lachlan. We're lying in bed with our bodies entangled around each other. My head is resting against his chest, and he's drawing circles on my bare back. The sun is rising, and we haven't slept a wink, but I can't find it in me to close my eyes. In a few hours, I'm going to have to get up and meet Willow, Jax, and Kinsley at the park for her soccer game, and I'm going to regret not getting any sleep. But right now, I just want to lie with Lachlan and learn all there is to know about him. I've been asking him random questions in between our heavy make out sessions—some of which end with him inside of me—and I love how he's an open book with me.

"On Christmas."

"Really?" I lift my head to look at him.

"Yep."

"That's cool. Kinsley and your birthday are both on holidays."

"It's not as cool as it seems," he says, his voice serious. "People always tried to give me one present for Christmas *and* my birthday." His lips turn down into an adorable pout, and I crack up laughing.

"Poor baby."

"Damn right. When's yours?"

"March fifteenth." I groan.

"What's wrong with your birthday?" He laughs.

"I'll be the big four-oh."

"Eh, don't fret. You're like whiskey, you get better with age." His chest shakes with laughter at his own joke.

"Ha ha, easy for you to say. What are you turning? Twenty-eight?" I roll my eyes, and even though he couldn't possibly know I did so, he laughs and says, "One day your eyes are going to get stuck like that."

"Wow, you're just full of jokes, aren't you?"

His response, of course, is to tilt my face up and kiss me. "We should start getting ready soon. Kinsley's game starts in a couple hours. I imagine you're going to need coffee and something to eat."

"You don't have to go," I tell him. "We were up all night and you have to work today."

"I'll take a quick nap later, but I'm not missing her game." He gives the tip of my nose a kiss and shifts me off him so he can get up. "Shower with me?" He waggles his brows.

"Sounds perfect."

TWENTY

QUINN

"I'LL MAKE the mashed potatoes, and you can make that cornbread casserole everyone loves." I'm having lunch with Celeste, Olivia, Willow, and Giselle, so we can discuss Thanksgiving, which is in a few days. We've decided to do one dinner at Celeste and Jase's place since their house is the biggest and has the largest dining room.

"Okay, great." Celeste types something into her phone.

"I'll bring the green bean casserole and sweet potatoes," Olivia adds.

"Perfect." I check the items off my list.

"I'll have my mom make the deserts," Giselle says. Her mom owns an upscale restaurant here in New York. The food is delicious!

"Jax and I can bring the rolls," Willow says with a laugh, and we all join in.

"I think that covers everything." I check my phone and see it's almost time for Kinsley to get out of school. Her babysitter, Ember, took the week off to visit family, and the backup one has moved out of the state, so I've been picking Kinsley up every day myself. Today is her last day of school before Thanksgiving break. With the snow falling, making the roads slippery, I need to leave shortly so I'm not late to get her. A text vibrates on my phone, and when I click into it, it's Lachlan: **I miss you. Send me a pic.** I shoot him back a text, telling him I'm at lunch with everyone, but he texts back he doesn't care, which makes me laugh.

"What's so funny?" Celeste asks.

"Every time I'm not around Lachlan, he's begging me to send him pictures."

Giselle laughs. "Killian does the same thing!"

"Really?" Olivia asks. "Do you send them?"

"Of course! Gotta keep his spank bank filled with me," Giselle quips.

"I would be so afraid of them getting lost in cyber space," Olivia says.

"I send them to Lachlan, but only ones of me clothed. He's asked for some nudes, but I feel like I'd need to edit them beforehand," I say, only half-joking.

"Oh! You should do a boudoir shoot," Celeste says. "That way he gets his nudes and they're done tastefully."

"That's actually a really good idea," I admit. "Lachlan's birthday is coming up. I could give them to him as a gift."

Celeste's face splits into a wide grin. "Well, look at you, getting all risqué in your old age." She winks teasingly. "You know Adam's husband, Felix, right? I think you've met him before." Adam is a model and one of Celeste's best friends, and Felix, his husband, is a huge well-known photographer. "Want me to see if he's available?"

"That would be great. Thanks," I tell her, feeling both excited and nervous.

"Have you decided yet, if you're going to Ireland with him?" Willow asks.

"Ireland?" Celeste questions. "You guys really are getting serious, aren't you?"

"He told me he's falling in love with me," I admit. "He asked me to go with him for a wedding."

"You should go!" Willow says. "You deserve a mini vacay."

"I do want to go, but I feel bad leaving Kinsley with you guys. He said I could bring her, but I hate for her to miss any days since she'll be out for Christmas break shortly after."

"That's what family is for," Celeste points out. "You have all of us. I bet Skyla would even stay with her if you wanted her to. It's okay to lean on us, you know." Hearing her say the words, knowing my family has my back, solidifies my decision to go.

"You're right. Thank you. I'm going to tell him yes." I send

Lachlan a text, asking if the invitation is still available to join him in Ireland. A few seconds later, my phone rings. "Hello."

"Does this mean you guys are coming?"

"This means I'm coming."

"No Kinsley?" I can hear his disappointment through the phone.

"She has school, but my family said they'll watch her."

"I'll book our flights tonight," he says with a smile in his voice. "If you change your mind about her, just let me know."

"Will do."

We hang up, and when I place my phone down on the table and look up, I see four sets of eyes smiling at me. "What?"

"You are so in love with him," Celeste says in a sing-song-y voice.

I don't even bother to deny it. "I so am."

"GOOD MORNING, BEAUTIFUL." Lachlan's words are accompanied by a kiss to my cheek. I snuggle deeper into his side, hiding my face so we don't have to wake up. I have no idea what time it is. The only thing I'm sure of is that I don't want to leave this bed ever. And then it hits me. Lachlan is in my bed...in my house... and Kinsley is home. Oh, God! We fell asleep again! We've been getting more and more careless lately. Lachlan keeps waking up a little later. And judging by the light shining in through the windows, unless a miracle has occurred and Kinsley is still asleep, she's going to see him leaving.

"You have to go," I stress.

Lachlan's body stiffens. "Shit!" he hisses. He shoots up into a sitting position and my head drops onto the pillow. "I set my alarm." He grabs his phone and swipes it open. "Damn it, I'm sorry, I set it for p.m. by mistake. You go down and distract her and I'll sneak out."

That's when I remember today is Thanksgiving. "You're coming back, though, right? For dinner?"

"Of course." He cups the side of my face and presses his lips to mine. "Declan said he and Venessa would be going as well, so I'll probably drive them over since I still have my vehicle."

"Okay." I pout, not thrilled that I won't see him until later.

"What's wrong?"

"What if I talk to Kinsley about us? She already knows you're my boyfriend."

Lachlan is already shaking his head. "No, you said you weren't comfortable with her seeing a man wake up here unless you knew it was forever. One day I'm going to make you mine, forever, and then we will explain why we're all living together. Until then, I need to do a better job at sneaking out."

My shoulders droop in relief at how perfect this man is. "Okay, I'll go distract her." I give him a chaste kiss, despite wishing I had the time to devour him. "See you later."

I find Kinsley in her room, still in her pajamas and playing with her Barbies. I close her door partially so Lachlan can sneak out without her seeing. We spend the better part of the morning playing and then Kinsley helps me make the mashed potatoes to bring with us for dinner.

We arrive at my brother and Celeste's place, and I see Lachlan's BMW is already parked in the driveway. When we walk in, Kinsley immediately spots him sitting at the dining room table and gives him a hug. She and Lachlan have become close the last couple months, and it warms my heart to know she has yet another person in her life who loves her. I take a moment to say hello to all the guys—and Declan's girlfriend—who are sitting on the couch watching football.

Both Nick and Killian are yelling at the screen, and I can't help but laugh. They both played several years in the NFL and always have a lot to say when a game is on.

After I'm done talking to Killian about the new ink he just got done, I walk over to Lachlan. "Hey you," I say, leaning down to give him a kiss. "Whatcha doing?" I look around and see several of the kids are drawing and painting turkeys.

"Painting my turkey." Lachlan laughs. "Hey, Mini-Q, want to draw one?"

"Yeah!" she exclaims, jumping into the empty seat next to him. He hands her a plate and explains how to trace her hand and then cut it out. I watch as she follows his directions to a T. When she starts drawing and painting the actual turkey, though, she frowns, her gaze flickering between Lachlan's finished turkey and hers. "Mine sucks." She pouts.

"Hey," he admonishes, cheekily. "You said a bad word. You owe me a dollar." The room erupts into a fit of laughter—well, everyone but Kinsley, whose brows knit together as she pulls a dollar bill from her pocket.

"Fine, but it's a waste of time because you'll curse soon and have to give it back." She slaps the dollar bill into his palm with an adorable glare. "My turkey looks so bad, and yours looks perfect." She crosses her arms over her chest. "It's not fair. You make tattoos, so you can draw." She huffs loudly.

"You're being kind of rude," I tell her. "Are you in need of a nap?" Every day after school, she goes home and takes a short nap to help her unwind from her day. We were busy cooking and playing today, so she never took one. It's about that time.

"I'm not a baby, Mom," she whines, her eyes darting around at all the kids at the table.

"I didn't say you were," I point out.

"Why don't I help you draw it," Lachlan says, taking over, "and then you can paint it."

"Okay," she whispers, covering her mouth to hide her yawn. "Thank you."

Leaving them to do their own thing, I head into the kitchen to deliver the potatoes. Celeste and Skyla are standing at the double oven, taking the two birds out, Giselle is getting all the sides in order, buffet style, and Olivia and Willow are gathering up the plates and silverware.

"What can I help with?" I ask, and everyone waves me off.

"I heard you're going to Ireland with Lachlan," Sky says, walking over to me. "Go you, Aunt Quinn!" She laughs, and I roll my eyes. "I told Dad and Mom, I can watch Kinsley at your place, so she can sleep in her own room. I can take her to school in the morning and pick her up."

"Have I told you how much I love you?" I take Skyla's face between my hands and kiss her nose. It's hard to believe she's going to be twenty-three next year, which makes me realize Lachlan is closer in age to Sky than he is to me.

"What's wrong?" Sky asks.

"Nothing." I fake a smile, pushing down the self-doubt. Lachlan told me he's falling in love with me. He spends the night, every night. No man jumps through the hoops he does, just to get laid by a woman twelve years his senior.

"Okay." She gives me a look that says she isn't quite buying it, but doesn't argue. "What time are you leaving Thursday? Do you need me to spend the night on Wednesday?"

"That would be great," I tell her, wrapping my arms around her for a hug. "I'm so proud of the woman you've become."

"Oh, stop!" She laughs. "I'm twenty-two and just recently moved out on my own."

"And you go to FIT full-time, and will be graduating in May, while helping to run a multi-billion-dollar company," I point out, which has Sky blushing with pride. "Like I said, I'm very proud of you."

DINNER IS SERVED, and everyone grabs a plate, piling food high, and then finding a seat at the expansive table. The kids have a separate table right next to us. Jase gives a small speech about being thankful for everyone here, and I can't help the tears that come. I don't know what I would do without my family. Jase and Jax have been there through everything: a dead father, a deadbeat mother, a cheating husband. Helping me to raise Kinsley. And now here they are supporting me as I find love.

"Hey, you okay?" Lachlan leans over and asks softly, giving my thigh a comforting squeeze.

"Yeah, just getting emotional." I laugh it off. "Thank you for being here." I press my lips to his cheek. "I love you." I still in my place, realizing what I said right after the words come out.

Lachlan turns to face me. "Do you mean that?"

"Yeah." I nod once. "That wasn't how I wanted to tell you, but yes, I do mean it. I love you."

He grins the most beautiful boyish grin, and cupping the side of my face with his hand, he says, "I've been waiting for you to catch up, beautiful. I love you."

TWENTY-ONE

LACHLAN

"YOU HAVE YOUR CELL PHONE?"

"Yes." She nods.

"Passport?"

"Yep." She nods again.

"Laptop to do edits during the flight?"

"Oh! I forgot that."

I chuckle as I watch Quinn run back upstairs, for the third time, to grab her laptop. It's four in the morning, and since our flight to Dublin leaves at seven, we have to get going, so we can get through security. Flying out of JFK is always a hassle, but during the month of December, it's exceptionally crazy. Luckily, it's the week after Thanksgiving and a few weeks before Christmas, so it shouldn't be too horrendous.

"Got it!" she whisper-yells, not wanting to wake up Skyla or Kinsley. "Oh! I need the adaptor!" She takes off running her sexy ass back up the stairs again, while I get the pleasure of watching. While she's up there, I spot Kinsley walking down the stairs, rubbing her eyes with her tiny fists.

"Everything okay, Mini-Q?"

"Yeah, I heard Mommy running around and I wanted to say bye." Her tiny mouth curls down into a sad little pout. "I'm going to miss you guys."

"We're going to miss you." I glance up the stairs and don't spot Quinn, so I kneel down in front of Kinsley and whisper, "I got it."

Her eyes widen. "Can I see? Please!"

Pulling the box out of my pocket, which reminds me I need to stick it in my luggage before we go through security, I hand it to her.

"It's so pretty," Kinsley murmurs with a giant smile on her face. She's staring down at the three carat, platinum, princess cut engagement ring I purchased the day after Quinn told me she loved me—that was after I spoke to Kinsley and asked if she would be okay with me asking her mother to marry me and the three of us becoming a family.

She hands it back to me. "I really want to go with you guys," she says with tears brimming her lids, breaking my heart. If it were up to me, she would be getting on that plane with us, but Quinn is her mom, which means it's up to her, and I have to respect her decision.

"I know, but your mom doesn't want you to miss school. After I ask her, I promise we'll Facetime you on your iPad, though. Okay?"

"Okay," she agrees.

"Kins, you're awake?" Quinn comes jogging down the stairs with her laptop under her arm and her cord in her hand.

"I wanted to say bye." Kinsley wraps her arms around her mom's waist. "I'm going to miss you so much," she says with heavy emotion clogged in her throat. It takes everything in me not to beg Quinn to let her go with us. She might not be my daughter, but I've grown to love her as if she's mine, and I hate the idea of her being upset in any way.

"Oh, sweetie. I'm going to miss you too. I'll Facetime you every day. I love you."

"Okay, love you more."

"C'mon, Kins," Skyla says, making her presence known. "Since you're up early, why don't we get ready and go to breakfast before school? We can go to our favorite donut shop." She waggles her eyebrows, and Kinsley's frown turns right side up.

"Okay! Bye, Mom! Bye, Lachlan," she yells, running up the stairs.

"Thank you," Quinn says to Skyla, giving her a hug.

"You're welcome. Have a good trip." She smirks at me, and I stifle a laugh. She was sleeping on the couch, so my guess is she heard Kinsley and I talking, and she knows I'm planning to propose.

THE SIX-HOUR FLIGHT to Dublin was spent with Quinn wrapped up in my arms while we talked, flirted, an even made out. Purchasing first class tickets was the best decision I could've made. With only the two of us sitting next to each other, the flight was actually enjoyable. Since Ireland is five hours ahead of New York, we arrive at six p.m., and after renting a vehicle—where I splurged and got a BMW M5—the same model as mine, only newer—we drive the two hours from Dublin to Galway.

When we pull up to the Glenlo Abbey Hotel, Quinn is lying back in her seat, but when she spots the two-story manor that's situated on several acres of lush green property, she pops up and gasps. I chose this hotel because I knew she would love the restored castle. It was originally a church, and then it was bought and turned into one of the most luxurious hotels in Galway. Tourists, who aren't even staying here, will make the drive just to get a look at the castle in person. I imagined Quinn taking a million pictures here.

"Lachlan," she breathes, "this place is amazing! This is where we're staying?"

"It is...but only for two nights. My mom asked that we stay with her the night before the wedding and the next night."

"We could've stayed there the entire time."

"I know, but I wanted some time with you alone."

We pull around to the side of one of the bays, and park, so we can go check in. Quinn, as I expected, pulls her camera out of her carry-on and starts snapping pictures as we walk up the steps. "I can't believe how gorgeous this hotel is. It looks like an old church."

"It's a restored church," I tell her. "Wait until you see the inside."

We're greeted by a butler who takes our luggage and guides us to the front desk. When I give the woman my name, she confirms we're staying for two nights in the Grand Suite. I hand her my credit card, and when she gives me the total, Quinn gasps. I was hoping she wouldn't know the Euro to US dollar rate conversion, but judging by the look on her face, she knows. Quinn and I haven't talked money—not what she or I have. I know she's well off by the car she drives and the designer labels she wears, but we haven't had an actual conversation about it. Truth be told, I don't really give a shit about money, which is why I rarely spend any, and is probably the reason I have so much of it.

After taking the key, and being told our luggage will be brought up shortly, we head upstairs to our room. Quinn is quiet the entire time, and I know she's itching to ask how in the world I'm able to afford luxuries like a BMW, a condo in Hell's Kitchen, first class tickets to Ireland, and a hotel that costs a night what some pay a month for their mortgage.

When we step into the suite, Quinn stops in her place to take it all in. The entire suite is over six hundred square feet with a separate living room and bedroom. In the living room, the furniture is elegant with mahogany wood and gold trim, giving the room an enchanting feel to it. The bedroom has a large king-sized four-poster bed with crisp white sheets and is topped with a plush duck feather duvet—and no, I don't actually know this shit. I read about it when I was booking it.

"Lachlan, I don't want to sound like some gold-digger—" Quinn scrunches her nose up adorably "—but how are you able to afford all of this?"

"I'm a damn good tattoo artist," I joke, and she laughs.

"I'm kidding...I sell drugs." When her eyes bug out, I crack up laughing. "I'm kidding! I'm an only child." I shrug. "Since I was old enough to walk, I've helped my parents with the distillery. I worked there all through high school. When I turned eighteen, my parents gave me one-third ownership of the business. I told you I owned it with them."

"Yeah, you did. I guess I didn't consider what that means."

"It means I get a five-figure quarterly check for as long as we're in business. Whenever they need me, like when my dad had his stroke, I'm there."

"Wow, that's awesome," she says. "I love that you're so involved in your family's business. If I could tattoo, I would've opened Forbidden Ink with Jase and Jax, but drawing is not my forte." She laughs.

Taking her hands in mine, I pull her into me until we're almost flush. "Family is important to me. Sure, having money is a positive since we need it to survive, but being with family, spending time with them is what's important. I could've worked full-time for my parent's distillery, but they knew inking was my passion. I didn't ask or expect them to give me a percentage of the business, but they did it because they wanted to make sure I'm always taken care of. The same reason your brothers wanted you to have that townhouse instead of selling it. It's part of being in a family. And one day I would really like for us to be a family."

Quinn nibbles on her bottom lip and nods. "I want that too."

BECAUSE OF THE time difference between home and here, Quinn isn't the least bit tired. I warned her she'll regret it tomorrow, but tonight she can't sleep, so we spend the next few hours lounging in the spa tub, talking about this weekend and the wedding, who she'll be meeting, planning our day tomorrow, Facetiming Kinsley, and getting fully acquainted with our comfortable as fuck bed.

The morning comes too soon, and while I want to stay in bed—and in Quinn—all day, I also don't want to waste the time we have here. So, after ordering breakfast from room service, I wake her up so she can jump in the shower and we can start our day. After we eat, we head out. We're planning to have brunch with my entire family tomorrow morning, but I already told my parents that today and tonight would be just Quinn and me.

We drive to the center of the city, to Eyre Square, and get out. It's not spectacular, just a typical downtown type of area with places to shop and eat, but it's a nice day out, and the walk over to the Salthill Promenade, which runs along the northern shore, makes it worth it.

"Lachlan! This country, this city, is seriously so beautiful," Quinn gushes as she takes picture after picture of everything she sees. As she watches everything and everyone around her, I watch her. I love seeing her excitement, her love for the city my family is from.

After checking out all the different shops, we eat at a bistro in the square and then walk hand-in-hand along the sidewalk that leads to Salthill. The closer we get to the beach, the more nervous I get. Quinn of course notices and asks if everything is okay.

"Everything is perfect," I tell her honestly.

When we get to the shoreline, we walk a bit farther until we're alone. Quinn takes pictures of the water, the pier, and the rocks. She gushes over everything, from the smell of the salty air to the beauty in the way the water hits the rocks. Briefly lowering her camera, she turns to me with the most beautiful smile and says, "Thank you for bringing me here," and my heart feels like it's about to explode. She's the best mom, the most selfless, caring woman. She loves with everything she has, and she has no idea how much she deserves, how much I want to give her. What I want, and plan, to give her, if she'll agree to spend her life with me.

She turns back to take more pictures, and I pull the ring box out of my pocket and get down on one knee. It takes her a second before she looks back over at me, but when she does, when her eyes glide downward and she sees I'm kneeling with an open ring box in my hand, her camera falls, which is thankfully hanging around her neck, her hands go to her mouth, and she gasps loudly.

"The moment I saw you walk through the door of Forbidden Ink, I knew you were the one. Not only were you the most beautiful woman I've ever met, but your sass was a damn turn on."

Quinn's hands remain covering her mouth, but I can see her shoulders shake with laughter, and the curve of her lips turn up around her hands.

"You were dressed all professional, but I knew, under those conservative pants and blouse, was a tattooed, sexy woman, waiting to break out of that shell she was hiding under." Tears shine in her eyes. She knows what I'm talking about, but I'm still going to tell her. She needs to hear how I feel about her. "I instantly fell in lust with your luscious curves and perfect tits...those dark, soulful eyes and pouty lips. And the way you blush over every emotion. I knew I needed to make you mine. And that was all before I even got to know you." I chuckle softly.

"I know we've only been dating for a few months, but I've fallen in love with you, Quinn, and I can't imagine there ever being a day that I'm not in love with you. All I want to do is spend every moment with you. When you cry, I want to make the tears go away. I want to be the one who makes you laugh, and be the one by your side while all of your dreams come true."

TWENTY-TWO

QUINN

I'M STANDING on the edge of the water, listening to Lachlan tell me all the reasons he's in love with me and wants to marry me, and the tears are threatening to come with each word he speaks. But then he stands and bridges the gap between us. With the ring box still in his hand, he closes it and pushes it back into his pocket, so he can take my hands in his. I'm confused why he put the box away, until his eyes lock with mine, and he continues to speak.

"But I didn't just fall in love with you," he says, his voice so strong, not wavering in the slightest. "I also fell in love with your daughter." And the tears that were threatening to fall, spill down my cheeks. "How could I not, though?" He laughs softly. "She's literally a mini version of you. And I want nothing more than to make her mine. When she asked me that day in the bounce house, if I married you, if I could be her dad, I wanted to tell her I would love nothing more than to be her dad, but I knew I couldn't do that. It wasn't my place to make that promise before I made a promise to you. It killed me having to wait for you to catch up, but I'm a patient man." He chuckles. "Kind of," he adds with a shrug.

"My point is, I knew one day we would get here, with me asking you to marry me, but I also knew I would have to wait a little while for you to get to this point. On Thanksgiving, when you told me you loved me, I knew we were *both* finally at the same place." His smile shines so bright, it's almost blinding. "You're everything I could ever want and need. I want you and Kinsley and me to be a family. And I promise you, I will spend every day for the rest of our lives loving the both of you with all of my heart." He pulls the ring box back out and opens the top, the ring sparkling in the sun, and takes it out. "Will you marry me?"

There's only one answer to give him. There's only ever been one answer, but I have a couple things I need to say before I tell him yes. "When I met you, I didn't realize how insecure I was. I didn't understand the damage my ex-husband did to me. I thought I was healed. I was happy and living my life. I had my business and my family and Kinsley. But it wasn't until you, I understood how unhappy I really was. With myself. I read once somewhere that nobody can make you happy. You have to make yourself happy. And I fully believe that. But what I also believe is through you loving me, despite all of my imperfections, I've learned to love myself. And once I was able to love myself, it allowed me to fall in love with you."

I don't even realize I'm crying again, until Lachlan reaches up and catches my falling tears. "Thank you for loving me unconditionally, and for loving my daughter as if she were your own." I brush a soft kiss to his lips. "Yes, I will marry you."

The corners of Lachlan's lips curve into a soft smile as he takes my left hand in his and slides the ring onto my finger. "You just made me the happiest guy alive."

After Facetiming Kinsley like Lachlan apparently promised, and learning my daughter already saw the ring and knew Lachlan was going to propose, we spend the rest of the morning exploring Galway. In the afternoon, we take a ferry over to Aron Island and explore over there. I'm absolutely in love with Ireland, with Galway. Everything is so lush and green and breathtakingly beautiful. The people are friendly, and there is so much to see and do. We end up having dinner at the hotel, and after making love, we fall asleep with Lachlan's body wrapped around mine. I told myself he wouldn't move in until after we're married, and since I can't see myself lasting much longer going to bed and waking up without him, I imagine the engagement will be rather short.

"WHAT IF THEY don't like me?"

"They're going to love you."

"But what if they don't?"

"They will."

Lachlan and I are driving over to his parents' place—because apparently, they visit so often, they own a home here—and it's just hit me I'm engaged to a man whose parents I've never met. My mind has been running wild all morning. What if they're like Rick's parents and stuck up? Or hate me like Rick's parents hated me? What if they think Shea is better suited for him? Or what if they think my tattoos look trashy? Okay, that's probably a dumb thought since their son is covered in them, but what if they're sexist and think ink should only be on men? What if they find out I have a daughter and are against blended families? They are still married after all.

I haven't asked Lachlan any of these questions, though. Mostly because I don't think he would tell me the truth. He loves me, and because of that, I think he would do anything to protect me, even if that means lying to me. But also because I'm afraid of what his answers might be if he does tell me the truth. My line of questioning also tells me something about myself... I'm still a work in progress. And with that thought comes one I've been thinking about more often lately. Maybe it's time I find someone to talk to. A professional. I want to be the best version of myself for Kinsley and Lachlan, but in order to do that, I need to be whole. And being whole means being healthy—emotionally and mentally. And while I feel like I've made strides in the right direction, I still have a long way to go.

We pull up the driveway, and even though I shouldn't be, I'm in shock by the extravagance of his parents' home. It's two stories with a three-car garage, a huge wrap around porch and second story balcony, complete with a freaking running fountain in the front yard.

"Tell me everyone's names again," I beg, suddenly feeling nervous over meeting his entire family at once. I've spent a lot of time with wealthy people like Rick's parents and know firsthand how unforgiving and judgmental they can be.

"My mom is Evelyn, and my dad is Matt," Lachlan says for the third time with the patience of a saint. Every time I do or say something I know would've aggravated Rick, I hold my breath, waiting for Lachlan to behave in a similar way, but every damn time he proves me wrong, making me fall that much more in love with him.

"My mom's brother is Anthony, and he's married to my Aunt Tracy. They have two daughters. You met Kiara, who's here with her husband, Kevin, and then there's Emily, who's getting married to Steven. My mom's sister's name is Patricia, and she's married to my Uncle Thomas."

"They're Declan's parents," I add, trying to remember.

"Yep, and Riley is his sister."

"Who's best friend's with Shea," I mutter, needing to remind myself she will be here because she's close with his family. Her mom is best friend's with Lachlan's mom, of course.

Lachlan smiles softly and turns my face toward him, leaning over and kissing me tenderly. "I love you," he murmurs against my lips.

"I love you too." I inhale and exhale, allowing his words to run through me like a soothing balm to my nerves.

"You ready?" he asks.

"Yes."

The minute Lachlan turns the ignition off, the large oak door swings open, and out runs a petite orange-haired woman. She's light-skinned with tiny freckles dotting her skin. When we step out, she wraps Lachlan up in a hug and her eyes briefly land on me. They're green just like Lachlan's. She must be his mom. She smiles sweetly, and my nerves come down a couple notches.

"Ay, my boy, it's so good to see ya!" Her Irish accent is thick—thicker than his cousin Kiara's—and I immediately fall in love with it, just like I've fallen in love with everything about this country.

Just as they finish hugging, an older version of Lachlan steps outside to join the party. Lachlan gives him a hug as well. Unsure of what to do or say, I stand here, waiting for Lachlan to lead.

Once the three of them have finished hugging each other, they step over to me, and Lachlan introduces us. "Mom, Dad, I would like for you to meet Quinn, my fiancée." Lachlan grins, and I choke on my saliva, shocked he just threw it out there. *Way to ease the family into it, buddy...*

His parents, though, don't appear to be surprised, like at all. Instead, they both smile warmly. His mom embraces me in a hug first. "We're so glad to finally meet ya," she says sweetly. "Lachlan, here, hasn't stopped talking about you and your wee one."

"Congratulations," his father says, giving me a friendly hug. "It's so wonderful to meet the woman who's stolen our son's heart."

"Thank you, it's nice you meet you, too," I say politely, in shock at how nice they are.

"You ladies go in, and Lachlan and I will grab your things."

The second we're through the front door, I can hear all the

voices. I must've been too nervous to notice the cars in the driveway, but just as Lachlan said, everyone is here. One by one, they each introduce themselves to me, and I take a deep breath when I don't see Shea here.

Evelyn tells us they were just finishing getting brunch ready and everyone is heading to the dining room to eat. Since it's the next room over, I don't get a good look at the house, but I do notice the striking crystal tear-drop chandelier hanging in the foyer. The living room is to the right, and looks like it's never even been sat in. The dining room is to the left. In the center is a large sweeping staircase, which leads to the second floor. When we enter the dining room, the huge rectangular wood table takes up the majority of the room. Intricately carved wood bench seats run down the length of the table with a matching armchair on each end.

As if Lachlan can sense how nervous I am, he pulls me to sit next to him and starts making me a plate of food. He's naming each of the foods, asking if I would like some, since I have no idea what any of this is, when the sound of the front door shutting, reverberates through the room, and in walks Shea. She's dressed in an adorable yet sexy olive-colored romper with her perky breasts peeking out on the sides. Her blond hair is down in perfect beach waves, and she's wearing cute nude heels.

She walks around the table with a bright smile on her face, greeting everyone with the confidence and self-assurance I wish I had. *You used to,* I remind myself. *You just have to allow yourself to get back there.*

When she gets to Lachlan, who has an empty spot next to him—although, it's not the only empty spot—she leans down and gives him a chaste kiss on his cheek. I can see him give her a disapproving look out of the corner of my eye, but he doesn't say anything to her.

She also makes it a point not to say anything to me. Simply sitting down next to Lachlan and making conversation with Riley, who is sitting across from me, as she loads her plate up with food. When Lachlan asks me if I'd like cheese on my eggs, Shea's eyes swing over to us, her brows knitting together as she watches us.

"That's sweet, Lach. You're making your girlfriend a plate." She says it softly, so only Lachlan and I can hear over the chattering that's going on all over the table. And then she adds, "But wouldn't it make more sense for her to make yours?" She grins evilly, looking right at me. "You are young enough to be her second child." She snorts at her own joke, and I want to hide, because just as she said the last part, the table got quiet and everyone heard.

My heart starts picking up speed, my fight-or-flight kicking in. Of course flight wins out—it always does—only I'm stuck on this bench between Lachlan and his mom with no way to get out without asking Lachlan and Shea to move.

Just as I'm seriously considering jumping over the back of the bench, Lachlan's hand lands on mine, squeezing it tightly. Calmly, yet loud enough for everyone to hear, he says, "I will not tolerate you speaking to, or about, my fiancée negatively. This is my home, and I will ask you to leave. I don't care who your mother is."

Without waiting for her to answer, he leans in so only I can hear and whispers, "I'm sorry."

Unable to speak without risking my voice cracking with emotion, I nod my okay, refusing to look over at Shea, then reach over and grab my plate Lachlan's still holding. There're only a couple items of food on there, and I know I'm still going to be hungry later, but I hate what she said about him making my plate. I shouldn't let it bother me, but she hit on one of my biggest insecurities about us—our huge age difference.

Lachlan's brows furrow, knowing he wasn't done making my plate, but I ignore him and start eating. The entire time we're eating, his gaze flicks over to my plate. I know he wants to add more to it, or tell me to, but he also knows it will only embarrass me.

His mom tries to make conversation, asking me various questions, but I'm too closed off to converse. I answer her every question, but they're short and cut off. The worst part is I know what I'm doing, and I hate it. I hate being weak. I want to be strong. I want to snap back at Shea and tell her to fuck off. I want to display my engagement ring, so she can stare in envy. And in my head, I totally do. Too bad, in my head doesn't count. It's moments like these I'm reminded of how much further I need to go to get back to being the person I used to be. The person I was before Rick. And then I curse Rick for doing this to me, and myself for allowing him to do this to me. And then I chastise myself for once again letting Rick into my thoughts. It's really a vicious cycle that needs to be stopped.

When brunch finishes, Lachlan excuses us so he can show me to our room. Refusing to let me help with the luggage, he carries both upstairs to the guestroom we'll be sharing. The room is beautifully decorated in cream and powder blue. There's a large king-sized bed in the corner, and the coziest looking reading nook I've ever seen under the window—complete with several fluffy pillows. Lachlan mentioned going out tonight for the bachelor party with all the guys, and since I didn't want to be that woman who prevents him from having a good time, even though the idea of me being here without him makes me feel sick, I told him he should go. Well, now I know exactly where I'll be tonight. Relaxing on that comfy bench, reading my book.

Lachlan sets our bags down and closes the door behind us, then pulls me over to the bed and sits me down on the edge, separating my legs and stepping in between. He grips my chin and lifts my head, so I'm looking at him. "Do not let that bitch get in your head," he commands, his voice taking on an edge I've never heard from him before.

And then his mouth is crashing down on mine, his tongue pushing through my lips and swirling against my own. The rough way he kisses me leaves my head spinning. My body heating. My insides sizzling.

He pulls me into a standing position, ripping my shirt off my body, reaching behind to unclasp my bra. We're ravenous, both of our hands working in a frenzy to remove every article of clothing from each other's body.

Lachlan drops to his knees and pushes me back onto the bed. His hands grip my knees and spread my thighs. His tongue delves between my pussy lips, licking and sucking on my clit. It feels so good, I release a heady moan, one that quickly reminds me where we are.

But I don't care because when Lachlan's mouth is on my body, everything else fades away. The entire world around us could be falling apart, but as long as he's touching me, I wouldn't even notice. I wouldn't even care.

And then his fingers are inside of me. Pushing in and pulling out. In and Out. In and Out. Deliciously slow and deep. A complete contrast to the way he was just devouring me with his mouth. Craving his roughness again, my hips push down on his fingers, meeting them thrust for thrust.

I can't get enough of him. Of the way he gives me all of him. Every ounce of himself is mine for the taking.

His pace picks up, pushing in deeper, harder, hitting that magical spot inside me. The man knows my body better than I do at this point. And with another thrust in, I'm exploding around him. My legs trembling. And then my entire body goes limp.

He doesn't even let me come down from my climax before he's dragging me up the bed and placing me on top of him. I have no clue how I'm supposed to ride him with numb legs. His fingers grip the sides of my ass, and he lifts me up and onto his stiff, pierced cock. He's so deep this way, my back arches. He grabs my hands and places them on the back of the headboard, on either side of his head. My body jerks forward, my heavy breasts going right into his face. He catches one with his mouth, sucking on the hardened peak. All the while, he continues to fuck me from the bottom. Powerful thrusts that have him in me so deep it feels like he's in my stomach.

Every. Piece. Of. Him. Is. Mine.

My legs finally get some of their feeling back, so I take over, riding him, trying to show him through my movements how much I need him. When he notices, his hands travel from my hips to my breasts, massaging and kneading them. And then his thumb hits my clit, flicking the swollen nub, and I detonate, coming so hard, my hands fall from the headboard, and my body slumps forward. My face nuzzles into the curve between his neck and shoulder, and Lachlan's face does the same. He kisses and suckles on my neck as he spills his warm seed into me.

I should probably get off him, so we can get cleaned up. I can feel his cum running out of me, but I can't move. I don't want to. I've come to the realization that Lachlan has imbedded himself within me. I'm no longer just me, I'm a part of him. When I'm with him, I feel beautiful, wanted, loved. I feel whole. He took all the broken pieces and somehow managed to put me back together. And then it clicks. There's no way he found all my pieces. I know for a fact Rick took several of them with him to the grave. Which means there's only one reason I'm complete. Lachlan replaced all the missing pieces with his own. The puzzle is only complete because he took pieces of himself and gave them to me. And I know the second we pull apart, I'll no longer feel as put together. I don't just love him, I need him. He completes me. Without him, I'm not whole. I'm not me.

TWENTY-THREE

Quinn

"I LOVE YOU SO MUCH, sweetie! Be good for Auntie Sky!" I wave through the phone, and my daughter waves back.

"Okay, Mommy! Love you too! See you soon! Bye!"

With one last kiss to the screen, Kinsley hits the end button, and her adorable face disappears. I drop my phone on the bed with a sigh. Lachlan's only been gone for a few hours, but I really wish he was already back. I imagine my need to be near him isn't healthy, but I don't really care all that much. Especially when he's out having a good time at the bachelor party Declan is throwing for the groom, Steven. He said tonight was perfect since Emily insisted they sleep apart the night before the wedding. She's here, along with all the other women, including Shea. I tried to hang out with everyone downstairs. I didn't want to be that person. The one who seems stuck up because she doesn't socialize, but when Shea droned on and on about all the fun times she, Declan, Lachlan, and Riley used to have, I excused myself to call my daughter. Now I'm dying of thirst and my stomach is growling, and the last thing I want to do is go down there, but it's going to have to happen.

Tiptoeing out the door of our room, I quietly glide down the stairs. I inhale a deep breath when I hear voices and deduce they're coming from the family room—the room just past the dining room and kitchen. When I get to the kitchen, I peek in, and once I see it's empty, I scurry over to the fridge to find something to eat and drink. The sound of women laughing and chattering rings through the house, but I ignore it as I quickly cut up some strawberries and make myself a roast beef sandwich. That is until I hear Shea's whiny voice mention Lachlan. Then I stop what I'm doing and listen.

"I can't believe he's seriously going to raise someone else's child," she says in her heavy Irish accent. Why does she have to have such a beautiful accent just to spew such nasty words?

"He's always wanted a house full of children," another woman adds. It sounds like Riley, but I could be wrong.

"Yeah, of his *own* kids," Shea volleys back, disgust evident in her tone. "What is she, like forty? She's not having any more kids. They'll never last," she hisses. "Lach and I are meant to be together, and once he learns we're on the same page, he's going to drop her like a bad habit."

"So, you've changed your mind?" a different woman asks.

"I didn't really think it was that important to him..."

"But have you changed your mind?" the same woman repeats.

"Lachlan will—" Shea's sentence stops abruptly. There's a quiet moment, and then she says, "Oh, Evelyn, you're back! Where were you?" I almost vomit at how different her tone is. What a fake bitch.

"With us leaving right after the wedding, I wanted to visit my garden one last time," Evelyn says sweetly. "What were you ladies talking about? I thought I heard Lachlan's name."

"We were just talking about how good Lachlan is with chil-dren," Shea says, her voice so saccharine, I'm going to get a toothache just from listening to her speak.

"He was definitely meant to be a family man," Evelyn says, motherly pride and fondness for her son in her tone.

"I bet you can't wait to one day be a grandmother," another woman says, but I'm not sure who it is.

"Oh, yes," she gushes. "I can't wait to have my own grandbaby to spoil."

My heart drops at her last word: *grandbaby*. She wants a grand-baby, and Lachlan wants his own children. He's meant to be a family man.

Having lost my appetite, and not wanting to hear another word, I drop my food into the trash, grab a bottle of water, and go back upstairs. I grab my iPad to read, but the idea of reading about someone else getting their happily ever after makes me feel that much worse.

As I cuddle into my blankets, I think about everything Lachlan has done to make my life better, everything he's given me, and the whole time, I didn't stop to think about his life. What his needs and wants are. Shea insinuated they broke up because she wasn't ready for a family, and it makes sense because Lachlan is a natural born father. He's amazing with Kinsley. While I don't think he'll end up with Shea, she still makes a valid point. I am turning forty. It took me nearly four years to get pregnant with Kinsley, and I was younger. The odds of me getting pregnant go down every year, and then there are the risk factors that increase the older the woman gets.

Lachlan deserves to have a family of his own. He deserves more than to only ever raise another man's child. Sure, he'll probably deny it when I ask him if that's enough for him, but what happens one day when reality hits and he resents me? He'll either stay with me out of guilt or leave me.

My mind goes to my father. He's not someone I ever try to think or talk about. But right now, it doesn't surprise me he's who pops into my head. He was with my mom for years, but when she couldn't conceive, he started to cheat on her. Jax and Jase were both born and then a couple years later I came. But by then he was fully living a double life...well, actually three lives, if you include his *other* wife no one knew about. He chose my mom over the others and sought custody of Jax and Jase, proving their mom to be unfit. She ended up committing suicide.

I feared Rick would do the same thing to me when I found out I was pregnant—try to prove me to be unfit. Only he died, and I was able to raise Kinsley on my own. Would Lachlan cheat on me if I couldn't get pregnant? Would he seek another woman to fill in the gaps I'm not capable of filling in? I want to say no, but I've seen what men are capable of doing.

Unable to fall asleep, my mind races with every doubt and insecurity, every worst-case scenario and what if, until the tears are racing down my cheeks as I mourn the loss of Lachlan and me and our future.

Just as my eyes are finally closing, the door creaks open. I know it's Lachlan without seeing him. I can feel his overpowering presence, and it takes everything in me not to lose it.

After he shuffles around the room, the bed dips down as he climbs in behind me, his strong arms wrapping around my torso. I let my lids flutter shut, reveling in the warmth his body and touch radiates. He snuggles closer to me and nestles his face into the back of my hair. "I know you're awake," he murmurs. "I can practically hear your mind spinning, and your body is stiff with tension." He runs his hand down the curve of my hip and over my thigh. "My mom said you've been in the room all night. Did something happen?"

I inhale deeply and exhale slowly, trying to decide what to do or say. I never want to lie to Lachlan. So, I answer his question with one of my own. "Do you want your own kids?" I stay lying with my back to Lachlan, and I'm surprised when he lets me. His fingers still on my thigh, and I feel him tense up. I already know his answer, but I wait for him to say it.

"No," he murmurs, and I close my eyes, the silent tears breaking out from under my lids and falling.

He lied to me. His answer should've been yes, but he said no. He chose to protect me with a lie, instead of breaking my heart with the truth. And by doing so, I now know what needs to happen next.

TWENTY-FOUR

LACHLAN

OVER THE NEXT two days I watch helplessly as Quinn pushes me away. She attends the wedding with me, speaks politely when spoken to, smiles at the right time—although every one of them is fake—laughs when someone says a joke, and takes tons of pictures of everything around her. But I can feel it, she's retreating back into her shell.

When she asked me if I wanted my own kids, I knew something was wrong. She wouldn't have asked that out of nowhere. Something was said, probably by fucking Shea. I don't know. I tried to further explain my answer after I said no, but Quinn wouldn't let me. She complained of a stomachache and retreated to the bathroom, locking it behind her. When she finally came out, I tried again, but she cut me off, telling me she was tired and wanted to get some sleep.

On the plane ride home, she faked sleeping for half the trip. The other half, she plugged in her headphones and worked on edits. I can literally feel her slipping from my fingers, and I have no idea how to fix this. I don't know what to ask, what to say.

Because we live in different parts of the city, after we get our bags from luggage claim, she insists we take different cabs home. I try to argue, but when she says she just needs some space, that she misses Kinsley and wants to spend some alone time with her, I know I'm stuck.

As she gets into the cab, she kisses my cheek and gives me a sad smile, and I can feel it in my bones, I've lost her before I ever truly had her. I close the door, in shock, and watch as the cab drives away. I take the next cab home, staring at my phone, wondering if I should text or call her. Debating if she just needs space. But then when I'm home and in my room, as I'm pulling my jeans off to change into a pairs of sweats, a diamond ring falls out of my front pocket, hitting the wood floor with a clink, confirming what I already know.

I've lost her.

TWENTY-FIVE

Lachlan

I WAKE UP, and for the first time in days, Quinn isn't lying next to me in bed. Her perfect, warm body isn't pressed into my side, and her leg isn't thrown over mine. Her hair isn't fanned out across her face and pillow. She's not waking me up and hurrying me out the door, so I can go get breakfast and come right back to eat with her and Kinsley.

I throw my legs over the side of the bed and turn my alarm off since I'm up before it's gone off. After showering and getting dressed, I head out to the kitchen to pop a K-cup into the Keurig so I can make myself a cup of coffee before I go to work. As I listen to the water heat up and then the coffee brew, I ignore the otherwise deafening silence. Kinsley's giggles are missing. The way she clacks her fork and knife against her plate. Quinn's voice isn't yelling across the house for her daughter to hurry up and eat so they aren't late. She's not begging me to make her a cup then kissing me when I hand it to her, already made.

Declan makes his presence known, half-asleep and scrubbing his face as he grabs a mug from the cabinet and moves mine to the side so he can make his own coffee. He flew back in yesterday along with my parents and Quinn. Nobody knows that Quinn and I have...fuck...what have we done? What did she do? Are we on a break? Did we break up for good? She gave me back the engagement ring. Does that mean she ended our engagement?

Grabbing the mug, I take a sip of the black coffee. When I notice Declan is silent too, I ask if everything is okay with him. Better to focus on someone else's issues instead of my own.

"I caught Venessa with another guy last night. I wasn't supposed to return until later in the week, but as you know I changed my flight last minute to get home to her." He shrugs nonchalantly, but it's an act. He cares about her.

"Are you sure it's what it looked like?"

"Yeah, unless shoving her tongue down a guy's throat can somehow be misconstrued." He takes a spoon out of the drawer, then slams in shut.

"Quinn ended our engagement last night," I admit.

Declan whips his head around to face me. "Are these women fucking possessed?"

I just shrug a shoulder and chuckle humorlessly.

"You're not going to just let her end it, are you?"

I've thought a lot about this since I found the ring last night. "She asked for space, so I'm going to give it to her. I don't want to. Hell, if it were up to me, I would throw her over my shoulder and lock her in my bedroom." I laugh without any humor. "Quinn is so fucking insecure, man." I take a sip of my coffee. "I've tried everything to convince her she's perfect. That I love her. That she's the one for me. But it feels like with every mole I whack, another one pops up in its place." I hate this feeling of defeat.

"What happened to make her end things?"

"I'm not certain, but I think while we were at the bachelor party, the women were talking. When I got back, she asked if I wanted my own kids."

"Have you asked your mom? You know, she was there."

I didn't even think about that. But Declan is right. "I'll do that. Thanks."

On my walk to work, I call my mom and she confirms the women—specifically Shea—were gossiping about how much I love kids and want my own family, but she says Quinn wasn't in the room, and she wasn't either during the beginning of the conversation. So maybe she overheard? Or she left before my mom walked in? I want to call Quinn and ask her, but that will go against giving her space. So instead, I go to work and lose myself in tattooing.

ON WEDNESDAY I wake up to my phone buzzing. I jump up and snatch it off the nightstand, praying it's Quinn. Only it's my mom, who apparently has been shopping. Not wanting her to judge Quinn, in case we get back together, I haven't told my mom Quinn called off the engagement. There are several pictures of little girl toys. Barbies, a Barbie mansion, tons of dolls and other shit. Under all the images is a message from my mom: **Christmas is in three weeks! I would like to meet my granddaughter before then!**

Not having the heart to tell her she may never meet Kinsley, I text back: **Ok.** Then I get out of bed and repeat everything I did yesterday. Only today, the ache in my chest hurts like a bitch. I consider calling Quinn several times throughout the day, but I don't do it. Space. She needs space. But fuck if I don't need her.

ON THURSDAY I call in sick, never leaving my bed except to eat and drink and piss. I'm fucking hurt and pissed at Quinn for doing this shit to us. All I want is to be with her. I turn off my phone and shove it in my drawer, so I don't call or text her.

ON FRIDAY I wake up and power my phone back on. It immediately dings with a text from Jax letting me know the new receptionist he *just* hired has called in sick and Quinn is filling in. He also added he'll reschedule my appointments today, so I don't have to come in. He didn't know when he asked her to fill in that we broke up, but since I'm sick I probably won't be coming in anyway. Without texting him back, I throw my phone to the side and get dressed. Since my car is still in the parking lot, I decide to drive it back to my parents' place today. I need to get the fuck away from here. Not only am I losing Quinn and her daughter, but now I'm probably going to lose my job. I spend the day working at the distillery, bugging the hell out of Salazar.

When my mom sees I'm here, she asks me to dinner, and when she invites Quinn and Kinsley, I lose it. It's probably the liquor talking, since I drank more today than I actually helped, but I end up telling her everything about Quinn and her ex. The emotional and mental abuse she's endured that have caused her insecurities.

"What if loving her isn't enough?"

"Oh, Lachlan," she says. "You can't possibly believe that. The thing about loving someone, being in a relationship, is finding the yin to your yang. When she feels weak, you be her strength. When you're lost, she'll be your beacon. When she feels insecure, you lift her up. Love is always enough, but you have to be willing to love even harder during those tough moments. Fight for the both of you when she's given up."

She's right. Whatever is going on with Quinn, she needs me. Even if things don't work out, I love her. She's become my best friend, and I'm not about to let her go through this alone.

"Thank you, Mom, that's exactly what I needed to hear."

After we eat dinner, I call a cab to go home.

ON SATURDAY I wake up with renewed confidence. I text Jax I'm coming to work before he can text me shit, and then I head out to go to Kinsley's soccer game. Aware that her game isn't the place to talk to Quinn, I hang back and watch from a distance. Quinn is sitting on a blanket, surrounded by her family, and even from where I'm standing, I can see she's sad. Her eyes aren't sparkling, and she has black circles under her lids. Tonight we're going to talk.

Needing Kinsley to know I was here, I snap a photo of her kicking the ball into the net and send it to her iPad with a message: **Good game!**

TWENTY-SIX

Quinn

IT'S BEEN five days since we've been back, since I slipped the engagement ring into Lachlan's pocket and kissed him goodbye. Five days since I told him I needed some space. Since I've felt his warm touch, smelled his delicious cologne, listened to his smooth voice. I don't even feel like I'm living at this point, just merely surviving. Kinsley, of course, doesn't understand what's happened. She thought him giving me the ring would mean he would move in and become her daddy. I didn't have the heart to explain it all to her yet, so when she asked where he was, I omitted the truth and said I wanted to spend some time with her. Thankfully, she accepted that answer.

I did call a therapist on Tuesday morning, and due to a cancellation, I was able to meet with her the same day. Her name is Fran, and she's very sweet but also straight forward. I spent the hour explaining my past, and she said she feels it would be best if we meet twice a week at first. I agreed. Honestly, with as many problems as I have, I'm surprised she didn't suggest we meet five times a week.

I met with her on Thursday, and we dove right in, head first. We talked about the person I used to be and the person I am now. She asked me to make a T-chart and list all of my qualities. On one side are the qualities before I was with Rick, and on the other side are the qualities after Rick. I noticed as I made the list, many of the qualities from before Rick were close to being added to the list after Rick, but only because they came back *after* Lachlan. So I added another column: after Lachlan. But then I deleted it...because it's time I'm responsible for my own qualities. I'm aware I'm not going to change overnight, but I'd like to think this is a good start.

I'm lost in thought as Kinsley and I walk down Delancey Street toward the Japanese restaurant we agreed to meet everyone at—after Jax assured me Lachlan wouldn't be there. I didn't want to go out, but Celeste mentioned going out for hibachi in front of Kinsley at her soccer game—the first game Lachlan has missed—and I had no valid reason to say no, especially since I've been sucking lately at the whole parenting thing and she could use a good meal.

So when someone calls out my name, I don't question it, simply turning around to locate the owner of the voice. And that's when I come face-to-face with the last person I ever hoped to see again. I'm in such shock over who I'm staring at, I completely forget whose hand I'm holding. That is until she asks, "Who's this?" and I glance down at the *who* in question. My heart pounds against my ribcage as my past and present collide. I try to think of a way to turn back time, but it's not possible.

"I'm Kinsley," my daughter answers for me, extending her hand to politely shake the woman's hand. I watch in fear as the woman eyes Kinsley. She's doing the math in her head, recognizing her bright blue eyes, her button nose, and her lips, the top one slightly fuller than the bottom. Her chocolate brown hair that's about five shades lighter than my black. She's putting it all together. I want to run, but I know it will only make matters worse.

I can tell when it all finally clicks. Her sharp gaze meets mine, and her lips—the top one slightly fuller than the bottom—form into a thin line. Her nostrils flare in anger as she says, "You had my son's child and never told me."

I flinch at her words, but don't deny it. Jacquelyn Thompson isn't a dumb woman. She knows that standing right in front of her, is in fact, Rick's biological daughter.

"There you guys are!" I hear from behind, breaking me out of my shocked state. Kinsley, having no clue what has just happened, releases my hand and runs over to Jax. Only when I turn around, it's not Jax she's running over to. It's Lachlan.

"Daddy! You're here!" she squeals. "I missed you so, so much." My eyes flit from Jaquelyn to Lachlan and Kinsley. I had no idea she was going to say such a thing, but I should've known. She flat out said Lachlan marrying me meant he would be her new daddy, and she's only six. She doesn't understand being engaged isn't the same as actually getting married.

Lachlan takes her in his arms and kisses her cheek, not correcting her. I knew he wouldn't. He would never say something to upset her. As I watch everyone talking and laughing, I feel like I'm on the outside, watching a train plowing forward without any working brakes, and I'm the only one who can see the collision that's about to occur. But I can't speak. I can't warn anyone. Who would I warn anyway? I'm the one on the train that's about to wreck. Just as I finish that thought, Jacquelyn makes her presence known, right in front of everyone.

"Why is my granddaughter calling that hoodlum Daddy?" She never was one to mince words. "All this time, you've had Rick's baby, and you've been hiding her from us, allowing another man to stake his claim on her. How dare you!" Her hand comes up, and I should block her, but I don't. Instead, I stand in my place as her palm strikes my cheek, and my face whips to the side from the force.

"Mommy!" Kinsley cries out. Damn it! She saw. "Don't hurt my mommy!" she screams.

"What the hell!" Jax yells, stomping over to Jacquelyn. "You better walk away right now before I call the cops on you for attacking my sister."

Jacquelyn doesn't even flinch, her eyes staying locked on me. "You will be hearing from my attorney," she hisses.

"For fucking what?" Jase asks. I didn't even realize he was standing on the other side of me.

"For keeping my granddaughter away from me," she says, and I don't have to hear what she says next to know where she's going with this. The entire reason why I never told her about Kinsley. "She's my blood, and I have the right to see her. Six years lost. I will see you in court." And with those words, my nightmare has come true. She's going to sue me for visitation, maybe even custody.

She turns on her heel and walks over to the town car waiting for her, taking one last look at me—or maybe Kinsley—before she slides into the backseat and disappears.

My chest rises and falls, my breaths quickening. My hand reaches up to my throat. It's hard to catch my breath. I feel dizzy, lightheaded. The world around me is blurry. I try to speak, but my vocal cords are cut off by the huge lump in my throat. I'm going to pass out. I can feel it. I can't catch my breath. I turn to my brother, trying to tell him something is wrong, but then everything goes black.

I WAKE up in my own bed with Lachlan's arms wrapped around me, and for a brief moment, before I have time to think about everything that is wrong, I feel complete again. Whole. Put together. His head dips down, and he presses a kiss to my forehead. An involuntary whimper escapes my lips, and the tears spill over the sides of my eyes.

"No, no, no, shh," he coos. "Don't cry, baby," he soothes.

"How is it I push you away, give you back your ring, and end things with you in the worst way, the cowardly way, and yet you're right here once again putting me back together?"

"Because I love you," he says simply. His words, for some reason, anger me, and I jump out of bed, needing space.

"You shouldn't be here," I tell him, standing at the end of my bed. I might be seeing a therapist now, but I'm far from fixed, and nothing between Lachlan and I has changed.

"There's nowhere else I should be," he says, his pierced brow rising in defiance. I take him in for a second, sitting on my bed, in his standard white T-shirt and jeans. He's sporting his sexy grey beany I love, and his shoes are off, his sock-covered feet stretched out. His arms are now crossed over his chest.

"We broke up," I tell him, fully aware I'm choosing to focus on us instead of dealing with the much bigger issue of my ex-mother-in-law.

"We're not breaking up," he says matter-of-factly. "I don't know what happened when we were in Ireland, but whatever it is, we'll deal with it."

"There's nothing to deal with," I snap. "I'm about to turn forty and you're twenty-fucking-seven. We were being delusional thinking we would ever work."

"So, we're back to our age difference again?" he says dryly. "Love knows no age." He shrugs like he's already bored of this conversation, and it fuels my fire.

"You're wrong!" I shout. "Love does know age, and it knows you have your entire life ahead of you. A chance to fall in love and create a family for yourself. And I love you enough to let you go." At my words, Lachlan stands and stalks over to me.

"You're not fucking letting me go," he growls.

"Yes, I am," I argue. "And what happened earlier is a perfect example of why. You deserve a fresh start. To meet a woman who will give you your own babies and create a loving home with you. You deserve more than a damaged single mom with a vicious ex-mother-in-law and a husband who continues to fuck her over from the grave. You deserve a woman who can give you her entire heart."

I slump against the front of my dresser, my vision blurry from the grief dripping down my face. "You deserve more than me." I shake my head. "And I would be selfish to hold onto you simply because you're everything I've ever wished for. You picked up the pieces of my heart, and when you saw it couldn't be fixed, you gave me parts of your own to make me whole." I look up at Lachlan. He's such a beautiful man on the inside and out. "You give me all of you, and I have nothing to give you in return," I admit defeatedly.

I close my eyes to release the built-up fresh tears, and when I open them, Lachlan is standing directly in front of me. His arms cage me in, and his face is only a hairbreadth away from mine. "You give me everything," he says, his voice low and serious.

"Shea said you wanted to have your own kids, and she made it seem like that's why you guys broke up."

"Shea and I broke up for a myriad of reasons, but, yes, our last fight *was* because I said I wanted kids, and she said she didn't want any," he admits.

"You told me you didn't want any kids."

"No." He shakes his head. "You asked me if I wanted my own, and when I said no, you wouldn't let me explain."

I open up my mouth to speak, but Lachlan places two fingers against my lips. "No, now you're going to listen. I gave you a few days of space like you asked, but I'm done. Family isn't blood. Family is heart, and you and Kinsley own mine. When I said I wanted a family to Shea, because neither of us had kids, yes, it meant having our own, but it's different with us. You have Kinsley, and even though she isn't my blood, she's still mine. Many couples can't conceive. They foster or adopt, and if they can't do that, they get a goddamned dog. With Shea, I couldn't imagine having a family with her, but with you, I can see it all. Even if it were only you and me, we would still be a family."

"Your mom said she can't wait to be a grandmother," I say weakly.

"Damn right, she can't wait. She's already sent me twenty pictures of the gifts she's bought for Kinsley for Christmas. She's chomping at the bit to meet her granddaughter, but I told her she has to wait because you need some time."

I gasp at his words, warm liquid gushing from my tear ducts. "But..." I don't even have anything to argue about anymore, but my insecurities can't stop me from trying. Why is it so damn hard just to let him in? Damn it!

"But nothing, Quinn. I love you, and you love me, and we're going to get married, and I'm going to adopt Mini-Q, and maybe we'll even get a dog. End of story." He grins. "No, not the end of the story. It's just the fucking beginning." And then he lifts me off my feet, and proceeds to show me exactly how the story continues—over and over again.

TWENTY-SEVEN

LACHLAN

IT'S BEEN three weeks since Quinn and I got back together, and she put my ring back on her finger. She's seeing her therapist twice a week, and yesterday I joined her for a session. It was hard as fuck listening to her talk about her insecurities, but her therapist seems to have her on the right track. I know it's going to take time for Quinn to finally be able to put her past behind her, but luckily, we have plenty of time.

With Kinsley calling me Dad, and the fact we're planning a wedding, we decided to move in together. I'm still keeping the condo for Declan, but I'm now one hundred percent living in the townhouse with my girls. *My girls.* Just the thought has me grinning like a damn fool. We've hired an attorney to handle the adoption papers for me to adopt Kinsley, and once we're married, he'll submit them to the courthouse to make everything legal. We're aware of Jacquelyn's threat to seek visitation-slash-custody of Kinsley, but we haven't discussed it. However, just because we haven't discussed it, doesn't mean I'm not handling shit. I have no doubt that woman won't try to take Quinn to court, but I'm going to make sure it doesn't come to that.

It's Christmas morning, and my birthday, and I'm lying in bed alone. I can hear the girls downstairs, though. Quinn is telling Kinsley she can pour the chocolate chips into the batter, and

Kinsley is questioning why she can't eat the batter if she can eat cookie dough.

Laughing at how adorable she is, I get out of bed so I can join them. There's a massive Christmas tree in the living room. Santa came last night. As Quinn and I put together several gifts so Kinsley would have them ready to go this morning, she kept apologizing for keeping me up until the crack of dawn, especially since it's my birthday. By the third time, I told her it was enough. What we're doing here means everything to me.

When Kinsley sees me approaching, she yells, "Merry Christmas! Santa came!"

"I see that! So when do we open presents?"

Kinsley pouts. "Mommy said after we eat breakfast." Then she perks up. "Oh! Happy Birthday!" She jumps off the stool and gives me a hug.

"Thank you," I tell her. Then I walk over to Quinn, who's standing in front of the stove, waiting to flip the pancakes. Pressing the front of my body against her back, I lean down and give her a kiss to her neck. "Merry Christmas, beautiful."

"Merry Christmas," she says through a smile. "And Happy Birthday."

After we eat and do the dishes, we spend the rest of the morning opening gifts. Kinsley squeals and shrieks in excitement over every gift. Quinn and I exchange gifts as well. I bought her a necklace with a mini camera on it, and she got me a new tattoo kit I'd mentioned wanting.

"I also got you something for your birthday," she says nonchalantly, but when her cheeks and neck turn pink, I wonder what it is she got me.

"Where is it?" I look around at all the ripped up paper and abandoned boxes. Kinsley is currently running each of her toys up to her room.

"In our room." She smiles sheepishly. What's she up to?

An hour later, Kinsley has conked out for a nap, and I've texted my mom to let them know we'll be coming over once she wakes up. We're doing lunch at my parents' place and dinner at Jase and Celeste's.

"Can I get my birthday gift now?" I ask Quinn, curious. She laughs and nods, pulling a square box out of the closet.

Setting it on the bed, I open the top to find what looks like a photo album. I take it out of the box and flip to the first page. It's a professionally photographed picture of Quinn. She's lying on her stomach, and her sexy ass is slightly in the air. She's wearing lingerie I've never seen before. And she looks fucking stunning. Slowly, I flip through page after page. Different poses, some in the same lingerie, some different, all fucking gorgeous. And not just because every image shows off her perfect tits or curvy hips. But because in every single picture she looks so damn confident and secure about herself.

"Quinn, these are perfect. You're so damn beautiful." I flip through the final pages, each one a tad more risqué than the last, but all tastefully done.

"It's because of you I was able to have this done," she admits.

"No, baby, it's because of you." I close the book and pull her into my arms. "Nobody can make you feel any way but yourself." I'm using the words her therapist has said to her several times.

"I know, but it was through your eyes, I was able to finally see that I'm enough. That's the tattoo I want to get. On my collarbone. I want you to tattoo it on me."

And without even meaning to, she just made this the best birthday ever. Because from those words alone, I know Quinn finally trusts me.

EPILOGUE

LACHLAN
Three Months Later

I READ over the papers Salazar has given to me. While he runs my family's distillery, in another life, he was in the Irish mafia and his connections reach far.

"Got you, bitch." I nod my head a few times, then thank Salazar. "I owe you. Whatever you need..."

"Your family took a chance on an ex-mafia fresh out of jail. You don't owe me anything." He shakes my hand. "The papers have already been submitted, so she will most likely be served any day."

I noticed that. I'm hoping I'll either get to them before they have her served, or we'll be out of the country. Either way, nothing will come of them, but I'd rather Quinn not be stressed unnecessarily.

Once Salazar leaves, I seek out Jase and Jax. Knowing I might need their backup, I've kept them informed of my plan.

"I got what we need." I hold up the papers, explaining to them what Salazar was able to find out.

"So why would they seek visitation or custody then?" Jase asks.

"My guess is they have no clue, but they're about to find out." I smirk. "I'm heading over there now."

"Let's go," Jax says, just as my cell phone begins to ring in my pocket. It's Quinn.

"Hey baby."

"Lach," she whispers, "I need you to come to the hospital." The hair on the back of my neck rises. Why the fuck is she in the hospital? Is Kinsley okay? When I left this morning, Quinn was packing, and Kinsley was getting ready for her last day of school before spring break.

"What's wrong?" I'm already heading to the front door when I remember I need to let her brothers know.

"I'm okay… Rick's parents served me this morning, and I-I kind of broke down and Kinsley called nine-one-one." She sobs into the phone. "Sky has Kinsley." Damn it! We were so close.

"I'll be right there." I hang up and tell her brothers what's happened.

"You go to my sister. She needs you. We'll give those pieces-of-shit a visit," Jax hisses, taking the folder from me.

Fuck! I wanted to see the look on their faces when they realized they were fucked, but Jax is right, Quinn needs me more.

QUINN

Two hours ago

I'M RUSHING around my room trying to finish packing. We leave in two days to Ireland for our wedding! After falling in love with the country, and getting engaged there, we decided to get married there. My brothers and their families will be coming, as well as Lachlan's family. We'll be there for a week since the kids are all on spring break, and my brothers can leave Evan and Gage to run the shop while we're gone. The latest receptionist is still going strong.

The doorbell chimes, and Kinsley yells up the stairs to let me know someone is here since she's not allowed to open the door. I check the clock. It's ten to eight. It's probably Skyla. She offered to take Kinsley to school for me this morning so I can get everything done.

I jog down the stairs and swing the door open without checking to see who it is, and standing there on my doorstep is a police officer.

"Quinn Crawford?"

"Yes."

"You've been served."

With shaky hands, I sign my name and take the envelope from the officer. I barely remember closing my door or opening the document. And everything after I open the flap and read "Notice to seek custody" is all a blur. I vaguely remember feeling like I was having a heart attack, and Kinsley yelling for me. My ears begin to ring, and my vision goes blurry. My first thought is I'm going to die, and my second is Rick's parents will get Kinsley because Lachlan hasn't officially adopted her yet. Once again, from the goddamned grave, my ex-husband is destroying another piece of me.

———

I COME to in the ambulance, where the EMT tells me my daughter called for help. When I ask where she is, he says her aunt showed up and showed proper identification, so they let her take her. Once I arrive at the hospital, I'm checked-in. Without my cell phone, I can't call Lachlan. Thankfully, Skyla shows up a little while later, while the nurse is drawing blood, and gives it to me, letting me know she dropped off Kinsley with Celeste on her way here. She was too upset to go to school. I call Lachlan, and he tells me he's on his way.

Once he shows up, I tell Skyla she can go. I'll be here for a while, waiting for the test results to come back, but I'm almost positive I just had an anxiety attack.

"Kenneth and Jacquelyn petitioned for joint custody of Kinsley," I tell Lachlan once he's sitting next to me by my bed.

"They will be recanting that petition," he states matter-of-factly. His fingers glide over my newest tattoo. The one he inked on me the day after Christmas. *You are enough.*

"How do you know?"

"Because after she threatened you, I had Salazar start digging for dirt on them." He smiles apologetically. I'm assuming for hiding it, not for actually doing it. "I didn't want you to stress over all this, Quinn." He brushes his knuckles down my cheek.

"Did he find anything?"

"He did, and your brothers are delivering the information to the Thompsons as we speak."

"What did you—"

"Good morning, Miss Crawford." A young gentleman, maybe in his late twenties, strides in. "I'm Dr. Fields." He extends his hand to shake mine, and I take it.

Then he extends his hand to Lachlan, who eyes him up and down like he's some sort of competition. I snort in amusement. "This is my fiancé, Lachlan," I tell the doctor.

"Are you old enough to be a doctor?" Lachlan asks.

"Lach!" I exclaim.

"I am," Dr. Fields says with a grin. Luckily, he doesn't seem offended. "We got your results back, and everything appears to be good. When you were brought in, your heartrate and blood pressure were both elevated, so we ran an EKG, and it came back negative, which leads us to believe your passing out was stress related.

"I did notice, though, you marked not pregnant on the nurse's questionnaire, but your HCG levels are significantly peaked, indicating you are pregnant. We would like to do an ultrasound just to confirm and make sure everything is okay. I've put the order in, and a tech will be by to take you to do the ultrasound. Once we get the results, and if everything looks good, we can let you go."

There is so much he just said. I'm pregnant...holy shit! I. Am. Pregnant. How is that even possible? Well, of course it's possible. I never got on birth control. But I didn't really believe I would get pregnant. But was I hoping to? My hand goes to my stomach, already feeling protective of the possible baby growing inside me. My gaze goes to Lachlan, who thanks the doctor, since I'm not able to speak, and closes the curtain behind him. My lips curl into a smile, and Lachlan's shoulders visibly slump.

"We...we might be having a baby," I breathe.

He leans over the rail of the bed and kisses my belly, then comes up to my face and kisses my lips. "I heard."

THE TECH WHEELS me in for the ultrasound and confirms I am ten weeks pregnant. I had no idea. I haven't felt sick or anything. When I convey my concern, she simply says every pregnancy is different, but everything looks good. She lets us listen to the heartbeat for a minute and then prints out a grey image of what looks like a tiny bean, but is actually our baby.

Our baby. Lachlan's and mine. We're having a baby!

When we get back to the room, Jax and Jase are both waiting for us with small smiles splayed upon their faces. I'm not sure what they're about to tell me, but I take a few calming breaths. I'm pregnant and I'm not going to allow myself to stress out. I've passed out twice recently from the stress, and I need to make sure to put this baby first.

"I'm pregnant," I tell them both before they can speak. "So, if it's something bad, can we talk about it later? I can't let Rick or his family ruin this moment." Tears prick my eyes. "I'll deal with it, whatever it is, but not yet." I feel Lachlan entwine his fingers with mine, and I'm grateful for it. I know with Lachlan by my side, we'll get through anything that comes our way.

"You're pregnant?" Jase grins, then pulls me to him for a hug. "Congratulations, sis."

"Congratulations," Jax says. "And we have good news. Jacquelyn has already called her attorney to remove her petition for custody. She and her husband will also be signing an agreement that they will never petition again, nor will they contact you or Kinsley."

"Wow," I murmur. "Whatever you found must be bad."

"There's only one thing those people love," Lachlan says with disgust. "Money."

"You paid them off?" But they're worth millions.

"No." Lachlan scoffs. "When I had Salazar dig, I wasn't sure what we were looking for. I was hoping to find something to blackmail them with." When I give him a disapproving look, he just shrugs. "I'm not even sure why Salazar thought to read your ex's will, but he did, and in it, it states if he has an heir, he, or she, will receive his percentage of the company along with all of his assets.

Holy shit! That would mean Kinsley would own fifty percent of the company and all the business accounts. She would be a millionaire, which would mean Rick's parents would have less.

"We didn't even have to threaten them," Jax says. "Apparently because there weren't any known heirs at the time the will was read, the attorney didn't mention it, and your parents never thought to ask. The second we brought it to their attention, they agreed to do whatever we wanted."

"They chose the company over their granddaughter," I say softly.

"They don't deserve to call her their granddaughter," Lachlan says. "Remember what I told you before. Blood doesn't make a family. Love does. Now let's get you the hell out of here and go get our daughter, so we can finally make us a family, legally."

LACHLAN
Sixteen Years Later

. . .

"DAD WON'T KNOW if you tattoo me. It's not as if he looks at my back," I hear my fifteen-year-old daughter, Kaylee, murmur from my office at Forbidden Ink. With Jase retired and traveling the world with his wife, and Jax and Willow retired and enjoying the quiet life, naturally it meant I would take over the family business. I wasn't supposed to come in this morning, since Barrett, my four-teen-year-old son, has a soccer game this afternoon, but I needed to place a quick order, since I forgot to do it last night before I left. And now I'm damn glad I did...

"It's not happening, Kay," Kinsley chides. I can't help the grin that forms. "Dad would kill me. You know his rule. No tattoos until you're eighteen."

"You're such a downer," Kaylee whines.

"Trust me, you'll thank me later for not doing it."

"Doubtful," Kaylee grumbles.

"Look at the bright side, I just saved a unicorn from being killed." Kinsley cackles.

"Whatever."

I should probably make my presence known, but I don't. It's obvious Kinsley has this under control. She's been officially appren-ticing with me for the last three years since she graduated from high school, and this weekend is her first time taking clients on her own. I'm so damn proud of her.

A memory surfaces from the past, when Kinsley was six years old and decided she wanted to become a tattoo artist.

"Dad! Look what I drew." I'll never get tired of hearing that three letter word come out of her mouth. She hands me a drawing of two stick figures with the words Dad and Kinsley over them. They're holding hands.

"Where's your mom and Kaylee?" I ask.

"At home. This is me and you." She points to the square behind us. "And that's Forbidden Ink. My teacher told us to draw what we want to be when we get bigger. I want to tattoo people like you." Kinsley beams up at me with pride, and my heart expands. "When I'm bigger, will you show me how?"

Her eyes are wide with hope, as if there's even a small chance I won't give her anything she wants.

"How about I show you now?"

She gasps. "Really?"

"Sure."

Kinsley's spending the day with me at the shop because there's no school and her mom is home with Kaylee. She's only four weeks old and sleeps a lot, and Kinsley gets bored hanging out at home, so occasionally she comes in with me while I tattoo. She's a great little assistant.

I grab my gun and hand her gloves to put on. Grabbing the black ink, I open the cap. I place my arm on the counter and Kinsley climbs onto the chair.

"You're going to let me tattoo you?" she squeals.

"Yep! But you can't tattoo anyone else until you're licensed."

"Okay!"

I walk her through how to hold the gun, turn it on and off a few times so she can see how it feels, then let her try it for herself. When she tells me she's ready, I point to a small spot on my arm. "Go ahead and give it a go."

"What should I tattoo?" she asks, her voice full of excitement. "A skull or a soccer ball?"

"How about we start small," I suggest. Anything too big will probably leave a hole in my arm.

"Okay," she says softly, "I'll draw a heart because I love you."

She presses the button to start the gun and dips the tip into the black ink. Slowly, she draws a heart on my skin. Tiny beads of red surface. When she's done, she jumps down and grabs a paper towel, wetting it with water and soap, like she's seen us do a million times. She drags the paper towel across my skin, exposing the new black heart tattoo.

"I did it!" she squeals.

"You did. One day you're going to make a great tattooist."

Sneaking out the back, I head over to the high school. I spot my gorgeous wife snapping pictures of Barrett from the stands. Next to her is Skyla and her husband, Sean, who are also here to watch their son, Victor, play since he's on the same team as Barrett.

"Hey you," Quinn says with a smile. "They just started." She leans over with the intention of giving me a quick kiss, but I grab her face with my hands and deepen it further, needing to taste her and feel her. I don't think there will ever come a time when I've had enough of her.

"What was that for?" She giggles, tilting her head to the side slightly.

"Thank you."

"For what?" Her brows knit together in confusion.

"For realizing we were meant to be together. For spending your life with me. For finally seeing yourself through my eyes."

FINDING OUR TOMORROW

IMPERFECT LOVE SERIES: BOOK FIVE

ONE

Jax
    Present Day

"WHAT'S ALL THIS FOR?" I step into the condo I share with my longtime girlfriend, Willow, and find rose petals and candles scattered all over the place. When I glance at our coffee table, two champagne flutes are sitting on top with a bucket of ice and a bottle of champagne next to it. I was only gone for a couple hours, having a beer with my brother, Jase.

Willow steps forward, and her lips curl into a shy smile, a look I rarely see on her face. My girlfriend isn't shy by any means. With her midnight black hair that has different colors running through it —this month it's blue, that same blue that matches her eyes—tattoos covering most of her arms, perky tits, and tanned, toned legs for days, she's sexy as fuck. And with her *I don't give a fuck* attitude, she's sassy as hell. With her heart that beats outside of her chest, she's giving and loving and selfless. But she isn't shy. So when she hits me with that rare smile, I know something is up.

"Today is our ten-year anniversary," she tells me, her shy smile splitting into a wide grin. I give her a shocked look. Not because I don't know what today is, but because Willow Montgomery doesn't celebrate anniversaries. So the fact that she's standing before me, suddenly celebrating our anniversary, definitely has my interest piqued.

"It is," I agree. "An entire decade of getting to spend every day with you."

Willow's eyes fill with tears, and my thoughts jump to a worst-case scenario. "Baby, what's wrong?" Whatever it is, we'll deal with it together. My girlfriend may live for today, but she knows I'm always going to be right by her side, living for today with her.

"Nothing is wrong," she says, taking another step forward. "I'm just...I'm kind of nervous."

Pulling her into my arms, I plant a kiss on her forehead. She smells like the lotion she puts on every morning after she gets out of the shower. Light Blue by Dolce & Gabbana. It's sweet and feminine and I could recognize the scent anywhere. "You're going to have to help me out here," I murmur. "You were just smiling and now you're in tears."

Willow pulls back and wipes the tears from her eyes. "Jax, you are everything to me. You aren't just my boyfriend, you're my best friend, my other half."

My heart pounds against my ribcage with every word she speaks. "I feel the same way."

She pulls something out of the front pocket of her jeans. A ring... No, not *a* ring. Two rings. "I'm ready, Jax," she says through her watery smile. "I'm ready to marry you. To spend the rest of my life as your wife. Jaxson Crawford, will you marry me?"

My gaze flits between Willow's hope-filled eyes and the two rings she's holding. The one I bought for her ten years ago, and a simple silver band that I'm assuming is meant for me. I want so badly to say yes, but before I do, I need to know one thing. "What's changed your mind?"

Smiling, Willow places the rings on the coffee table and grabs a small, square black book. "This."

She hands it to me, and I turn to the first page and then the second and then the third. Each page is filled with pictures of us, of our life, starting with the first night she took pity on me and took me out with her.

TWO

*J*AX
  Ten years ago

"I'M OUT, BRO," Jase, my younger brother, says, popping his head into my workstation. While I'm waiting for my last appointment of the day to arrive, I'm working on a sketch for another client.

"Already?" I glance over at the clock and see it's only six o'clock.

"Promised Celeste and Sky I would pick up dinner and bring it to them. They're getting ready for that fashion show coming up. You want to come over for dinner?"

He asks the same question every day, and every day I tell him the same thing. "I'm good, bro. Go be with your family."

For as far back as I can remember, Jase, our sister Quinn, and I have lived together. Whether it was in North Carolina where we grew up, or here in New York, where we've been living for the last several years. We've always stuck together. Until recently, when both my siblings moved out and in with their significant others. It's weird living on my own. I'm almost forty years old and I've never had a place to myself. I imagined the townhouse would become a bachelor pad. I would throw parties every night and have women over without having to worry about the innocent ears of my niece hearing anything. But after a couple months, the partying got old, and the mindless sex got even older.

As much as I would love to spend time with Jase or Quinn, I don't want to impose. They moved out for a reason. To start their own lives. It's not like I don't see them every day. Quinn helps out occasionally by running the front desk at the tattoo shop Jase and I own: Forbidden Ink. And since I work with Jase at said tattoo shop, I see him every day.

"You sure?" he asks.

"Yeah, man. I'm going to head home after my appointment and get some shut eye. Late night, last night." Late night watching reruns of Breaking Bad on Netflix...

"All right, well, if you change your mind..."

"Yeah, yeah, I know. Get out of here, and make sure you give my favorite niece a kiss."

"She's your only niece," Jase volleys.

"For now." I laugh. Celeste recently found out she's pregnant and they're expecting twins. Nobody knows the sexes yet.

A little while later, my client shows up. She's a twenty-five-year-old breast cancer survivor and gets a pink ribbon with a quote down the side of her ribcage. By the time I finish and clean up, it's just after eight o'clock.

Gage, a tattooist who works here, and Evan, who answers the phones while apprenticing with us, stop by to let me know they're leaving for the night.

When I unplug my phone from the dock and switch off my music, I hear the soft sound of pop music playing somewhere. Willow must still be here. She's the only one of us who listens to that girly shit.

Walking down the hall, I check her workstation, but it's empty. I follow the music, until I find where it's coming from. The bathroom.

As I raise my fist to knock on the door, her voice rises several octaves as she sings completely out of tune with the singer. The horrible sound has me laughing out loud.

"Hey, Beyoncé." I bang on the door. "I think you're late for your performance."

I'm still laughing when the door swings open and Willow steps out, dressed in a pair of skintight dark blue jeans with more holes up and down her legs than there is material, and a blood red shirt that covers her tits, but exposes her entire midriff, showing off her pierced belly button. Her black hair is straight and bits of hot pink peak out from underneath.

She's only been working here for a short time, but I've never seen her dressed in anything but our business shirts, which cover her completely, and regular jeans or shorts.

"Like what you see?" She winks dramatically. My eyes meet hers, and I can't help but stare at the gorgeous woman in front of me. Her face is usually free of makeup, and she always looks pretty, but with whatever she's done to her eyes and lips, she looks fucking hot as hell. And older. That's the problem. The makeup and clothes make her look older.

"Playing dress up?" I joke, trying to play off how attracted I suddenly am to her.

"Funny." She rolls her eyes. "Can you do me a favor and button the back of my top?" She turns around and lifts her silky hair, exposing her slim neck and artfully tattooed back. I step toward her and quickly button the couple of buttons she couldn't reach, making sure not to touch her in any way.

"Thanks." She turns back around, hitting me with a bright smile. "So, what are you up to tonight?"

She sits on the couch and grabs the tallest pair of black fuck-me heels I've ever seen, slipping each one onto her slender feet. Jesus, I need to stop eye-fucking her. She's ten years younger than me and I'm her boss.

"Jax?" she prompts. Shit, she asked me a question.

"Umm... just going to watch Netflix." I flinch as the words come out. Can I sound any more like a loser?

She laughs. "It's Friday night and you're a single guy. Netflix is for teenagers who need an excuse to make out, or old people who have nothing better to do with their time."

"I am old," I say dryly, which causes her to laugh harder.

"What are you, like thirty-five? That's hardly old." She sets her foot down and stands.

"Thirty-seven," I correct her. "And I've done my fair share of partying. I guess I'm just over that scene."

"Have you ever been to Flora's?" She steps towards me, so close I can smell her perfume. It's sweet and soft. Delicate.

"Jax." She smirks, knowing I'm all caught up in how she looks and smells. "Flora's?"

"No." I shake my head. "Never heard of it."

"Come with me tonight."

"Ehh..."

"Come on." She smacks my bicep playfully. "You're too young to be home on a Friday night... or any night for that matter. Life's too short." She hits me with her pearly-white smile. "Please."

I don't think it would matter what she's asking me for. Dressed like that, smelling like that, smiling like that. I would say yes to anything she asks.

"Sure. I think I have an extra shirt in the office."

THREE

Jax

WE GET to the club and Willow seems to know everyone. She doesn't wait in the long as hell line like everyone else, and the bouncer not only lets us in, but tells her to head up to the VIP section. When we get to the roped off area, there are about two dozen people drinking and dancing. They greet Willow, all wanting to hug her and offer her a drink. I watch quietly as she laughs and flirts with everyone who approaches her. She doesn't do it in a tease sort of way, but more of a friendly, she just loves everyone sort of way.

She introduces me to everyone as her friend, then hands me a shot. "To today!" she yells over the music.

"To today," I agree. We both down our shots and then she hands me another and then another. Her friends join in, and we spend the next however long drinking and laughing. Willow does most of the talking and I find myself just listening. Soaking in every word she speaks. She talks about work, the different customers she had. About visiting the Farmer's Market this weekend. One of her friends complains about a co-worker and Willow tells her not to stress. Life is too short.

When she catches me watching her, she asks, "What?"

"Nothing. I'm just enjoying learning about you," I tell her honestly. She's the most care-free person I've ever met.

"And what did you learn?" she asks.

"You like to have fun."

She smiles. "We only have one life, Jax. We have to make it count."

After downing another shot, she pulls her phone out and insists we take a selfie together. Then she grabs my hand and guides me onto the dance floor.

"I love this song." She smiles wide and wraps her arms around my neck. I'm not sure what this song is or who sings it, but neither matters as Willow separates her thighs and grinds down on my leg. My hands find the curves of her hips as she shimmies up and down to the beat of the music.

She throws her head back, and her fingers tighten around my neck to hold her up. My eyes go straight to her slender throat, and my only thought is what her skin would taste like. It's glistening from the hot club and the dancing and drinking, and I wonder if I licked down her throat if it would taste salty, or if it would taste sweet like she smells. *Probably a mixture of both.*

But before I can find out, Willow's head snaps up and her blue eyes meet mine. Her lips curl into a beautiful smile before she turns her body around, giving me her back. Without missing a beat, her arms go over her head and she shakes her ass. Briefly, I wonder if she has any idea that I'm not dancing, but instead standing here like a horny teenager, watching the show.

Willow backs her ass up and hits my crotch, and it's then I realize I'm sporting a semi. Fuck, there's no way she didn't feel that. Her face turns slightly so our eyes meet once again, and she hits me with the sexiest smirk, telling me she definitely felt it.

She backs up until our bodies are flush and then she grinds her ass against the bulge in my pants. Her arm comes up and hooks around my nape, and she pulls my face forward. Her soft lips find my ear, and she murmurs, "Let's take this elsewhere."

Jesus, fuck. I want to say yes, but I can't. It's one thing to drink and dance with her. It's another thing to fuck her.

"Don't do that," she says. She turns back around, so our mouths are only inches apart. "Don't overthink this."

"I'm your—" I attempt to argue, but her tongue darts out and traces my bottom lip, effectively shutting me up. Her tongue then moves to my top lip before it slips past my parted lips. Stroking, teasing, caressing. Our kiss deepens. My hands find her ass, and then I'm lifting her into the air.

"Bathroom," she murmurs across my mouth.

I do as she says as she continues to kiss me with abandon.

I don't think about how crowded this place is, or who's watching us. I don't consider how many people will be in said bathroom, or how this is going to work. I'm too lost in Willow and her kisses and touches.

When we get to the bathroom, there are a couple of women, but neither of us pay any attention to them. We enter the handicap stall and Willow drops to her feet. She unbuttons her pants and pushes them, along with her underwear, down.

My mind is telling me this is wrong, that I should stop this. At least take her home and do this on a bed, but Willow's voice pushes my thoughts away when she turns around, slaps her hands against the bathroom stall wall, and says, "Fuck me, Jax. Please."

I unzip my pants and pull my hard cock out, stroking it a few times. Willow's luscious ass is perked up in the air, and she shakes it back and forth, silently begging me to take her.

"Willow, are you sure?" I hate that I'm being such a downer here but fuck, I'm in over my head with this woman. People talk about hooking up in bathrooms, but I've never seen or done it. My alcohol-filled brain is telling me to do it, but the adult in me is telling me this is irresponsible as hell and I'm going to regret it when the alcohol is out of my system.

"Jax, now," Willow growls, pushing the responsible part of my brain aside.

As I'm lining up the head of my cock with her entrance, there's a knock on the door. "Hurry up! I need to go pee!" a woman screeches. And just like that, the moment is gone. I pull back and Willow turns around with the most adorable pout on her lips.

"Jax." Her brows furrow as she watches me tuck my rock-hard dick into my pants the best I can.

"I can't do this," I tell her. "Not here...not like this." I step towards her and bend at the waist so I can pull her pants up. She swats my hands away and finishes herself.

"Come home with me," I whisper against her ear.

She glances up at me and shakes her head. "No, I don't know what I was thinking." She closes her eyes.

"Willow." When I say her name, her eyes flutter back open. "I'm sorry..."

"You have nothing to apologize for." She plasters on a fake smile. "You're my boss and it would've been a mistake."

I nod in agreement, but my insides are tightening in disagreement. "Why don't I walk you home?"

She shakes her head. "That's okay. I'm a big girl." She winks, but it's not carefree like before.

We exit the stall, and a couple of women gape at us, thinking we just hooked up in there.

Instead of going back up to the VIP area, Willow heads to the exit, and I follow.

"Please let me walk you home," I insist. I'm not sure where she lives, but it's late, and nowhere in New York is really safe at this time.

"Jax, really. I'm fine." Her voice is rough in frustration.

As much as it kills me to let her walk away, I don't want to piss her off, so I tell her okay and that I'll see her tomorrow at work.

And then I watch her walk down the street, wait a minute so she doesn't know I'm following her, and then head in the same direction. She walks fast as hell, especially for a woman who's been drinking and is walking in tall as hell heels, but I easily keep up. Making sure to remain far enough back, so she won't see me, I follow her several blocks. When she stops at a quickie mart, I hide in the shadows. A few minutes later, she comes out with a large duffel bag over her shoulder and continues on her way.

She walks a few more blocks and then she stops in front of an abandoned building. Pulling a blanket out of the duffel bag, she shakes it out, spreads it out in front of her, and then drops down onto it. She fluffs the bag to use it as a pillow, then lays her head on it.

What the fuck is going on? I wait for her to jump up and tell me she knows I've been following her. Tell me she's joking and laugh in my face. But she doesn't. Her eyes close and her breathing evens out. As I watch her sleep, it hits me that Willow is homeless.

When I met her, she was drawing pictures in Central Park along the bridge. She was dressed in a ripped T-shirt and jean shorts, and I could see a couple of tattoos peeking out. She was laughing with a couple who were checking out her artwork, and I was immediately drawn to her. I could tell right away she was talented and knew she would make a great addition to the shop. When I asked if she could tattoo, she told know me she would love to learn, so I taught her. She caught on quickly and has been working at Forbidden Ink ever since. So, I know she makes enough money to survive. To live in an apartment.

She mentioned a while back that she and her boyfriend broke up, but I didn't think much of it. Is it possible he kicked her out? But then why wouldn't she just get another place? It doesn't make any sense.

Well, whatever the story is, there's no way I'm going to let her sleep out here all night. Not wanting to startle her, I call out her name. She squirms but doesn't wake up, obviously already in a deep sleep.

"Willow, wake up," I say louder. This time her eyes open. It takes her a second, but once she realizes she isn't dreaming, her body pops up and she looks around.

"Let's go," I tell her before she can even think of an excuse or a lie to feed me.

She considers arguing, I can see it in her eyes, but she must realize I'm not playing around, because she lets out a deep sigh, shoves her blanket into her duffle bag, and then stands.

FOUR

WILLOW

WHILE WE WALK to the subway station, Jax doesn't say a word, and I greatly appreciate it. I've already made enough of an ass of myself for one night. When we get on the subway, he continues with his silent treatment, but the longer he doesn't talk, the more I just want to get the conversation over with. Like ripping the band-aid off. Why prolong it? We get off in Cobble Hill and walk a couple blocks through a small suburbia neighborhood lined with cute brick townhouses.

When we arrive at his place, he unlocks the door and holds it open for me to walk through first. It's fall in New York, so the temperatures tend to fluctuate. This week has been on the cooler side, but when I step into Jax's house, it's nice and warm. I take a look around and find the place to be neat and tidy. The furniture is nice, nothing fancy, but it's all good quality.

"The bedrooms and bathrooms are upstairs," he says, walking toward the stairs. I follow him up and he stops at the first door. "This is the guest bedroom and it has its own bathroom. It's stocked with toiletries and towels are under the sink."

He steps back to walk away, but I stop him. "Don't you want to talk about it?" After thinking about it, I'm going with ripping the band-aid off.

"About what? The fact that I almost fucked my employee in the bathroom of a club? My employee who is over ten years younger than me." His eyes shoot to the ceiling like he's praying to God to help him before he looks back down at me. "Or the fact that you've been living on the streets for God knows how long and haven't said a word to any of us?"

"All of the above." I shrug, unsure what to say.

"I'm tired, still half-buzzed, and it's late..." He glances at his cell phone. "Or I guess early since it's almost four in the morning. We have to be at the shop in a few hours, so how about we shower, get some sleep, and we can talk in the morning."

"Okay." I give him a half-smile, hoping to knock his evident frustration down a few notches. "I'll see you in the morning—er, in a few hours."

Closing the door behind me, I strip out of my clothes and head straight for the shower. It's been a few months since I've had a shower that's not in a women's shelter, and I find myself relaxing under the hot spray until the water goes cold. Hopefully Jax already finished his shower. I grab a fluffy towel and dry off, then grab my pajamas to change into.

Since I have a couple hours before we leave, I wonder if Jax would mind if I do a load of laundry. I can do it at the laundry mat, but they're freaking gross. Tiptoeing over to the room I saw him go into, I knock lightly in case he's already asleep. If he is, I'll just find the washer and dryer and do a load before he wakes up. I doubt he'll even notice.

"Come in," he calls out. My hand grasps the knob to open the door when he pulls the door at the same time. My body stumbles forward, and just before I think I'm going to faceplant, Jax catches me in his strong arms.

"Jesus, you okay?" He chuckles, the sound reverberating through my body and going straight to the apex of my thighs.

"Yeah." I laugh softly. "I didn't realize you were opening the door."

"Everything okay?" He looks me up and down.

"Yeah, I was just wondering if you would mind if I used your washer and dryer to do a load. I'll have it done before we leave in the morning."

Jax's jaw ticks and I worry I've overstepped. He's already been kind enough to offer me a bed and a shower. "You know what... never mind..." I turn to leave when he grabs my wrist, twirling me back around.

"Are you homeless?" he asks, even though he already knows the answer.

"Yes."

"For how long?"

"For about a year now."

"Fuck," he curses under his breath. "Why haven't you said anything?"

"You're my employer. It's not your problem."

"I'm also your friend." His eyes bore into mine.

"Not really," I say honestly. I've never been one to beat around the bush. "I mean you're nice and I love working for you, but we aren't friends."

When his brows furrow, I add, "Where did I live before I became homeless?" When he doesn't answer, I continue. "What's my favorite color? My favorite food? Where am I from? What's my ex-boyfriend's name?"

Jax's shoulders slump, and I give him a reassuring smile. "I'm not saying all that to blame you. I'm just explaining that we aren't friends. I used to have friends... when I lived in Michigan, where I was born and raised. Then I met Henry, and after dating for a few months, he got a promotion and was transferred to New York, so I moved with him. The friends I made here were all his, and when we broke up, they remained his."

"Why didn't you move back home?"

"Both of my parents died from cancer. My mom from breast cancer, and a few years later, my dad from colon cancer."

"What about all those people at the club?"

"Those aren't friends. They're acquaintances. I don't do friends, Jax." Stepping out of his grip, I head back down the hallway to grab my dirty clothes. "Is the washer upstairs?"

"Down," he says. I jump when his voice comes out right behind me.

"You can go to sleep."

"Thanks for letting me know," he replies dryly, following me down the stairs.

After I throw my clothes in, along with some detergent, I close the lid, then go straight to the kitchen to get a glass of water. When I can't find the cups, Jax opens the correct cabinet and hands me a glass.

"Thanks."

"Why are you homeless?" he asks, settling his back against the edge of the counter.

Not wanting his pity, I consider lying to him, but something tells me he's not going to stop until he gets the truth out of me. He already stalked my ass 'home.'

"Long story short, a year ago, the gynecologist found cancer cells in my uterus. I could've gone through chemo and all that, but instead I chose to get a hysterectomy. Henry didn't agree with it because it meant we could never have kids. When I told him kids were no longer in my plan, and neither was marriage, he dumped me. Since the apartment was his, I had to leave."

Jax's eyes go wide, and his arms which are crossed over his chest, flex. "When you said you needed a couple weeks off to go on vacation you were having fucking major surgery?"

I nod.

"My insurance covered a portion of it, but not all, and then there were follow up visits and radiation and the medications. Unlike the hospital which allows you to make payments, the private facilities require payment at the time of visit."

"Jesus, Willow." Jax sighs. "You should've said something. Are you okay now?"

"I am. I'm done with all the treatments and as of right now, I'm cancer free. I'm saving for a place now."

Jax stares at me for several beats before he says, "You're staying here."

"Tonight?" I ask, confused.

"No, indefinitely." I open my mouth to argue, but he shakes his head. "I have a three-bedroom, three-bathroom place to myself. I'm not taking no for an answer." He lifts a brow, daring me to argue.

"Okay, on two conditions."

"You're giving me conditions when I'm offering you my home to live in for free." He throws his head back in a laugh, and I find myself smiling at how sexy he looks when he laughs.

"My first condition..." I raise my voice so he can hear me over his laughter, and he stops. "My first condition is I pay for half of the bills."

Jax is already shaking his head. "Not happening. Next condition."

I huff in frustration. "My other condition is that you're not allowed to get attached to me. It's inevitable we'll hook up, and I have no doubt it will be hot as hell, but that's all it can ever be. No friendship, no relationship."

Jax stares at me for several seconds before he busts out laughing again. "Are you serious right now?"

"Yes, very." I give him a dry look, so he knows I don't think what I said is funny, nor do I think it's necessary he laughs at what I said.

"Oh, Willow..." Jax steps forward. "One, we're not hooking up. In case you forgot, I stopped it from happening tonight, and two, we are going to be friends. I know exactly what you're doing, and unlike your piece of shit ex, I'm not going to allow it to happen."

When I give him a *what the hell are you talking about* look, he says, "Your mom and dad died from cancer. Then you got cancer. Now you don't want marriage or kids. You don't want friends. You would rather be homeless than lean on other people..." He steps towards me. Out of instinct, I step back, but the kitchen is small and my back hits the edge of the counter.

Jax presses his body against mine and pushes a wet strand of hair behind my ear. "You're pushing everyone away, Willow. If you make no connections, nobody can mourn your loss if you die."

I swallow the boulder-size lump in my throat because he's right and we both know it. Breast cancer wasn't the first cancer my mom was diagnosed with. It was just the one that killed her. Then there's my aunt who died from ovarian cancer, and my uncle who died from brain cancer...

"I'm not letting you push me away," Jax says, his voice filled with conviction. "You're going to live here as long as you need to, and I'm going to be your friend. When you need someone to lean on, I'll be here. Got it?"

My head is telling me to run. Run far and run fast. But my heart, the organ that's craving a connection I've denied myself for too long, is begging me to stay, and like the fool I am, I go with my heart. "Got it."

We head back upstairs, but before I can enter my own room, Jax's hand lands on my shoulder. "You've been alone long enough, Willow. Why don't you come sleep in my bed with me?"

Wordlessly, I allow him to take my hand in his and guide me down the hall to his room. We both climb into his bed and shuffle under the covers. At first, it's awkward, especially since not even a few hours ago we were very close to fucking. But then Jax lifts his arms and scoops up my body, dragging me closer to him. My arm drapes across his torso and my face snuggles into the curve of his shoulder. His fingers run up and down my spine and my eyelids begin to flutter closed. For the first time in too long, I not only feel connected to someone, but I feel safe.

FIVE

Jax

WHAT KIND of fucking man kicks a woman out when she's already at her lowest point? When she's just found out she has cancer and is scared for her life? A selfish piece of shit, that's who. I never met Willow's ex, but if I ever find out who he is and see him somewhere, you better fucking believe I'll beat the shit out of him.

I hate that Willow went through having cancer, having surgery, and then all of the treatments alone. Looking back at the last year, it all now makes sense. So many times, I would find her at the shop early in the morning. She was given a key for early appointments, and I would bet she's used the bathroom to rinse off and brush her teeth. After she came back from her vacation, she didn't look well rested at all. Not like you should look when you've just spent weeks relaxing and enjoying your time off. She looked tired, but I didn't even think to ask questions. She's always kept to herself. Sure, we all get along. She's one of us. But looking back, she's always kept everyone at a safe distance. Close enough for us all to know she's a good person, but far enough away that we never really got to know the parts she chose to keep hidden.

Tonight, at the club, she laughed and joked with everyone. They all knew her name, and it was clear she got along with every- one, but she never actually conversed with anyone. She uses them to have a good time. To have a connection without actually connecting. She's so scared of dying, she won't let anyone in.

"When I told him that kids were no longer in my plan, and neither was marriage, he dumped me."

Any smart person can see that Willow was pushing him away in hopes that he would pull her closer. She needed someone strong to hold her tight when she felt like she was drifting away, but instead he cut the rope and let her go. Because he's weak and doesn't deserve her.

My alarm buzzes letting me know it's time to get up. I have an appointment coming in first thing this morning. Willow's side of the bed is empty, so she must have gotten up earlier.

After showering and getting dressed, I head downstairs. The aroma of coffee wafts in the air, and when I reach the kitchen, I find Willow standing in front of the machine with two cups of coffee in her hands.

"Morning," she says, handing me one of the cups. "Black, just like you like it."

"Thank you." I take a much-needed sip.

While we drink our coffees in silence, I take a moment to check out Willow. She looks the same as she did yesterday before she changed into her club clothes. She's wearing a black Forbidden Ink T-shirt, ripped jeans, and a pair of Converse. On the outside, she looks like she's always looks. But after everything she's told me, it feels like I'm seeing her in a new light. She's no longer the sweet, delicate woman I always assumed her to be. She's strong and determined and kind of badass. She hides her insecurities and only allows the world to see what she wants them to see. And instead of allowing herself to wallow in what she's been through, she chooses to live life for today. She laughs and smiles and never lets anything bring her down. She may be ten years younger than me, but with her parents' deaths and having to face cancer on her own, she's far more mature than other women her age.

And then it hits me. I told Willow I wanted to be her friend, but the truth is I want to be more than that. I want to be the man she turns to, leans on, depends on. I want to be the one she lives her todays with. But more than that, I want to be the man who shows her how to find her tomorrow.

"Your face looks like you're thinking so hard you're going to explode," Willow jokes.

"I was." I laugh. "What do you say after work tonight we grab dinner and a movie?"

"You were thinking that hard about asking me out on a date?" She raises a single brow in question.

I want to tell her everything that was really going through my head, but I can already tell Willow is the type of woman to spook easily. I told her I would be her friend, and I'm going to be just that, and over time, once she knows I'm not going anywhere, I'll show her that I not only want her today, but her tomorrow as well.

"Not a date," I correct her, so she won't have an excuse to say no. "Just two friends going to get something to eat and see a movie together."

She rolls her eyes, but when a hint of a smile splays across her face, I know she's going to say yes. "Okay."

———

THE DAY CRAWLS by and I know it's because I'm looking forward to taking Willow out tonight. Lunch finally rolls around and Evan orders subs from the deli next door. Since Willow and I don't have clients at the moment, she eats with me in the office.

"What movie do you want to see?" I ask her, pulling up the listings on my phone.

"What is there?"

"Romantic comedy, action, horror..." I flip through the different movies. "*The Breakfast Club* is playing too."

"What's that?"

My finger stills and I glance up at her. "You don't know what *The Breakfast Club* is?" And then I remember she's ten years younger than me. "*Pretty In Pink*?" She shakes her head. "*Grease*?" Another shake of her head. "*Stand By Me*?" She shakes her head. "*Sixteen Candles*...every girl has seen that damn movie."

"Nope, haven't seen any of those."

"All right, that's it." I click on the movie and place an order for two tickets. "Your movie education begins tonight with *The Breakfast Club*."

Her smile is wide when she says, "I can't wait."

Jase leaves around three, and then Gage leaves shortly after. Evan stays until around five, when I tell him I'll handle the phones since I don't have any more appointments today. Willow finally comes out of her workstation a little after six. The guy she tattooed is grinning ear-to-ear and talking her ear off about what he plans to get next.

"Everything good?" I ask him as he pulls his credit card out of his pocket to pay.

"Yeah." His eyes stay trained on Willow. "That woman is seriously talented."

"That she is," I agree, pulling up his appointment in the computer, so I can find how much he owes.

Willow points to his name, and when I look up, I notice she's leaning over my shoulder. Her shirt is a V-neck, and her ample cleavage is peaking out of the top. My eyes flit over to her client, who is zeroed in on her tits as well.

"Willow, why don't you go clean up your station while I check this guy out? That way we can leave to go to dinner. We don't want to be late for the movie."

She stands up straight, and in my peripheral vision, I see she's looking at me like I'm crazy, and maybe I am, but I'm not about to sit here and watch this fucker eye-fuck her.

"Thank you for your business," she tells the guy. "Here's my card for when you're ready to schedule your next appointment."

"Does it have your personal number on it?" the guy asks.

His card gets approved, and I hand him his receipt so he can sign it. "No, it's the business number because we're professionals here and don't date clients," I say as I drop a pen onto the receipt for him to use.

The guy signs his name, leaving Willow a decent tip, and takes his card. "Well, if you change your mind—"

I don't let him finish whatever he's about to say. "She won't."

The guy looks over at Willow, probably hoping she'll correct me, but when she doesn't, he just nods and then exits the shop.

"What the hell was that for?" Willow hisses, getting into my face once the door is closed and locked. "I'm pretty sure I have a voice, which means I can speak for myself." She pokes the front of my chest with her pink-painted fingertip that matches the streaks in her hair.

I scoff. "That guy was practically stripping you naked with his eyes."

"And he also tipped me forty percent," she volleys.

"Your work speaks for itself. There's no reason to flirt to get more money. This is a tattoo shop, not a strip club." I eye her shirt, and she glances down. When she looks back up, heat is practically steaming from her ears. Her eyes glaring daggers my way. "It's no different than when you guys let women flirt with you. It keeps them happy and gets you a good tip." She's not wrong, but I'm not about to tell her that. I'm too jealous thinking of all the men who probably ask Willow out. She's young, tatted up, pierced, and beautiful.

Without thinking about what I'm doing, I grip the back of her head and pull her face towards mine, claiming her lips. The kiss starts out soft and slow, but quickly progresses. Teeth clash, tongues duel. Willow's fingers quickly find the button to my jeans at the same time I'm yanking hers down her thighs. This is not how this was supposed to go. I was supposed to befriend her, show her I'm here for her.

Her tiny fingers wrap around my hard dick, and I groan into her mouth. Why is it all this woman has to do is touch me and all rational thought flies out the damn window?

Using my dick like it's a rope she can pull on, she guides us backwards until the back of her legs hit the couch. Needing to taste other parts of her, I wrap her hair in my fingers and tilt her head to the side. As I trail open-mouthed kisses down her slim neck, she strokes my dick. I focus on how sweet she tastes so I don't come in her hand. My nose sniffs her scent. It's sweet. The same perfume she always wears. I already know I'm fucking addicted.

My mouth descends to her collarbone, and I push her shirt and bra strap to the side so I can bite down on her shoulder. She moans in pleasure, so I bite harder.

Not liking her shirt in my way, I yank it up and over her head, then take a second to check out her perfect fucking tits. Scooping one out of her bra cup, I lift it to my mouth and wrap my lips around the pointed, pink nipple. Then I bite down on it. Hard. Willow groans, and her hand squeezes my shaft. *My girl likes it rough...*

"Do it again," she breathes.

Pulling her other tit out of its cup, I take both in my hands and squeeze them together. I can feel Willow's eyes on me. She's watching. Opening my mouth wide, I take both nipples into my mouth and suck on them. Willow squirms, wanting more. I'd bet my left nut, if I dipped my finger into her pussy, she would be dripping wet.

I suck on her nipples again, but this time I scrape my teeth across the hard buds.

"Jesus, Jax."

"I love your fucking tits," I growl just before I suck on them again.

"My turn," she murmurs. Before I can ask her what she means, she drops down onto the sofa, so her face is parallel with my dick.

She takes my entire length into her mouth until the tip of my dick hits the back of her throat.

"Willow, fuck. Wait..." I try to get her mouth off me. I'm going to shoot my load right down her pretty little throat. It's been too long since my dick's seen any action aside from my own hand.

She shakes her head and mumbles something with my dick still shoved down her throat, and the vibration sends me over the fucking edge. I watch as Willow swallows down every drop of my cum, then licks the head clean. With hooded eyes, she glances up at me shyly, and if I hadn't just come, I would be now.

Hating that she made me come before I pleasured her, I lift her and throw her onto the couch. Her back hits the leather, and she laughs at my caveman behavior.

"I'm supposed to be a gentleman," I growl, ripping each of her shoes off and then tugging her pants and underwear down her legs and onto the floor. When I drop my body on top of hers, she giggles, something I've never heard from her before. The sound does shit to me, hitting me in places I've never felt.

Taking her bottom lip between my lips, I suck it into my mouth then bite down on it. "A real gentleman always makes sure the woman is taken care of before he is." I kiss my way down her neck, over her breasts—only stopping long enough to give each nipple a lick—and down her belly. I stop when I spot a horizontal scar several inches below her belly button.

She tenses up. "That's from my hysterectomy," she admits.

I give it a kiss. "A beautiful battle wound," I murmur before I continue my descent. When I get to the hood of her neatly trimmed pussy, I give it a soft kiss. When I spread her thighs, I notice two things: one, she's just as I thought—wet as fuck. And two, her clit is pierced.

"Who did this?" I pinch the tight bud between my fingers. The thought of Gage or Evan seeing her sweet pussy has me seeing red.

"I had it done before I started working here."

Dipping my head between her legs, I suck the silver piercing into my mouth. Her back arches and she begs me to make her come.

Not wanting to make her wait any longer, I push two fingers into her pussy at the same time I flick her clit with my tongue. My fingers and mouth work in tangent—licking, fucking, sucking until Willow's body is trembling and she's screaming out my name.

Her hands find my hair and she tugs me against her pussy, grinding herself on my face until her orgasm has passed. When she lets go, I look up at her. Our eyes meet, and I swear my heart actually skips a fucking beat. Her lips are swollen from our kissing and her sucking my dick. Her nipples are red from me biting them. Her eyes are hooded over. Her hair is ruffled like she's just been fucked even though she hasn't been. She looks gorgeous, and my only thought is I need to make this woman mine.

Crawling up her body, I take her face between my hands, careful not to press my weight on top of her. As if she knows exactly what I'm thinking—or maybe she's just thinking the same thing I am —she reaches down and grabs my dick, guiding me into her.

Her pussy is wet and warm, and even though I just finished fingering her, my dick still stretches her out good. Our mouths fuse, and our tongues unite. With my arms on either side of her head, and my hands still cradling her face, I kiss and fuck Willow slowly, deeply. And unlike the frenzied way we both came a few minutes ago, this time we take our time. I make sure I don't come until Willow does, and only once she's moaning and her insides are clenching around my dick, do I let myself follow behind.

When we both come down from our orgasms, and our breathing has calmed, I pull out of Willow and roll to the side so we're both lying on the couch. It's not big, but that's okay because I like her body snuggled up against mine.

After a few minutes, Willow breaks the silence. "I think this was a mistake, Jax."

I take her face and tilt it up to look at me. "No, it wasn't."

"We were supposed to be friends," she says. If I thought she really meant that, I would backtrack and apologize, but I know why she's saying this—to push me away. She felt what I felt. The connection. I watched it happen with my brother and Celeste when they were younger, and then later when they found each other again, but I never thought it would happen to me. I had accepted some people just aren't meant to fall in love. I have my family, my friends, my tattoo shop. I thought I was okay being unattached. Until now. Until Willow.

It's only been twenty-four hours since she stepped out of the bathroom in the shop and opened my eyes, but I already know she's the one.

"Jax," she prompts when I don't say anything—too lost in my own thoughts. "This thing—"

Not wanting to hear every reason she's about to spew in an attempt to push me away, I cover her mouth with mine. We kiss for a brief moment before I pull back.

When she opens her mouth, I cover it with my hand. "No, I

have something I need to say and you're going to listen." Needing to look her in the eyes, I sit us up and pull her naked body onto my lap.

"This is probably the craziest thing I've ever said to anyone," I admit. "And I don't know what's come over me, but I know the words I'm about to speak are one hundred percent true, and I need you to know that." She nods once, but thankfully keeps quiet.

"Willow, you've been through so much, and you went through it all on your own. Your parents having cancer. Then you having to make the scary decision to have a hysterectomy when you found out you also had cancer. I don't blame you for pushing people away. I get it. You're scared. What if you get cancer again? What if someone else you love gets cancer?

"The thing about life is that nothing is a sure thing. We could walk out on to the sidewalk and get hit by a car. But that doesn't mean we live our life alone. You toasted last night to today, but are you even living for today if you don't let anyone in?"

Willow's face softens. She swallows thickly, but doesn't say anything, so I continue. "You don't have to be alone... *We* don't have to be alone. I'm almost forty years old. I've dated dozens of women, but I never saw a future with a single one of them. It wasn't until you stepped out of that bathroom that I realized it was because I was waiting for the right woman. You. I want to be the guy who you live today with. But more than that, I want to be the man who helps you find your tomorrow."

Willow gasps and a tear trickles down her cheek. "I don't know if I can give you that," she admits softly. "I'm so scared."

Framing her face in my hands, I give her a soft kiss to her lips. "How about you just give me today? We'll take it one day at a time, but instead of doing it alone, we'll do it together."

"Okay," she whispers. "Today. Together."

SIX

WILLOW

MY HEAD IS SPINNING with everything that's happened. Everything Jax has said. I don't know where up is at this point, but I think I'm okay with that. He wants to live in today with me, and if I'm honest, I really want to live in it with him. I was never one to believe in love at first sight, and I'm not saying I'm in love with him, plus, I've known him for two years... But there's something there between us, and I would be stupid to allow my fear of the future to stop us from seeing where things go. But first, he needs to know a couple of things.

"No marriage," I blurt out. When his brows furrow, I explain. "Marriage means forever. I can live in today with you, but marriage is off the table. So, if that's something you want, you need to know it's never going to happen."

Jax nods once. "I understand. No marriage."

"And I don't want any kids."

"There are other ways of having kids," he says softly.

"If you want kids, you need to walk away now," I tell him. "I don't want kids. Kids are attachments, dependents, and if something happens to one of us, they will be left without a mom or a dad. No kids. Ever." I choke out the last word.

Jax's gaze flits back and forth between my eyes, then he nods. "No kids. Just you and me. Today."

My chest tightens, squeezing my heart. "If you change your mind, it's okay," I tell him, needing him to know he always has an out. "I'll never change my mind, but if you do... if you want marriage and kids, all you have to do is tell me and I'll understand."

"Okay," he says, wrapping his arms around me. "If anything ever changes, I'll tell you." He presses his lips to mine. "We already missed the movie, but how about we get cleaned up, go grab some takeout, and we can go home and rent a movie."

"That sounds good."

When we get home, we both run upstairs to change out of our work clothes. When I go to enter my room, Jax stops me. "I want you in my room with me."

"Do you think we're moving too fast?" I ask, worried we're going to lose control and crash and burn.

"We're living in today," he says. "Today, I want you in my bed with me."

After moving my duffel bag of stuff into his room, we change and then go back downstairs to eat our Chinese and watch a movie. He doesn't find any of the movies he mentioned before, but he seems stoked when he apparently finds another movie he swears everyone needs to watch before they die: *Top Gun*.

While we watch the movie, Jax holds me close to him. We laugh at the funny stuff the guys do and say. Jax recites his favorite lines along with the guys when they say them, and then when Maverick and Charlie make love, he picks me up, and forgetting about the rest of the movie, carries me up to his room and makes love to me until we're both unable to move. And then once we're both completely sated, we fall asleep wrapped in each other's arms.

Today, I think to myself, *was a really good day*. And then for the first time in over a year, I allow myself to think about tomorrow.

SEVEN

THE FEEL of something rubbing against my dick has me waking up. I glance down and grin at the sight of Willow's perfect round ass currently rubbing up and down my dick. I take a moment to appreciate the sight in front of me. She's in a tiny black tank top and an even tinier black thong that leaves her plump butt cheeks completely exposed. She wears the same thing to bed every night—only the colors changing. And every morning she wakes me up in the same way. With her ass against my dick.

It's been a week since she's moved in here. A week of going to bed and waking up together. A week of flirting and fucking. A week of watching classic movies and getting to know each other. She asked that we keep what's happening between us quiet until we know for sure it's going somewhere. Today is a family barbecue, though, and there's no way I'm keeping what's happening between us quiet. It's been hard enough trying to keep my hands off her at work every damn day.

Pushing my boxers down, I release my dick so she's now rubbing skin to skin. My hand grips the curve of her hip, and she stills, knowing I'm now awake. Then she picks up her ministrations again. Rubbing along my length, which is hardening by the second.

My hand glides up her side and over her tit. I squeeze it hard, and she arches her back. I push the top of her tank down and pinch her nipple. Willow tries to remain quiet, but I catch the tiny sigh that escapes her lips, and it makes me smile.

I love her sighs and moans. Anything that tells me I'm making her happy or satisfied. Pleasuring her. Making her feel good. Until Willow, I never much cared about how a woman felt. They were all just warm bodies to sink into. And I never allowed them to spend the night. With my little sister living with me, and then my niece, I never wanted to set a bad example. And if I spent the night at their place, I'd usually leave before they woke up. But with Willow, all I want to do is spend my days and nights in bed with her.

I push Willow's hair out of the way, and then her thong, and then leaning forward, I spread her thighs enough that I can sink my dick into her from behind. She helps me by propping her foot up onto the side of my thigh. My lips trail kisses along her delicate neck and collarbone as I slowly move in and out of her.

Her soft sighs turn into loud moans. Her ass pushes back against my pelvis, and she meets me thrust for thrust. I grab ahold of her tit again, pinching and pulling on it, before I go lower, dipping my hand beneath the front of her underwear. She's soaking wet. I press my thumb against her swollen clit and massage circles. It only takes a few seconds before she explodes. Her pussy clamps down on my dick and her juices soak my fingers. Knowing she's come, I let myself come as well, shooting my hot seed deep into her.

For a brief moment, an overwhelming sense of sadness hits me, knowing that no matter what we do, no matter how many times I take Willow raw, she'll never be able to get pregnant. Not because I need a child of my own, but because I've seen the way she is around other people's kids, and I know she would make a damn good mom. And because of something out of her control, whether it's genetic or science or whatever, she's been robbed of that chance.

And I vow in this moment to make sure every today with Willow is filled with so much love and happiness, she'll never for a second miss what she can't have.

***

"SO, YOU AND WILLOW, HUH?" Jase asks, leaning up against the wall of his back patio. I was going to announce our being together at the barbecue, but then I got worried of how they might react. So, instead, I texted him and Quinn to let them know, so when we showed up, they wouldn't be shocked and make Willow feel uncomfortable. I should've known, though, they would have my back. We always have each other's back.

"I didn't see it coming," I admit, watching her, Celeste, and Skyla wading in the pool, probably gossiping about God knows what. "But she's fucking amazing."

"And young," he adds, his tone clear of judgment.

"Ten years younger, but she's been through a lot. She's probably more mature than the both of us combined," I joke. I'm glad when he doesn't ask me to explain because it's not my story to tell, and I won't tell Willow's story unless she tells me it's okay.

"If you're happy then I'm happy." He pats me on the shoulder. "I have to ask, though. What happens if it doesn't work out? How will that work with her being employed by us?"

"It will work out," I tell him. "She's the one, man. No doubt about it."

Jase's cell phone goes off and he pulls it out of his pocket to check it. "Quinn can't make it. Rick needs her at some function." He rolls his eyes.

"Leave her alone. She's in love, and they're still newlyweds."

"She can be in love, and they can be newlyweds... Doesn't mean she has to completely cut us out of her life."

"Dad, come in the pool!" Skyla yells.

"Duty calls," Jase says, shrugging his shirt off and running towards the pool. With his legs tucked under him, he jumps into the water, splashing all of the women. Celeste shrieks, Skyla laughs, and Willow splashes him back.

Willow's eyes meet mine and I nod toward the door. Her eyes light up, but she shakes her head, knowing exactly what I want. I nod and her grin gets wider. I make sure she's going to follow me in and then I head inside to wait for her.

When I hear her bare feet slapping against the marble floor, I reach out and grab her arm, pulling her into the bathroom and slamming the door behind us.

"Jax, we can't do this here!" She giggles.

"We can and we are." I lift her onto the edge of the sink, and waste no time pulling her wet bathing suit bottoms down her legs and pushing the tiny triangles covering her pert tits to the side, exposing her taut pink nipples. As I lean down, taking a nipple into my mouth, Willow's nails scrape along the scalp of my newly shaved head. I suck on her nipple then give the other one attention.

"Jax, you have to hurry up," Willow whines breathlessly. She's afraid of getting caught. While I don't really give a shit, I don't want her to feel uncomfortable.

I push my swim trunks down enough my dick pops out, hard and ready to be inside Willow's perfect pussy. She spreads her legs open for me, and I pull her to the edge of the counter. She grips my shaft and guides me into her. The feeling of her tight pussy wrapped around my dick is absolute fucking perfection. I could live inside this woman.

Once I'm completely seated in her, she wraps her arms around my neck and kisses me. Knowing we don't have much time, my thumb goes straight to her pierced clit. As I fuck her slow and deep, I massage circles along her swollen nub, once in a while tugging on the metal jewel. She's soaking wet, and I can feel her juices dripping down my balls.

"Oh my—" She begins to scream out her climax, and normally I love the way she lets go, but I know she'll regret it once she's come down from her orgasmic high. So, I fuse our mouths together, muffling her screams, as we both find our release.

EIGHT

Willow

I ALWAYS THOUGHT Jax was a boring old man. Sexy, but boring. But I was wrong. He's anything but boring. And he's an animal in bed. He loves to fuck me everywhere. All over the house, in his office at the shop, the bathroom in his brother and sister-in-law's house, and right now, in the movie theater.

"Baby," he whispers into my ear, "just pull that skirt up and sit on my dick."

I stifle a laugh, not wanting to draw attention to us. The theater is almost empty since we're seeing an older movie that's on its way out. There's only one younger couple in the middle and one more all the way in the front. Jax and I are sitting in the back corner. It's dark, and nobody would probably notice...

"C'mon," he purrs, running his hand up my thigh and under my skirt. He pushes the thin material of my panties to the side and inserts a couple of fingers inside me.

When I moan softly, he shakes his head and pulls his fingers out of me. I pout, wanting him back inside me. With those same fingers, he brings them up to my lips. "Shh... You have to be quiet." He rubs the pads of his fingers along my lips, wetting them with my juices, and I squirm in my seat.

"Come here, Willow," he whispers, and this time I do as he says.

He lifts my skirt up slightly and pushes my panties to the side, and when I sit in his lap, his dick impales me.

He must know I'm going to moan or scream because he covers my mouth with his hand. It's the hand that was just inside me and I can smell myself on his fingers. "You have to be quiet," he warns, just before he moves his hand and pushes into me from the bottom. I hold onto the armrests as Jax slowly thrusts in and out of me. My eyes flit between the two couples who oblivious to what's happening behind them and the front door, afraid an employee will walk in.

Jax reaches around and finds my clit. Using my juices to help create friction, he rubs my clit until I'm coming all over his fingers and dick. A couple more thrusts and I can feel his warmth shooting inside of me.

He lifts me from his lap, and I feel the cum trickling down the inside of my thigh. Grabbing a napkin, I wipe it up the best I can, then excuse myself to the bathroom to clean up better.

When I get back, Jax is watching the movie with a big grin splayed across his face. I sit back down, and he feeds me a piece of buttery popcorn. "What's happening in the movie?" I ask, trying to play catch up.

"I have no clue." Jax shrugs. "I guess we'll have to see it again."

NINE

WILLOW

PINK BALLOONS. Pink streamers. Pink cake. Pink cupcakes. Pink is everywhere. Which makes sense, since Celeste and Jase found out they're having twin girls. I've just never seen so much freaking pink in one place before.

I watch Celeste laugh at something one of her friends is saying. She throws her head back, so carefree and happy. She looks adorable, dressed in her designer pink and black dress, with her baby bump popping out. Jase is standing next to her, with his arms around her—one of his hands rubbing the bump. I swallow a bitter tasting lump in my throat. I'm happy for them, but it's still a hard reality to swallow that I'll never be pregnant. I'll never have my own baby to love. I've accepted my decision to never have kids, but it doesn't mean I don't occasionally feel sad or envious of others.

"I got you a cupcake," Jax says, sitting next to me on the couch. I jump slightly, lost in my own world, and he gives me a curious look. "You okay?" he asks, his tone laced with worry. Not pity, though, which is one of the reasons I love being with Jax. It's been four months since we've been together and not once has he ever looked at me with pity over my situation.

"Yeah," I tell him, taking the pink cupcake from him and giving him a fake smile.

He can see right through me though, and he frowns. One thing

I've learned about Jax is he doesn't like to see me upset, ever. When I don't give him anything more, choosing to focus on my cupcake instead, he doesn't say a word.

We spend the next hour talking to everyone we know. Quinn and her husband, Rick, show up late, and when he tells her they need to get going, Jax and I decide to leave as well. We say our good-byes to the happy couple and then walk outside with Quinn and Rick.

"How's the photography business going?" I ask Quinn as we walk down the sidewalk to their vehicle. She started a photography company a few years back and has been working hard at building it up.

Quinn glances back at Rick then says, "I've actually decided to put that on hold."

"What? Why?" Jax asks.

"Well, with Rick and I trying to have a baby, we felt it would be best if I stay home."

"*We* felt or he felt?" Jax accuses, glaring daggers at Rick, whose jaw tightens in anger. "You know you can have a family and work." He points towards the house. "Look at Celeste and Jase. They're doing it."

"What my wife and I decide is between us," Rick says, taking Quinn's hand in his. "We need to go."

Quinn opens her mouth to argue but then closes it. "Bye," she says softly.

"She's changed," I tell Jax, remembering how lively Quinn used to be. In the past, we'd been out a couple times together and she was the life of the party. Laughing and drinking and having a good time. Now, it's as if she's a scared turtle hiding inside her shell.

"Yeah," he agrees. "I just don't know what to do about it."

Taking my hand in his, we walk down the street to the subway station to go home. Jax is quiet the entire ride home, and once we're inside, he remains quiet.

"What's going on?" I ask him, climbing onto his lap and strad-dling his thighs.

His eyes meet mine and he frowns, almost as if he's warring with himself as to whether he should tell me what's on his mind.

"Talk to me," I insist. Jax has quickly become my go-to person and I would like to think he feels the same way. He's not just the guy I'm sleeping with. He's my best friend. The person I wake up with every morning and go to bed with at night. He's become a part of me.

"You could have what Celeste and Jase have," he says softly. It takes a couple times of repeating his words in my head to properly string them together. And when I do, I try to back up. But Jax wraps his arms around me and holds me close to him.

"Just hear me out," he says, but I'm already shaking my head. "Please," he begs.

"Jax..." I begin, but I'm stunned into silence when he reaches into his pocket and pulls out a diamond ring.

"I love you, Willow," he says, his eyes locked with mine. "We could get married and adopt a couple of kids. I make enough money. We could have a house full of kids if that's what you wanted."

A golf ball-sized lump blocks my airpipe. I can't talk or swallow or even breathe. I told him what I wanted and he said okay. So, why is he doing this now?

I scamper off his lap and stand, crossing my arms over my chest and willing myself not to cry. "I told you I didn't want to get married or have kids. You know this. Why are you doing this? You're ruining everything."

Jax leans forward, and gripping me by my hips, pulls me back into his lap. "Willow, I know what you said, but I saw the look in your eyes today. You can't tell me deep down you don't want that. The marriage, the kids, the family."

"Is that what you want?" I ask.

"I want whatever you want." He takes my face in his hands and kisses me softly before he pulls back. "This ring isn't a proposal."

When I give him a confused look, he continues, "I'm okay with what we have. I'm more than okay with it. I love you and I love our life together. But I need you to know that if you ever change your mind, if you ever want more, I want to be the one to give that to you."

He takes my hand in his and opens it up, so my palm is facing up. Then, he places the ring in the center. "I bought this ring because I want you to know I love our todays, but I also want your tomorrows. If you never decide to put it on, that's okay. I'll still be here. Always."

He pulls a chain out of the box and loops the ring through the chain. Then he puts it around my neck and links it together. He leans forward and kisses the ring, which is resting against my chest. "I love you, Willow."

Tears burn my eyelids and then fall down my cheeks. Jax uses his thumbs to wipe them up before he kisses me again. The kiss is intense, as if he's trying to convey through his lips and tongue how much he loves me. And I let him. I get lost in our kiss until our lips are numb and our bodies are entangled in one another. We shed our clothes until we're both naked and then Jax makes love to me, whispering how much he loves me and needs me. And it hits me that somewhere along the way I stopped living for today and started looking forward to tomorrow.

And with that thought, I want to run, because looking forward to tomorrow is scary. It means I'm feeling. Letting someone in. It means I'm setting myself and him up for heartbreak when something goes wrong.

As if he can feel me drifting, Jax pushes himself into me deeper, and his lips finds my ear. "You're not going anywhere, Willow. You're going to stay right here with me and live for today."

"Jax," I whimper, finding my release.

He grunts out his own release then stills. "No, baby. If we never get married, that's okay. I just need you to know that whatever you want, I will make sure you have it. Always."

He rolls off me and pulls me into his arms, my back against his chest. His scruffy face nuzzles into my neck, and when his breathing evens out, I know he's asleep.

I consider leaving. Running. And I should. He might not have officially proposed, but it's still a proposal. There's a ring hanging from my neck with the promise of tomorrow.

But instead of running, I snuggle back into Jax and close my eyes, needing him to hold me while I figure out what to do next.

TEN

Jax
   Present Day

"I REMEMBER when I gave you that ring." I find myself grinning at the memory. "I thought for sure I was going to wake up and you would be gone. But you weren't."

Willow smiles. "I considered it, but I loved you too much to let you go."

"But you didn't say yes," I say, remembering the next morning when we woke up.

ELEVEN

Jax
   Nine and a Half Years Ago

"MY ANSWER IS NO," Willow tells me, holding the ring and necklace out to me.

"I didn't ask you to marry me," I say, taking a bite of my cereal. "I told you when you want to, I'll be here. That ring is for you to wear around your neck as a reminder of how much I love you, and one day, if or when you're ready, I hope you'll wear it on your finger."

Willow's brows furrow. "I don't want to have kids, Jax."

"You already told me that." I take another bite of my cereal.

"I know, but I really meant it."

"Okay, then you meant it." I shrug.

"That means no kids for you as long as you're with me."

I know what she's trying to do. Push me away. But it's not going to happen. What Willow doesn't understand is that all I need in my life is her. I'm completely content to spend my days with—and in—her. Kids, no kids. Marriage, no marriage. It doesn't matter. I just needed her to know that whatever she wants, I want that too.

"Willow." I set my spoon down and look at her. "I already know all of this, and I don't care. As long as I have you, I'm good." I push my chair back then pull her onto my lap. "Do you like the ring?"

A tiny smile curls on her lips. "It's beautiful," she breathes. "I just can't do it." Her eyes land in her lap and I lift her chin so she's looking at me.

"That's okay, baby. It's an open invitation."

"An invitation to what?" she asks.

"To share my last name." I shoot her a playful wink.

TWELVE

Jax
Present Day

"I'VE SPENT the last ten years living for today with you," Willow says. "You've given me everything I could ever want or need. A family. Nieces. Sisters. A home." Tears flow down her cheeks like a beautiful waterfall. "But I'm ready for more. I'm ready to share your last name. I'm ready to finally find our tomorrow."

"Oh, Willow." I cup her cheek with my hand. "What do you think we've been doing for the last ten years?" I peck her lips. "We already found it, baby, but it's nice to hear you admit it."

"So, will you marry me?" she asks.

Taking the ring from the table where she set it down, I slide it up her ring finger. Over the years, I've gotten used to seeing it around her neck, but fuck if it doesn't look even more gorgeous on her finger. "Yes, Willow, it would be my honor to marry you."

Willow grins wide. "When?"

"When, what?"

"When can we get married?" Her smile widens.

I laugh at her excitement. "How about tomorrow?"

"Tomorrow?" Her eyes go wide.

"We have nothing holding us back, baby. Let's book a flight to Vegas and say I do."

Willow laughs. "Okay." She nods up and down. "Tomorrow."

ABOUT THE AUTHOR

Nikki Ash resides in South Florida where she is an English teacher by day and a writer by night. When she's not writing, you can find her with a book in her hand. From the Boxcar Children, to Wuthering Heights, to the latest single parent romance, she has lived and breathed every type of book. While reading and writing are her passions, her two children are her entire world. You can probably find them at a Disney park before you would find them at home on the weekends!

Reading is like breathing in, writing is like breathing out. – Pam Allyn